Lawrence Schimel was born in 1971. He is the author of the short story collection *The Drag Queen of Elfland* and the editor of twenty anthologies, including *Switch Hitters: Lesbians Write Gay Male Erotica and Gay Men Write Lesbian Erotica* (with Carol Queen), *Two Hearts Desire: Gay Couples on Their Love* (with Michael Lassell), *Food for Life and Other Dish*, *Southern Blood: Vampire Stories from the American South* (with Martin H. Greenberg), and *Kosher Meat*, among others. His stories, essays, and poetry have been included in more than 100 anthologies, including *Best Gay Erotica 1997* and *1998*, *The Mammoth Book of Gay Short Stories*, *Gay Love Poetry*, *The Mammoth Book of Fairy Tales*, *The Mammoth Book of Comic Fantasy*, *The Random House Book of Science Fiction Stories*, and *The Random House Treasury of Light Verse*, among others. He has also contributed to numerous periodicals, from the *Saturday Evening Post* to *Physics Today* to *Gay Scotland*. Educated at Yale University, he lives in New York City, in one small room with many, many books.

The Mammoth Book of

GAY EROTICA

Edited by
Lawrence Schimel

CARROLL & GRAF PUBLISHERS, INC.
New York

Carroll & Graf Publishers, Inc.
19 West 21st Street
Suite 601
New York
NY 10010–6805

First Carroll & Graf edition 1998

First published in the UK by Robinson Publishing 1997

Selection, introduction and editorial matter
copyright © Lawrence Schimel 1997, 1998

The moral right of the editor has been asserted

A copy of the Cataloging in Publication Data for this
title is available from the Library of Congress.

ISBN 0–7867–0476–4

Printed and bound in the EC

10 9 8 7 6 5 4 3 2 1

CONTENTS

ACKNOWLEDGEMENTS

THE QUALITIES OF LETTUCE © 1997 by Paul Allatson. First published in *Hard*, edited by Tony Ayres (Blackwattle). Reproduced by permission of the author.

LEARNING HOW TO CRAWL © 1997 by Tony Ayres. First published in *Hard*, edited by Tony Ayres (Blackwattle). Reproduced by permission of the author.

THE ROBBER BRIDGEROOM © 1996 by James Ireland Baker. First published in *Happily Ever After*, edited by Michael Thomas Ford (Richard Kasak Books). Reproduced by permission of the author.

COUPLE © 1990 by Neil Bartlett. First published, in a different form, in *Ready to Catch Him Should He Fall* (Serpent's Tail). Reproduced by permission of the author.

BODILY FLUIDS © 1997 by Kerry Bashford. First published in *Hard*, edited by Tony Ayres (Blackwattle). Reproduced by permission of the author.

NEW YORK 1942 © 1986 by Christopher Bram. First published, with some changes, as part of the novel *Hold Tight* (Donald M. Fine). Reproduced by permission of the author.

TO/FROM © 1997 by Matthew Rettenmund. Reproduced by permission of the author.

BILLY CROW © 1988 by Philip Ridley. First published in *Crocodilia* (Brilliance Books). Reproduced by permission of the author.

GHOSTS © 1997 by Paul Russell. Reproduced by permission of the author.

DO AS THE ROMANS DO © 1987 by Steven Saylor. First published in *Advocate Men*, December. Reproduced by permission of the author and Masquerade Books.

BURNING BRIDGES © 1994 by Lawrence Schimel. First published in *Honcho Overload*. Reproduced by permission of the author.

TATTOOED LOVE BOY © 1995 by D. Travers Scott. First published in *Stallions and Other Studs* (PDA Press). Reproduced by permission of the author.

HOW DO WE COMMUNICATE LOVE? © 1997 by Aiden Shaw. Reproduced by permission of the author.

ADONIS: A PERSONAL HISTORY OF THE PORN PALACE © 1996 by Don Shewey. First published in *Flashpoint*, edited by Michael Bronski (Richard Kasak). Reproduced by permission of the author.

E VERO? © 1985 by Edmund White. First published in *16 Tales* (Gay Men's Health Crisis, Inc.). Reproduced by permission of the author.

INTRODUCTION

For gay men, our erotic literature provides more than mere titillation – it is a vital and important part of our culture, a manifestation of our sexuality-based identities that reassures and educates, comforts and excites us. Erotic or pornographic writing (a distinction based on marketing rather than content or quality, *per se*) is one of the few times when we are not looking for outside acceptance, approval, or validation from the mainstream culture, we are not apologizing for our sexuality or saying "we're just like you." We are writing about ourselves, our desires, our lives.

In a society which constantly tells us our sexuality is wrong or bad, or ignores its existence altogether, there is a hungering among gay men for literature which describes and exults in our sexuality, thereby affirming our sexuality-based identities. And pornography is really one of few mediums where we can communicate, directly and unapologetically, as gay men to a gay audience – it is, in many ways, our vernacular. Writing is an act of communication, and pornography has a very specific goal – arousal – it hopes to evoke in its reader.

For many of us, pornography is how we learn about sex: what we should do and how we should do it. It is educational, if also deceiving. Because pornography is not sex; pornography is a simulation of sex, for the benefit of the reader/viewer. (Although, because its intent is arousal, the *reading* of erotic writing can arguably be considered a sexual act.)

People often complain to me about how badly-written or cliched so much pornography seems to be, as if I am supposed to be impressed by their honesty. Like any genre, it has its share of hacks, who churn out formulaic fantasies to meet the voracious need of magazines like *First Hand* or *Vulcan*. There are some who dismiss all erotic writing because of its physical side-effects (or, more properly, consequences, since arousal is intended rather than accidental) claiming that "art" appeals to the soul and the aesthetic and not to the body. I beg to differ, believing that stories – such as those I've collected here – can do both.

The noted playwright Tony Kushner wrote, in an essay for *Esquire*, "It is impossible to write about sex and not reveal too much of yourself. Whereas I think it is possible to have sex and reveal nothing of yourself whatsoever."

I couldn't agree with him more. Too many men, I think, have sex so unthinkingly, going through the motions perhaps but not really understanding or even enjoying what they're doing.

Gay men, contrary, to popular belief, find it hard to talk about sex in our lives. Sure, we're quick to use the locker-room bravado of how big last night's trick's dick was, or how many men we sucked off in the good old days of glory holes.

But most gay men are afraid to talk about their real desires, especially if these desires challenge conventional stereotypes about our gay identities and sexualities, and many men are even afraid to talk at all during sex – with the exception of those men who recycle bad porno-movie dialogue and ought, really, to keep their mouths shut or else keep busy sucking or biting something.

And, perhaps more importantly, most gay men are afraid to talk about their anxieties and concerns. They are usually afraid, in the heat of the moment, to say, "I'm not comfortable doing that." To say, "I want to know you better first." To say, "That's too big," since every piece of gay media tells them they are to exult and adore the largest cocks, and to be ashamed of anything smaller than gargantuan.

Especially, most men are still afraid to talk about AIDS during sex. We are still living in a state of crisis, and a negotiated safety needs to be a part of every sexual encounter. It is one thing if the stories you jerk off to ignore safer sex and this disease, if your fantasies while you masturbate – or even while you're having sex with someone – forget about AIDS; in your actual sex life, however, it is important to be aware of and to talk about this disease, openly and honestly, before sex and during sex and after sex. It should be impossible to think about sex and not also think about AIDS, to at least consider it; our lives depend on it.

While there is talk these days of reducing viral load to virtually nil, this is not yet the end of the disease. There is so much we still don't know or understand about AIDS – or about this new "miracle cure" of protease inhibitors. We don't know how these inhibitors will work over the long term, what will happen if you accidentally skip taking the treatment, or any of a hundred other important questions. The existence of these drugs is wonderful, but they are not the end of AIDS. They suppress some effects of AIDS, but they do not eradicate the disease completely from the body or reverse the damage the disease has already wrought. And just because this drug exists does not mean it is available to all the many men and women who need it, or that it ever will be.

Because of AIDS, we've had to change how we gay men have sex. We wear rubbers now, much as we dislike this barrier between our skins. We don't, for the most part, taste cum.

And more often than we used to, we turn to pornography and erotic literature to get us off.

This does not mean we've stopped having sex.

We like the erotica we respond to because it's about the kind of sex we like to have, or the kind of sex we'd like to have, or the kind of sex we like to fantasize about. While our sex lives have changed because of this disease, our desire for certain kinds of sex have not changed, and we turn to pornography as one safe way of fulfilling these desires. Sometimes, we like to get off reading about or watching things that we don't actually like to do ourselves. Reading a hot rape fantasy can turn me on in a way that actually being raped would not.

Reading about physical intimacy, too, can turn me on.

This collection encompasses a broad range of representations of gay sexualities and sexual activities, as well as various styles of writing. The authors range from best-selling and well-known writers such as Alan Hollinghurst, Neil Bartlett, Edmund White, and Andrew Holleran, to those whose first stories are being published in this volume. While most recent collections of gay erotica have been national in scope (due mostly to myopia than any sense of purpose or intention), writers from England (Philip Ridley, Aiden Shaw), Canada (Stan Perksy, Robin Metcalfe), the United States (Paul Russell, Lars Eighner), and Australia (Kerry Bashford, Tony Ayres) all rub shoulders in this volume, for desire does not restrict itself to our territorial boundaries (and often seems to purposefully thwart or exult in transgressing such boundaries).

In selecting stories for the volume I have chosen to restrict myself to contemporary and living authors, in an attempt to give a cross-section of current erotic writing; this also allowed me to avoid some complications of writers whose estates are in confusion or disarray and otherwise freed me from feeling compelled to arrange the book historically, and to include pieces for historical rather than literary merit. Had I not made this somewhat arbitrary decision, I would have liked to include work by Phil Andros, John Preston, and Robert Trent, among various others. Likewise, I have decided not to include in this collection the work of the many women writing gay male erotica, under their own names or pseudonyms, else I might have included Pat Califia, Carol Queen, Laura Antoniou, Lucy Taylor, etc. (though readers interested in the subject can check my previous collection on the subject, *Switch Hitters: Lesbians Write Gay Male Erotica and Gay Men Write Lesbian Erotica*, co-edited with Carol Queen).

The stories I have included are a celebration of gay men and gay sex, in all its complexity – from the delights of the flesh to anxiety about disease, from ephemeral anonymous encounters to long-term relationships. But each is unquestionably and unapologetically the story of desires between men.

BILLY CROW

Philip Ridley

THE DAY AFTER Steven's drunken return there was a knock at the door. It was about midday and Steven was still asleep with a hangover. Anne and Garreth were out doing some shopping.

I opened the door.

It was the guy from next door. My sister was right about his appearance. But the first thing I noticed were his eyes – a bright green. I'd never seen a colour quite like it. He was wearing a ripped T-shirt and black leather trousers. There was a diamond and silver brooch of a crocodile pinned to his shirt.

"Dominic! Right?" he said.

"Yes."

"Thought so. Listen, Dom, have you got a camera?"

"I've got a Polaroid."

"Oh, great. Look, come and take a photo of me."

"Sorry?"

"I need someone to take a photograph of me. I haven't got a camera. And I need someone else as I can't have me in the photo and take it. Get me?"

"I get you."

"Where's Steven?"

"Do you know us all?"

"Walls are thin, Dominic."

"Asleep. He was out getting pissed last night."

"I know. I heard him come back." He smiled. "Is the kid his?"

"Yes."

"Pretty kid. Pretty dad."

"He likes girls."

"Each to his own, Dom. Now I need a camera."

"I'll get it. Give me a second."

"I promise I won't throw anything at you this time."

"An offer I can't refuse."

And that was how I met Billy Crow.

In that first photograph I took of Billy Crow he is sitting in a black chair against a white wall and he is looking directly at the camera. He is stripped to the waist and his body is tanned and muscular with a few blond hairs around the nipples and navel. His legs are crossed, right over left, and his arms are folded, left over right. He is both smiling and frowning – as if amused, yet somehow puzzled. The floor is bare and the floorboards are littered with dirty cups and torn pieces of paper. There are one or two used matches by his foot. On the wall behind him is a mirror. And in the mirror is the reflection of the flash obscuring my face.

"I've been sitting here all morning," said Billy. "Alone. And suddenly I thought, I must have a photograph of myself. Sitting here alone. A photo. So I'll always remember that I did it. Because sometimes you forget. And I didn't want to forget. And photographs are like little pieces of memory. They help you have a past. Now I'll always remember that I once felt so alone."

"Yes," I said. "I see." Although I didn't.

The room was quite bare; wooden table, gas cooker, a few cups and sketchbooks.

"I've been watching you," said Billy.

"Really."

"Watching you in the garden, watching you walk down the street. I even watched you undress one night. You forgot to pull the curtains. It was a nice sight. I wanked while I watched you."

"Did you? Well, well, well . . ."

"Tea?"

"Yeah. Thanks."

He went to put the kettle on.

"Let me tell you a little about myself," he said, running his hands over his chest and stomach. "My name is Billy Crow. William Lester Crow to be exact. I'm twenty-four. The real colour of my hair is fair." He pulled down the front of his jeans to reveal some pubes. "As you see."

"I see."

"I moved into this squat a little while ago with my boyfriend Dave and his brother, Theo. But that didn't work out. Some things just don't. Dave left and took everything that we possessed. Meaning he took one lamp, his clothes and a teapot. Which is why we're having tea-bags. OK?"

"OK. By the way," I added, for want of something to say, "I like that crocodile brooch of yours."

"Yes. It is nice, isn't it. It was a present from a friend. But I might have to sell it to get some money. I think it's probably worth quite a bit. There's a kind of antique shop near here and it's called – wait for it – 'Crocodile Tears'. And that seems a perfect place to sell it. I suppose the name of the shop is supposed to imply a kind of false sentimentality. Because it deals with people's antiques . . . or junk. But I don't look on it like that. If I were really in love with someone I would buy them a gift from that shop. You see, for me, crocodile tears are honest. A present bought from that shop would be an omen. A magic sign. It would mean something."

"OK. You've made your point."

He smiled. "Right. On with business. I like music and films and dyeing my hair different colours. I like people and food. Not necessarily together." He gave me my tea. "And I like you. Very much, Dominic."

"Thank you, kind sir."

"And you like me?"

I touched his stomach. "Yes."

"Good. We begin on equal terms and proceed in light." He sat down. "What's the set-up next door? Your sister and all that."

"I was living at home with Mum and Dad. Things were getting bad between us. Anne suggested I move in with them. And that's it. I've got my own room. I live my own life. I just lie in bed at night and listen to them screw each other to kingdom come."

"Ahhhh . . . Steven screwing. I bet he's noisy."

"Like an animal."

"I knew it. Do you fancy him?"

"Of course."

"Of *course*?"

"But he likes girls, Billy."

"OK. Fair enough. That's the way it goes, Dom. I'm sure there's plenty of girls that he fancies who like girls, and plenty of girls who like guys but not him. It's the way of the world. Some things are just not meant to be." He sipped his tea, looking at me the whole time. "Have you ever spoken to anyone about sex before?"

"No. Not really," I said.

"Not *really*?"

"Not truthfully."

"Oh, I see. So all this is by way of initiation."

"Correct."

"And you've never . . .?"

"No. Never."

He laughed out loud. And I laughed too. I had never felt so relaxed and contented.

"Here," he said. "Let me take a photograph of you. Against the wall. I want to remember this day. This meeting."

He took the photograph.

"Look, Billy," I said. "I best get back. I promised Anne I'd cook Steven's breakfast when he gets up."

"The pleasures of servitude, eh?"

"Sort of."

I went up and kissed him full on the mouth.

His tongue probed between my teeth and his hands felt between my legs. I was instantly erect.

"I'm new to this," I said.

"Nonsense. You've been doing it for a thousand years."

I kissed him again. And felt between his legs.

I almost fainted with excitement.

As I turned to leave, I said, "You can have the camera and the rest of the stuff here. Just in case there's anything else you want to remember."

"The memory-maker," he said.

I opened the door.

"Dominic," he called.

"Yeah?"

"Come back tonight, eh?"

In that photograph of me I am sitting in a black chair against a white wall and I am looking directly at the camera. I am wearing my usual black T-shirt and my stomach appears soft and flabby over the belt of my jeans. My hair is black and very long at the back, short and spikey at the front. My legs are crossed, left over right, and my arms are folded, right over left. I am looking blankly at the camera. The floor is bare and the wooden floorboards are littered with dirty cups and torn pieces of paper. There are one or two matches by my foot. On the wall behind me is a mirror. Beside the mirror is the photo I took of Billy.

I lay in bed naked and hot and I wrapped my legs round Billy's waist. He kissed me and thrust his tongue deep into my mouth, his right hand squeezing my nipples until they were hard and tingling. His body was as smooth as marble and slippery with sweat. He felt like some sleek seal, lithe and playful between my legs. Whenever I moaned or gasped with a sensation so new I felt my fingertips glow, he cooed my name and whispered "love" and "darling" into my ear, leaving the word to float around my head like a halo of tiny tadpoles or fish.

He grasped my cock, clutched it tight, then started to wank me. All the time his tongue flickered in and out, in and out, and I was torn between the desire to close my eyes and scream out loud, and the need to watch my Billy, watch everything he did, study his beautiful, hard shoulders, watch the caterpillar of his spine arch and contract in the spasms of ecstasy. I wanted my eyes to look at everything he did, everything he had, his firm flat stomach with muscles like tightly packed walnuts, the mound of blond, pubic hair, his cock, his balls, his smooth, round arse, his green eyes, Mohican haircut, shaven head, pointed nose, white teeth, smooth skin. I wanted to remember everything, everything. As if my very eyes were hungry for him, wanted to capture his image, burn it deep into my iris and mind.

Sex made me what I was supposed to be. Before that night, before Billy Crow held me in his body and cooed my name like a melancholy pigeon, before Billy Crow possessed me and told me who I was, I did not know my identity. It was hidden from me, concealed in the shadows, indissolubly fused with other people's lives, the million, million stories of which I was a part but not the whole.

Billy made me whole. He took what I was, digested it, then gave it back to me, richer, fuller, somehow honest. I had been masturbating thinking of doing this for as long as I could remember. But it felt like nothing I could have ever imagined. Sex was not something separate from what I was. Not something I did only when I was randy and erect. Sex was part of me, part of everything that I aspired to be, part of every decision I made. Sex was with me every second of the day, controlling me and smiling at me. It wasn't something to be feared. On the contrary, it took away fear. It made me Dominic Niel.

Billy Crow said, "Wank me. Please. Wank me."

He lay on his back and thrust his hips forward. I ran my hands over the hard continent of his stomach. His skin was cool and smooth. Like ivory, without blemish; the skin of a Giotto icon.

Billy closed his eyes. Clenched them so tight his face became wrinkled and red.

"We could be anywhere," he said. "Anywhere at all. We could be doing this any place on earth. Other people could be watching. Anything."

I grabbed his cock. It was both hard and soft; tusk in velvet. Slowly, I rubbed it up and down, up and down. His penis grew hot in my hand.

Billy started to breathe faster. I watched his stomach muscles quiver, his eyelids flicker. He licked his lips, threw his head back, clutched at the sheets.

"Where are we?" he panted. "In your fantasy. Where are we? Ice or jungle? Sand or swamp? Tell me."

I was too busy watching to reply.

I was Dominic Niel and this was Billy Crow and sex had given us names and purpose.

I rubbed him slowly. Up and down. Watching everything, everything. I moved forward so that my stomach lay sticky with sweat against his thigh.

"We're in a jungle," whispered Billy. "It's a tropical night. The moon is full. The sky glitters with stars. And all the creatures of the forest are watching." His breathing grew faster, his skin turned pink, shimmered with sweat. "I can see them," he hissed. "Watching, watching."

I rubbed him harder.

"Their eyes are expressionless. They don't understand."

Still I pumped at his cock.

"They're watching!" he cried. "They're watching! The . . . crocodiles!"

And then he came. Came in glorious fountains of spunk, like a whale rising for air. His spunk landed warm and white on his stomach and chest. And, as he came, so I came too. Came without even having to touch myself. Spat my desire down the length of his legs. His spunk mixed with my spunk in a strange potion of purification and contentment.

He opened his eyes and kissed me.

The sounds of the room seemed to change now and surrounding objects, that had seemed distant and ethereal during sex, regained their presence and solidity. It was like clicking back into another time, another world. I became aware of a dog barking, of my breathing, of a slight chill in the air, of myself as monster and angel in the world of reasonable delight.

"You know something," said Billy.

"What?"

"After sex, I always think of the same thing. An image, I suppose. I've had it ever since I first started to come."

"What image?"

"I see a castle. A castle with a tower. It's night. There's candle light in the tower. Inside there sits a king. He is talking to a creature. A creature that is chained to the centre of the room."

"What kind of creature?"

"Oh, you know."

"No. I don't."

He sat up and looked down at me.

"Tell me," he said. "What did you think about while we were having sex?"

"Think about? Well, you."

"Me?"

I nodded.

"But didn't you have a fantasy? Think about something else? Didn't you go into your own little story?"

I blushed. I felt as if I had done something wrong. Cheated him somehow.

"No," I whispered. "I just thought about you."

Billy grinned and grabbed my limp and sticky penis.

"Well," he said. "We'll have to do something about that."

BY THE NUMBERS

William J. Mann

SPREAD OUT ON the table in front of me are numbers. Phone numbers. This one, the one most wrinkled and torn, is the oldest. I got it in Los Angeles when I was 18. His name was Philip. I've kept it all these years, more than a decade, a relic of an earlier time, a physical remembrance of a special night, a beautiful man. I really started collecting numbers once I became an activist, when rallies and protests and marches took me all across the continent. This one is from Montreal: I have a thing for French boys. This one, from Seattle, I keep purely for sentiment. Teddy's not around anymore. But I keep his number anyway.

They give me some sense of belonging, these numbers. They're my connections throughout this vast land: lines drawn across the map from heart to heart, from dick to dick. For a while, I was traveling a great deal. Back in the days when it seemed we all were activists, when there was always some new action, some new march to attend, I got around quite a bit. I collected dozens of little slips of paper, with the requisite seven digits plus area code scrawled upon them. "Do you want my number?" they'd usually ask, as I'd be lacing up my boots, sitting on the edge of their beds. Of course, I'd always say. I might be leaving the next day, or that very night – but you never did know when I might pass through this way again.

And it did happen, once in a while. And once in a while, they'd surprise me, too, when they ended up in New York. "My second cousins are in town," I'd say. And they are kin. They're my unseen family, the libidinous network that makes up the queer nation, the collective conscious that lives on in that queer little place way down in our souls. "Do you want my number?" they'd ask. Of course I do: that's what it's all about.

Five cities in six days. Then four cities in three. Of course, I knew when I signed on that we'd be constantly moving, but the idea, back then, back in those sad, depressed days in my cramped apartment in Hell's Kitchen, seemed invigorating. Inspiring. Rejuvenating. Just what I needed.

I needed to connect. It had been some time since I'd been out there, collecting numbers.

"Oh, you know those activist boys have lots of sex on road trips," my dyke friend Cassandra had assured me. "It'll be one long orgy."

Only that's not the way it was. At least, not at first. Surprising that even the most radical queer – screaming his lungs out about a homophobic, racist, sexist system of government – can hold such traditional views about sex. Funny how by being out, you're able to see just how smothering the closet can be – and how terrible that realization can make you feel.

Here's how this particular realization began for me: the four guys in our particular contingent packed into a two-door compact, the heavy fragrance of our leather jackets and sweaty bodies quickly triumphing over the scent of new carpet on the long ride out of New York. We were wedged in pretty tight, given the luggage we carried with us (even activists can be queens – or maybe, especially activists can be queens.) We listened to old 1970s' disco tapes as we cruised up I-95, and I liked how our knees kept knocking and how, when we took turns driving, one of us always had to climb over someone else. We stopped off in Hartford for an hour, to chant in front of one of the insurance companies, and then we headed north again. That night, we pulled over to sleep in a dusty motel room, doubling up in the two beds. But the nightcap I'd expected was not to be. "I've got a boyfriend back home," the boy I'd been lusting after all day whispered when I came on to him under the sheets. "We're monogamous."

That first night, it was very difficult to sleep.

Because the boys I was traveling with – living with, eating with, sleeping with – were cute. Really cute. Wide-eyed and eager, still innocent in some quirky way despite – or perhaps, because of – their disillusionment with the government. We shared the same sadness and the same anger: the loss of friends, the fears about our own futures. I'd heard that these bands of protesters, running around the country chasing after the presidential candidates, were able to transform that grief and rage into passionate sex, or at least use fucking as an outlet for their emotions, to bond with one another in a common struggle. But this band (just my luck) seemed passionless after the protests died down.

The boy I lusted after was Craig. Dark hair, dark eyes, big lips. A mole just above the upper lip, like Madonna. Hard body, little body hair, tight round ass. The sideburns, the earrings, the Doc Marten's, the Action=Life stickers on his black leather jacket. Too perfect, too trendy, too cloney. But lying there next to him in bed, unable to touch him, listening to him snore in a baby buzzy way, all I could think about was rolling him over and pushing my stick up his hole.

We would've made a good pair: Craig being so dark, me being so fair. I'm not really blond, but not really brunette either: somewhere in between. Blue eyes. A body not as hard as Craig's, but not soft either. And I've got a lot of hair on my chest, thinning out down to the happy trail that leads from my stomach to my dick. We would have contrasted nicely, Craig and I.

As it turned out, the contrast became more than apparent.

The other boys were Emilio and Sam. Emilio would have been more my type under different circumstances: Latin, short and beefy, with olive-brown skin and strangely green eyes (he assured me they were not contacts). Big arms and a pumped-up chest, short legs and a flat stomach. Had we shared a bed, instead of Craig and I, there would have been considerable more difficulty in restraining myself. Sam was cute, too, but in a nerdy sort of way. Slightly built with dirty blond hair and glasses, he was quiet and solemn, except when he was chanting about the government having blood on its hands.

We were all pretty mouthy in the demonstrations. After our second one, in front of Pat Buchanan's primary campaign headquarters in Manchester, New Hampshire, I knew we had a good team. It was our first stop after Hartford, and the nation's first presidential primary – held in New Hampshire – was just days away. We chanted "Heil! Heil!" in front of Buchanan's office, making me feel strangely uneasy, especially seeing the fierce glazed look that grabbed ahold of Craig's pretty face. There was something in his eyes that frightened me, as if he'd become possessed by the ghost of some long-dead SS. And from an upstairs window, his opposite image peered out at us: the soulless eyes of a young Buchanan volunteer, staid and handsome in his jacket and tie, his hair combed just so, staring down in an uncomprehending emptiness at the angry, leather-jacketed protester chanting Nazi slogans in the street.

"Did you see them looking out at us? Did you see their scared little Republican faces?" Craig laughed as we crowded around a table at Burger King afterward, eliciting stares from the staid New Hampshire folk with our leather jackets and slogans plastered all over them. "They didn't know whether we'd storm their front door," Craig said, slapping the table, causing the family at the next table to get up and move.

"This isn't about spreading fear," Sam said to him, unwrapping his Whopper. "We aren't storm troopers, although we might look like it."

Craig frowned. What beautiful lips, I thought. "I'm not averse to making Republicans afraid," he said. "Did you see that pretty little closet case looking down at us? I especially enjoyed seeing him squirm. Republican pretty boys are especially pretty when they're squirming."

Sam shook his head. "It's not a Democrat-Republican thing. It's the system. Both parties. Both liberals and conservatives. We should be targeting all of them. Raising their conscience and their consciousness. It's not about spreading fear. There's too much of that already."

I looked at Sam with new eyes. Next to big pouty lips, brains really turned me on. I liked his analysis. He was serious, and for good reason. Craig was your typical activist: all passion, all mouth. Why was he so angry, I wondered. Why were any of us?

But with Craig, it went deeper: I imagined him to be the kid on the playground who always got picked last for sports, the son whose father always chided for being a sissy. I'll show them, I imagined Craig saying: I'll show them how tough I can be.

Sam, on the other hand, thought about the significance of it all. He was angry, and mouthy, too, but always with a motive, an ulterior strategy. Without Sam along for this ride, I realized, we'd be nothing more than a pack of rabble rousers. Or wolves.

Because it was precisely at that point when I felt a hand under the table, without warning, take a firm hold of my crotch. I nearly spit out my French fry. I looked to my right, where the hand seemed to come from. And Emilio grinned over at me.

It was his turn to unwrap his Whopper. And I don't mean his burger.

Manchester is a quiet little town. The gay bar is pretty much in the center of a residential area, but no sign marks it. We found our way there by gaydar. Emilio and I hadn't stopped looking at each other. I'm not sure if the other boys noticed. As we walked, a light, dry snow tickling our faces, Emilio and I kept bumping into each other, brushing our hands together, rubbing shoulders. We had not yet articulated any attraction, just let our eyes raise the ante. Sam and Craig were still arguing, but I held my interest in check: after suffering through blue balls last night, I wasn't going to go sexless again tonight.

"Hold on a minute, Mike," Emilio said to me, just as the other two ahead of us slipped into the yellow light of the bar. He tugged at my hand, pulling me back into the snowy blue night. "Let's go for a walk."

I saw Craig look back at us and I shrugged, letting the door swing closed. Too bad for you, buddy, I thought.

Under the moon and the softly falling snow, on somebody's back lawn, behind a thicket of blue spruce trees, the kind my Dad and I would chop down every Christmas back in Michigan and drag all the way home to decorate, Emilio and I made love.

He surprised me with his gentleness. For such a strong man, he was endearingly tender. There was no question of who would mount whom, who would be the top and who would be the bottom. I'm comfortable in either role, but that's what they are after all: roles. And it's usually pretty instinctive for me who will play which one when I first meet someone new. I just know. And I knew from the moment Emilio grabbed my crotch under the table at Burger King that he was going to fuck me.

We spoke not a word. I remember the cold of the crisp new snow against the back of my neck, his warm lips, still smelling vaguely of ketchup and mustard, pressing down onto mine. His hands were rough but gentle, inching up under my shirt to play with my pecs. I flexed for him, and he purred in appreciation. Then he slipped one hand down between my legs, finding my swelling dick outlined in my jeans. He stroked it through the denim. I knew I was already wet, and he probably felt it. With his other hand, he moved around to cup my butt, and I instinctively lifted myself up off the ground, positioning myself. This was it: this was why we yelled and screamed; this was the passion. How else do we stay alive except by making love to one another?

I've come to eroticize the sound of tearing cellophane. It makes me jump, catch my breath. Call me Pavlov's bottom. I know what it means: within seconds, I'll feel the hard sting of a dick head invading my asshole, as I felt Emilio's that night in the snow. I don't know why I was tense that night; maybe I was just cold. But he had to reach up under my shirt and my leather jacket and start pinching my nipples for me to relax enough to let him in. Once he was up there, however, I was meeting his every thrust with my own hip movement. I hadn't yet seen his cock, only felt it, and it felt great. Big enough, not too big that it hurt beyond the expected pain. It filled my guts nicely, and the movement in and out reminded me of how beautiful it was the first time I was ever fucked: by my cousin Randy, when I was sixteen, out on my grandfather's farm in Michigan, behind the barn, in the snow just like this. Randy was married, and we never talked about it now. But he was gentle, just like Emilio was being, and he'd played with my nipples too.

Finally Emilio spoke: "I've wanted to fuck you every since we got together yesterday. Sleep with me tonight," he said. All I could do was nod. It's hard to talk with a cock up your butt.

He rammed it up inside me one final time, and I heard him inhale deeply. The tip of his dick gave my prostate one final assault, and I felt my own cock, in my fist and itself pumping feverishly, get ready to explode. Emilio pulled out and tore off the condom. Then he shot his load of cream all over the front of my leather jacket.

"Sorry, man," he murmured.

I laughed, thinking: that's what gives my jacket that great weathered look.

I fully expected to jerk myself off then, but he surprised me. Tenderly, he bent over my dick, spearheading the night air, and swallowed it. I groaned in sweet surprise, feeling the warmth of his silky mouth suck my cock far down his throat. I lifted my hips to fill him up, and pumped his mouth slowly. Then he took over the work, lapping at my rod as if it were a big stick of candy and he a sweet-toothed child. He circled the tip of my cock with his tongue and played with my still raw asshole with his finger. Then he licked all the way down the shaft and took my balls into his mouth, one at a time, gently, delicately, holding them there, savoring them.

Then his warm, wet tongue made its way down below my balls to that precious little spot between the scrotum and the anus, the very bottom of the human body, its soft pink underbelly, and he kissed me there. Then his tongue darted into the hole he'd forced open just moments ago, and finally, like a geyser, I came, without even touching myself.

We did it again later that night, after Sam and Craig had fallen asleep in the bed next to us in the Howard Johnson's Motor Lodge we crashed in for the night. The fact that we had to be quiet and fuck slowly so that the bed didn't squeak just turned me on all the more. At one point Emilio covered my mouth and I could hardly breathe: as near to living out an S/M fantasy I have (so far) experienced. His dick felt even better up my ass the second time. He kissed me hard, hurting my lips, as he fucked me equally as hard.

We both slept incredibly well.

Next stop was Boston. I think Craig and Sam suspected something was going on between us. Emilio falling asleep on the bed next to me so that Craig wouldn't reclaim his spot the night before hadn't fooled anybody. And then, in the backseat, we sat awfully close together. It was a few hours' drive from

Manchester to Boston. We were listening to an old ABBA tape, getting off on it: "You are the dancing queen, young and sweet, only seventeen . . ." Emilio and I were especially giddy. The pheromones we'd let loose the night before were still making us high. By noon, we were all pretty hungry, and Emilio suggested we stop and get something to eat. He winked at me, saying he also wanted to use the men's room. I think Craig noticed.

We pulled off at a McDonald's. We weren't far from Boston now. "Hey," Emilio asked the kid behind the counter, a thin black guy with smooth, glowing skin, "how come the rest room's locked?"

"Hold on," the kid said back, and I saw it in his eyes. He and Emilio locked stares, and I was amazed. How do we find each other? How do we know? What secret scent do queers emit that only we can detect? "I'll bring over the key," the kid behind the counter said, his voice catching in his throat.

Sam and Craig ordered their Big Macs and fries and settled into a booth. I followed Emilio as he followed the kid to the men's room. No, I kept telling myself: this isn't really going to happen.

But it did. Once inside, the kid turned and smiled. "Hey," he said. "Act up."

"Anything you say," Emilio said, and grabbed the kid, who couldn't have been more than 18, and pulled him in close for a savage kiss. I moved behind him, feeling his round, hard butt beneath his orange polyester McDonald's uniform pants. He smelled like vegetable oil. I bit his neck, and his hands came around back to squeeze my crotch through my jeans.

Emilio shrugged off his leather jacket and peeled off his T-shirt up over his head. The kid began licking his bronze, hairless chest, following the shapely definition of his pumped-up pectorals. Then he sucked onto Emilio's left nipple and just hung there. His McDonald's cap slipped from his head, and I pulled down his pants, revealing the most beautiful ass I'd ever seen: round and hard, with deep cleavage. Down onto my knees I went, thrusting my nose and my lips between his cheeks. Tongue-first, I found his hole, and began rimming him with a ferocity that surprised even myself.

I mean, it wasn't as if I hadn't gotten any lately.

"Aw, yeah, Mike," Emilio said, "eat his asshole."

I loved dirty talk. I wanted Emilio to say more, to describe how the scene looked, but I realized that he'd gone to his knees too, and was blowing the kid. He was moaning pretty loud, and for a fleeting second I wondered if Sam and Craig might hear what was going on. But I was too into my work to think about much else: the kid's ass tasted so sweet, so tangy, and I really wanted to fuck him. I pulled out of his crack just long enough to get a glimpse of his massive tool plunging in and out of Emilio's face. Energized by my own raging hard-on, I went back to my feast.

But any hopes of fucking the kid evaporated when I felt his whole body tighten, and he yanked his dick from Emilio's mouth, shooting the kind of load I remembered shooting when I was his age, nearly a decade ago. I stood up and helped him regain his balance. He looked slightly embarrassed, but Emilio kissed him lightly on the lips. "Hey, great show, man," Emilio said.

"I need to get back to work," the kid said awkwardly.

"Sure," I said, and smiled at Emilio as we watched him hurry out the door.

Back at the booth, Sam was blissfully eating the last of his fries and reading the *New York Times*. But Craig eyed me with an accusing glare.

"Where were you guys?" he asked.

"Getting directions," Emilio said, and I laughed.

"That kid—" Craig said, checking him out behind the counter. "You just did that kid!"

"Yup," I said, meeting Craig's eyes, which were burning with envy.

"Christ," he said, dropping his gaze. "Thanks for letting us know."

"Hey," I protested. "You're monogamous."

He didn't respond.

I walked cockily up to the counter. The kid grinned at me. I ordered a Coke to go. "Hey," the kid said, handing me my Coke and the receipt. I looked at it. In blue ink there was written: "Call me next time you're in Boston. Earl." And then his number. Area code first.

*   *   *

Back on the road, we sang along with Jimmy Somerville ("Never can say goodbye, boy" – emphasizing the boy.) We tailgated a car with a Bush/Quayle bumper sticker for a while, then passed them so they could see our Silence = Death. "You guys are so immature," Sam kept saying.

I'd never been to Boston. The boys sure were pretty, in a WASPy kind of way. There was a big action in front of Bush's headquarters, and standing there, in that sea of leather jackets, the anger and the pain and the determination giving us all hard-ons, I felt as if I wanted to fuck each and every one of the guys there, and maybe the women, too. It's a great, secure sensation to be surrounded by those who believe as you do, all of us united in one common passion, one single purpose. There's a ton of cruising going on: eyes darting from this one to that one, dicks getting harder with every increased decibel of our chanting. Sometimes I hook up with someone after an action. Other times I take my horniness away with me, to the bar or to the sex club. But all that passion can be deceptive, too: later, when everyone had dispersed, we sat in Quincy Market alone, the four of us, shivering in the gray winter dusk.

"Now what do you want to do?" Emilio asked.

"I guess go back to the motel and get a good night's rest. We have to be up very early tomorrow morning to get on the road so we can be at the action at City Hall in New York by 11," Sam said.

I'd come to appreciate Sam's wisdom, but not right now. "I don't want to go back to the motel," I said. "Not yet."

"Me either," Emilio agreed.

Craig had been silent. Now he spoke. "Let's go zap Buchanan's HQ."

"What?" I asked.

"That wasn't scheduled for today," Sam pointed out.

"So?" Craig asked. "All the better. They won't be expecting us."

"What good's that gonna do?" Emilio asked. "We'd be the only four there."

Craig had that scary look in his eyes again. "I'm going," he said.

So we went with him. We were, after all, a team. It wouldn't be safe for him to go alone. We decided we'd go inside the office, pass out some leaflets, and then chant for a few minutes on the sidewalk outside. "Maybe we'll get through to someone in there," Craig said.

We were surprised to see who was there. The pretty, empty-eyed closet case we'd seen the day before in Manchester. He was dressed in a blue suit and a red and blue tie against a white shirt. His eyes registered nothing when we entered, our leather jackets hidden behind a snowdrift outside. I handed him a leaflet and he looked at it, not comprehending. Two old ladies with white hair and pearls, sitting at a table drawing lines on voter lists, took leaflets from Sam and read them. One of them shouted: "Oh! They've got AIDS!"

Then a flurry of papers began. Leaflets were thrown into the air. I'm not sure who did it: probably Craig. This caused the old ladies to push back their chairs, accidentally toppling over their table, sending the voter lists into the air like big white moths. The closet case remained still, until he looked around and realized he was the only man in the room. Then his face shifted, as if he figured he had some sort of responsibility to act, and he stepped one foot forward. "Do something, Chester," one of the old ladies screamed.

We, meanwhile, had beaten the hell out of there, standing on the sidewalk outside their storefront chanting: "Buchanan preaches while people die!" Chester—what an appropriate name, I thought – stood in the doorway, watching us, emotionless.

"Hey, Chester," I called. "Why don't you come out and join us?"

"Or maybe you can just come out," Craig shouted.

Finally, there was a spark of something in his eyes. Emilio said later he saw it too. It was as if Chester's eyes reflected the glare of a streetlight all at once. But then it was gone. His eyes went right back to nothing. He didn't say a word. One of the old ladies thrust her ugly neck out from the door behind him and squawked: "We're going to call the police!"

Chester turned then, as if to calm her. He closed the door behind them.

I could see them straightening up the tables, reordering the voter lists. Every now and again Chester would look up through the window and see if we were still there. Once, I waved.

"Fucking Republican closet case murderous self-oppressed Uncle Tom," Craig spit.

"How can you be so sure he's gay?" Emilio asked.

"Same way you knew that kid in McDonald's was," Craig said, and he had a point.

"Why don't we wait for him?" I suggested. I wasn't sure what we'd say or do, but that glint in his eye had intrigued me.

"I don't think that would be a good idea," Sam said.

Craig's eyes had lit up. "Sure it is," he said. "We could jump him. Beat the shit out of – "

"No," I said firmly. "That's not what I meant. I meant wait for him, talk to him."

Emilio laughed. "You think you can get him to come out?"

"Why not try?" I asked.

Sam stretched. "I'm beat," he said. "This is where the team will have to split up. I'm going back to the motel and crash."

Craig nodded. "Sure, Sam. You go on back. You too, Emilio, if you want."

Emilio looked at him suspiciously. "No," he said. "I'll stay."

So it was just Sam to clump on off alone through the snow to find a cab. We settled down behind a statue of some New England patriot and waited. It got pretty cold, and we didn't say much. Craig kept an eye out on the Buchanan headquarters. Emilio and I sat close together, kissing for both passion and warmth in the shadows. We both had erections, but the kind that feel good to keep around for a while, not the kind that need immediate release.

"Hey," Craig whispered. "Why don't you guys go get us some coffee? It could be a while before he comes out."

I looked at Emilio. "Sounds good to me," I said.

Emilio looked up at Craig. Then back at me. "All right," he said, but he sounded uneasy with the idea.

The streets were quiet. A new snow had begun to fall, and an eerie stillness had settled over the neighborhood. It reminded me of some movie I'd seen a long time ago, back in Michigan, at the old Rialto Theater on a Saturday afternoon on Main Street, back before I'd lost 15 friends and one very special lover to this plague. The movie was about space invaders who take over a town and kill everyone in it so when the hero returns after some time away, he walks down the street confused by the solitude, with the dawning horror that he's the only one left alive.

"Where is everybody?" Emilio asked, while I was thinking this.

"That's what I want to know," I said.

We found one man, probably Korean, a slight sad smile on his face, behind the counter of a delicatessen. We ordered three coffees. "Should we get one for Chester?" Emilio asked.

"He can drink out of mine," I said with a wink.

"You know," Emilio said, as we trudged back out into the snow, "I wonder if we're really ready to keep up this pace."

"What do you mean?" I asked. The coffee burned my tongue.

"I mean, five cities in six days. Then four cities in three. I'm already getting tired."

I laughed. "Maybe we should stop boinking McDonald's clerks in the middle of the afternoon."

He smiled. "I've got to watch my pace," he said. "I can't get run down."

I put my arm around him. "Hey, that's why we travel in teams. I'll watch out for you."

We kissed. Snowflakes landed on our noses and foreheads.

Back behind the patriot's statue, there was no Craig. And the Buchanan HQ was dark, closed for the night.

"Hey, where the hell — " Emilio started.

Then we heard the clatter of metal. Something moved in the alley beside the headquarters. We heard a muffled shout. We looked at each other for just a second, then dropped our coffees and ran.

In the darkness, next to a line of garbage cans, Craig had Chester in a headlock. The young Republican was struggling, trying to break free. His tie was askew now, and snow covered his blue suit pants. Craig's eyes were wild.

"Hey, guys," Craig called to us. "Come on over and make this closet case suck your dicks."

"Let him go!" I shouted.

"No fucking way," Craig shot back.

Emilio was speechless. The sight, I have to admit, was intriguing. Leather-jacketed queer militant overpowering suit-and-tie Buchanan boy. Both pretty. Both needing a good hard fuck to wake them out of their ignorance and denial. Maybe we should just let it happen. Maybe the closet case should get fucked over for the way his master and those like him have fucked us over. Maybe then he could turn and fuck some sense into Craig as well.

But that's crazy.

"Let him go," I heard from behind us.

It was Sam. Craig tensed, then made a horrible face. "Fuck you," he said, releasing Chester, who stumbled and fell into a snowbank.

"You're a fool," Sam said to Craig, who shoved him. With unbelievable speed, Sam took hold of the front of Craig's shirt and pulled him up to meet his eyes. I couldn't believe our little nerdy voice of reason could exert such physical strength. But Craig seemed in awe; so were Emilio and I. Sam spoke just two words into Craig's face: "Go home." And Craig, upon being let go, ran off into the snowy night.

"And then there were three," Sam said, more to himself than to us. He bent down and helped Chester up from the snow.

"Thanks," Chester said, the first time I'd heard his voice, a shy, low sound.

"Just so you know," Sam said, staring at him. "I didn't save you because you deserved it. I saved you because it was the right thing to do."

Chester stared at him.

"We aren't thugs. But the people you work for are," Sam told the boy.

Chester seemed to seek me out. Our eyes connected. Even when Craig had him in the stranglehold, his eyes had registered nothing. But now there was something: fear, perhaps, but more than that. Anticipation. Even excitement.

"I know that," he said finally. "If anything has become apparent these last few months, it's that."

"So get out of there," Emilio said. "Leave."

"It's not that easy. My father is a party official. When I graduate from school, I'm getting a job – "

"And a wife," I said.

He looked at me. "You wouldn't understand," he said.

"No," I said. "I wouldn't."

"Please," Chester said, and now it looked as if he'd cry. "Leave me alone."

So we did. We left him standing in that alley, pitiful little thing. I figured that would be the last image I'd ever have of him, standing in the snow, his clothes all disheveled, hanging his head in the shadows.

But it wasn't. Emilio, impressed by Sam's show of strength, was all over our fearless leader. I didn't mind. I figured we'd all get around to sharing each other before this trip was through. Except, no doubt, for Craig. I lingered a bit, watching Emilio and Sam walk ahead of me. I glanced over my shoulder once, and I saw Chester still standing there, looking after me. I slowed down my pace and looked around again. He stared at me with those lifeless eyes. I called out to Emilio and Sam, telling them to go on without me, that I'd come along soon. I stopped walking, and turned around to face Chester.

He was so young. Even at this distance, that's what struck me. So young. So misguided. In the sad spilled light of the yellow streetlamp, he looked for all the world like a character out of Dickens: alone and cold, lost and forgotten, on a snowy winter night.

Don't feel for him, I told myself. He's the enemy. But when he walked back into the alley I followed. There, in the deep blue shadows, I put my hands out to him, and felt the warmth of his body against mine. Our lips sought each other across our faces, and we locked our mouths in a ferocious kiss. Part of me wondered, just for a moment, if I was imagining this, if I was really still standing there on the sidewalk, pitying the sight of the boy in the glow of the street light. But then I felt his swelling cock through his thin suit pants. It jumped when I stroked it, and I let my lips slip down from his mouth along his neck, feeling him tremble in my embrace.

We said nothing to each other. He silently fell to his knees, making a soft thump in the blanket of snow. He undid my jeans with shaking fingers. I took hold of his shoulders, as gently but as firmly as I could, and pushed him onto me. I felt his warm breath on my dick, and then the sweet caress of his lips. I felt my dick slip down the silky length of his tongue, and I felt him lick its underside, struggling inside my underwear to kiss my balls.

I pulled him to his feet and turned him around, so that he was facing away from me. I roughly undid his belt, yanking down his pants. Folding up the flaps of his sport coat, I slipped on a condom and entered him effortlessly, both of us standing up. He shuddered with what could have been either agony or ecstasy, or a combination of both. All he said was: "Yes." I plunged into his tight young ass, feeling the grip of his muscles as I pumped back and forth. His hands reached around behind him to hold tightly to my arms. In a move that surprised me, I kissed the back of his neck as I fucked him, and then we both came, near simultaneously.

I allowed the silence to continue as we pulled our clothes back on. Finally, when we were done, he turned, and I saw the glint in his eyes again. "Hey," I said. "Come on with me."

"No," he said. "I can't."

"Why not?" I asked.

"You wouldn't understand." He looked away.

"At least give me your number," I said. "Or take mine."

He turned back to face me. The light in his eyes had disappeared. He once again possessed the vacant stare with which I had first seen him. I looked at him for several seconds to be sure. Then, in a resignation to the sorrow I felt welling up inside, I left. And I didn't dare look back and see him again.

Emilio and Sam were sound asleep in each other's arms when I got back to the motel room. Craig wasn't there. He had gone out to a bar and gotten laid. Overcome with guilt, the next morning he hopped on a bus back to his boyfriend. So it really was now just three.

I didn't tell them about Chester. How could I have explained it to them?

The trip to New York was a quiet one. We didn't play any music. I watched as we passed the backs of shopping centers, the bad side of tenements, the littered back yards of suburban homes. Sam drove the whole way. Emilio slept. I stretched out in the backseat, unable to sleep. Once, stopping at a McDonald's to pee, I spied a cute guy mopping the floor and he looked back at me and smiled. But I didn't do anything about it.

Tomorrow would be Philadelphia, but for now we were back home. I'd even have the chance to pop up to my apartment, collect my mail, and check in with Cassandra. "So how's the sex?" she'd no doubt ask. "That orgy started yet?"

How would I answer? All I could think about were Chester's sad, lost eyes: more lost than any of the friends for whom I grieved.

At City Hall, we fell into the large contingent, allowing the warmth what passed from body to body to enliven us, inspire us, revitalize us. But even this, that old sense of comfort and affirmation that always came when I stood among dozens of other angry, chanting queers, was fleeting. Even as I reveled in it, I knew it was temporary, that this too would pass.

And it did. Once again, the three of us were left alone sitting on the steps of City Hall, our voices hoarse, our heads aching.

"Hey," Emilio said. "We'll meet up at six then, to head to Philly?"

"Five cities in six days," I said as way of reply.

"I'm going home to shower and rest up," he said. "I'll see you then."

After he left, Sam turned to me. "You going to be all right?" he asked.

"I don't want to become like Craig," I said.

"Don't worry," he assured me. "You won't." And then he kissed me, full and deep, the best kiss I could remember in a long, long time, right there in front of City Hall.

"Hey," I said, awakening, not letting him pull away. "This could be a fun six days after all."

Sam smiled, and for the first time, I saw how beautiful he was. "And don't forget – four cities in three days after that," he laughed.

"The more the better," I said, pulling him in for another deep, wet tongue kiss.

My dick was straining against my jeans. I would've done

him right there on the cold marble steps if he'd have let me. Fuck whoever saw us. But Sam eased himself out of my grasp. "Tonight," he said, "let's all share a bed."

I agreed. Then Sam hurried off among the throngs clogging the street, back to his little nest, to shower, to rest up, to get ready for the next leg of the trip.

Which I should do, too, I told myself. The next part of the trip would be even more tiring: Philadelphia, Baltimore, Washington. So much had already happened. We'd lost one of our trio. We'd fucked, we'd fought, we'd found other souls. And lost them, too. What would happen in the next week? And the week after that?

I was horny. I had to get off before we started out again. It was cold and people were dying and some were closed off forever – but I could still come, I could still shoot, I could still find a boy to fuck, who would fuck me.

At Prince Albert's Theater in Times Square, I found who I was looking for.

He was pretty, as I wanted him to be. Young, too. College age. He would have looked good in a suit and tie, with his hair combed back neatly instead of falling into his eyes, as it did now.

In the dark space, I couldn't see his face precisely, but enough: his features writhed every time I slipped my cock in and out of his ass. His legs were in the air, and he threw his head from side to side in rhythmic pleasure. I watched as my cock slid in and out of his tight little asshole. I marveled at the beauty of it, how perfectly we fit. Those damned Bible thumpers who claimed that the anus and the penis were not made for each other had never known this bliss, never seen how expertly this worked. I raised my face to the water-stained ceiling and moaned in deep, profound pleasure. The boy beneath me pumped his own dick in his hand.

Gently I eased him up, so that his sweet young mouth could suckle at my nipples. He lapped eagerly, like a kitten, and my chest hair became matted with his saliva. All the while I stayed inside him, fucking his silky succulent little hole. I bit his ear and his neck, feeling the gooseflesh rise all over him in cold little bumps.

Then I was ready to shoot. I wanted to see it, wanted him to see it. So I pulled out, and barely had time to peel off the condom before I came in long, stringy white spurts. The boy's eyes widened in amazement, as if he'd never seen such a thing before.

Maybe he hadn't.

Then he came himself, in a bubbly white eruption that frothed over his fingers and ran down over his fist. He took a glob of it and placed it on his lips, licking hungrily.

"Sweet thing," I said, tousling his hair, standing up to pull my pants back on.

"Hey," the kid said. "What's your name?"

"Mike," I said.

"You want to get together again?" he asked.

"I'm hitting the road tonight," I said. "I'll be back in a few weeks." Then I added: "Maybe."

He looked sad. I felt sad, too, but only for a moment. "Hey," I said. "Here. Take my number."

I handed him my card. His face brightened. "You want mine?" he asked.

"Of course," I said to him. But of course.

Now, with their numbers spread out all around me, I remember them all. Philip in Los Angeles. Teddy in Seattle. Raphael in Montreal. Earl in Boston. Chris, who I met in Philly. Miguel, who I did in D.C. Steve, the guy from Baltimore.

And I've got Emilio's number here, too, for keepsakes. And Sam's. Even Craig's, although he's still monogamous. I see the kid from Prince Albert's Theater a couple times a month. His name's Tony. I keep his number on my mirror.

There's only one number I don't have, and I think about that every time I spread them all out around me like this. I think about that, and I think about him. His soulless eyes. The life I didn't understand. And I wonder how it must be not to have any second cousins, no lines drawn from heart to heart, dick to dick.

Then I gather up my numbers, and put them away.

BODILY FLUIDS

Kerry Bashford

THE FIRST TIME I met the man his beard was crusted with cum. I never did find out whose it was. There are some things you don't ask on a first date.

By the second date it was my load he was wearing, preserved in the confused mess of his beard. When he arrived for the third date with his whiskers unwashed and still carrying the scent of my loins, I felt almost touched. It seemed an uncommon expression of commitment.

I shared this with my friend Trevor but he was not so moved.

"I think I'd prefer flowers. How can you possibly find romance in a lapse in personal hygiene?"

"Well, I know it's a bit obsessive and strange but . . ."

"Strange? Look, most of your lovers have been strange, but this guy sets new standards."

By the fourth date the man arrived, his facial hair smelling of nothing more than jojoba and lavender. I was somewhat relieved. At least he had a life outside being my cum rag. My confidence was shortlived. Stepping out of the shower after sex, I found him drying himself not with the towel I'd left on the side of the bed but with the towel I kept beneath it. I tried not to notice as he made a sham of the soap and water, stale cum foaming in sticky swirls on his abdomen.

It seemed like a helpful gesture, a little too domesticated for this stage of the relationship but generous nonetheless. He would take my laundry with him when he left, returning days later with sheets and handkerchiefs crisply folded, shirts clinging tautly from their hangers.

One day I found him at his house, sitting on the floor sorting my laundry. At least I thought he was sorting my laundry until I noticed through the half-opened door his own clothes in a disarray, his pants wrapped around his ankles, his T-shirt gathered up around his armpits. He fell back, thrashing his cock, rolling around the half sorted piles, burrowing his nose through my underpants, frantically drawing in their odours like oxygen.

I didn't know what to do. I wanted to run but I wasn't sure I should leave this man alone with my laundry a moment longer. I crept closer and, after a few discreet moments, knocked. He answered as if nothing was amiss, the washing machine buzzing innocently in the background as he muzzled his beard into mine.

He smelt like a toilet. My toilet, in fact. It was like he'd smothered himself with all my rank and filth, as if he'd been plying my underpants like a perfumed towelette. At first I felt repelled, but almost in awe of this clandestine act of devotion. What more, I wondered, could a man want than a lover who was prepared to take him at his worst? Could anything be more flattering than someone who's willing to wear your waste?

Trevor was not so sure.

"Congratulations, you've just discovered the Casanova of crotch rot. I wouldn't trust him, he'll leave you for the first grubby little groin he can sniff out. I mean, he's already committing an infidelity with your jockey shorts."

"Don't be ridiculous, he was just having some innocent fun."

"Honey, check your washing machine. Where on the spin

cycle is there any mention of self abuse? I would still prefer flowers."

When the man would open his mouth to kiss me, I sensed he wanted more. His mouth moved inside mine as if he was trying to drink me in or draw something out of me. It was not until he lay beneath me, his eyes closed and his lips apart, that I guessed what it might be. He only wanted my mouth for its moisture. At first I ignored him but his tongue tensed, stretching out further as if expecting refreshment.

I could have spat on him with force or suddenness, meeting mock humiliation with mock contempt. He would revel in that if I did. But I had come to think of him so fondly that any kind of abuse, no matter how playful or pantomime, seemed too real to me.

I soon realized that it was not the gesture but the substance that excited him. One night I let the saliva drip from the side of my mouth, holding him in anticipation until it stretched like a gossamer thread. He sighed as it splashed on his tongue, smoothing the thick resin around the edges of his mouth.

He didn't ask much of the relationship. I thought I could afford a little drool. Trevor was not so sure.

"Can't you just kiss?"

"Yes, we could. We do."

"So when you want to express affection, you just fling a bit of phlegm in his direction. Cute. Daffodils would be nice, pansies perhaps. Lilacs are in season . . ."

It didn't take me long to realize the man also had an unnatural interest in my armpits. At first this went unnoticed. As he curled on my lap and burrowed his head into my shoulder, I wasn't aware of anything more disturbing than the uncomfortable scrape of his beard on my chest.

One night in the living room, he lay as always in my lap, his face buried beneath my arms. I assumed he was snoring when his breathing became measured and heavy. Soon I realized he was in fact sniffing. It seemed a fairly innocent gesture so I cupped the back of his head and pushed his face deeper into the sweaty recess.

I discovered this was an encouragement I could not afford. His obsession gradually became the focus of our social life as he ignored any amusement other than my armpits. We could barely greet each other without him lowering his nose into my shirt to inhale. I didn't mind being objectified. I just wished it was for something other than my body odour.

During sex, it was the same. As he lapped up all the stink he could swallow, I wasn't sure what was more disconcerting – the fact that I felt secondary to my own sweat glands or the fact that it's so difficult to remain masterful when you're being tickled.

Trevor arched his eyebrow knowingly. He knew I'd done nothing about the man's illicit affair with my laundry. I decided to put a stop to it. The next time I saw the man I thanked him but suggested I look after my own underwear from then on. I took my washing to the local laundromat and watched as the sober green bag sagged dejected in the corner.

When I found him secretly pocketing a particularly rancid pair of Calvins, I realized that my underpants drawer was beginning to look a little lean. I started to become obsessive myself, hiding the garments from view, changing them at the vaguest threat of soiling, washing my genitals after every trip to the toilet.

I felt awful but I couldn't renege. I wanted this man to realize there was more to me than the mess I left in my knickers. The next time we met, I made sure I was wearing a pair of shorts so sanitary I could visit casualty without shaming my mother. As I undressed, he knelt eagerly at my groin, burying his face into my fragrant and fabric softened cock and balls.

He looked up at me like a child denied his Christmas present. I felt a remorse burn through me. Then a warm wetness formed in my lap. He watched as a jaundice stain spread across my white underpants, my cock taking shape under the clinging damp. I stroked his sodden beard as streams of piss leaked through the cotton, saturating his ecstatic face beneath.

"Chocolates would make a nice statement. Even a card," Trevor said.

He likes to fuck me with his arse. He lowers himself onto my lap, slams himself down upon my thighs, clutching my cock tightly within his. It is the only time I indulge him. I allow him this control because I like to watch him lose it.

I have become his master but we are not equal. He would sit in my shit if I suggested it, but the fact that I can often makes me feel subordinate. I can barely conceal my shock at the capacity of his body for desecration and damage. It takes nothing to inflict, everything to receive.

He has many pleasures but the greatest is when his hole is heavy with my cock. And it is a pleasure that's easy to impart. I needn't do more than sit back and watch him jerk me off with his arse.

There isn't an inch of his insides that hasn't been beaten, that hasn't been contorted beneath the weight of my thighs. When I tire of the pounding, I roll my cock around the rim of his guts, stretching them to a point that only a fist could satisfy.

If he is hungry for my cock, then he is greedy for my wrist. I can feel his muscles massage my hand, moulding themselves around the curve of my closed knuckles. Sometimes I slide my cock across my palm and I jerk off inside him. And sometimes I jerk him off with the blood from his battered behind.

Most of all I like to watch his arse explode. I know when it is about to happen and how to make it so. The walls of his arse seem to melt and it feels like I'm fucking buttery air. At that moment I withdraw and sit back, my dick dripping, while his hips go into involuntary and volcanic spasms. I spread his damp cheeks apart and watch the lips protrude like mutant petals, his arse juices erupting like an alien bud spitting out nectar.

I always did prefer flowers.

ADONIS: A Personal History of the Porn Palace

Don Shewey

> "APHRODITE SAW ADONIS *when he was born and even then loved him and decided he should be hers. She carried him to Persephone to take charge of him for her, but Persephone loved him too and would not give him back to Aphrodite, not even when the goddess went down to the Underworld to get him. Neither goddess would yield, and finally Zeus himself had to judge between them. He decided that Adonis should spend half the year with each, the autumn and winter with the Queen of the Dead; the spring and summer with the Goddess of Love and Beauty.*
>
> *"All the time he was with Aphrodite she sought only to please him. He was keen for the chase, and often she would leave her swan-drawn car, in which she was used to glide at her ease through the air, and follow him along rough woodland ways dressed like a huntress . . ."*
>
> – Edith Hamilton, *Mythology*

1

The other night I went to the Adonis for the first time. It's a huge theater, an old-fashioned glamorous movie palace with

an ornately plastered balcony and wallpapered lobby, now
gone seedy from a decade or two of unreplaced light bulbs
and neglected plumbing. Besides the seats and the back of the
balcony, fuck places include the bathrooms on the balcony,
ground, and basement floors and two curtained alcoves on
either side of the balcony lobby. Lots of looking and walking
around, not much doing. I got unthrillingly sucked off in the
john. Had one big dick in my mouth, though he didn't come.
Movies for shit.

2

My Porno Life – I've been exploring the Adonis, the New
David Cinema, the 55th St Playhouse, the Loading Zone,
Show Palace, the Glory Hole, and the Bijou. My curiosity
won't be sated until I've investigated each stop on this dirty
moviehouse circuit. However, I may die of guilt beforehand.
Words from my lover H. to the opposite effect are at once
consoling and alarming: he sets me free to follow my lust,
therefore it's all up to me. I'm addicted to this perverse quest
and can't stop it. The sensation is so rewarding of having a
fat, juicy cock filling up my mouth that I pursue it again and
again. A dyed-in-the-wool cocksucker, that's me. Constantly
turned on. I used to let people suck me off but wouldn't
want to reciprocate; somehow even kissing someone would
constitute infidelity, while the sex act remained impersonally
faithful. Now I only chase cock and save my own juices for my
lover. Should I be doing this? What if I get caught? What if I
catch the dread amoebiasis? I worry about it constantly . . .

3

Last night I went to see one act of a terrible play at the
American Place Theater. Afterwards I went to the Adonis
and saw *Sextool*, that porn classic. It really is the precursor of
Taxi Zum Klo. It has the gamut of gay life: drag, beatings, piss,
tit-piercing (I couldn't watch). Fred Halsted is so gorgeous –
a beefy Richard Gere. I watched the whole movie without
moving.

The second feature, *Sex Garage*, was a bore. I wandered around and finally up in the balcony blew a once-attractive older guy with an unremarkable cock and then another guy with a prize-winner who'd gotten hard watching. That was it, except later, in one of the curtained niches, there was a stand-up orgy centered on two tall guys with lovely meaty cocks, both of which I got a hand on for a little while. It was so cute – these two big lugs took off together . . .

4

Being unemployed and freelancing is a bore, a constant anxiety. Beating the depression is half the work. The other day I was especially down from spending the morning in the bewildering atmosphere of Sidney Lumet's movie set, where you can't sit down without being yelled at and where a five-minute chat about nothing with Paul Newman is called an interview. How do I cheer myself up? I take myself to the dirty movies to see the new Joe Gage movie *Heatstroke*, which I'd been saving until I was horny for it. This cheered me up immensely. God even rewarded me by sending my way exactly what I wanted: a curly-haired man with intelligent green eyes, movie-star cheekbones, and an immense but deliciously suckable dick.

First I went upstairs and watched the movie. It was about halfway done so I watched it until it was over. The best scene was the first, a drive-in movie where a cowboy initiates our innocent narrator to sucking cock by pulling his head down on his giant boner. Then between features they started showing a bunch of dated shorts, so I prowled. I went over to my lucky spot in the balcony on the right in the top section. Before long the aforementioned hunk trooped up the stairs, gave me the eye, went and stood behind me by the fire exit. I wasted no time in depositing my chewing gum on the railing and approaching him. He was friendly. We groped each other. He was soft but obviously huge. I quickly unzipped him and went down on my knees and took his soft prick in my mouth. It got hard soon, and for the next ten minutes or so I adored it lovingly, licking it up and down, stroking it with my spitty hand, licking his balls at his request. He had a smooth, muscular, hairy stomach which

I stroked. He moaned occasionally, and he didn't seem to be in a hurry.

The specimen in my mouth seemed like the kind of treasure you hunt in antique stores for hours and stumble across under a pile of dusty baby bibs. I wanted to inspect it with my eyes. But I always hate to pull away from sucking a good dick for even a moment. I'm afraid they'll think I've lost interest, or someone else will horn in on the action, or they'll panic or get bored and go away. So I only allowed myself a few chances to sneak a look at his dick. It was a beauty. At least ten fat inches long but maybe more, hard and taut, pointed up, not straight out at 45 degrees but up in a curve. Finally I took it all the way down my throat as far as possible. He loved that. He said, "Hold it there," but I couldn't breathe. Every time I pulled back to breathe, I went back in a little deeper. Finally with me just staying still, he came copiously. I choked and sputtered a little bit but drank all of it down. It was seven flavors of spunky heaven. In a trance I continued stroking his big squishy meat after he put it back in his underpants and then patting his ass. He had a nice meaty ass, and he was wearing very thin, soft pants so you could feel every bit of his body through it. I had the feeling he was maybe straight or from out of town or in any case didn't do this often. It was so amazing I just sat in a daze for a while, thanking the goddess.

After he came and I stood up, I nuzzled his cheek but gathered he didn't want to kiss, which was OK with me. But I wish I'd gotten his name. Just writing this makes me want to go back there in hopes of a second chance.

The rest of the evening was distinctly anticlimactic. A young black boy came and sat down next to me. I felt him up, and he seemed to have a big one so I took him over to my favorite corner and went down on it. It was very thick at the end but not so thick at the base, oddly, so when you took it in your mouth you had a mouthful but you could easily close your lips around the base. He took longer to come than I was interested in. Then he wanted to suck me, so I let him. A blond boy came up to us and was eye-ing me. I gestured to him, and he came over and got down and started sucking me at the same time as the black boy. He started to inch around as if to rim me but I wasn't into that. He started sucking and jerking me, and I came rather quickly – in his mouth, I think, but maybe just on the floor. Not very satisfying.

Then I watched the rest of the movie, the first half. I wanted to suck more cock, but there was more competition and less action at this point, and it was getting late. Suddenly I discovered a little dark room under the stairs I'd never seen before. I went in, and there was lots going on. I went down on this short white guy. He started fooling around with a black guy next to him, eventually pulled out of my mouth and drifted away. The room was pitch dark. Nothing else developed.

Earlier in one of the bathrooms there was a black guy with a hard dick pumping in his hand, and I had the choice between him and a tall white guy who walked in and took the vacant booth. I chose the latter, and it was a mistake: he wanted to suck. I figured he was tall so he must be well-hung and wanted to get sucked. He started to unbutton my vest, and I split. Later in the same bathroom I spied a balding curly-redhead stroking a big wiener inside his pants. Hot men there, not all willing to leap into action, though.

One time in my lucky section I sat down next to a guy and pulled out his fat honker and sucked him off there in the seat. He loved it and I loved it. Another time I stroked, hugged and sucked a balding redhead for a long time standing up on the opposite side of the theater. He looked on with an amused but distant grin, not interested in coming or anything, just letting it happen. Not stoned, either.

5

Yesterday was such a gorgeous preview of spring that I couldn't work, so I took myself to the Adonis to wile away the afternoon in the apprehension of cock. The movie was *Heatstroke*, which I'd seen before. The audience was mostly uglies, but in the upstairs bathroom an athletic, gorgeous black man with an immense erection was lying in wait, and I bit. I proceeded to spend 15 or 20 minutes gulping his humongous thing. It was fleshy, rather than rock hard, so I found I could take it all in, even though it was very thick. He had stripped off his pants so was wearing just gym socks and a thin yellow T-shirt. He stood up straddling the toilet, and I went down on him. After a while, the adjacent booth vacated, and he had me go in there and suck him through the glory hole – a little awkward because he was tall. We did that for a long time. He didn't come. Eventually I moved back to his stall, but then he said he needed a rest. It was the closest I've gotten to the proverbial "baby's arm holding an apple".

Later in the balcony I fiddled with and sucked another black man, a scroungy-looking guy named Tom. He didn't come, but he sucked me off, not very adeptly. Then I left.

6

I went to the Adonis at dinnertime to stimulate my waning sex drive and was amply rewarded. I had a long pleasant encounter with a sexy dark-haired boy in a T-shirt named Richard. Sitting downstairs at the very back by the door, I sucked him and played with his balls and eventually jerked him off. "There's nothing I like better than a good handjob," he said. I sucked off a chubby, not very sexy Spanish guy in the john. Then later, ready to leave, I went into the john and decided to take the empty stall and eventually landed Tom, a cute redhead I'd been exchanging interested glances with all night. He'd been getting lots of action, I noticed. We sucked each other off but with lots of playing and kissing. He had a very good hairy body, and he was in a business suit and tie and had a briefcase. But he was basically a clone – mustache, short hair, balding, cute. If I were looking, I'd go out with him more than once.

7

I've just met the perfect dick, and it was attached to a man named Kevin Keller. I felt rotten all day, just horrible, hot, depressed – vacation's over, back to work like how. So I decided I needed a porno lift. I went to MOMA to see Genet's tiny little erotic fantasy *Chant d'amour*, and then ran six blocks in the rain to the Adonis, which was hopping, as I somehow knew it would be. Quite quickly I got down on a lovely hard hard dick in the balcony belonging to a blond bespectacled blank-looking guy in shorts, which easily pulled aside to release his cock and large balls. Kevin Keller I discovered downstairs. In the dark he looked older, sort of fading, balding, maybe chubby but with a handsome face. When I sat down next to him, I quickly realized he was a total hunk – bearded, green eyes, hairy chest. He liked his nipples worked, and he had a lovely, not-too-long but thick beautiful tool with a perfect, delicious mushroom head. I worked on it for a long time but he had a cockring on and never came. He gave me a handjob and I quickly came. He leaned over and took it in his mouth but then spat it out. We sat for a while longer. I wanted to kiss and neck with him. He wasn't inclined to kiss and eventually stood up to move along. The man that got away?

The last one was Greg, who beckoned in the bathroom with a beanpole in his trousers – long and hard, also wore a cockring, also never came. He gave good head, too, but I'd already come. He had firm tits & wonderfully pliant ass.

8

I went to the Adonis yesterday. It was quite busy, good movie (*Games*, with Al Parker and Leo Ford). There was action, but I wasn't getting any. Finally, I took an empty stall in the first-floor john. One guy stood across from me staring through the crack. He didn't seem very attractive, so I ignored him at first. Then he started stroking himself through his pants, so I invited him in. He turned out to have a lovely muscular body and a hard cock, which he let me lick through his shorts but not suck. It was so gorgeous-looking I was very frustrated, even annoyed, that he wouldn't let me suck him. At one point I almost kicked him out, but I got into it. It was the first time I've had such a phobic sex partner who prohibited everything but j/o. I was sitting on the toilet, my T-shirt pulled up baring my rippled torso while he beat his meat. I finally shot a huge load across my chest, and in a few seconds he came too, thick and juicy. It was a mess, though – no toilet paper to wipe it off my shirt and chest. I wanted to chat but he rushed off. Maybe he was diseased and wanted to spare me. When I stood up to hug him and dress, I pointed to the semen on my T-shirt and said, "What am I gonna tell my mother?"

9

He felt horny, or perhaps in need of a little sexual esteem, so he went to the dirty movies, which was a mistake. It was a Tuesday, not the most lively day of the week (in fact, he sometimes thought Tuesdays were malevolent, secretly evil), and he went around seven, just past the businessman's rush. When he arrived, a movie he'd seen before and liked a lot was on but nearly over. It was about an athlete who gets injured on the way to the gay Olympics and ends up in the hospital apparently comatose. He's tended by a very cute young doctor who has the hots for his patients. The movie shows him actually carrying on with the boy who shares the star's hospital room, who doesn't look very sick when the doctor comes in, throws off the sheet, and starts sucking his cock. One of the most pleasing images is the doctor on his stomach, his ass in the air getting fucked while his face is buried in the pillow, an expression of ecstasy all over it. Later, the doctor fantasizes getting it on with the star of the show.

He had missed the best parts of that movie when he arrived and circulated through the theater, but he quickly came upon a scene as good as one in any movie. In the front row of the upper balcony one man had stripped naked and was sitting next to another man who was clothed and jerking off the naked man, who was very muscular and sexy in a conventional gay-porno way. Then the naked man crouched in front of the clothed man and went to work on his cock, expertly it seemed from the careful rhythm of his bobbing head and the apparent pleasure of the clothed man. The naked man had a broad back and wide but muscular, not flabby buttocks, and he wore work boots and wool gym socks which he rested his ass on while sucking.

Watching the two of them, he became very excited, as did others who gathered in a circle to watch. He kept his eye on another excited voyeur, a blocky blond in a denim jacket. They stood nearby, stroking themselves while watching the two men in the front row carry on quite uninhibitedly. Finally, the naked man and the clothed man sat back and jerked themselves off. It was spectacular, just like in the movies, with great gobs of flying cum. The naked man came several large gobs onto his knee and the floor; the clothed man directed his ejaculation toward the naked man's torso. They seemed very happy and for the next hour continued to neck in the theater. He was so hot watching them – he'd tried to get involved, but was pushed away, no third parties allowed – that he pursued the denim jacket until they settled in a dark corner. When the denim jacket started sucking him, he came almost immediately. The denim jacket didn't want reciprocal satisfaction and walked away. He felt ridiculous to have released his pent-up sexual energy so soon.

By now the movie had changed to a dreary cheap film set in a succession of undisguised hotel rooms. Though he spent nearly an hour trying to drum up some oral action in the theater, the crowd had thinned. He left feeling worse than he had when he arrived. He had made no connection but had inhaled the rancid smell of the porno moviehouse, a stale stench of toilet disinfectant and amyl nitrate. He vowed that he would not succumb to this temptation again, a vow that would surely be broken in a month, or a year, on another afternoon when he felt horny or in need of sexual self-esteem.

10

It was a lovely afternoon, a tiny bit breezy. I walked to the Adonis. The movie's gone up to six dollars. The theater was relatively busy – business as normal, AIDS or no AIDS. I didn't witness much action, and when I thought about it, I realized that for all the wolfish prowling not an awful lot does go on at the Adonis most of the time. Except for me; I insist. I started off as usual, watching the movie from the balcony, but the second feature was on, *Malibu Days – Big Bear Nights*, one of those skinny-boys-with-big-dicks-fuck-each-other movies. So I got bored very quickly. I wanted to see the main feature, *Job Site*, because I assumed it was about construction workers, but it turned out to be a crude silly thing about a male brothel. Anyway, the aisles were full (not full – a trickle) of prowlers. A Hispanic-looking guy sat down next to me. We took our dicks out and played with them a little. He had a very loose foreskin (I had the feeling I'd encountered this dick at another moviehouse before), but he got up and left before long. A black-haired fellow smoking a cigarette sat down two seats away, and finished his cigarette with stealthy glances at me. Finally he moved over. We felt each other up. His dick was pretty small, his hair was very sprayed, possibly a wig, he sort of turned me off, but I idly went along. He bent over to blow me, and he had such a silky smooth mouth that I was ready to come in about a minute. I made him stop, but my orgasm had already begun. Some leaked out, some I choked back. I lost my erection, but he gobbled my dick for another five minutes before I stopped him. He was very sweet, spoke with a foreign accent, and wore designer jeans.

Then I walked around, checked out the johns, and settled on an older guy, whom I followed around a bit. He didn't seem to pay any attention. When I saw how duddy *Job Site* was, I was ready to leave. I took a last spin, and I locked eyes with another older man, short with white-blond butch haircut. He came right over and stood next to me. I couldn't tell from his baggy shirt (in the dim light) whether he was a troll or a doll. As I watched four skinny legs and two skinny dicks flail against each other on the screen, I thought, "Should I go along with this, or should I just leave?" The impulse to leave was strong – my half-orgasm with the pompadour had almost entirely sapped my sex drive. On the other hand, I hadn't gotten what makes me happier than anything else in the world – a big hard dick in my mouth.

So I went for this guy's crotch, and he grabbed my hand, and we stood there holding hands like teenagers. I finally turned to him and croaked "How ya doin'?" He said, "What?" The usual witty openers. He wanted to sit down, so we sat down and, as if at dinner, went to work. He felt my body all over: my stomach, chest, dick, balls. He had a muscular-going-to-pot body like J.'s, not bad, big nipples, OK dick. He was very cuddly, so we nuzzled, kissing chastely, no tongues. I went to take his cock in my mouth, and he said, "Let's just use our hands." He told me he liked "hot talk," and I told him I wasn't very good at it. He said he'd love to be naked in bed with me (I wouldn't have minded), and he'd like to have me shoot all over his stomach. He also notified me that he didn't have very much time because he had to meet some people. So I told him I wanted to make him come – his dick got very hard as I jerked it, pinching his tits, biting his earlobe, and he came before too long. He asked me if I wanted to come. I said not really. We exchanged names – his is Phil. He was a bit coy about particulars; said he lives in the West Eighties. He asked if I wanted to meet again. I said I lived with someone; he also has a boyfriend. I figured if I run into him on the street, it's OK, if not, also OK. He seemed a bit crestfallen, but there we were. I left right after him.

11

Today is the eighth anniversary of my relationship with my lover. I celebrated by going to the Adonis for the first time in maybe two years. Very busy on a rainy Friday afternoon. In the balcony the first thing I noticed was a bunch of people standing around a guy on his knees sucking someone off. I felt shocked and disturbed – don't they know what danger they're in? Still it was sort of exciting to be a part of this taboo scene. A pretty Spanish boy with a big dick came on to me. I played with him, he didn't get too hard, I did, he wanted to suck my cock, but I didn't feel comfortable letting him. I cruised around for a while, and a scruffy-looking guy kept cruising me and finally started groping me. He had a big dick and was sweet and tender. We sat down and eventually pulled our pants down and played with each other's dicks. He was very careful, he took my dick all the way in his mouth but only for a second to get it wet. His dick was cut but with a very loose skin. He got very hot and close to shooting very quickly. We took turns a couple of times, and then he pulled up his shirt while I jerked his cock till he shot all over his stomach. It was beautiful. But quickly after that I lost my erection, so I didn't come – partly because a fat, crazy queen sat down next to me and started touching me, which turned me off. And in general sitting there in the theater, site of many lovely exciting sexcapades in the past, I felt queasy, particularly observing guys sucking cock all over the theater – something I long to do indiscriminately but firmly feel would be disastrous healthwise. I know that I'm not comfortable anymore having sex with total strangers – I feel on guard and incapable of the spontaneity of great sex.

12

I went to the Adonis Saturday afternoon – things were hopping. The theater was in serious decline: the movies had changed from projected films to projected video (terrible quality, practically devoid of color), the balcony had been closed off, and besides the safe sex sign at the door there was a sign about the presence of policemen on hand to arrest people using or selling drugs. The weird thing about all this is that it has made the subtext of going to the Adonis (for sex) the text, since going to see movies was out of the question. Up and down the side aisles were dozens of men – black, white, and Hispanic – sitting in seats sucking each other off. The center section, more well-lit (though still dimly) from the screen, was deserted. I cased the joint once, then zeroed in on a dark-haired big-eyed fellow who looked like Eric Bogosian. We stood next to each other at the back of the theater. He groped my hardening cock. I played with his butt. I suggested we find a corner; he led me to a seat. He took out his dick – uncut with a loose skin – and with his hand on my neck indicated he wanted me to suck it. I weighed that back and forth, licked his balls, talked some dirty talk with him, then went down on his cock. After three good gulps, he was ready to shoot – pulled his foreskin closed and held it, though he did halfway come (not in my mouth). After a while I resumed sucking his balls extensively, which he liked. A crowd gathered to watch. After a while he stopped and said he had to pee. His name was Steve; we parted in a friendly manner.

I walked around. One studious but handsome guy trailed me a lot. I watched one lad very expressively fucking another guy's mouth down front; the sucker kept stopping to spit out huge gobs – he did it several times, so I assume it wasn't come.

On a stroll I locked eyes with a handsome balding redhead and followed him upstairs. He made a phone call; I stared at him from outside the booth, and he took out his dick. When he got out of the booth, we gravitated to a corner. I played with his dick, he with mine, but he really wanted me to suck him. He was a little rude about it, and he had a smaller-than-average dick. But he had a muscular body, and I played with his tits. He pulled my pants down and played with my ass. He wanted to go somewhere and fuck – or have me "work on" his tool, his mighty sword. But I had an hour to get home, change, and go out with my lover H. His name was Ted, he said, and he lived on 36th Street He went off to check with his roommate that it was OK to go to their place. He said, "If I'm not back in five minutes, it's not OK." I took that to mean he didn't care one way or the other. I calculated it would be a 15-minute fuck at best, so I just left the theater.

13

I went to the walk-in bereavement group at GMHC, mostly to get pointers on visiting the parents of someone who'd died. No one had anything helpful to say at all. Afterwards, to reward myself with life affirmation, I went to the Adonis, which was really hopping. I had to pee, so I immediately went to the john. All the stalls were taken and a lot of commotion was taking place in one. After I peed, I went to look. In the far stall a naked guy was on his knees being forcefully face-fucked by a guy in cutoffs, who was wearing a rubber. Just in front of the stall, two guys watching had gotten so hot they started, too – the mustachioed one on his knees, sucking off a young guy in blue shorts with a shapely very hard dick. He was very interested in me so I stood there playing with his tits and his butt while he was being blown. This went on for a while and got to be quite a scene, drawing a crowd. Eventually I realized I was violating my vow not to have sex in bathrooms, so I wandered away.

I fooled around some with several other people, watching a fairly good Al Parker video. But I never came, so I left horny. I saved it for J., and we had hot sex that night.

14

Horny these days, looking for good sex to make me alert, to ground me in the moment, to give me something to look forward to. No luck recently. Friday sundown spin through the park a bust; the gym no fun. Yesterday afternoon I went to the Adonis, which was crawling, but it was disgusting and dispiriting: hot, smelly, bad films, bad projection, ugly guys made uglier from desperation, lots of street people just trying to stay off the street.

15

I visited the new Adonis Theater for the first time yesterday. The old one is clearly scheduled for demolition; the whole block is boarded up. The new location is at 44th and 8th in what used to be the Cameo. It's much smaller, but clean and neat and in good shape. It has a balcony, which I like, and the men's room is downstairs from the main floor. I went at five p.m. on Friday, to see what the after work crowd is like – as expected, lots of older men in raincoats, suits, and briefcases. Lots of blowjob action in the seats. Very soon after I settled down in the balcony I got to playing with a cute, curly-haired, slightly dissipated Jewish accountant from the Bronx (he now lives in Queens) named Stuart. We played with each other's dicks, he sucked mine, but his was leaky so I didn't want it in my mouth. He wasted no time in pulling his pants down to his ankles and unbuttoning his shirt to the neck. He had a thick dick, average length, big balls. One of his nipples was divided so it's like there were two on one side. He mostly wanted to kiss and clamped his open wet mouth over mine, but I didn't want to swap spit – he was a little too eager. Feeling his butt, I noticed he had a dry scabby section just above his coccyx – probably from doing situps on a hard floor (H. sometimes gets this). He kept telling me how beautiful I was, and when I would respond with the obligatory reciprocal compliment, he would visibly glow as a result.

This went on for a little over an hour which made me eventually bored and tense. I always like to see what else is going on and check out the movies. At first I didn't want to exchange life histories, but I'm glad we did. I figured he was an other-boroughs kind of guy with a non-gay lifestyle. He said something about problems, to the effect that "Being gay is my only problem." I asked him why it was a problem for him. He said because it wasn't accepted in society, because relationships don't last, because of drug problems, etc. He admitted that straights have many of the same problems but regretted that he couldn't walk down the street holding a boyfriend's hand. He said he was bad at picking boyfriends – one turned out to be a suicidal alcoholic, another a minister who was always too busy to see him.

Since we were sitting right on the aisle with our dicks out (I didn't take off anything), a lot of people stopped to watch – unattractive, lonely older guys. But I saw one guy, a graying bespectacled older black man, sucking off a big hunky cock in the front row of the balcony. I saw it all in silhouette. Funny, isn't it? Any blowjob in reality is more riveting to watch than any on the screen.

"One sad day Aphrodite happened not to be with Adonis and he tracked down a mighty boar. With his hunting dogs he brought the beast to bay. He hurled his spear at it, but he only wounded it, and before he could spring away, the boar mad with pain rushed at him and gored him with its great tusks. Aphrodite in her winged car high over the earth heard her lover's groan and flew to him. He was softly breathing his life away, the dark blood flowing down his skin of snow and his eyes growing heavy and dim. She kissed him, but Adonis knew not that she kissed him as he died. Cruel as his wound was, the wound in her heart was deeper. She spoke to him, although she knew he could not hear her: –

> *You die, O thrice desired,*
> *And my desire has flown like a dream.*
> *Gone with you is the girdle of my beauty,*
> *But I myself must live who am a goddess*
> *And may not follow you.*
> *Kiss me yet once again, the last, long kiss,*
> *Until I draw your soul within my lips*
> *And drink down all your love.*

"*The mountains all were calling and the oak trees answering,*

    Oh, woe, woe for Adonis. He is dead.
    And Echo cried in answer, Oh, woe, woe for Adonis.
    And all the Loves wept for him and all the Muses too.

"*But down in the black underworld Adonis could not hear them, nor see the crimson flower that sprang up where each drop of his blood had stained the earth.*"

PETER AND THE DRUNK

Andrew Holleran

HE WAS ALL alone in the park when Peter saw him – sitting on the picnic bench where usually old men sat on the weekends playing cards and gambling. It was a Tuesday night and it was very late when Peter, fatigued from a proof-reading shift at a midtown law firm and several long dull hours in a couple of bars after that, entered the park. Drifting home in a state of dejection and ennui, he noticed the man seated in the southeast corner of Stuyvesant Square singing. He had black curly hair, glasses with black frames, wore navy polyester pants, a blue short-sleeved shirt and tennis sneakers. In his right hand was a bottle of beer. He was singing "Ya no estás más amilado, corazón."

He did not look like one of the queens who cruised this park – he did not look homosexual. He looked like one of the young Puerto Ricans who lived with their families on streets to the east. Peter stared at him from a safe, noncommittal distance for some time – the two of them the only inhabitants of the park at four-thirty on a Tuesday night in the middle of July – before he made an important discovery: the man's penis was protruding from his fly. It was not a large penis but Peter didn't care. He sat down on the adjacent picnic table. The man hoisted his bottle of beer in salute. Peter walked over. The stranger had a friendly, open, cheerful expression on his handsome face. He seemed about 22; a drunk who had strayed into the park on his way home from some party or bar. He stood up and held out a pack of cigarettes toward Peter, but then lurched forward so suddenly the cigarettes all fell out onto the ground. Then his knees buckled and he sat down, like a marionette, as Peter knelt on the ground and began picking up the cigarettes. "Forget it," the man said, but Peter finished his task and inserted all the cigarettes into the pack, as the man said: "I gotta get home, my wife will kill me. I was with my friends, you know, we started to drink. You want some beer?"

Peter shook his head. About some things he was not shy. He said: "I want you."

At this the man's head jerked down so that he was looking at his penis. Peter was not sure if this indicated assent, or shock, at realizing he had forgotten to close his fly after urinating in the flowerbed. Peter knelt down again nevertheless and took it in his mouth as the man put his head back and guzzled some more beer. Then he said, "It gets bigger."

"I'm sure it does," said Peter, standing up. "Why don't we go down the street to my apartment? It's just seven blocks south, it'll be more comfortable there."

The man rose and lurched into forward motion and, once underway, tilted forward, so that Peter had to hurry to keep up with him, as if there was a wind at their backs pushing them along. Neither of them spoke. It was a cool night for July. The seven blocks down Second Avenue were deserted; they might have been the sole inhabitants of the city. When they reached his apartment, he lighted five candles and set them on the table in the front room, then took his bottle of poppers out of the refrigerator and set it on the table beside the candles. The drunken stranger lay down on the low bed beside the table – stretched out as if upon an altar, the flames of the candles reflected in his glasses. Peter liked men with glasses. He unbuckled the belt, unbuttoned the pants, gently moved them down to the stranger's ankles, and then pushed the underpants down. The penis bobbed on its thatch of pubic hair. There was a cool breeze stealing under the windowpanes in the back room, moving through the apartment to the windows on the airwell. The moon floated, a slender scimitar of silver in the sky behind the building, so bright the water tower stood out in detail on the adjacent roof. A woman sat at one tall lighted window of the building behind his smoking a cigarette. It was the holy hour – cool and late; it was the peace that lay beneath all things. He took the penis in his mouth and sucked it with little effect except to turn it on its side. But Peter was a patient man. He unscrewed the top on the bottle of poppers, carefully inhaled the fumes, screwed the cap back, and reapplied himself to the task at hand. The only thing that tinged the joy he felt at finding his deepest dream realized was the suspicion, as he knelt there on the hard wooden floor beside the supine stranger, that his visitor was asleep. *I am having sex with a corpse*, Peter thought as he raised his head, letting the penis slip out of his mouth, and looked at his guest.

"Man," the stranger moaned, lifting his head up and simultaneously taking his penis in hand and giving it a shake. "When this happens with my wife – she slaps me."

"She *slaps* you?" said Peter, shocked.

"She don't fool around," the stranger said. "She don't got no patience with this shit." He shook his penis back and forth as he continued to look down at it, and Peter moved a pillow over behind his visitor's head.

"Is it that she thinks you don't desire her?" said Peter, whose curiosity about life equalled his lust. "That you no longer love her?" By the time he finished the sentence the man was snoring. Peter looked at his face with a certain sympathy, a certain tenderness. He hadn't, Peter could tell, a mean bone in his body. He was one of those good-natured people who would live till the end of their days with an unimpeachable cheerfulness. He was just a nice guy. He wondered what the wife was like, and why she took it as a personal affront when he did not get an erection. No doubt because it reflected on her own sexual charisma. And because the world depended on this magical occurrence, he reminded himself as he stared at the penis; unless blood rushed into its capillaries, unless the member engorged, insemination would not occur, and consequently Life. Perhaps that was the source of the slap. He travelled down the smooth white torso with his lips a centimeter above the flesh until he found himself face-to-penis again, and there he paused to contemplate the darling member: the source of Life, the only organ which changes shape, the amazing appendage on which everything (Peter's, the wife's, pleasure) rested. What a burden, when you stopped to think about it; one he himself had excused himself from years ago. *Oh, let me do what the wife could not*, he thought, then picked up his bottle of poppers, inhaled, and took the penis in his mouth while the warm exciting rush spread throughout his head and chest.

Then he climbed onto the mattress and lay down beside his visitor to examine him in the candlelight: the soft blue shirt unbuttoned to reveal the smooth white chest with just a dusting of black hair across the chest and nipples, the solid thighs, the beautiful point at which the trunk joined the pelvis, the Greek muscle so exaggerated on the statues at the Met, where he loved to linger. Suddenly the stranger made a gurgling sound, lifted his head, rolled over on top of Peter and began to hump him, until, exhausted by the brief effort, the river of Lethe flooded his form and he went limp on top of his host. "Is it because your wife thinks you no longer desire her?" Peter said again. "That you are sleeping with someone else?" But he received no answer. He lay quietly under the dead weight of this handsome husband for a few moments, then gently turned him over by raising himself up on his elbows, and got up off the bed. This woke the visitor. His hand went down to grasp his penis and shake it back and forth, as a man who has just urinated removes the last drops. At that instant a heavy object – a body – thudded against the wall of the next apartment. The couple next door – a construction worker who came in at odd hours and his waitress wife – were fighting. The noise brought the cat out of the back room, which walked slowly over to Peter and his guest and stopped beside them. Peter looked across the white penis at the cat looking at him. The candle flames gleamed on the surface of her eyes. She meowed. He meowed back. The voices next door rose, then subsided. Then Peter lowered his face to the penis and took it in his mouth.

Perhaps this is best, he thought. With someone who's asleep there is no competition or anxiety or failure to communicate, no wondering what it is the other really wants, no feeling one has to bring things to a climax, no sense that one is only at an audition. Sex with someone asleep is sex outside of time and human limitations. He licked the penis gently, as the cat came close, put her nose delicately to Peter's face and sniffed the air around his lips, drawing back abruptly when he bobbed too close to her own whiskers. At this Peter stopped, the penis still in his mouth, and looked at the cat. The cat, a Russian Blue with a beautiful grave face, stared at Peter with an inquiring expression he had come to recognize, an air of curiosity equal to his own. It said: What are you doing? "It's not a mouse, Emma" he said. "It's a penis." Then he sniffed the poppers, and resumed slurping. Another body thudded against the wall. The cat began to lick Peter's forearm, then bit his flesh with a series of quick, brief bites, and then finally settled into a rhythmic blend of both activities, which constituted nursing, as the cat's throat began to throb like the motor of a water fountain late at night: a deep and powerful purr. The world was joined. The cat was in the magic circle, the great chain of being. While the man threw his wife against the wall, or she threw him, the cat sucked on Peter and Peter sucked on the drunk. Only the drunk had nothing in his mouth. Only he lay outside the world as Peter's saliva began to festoon his pubic hair in gluey strands, and glisten on the surface of his groin. *What every house needs*, Peter thought as he bobbed up and down, *is a penis. You need a refrigerator, a fan for hot nights, a stove, a shower, and a penis. That's about it. You didn't really need furniture, and you didn't have to have a telephone, in fact you were probably better off without one, but you need a penis.*

This was a penis and nothing more; the person connected to it might as well have been dead – and it made Peter feel vaguely necrophiliac as he soldiered on, pausing now and then to survey the supine, inert form. Nevertheless, he was grateful to have this man in the apartment – two people from different worlds joined together in the dead calm of a summer night. It was like having a mermaid in one's bed. The sea of New York City had tossed him improbably up, as it always did if you were patient, and tomorrow would take him back down to its depths. The man was married. He had simply strayed over the line momentarily into this other world, and tomorrow, hung-over, he would go back – back to his set of young Puerto-Rican couples who went to Jones Beach (the heterosexual section), barbecued, played boom boxes very loud and went dancing afterwards at clubs he, Peter, had never heard of, in the Bronx. Exotic creature! He would not have him for very long, he realized as the air outside the window began to change its hue, and he wondered if he should ejaculate onto the smooth flat stomach and give up on the man's participation. No, that was silly, he decided; like drinking alone. At which point his dilemma was solved by the cat licking the man's face with its rough tongue; the man awoke with a snort and raised his head. "Why does she slap you?" said Peter. "Is it because she thinks you no longer desire her?"

He yawned and said: "Because she wants to have sex." He reached down, grasped his penis and shook it violently.

"Don't worry," said Peter.

"I gotta worry," he said. "I got a wife."

"Have you been married very long?" said Peter.

"Two years," said the visitor. "She just got a job as a nurse's aide, so our hours are different. She don't go dancin' with me no more."

"Where do you dance?" said Peter.

"At this club on King Street," he said. "I don't know the name. Just a red door. This guy who sells me my drugs runs it. He knows my wife."

"You do drugs?" said Peter.

"Yeah," he said. "But now it's different with my wife since she has to work the next day. She does some poppers now but nothin' else."

"She does *poppers*?" Peter said.

"Yeah," said the visitor. "I saw you sniffin'."

Still, thought Peter, *it's OK for us, but straight people shouldn't use them. We're supposed to be decadent, but they're supposed to be . . . parents.*

"She doesn't do 'em so much now," the visitor said. "She is calming down, you know? But I still like, you know, to just go out, sometimes, and fool around."

There was a silence and then Peter said: "That's *all* I do is fool around. And frankly – it gets tiring after a while. After a while you get tired of going out."

"I know," said the visitor. "Like I wish right now I had not, you know?" He closed his eyes and lay back again.

"Your wife slaps you because you don't get hard," said Peter, "but gay people don't even have to slap you. They just put on their clothes and leave, and don't give you their phone number. That's the slap. Gay people can be very critical too. There's no pleasing some of them at all."

"Well, I would like to please you," the visitor said.

"That's all right," said Peter.

"I would like to give you a nice time," he said.

"Don't worry," said Peter.

"But I think I drank too much," he said.

"No problem," said Peter, reaching for a baby carrot in the bag on the table and putting it in his mouth. "Carrot?" he said to his guest. "No, thanks," said the visitor. Peter finished eating the carrot as he stared into space, and then he said: "A friend who used to live in this apartment once said to me, 'A man is the size of his cock.'"

"That's right, that's right. And it better get big. Otherwise – " he said, "your wife slaps you."

"No one slaps me," said Peter.

"You don't have nobody special?" said the visitor.

"No," said Peter.

"Why not?" he said.

"I don't know," said Peter with a sigh. "Sometimes I think it's New York. It's too easy to keep on moving in this city, you know? There are so many people to pick up – like you. In gay life you need a penis that brings people to a *halt*. That says: This is it. Go no further. You'll never find bigger. When are you moving in? How do you like your eggs in the morning?" He looked at his visitor. "How do you?"

"I don't eat eggs," he said. "I got cholesterol." He put a hand over his face and moaned. "I gotta get down to the store and open the register. What time is it?" he said as the room brightened around them.

"Five forty-five," said Peter. "What store is that?"

"Confetti, on Court Street," said his guest. "We sell, you know, confetti and hats, horns for parties. Basic party toys."

"That's what your penis is," said Peter. "A basic party toy. It's perfect."

"How can you tell?"

"Gay people can read penises very well," said Peter. "We don't have to see them hard to know just what they're like. And I'm certain too that you are a very nice person."

"Thanks man," said the guest. "I mean, a man is not just his dick."

"I'm afraid you're wrong – at least in the circles I run in," Peter said as his guest sat up and began to button his shirt. Then he raised his right arm and smelled the pit. Then he stood up – Peter always hated this moment; the ship was sailing, the men were climbing the rigging – and put his pants up and buckled his belt. The room was light now, the cat sat on the radiator waiting for Peter to pull back the window-gate so she could go out onto the fire escape and watch pigeons. "Would you like to take a shower, or have coffee?" said Peter. "No, I gotta go," said the visitor. "My boss is worse than my wife." He went to the door and held out his hand. "Thanks man, sorry I was so wasted," said the guest. "No problem," said Peter. It was one of those encounters, he realized, when sex was not important; when something else had been given in its place. "Just go all the way to the bottom," he said, as he opened the door, "and turn right." The man went into the hall, and pushed the glasses up his nose.

"By the way," said Peter, attempting to retain some fragment of this person he would probably never see again in his entire life, "Where are you from originally?"

"Ponce, Puerto Rico," said the man, and disappeared around the corner.

A lovely colonial city, Peter thought as he closed the door on his echoing footsteps, *in which the women slap the men for not getting hard. No wonder there are more Puerto-Ricans in New York City alone than on the entire island – that's why*! He opened the window gate to let the cat out and stared at the pale blue and pink sky behind the water tower. Something holy and wonderful had happened: two lives, so very different, had touched. Two men had been kind to one another. Two strangers had met, like the soldiers in the Iliad, on the field of battle and told each other their stories. Hours later, that night, he was walking home again quite late through the park after yet another dinner with friends whose conversation was so familiar, so stale, at this point, that only the memory of the angel God had given him the previous night made him think there was any point in remaining in New York, when he noticed some dark figures standing beneath the trees as he glanced in through the wrought-iron fence. They were all staring at the same thing: There on the picnic bench sat a young man, a bottle of beer in his hand, singing "Ya no estás más amilado, corazón!"

DO AS THE ROMANS DO

Steven Saylor
writing as Aaron Travis

"THE IMPORTANT THING to keep in mind," Simon said, "is that all Italian men are obtainable. All of them."

On the word *all*, Simon suddenly flung both hands up in a wide arc, as if he were trying to embrace the whole world – or at least that part of it containing Italian men. If I'd been standing any closer, he'd have knocked me down.

Simon had always been the melodramatic type; two years of living and studying in Rome had made him even more so. He had always talked with his hands; now they became virtual deadly weapons every time he opened his mouth. I was learning to keep my distance.

Simon and I had been roommates in college. In those days we'd shared everything – plans, dreams, expenses, boyfriends. Life after graduation drew us apart; I hadn't seen him for five years. Now we were together again. I was several thousand miles from home, suffering a bad case of jet lag and culture shock. Simon was in his element and eager to show it off, waking me early every morning and dragging me still half-asleep from his room in the boarding house on Via Palestro to begin another day of discoveries in Rome.

I couldn't have asked for a better host. Simon knew everything about ancient Greek and Roman art (his specialty), spoke fluent Italian (with his hands as well as his mouth), and always knew just what to order in every restaurant. Simon knew a Rome that only natives know and that I could never have found on my own, wandering through the narrow, winding cobblestone streets.

Equal to any other tourist attraction – as Simon was quick to point out – were the men. Simon had raved about them in letters. I now saw why. From the moment I landed at Da Vinci I was thrown into a constant state of heat – not from the blistering August sun, but from being surrounded by such an overwhelming abundance of masculine beauty. At times Rome seemed to be a city populated exclusively by young male models, all of them lean and impeccably groomed, dark and broodingly handsome.

At night the streets were their promenade. Women seemed to vanish – mothers and married women had no business being out, Simon explained; single girls did not go out alone. This left the streets to the young men, of whom there seemed to be an unending supply. Roman boys, I discovered, love to dress up, to show off and swagger, to watch and be watched by each other. None of them seemed the least bit shy about making eye contact – a smouldering, check-it-out kind of macho glare: defiant, cocksure, mysterious.

Nor were they afraid to touch one another. There is no sight in Rome quite as thrilling as that of two young Italians strolling down the street in a public embrace. Not just casually holding hands or with arms slung across each other's shoulders – instead, the older and larger cradles his arm protectively around his partner's shoulder, lightly clutching his hand, practically cooing in his ear. ("Not quite what you think," Simon had explained, laughing at my bug-eyed stare. "Country boys from the south. Traditional bonding. In a few years they'll both be married, with a house full of screaming Italian brats.")

Which was not to say that Italian men were necessarily, as Simon would say, "unobtainable." In the neighborhood around Via Palestro, Simon seemed to be on suspiciously friendly terms with almost every young man we passed – waiters, shop boys, students. Seeing us approach they would smile, wave, bark a friendly "*ciao*." Once around the corner Simon would lean toward me and talk dirty with his hands, spreading his palms apart: six inches, seven, eight. I would shake my head and jab him in the ribs, not believing a bit of it.

After all, we were in the very heart of the most Catholic country on earth. Impossible, I told myself, that Simon could have known all these beautiful, tight-bodied, curly-headed hunks in a biblical fashion.

"*All* of them," Simon was saying again. I automatically ducked. His arm-waving was purely semantic; at the moment there were no discernible Italians nearby to be included in his sweeping embrace, only a hoard of foreign tourists. This was my eighth day in Rome, the morning that Simon had reserved for the Vatican museums.

In what must have been record time, we had already seen the Sistine Chapel, the Raphael loggias, the Borgia suites. Simon sped me through at a breakneck clip; Simon had little use for Christian art. It was the pagan collections, where we were now headed, that drew him like a magnet.

"All of them?" I said, raising an eyebrow. "I suppose you're speaking from personal experience?"

"Actually, Steven, yes. Though I'm sure they prefer to have sex with each other. With their own kind, you know, rather than a foreigner like you or me. It's part of their culture. No puritan hang-ups, like back in the States. Italian boys are horny as goats all the time – I don't know, it's their Latin genes or something, maybe the heat. Who wouldn't be hot, living in Rome? Italian men are the most beautiful on earth."

I was inclined to agree. "But so macho – "

"*Molto maschio*, indeed," he said. "*Molto gagliardio*. How they love Sylvester Stallone!"

"I mean, I can hardly imagine them . . ."

"Oh, can't you? You see, up to a certain point the girls are simply inaccessible. No sex before marriage – no birth control, no abortion, you understand? And after marriage, where's the mystery? So a young man at the peak of his sexual prowess can either masturbate until he's blind, or use a prostitute – awfully expensive with Italian inflation – or he can simply do what comes naturally and share with his buddies. Believe me, all the guys you've seen under twenty-five are sticking it in to each other, constantly."

"You're saying it's a phase they go through."

"No, just a natural, inexpensive way of having fun. Most of them aren't consciously gay. They don't think of it as sex. Recreation. Friendly relief. Cheap thrills."

"Sounds like sex to me. And I'll bet it sounds like sex to the Pope, too. Or haven't these pious Italian boys gotten the latest word about what they may and may not do with their dicks?"

Simon made a hand gesture so bizarre and disparaging it must have been native Italian. "*Fa!* The Romans get as pissed off at the Pope as everybody else. Maybe more so – he's not even Italian! And why do you think he bothers to issue those anti-gay broadsides, anyway? Where there's smoke, there's fire, eh?"

"Simon, please. We *are* in Vatican City at the moment."

"Ummm. So, Steven – have you scored yet?"

"Simon, between jet lag and five pounds of pasta a day and you running me ragged – "

"Yes, I haven't given you much time alone, have I? And it can be hard for the casual tourist. Me, they trust – I speak Italian, I've been living on the same street for two years. Don't worry. You've got another week to go. Watch your step."

We descended a marble stairway, passed through a wide vestibule, walked down another flight of steps. The crowd thinned. The temperature dropped from sweltering to balmy. Someday the Italians will discover air conditioning.

We entered a wide, long gallery with a high vaulted ceiling and a checkerboard marble floor. Tall, narrow windows flooded the room with beams of mote-filled sunlight amid patches of deep shadow. Set against the plaster walls, extending hundreds of feet into the distance, were more marble statues than I had ever seen in one place before.

The entire wing, except for its population of gods, demigods, fauns and heroes, was virtually deserted. There was only one other visitor in the room, a young Italian standing near the entrance, his hands clasped in front of him, gazing up at a statue of Hercules in combat with a centaur. As we passed, he turned his head, caught my eye and then looked quickly away.

"Beautiful!" I whispered. The word was involuntary, like a gasp or a heartbeat. And he was: smooth olive skin, a long graceful nose, sensuously molded lips, deep brown eyes, all framed by a mass of jet-black curls. Not a day over 19, with a slight but solid build beneath his loose cotton shirt and tailored brown slacks – the epitome of every beautiful Italian boy I had seen during the last week.

I followed Simon, feeling shaky. Why is beauty so painful? A single glance had been enough to knock the wind out of me. I looked over my shoulder. The young Italian was across the room now, his back turned, staring at a frieze of Roman soldiers in combat. The outline of his ass inside his slacks took my breath away. I said it again: "Beautiful."

"Yes, isn't he?" Simon sighed – but he wasn't looking at the Italian boy. In fact, he seemed not to have noticed him at all. Instead, Simon was standing with his arms folded, gazing up at a statue of a nude young Apollo. He slowly circled the pedestal, then reached out, cupped his hand around one of the statue's sleekly moulded buns and trailed his fingers up to the dimples in the small of Apollo's back.

I glanced nervously behind us, and caught the Italian boy looking quickly away. "Simon, don't. You can't touch these things. They'll kick us out!"

Simon laughed. "Don't be silly. This isn't New York or Paris. This is Rome, and Rome is an old whore who's seen it all, where every good-looking ass is fair game. Even the ass of Apollo. Besides, what do you think these statues were made for in the first place? To be worshipped."

I looked around again. The Italian boy was definitely watching us. Our eyes locked for an instant, then he went back to studying the frieze, or pretending to, clasping his hands behind his back and shifting from foot to foot.

When I turned back, Simon had walked on to the next statue, a muscular Hercules, nude except for a lion skin slung over his shoulders, the paws crossed over his chest and resting atop each sublimely muscled pectoral. Simon was balanced on one foot, one hand on Hercules' thigh, leaning around to get a better look at the statue's ass. He slid his fingers upward, cupping the sleek marble buns in the hollow of his hand as if he were weighing them.

Simon's eyes were narrowed, his brows drawn together in an expression of muted ecstasy. "*Mama mia*, what an ass! Really, you should try it, Steven. You like asses, don't you? Believe me, they don't come any more perfect than this."

"I wouldn't be too sure of that, Simon." The Italian boy was standing with his back turned – allowing me another look at the buttocks straining taut and round against the seat of his pants. He glanced over his shoulder. Our eyes snagged for an instant, then we both looked away. "Look, Simon, you're making me nervous. Maybe we'd better head back to the religious art."

"But this *is* religious art. I mean, you can bow down to a Madonna if you want, Steven, but I'd much rather bow down to this." He was referring to a monumental statue of Jupiter, just across from the Hercules. Larger than life, lofty-browed, one hand raised and the other holding a scepter, the father of Olympus was seated naked in his throne except for a rather skimpy loincloth draped across his lap. Jupiter was even more massively built than Hercules – immensely broad across the shoulders with wide, flat pectorals and thickly muscled limbs.

"Doesn't it take your breath away? Even more amazing, when you think that they sculpted these from living models." Simon slowly circled the statue, gazing up at it in genuine awe. Since Jupiter was seated, there was no way Simon could cop a feel of the god's ass; he settled instead for a lingering caress of each of the thickly corded calves.

"You know what the Greeks said, Steven – man is the measure of all things. The Romans took them up on it. This is how they invested their highest aspirations, their loftiest passions – celebrating the glorious perfection of the male physique. Here it is, right in front of you, in this very room. The highest beauty imaginable – the ideal male form."

I looked around, and thought for a moment that the Italian boy had disappeared – until I spotted him standing half-hidden behind a monumental bronze Mercury. He was staring straight at me.

Simon, meanwhile, had moved beyond Jupiter, to a statue

of Antinous. "The emperor Hadrian's beautiful young lover," he was saying. "After he drowned in the Nile, Hadrian made him a god – as if he wasn't one already. Oh, that Hadrian knew how to pick them. This is the other side of Rome, Steven, still as strong today as anything that came afterward. The side that recognizes beauty, and worships pleasure . . ."

The Italian boy was biting his lip, raising his eyebrows, looking both nervous and determined. Deceptively innocent. Irresistibly inviting. Simon's voice receded behind me as I stared back into the boy's eyes and began to step toward him.

Beside the statue of Mercury, there was a small door recessed into the wall and hidden in shadow. How it happened to be unlocked I'll never know. Perhaps the Italian boy could have told me, had I spoken Italian, or had he known any English. All I know is that when I stepped around the statue he was waiting for me, and then suddenly pulling me through the door. It closed behind us. He reached toward it. I heard a click.

It was a small, dark, musty room, ventilated and lit by a metal grating set high in one wall; a storage closet of some sort, lined with shelves cluttered with odd bits of marble and bronze, fragments of broken sculptures. A naked light bulb hung from the ceiling; I never found the switch.

His hands were on my chest, his lips on my neck. He grabbed my hand and guided it into his shirt, somehow already unbuttoned. My fingertips made contact with the taut, silky flesh around his nipple. He shivered and I felt his breath, warm and gasping, against my neck.

He was electric, surrounded by a kind of static charge – pure ozone. Or maybe the charge came from me, all the erotic energy that had been building up inside me since the day of my arrival, abruptly released.

The shirt slid over his shoulders and dropped to the floor. The faint light shone over the firm, sleek definition of his chest and abdomen, casting the cleft between his pectorals into deeper shadow, highlighting his nipples with a lustrous sheen. I bent down and licked his chest, dragging my tongue from nipple to collarbone, dabbing into the hollow at the base of his throat, feeling the vibration of his groan against the tip of my tongue. I leaned back and stared down at the glistening track of saliva trailing across his dark, satin flesh.

His eyes were bright in the darkness, his lips smooth and glossy. I pulled him toward me, ran my hands over his warm shoulders, down the silky furrow of his back, onto his buttocks, firm and full inside his pants. He was busy with his hands, opening my shirt, unbuttoning his pants and mine, pushing them down around our hips, until suddenly my naked chest was pressed against his and my hands were filled with his smooth naked ass, as perfect as the polished marble ass of Apollo and infinitely more supple. At the same time I felt his cock pressing warm and solid alongside my own, jabbing at my thigh and sliding upright against my groin. I reached for it, keeping one hand on his ass – a warm, sturdy mallet of flesh, unexpectedly thick, his foreskin making it slippery and elusive in my hand.

From somewhere far away I thought I heard Simon calling my name, his voice baffled and a little perturbed. Then another voice, my own, saying: *You must be out of your mind – don't you know where you are?* In Rome. In the Vatican Museum. In a dark and musty closet, with a Roman boy who at that very moment was sliding onto his knees and taking my cock in his mouth . . .

I threw my head back and my pelvis forward, pulled cock-first into a hungry and devouring ecstasy. I cradled his head lightly, letting it rock back and forth, feeling the tight, crisp curls brush and tickle the palms of my hands.

He brought me close, but I wasn't ready and neither was he. I pulled him back to his feet and clutched him close, grinding him into me with my hands planted firmly on his ass. The kind of ass that makes your heart skip a beat and your stomach knot up in desire – he was hard, lean and muscular everywhere, not a hair on his body, slick and smooth as silk; but it was his ass that took my breath away. For days afterwards I had only to shape my hands in the air to feel it again.

I spun him around, knelt behind him, cupped and fondled his ass in my hands. I ran my tongue up his flanks, over flesh taut with muscle and smoother than marble. I lapped at the dimples in the small of his back, nuzzled each solid globe of muscle, traced my tongue along the contours at the base of each cheek where buttocks melted into thighs without a crease.

He was pulling me up then, onto my feet, drawing me into him, a vacuum demanding to be filled. I bit my lip, shook my head. If only we had the time. If only I had a condom – and then I reached down and felt it, deep in the pocket I never use. There since I left the States, neglected, forgotten, like a teenager's mad money hidden away. I quickly pulled it out, fumbled with the foil, slid it over my cock, and then slid deep inside him, swallowed by clutching warmth. He welcomed me with a satisfied gasp, and in the darkness I could almost see the sparks dancing off his sweat-shimmered back.

He left without speaking a word, only giving me a tender kiss as he hurriedly put on his clothes, and then an oddly bashful smile as he opened the door and closed it silently behind him. I buttoned my shirt, pulled up my pants, found a piece of rag to wipe my warm, sticky fingers. The condom was lost somewhere on the floor. I smiled, wondering who would find it and what they would think, and stepped into the gallery. Simon was nowhere to be seen.

As I headed toward the stairs, I passed a group of monsignors, resplendent in their robes, chattering in Italian, gesturing with their hands. Despite their scandalized frowns, I couldn't resist reaching up and giving a farewell caress to the polished marble ass of Apollo – in deference to Simon's brash encouragement; in memory of an Italian youth whose name I would never know but whose beauty I would never forget.

LEARNING HOW TO CRAWL

Tony Ayres

NEVER CALL YOUR mother a cunt. Well, not to her face, anyway.

Mum and I were going through a bad patch. This was partly because she refused to accept that her baby boy was growing up. But it was also partly because she found the stash of porn hidden under the lining of my sock drawer. I guess it was my own fault for not finding a sneakier hiding place. But, truth be told, short of digging a hole in the neighbour's backyard, there was not a square inch in the house safe from my nosy mum.

According to her, 22 wasn't too old for a good wallop. She chased me around the sofa with her favourite silver-plated hairbrush, the one with my butt impressed upon its shiny enamel embossing. I ran out the door, hands protecting my head. From experience I knew she couldn't match me on the open road.

There was no point going back until the Serapax kicked in so I decided to kill some time at the park. The park was a significant place for me, a sacred site. It was where I discovered one of life's great joys – in the far cubicle of the toilet block with a so-called "jogger". Afterwards, he asked me if the school uniform was for real. I couldn't answer because I was also discovering one of life's great dilemmas – swallow or spit? In my final year at high school, the park became my favourite playground, which pleased Mum no end.

"You need to spend more time outside. Not all the time watching TV."

Of course, everyone's got to grow up. Or at least move on when the cops start patrolling. In recent years, the park has been about as thrilling as a Tracy Chapman concert. The more discerning gents have shifted their allegiences to a toilet block near the Richmond Cricket Ground. Hardly anyone went to the park anymore. But there were exceptions.

Like that morning, while I was at the urinal, catching up on the local news scribed at reading height next to the cistern:

Horny sucker swallows it deep. Leave time and place.

Big cock, 10 inches, 8 p.m., 2/11

4/11 Sorry I missed you, you sound like my kind of man

Big cock, meet here 8 p.m., 17/11

18/11 No good for me, can you make it earlier?

19/11 How about tonight?

20/11 Got your message too late. Tomorrow?

20/11 Sure. What time?

22/11 Sorry, couldn't make it . . .

It read like the script of a Meg Ryan movie. I was about to zip up and leave when this young guy walked in. There was something familiar about him. Maybe it was his leather jacket, an old biker jacket with patches and badges all over. I'd seen one just like it in *The Face*. He wasn't so bad himself. My age, maybe a bit few years older. Crew cut. Three earrings up the right ear. Ring through the left eyebrow. Big nose – good sign.

I hung around to see if he liked Chinamen or not. Wth the feral guys you could never tell. Sometimes they looked at you with interest, sometimes they didn't. It depended on which way the wind was blowing. This guy was looking, alright. He was standing beside me at the urinal, having a really close inspection.

"Simon?"

I tucked my dick back into my jeans as I turned.

"Robert?"

I knew Robert from high school. He was the brother of my best friend, Benny. Benny and me used to terrorize the younger boys together. Steal their lunch money. Stick their heads in the toilets. Kids stuff. I hadn't seen Benny since I said the "H" word. I didn't think it would upset him because of the number of times we'd wanked off together. But I was wrong. Some guys are sensitive that way.

Anyway, that was how I first met Robert. No wonder I didn't recognize him. Four years ago, he wore thick black glasses, had greasy long hair and spent all day in front of his computer. That was before Courtney Love gave him a make over.

Robert had a boofy smirk plastered over his face.

"I didn't know you were a poofter, Simon."

"You should have asked Benny."

Robert scowled.

"He's a cunt."

We continued our reunion outside. Robert pulled out a thin little joint as we walked.

"Want some?"

He offered it without waiting for an answer. Out of politeness, I took a long toke and spun out before the smoke left my lungs.

"Good stuff, huh?"

"Yeah . . ." I croaked.

"I got more at my place if you want . . ."

There was the hint of a grin on his lips. I couldn't tell what he was really offering, but it seemed more attractive than mum's hair brush. We headed towards his car. I took another drag on the joint and my legs went wobbly as if the lawn had turned into a quicksand. Oh well, never mind.

We arrived at Robert's vehicle, a clapped-out, faded bronze 1976 Mazda 323. It was a ridiculous vehicle for a grungy skinhead. I managed not to giggle by biting down on the inside of both cheeks at once, a trick I had learnt at my Auntie Winnie's wedding when she and Uncle Peter made their own vows.

As we drove, Robert was bobbing his head up and down like he was wearing an invisible Walkman, a bright, vacant smile on his face. Not comfortable with silence, I tried to make conversation.

"How's Benny?"

"Who cares?"

Robert cleared his throat and spat out the window.

"What about your mum? How's she going?"

"Don't know."

To shut me up, Robert turned on the radio and twiddled the knob till he found a sign of life. It was a Hits and Memories station. Elaine Page wailed Andy Lloyd Webber. Robert apologized.

"I don't get FM."

This didn't concern me as much as the bus which was looming head on towards us. In attending to the radio, Robert had let the Mazda drift careless towards the oncoming traffic. At the last minute, he veered to safety, only to slam on the brakes to avoid running into a pedestrian at a crossing. He barely flinched.

"Hey, I love this song."

It was Air Supply, "Love and Other Bruises". He sang along in a shrill falsetto at the top of his voice, sounding like Olivia Newton John at the proctologist.

By the time we reached Punt Rd, we had had several near-death experiences, swerving at the last minute past trams, right-hand turners and irate cyclists. I remembered how thick Robert's glasses used to be, and my palms started to sweat. Fortunately we pulled into the front of his house before I had a full coronary.

It was a rundown terrace in Windsor. When Robert unlocked the front door I expected to be greeted by a swarm of rats. Instead, we entered a refined hallway painted in pale grey with framed Herb Ritts posters on the walls. In the living room, there was a porcelain lamp in the shape of a harlequin and a black leather three-seater sofa. Maybe Robert had become a hairdresser since I saw him last? He beamed proudly.

"My flatmate's doing it up."

Robert lived with Frank and Angelo. Frank worked for Qantas, though Robert assured me that he wasn't a trolley dolly. "He's a systems analyst. Gets paid a fortune." Robert raved about Frank. They met at a bar six months ago. Frank took Robert home for a threesome with him and Angelo. After a while, the sex fizzled but they remained the best of friends. Frank was helping Robert till he found a place of his own.

"Great, huh?"

I nodded politely, staring in disbelief at the foot-high ceramic replica of Michelangelo's David in a frilly red gingham apron on the mantelpiece.

"Wanna drink?"

Robert poured two Bailey's Irish Creams into pink crystal tumblers at the customized white vinyl bar.

"You ever had this stuff? It's like a milkshake."

Actually it tasted like the medicine they gave you when you got an ulcer. I swallowed half a bottle of Mum's once in the hope that it would do something more exciting than loosen my bowels.

Robert directed me into a leather armchair and sat cross legged on the floor opposite. I was glad that he was making the moves because quite frankly, I was out of my depth. Up to this point, my relationships had primarily been conducted in the upright position, crammed into a toilet cubicle or side by side at the pissoir. Whilst I considered myself an expert in the art of avoiding cum stains when you zip up, I was a novice when it came to the more refined details of seduction.

Opening a pink porcelain pig on the coffee table – the mull jar – Robert rolled another joint. I was already close to hallucinating but accepted nevertheless. The Chinese hate to lose face even when off theirs.

"You got a boyfriend, Simon?"

"No,"

"Me neither."

Robert stared at me through heavy glazed eyes.

"You ever had a boyfriend?"

"No,"

"Me neither."

He jumped up like he'd been hot-wired, turned on the CD and played a Frankie Knuckles mix, real loud. Spinning towards me like an out-of-control top, he signalled for me to join him on the vertical. The prospect was too scary.

"No way."

He tried to hoik me to my feet. Instead, he toppled forward and landed in my lap. His face was only centimetres from mine. I fell as well, not onto the floor, but into the hypnotic depths of his pale blue eyes. Our breathing was slow, like anchors dragging against the furious white water of the music.

Then he was up again, a jack rabbit. An evil leer crossed his lips.

"Wanna see something?"

He lead me by the hand down the corridor. I followed, will-less and floating. At the rear of the house, next to the kitchen was a locked door. Robert, on his tiptoes, fumbled above the door frame for the key.

The walls were painted black and there was black plastic covering the floor. In the middle of the room, in the pride of place, was a leather sling hanging from heavy rings drilled into the ceiling. Lining the wall next to the door were open shelves which housed a menagerie of pink rubber. On the far wall, hanging off hooks, was a display of whips, riding crops and paddles.

"Amazing, huh?"

Actually, amazing wasn't quite what I was experiencing. I didn't know whether it was the gunja or the episode of Oprah where they interviewed Jeffrey Dahmer's neighbours, but a chill of apprehension travelled up my spine. Robert used to do very strange experiments with insects, if I remembered rightly. And then there was that guinea pig he tried to teach to fly. Mum's hairbrush was not looking like such a bad option after all . . .

In the meantime, Robert was fizzing like a shaken-up can of Coke.

"Frank's still doing it up. He wants to buy a set of wooden stocks next."

He pressed a switch on the wall and the overhead bulb was

replaced by a bloody red glow. In this light Robert's features took on a sinister angularity. I felt like Laura Palmer (not an unattractive simile, to tell the truth). My mind whirred, orchestrating an exit which would not ignite the axe murderer's fury. I wished that I hadn't had that second joint.

Robert picked up a cone-shaped object from the shelf. There were several of them, in order of ascending scale.

"You ever used one of these?"

"Sure," I bluffed, eyeing the door.

"Which one?"

I pointed at random. Robert was dumbfounded, "Amazing." I had inadvertently chosen the second largest. He stared at the rubber cone, then at me. Then he cracked up, a manic cackle like Bob from *Twin Peaks*.

"You're shitting me . . ."

I didn't answer. As soon as he turned his back, I was planning to run.

"This is the best I can do." He picked up the second smallest, "Frank says it takes practice, but I read somewhere it's got something to do with your natural hip girth . . ."

This nature/nurture argument would have been the perfect cover for an exit, but unfortunately, my idiot curiosity tripped me up.

"So what is it, then?"

"A butt plug."

"Yeah?"

"You stick it up your ass."

"Fuck off."

"No bull!" He pointed to the narrowing at the bottom of the cone which widened into a flat base. "Your sphincter muscle grips it here and it stays in. It feels fantastic. You can wear it around for hours. Great for dinner parties. I got one in now. Wanna see?"

"No way."

Robert cackled again. "Fell for it!"

He grabbed the plug I had indicated.

"Frank can get this up him. You should see it. His arsehole opens up like a flower."

"Why would you want to?"

"It's the challenge. You know, like climbing Everest from the inside."

I was aswirl with conflicting emotions. Part of me felt like a poddy calf trapped in an abbatoir. Another part wanted to slide to the floor and bury my face in Robert's crotch. I made an executive decision. Discretion was the better part of valour.

"I got to get going, Robert. I promised Mum I'd help her cook."

A dark cloud passed over his face. Convinced that there was violence in those eyes, I searched for potential weapons. The biggest butt plug was two feet away. If worse came to worse, I could conk him on the head with that.

"What's wrong? Aren't you into this stuff?"

"It's interesting. Honest. But Mum'll chop me into little pieces if I'm late."

Woops, Freudian slip.

"You don't want another joint?"

I shook my head, edging around him. There was a clear line between me and the door.

"Another drink?"

"No . . ."

My escape would have come off without a hitch if Robert hadn't chosen that moment to throw himself at me. Despite innumerable late night viewings of *Ten Rillington Place*, I found myself reciprocating. The way I figured it, a cold-blooded murderer couldn't have a cock as fat as the one I felt shoved up against my thigh.

Robert fumbled at his belt buckle and wriggled his jeans down. I tore off his jacket, and lifted his T-shirt. His torso was skinny and pale, left nipple pierced. I licked down his body from nipple to navel and knelt before his hooded cock, peeling it back like a ripe banana.

"Er . . . yuk!"

There was a rank smell emanating from under his foreskin, the head coated in worms of dick cheese.

"What's wrong?"

"Your dick is foul."

He looked down at me, embarrassed, his cheeks blushing. He mumbled. "I thought guys got turned on by cock cheese."

"It's like the Kraft factory down here. Go and wash it. Go on."

Obediently, Robert pulled his pants up halfway and waddled towards the bathroom. I watched the dimples of his skinny white arse as he went.

Left alone, I turned the overhead bulb back on and inspected this homemade chamber of horrors. It wasn't so scary when you took a closer look. All the shackles were lined with lambs' wool, the handcuffs were the cheap magic-shop variety and the paddles doubled up as ping-pong bats. I inspected the butt plugs, trying to imagine one of those things up my tight Oriental browneye. Ouch!

Robert returned, zipped up and sheepish. He smelt of Palmolive. We got back to it.

Cleared of the grunge, his dick was beautiful. Velvety and smooth. He especially liked it when I licked his balls and tickled the silver ring at the base of his scrotum with my tongue. He tried to get me to tongue his arse but I resisted, not trusting what I might find. If the front was anything to go by . . .

We were lying on the black plastic floor, him on the bottom, me on top. He'd swung me around so that we could 69. Then he strained his neck forward and poked his tongue up my crack. I must have jumped a million miles. I didn't know it was so sensitive back there. He grabbed me back down by the thighs and shovelled his face into my arse cheeks, grunting and snorting. His tongue penetrated me. I gave up trying to suck him and instead pushed back harder into his face, which sent him over the edge. He wanked his cock furiously and spattered a load over his stomach and my chest. I tobogganed down his torso then leant back and sat on his face again. I felt like a space shuttle about to take off. Ten, nine, eight, seven, six . . . Lift off! I exploded into the stratosphere.

Robert wiped up our cum with his T-shirt. I lay next to him, exhausted and spent, my legs like jelly.

"I've never done that before."

"What?"

"When you licked my bum."

"Wild, isn't it? You're not supposed to because of germs but I couldn't resist."

"It's like owning a doberman."

He ran his finger along the line of my thigh, over the round of my arse. He touched his finger against my saturated arsehole, pushing against the unyielding bud.

"You've never been fucked, have you Simon?"

"Nup."

Robert was incredulous.

"Jesus, a virgin . . ." His expression became beatific. "It's the best thing in the world, man. Better than dancing all night on eccie, or a Big Mac when you're really stoned. You feel so . . . I don't know . . . so complete . . . It's the best . . ."

He whispered into my ear, soft as lamb's breath.

"Next time, let me fuck you, Simon. I want to be the first. I'll take care of you, promise. It'll be fantastic. Will you let me?"

I didn't get a chance to answer because we were rudely interrupted by an electronic beep. Robert fumbled around his jeans' pocket, selfconsciously.

"Shit! . . . Frank makes me use this because I keep forgetting."

He turned off the beeper and opened a small tobacco tin filled with blue and white pills. He swallowed one of each.

"What are they for?"

"Drugs I have to take . . ."

I was too polite to ask more. Or maybe I didn't want to know. Robert looked troubled, though.

"There's something I should tell you, Simon."

He didn't need to say it. His expression said everything.

"I'm HIV positive."

Robert put on a big phony grin. This time it was his turn to bluff.

"It doesn't matter, does it? . . ."

"No, of course not."

"Some guys freak out about it."

"No, it's fine by me."

The edges of Robert's smile began to sag. For once, he seemed at a loss for words. I should have been grateful but I was too busy trying to remember if there was cum on his finger when he touched my asshole, whether I had a paper cut on mine, whether I swallowed his precum . . .

We sat in silence. I was trying to think of something to say but everything I could think of sounded like the season's finale to *Home and Away*. Finally, he broke the impasse.

"I'll drive you home."

I remembered the trip over, and my voice cracked in panic. "No!" Then calmer, ". . . I feel like the walk."

Robert was blushing again, this time a deeper shade of crimson.

"I was gonna tell you . . ."

"It doesn't matter. I've had sex with lots of positive guys." I sounded as convincing as Elton John on his wedding day.

"Everything we did was safe."

"Yeah, yeah, I know."

All I could think was, "I gotta get outta here". He saw me to the door, still naked. His skin was white as ivory and for the first time I realized just how beautiful he was. I resisted the urge to run. He jotted his number on a piece of paper.

"Call me, Simon."

"Yeah sure . . . You're Simon."

I looked at my watch as if I was really late. Robert watched from the doorway as I ran down the street. A block away, I slowed to a walk.

I'd told Robert the truth. I had promised mum I'd help her cook. She had invited Auntie Poong and her only daughter Precious over for tea. In spite of the overwhelming weight of evidence indicating that her son was a flaming homosexual, my mother still had hopes of marrying me off to a nice Chinese girl. Not that Precious was your typical China doll. She was a foul-tempered creature the size of a giant panda who would undoubtedly remain single forever. But Mum and Auntie Poong loved an excuse for a gossip, and Precious and I got on famously, so we all keep the pretence bubbling along.

I hurried past the living room and headed straight for the bathroom. I was in no mood to deal with Mum's whinging. Over the basin, I pulled my jeans to my knees and washed my cock. Then I worked on my tail end, scrubbing furiously at the crack of my ass till it was raw. I had read enough to know that this was entirely superstition but it made me feel better.

In the midst of my purging, the door opened. It was Auntie Poong who had never been afflicted with the Western habit of knocking. She took one look at what I was doing and slammed the door shut without a word.

I joined the others at the table. Auntie Poong was red as a slab of barbecued pork. Mum acted like she was pleased to see me. (The Serapax must have kicked in.) Precious looked like a dugong surrounded by hungry Eskimos.

Mum force fed me her famous sweet dumplings. For some reason she thought that Precious and I were more likely to hitch up if we were roughly the same size. This was almost impossible because on most occasions Precious would match me dumpling for dumpling and pull away in the home straight, consuming two to my one. Normally, I made a better fist of keeping up, but that night, I had no appetite. Auntie Poong watched her daughter's pigheaded eating, moaning with each mouthful.

"Look at her. She does this to humiliate me. Soon she'll be so big we won't be able to leave the house. Who ever saw a Chinese girl this big?"

"She's a healthy girl. Look how strong she is. She'll be worth two wives to a lucky husband." Mum was staring pointedly at me.

"She's the size of two wives! Ai-ya! If someone would take her off my hands, I would give them every cent I own. Every cent!" Auntie Poong was also staring pointedly at me.

Neither Precious or I gave a sign of response. We knew better than to encourage them. Soon enough the ladies lost interest in us and retired to the balcony to gossip about Mrs Feh, the pretty young wife of a powerful neighbourhood mogul. Our local Anne Nicole Smith. Once they had gone, Precious lost interest in food, proving my theory that she spent so much time with her mouth full to avoid speaking to her mother. She noticed my mood.

"What's wrong with you?"

"Nothing."

"You look like someone shat in your lunchbox."

"Don't give me a hard time, Precious."

"I was just trying to be considerate. Fuck off then, you touchy little slope."

Precious was prone to these outbursts. True to form, she continued the conversation without dropping a stitch.

"Mum's been buying all these books about bulimia. She hopes that I get some ideas."

"Why don't you tell her to mind her own business?"

"I scream at her, 'It's genetic. If you weren't so *fat*, then I wouldn't be so *fat*! It's your fault.' That shuts her up for about 15 seconds."

"Maybe we should get married, Precious. That'd give them a shock."

"They'd both have heart attacks, and we could collect the insurance."

"I'm serious. We could set up a flat together. Get some peace and quiet. We wouldn't have to eat rice every night."

Precious rolled her eyes. "You've been watching *The Wedding Banquet* again, haven't you, Simon?"

"Fuck off"

"If we got married, they'd move in with us, stupid. We'd have both of them at us, 24 hours a day. I'd rather kill myself."

The tone of her voice changed.

"Anyway, I can't marry you. I'm in love."

I tried not to look incredulous.

"Who with?"

"Johnny Spiros."

My jaw dropped. Johnny Spiros was the greengrocer's son. A star athlete at our school. Totally gorgeous. A fucking God.

"Yeah, I know, I can't believe it either. But he's got this thing for Asian girls. Big Asian girls. It's this *perversion* of his. And like, how many fat Chinese girls do we know? I feel like I've just won the lottery. I never realized that being someone else's perversion could make you so happy."

"How come you haven't told your mum? It'd get her off my back."

"No way. She hates Greeks."

It still didn't compute but I wasn't going to say anything. I'd never seen Precious smile like that before – without a sneer. It wasn't up to me to spoil it. Her news didn't make me feel any better, though. I mean, if even Precious could get a boyfriend . . .

"What about you? You seeing anyone, Simon?"

"No way."

For the next few weeks, I avoided the park. I was too busy getting on with life. You know, going to the dole office, watching Ricki and Phil and Oprah, reading *Who Weekly*, driving mum up the wall. She used her influence in the yumcha set to get me a try out at a Chinese restaurant. My brilliant new career almost went bung on the first night when I dropped a bowl of chilli beef on this guy's head but for some reason they gave me another chance.

With me working, Mum was cheerier than she'd been since the death of Chairman Mao. She thought I finally had prospects, even if it involved slaving for $5.00 an hour with the restaurant keeping 50 per cent of my tips. She'd probably have me work for nothing if it meant getting me out of the flat. Personally, I didn't mind the distraction. It was only one night and one day a week (Mr Feh refused to give me more). And my appetite for the park had taken a dint after the Robert episode. Maybe a change wasn't such a bad thing.

As long as the restaurant didn't distract me from my real vocation, *Chang the Invincible*. This was the underground comic I self-published once a month. *Chang* was a cult classic sold around independent record stores and comic book shops throughout the inner city with a current circulation of around 250. It told the true-life adventures of a young Chinese poofter living in a housing commission flat in Richmond. Life on the edge, you know, inspired by the Hernandez Brothers' "Love and Rockets". Of course it was purely fictional. Like Episode 11, where Chang got fucked for the first time by a skinny white skinhead, Robbie.

I had just returned home with the said masterpiece, hot off the press, clutched to my bosom, when I heard two voices and realized that mum had a visitor. A male visitor. This was as rare as the appearance of Brigadoon. I was flabbergasted to see who it was. Perched on the sofa with a cup of tea balanced on his knee, dressed in tiny black cut off denim shorts, blundstones and skimpy white string singlet, was my old mate, Robert.

Mum greeted me tight-lipped. Obviously, she hadn't had a chance to reach for the happy pills.

"Your friend come to visit."

Robert grinned wickedly.

"I got your address from Benny. He sends his regards."

I was at a loss for words. Mum's gaze shifted from Robert to me and back again. He turned on the charm.

"I was just telling your mum what a nice cup of tea she makes. And these biscuits are just gorgeous. They've got peanuts in them, haven't they?"

Wearing a grin fixed with Araldite, Mum addressed me in Cantonese.

"He smells like the bottom of the rubbish bin. Is this the kind of no-brain you went to school with? No wonder you learn nothing."

Robert nodded affably, not understanding a word. As he spreads his knees I could see his left testicle squeezed out the bottom of his shorts. I decided that enough was enough.

"Come on, Robert, let's go for a walk. See ya later, Mum."

"Nice to meet you Mrs Chang. I hope to see you again sometime. Maybe you could write down the recipe for these biscuits for me."

I grabbed my bag and whisked him away before he offered to show her his piercings. The intensity of Mum's parting glare was like a magnifying glass in the sun on my back.

Outside, I cuffed the little turn on the head.

"Dickhead."

Impervious to insult, Robert bounced around like he was on fire.

"I thought you'd be glad to see me."

"Listen Robert. I've got a lot happening at the moment. I don't want any complications."

"Your Mum says you're a lazy good-for-nothing."

I had learnt not to take offense at mum's indiscriminate public betrayals. It was just her way of making conversation. I walked ahead, angrily. Robert was persistent.

"Listen, I went to a lot of trouble getting your address. I had to call home eight times before Benny answered. Then the little cunt hung up on me. So I sent this fax to his work."

He unfolded a photocopy of his ass. Across the bottom was scrawled the warning threat. "If you don't send the address, I'm turning over . . . PS – it's hard!"

I imagined it arriving at Benny's garage, him surrounded by his beer-swilling mates. In spite of myself, I smiled. Then Robert's tone became serious.

"I wanted to tell you . . . I just wanted to say. Just because of what happened . . . You know, we don't have to . . . you know . . . we could just be friends."

The way he sounded, the way he looked, I could tell it really mattered to him. The same thought occured to me as before. He was really beautiful.

"All right."

"Yeah?"

"Yeah."

Neither of us had anywhere particular to go so we walked through the neighbouring suburbs which became progressively leafier and greener. This was where the rich people lived. Usually I steered clear because nature made me scratchy but on this particular afternoon it felt like the right thing to do. Robert accentuated the picturesque mood by running a coin along the duco of the parked Mercedes and BMWs as we passed.

He took on that chirpy tone again. His eyes were bright and shining. I felt like I was chatting to Alvin the chipmunk.

"How come you haven't got a husband, Simon? A pretty boy like you."

"I never met the right guy."

Truth be told, most of my past relationships had lasted about seven minutes. After that (as they were pulling up their pants) they would start talking. "Oh, where were you born? You speak well for an Oriental. I've just come back from a holiday in Bangkok . . ."

Robert told me about his own chequered history. He'd lied about never having a boyfriend. He's had about forty.

"I didn't want you to think I was some kind of slut."

"Which you are."

"Yeah, but I've never been with anyone who didn't fuck me over. Frank says it's because I'm into being emotionally abused. I set up situations where people use me. Which is why the whole s/m thing is so good for me. I play out my masochism in this ritual way so I don't have to do it in my relationships anymore. It's incredibly empowering."

"You should be on Oprah."

Robert punched me on the arm again. Something told me that he liked doing that.

"Who are you to talk, you fucking *virgin*. Twenty-two and never been fucked. That must be some kind of record."

I took Robert to my favourite place, "Red's Comic Book Shop". It specialized in the obscure and grotesque, just like Red himself. Red was this oddly shaped 40-year-old hippie who spent most of his time stoned out of his skull. He would make a lot more money if he took down his "Shoplifters Welcome" sign.

I took Robert on a lecture tour of the independent comic world, stopping at milestone works such as Alan Moore's *Miracle Man*, Frank Miller's *Hard Boiled*, Howard Chaykin's *Big Black Kiss*, and my favourite, the Hernandez brother's *Love and Rockets*. I described the essential struggle between the valiant independent publishers such as Dark Horse who battled the evil empires of Image, Marvel, and DC in a vain attempt to stop them flooding the market with their mindnumbing drivel.

"How's it hanging, Simon?" Red addressed me from the counter, swaying in time to "Everything but the Girl". "When are we going to see Issue 11?"

Red was my number one fan. I handed him the mint print from my bag. Robert was puzzled. Red pointed out the previous episode of *Chang the Invincible* sitting in place of pride on the counter.

"This is you?"

I nodded, pleased.

"A published author."

Red flicked through the comic.

"Beautiful work, Simon, I think we'll sell out this issue."

Robert picked one up as well. He stopped at the page where Chang got fucked. He looked up at me, a sad, sweet expression on his face. I half expected him to declare his love, but instead he asked Red where the toilet was. A minute later, he came back with a bulge in his right pocket.

"Phew, that's better. It was beginning to chafe."

I couldn't believe what I was hearing.

"You visited my mum wearing a buttplug?"

Robert was defensive. "Well, I didn't know if anyone was gonna be home . . ."

This time, I punched him in the arm. He looked at me, as if daring me to do it again.

"You wanna punish me?"

"In your dreams."

We were back on the street. It was twilight, a cold blue grey light tinted the neighbourhood. Robert led us towards a gay bar at the fag end of town.

"I said I'd meet Frank and Angelo at the Cockpit. Come on, you'll love them."

"I hate gay bars."

On the rare occasion that I'd visited, I'd either been totally ignored, assaulted by UFOs (Ugly Fat Old) or eyed suspiciously by silly little Asian boys who run around all night quoting *Absolutely Fabulous*. Patsy and Edina were at the top of the list of my pet hates. Closely followed by Kylie, Madonna, the Petshop Boys, Sandra Bernhardt, drag queens in any shape or form, CK One, tans, pectorals, washboard abs.

"The Cockpit's different."

"How?"

"Find out for yourself."

He pulled me close to him. We were walking arm in arm. I'd never done that with a boy before. I was beginning to be swayed. What was I rushing home to anyway? 90210 was just repeats.

"You sure you want me to come?"

"Frank wants to meet you. I told him all about you."

"I don't know . . ."

In response, Robert kissed me. Long and hard.

The Cockpit was a converted Spanish restaurant which, in spite of the machismo makeover, still resembled a hacienda. Even though it was early, there were quite a few stray cowpokes come in for a graze. I realized why the Cockpit was different to your regular gay bar – we were the youngest guys there by at least two decades. Robert reached into his left pocket and pulled out a studded armband, which he clipped onto his right arm with a wink.

"Image is everything."

This made me conscious of my own attire, the baggy shorts and oversized Mambo T-shirt. Robert headed for two guys, decked out head to toe in leather. He greeted the first man with an exaggerated hug, like they had fought in Vietnam together. Frank was old enough for that. He was in his late forties, ginger beard and fine, plucked eyebrows. Robert had neglected to warn me that Frank was a dwarf. Not technically I suppose. He was about five foot two, but looked smaller because he'd spent a lifetime at the gym compensating for lack of height with increased breadth. The end result was that in his leather shirt and pants he looked like a shiny black cube.

Robert hugged the other fellow, a tall skinny, pockmarked Italian man in his early thirties. He was wearing a leather vest and no shirt. No chest either. This was Angelo.

Robert introduced me. Frank shook my hand with a firm grip.

"Pleasure to meet you, Simon. Any friend of our Robert, is a friend of ours . . ."

Angelo nodded. He was sniffing and his nose was red, like he'd been crying. He got out his hankie and blew loudly.

"I've got shocking hayfever."

Frank chastised him. "You should have worn a shirt."

"It's hayfever, not a cold, all right?"

Someone puts his arm around Robert and lifted him into the air. A handsome man in his late thirties with a black beard. He tongue-kissed Robert forcefully. Robert pulled himself away and introduced me.

"Simon, this is Duane."

Duane gave me one of those looks I've gotten used to in gay bars, automatically assigning me to his peripheral vision. He turned his attention to Robert.

"How's it going, Tiger? When you going to come and visit?" Duane rested his big mitt on Robert's butt and kept it there.

"You'll have to wait your turn, Daddy," said Robert playfully.

"Daddy doesn't like to be kept waiting."

Obviously Robert was a crowd favourite. Another pair, Lex and Colin, joined the gang. They were in their mid-forties, overweight and squeezed into black rubber like two packets of tightly packaged donuts. They squealed upon seeing young Robert who was passed around the group like a toy poodle. They took turns patting and pinching him. He lapped it up. Meanwhile, I clung to the edge of the group like Casper the friendly Ghost.

Angelo whispered to me.

"My boots are killing me. I've been rubbing Dubbin into them all week and the leather hasn't softened at all."

"I thought you guys got aroused by pain."

"Darling, bunions are not a turn on."

Colin had overheard us. "You put them in front of a heater?"

"Doesn't that dry them out?"

"Oh no, just the opposite, it opens up all the pores . . ." I was not up to an in-depth discussion about the care and upkeep of leatherware so I distracted myself at the pinball machine. As I struggled to keep the ball in play, a whisky voice tickled the nape of my neck.

"You're a good player."

It was Frank, pressed up against me so that his crotch pressed my thigh.

"Thanks."

"Games can be a lot of fun, can't they?"

"Yeah."

"You know, what happens between two people is a game, too. You set the rules and the boundaries."

There was a compelling intensity to Frank's voice. The second ball went whizzing down the side alley.

"Shit!"

"Robert says you didn't like our little play room."

"I didn't say that."

"Let yourself go, Simon. You'd make a beautiful slave if you'd only learn to relax."

I felt a gloved hand brush my bum. I jumped, startled. The last ball flashed down the centre lane. Game over.

I interrupted Robert who was laughing girlishly at one of Duane's jokes.

"I'm gonna go."

"One more beer?"

"No. You stay if you want."

"Wait, I'll come with you."

I could tell he was reluctant. He disentangled himself from Duane, who gave him a "sure you're doing the right thing?" look. Then he bade everyone a gushy, kissy, extravagant farewell, like the end of a Diana Ross concert. As I waited for her highness, I overheard Duane comment to Colin, "Looks like our Robert's turning rice queen".

We hit the night air. Robert was doing his Chipmunk act again.

"What did I tell you, it's a great place, isn't it?"

I nodded coolly.

"Didn't you like it?"

"It was all right."

"It takes a couple of times to feel at home. But all that leather and those hunky guys. It's a major turn-on."

I wondered if we were accidentally warped into different dimensions. But Robert insisted upon my approval.

"Makes you want to go out and buy something shiny, black, and sexy, doesn't it?"

Yeah, like a gun.

We ended up back at Robert's place. Frank's place. I had gone quiet. Robert, of course, hadn't noticed. We were in the kitchen because he wanted me to try out this new dish he had been experimenting with, tamarillo soufflé.

"I'm still getting the combination of flavours right."

I tried not to retch. Robert stared at me with a sexy glint in his eye.

"What do you want to do now, Simon?"

I braved another mouthful to avoid answering. I didn't know what I wanted or what I was feeling like. All I kept thinking was that Robert's leather mates were disgusting old perverts who treated him like a chihuahua.

"I mean, you could just go home and we could just be friends . . ."

Robert moved closer, his eyes unwavering, holding me in their tractor beam. He ran a finger along the front of my T-shirt, all the way down to my board shorts which started to tent frontwards, involuntarily. Damn that thing! I closed my eyes.

"But you don't want to do that, do you?"

In spite of all the reasons I had not to, or maybe because of them, I found myself on the floor of the kitchen with Robert climbing all over me, pulling at my clothes, trying to tear them off.

"What if Frank comes back?"

"He'd probably join in."

This wasn't what I wanted to hear. Robert was licking, pawing and scratching me, like a beagle who'd been trapped in the house all week. He had my shirt above his head, vacuum-pumping my nipples.

"Ow! Not so hard."

"Don't be a wooze."

"Too hard!"

He eased off, and slipped my board shorts down. My cock was half hard and deflating by the second. He continued sucking on my tits whilst frigging my dick like he was conducting Beethoven's Ninth with it.

"That hurts!"

"Sorry . . ."

He relaxed his grip, but lay on top of me again. He tried to kiss me but I flinched. He licked my neck instead. He whispered in my ear.

"Can I fuck you? Can I? I want to be the first."

My sphincter clenched tighter than a fist and the blood in my dick started to flow towards stomach so that it looked less like an erection than a dead mouse.

"Not tonight."

"You want to fuck me, then? Come on, come to my room."

"No . . ."

Robert's rock-like cock began to soften as well. He went down on me, trying to blow some life back into the shrivelled creature between my legs. I closed my eyes, willing the blood back. He was running his tongue around my balls, then lower towards my ass. But I was like a born-again virgin, my knees locked together, restricting his access.

He shoved them apart in frustration, pushed me on my back, knees around my ears. He lapped at my hole with his scratchy tongue and jerked me off at the same time. No go. The mouse refused to be resuscitated. I pulled myself upright, out of his reach. He stared at me. I put my hand on his lean white torso.

"Can't we just wank together?"

"What, in the same room?"

"It's too much, all right? I wasn't expecting it . . ."

"Yeah sure."

We played with ourselves for a while but neither of us got hard again.

I was at the door. Robert was staring at me, confused. I pecked him on the cheek goodbye, sad but kind of relieved.

"I'll give you a call, all right."

"Yeah."

"See ya."

"See ya."

About 20 metres away, Robert yelled at me.

"Fuck you, Simon!"

I don't know why, but I screamed back, "Fuck you, too, Robert!"

"You fucking loser!"

"Well at least I don't have AIDS!"

"I hope I gave it to you!"

"Yeah, well I hope you get sick tomorrow! I hope you die next week!"

I visited Precious at the milkbar. She was in a mopey mood too. She'd found out what everyone in the neighbourhood already knew. Johnny Spiros already had a girlfriend – pretty, blonde, slim Karen Casey who was the head girl at our high school and now managed the Body Shop in the mall. Apparently Johnny only went out with Precious on a dare from some of his mates.

They got the idea from this video called *Dog Fight* where these Marines have a competition to see who can find the ugliest date for the night. Precious shrugged.

"I had the last laugh. I gave him crabs."

That what I liked about Precious. She was the eternal optimist. Then I put two and two together.

"How come you had crabs?"

"You may not have a life, Simon, but it doesn't mean the rest of us have to live in a monastery."

I told Precious about Robert. She was philosophical.

"You shouldn't fall in love with someone just because they lick your ass."

"Yeah, I guess so."

"You gonna call him?"

"I don't know. There's no future in it."

"That's not such a bad thing."

"I suppose not. What do you think I should do?"

"Don't ask me, I'm your *fiancée*."

To cheer ourselves up, we went to the mall. Pretending to admire the window display outside the Body Shop, we watched as the pretty, blonde and vivacious Karen Casey served a long queue of customers. Only Precious and me could understand why there were beads of sweat on her brow. Only Precious and me were witness to Karen, after the last customer was gone, clawing at her fanny like it was on fire.

Apart from this moment of divine inspiration, though, the next while was pretty bleak. Mum noticed my funky patch and ground a little Serapax into my rice to try to cheer me up. All this did was send me to sleep during *Sale of the Century*. I woke up, stone-cold sober and grumpy as all hell at 3 a.m. and stomped around cursing loudly until dawn. She abandoned this tactic and consulted a fortune teller in Chinatown to see if I was possessed.

In spite of myself, I couldn't stop thinking about that no good Robert. Thanks to him, rimming became a welcome addition to my limited repertoire. But every new tongue up my winking brown hole reminded me of my skinny friend. I guess I was sentimental that way. Really, the toilets weren't the same anymore and in my idle hours I found myself daydreaming about sex that was more horizontal than vertical.

In these daydreams I imagined what it would be like to be fucked. To feel Robert's fat cock nudging against me, pushing the tight fold of muscle open. I pushed my own finger there, and dreamed of Robert's cock, opening me up, tearing apart the barriers of fear and suspicion that separated me from the rest of the world. To be open, to be vulnerable, to be touched inside – it was only in a daydream that I admitted to myself how much I wanted this. I slipped a second finger next to the first and imagined it was Robert doing this to me, all the veils of pretending pushed aside so that, for just one moment, I could look someone in the eye and see him as he really was, nothing else, none of the bullshit, just him. Me and him. Me and Robert. The two of us. And then I would cum, and I'd take my fingers out and feel empty again.

Finally, on a cold, grey autumn afternoon, about four months after I saw him last, I found myself back at Robert's house. Frank answered the door, all smiles. He wasn't quite so daunting in a kimono. Behind him in the corridor Angelo was on his hands and knees. He was wearing a dog collar and baggy track-suit pants, polishing the floorboards with French wax. Frank winked at me.

"That's the real reason I'm a master. I hate cleaning."

When I asked if Robert was around, Frank's expression became sober.

"Robert's in hospital."

"Oh . . ."

"He drove his car into a bus shelter."

I took flowers. Because of his HIV status, they put Robert in the AIDS ward, even though he had a broken arm. I passed rooms with men plugged into tubes and machines, some so brittle and translucent they looked like they were made of bone china. It must have been pretty freaky for Robert.

But if it was, he didn't show it. He was propped up in bed, reading comic books.

"I was just thinking about you. Look." He showed me Alan

Moore's *Miracle Man.* "Duane's into comic books too, and he leant me these. It's so cool."

I gave him the flowers. Hydrangeas stolen from the park.

"You want me to put them into something?"

"Nah, they'll just die, anyway."

I sat next to Robert, happy to see him. He had a ring through his nose and another couple in his left ear. Otherwise, he looked the same. I didn't know what I was expecting.

"I like the ring. It must be weird when you pick your nose."

"You get used to it. Learn not to pick too hard."

Robert put down the comic book. There was a change in him. His eyes were more blue than ever.

"You having a scene with Duane?"

Robert nodded. "Yeah . . ."

"Cool."

I probably should say, "He's a nice guy" or words to that effect, but what was the point? Robert looked at me sadly.

"I was wondering, Simon, why we fucked up. Whose fault was it?"

"I guess I'm too sensitive."

"Me too."

"It was the HIV, wasn't it? You couldn't handle it."

"I guess not. I don't know . . ."

I looked down at my hands. They were sweating again and we weren't even in a car. I'd never been in this position before.

"I was wondering, Robert. You know, if you want maybe we could try . . . Maybe we could be friends again? Just friends, you know."

There was no response. Finally I summoned the courage to look up. Robert was studying me, coldly.

"If you do two things."

"Yeah?"

"First, go and close the curtain."

I did as he asked, closing the curtain to the glass window in the door. Well, that was pretty easy.

"Now, get down on your hands and knees and crawl towards me."

I looked at him, puzzled. A faint hint of a smile played on his lips.

"I lied about Duane."

I broke into a broad grin as well, but only for a moment. Then I sank to all fours and crawled. Robert swung out of bed. The front of his pyjama pants were tenting out. He stared at me. I didn't take my eyes off him.

"Come up here, boy."

I knelt in front of him. He felt my face with his good hand.

"Open your mouth."

He stuck a finger in my mouth. Then two. I sucked them hungrily.

"You have to give yourself to me, you have to trust me."

He put a third finger into my mouth, probing, taking control. Choking me. I opened up further, wanting more. With each thrust, my cock strains against my jeans. I wanted him do whatever he wanted. I wanted to be his.

Without taking his eyes off me, he held my face in his hand.

"You're my boy, aren't you?"

I nodded. He slapped my face. Hard.

"You trust me, don't you?"

I nodded. He slapped me again. Harder. Then again. I couldn't help it. I started to laugh. This wasn't what Robert was expecting.

"What's wrong?"

"You remind me . . . of my mum."

Robert shook his head.

"Jesus, Simon, if this is going to work, you have to take it seriously."

We tried again. This time, I didn't laugh.

ONE THURSDAY
IN NOVEMBER

Michael Lassell

WHEN YOU FEEL like an outsider wherever you go, darkness is
a comfort, a . . . what? – cloak, blanket, mantle of anonymity
that hides you (from the persecution of the day, from detection,
from unwilling revelation). In the dark you are a kind of warm
no matter what the temperature. And the warm, wet darkness
of the bathhouses where men come together for sex are a special
kind of darkness – or near darkness – a particular safe harbor
where risk and danger are safety nets that keep you from falling
absolutely into yourself, where privacy is an interior matter in
a naked world. Here – whatever "here" is your favorite – the
bleachy scent of ejaculate floats on waves of pulsing music,
music that throbs in the floorboards and walls, familiar and
completely new at the same time. It floats, too, on the smoke
of cigarettes without filters and on whispered conversations that
are the same no matter what language is being spoken, spoken
by an older, fleshy man with a gold bracelet, perhaps, leaning
against a door frame, holding himself with an arm high against
a wall while he slowly rocks his body closer to the sleek, small
body of a young man with eyes the size of a llama's. No matter
where you are, no matter what the time of day, this dark spreads

its legs to you even if the boy you'd kill for wants nothing to do
with you, nothing whatever.

Time stops.

Thought stops. Rational thought.

Only desire does not stop. Your head fills with it. Your mind
simmers in desire (the comforting inflammation of a childhood
fever, a mother tending you with cinnamon toast and sugary
tea, wrapping you in the thin cotton quilts her mother sewed
before the bone cancer took her arms).

Kosta.

1

He stands in the doorway, leaning on it with his right shoulder.
Tall and lean and dusted with a brush of fine dark hair. He is
smoking and has his head turned down to the left. He's wearing
a towel, blue and ancient; a key on an elastic band around one
ankle. He puts the cigarette to his lips, takes the smoke into
his expectant lungs. He looks up and catches my eye.

Here is how it will be for you if it is for you what it was for me:

You arrive in Piraeus, the Athenian port, on the morning of a
clear day as full of sunshine as your imagination is of ancient
Greece. The night was stormy, sailing from Istanbul – Istanbul
of 16th-century Turkish baths, of the waiter from the hotel near
the Blue Mosque, the twin Arabs who cleaned your room, a rug
merchant in Armani named Taygun – sailing from the placid
Sea of Mamara into the rapid Dardanelles (once the Hellespont,
where poor Helle drowned when she fell from the back of the
golden ram as he flew over these waters), sailing past mournful
Gallipoli and out into an angry Aegean, tossed all night, battered
with fists of black waves. The captain confined all passengers to
their staterooms. "Your safest place is in bed," he said over the
public address system. It was Poseidon's greeting, a reminder
not to take him for granted. You spent the rough night glued
to the window watching the storm rage, filling your chest with
a thrilling fear as watery hills crashed over the deck. It was the
danger that made the voyage memorable. Suddenly, Homer
makes sense, the *Odyssey*, why it took Odysseus 17 years to sail

from Troy back to Ithaca, back to the arms of faithful, weaving Penelope, and to the arms of his vengeful son Telemachus, a mass of muscle in every 19th-century neo-Classical painting (the Louvre is full of them).

In time, the storm passes. At dawn – Homer's "rosy-fingered dawn" – you are refreshed and ready.

You dock. It is Thanksgiving Day back home. Here, in this ancient port, it is only a Thursday, and the day of a national strike in sympathy with the country's taxi drivers. Nonetheless, you manage to find a car. "Of course," the driver says with a shrug. Of course he knows your hotel.

You settle into the back seat, waiting for Greece.

It reveals itself slowly, in glimpses just beyond and between modern buildings as you crawl through clogged streets, which are not crowded today, the driver tells you, because of the strike. He is young, dark, his hair a mass of ebony curls caught in the light at every turn. He stares into your eyes in the rearview mirror as he drives. You stare back. His eyelashes are a conversation.

At the hotel you give him a tip, a big one. He gives you his card and scribbles his name and telephone number on the back of it. Then he shakes your one hand in his two.

You feel welcomed.

From the landscaped patio of your room on the seventh floor of the HOTEL GRANDE BRETAGNE (below the second T) you face the Acropolis, a white marble shard of which sits on your desk at home, a gift purloined by a friend now long dead. Yes, there the temple sits, not quite white, but a kind of pink, a kind of gold, its millennial buildings sharp in the daylight: the Parthenon, Erechtheum, Propylaea, Porch of the Caryatids, Temple of Athena Nike . . . Icons, symbols for a kind of perfection long abandoned, even in the attempt.

A blond boy in a green tunic and loose, cream-colored pants, is sweeping the terraces. He approaches slowly, sweeping, sweeping the dried leaves that have fallen from the manicured plants that define the balcony of each guest room.

You watch: Acropolis, blond boy . . . Acropolis, blond boy . . .

His work is deliberate, but he glances at you from time to time, until it is most of the time.

"Good morning," you will say when he begins to sweep your own landscaped patio on the topmost floor but one of the Hotel Grande Bretagne.

He locks you in his eyes (they are blue) and smiles. "No speak," he squeezes out, abandoning his muffled attempt at the word "English" somewhere in the course of its second syllable.

His sweeping slows as he comes near you. Keeping your eyes locked, he approaches as you lean your butt on the concrete balustrade. How many "dignitaries," how many "personages," you wonder, have stood on this same spot, in this same position, since the hotel was built, over a century ago, when it actually stood on the grounds of the royal palace?

The blond boy's broom is brushing your shoes now, the comfortable ones you wear for walking when you travel. He looks behind him. There is no one to see, no witnesses (except for the population of Athens, tourists in nearby cafés, accountants in the office buildings opposite, construction workers in the square below). You put one hand on his arm. He moves in closer. The brass buttons of his tunic are brushing your shirt now. You lean in to kiss. His eager lips move in to meet yours, still dry and cracked from too much Mediterranean sun. You slip your tongue into his mouth and pull his hips into your hips. Strangers – *foreigners* – don't need to be cautious. You are both engorging quickly now. His cock, you can tell, is long and thin. You put your hand on his hard/soft man/boy ass, and he starts to sigh while he kisses . . .

There is a knock on the door. You have not put on the security bolt. The door begins to open. You brush past the boy into your dark, cool room, arranging your shirt in front of your full fly. The housekeeper is startled.

"Oh, I am sorry, sir," she says with a thick accent, a pretty girl with the eyes of a martyr and the oversized lips of Melina Mercouri. "Do you require any assistance." Sir does not. Not from her.

Outside, on the balcony, the boy is gone.

Or transformed into the dove that sits on the back of your patio chair, the dove that doesn't move when you sit in the other but hops onto the glass-topped table, and finding nothing there, flies up and roosts in its usual T.

You walk through the polished door of the hotel, held by a doorman in green, and walk to the Tomb of the Unknown Soldier. It is at street level in front of the elevated Parliament Building, once the Royal Palace, which occupies one side of Syntagma (Constitution) Square, which is closed now for massive "improvements."

On the "tomb" itself is set in a wall fronted by marble frieze. It depicts an ancient Greek warrior in profile, nude. He lies on his back, arched over a large stone from knees to shoulders. The rigid crest of his helmet rests on the ground behind him, keeping his head heroically high. His shield, behind him, sets like a carved sun over the hollow of his belly, the muscled mounds of his thighs. Perhaps it is Patroclus, you think, the boy Achilles so loved and grieved he wreaked his vengeance on the Trojan army, slaying heroic Hector – who slaughtered the boy – and, defying the gods in his superhuman grief, dragged the prince's body behind his chariot by way of unspeakable desecration. And you imagine their lovemaking, the young Achilles and his warrior lover, and you think of them as hairless and smooth as marble, as cool in the night, their oil-scented bodies slick with torch light as the general enters the body of his aide-de-camp, his cock a marble pillar, a wet shaft of marble that slides in and out of its home like skates on ice.

In front of this wall, as always, two armed *évzones* stand watch in canopied stations. At hourly intervals, the guard is changed: hoisting their rifles, these most élite of all soldiers change places in slow goose step to the shouted commands of their superior officer. As stiff in the spine as the weapons they carry, they raise their muscular legs to right angles with the ground. They are dressed in skirted white blouses, their legs bound in white tights; their wooden shoes, decorated with pompoms, thud on the marble as they bring their disciplined legs back to the ground. They are dark and fierce and splendid in their ritual.

The day is warm and cool at the same time: warmer than you expected, cool enough to hold a trace of November in it. The archaeological sites are closed because of the strike, except for the ones that are open, and you walk slowly through this faceless modern city built on an ancient place. Your mind is filled with architecture and desire.

Doric, Ionic, Corinthian . . .

Parthenon, Erechtheum, Temple of Athena Nike . . .

A blow job in the ruins of the Baths of Caracalla in Rome . . .

At the entrance to the National Garden are two news kiosks. Many things are sold here, from cold drinks to small magazines in which circumcised boys who look American are fucking. You cannot read the text, of course, but you buy the magazines anyway (they're Greek to you). The news vendor, a film star of a rough-shaven man, does not meet your glance. He already knows what you want from him.

You walk through the park sipping from a bottle of icy mineral water. When it touches your lips, you are reminded of the lips of the blond boy on the balcony (*the Egyptian teenager at the Cairo museum, the miniature Sikh waiter in Delhi, the Brazilian dancer overlooking Lincoln Square*). It is one of those days, one of those days when your mind becomes a Möbius strip of new experience and memories, an impossible band of your life turning on itself infinitely.

You sit in a patch of sun poking momentarily through the shade trees. (Are they chestnuts? Or is that only France?) There are children in the park, nannies, gangs of school friends. And men. In what park in the world are there not single men? And in what park in the world are they not doing what they do in this one? They watch. They wait. It is a microcosm of life, of your own life, as you age now out of the last year of your forties. You wait. You watch. You travel. Are you running? Is it away or from? Are you collecting anecdotes in place of a life? Are your string of boys a trophy case from which you take meaning, now that you are no longer young, no longer strong, no longer as beautiful as you once were. And your body was never a statue, never Adonis, in any case. Rodin's Balzac, perhaps, at best.

The hard questions come in silence, in parks around the world, but only during the day. Nights are full of softness, fogged notions, approximations. And answers, at least temporary ones.

*   *   *

At the far side of the park, you cruise the guard at the president's residence. He sneers. You stop to take photographs of the nude statues that face the century-old Olympic Stadium, and as you walk once around its oval, you conjure visions of bronzed naked athletes, gleaming under sweat and oil in competitions for laurel leaves and the lavish attention of older men, who watch the contests – themselves nude and shamelessly erect – who pull these unwashed champions onto their laps while other games are played out on the field before them, their grunting mixing with the cheers of the crowd and the roars of nude boys running, wrestling, blood on their lips, bruises on their arms and thighs. The ideal. And there's evidence of them everywhere in this land without fig leaves, of statuary genitals that hang and droop, of painted vase cocks that stand into the air, of bronze phalluses of satyrs that are as big as the goatlike creatures themselves (the pouring spouts of vessels, some of them, to drink from).

At the sun-drenched Temple of Zeus, a boy tosses historic stones, then straddles a fallen column. You wonder what he will be like when he is old. You realize with a small shock that you will, by then, be dead. Without a monument.

At Hadrian's Arch, a man in a red-leather jacket dips space-age sunglasses down onto the prominent bridge of his broken nose as you pass. You would like to break it again. You want him to *beg* you to break it again as he looks up into your face from his knees.

(The dark, open-faced Algerian boy outside L'Orangerie in the Tuileries, who turns as he passes and slyly asks if I am staying in a hotel nearby.)

You are wondering why you feel so free in your body. You seem desirable again in ways you never feel at home. Almost anywhere you go, you feel free of the body prejudices of your country. It is freedom, always, that makes you happy to the core.

In the Plaka, you buy a souvenir book from a chubby boy in a gray sweater. A grandfather sits behind him. The small spiral-bound volume you buy contains photographs of the great ruins of Athens, overlaid with acetate pages of fanciful restoration drawings. Athens now, Athens then. Instant history. The boy manages to hold your hand as he puts the drachma coins into your palm. His own nearly tremble. Is it fear? Or desire?

(A Thai boy in a gift shop in Chinatown in downtown New York, who speaks no English at all, but manages, in an upstairs room, where we are alone, to communicate his desire as he rakes long manicured nails over my palm and stares into my eyes through Asian eyes.)

At the Acropolis, you sit on the Aereopagus, the rock where law was first practiced when Orestes stood trial for the murder of his mother, Clytemnestra, and her lover, Aegisthus. (Was it moral indignation and righteousness that led him to the crime, or jealousy? you wonder, or had she bathed him so long into his adolescence that his hatred was mixed with lust for the woman who bore him?) Here the Apostle Paul, a man who is called a saint, once preached his anti-body brand of Christianity, the doctrine that decimated pantheistic pagan naturalism, at least officially (those dogma-crazed prelates in the censorious Vatican having shared more than prayers the whole Dark Ages long). You feel the old gods here, in a Japanese boy who scratches his sandaled foot absently as he looks down on the Agora and the Temple of Hephaestus (crippled cuckold and forger of Zeus's lightning bolts). You watch the subtle flexing of his legs, which disappear into loose shorts. You want to take his dick into your mouth on this very spot and preach a gospel of your own. You want to fuck him hard in the olive and cypress grove below, but he is not alone, and you descend, following the directions of a pair of teenaged Greek boys walking hand-in-hand.

(The Irish boy from the concert in Dublin I met a week later at a hotel next to the Castle at Bunratty, and the tattoo artist from Limerick the same afternoon.)

You want to see the Theater of Dionysus, the place where drama was born 25 centuries ago by Aeschylus, Sophocles, Euripides. But it is closed today, because of the strike. You want to mummify a striking taxi driver in thick, black electrician's tape and set him in the sun with a small straw up one nostril. Instead, you head to the toilet, where a redhead with a huge, freckled dick (he's from Cincinnati, it turns out) tells you the National Archaeological Museum is open today, despite the strike. Your mood lifts. You fly across Athens on foot.

"Is the museum open?" you ask, wondering if the woman at the desk speaks English.

She looks up through black-rimmed glasses that pinch upward at the outer edges. "Yes," she says with a sweep of her arm around the empty foyer, as if it were the most obvious thing in the world. You have an hour.

An hour.

In the home of virtually every major piece of sculpture you've ever seen in an art history book.

Alone, it is almost enough.

You walk from room to room, amazed. They are all here, all nude: the Artemision Poseidon, bearded and muscled, caught hollow-eyed, mid-hurl; the tiny boy from Euboa on his massive galloping horse; the bronze youth of Marathon, who holds up a right hand, as if to silence applause, his left held open to receive (a prize? his lover's hand?); the fourth-century BC youth of Anticythera, his arm stretched out over a moulded torso as if to pluck an apple from a forbidden tree. *(The bartender from the Elgin Marbles room at the British Museum in – Christ! – '68, a rainy afternoon when the old Y still stood just down Great Russell Street, and the poet in the manuscript room in '96 when it didn't.)*

You walk into a room and are greeted by a towering kouros, a sculpted boy with long braided hair. His eyes are closed, his arms by his side in loose fists, one foot slightly forward. He is nearly Egyptian. But, no, it's not one kouros but a large terracotta gallery filled with them, these strange funereal sentries, guardians of grave sites and tombs. And how they evolved over eons from simple, abstract forms to realistic boys who wear shoulder and chest muscles like the lion-skin stole of Orion. Their smooth torsos are wonderlands, the deep crevices at the top of massive thighs plunging to simple but intriguing organs. You want these boys, one by one in the dark, which is on its way, you see, the mullions of ceiling-level windows casting high shadows on this clutch of powerful boys. You could spend eternity with them, of that you are sure.

(Owl-bespectacled Mark in a cabin cot beside a cold lake we had swum in, had jumped into from a rowboat, the water mountain-lake cold, his lips so warm . . .)

And then you are blindsided in a deep-red hemisphere of a chamber lined with white marble busts of men set on pedestals that allow you to look each of them in the eye. Light through an oriel window in the ceiling dome could be a sun dial, each of these heads a moment in time on a celestial clock. I scan them left to right. It is so quiet here. The guard in the next room doesn't even bother to get out of his chair. I scan the faces until I come to a pair whose names I recognize: for here is Antinous, the boy beloved of the Emperor Hadrian, who drowned himself in the Nile in AD 130 that he might be young and beautiful forever in his imperial patron's eyes, and whose death Hadrian mourned so mightily that he declared the lost boy a god and ordered his likeness erected at every crossroads in his wide realm. And here the boy looks down toward the ground, shy, perhaps, or sad, his beauty in his lips and downcast eyes, the heft of a shoulder muscle cut off by the ungenerous sculptor. His curly hair is arranged over a thin fillet band of leather or gold. He is the ultimate lover: compliant, faithful, passionate.

And here, beside him, you now see, is Hadrian himself (handsome as a god, bearded, old, and so in love – or in grief – that your own heart aches for him and his loss, the loss of your own Roberto, your Kenny, your Clark, the men who helped you become what you are before the plague washed them away and left you standing there like a lone palm in a desert). And you find the tears welling up in your eyes with the enormity of their ancient Greek love, and their beauty, and their pulsing masculinity (old and young), which survives even this aesthetic rendering, and with gratitude for a sympathetic curator who reunited the two without apologies to modern mores and made them what they are: Antinous and Hadrian, lovers eternal, made one again by proximity.

*   *   *

And that is when time changes, and desire starts to rise in earnest, and you grab up a sheaf of images from the souvenir stand as it closes, and head out into the dusk, the building in deep shadow now, a golden sun hitting only the miniature replicas of Periclean statues on the triangular roof pediment above the columned entry.

Parthenon, Hadrian, hunger, loneliness, desire . . .

Athens, Thanksgiving, a Thursday in November.

The man feeding pigeons is not responding. You get up from your bench and through the gates and head down Eólou, the boulevard that leads directly to the Acropolis, which rises a mile or two in front of you. You are walking the New York City walk, and the crowds around you do not understand why. The foot traffic thickens as the sky turns darker and darker blue. At Konstantínou, you do not turn left on Panepistimiou (the road past the National Library, the Academy of Science, and the residence of Heinrich Schliemann, excavator of Troy, the road back to your hotel). You turn instead toward Omónia Square, a huge neon-lit circle of night life and heavy construction. You have never seen this place, and yet you know it from other cities: Times Square, the Ginza, Piccadilly Circus *(waiting impatiently for a Brit named Steven under the Eros Statue on a rainy Saturday night in spring)*.

Here the cafés and restaurants are filling fast. Music blares from the music shops. Gangs of boys congregate in any open space between buildings. Videos show on the television sets displayed in shop windows. Christmas decorations are already for sale among clothing, dinnerware, and souvenirs (plaster Acropolis models, Orthodox candles, fishermen's hats).

Here the news kiosks are bigger, more comprehensive than the ones at the National Garden. They bulge with foreign publications: *The International Tribune, The Times* (London and New York), *Der Stern, Le Figaro*. And magazines, too, of course, from beauty, fashion, and news to *Playboy* and its global clones. Here the male-on-male magazines are large and glossy, the uncut models clearly European. You buy a bilingual *Guide to Gay Athens* and your fingers begin to walk its pages. Restaurants and cafés (one just across the circular "square"). You sit in a window seat over a Snapple and something wrapped in filo dough and flip the pages as the beautiful boys around you watch you watch them, beautiful Greek boys who become (unaccountably) unbeautiful old Greek men, men like yourself.

Balding, graying, grizzling, thickening . . .

You find a page, a page on which a "spa" called the *Athens Rest* is advertised. You unfold your map. It is only blocks from where you sit, staring out the second floor of a huge café into the rigging of the cranes that install the new Omónia metro stop, the vowels of its name a euphuistic echo of "harmony".

The multi-folded plastic map is easy to follow, and it isn't long before you stand at the entrance to an alley, a dark alley off an ill-lit small side street. A dark alley in a strange city frightens you, a wet alley full of trash where ill-dressed men smoke and pace-slowly. You walk past it, knowing you have no power over this urban crevice in the hypocritical social façade. In these alleys some kind of authenticity collects like motes of truth, like dust in the cracked mosaic tiles of a palace floor in Rhodes. A single bulb above the door you are looking for lights nothing but the number 8. The address. You enter.

(You enter the bathhouses of New York, Los Angeles, Dublin, London, Honolulu, Istanbul . . .)

There is something in your mind, and you don't know what it is. But then you see it: Kosta standing in a door, his right shoulder up against the frame, his head declined like the bust of Antinous, dead these 1,866 years. He is smoking, this tall, lean, towel-clad Greek man in a doorway. He appears to be what you mean by the word straight.

You keep him in one corner of your eye as you pay the desk man, an older Greek who speaks no English except the price of a room. The desk man looks up at the *kouros* in the door, who on the old man's cue comes forward in English, counts out your drachmas, picks up a threadbare towel from the stack and a small bar of soap. The old man smiles.

"I'm Kosta," your translator tells you. "It's short for Konstantinos," he adds, holding out his hand, the wrist of which, like yours, is circled in silver, yours from an antique market in Agra the day of the kohl-eyed boy near the dancing bears.

Already you feel at home. The music. The damp heat. The elusive something in the air that is men having sex with other men. Kosta leads you to a stair. You wonder how long this building has been here. The treads of its steep ascending stairs are so worn they could have been made of mud. Was it always a place of disrepute, you wonder, a boy brothel? Was it here when Cavafy wrote his poems in the cafés that came before the ones that stand in this neighborhood now, lusting after the young men (perhaps the grandfathers of today's young men) who seemed to him so unavailable, whose American counterparts seem so unavailable to you in city after city any place at all? You have followed the melancholy poet's path from Alexandria to Constantinople, now here. You think of stooped and balding Cavafy climbing these same stairs that you climb now, paddling down these hallways in worn slippers. Who else has climbed them? Schliemann, weary from his dig in Asia Minor's lost Troy? The dignitaries and personages of the Grande Bretagne who resurrected the Olympics in that hotel in 1896? Tourists, certainly, workers from the construction site nearby, businessmen, men with money and time and desire.

Kosta takes your key and shows you how to unlock the door, as if you have never seen a key before, or a lock you could open with a matchbook. His smoke floats around his head like a nimbus. You forgive him.

The "room" is two feet wider than the platform on which a vinyl pad has been placed as a bed. There is a chair, a crate with a battered aluminum ashtray on it (it has been emptied many times but never washed).

Kosta shows you the hooks on the wall for your clothing.

"If you need anything later," he says, "just let me know."

"What kind of thing?" you ask (strangers need not be cautious).

"Some lotion, perhaps . . ." Kosta says, pretending to be offhand, as if thinking of the menu for the first time. ". . . a massage, or sex."

He looks into your eyes.

"Perhaps," you say, by which, of course, you mean *yes*.

Here is what will happen:

2

You will ask him the price of a massage and the price of sex. The price of a massage is fixed and cheap. The price for sex depends on what you want and is not, if you want what I want, cheap at all.

"I want to fuck you," you will say to Kosta, a man who smokes cigarettes in a bathhouse/brothel and who appears to be that thing you mean by the word straight. He seems surprised, but says, "OK, we do everything."

Then he says, "Wait here," and goes back out the door.

You take off your clothing, which is not the same thing as waiting at all. You peel off the day piece by piece until you are naked except for the towel, grateful it finds its way around your middle.

Kosta returns shortly with a vial of oil in his hand and another towel, which he spreads as carefully on the vinyl mattress as a set decorator detailing a cashmere throw for an over-the-shoulder shot.

"You lie," he says, and you do, you lie down as he unwraps his hips and hangs his towel on the wall.

His cock is long, thick, uncut. Nothing like the statues you have been admiring all day. His balls are big and hang between decent thighs brushed by hair that is lighter than the hair on his chest.

You stretch out on the bed, and this Kosta of yours begins to rub gardenia-scented lotion into your back, sore from the long walking day, the stormy sleepless night, the general disappointment with life you carry there as tension. You feel his cock as he straddles your ass, rubbing your tight muscles, raising up on his knees, dog-style, to reach your neck, insistently pushing his growing cock into the crack of your ass, rubbing oil into the crack of your ass, carefully massaging the hole, running his slick hands below you to pull out your own stiff prick and thickening sack, rubbing the oil onto his own dick as he works your hips into motion.

You could lie here for hours just accepting the pleasure of it, but Kosta is on a tight schedule.

"Turn over," he says. You . . . obey. Is that the word?

Now he kneels between your legs and rubs oil onto your chest, tweaking your nipples. You reach up and grab his, too, and squeeze them hard, pull them upward toward his chin, while this naked man between your legs rubs his slick cock against yours, against your ass crack, against the palm of his hand. Before you get the rhythm of it, he sinks down and takes your dick in his mouth. You are fully sweating now and are carried now weightless on the soft pulsing music that drifts in over the top of the walls from the halls and up through the ancient floors. His mouth seems to be without teeth, it is so vast and soft and wet a cavern.

"You want to suck me?" he says, standing now beside the bed where you sit. You take his balls into your hands and his spongy semi-hard dick in your mouth, working the foreskin back and forth over the shy and sensitive head of it. He holds your hair in his fists, arching backward like the frieze of the Unknown Soldier, rolling his head from side to side. You hold his cock in your mouth, working one hand up and down the shaft, cupping his balls with your other hand, cupping his balls and pushing upward with your knuckles in the sacred grove between balls and asshole. Then you rotate your hand and draw one finger, *the* finger, along his asshole and flirt with it and push into it, first with a knuckle, then with fingertip, until he begins to open and the whole finger slips (welcomed) in and you can feel that equatorial inside of him, the hard flat disk inside that is the button of all male pleasure, and he is groaning aloud now, his long hands caressing your beard. You bite down hard on the heel of one hand, and he draws his breath in sharp, rasping the air over the organs of his throat.

You stand and push your cock at him. They flatten, yours and his, up against your bellies, his flat, yours not. You pinch his tits. Hard. He grabs the muscles at the top of your shoulders as if they were handles. You have him up against the wall.

He pushes past you and kneels on the edge of the bed. You

step between the dirty soles of his long, thin feet and put on the rubber you always carry. He reaches up as he feels you begin to push and spreads the cheeks apart for you to enter. You slide inside like wet marble as he grips you, and you know this will not be long.

You push into him and he groans that groan that is every ounce of who he is and that makes you every ounce of who you are. You are not gentle but push and push and push, until a high whimper comes out of him from somewhere inside his sinus cavity and he points the cock he's been jerking toward the mattress below him and comes.

You pull out of him and flip him onto his back, holding his feet in your hands as you plunge in again, his dick already softening, the wet spot on the bed a mere dribble. You pump into him, the muscles of his torso rippling, the tendons of his groin stretched to breaking, and when you think you have gone too far past the point, you pull sharply out of him, rip off the bag, and with three fingers inside his ass and your other hand on your cock, you come and come and come, and the stuff drenches your Kosta, and splashes on the wall behind his head, and drips into his hair, and falls onto his face and across his lips, soaking into the hair of his chest, his crotch, the extra towel beneath him. Eight, ten, twelve shots that come from so far up inside you your balls are aching already and your ass muscles sore before you've even stopped shooting.

"My God," Kosta groans and makes a move as if to wipe himself off.

You push him down onto the bed and massage your cum into his chest and belly. You lick it off his face and kiss him with it on your lips. He turns his head. You suck on his neck, hard, then lower yourself onto him, two human stones joining perfectly, stuck together with the mortar of your fluids. You do not soften quickly and poke what is left of your erection between his legs and push against the used hole of him, all the while smelling the used smoke smell drift from his much-ruffled hair.

You want him to stay there with you for hours. But he is up on his dirty feet again.

"Come," he says. "I show you where is the shower."

Strangely, he is more affectionate in public than he was alone in the room. He drapes his arm on your shoulders as you walk to the shower room downstairs. Older men are sitting on marble risers in front of the shower, where several slim boys are soaping themselves and their semi-erections. You hang your towel where Kosta hangs his. You, too, begin to shower. He surprises you by reaching over and rubbing soap into your back, all the way down to your ass. You reciprocate, slipping your hand deep between his asscheeks, which is too intimate for him in this tiled and public space where older men than you are watching, their eyes twinkling at your sated lust.

When you are done, he dries your back. Then bends to kiss you on the lips. "I see you upstairs in the café, perhaps?" he says, clearly in need of a cigarette.

"Perhaps," you will say, by which you mean yes.

That is the way it was done. But it is not the way it is meant to be done. This is how it is meant to be done:

3

You pay at the door, you take a towel, a key, a bar of soap. You change in your cubicle, then walk the hallways, looking into open doors at the customers, wondering which of the boys in the halls and lounges are working. You shower, perhaps, or have a steam. Then you head for the café, where you order a coffee from the dark mustachioed man behind the counter.

While you drink coffee, the boys who are working will wander in and out. You will chat, size them up, make a choice. In fact, there are many boys here, boys or men, whatever the term is, who are closer to classic statuary than Kosta was even in his youngest days. Young men in the bodies of young gods, of Olympic athletes, men more beautiful, men you desire more than Kosta. From these men you make your choice. You can have them here, in your room, or they will meet you later at your hotel.

You find this out later, the proper way to have done the thing.

*   *   *

After your shower, you stumble into the café by chance. Seated there are three gorgeous strangers and one man you know, Chad, the choreographer from the cruise ship you have been sailing on these last two weeks, the American dancer with dark brown skin who ignored your attentions every day on the ship. He is suddenly friendly and you begin to talk. He is horny, he says, and wants to have sex, but he can't bring himself to pay the boys who work here. He's hoping for "old-fashioned" sex with another patron. (You can tell the difference, he tells you, because all the patrons are wearing the same color towel, a dark rose that might once have been red; the rent boys, as he calls them, bring their own towels, so they are any color *except* red.)

Chad has short hair in a classical mode slicked down à la Josephine Baker. He reminds you of a statue from the Archaeological Museum, a muscled bronze boy grown dark with the patina of age. You show him the postcard from your backpack. He finds this a compliment.

"I think you're beautiful," you say. (*Alonzo in your California dorm.*)

"I think you're cute, too," he says, using the one generic word that probably describes you least accurately of all.

"Then why did you ignore me on the boat?" you ask, suddenly out of character, speaking the thing that it is your mind to say.

"Oh, I was so busy . . . I . . . I was involved, with one of the Italian crew members. Straight, of course. Whatever. Wife and kids in Rome. He was beefy, like you."

And then Kosta is in the doorway and comes over to where you are sitting and sits, too, smoking. You introduce him to Chad. Kosta has written his name and phone number on a piece of paper and asks you for the same. You oblige, then ask him to write his again, in Greek this time. Does he think he will be traveling to New York soon? No, but you never know.

"Would you like me to come by your hotel later," he asks. "Not for money."

You find this touching, but you decline. He is not what you are looking for. He is efficient, surprisingly accommodating, but as passionless as a stripper, as the tile of the sauna a boy followed you in after you had already finished with Kosta. Finished with Kosta . . . Are you so callous? Or just so unsatisfied? Yes, this Kosta of yours is a rest stop only, not a destination. Not the other country you look for in every passing eye, the other country that is you.

"I think I'm done for tonight," you say, knowing that this body of yours, half a century old though it may be, is already building energy for later in the night.

So you sit and you chat there, Chad and Kosta and you and some of the other, more beautiful boys, Kosta's hand draped territorially across your thigh, until he catches the eye of another customer walking into the door dragging his interest in Kosta behind him like a scarf. "I see you soon," he says, and bends to kiss you gently on the lips and tousle your still-damp hair.

"Well," you say to Chad. "What are you doing tonight?"

"Nothing much."

"When do you have to be back on the ship?"

"Not until tomorrow."

And there is a pause while you consider Chad, who is considering the muscular Greek across the room, a short-haired, muscular boy who pulls at his stiff dick poking of his towel. You can see the desire in Chad's eye, can feel the heat of it coming off his skin. Suddenly you feel desire, not in general, but desire for this particular boy, a dancer from New York who lives in California, who is tall, and beautiful and black and sitting beside you in a bathhouse in a foreign land.

"Would you like to have dinner," you ask.

And Chad says yes.

4

"And he's straight?" Chad will say in the English pub of a restaurant in your luxury Greek hotel. "That's not what I call straight."

"No," you will say, over the remains of your turkey dinner with all the trimmings, the unaccountable menu, meant, no doubt, for the Americans staying here. "But maybe I was just wrong. Maybe he's not."

"Or maybe," Chad will say, taking the last bite of fish from his plate, "the word is meaningless."

Chad stands on the balcony of your room as you step out of the bathroom. The duvet has been turned down, four down pillows propped against the headboard, small linen damask mats are laid by the sides of the bed. A single lamp casts an orange glow on the room.

You step outside.

Chad wears a white T-shirt over red jeans. He is staring at the Acropolis, lit now under a crescent-moon sky.

"It's spectacular, isn't it?" you say.

"The Acropolis?" Chad asks.

"Yes, of course."

"I guess," he says.

"You don't think it's magnificent?"

"I think if you had come from a slave people, you might not have such a high regard for the Greeks."

Chad turns his back on the Parthenon and looks into your eyes.

"So," Chad says, "am I your first black man or are you one of those who only have sex with black men?"

You hear the sound of the traffic below, can see the neon city behind him. You have no idea what to say. You lift your arm and put the palm of your right hand on his chest, over the heart. Your hand looks brown against the white cotton shirt.

"Neither," you finally manage, saying for the second time today what your mind is thinking, saying what you should be saying.

Chad reaches down to his waist, pulls the shirt off his chiseled torso and puts your hand back on his chest.

His lips, when they touch your lips, are soft, soft and warm. They are the melting yes to the "work-for-hire" of Kosta's dry and closed-lip "kiss." When you kiss this Chad, this dancer from an American cruise ship, his body sinks into the body that is you, and the two of you enter a country where thought is not allowed.

You draw your lips over his lips, his neck, his cheeks. You

brush his eyelids with your lips, or perhaps your breath alone. You kiss one eyebrow hair into your mouth. You draw the tip of your tongue across his forehead, the place whose wrinkles will someday grow. You rub your beard along his cheek, his neck, his neck, his neck. He groans. You rub your head into his neck like a colt tossing back his mane. You bring your breath to his neck, your lips, your tongue, your teeth. You leave the imprint of yourself there, the purple mark of your having put your mouth here.

Your mouth works slowly down his body. Your body follows. His hard, full cock is nestled against your sternum while you lap his nipples up to full attention, drawing your beard along his belly past the complex knot of his navel until your chin reaches his neatly trimmed patch of black crotch hair. You grab his cock in the fist of your throat. He sighs. He undulates (the wild Ionian Sea).

You push up on his balls with your nose, place the tip of your tongue in the place behind them. He shudders.

You pull up onto your knees and kneel before him, pushing upward on his thighs, licking his balls, and the place where the balls hang from the thighs. He squirms. You draw your wettest tongue along the shaft of his thick cock to its tiny head, then down, then up again, holding his cock in your lips, in your hand, in your lips. You slip your mouth over the top of his dick and pull down on his skin as you swallow him whole.

"Oh, God," he says. You feel his body moving on the bed in many slow directions at once and wonder which God or gods he means.

You swallow, release . . . swallow, release . . .

You push back on his thighs until his knees approach his nipples.

You put your tongue on the dark pucker of his asshole. He is the noise he makes. This drives a groan out of your own mouth.

He pushes his legs down you, shifts you both. He stretches you on your back and throws his legs across your chest, kneeling over you, your cock instantly in his mouth and his asshole inches from your mouth.

You put two glowing hands on his ass and push your thumbs

into the nub of sensation you know where the thigh and buttocks meet and spread the cheeks with your hands. He shifts back toward you and you start to circle the hole with your tongue. Concentric inward movements. You put your tongue on his asshole while he sucks your cock and push the point of it in to him as far as it will go, wetting it as much as you can and pulling the cheeks further and further apart and widening the opening of him until he drops his elbows behind your knees and bends you back on yourself until your own hole is available to his lips, his mouth, his tongue. Your bodies are beginning to flow with sweat.

You can't keep up. You pull him off you, pull him around, attack his mouth with your mouth.

"What do you want?" you ask.

He does not answer. He just looks into your eyes.

"You want to fuck me?" you ask.

"No, baby," he says, "I want you to fuck me."

He sits above you, straddling your hips. He takes a palm full of lotion and rubs it up and down the shaft of your rubbered cock, sliding one long finger down into your asshole, and pulling up on your scrotum with his nails. And then he puts you in, and then he starts to rock.

And for a moment you have a flash of thought, something about color and race and home, but it is alien, fleeting, and soon you stop thinking of anything at all. You are feeling nothing but your cock up the ass of this beautiful man, the sweet hot pain of your nipples gripped between his fingers, the smell the sweat of him and the Versace cologne, the taste the salt of his palms as you pull him toward your mouth, the sound of his breath coming faster and faster between the groans that from deeper and deeper inside him while he rocks faster and faster, pushing down onto you as you arch your back and push higher and higher into him, his cock in your right hand, your left hand pulling his nipples nearly off his smooth and perfect chest, until he starts to cry out in little whimpers like a child who thinks his transgression will soon be found out. And the sound of it slips further and further into his throat and the wave of him ripples the ripples of him and the water pouring out of him runs in rivulets over the hard curves of him until he snaps his head back and down and back again and pulls your hand off his cock (your hand surprised the two are separable) and he grabs his own cock and pulls the skin of it down to his balls and then shoots straight up in the air and then again, both hot spurts of white cum hitting your body simultaneously, and the next and next, hitting you in the chest, neck, face, hair. You hear it hit the pillow behind you. It hits your stomach and fills your navel and gathers in the graying hair of your chest while he groans like the war wounded, until he collapses onto you.

And you pull out of him, which makes him take a sharp swallow of air, and you cradle him into your left arm, pull the rubber off your dick by the tip, tossing it across the room as it snaps, and you pull until you cum, the hot white fluid splashing your chest and stomach, splashing his shoulders, waist, hips. And you let out an animal groan of your own and shudder so hard its almost a spasm, your balls so high into your body you think they must be squeezing out your asshole, and this surprises him, and he puts his hand over your heart as you turn to him and kiss him again and again.

And you lie there, your bodies slowing down, growing silent.

And are you thinking now? You believe you are not. But you are wondering if he will go and hoping he will not go.

"Do you want a towel?" he asks.

"I'll get you one," you say.

"Oh, I'll need more than a towel," he says. And you both laugh.

You let the hot water run over you forever as you stand in the hotel bathtub wrapped around each other in the Greek night.

In bed, you wrap the smooth hotel sheets around his satiny skin. You turn out the single light. The Acropolis has long been dark. Soon it will be dawn. The rosy-fingered dawn will creep over the hills of Athens and will find you both asleep there. You, at least, will be giving thanks.

E VERO?

Edmund White

HAROLD MOVED INTO suite 108 of the Duomo Hotel in Milan
and took it for a year, on condition that he could remodel
it. The suite was two stories high, with a sitting room below
and a bedroom above. The window overlooked the side of the
cathedral (a hundred spires of newly washed ancient stone)
and the line of teenage boys who sat along the rail beside the
subway entrance below. Harold knew that almost all of them
considered themselves straight, but he thought he had found
a way around their objections.

Bettina, his Italian secretary and a woman of striking, severe
looks, stood in the window with Harold, behind the drawn
curtains. Harold pointed out the young man who had caught
his fancy. Bettina then sallied forth to explain to the young man
that she could pay him 100,000 lira (50 bucks) if he would
be willing to make love to her boss, a woman so famous he
wouldn't be permitted to see her. Bettina hinted that her boss
was an American movie star.

The whole process of lining up their pigeon took an hour. It
included a stroll through the Galleria and a drink in a café. At
first the young man thought Bettina herself was picking him
up. But when he was relaxed and moving in on her, Bettina,
with feigned timidity, sprang her odd request on him. He was

Harold's type: a big, young peasant ill at ease in his new city clothes.

He was led back to the impressive hotel suite and upstairs to the bedroom, which had been cleared of all furniture and outfitted with a floor that was a one-way mirror. Even the floor of the adjoining bathroom was such a mirror; Harold could see the young man, but the young man couldn't see him. Harold had installed a false ceiling in the downstairs room and between this ceiling and the mirrored floor he'd arranged a dark, mattress-lined cubbyhole for himself. He was already hiding in there when Bettina returned.

Once Harold had attended a concert given by Laurie Anderson in which she had used a microphone that had lowered her voice electronically so that she sounded like a man. Now Harold seized on a similar device to transmit his voice into the upper bedroom – and make it sound like a woman's.

While Bettina made Massimo a Campari and soda, Harold spoke to him in an Italian that was fluent, although his American accent was quite heavy.

Bettina went downstairs and left the suite. Harold said, in his woman's voice, "I hope you'll forgive me for this odd arrangement, but I have to keep my identity secret. Maybe next time, when I know you better, I can come out of hiding. Do you understand?

"Sure, sure, I understand."

"But you know I was looking out the window at you and I just had to meet you. You're so handsome. You can call me Diana."

"*Ciao*, Diana."

"Why don't you just take your clothes off? I'm lying here below you, and I'm all soft and hot and naked."

"*Below* me?"

"Yes. I like looking up at your strong, masculine body. You know what I mean?"

"Sure, sure, I can guess."

Massimo was obviously an unusually bright lad with a touch of kink in him. Despite traces of a Sicilian accent and his swarthy looks, apparently he had lived in the northern city long enough to adjust to big-city eccentricities. However, he was still enough of a Sicilian village peacock to enjoy a woman's flattery.

He unbuttoned his beige short-sleeved shirt and tossed it to one side. Sure enough, he had a guinea T-shirt on underneath. Even from this odd angle Harold could see that Massimo had massive biceps and flossy black silk under his arms. Harold could see everything – even the run-down heels on his shoes and the hole in his left sole.

"You look real good, Massimo, Take off the rest of your clothes. You're getting me real hot." Harold was speaking in his best imitation of a breathy Marilyn Monroe voice, and the microphone was working perfectly.

Pretending to be shy but showing all the confidence of a handsome young man who has never disappointed anyone by undressing, Massimo ran a callused palm through his hair and pulled off his T-shirt, slacks, and his black bikini underwear.

He had a great big uncircumcised dick, heavy big balls (one heavier than the other), hairy legs with rugby-sized thighs and calves, and a big hairy butt. Like a country boy, he left his dirty argyle socks on until "Diana" begged him to take those off, too. And, like a country boy, he folded everything neatly and piled his clothes in a corner.

"Oh, Massimo!" Diana groaned. "*Che bel uomo*! You sure are great looking. You know, my juices are flowing and my pussy's real wet just looking at you."

"*Vero*? For sure? I'd smile at you if I knew where you were."

"You can do more than that, Massimo. You can kiss me. Lie down on the floor, facedown. I'm right under you, just a few inches away from you."

Harold had already been admiring the big peasant feet just above his head, the soles white where the maximum pressure was exerted by this massive 200-pound, six-foot-three brute. He certainly deserved his name: Massimo. Now he lay down on the glass and for a moment squeezed his face into a horrible distortion, clowning like Jerry Lewis and then laughing, misting the glass with his breath. The mist cleared to reveal his beautiful white teeth, clean pink tongue, the shaved black beard that appeared to be sprouting hairs before Harold's very eyes.

Harold noticed that Massimo had pressed his cock against his belly. Harold licked the glass the length of the full ten inches.

"Right now, Massimo, I'm licking your cock. Can you feel it?"

For a second, Massimo's diaphragm lifted off the glass with a little chuckle, but then he whispered, "Yes, I can feel it. It feels wonderful, Diana, when you take it like that in your mouth." And indeed, the big cock was getting bigger, the sticky head emerged from its sheath and the balls tightened a notch, shifting slightly forward. Harold noticed the hard brown nipples pressed to the glass and the glossy chest hairs ringleting around the gold cross. A drop of sweat was running down from his armpit, and it splashed just over Harold's mouth.

"Now my lips are just below yours, Massimo. Why don't you kiss me? I'm just a little blonde girl – I hope I'm not crushed by your big male body."

"*Oh, mia cara Diana, ti adoro,*" Massimo breathed, his long black lashes fluttering shut, his lips wet and open, his hands clutching against the glass with frustration. "Diana, why don't you let me touch your body? I'll close my eyes. I won't try to find out your identity."

"Next time, Massimo, next time. Massimo, please, let me see your big hand wrap around your cock. Why don't you lie on your side?"

Massimo turned obediently onto his left side. His right fingers came down and grasped the big cock and worked it slowly, just inches away from Harold's mouth. He followed "Diana's" instructions on how to show the head, how to nestle his balls, how to wet the head with spit.

"Think of it as my own juices, Massimo. Oh, I'm so excited! I'm close to coming, but I'm waiting for you."

Massimo was biting his lower lip and beating his meat furiously. Harold watched his slender waist rise and fall as his diaphragm lifted and his breathing grew more rapid. At last he pounded the glass with his fist and laughed and said embarrassedly, "Diana, I have to make pipi first. The Camparis, you know?"

"Sure, Massimo, sure. But, *caro,* will you think I'm crazy if

I tell you I'd like to share everything, absolutely everything, with you?"

"Like what, my Diana?" He'd already stood up, his soles pressing white above Harold. His balls, which looked as big as apples, hid the view of his erect cock until it began to melt.

"Why don't you piss right here? Let me see that, too? I've never seen a man piss, specially not such a big, strong man. Why don't you take just a step backward. Oh, Massimo, I'm lying right under you, and you're looking like a god. Your strong hairy legs, your big cock, your beautiful balls, your tight stomach rising and falling. Why don't you give me everything, Massimo? You're not afraid to, are you? Foreign women don't frighten you, do they?"

"No, no, Diana darling. But if only I could see you . . ."

Harold instructed Massimo to go over to a shelf built into the wall and pick up a photo there of an exquisite blonde woman with high breasts, wasp waist, a hairless cunt, long shapely legs. "That's my picture, Massimo. My face is in shadow to protect my identity."

Massimo looked at the picture while he pissed in a strong, hot jet up and down the mirrored floor above Harold. The water splashed with force and ran in pools. Harold licked the other side of the glass with his tongue. Then Massimo, following "Diana's" instructions, legs spread and looking like one of the bronzes of Riaci, jerked off, the picture slipping from his hand, the gobs of cream leaping and splattering six feet away from where he stood. Harold shot at the same moment, his come splattering on the other side of the glass. Massimo's body was still pumping come, like a well spurting oil, as he sank to his knees in a swoon.

THE DAY I WENT GAY

Lars Eighner

A TREE FELL on the garage during a thunderstorm the day they took Rhona to the loony bin. It did not do much damage except that I would have to ask Loogie and his stepfather Arthur to help me get it off the garage, and I hated to ask Loogie for that kind of help. I mention it only in case you believe in omens. It turned out to be the most significant day of my life.

I suppose I ought to call this how I found out I was gay, seduced my best friend and a cop and found true love – well, at least for the summer. I wasn't doing any of it on purpose, you know. I don't know whether I was in the closet because my whole sex had been entirely theoretical. Sometimes I am asked how I could not have known because I must have fantasized about something when I choked the chicken, spanked the monkey, polished the knob, lubed the tube, or whatever the politically correct expression is for jacking off. But I did not have time for fantasy because I was working on technique. And those hours and hours of practice paid off because I learned to give a handjob so good it would bring tears to your eyes, and thus I was ready when Rhona went nuts.

I spent most of my days in the hole, which was the basement if you came at it from the front of the house, but was the first floor if you came from the back of the house. I believe my parents had meant, one day, to put in a pool and the hole was supposed to be a kind of pool house. There were two bathrooms in the hole, each with a shower stall. Since the showers were down there, I did not have to go upstairs, and most nights I slept on the sofa in the game room. By the time Rhona went off the deep end I was practically living in the hole.

And practicing with my dick. I practiced with my dick in the hole almost every waking moment except when Loogie and Arthur, who is Loogie's stepfather but only a couple of years older than Loogie, would come over to play cards or video games or whatever to pass the time while they hid out from Loogie's mother. They would bring beer and chips and dips and I had a little fits-on-a-shelf refrigerator down there, so mostly that was what we lived on – beer and chips and dips and delivery pizza which we got when Loogie's mom gave one of them some money, although for reasons I did not understand the delivery guy would often give us the pizza "on the house" as he would say.

Now, of course, I see there was a better way for me to have gone gay. But I didn't do it. Arthur and Loogie pretty much let themselves into the hole when they came over. Somehow they never caught me jacking off, which seems odd because I was jacking off so much the law of averages would say they would. But they thought they did one time when they didn't.

I had fallen asleep on the sofa in my underwear. They woke me when they opened the door, and I hopped up. Nothing peculiar about that; I often wore my underwear when they came over and when it was hot they would strip down to not much more. The hole wasn't air-conditioned because it was supposed to be a changing room if there had been a pool. But when I got up I had a stiffy and Loogie said, "Nice boner, dude!" I never can tell when Loogie means to be sarcastic. But Arthur said, "Sorry man, we can walk around the block or something while you finish."

They could not really have walked around the block because Loogie's mother would have spotted them and all their efforts to sneak out of the house would have been wasted. But I said "Finish what?"

I had left all my lubes out on the little table by the sofa. Loogie and Arthur looked at the table. Then they looked at my boner which was obvious in my underwear, then they looked at each other and the ceiling. And they said, more or less, "Sorry, dude, we didn't mean to accuse you of the heinous crime of jerking off. We know you'd never do such a thing and heaven knows we never do any such thing, and we wouldn't even hang out with a guy who would think of touching himself down there, but ya have got a nice boner on, dude."

And I'm like, "Fuck you both. I jack off. I practically live on my back. I just didn't happen to be doing it this time."

"Whatever you say, dude," said Loogie.

But Arthur was looking at the lubes, handling them. I had some of those therapeutic hand lotions, baby oil, Vaseline, hair-styling jell, a couple of tubes of stuff that is actually made for jacking off that I got in the mail. Arthur picked up the Corn Husker's lotion. "Aw, this is great stuff man," he said and he was almost misty-eyed about it. "I wish I could keep some of this at the house."

That was a hot afternoon and it turned into a hot night. While Loogie and I were playing a few rounds of some stupid video game, Arthur picked up the Corn Husker's lotion and went to the showers. We often did that – just step in the shower to get wet – when it was hot. But of course Arthur was in the shower awhile. So if I had a hint I was gay, that was it. When Arthur came back from the shower, he had put his little safari shorts back on, but not his shirt, and his chest was still red, and I knew he had shot off in my shower stall and used my Corn Husker's lotion. My boner came back, but we had moved the card table to play spades and wait for the pizza, so neither of them noticed my new hard-on.

After that I always left my lubes out, and Arthur and once in a while Loogie would borrow them and take them to the shower or one of the toilets. And Loogie and Arthur would mention it sometimes and comment as to whether it had been real good or not. This bothered me a little because after all Arthur was Loogie's stepfather, although only a couple of years older than us, and by a couple of years, I mean he was almost exactly two-and-a-half years older than Loogie and that is fifteen months or so older than me.

And once when Loogie went to the store for beer, Arthur went to one of the showers, but came back out dripping, naked, with a hard-on. He picked up the Corn Husker's from the table. "Forgot this," he said.

"Yep," I said.

"I mean to give you money sometime because I use so much of this."

"It's OK." I had a trust fund and he didn't have any money of his own and he was always promising to pay me back for things whenever he got some money.

"Well . . ." he said. "You got any porn?"

I didn't. I had a couple of tapes I made of me jerking off, but I didn't think of them when he asked about porn. I wondered why I didn't have any porn. I thought, yeah, I ought to get some. But I didn't have any.

"Well . . ." he said, standing there with his hard dick bobbing up and down in front of him and my Corn Husker's lotion in his hands. "I've been doing sit-ups again," he said, and punched himself in the belly.

"It shows," I said, although I couldn't really tell any difference because he had always looked pretty muscular to me.

"Well . . ." he said. And he went back to the shower which he had left running.

So unless you are as stupid as I was then, you see what I mean about my having the opportunity to go gay in a better way. But I didn't until Rhona went nuts.

Rhona had been mean as a snake since Mom and Dad were killed. She'd been mean to me for nine years running. I think she blamed me because I was in the car at the time of the accident. I wasn't driving. If people could get put away somewhere for meanness, Rhona would have gone there a long time ago. When she went bonkers I think it was all that meanness building up in her and she deserved it. I don't want to offend any innocent victims of mental illness. Since Rhona's living with them, they have enough problems.

She cut off her hair and said she was giving up sex. Shaved her head clean. Her scalp was real white because it didn't get any rays when she went to the tanning place. She broke stuff and made a lot of noise, and she called up people at random and saying "Fuckshitpisscuntcocksucker!" to them. So Nana called the sheriff. I guess Nana thought she was living out in the country again. So even though she called the sheriff, the police came and then Nana pretended she couldn't hear at all and they were going to send for a sign language interpreter but I prevailed upon Nana to admit she could hear when Rhona came downstairs.

"I'm gonna git my lopping shears and I'm gonna lop off your balls," she said to the man cop. "Yup, gonna lop 'em right off." And this was especially odd because Rhona usually enunciates very clearly and doesn't talk like John Wayne except when she is crazy.

The man cop moved his hand suddenly. I thought he was going for his gun. But it was like an involuntary thing. He was going to cover up, you know. It was just a split second motion. Rhona is very convincing when she is crazy, and she never does anything, but the convincing way she says things like "lop 'em right off" tends to spook people so bad that probably she does belong in the loony bin.

"I bet you want me to jack-off your dick," Rhona said in a somewhat too familiar way to the man cop. He began to blush and was more than a little flustered. "You want me to jerk off your dick, too?" Rhona said to the female cop. "Stay the hell out of it or ah'll lop your nuts off too. Yup, I'm gonna get my lopping shears."

That tore it. Rhona was on her way to the rubber room at la-la city, singing "Fuckyoufuckyoufuckyoufuckyou," and so forth as she went.

Rhona bade me farewell with: "Faggot cocksucking queerbait, you just want to suck that cocksucking cop's dick." This is the gift of prophecy that is the compensation for being bonkers. When she said it, the man cop and I sneaked a peek at each other. We both looked away quickly. I did not yet quite want to suck his dick, but I pictured myself kneeling in front of him, with his nightstick at the back of my neck, pulling my head nearer and nearer to his crotch. And if that picture did not turn me at just that instant, at least I didn't see anything wrong with it.

Nana didn't say another thing to me, but went to her room

and rocked and giggled for the rest of the day, and every so often she would cackle "Les secateurs de lopping, ha, ha, ha!" This was odd because I did not know she spoke French at all. In fact Nana was, or actually her parents, who were my great-grandparents, were pretty much German sympathizers, not just before the Second World War but during it. That seemed to have caused a little trouble and they had to move from one town to another several times.

She was taking too much Halcyon again and had made me talk to the doctor and swear that I had seen her accidentally spill almost a whole bottle into the sink. And the doctor okayed another refill, but I thought he smelled a rat and it would not be too long before Nana would have to find another doctor again.

I had, however, found a way to get her to drink her Ensure. When the liquor store guy would come with her Bailey's I would open the bottles and pour half the liquor out into a big pickle jar and top the bottles off with Ensure. Thus, I always had a large amount of Bailey's on hand in a big jar because I didn't often drink it.

As soon as Rhona was carted off, the phone in the study began ringing. That had been Dad's line for his home office. We never had it taken out. Rhona had kind of taken over the study the way I had taken over the hole and she had taken over that phone line too. It may have been ringing a long time before I answered the first call. Nana is not deaf, but she is hard of hearing enough not to hear the phone in the study and I couldn't hear from the hole.

I answered it the first time and got hung-up on. As soon as I put the phone down, it rang again, and this time someone asked for Rhona. He wouldn't believe – maybe he didn't want to believe – Rhona wasn't there and wasn't expected any time soon. So it went for a while, ring, click, ring, curses, ring, is Rhona there, until I recognized the voice that asked for Rhona.

"Loogie?"

"Yeah."

"You're calling Rhona?"

"You didn't know? No, I guess you didn't."

"Know what?"

"Ahh . . . umm . . . where is Rhona?"

"Lost her shit. Went to the funny farm. You know, committed. Probably won't out get for 90 days, at least. Now you. You tell me what I don't know."

"I'm coming over."

Loogie told me. His real name is Hugh Kroughk. We call him Loogie. We always did.

Rhona, he said, was very popular since she took over the study. I asked him, popular how? Popular, he said, like she would give anyone a handjob – anyone, any time.

He said he had to take a whiz before I could ask the next question. I said use the bathroom under the stairs. But sit down for christssake, don't try to use it standing up. "I know," he said.

It wasn't really a bath, just a crapper and a lavatory. The way the ceiling slanted, if you were more than about five foot six you couldn't pee in the crapper like a man – at least you couldn't get close enough to have but about a 59 per cent chance of hitting the bullseye with more than about 43 per cent of what you're aiming at it. Sure, it's great to be able to whiz standing up. Most of the time it is. But it's like a guy forgets how to whiz any other way. But they don't really forget. It's just every time they have to whiz, it's like one more chance to prove they've got a dick. And they can't pass that up, most of them can't.

And that is why the hall bathroom was always a mess, I thought. But then I thought – wait, who uses the hall bathroom? I don't. When Arthur and Loogie come over, they never go upstairs. And how did Loogie know he had to sit down in the hall bathroom. Maybe years ago, when we were both little kids, Loogie had come over and come in the front door – I don't remember – but he wasn't a tall, skinny, pasty-colored goth or vampire or whatever-he-is then. Then, he was a little kid who could have used it standing up.

He'd been my friend a long time. I thought he hated Rhona. But then I realized I was remembering him like he was when we were ten years old, and he thought all girls were icky. I realized that he grew out of that, not that it mattered much because once he did the girls returned the favor and generally thought Loogie was icky, with the exception of Vladia, queen of the goths or vampires or whatever, and I guess she didn't find him too icky because they had drunk each other's blood.

When he came out I said, "When you said Rhona jerks off anyone, what did you mean by anyone?"

"Anyone."

"Including you."

"Sure."

"Including Arthur?"

"Well, no. He asked me about it. But he said he had too much respect for you."

"He had too much respect for me, but you didn't."

"Aw gee, man. It was only handjobs. Don't be so bourgeois."

Loogie told me how it worked. Rhona gave guys handjobs in the parlor. They would come in through the sliding door to the patio. They would leave that way too. If the patio light was on, it meant Rhona wasn't occupied. If the light was on, a guy would push through the hedge and just go into the parlor. Sometimes Rhona would forget about the light, and a guy would go in but Rhona would be working on another guy. Loogie was real careful to be sure the light was right when he visited Rhona because once when Rhona was doing him this other guy came in, and the other guy was real good about it and pretended to look at the picture of the geese while he waited for Rhona to finish off Loogie. But it freaked out Loogie and he had to leave and finish himself off in the bushes. So he didn't want that to happen again.

According to Loogie, Rhona was busier than a two-dollar whore at a Shriners' convention – except she didn't charge two dollars. I told Loogie he shouldn't tell a guy his sister gives handjobs. Loogie said I was a middle-class moralist. And besides, he said, he thought I ought to know under the circumstances.

I would have unplugged the phone in the study, but I discovered it had been there so long that it had never been converted to a plug-in jack. It was still wired into the wall. I could have gone back to hole where I wouldn't have heard it. But I couldn't help answering it – some sort of morbid curiosity, I guess. I'd have to explain to them that they did get right number, but Rhona wasn't here, and she wasn't coming back very soon. Some of the guys were real suspicious of me. A lot of them had no idea Rhona had a brother. Some of them were whiners. A few asked me if I knew any other hot numbers.

I got the jar of Bailey's and took it to the parlor and sipped on it while I answered calls. Before long I got the first of the calls that when I had explained about Rhona, being gone, the guy on the line said, "How about you? Will you talk to me?" I talked to him. I talked to him about his dick. Guys on the phone always have big, hard dicks. That first call when he asked me if I was jacking off too, I lied and said I was. I was lying that first time. I had some more Bailey's. The sun went down.

I had washed the pickle jar, but the Bailey's still tasted a little of garlic and dill.

About eleven o'clock I heard a crash out on the patio, and I went out to look. One of the neighbor's cat had knocked over a plant. I set the plant upright and went back into the study. But of course I wasn't thinking what I was doing and I left the patio light on. The patio used to be the outside entrance to Dad's home office.

I had just settled back down on the sofa when this guy's shoe caught the runner of the patio door and he stumbled into the room. He was letting his pants down as he came in, but with the bottle in one hand he'd lost control of his pants. He saw, of course, that I wasn't Rhona. He was helpless to alter his trajectory and he plopped down on the sofa next to me. I had noticed he wasn't wearing any underwear, and I was a little worried about hash marks on the sofa, because he was bare-butt by the time he hit the sofa. He sat still for a moment so the room could stop rotating. His erection was sort of mixed up with his uniform shirt, but I could see that it was there.

"So," he said.

I said, "So?"

"So," he said, "I guess you are a real special guy."

I explained about Rhona being crackers, a couple of times, but at first he didn't quite understand that she had not just left the room for a moment and that she wasn't coming back, and when he did understand that, it was as if he had been kicked in the nuts. He balled up, squeezing his forearms between his thighs, and screaming silently. I patted him on the back. That's when I went gay.

My hand touched the moist shirt on his back. That was like testing a hot iron with a wet finger and it was the first time I realized that hot was not just metaphor when it came to horny guys. I had to swallow a couple of times before I could speak.

"Look, man," I said, "don't feel so bad. If you want, I'll jack you off."

He sat up and leaned back in the sofa. This time his erection had found it's way through the part in his shirt. I admired it.

"You?"

"Sure, I'll be glad to. It's the least I can do."

"You're a guy."

"I'm Rhona's brother. It'd kind of be like the same thing."

"So, you a fag or something."

"Maybe." If he had asked me if I was gay, I probably would have been ready then to say yes, but fag? I mean, yes, it is not a very nice word for a gay guy, but also it is just a word for a geek or dweeb or someone like that. I don't identify with it. "But it's me or nothing," I added.

"You ever jack a guy off before?" He began to tweak his penis, sort of like grooming it around the head.

"Sure I've jacked a guy off."

"Who?"

"Who what?"

"Who have you jacked off?"

"Actually only me. But I'm a guy. I know how to do it."

He took his hand off his penis. He felt around the sofa and found the long brown sack with his bottle in it. He pulled the sack off the bottle and looked at the level of whiskey left in it. He started to unscrew the cap. I was admiring him the whole time. He had the bottle up to his lips when he noticed that I was admiring him.

"Oh. Well, yeah, sure. You can jack me off." He took the bottle from his lips and sort of motioned with it. "There's some stuff in there."

"In there" was a piano bench which was used as a coffee table in the study and I found a bottle of baby oil, along with a lot of other stuff I didn't take the time to sort through. While he took a real big drag on the Turkey I squirted the oil on his penis and on my hand, and then I took a deep breath, and wrapped my fist around his penis.

Now probably I should say it was about two feet long, hard as steel pipe, and thick as a beer can. It wasn't. It was more than adequate, although I suppose anything you can get a fist around and still have some room to stroke is adequate for handjob purposes. Of course it felt enormous to me. I imagine the first penis anyone ever jacks off except his own feels enormous. But the major impression was hot, physically, literally, Bunsen-burner hot.

He lay his head back and closed his eyes and he moaned softly "Oh, yeah, that feels good, you have nice soft hands, feels, good, feels, your doing fine, yeah, you OK . . ." But for a while he didn't seem to be saying it with much conviction but more the way you say "Oh, yes, very good, I like it a lot" when someone has read you some of their own poetry. But I shifted in the sofa and got a better grip and he shut up for a little while before he started gasp. He started tugging at my T-shirt, stretching it all out of shape, and finally got it all off of me except for the hand I was jacking him off with, so I was jacking him off through the armhole and the rest of it was wadded up on his lap. It was one of my favorite T-shirts. He started kind of fondling my shoulders and he ran a finger along my clavicle, before his hand headed south.

I'm not very muscular, but I do have big tits, all out of proportion with my arms or deltoids or anything, but they don't squeeze very good. He squeezed. He ran a finger around my nipple and then he tugged at the little knob of my nipple. He squeezed my whole tit again. Then he sat up like Dracula from the coffin and opened his eyes and looked at me.

I stopped moving my hand on his dick, but I didn't let go.

"Oh yeah," he said, "you're a guy."

"It's OK. You can play with my tits if you like."

"They're hairy."

"Two hairs, and none, well OK one on the other one."

"Yeah, fuck. Three little hairs. What does it matter." He flicked the tips of my nipples with his thumb. "You a fag?" he asked again.

"I'm playing with your dick," I said, except I wasn't so much playing with it as holding it.

"Yeah, I guess so. You want to see a real hairy chest?"

"Uh, sure." I said.

While he ripped off his shirt Superman-style I let go of his dick long enough to toss my T-shirt out of harm's way. He didn't have a really hairy chest but it was hair, with a big patch in the center and two hairy circles around his nipples, with a sort of fluffy splotch on his belly that merged into a four-lane highway above his navel and then ran down to his pubes. He ruffled the hair up with the flats of his hands.

He became pretty much lost in himself for a while and I thought if he had a mirror it would be over in a hurry although I wasn't really doing much good in the handjob department because I considered myself stunned by his awesome beauty and manliness, which were pretty much the same thing to me. He wasn't really all that gorgeous, although he was way better than average, but he was my first, if handjobs count for anything.

He was actually reeling drunk, but I had never been very drunk, and I attributed most of his behavior to lust. He snapped out of it and sat forward again. He killed the bottle. He felt my chest again, this time very gently. He lay back again. I began to stroke him again like I meant business.

"Oh, fuck," he said, "I am afraid this was a bad idea. If my dad saw this he'd kill me, if seeing it didn't kill him first."

I hesitated. "You want me to stop?"

"Oh god no, don't stop. Please don't stop. It won't take much longer. Please."

"OK." And I went to work again.

"Please don't stop."

"I won't."

"I'll try hard to come. It's almost there. Don't stop."

"I won't," I said again.

It was not, of course, almost there. But after five sweaty minutes, I clearly was getting somewhere. He began to thrust into my fist, although in no particularly coordinated or effective rhythm.

"Please," he moaned, "please take it . . . just this one time . . . suck my dick . . . just once . . ."

I bent over and put my mouth around it. I had wanted to do that anyway. Instantly I had to swallow or drown. I knew it had been close. But I didn't know it was that close.

From the moment I decided to do that I was worried about how I would react to the taste. The taste wasn't bad, but I don't think anyone does it for the taste. While Mark panted and caught his breath I had a very large swallow of Bailey's from the pickle jar. The combination was great.

"Oh fuck, you did it," he said.

"Yeah. I mean, wasn't I supposed to?"

"I've never gotten . . . Not once. No matter how much I begged. Oh fuck, you did it."

He was deeply touched and pulled me toward him. I could feel every hair on his chest against my hairless chest, every single one.

"I want to kiss you," he said.

"Go ahead."

"I can't kiss you. You're a guy."

"I'm the guy who sucked your dick," I said. I thought that I had. It would be awhile before I understood that really sucking dick was much different.

So, he kissed me.

"Sweet," he said.

It was the Bailey's.

The human body is sometimes a very uncontrollable thing. I would not have done it if I could have controlled it. But as he held me against his chest my pelvis thrust against him and even as drunk as he was he could feel the hard lump in my pants. His hand went to my belt, and with a little fumbling he pulled my pants half down my thighs, taking my underwear with them. This surprised me, but it seemed to shock him more, as if he had not been sure what that lump had been before.

In the moment's hesitation, I got my hand around my own dick and began to stroke it to the beat of the band. I had hardly realized how aroused I was until my dick was out of my pants, but now that it was I had to deal with it the only way I knew how.

"I can't suck you," he said.

"I know," I said. "Just hold me."

"I should eat you all night if I had to, to make you come."

"Shut up," I said.

He grabbed my wrist. My hips continued to thrust involuntarily. I couldn't believe it. He began to bend over. He wrapped a hand around the base of my dick. His face got closer to my crotch until he was staring at my dick, eye-to-eye.

Oh, my God, it's going to happen I thought.

"I . . . I . . ." he said, and then he threw up on my dick. He threw up pretty much all over my belly and thighs. Then he rolled onto the floor and passed out.

"Oops, pardon me, I didn't mean to interrupt anything." It was Loogie. The guy had not turned off the patio light when he came in. Loogie, who had known Rhona had been carted away, saw the light and thought Rhona had escaped or something and gone back in business. The patio door was open and he had walked in just as Mark hurled on my manhood. What is more he had been whipping out his dick when he walked in.

Loogie zipped his pants back up. "Kinky," he said. "Smells like home cooking!"

Vomit doesn't faze Loogie much. His mom's a bulimic.

He knew where the paper towels were but that wasn't nearly good enough, so I sent him for a towel. When we got enough vomit off me so I didn't actually drip, we stood the stranger up and marched him to the shower next to my bedroom, my real bedroom upstairs, not the hole. We threw him into the shower and then all the clothes and the towel and I turned on the water. That left me naked so I stepped into the stall and rinsed the vomit off me.

When a guy blows beets on your crotch, that's pretty much a mood breaker, but I was still fairly bloated in the penis department and positively swollen in the testicle department, and I would have given the guy a creme-rinse for his hair, which I figured he deserved, if Loogie had not been standing there, propping the shower stall door open with his very skinny body and staring at the whole scene pretty intensely.

At best Loogie looks like death – not death warmed over, but death very badly microwaved. I left the shower running on the coolish side of tepid, wrapped a fresh towel around my waist, and grabbed another fresh towel in case I'd need it for whatever stuff might have got splattered around the study.

The study it turned out was not so bad. But the smell was awful. Loogie opened the piano bench and pulled a little spray can of something out.

"What's that?" I ask.

"Stuff they use at hospitals and mortuaries to kill the smell."

Rhona had wanted something like that and Loogie had nicked it from the funeral home where the guy on night shift lets Loogie look at the bodies. Loogie makes doughnut runs for the guy, and I guess if you work there on night shift even Loogie is a lively conversationalist. Anyway the spray worked like a charm. So since Loogie showed the spray to me and he had ripped it off to begin with, I offered him half of the Bailey's that was left in the pickle jar, reminding him to only take half.

"No, you drink what you want, and I'll take the rest."

"You don't want to drink after me," I said, forgetting that I had taken a big hit of it after I let the guy come in my mouth.

"Why not?"

"I sucked that guy's dick."

"And . . .?"

"He came in my mouth."

"Well, duh, you said you sucked him."

"So you don't want to drink after me."

"Fuck it," he said. He drank, as precisely as he could, exactly half the Bailey's. Then I downed the other half.

Loogie wanted to know how long I'd been sucking cock and all. So I told him the whole story.

"So you sucked a dick and got liquid pizza on your lap. And this is your sex life, so far?"

"I liked it."

"You liked it?"

"Yeah, I liked it. So how many dicks have you ever sucked?"

"Well, none," Loogie admitted.

"How many guys have come in your mouth?"

"Well, none."

"Have you ever touched another guy's cock?"

"You mean a guy who was alive?"

Oh, shit, I wasn't going to ask. I was real sure, I didn't want to know. "Let's not go there, Loogie. I mean, how many guys, I mean living guys, have you ever wanted to have sex with?"

"Well, none. You know I'm straight. I mean like heterosexual."

"But that is just it, Loogie. I'm not."

Just then there was a knock at the front door. I still had a clean towel, so I wrapped it around my waist.

It was the man cop, the one who had taken Rhona away.

"I noticed your patio light was on," he said, "and I thought I ought to advise you to turn it off."

"And why is that?" I asked as innocently as I could. He was wearing a grey cop T-shirt which was about two sizes too small and his pecs were about to burst it. He had blue nylon running shorts. I couldn't see his legs in the dark, but from the dark circles under his arms, I supposed he had been jogging by.

"You sister sometimes has . . . um late callers, and perhaps with the light on . . ." He couldn't quite form the words.

"Perhaps you had better come in and tell me about it."

As the cop came in I stuck my head into the study and shooed Loogie out the patio door.

"Oh, I think we can talk in here," I said.

He perched gingerly on the edge of the sofa. I sniffed to be sure he couldn't smell anything. He was just nervous about what he had to tell me.

"I'll make it easy," I said. "I know Rhona gave half the city handjobs in here. What I want to know is how you know that." My towel fell open as I sat on the sofa next to him, and I did not adjust it completely.

"Some guys . . . guys at the precinct brought me here one night."

"And did she jack you off."

"No."

"No?"

"I didn't really want . . . well, there were a lot of us and the other guys went first. And then, well, the moment had passed for me."

"You got hot and jerked off on the patio."

"Well, something like that."

"So I guess that's it," I said, "unless . . ." I was whispering, "you'll let me suck your dick." I thought maybe I'd seen something working in his shorts.

"What?" he said.

"You heard me."

"Yeah, I did." He sat quietly for a second. I didn't know whether he would bust me. I didn't know if he could bust. Then he leaned back on the sofa pushing his shorts halfway to his knees. "Is this what you want?"

It was a bloated slab of meat far larger than any I had seen before, not yet hard. He lifted it with a finger. His pubic hair was as blond as the hair on his head.

"Yeah, I want to suck your dick."

He flipped the loose towel off my lap. My dick was hard. He touched it.

"You're pretty fucking horny," he said. "Does the idea of sucking my dick turn you on like that?"

"Yes."

"Then, go ahead and do what you want, but you better be ready to take it because I haven't come in two days."

He leaned back on the sofa and in a couple of twitches his cock was completely hard.

I put my hand around his cock.

"Suck it," he said, "suck it fast and hard."

I felt it with my hand. I ran my fingers over its tip. "Suck it now," he insisted.

I put my lips around it, got it wet, and tasted the slit, and then he thrust up into my throat. I kept my mouth locked on his cock while I peeled the shorts off of his legs, rolled off the sofa and knelt between his knees. "Please, hurry. I want to shoot off in your mouth," he said.

One of his hands had slipped up under the gray cop T-shirt. I put his other hand on the back of my neck. He hadn't brought his night stick with him.

I wrapped my arms around his back, and sucked. I could hardly move my head for he had clamped my head to his crotch, and yet somehow the thrusting of his hips made his cock swell and slide against the back of my throat.

"Do you want me to come?" he asked.

I tried to nod.

"Do you want me to come in your mouth?"

I tried to nod again.

He released the back of my neck and took my ears in his hand. He moved my head up and down his shaft rapidly. Moaning, threatening to shoot. And then he almost pulled my ears off, pulling my head tight against his pubes. He was still, and his cock was hard and thick in my mouth. I thought it was over, a dry come, and then the jets started pulsing up his shaft.

It was thick, thick as tapioca. I tried to swallow. I sucked, like sucking Jell-o through a straw. More came. I guessed he really had not come in a couple of days.

Slowly he relaxed. His cock shrank a little, not much. I had to breath and pulled off it.

"Like that?"

"Yes," I said.

"Like it as much as you thought you would?"

"Yeah."

He pulled up his T-shirt. "Suck my tit," he said. He indicated a dark brown knot on a mound of muscle.

I licked it. He pressed my head against it. I bit. I sucked. He grabbed his cock and began stroking it and after about ten strokes he said, "Get another wad if you want it."

I moved my mouth to his cock and just as my lips covered it, he shot another, more fluid wad in my mouth. I was dazed. He was gone in almost no time with a final reminder to turn off the patio light.

Now, my nuts were really heavy. I lay back on the sofa thinking of having a first rate jackoff in just a few minutes. I must have had the greatest boner I had ever had up to that time. I was going to feel it throb awhile before I started beating it.

"I don't mean to startle you."

I had forgot about Loogie. I opened my eyes.

Shit! I thought. Loogie had lost his pants. But instead of the sickly white worm I had seen between Loogie's legs when he changed, there was a big, purple-headed pole. Yeah, his chest was still so pale it was practically green and he was still skinny. But he was – what? – not disgusting with that hard-on.

"Nice boner," I said.

"You, too. He shouldn't have left you like that."

"It's OK. I was about to jack off."

Loogie was stroking his cock slowly and it was weeping sticky strings of precome. "Would you close your eyes," he said. "I don't think I can do this while you're watching me." So I guessed he was going to jack off on the spot, which I thought was rude, but I didn't want to argue. I closed my eyes.

Loogie's hand closed around my dick. It was slick, perhaps with lube from the piano bench or perhaps from Loogie's own personal lubricant. When I opened my eyes, I saw his mouth just above the tip of my cock. "I don't suck good," he said, "but I'll jack you off into my mouth."

"Oh, fuck, go on," I said.

His lips pursed against the tip of my dick as his slick hand churned up an down my shaft. Slow and steady. It didn't seem like much at first, but he kept at it, in the same steady rhythm, beat after beat, until I felt the spurt building up with in me and only at the last second did his mouth slip down over my whole cock. I shot off and Loogie took it.

"Squeeze my nuts," he said, "you know, hurt 'em. And watch." I squeezed Loogie's nuts and watched him lay a load out that drenched his chest. And I fell asleep.

Loogie or somebody got the guy out of my shower. I slept until ten, on the sofa in the study. I woke up when the phone started ringing. I wasn't quite ready to yank it out of the wall, so more or less the first thing I fled to my refuge in the hole. Loogie and Arthur were having a party, which wasn't very much distinguishable from any other day in the hole with beer and chips and stuff.

I finally understood that this was a celebration of my decelibacy or something. What is more, Loogie had given Arthur a detailed account of the night before including Loogie's sucking my dick, which seemed to me nothing for a guy to be telling his stepfather about. They were laughing and talking about the taste and Arthur was telling about the first time he ever sucked a guy.

"Wait a minute," I said. I was a little pissed. "I go to the trouble of going gay and you guys are talking about the dicks you've sucked. What, has everyone else been gay all this time?"

"No," Arthur said. "Loogie isn't gay. He just felt like doing you a favor."

After a while Loogie whipped out his cock and said, "How 'bout a circle jerk." But I said, "no" and Arthur said it was whatever I said which was "no."

But when Loogie went for beer Arthur got naked and picked up some lube from the table.

"Well . . ." he said, "have you ever fucked a man?"

"No," I said.

"Well . . . do you wanna learn."

And when we got to the shower, he put his arms around and said, "Before I let you plow my ass I gotta tell you that I've loved you for a long time. I'd like you to be my lover."

And so, for the rest of the summer, except for squeezing Loogie's nuts once in a while when he jacked off, I was Arthur's lover. Which was OK except when Loogie would call me his Step Ma.

THE SHED

Robin Metcalfe

FUNNY, HOW A sunny morning can make the world fall silent. As if the bright hazy air had swallowed all sound. Gordon straightened his back and stood in the flower bed, gazing out over Frenchman's Bay. White sails shimmered in the distance, beneath the twin grey humps of Champlain and Cadillac. A sudden breeze rose off the water, ruffling the edge of his T-shirt, exposing a pale glimpse of skin. The wind was chill with the breath of the departing winter, but Gordon was warm from his work and from the sun that bore down through the lingering mist. With an ungloved hand, he pushed back clammy blond curls from his forehead. This first bed would soon be ready for planting.

Flower beds: so much effort for such fleeting pleasure. Before summer was out, this patch of earth would be turned under and planted twice again. Gordon would choose the tender young plants, prepare a bed for them to bloom in, then make it over for the next display of mums, marigolds, impatiens. Growing a little older himself with each passing show of colour. There were worse ways to pass the time, he reflected: fading away behind a desk in some fluorescent office.

Across the broad lawn, through an open window in the hotel kitchen, Gordon heard the muffled clatter of dishes, the sound of the season beginning. The first busload of senior citizens had already arrived from New Jersey. The students had appeared the week before to claim their summer sinecures as waiters and chambermaids. Sassy girls who traded playful insults with Gordon on their way to the boat dock. Awkward boys with the faces of children and the husky bodies of men.

A spectacular crash of falling glassware made him look up. Another novice learning the ropes. Gordon grinned. He arched his back and stretched, his arms uncurling skywards. A delicious feeling, this, his T-shirt sliding up and the cool air playing against his belly. He ran a hand across the smooth skin, studying the wiry hairs that sprouted from the waistband of his workpants. That's enough for the morning, he thought. No sense busting my ass.

Gordon turned towards the shed at the end of the garden. Bare shrubbery, like delicate latticework, enclosed it in a cage of twigs. The shiny branches had begun to blush a deep red and thicken with buds. Soon the shed would be hidden behind a dense screen of leaves. He loaded his tools in the wheelbarrow and loped off across the spongy turf.

Stephen stood in the sunroom, surrounded by flowering cacti. He was alone in the deep enclosed porch, except for two older women in painted wicker chairs at the far end, part of the blue-rinse set he had waited on at breakfast. They had peered interminably at their menus, he remembered: the one with the knitting had asked for diabetic marmalade. Her companion, draped in a sweater, dozed in the sun with her mouth open. Stephen was free until the first lunch setting.

Giant red and purple blossoms spread themselves lewdly before him, like velvet slippers hung in the warm air to dry. Stephen ignored them. He was watching the man outside, working on the flower bed, his body intent upon its task. When he bent over, his grey T-shirt rose from his grimy green workpants and a pink band of skin winked at Stephen. His trousers stretched tight across his ass and his arm muscles moved within his shirt like whales sliding beneath the surface of the sea. Now he stood up, looking out across the bay, towards Bar Harbor.

Stephen remembered the eyes, although he was too far away

to see them now. A grey as soft as the bank of fog that hesitated offshore, just beyond the mouth of the harbour. He had surprised those eyes once, last summer, in a bed of ferns by the shady hotel entrance. They had glowed in the shadow, holding his gaze until Stephen had turned away, flushed and embarrassed.

Those eyes might not recognize him now. Stephen had grown over the winter: taller, and wider in the shoulders. In a late growth spurt, he found himself suddenly in the body of a man, in awe of his own mysterious flesh, like a boy at the reins of a team of powerful horses, not fully tamed. Steering himself across the baize green carpet of the hotel dining room on long, unfamiliar legs, he had the sensation of walking on stilts. Quite without intending it, he had adopted a rigid military bearing. Meant only to control his unruly limbs, it had the effect of intimidating his co-workers. The greatest change in Stephen, however, had taken place inside. His body might be uncertain of its balance, but it was quite sure now of what it wanted.

Gordon leaned back in the wheelbarrow, letting the sun soak into his face and arms. A pair or workgloves stuffed behind his head served to pad where the ridge of metal dug into his neck. Otherwise, the wheelbarrow made a passable chair, tilted against the side of the shed beside a stack of peat moss bales in tight plastic wrappings. Protected from the wind here, he could enjoy the full warmth of the sun. He spread his legs and hunkered down. One hand rested lightly near his crotch, the other pushed up his T-shirt to let the sunlight gild the fine hairs that ran in a line up his belly. His eyelids hovered half-open. He was drifting off into a horny haze.

There were a couple of muscle magazines stashed inside the shed. Maybe he'd go inside and jerk off, nice and slow, stroking himself gently almost to the point of coming, seeing how long he could hold off before his come broke free and gushed in hot urgent spurts up his belly. Gordon's cock lengthened down the leg of his pants, like a gopher burrowing under a lawn.

"Coming in, one hot beef. Hold the gravy."

Stephen glanced at the clock. Another 15 minutes, and Mid-Meal Madness should begin to slow down. Right now, waiters and waitresses surged in a continuous stream through one door and out the other. Andy, the busboy, wheeled dirty dishes in on his trolley, from which they speeded through the dishwasher, across the drying racks and back out to the dining room still hot and wet from the rinse. Monica struggled with a bobby pin in her frizzy copper hair and blared out, "Picking up two seafood chowder and a cheeseburger no pickle!" She managed a friendly wink for Stephen before turning and deftly avoiding a collision with Andy's trolley. "Watch yer back, cute stuff," she sang out. Little Ricky dashed under Stephen's elbow to snatch a plate off the slide.

"Picking up two chicken salads." Stephen himself was the eye of the storm, surveying the kitchen from his imposing height and calmly loading his tray over the heads of the others. From the corner of his eye he watched Andy unload his cart. The busboy's white shirt moved in counterpoint to the muscles of his back, criss-crossing in diagonal folds as his weight shifted from foot to foot. A deep furrow plunged from his shoulders to the mysterious cleft between his – oh, yes! – buttocks, round and firm in close-fitting dress pants. "Watch your back!" Stephen had almost tripped over Little Ricky. Better watch your own back and not Andy's, Stephen scolded himself.

Stephen was not the only one distracted by Andy. Monica called him Dandy Andy and liked patting him on the butt for the pleasure of seeing him blush. Last year, Andy had been a scrawny kid whom Stephen had hardly noticed, but now maturity had begun to define his features, which were set off by straight black hair and a recent, but already thick, mustache. A quiet sort, Andy was nevertheless learning the effect his beauty had on others.

Halfway out the swinging door, his head lost in his own thoughts, Stephen became aware of giggles behind him. Glancing back, he just caught a glimpse of Little Ricky doing a savagely accurate imitation of his own ostrich walk, nose stuck high in the air. Ricky quickly evaporated behind a frowning Monica, but the busboy wasn't as fast. He was still in mid-laugh when Stephen's gaze fell upon him. A blush of complicity darkened his features and he glanced away, pretending to busy himself with the trolley he was unloading. Stephen felt his eyes grow suddenly hot and full before he turned on his heel and pushed through the door into the dining room.

Masses of fog rolled across the lawn, a ghost of the distant surf Gordon could hear off to his left. The grey bank that had slumbered off the coast all day had moved in with the tide. Beads of water dripped from budding branches. The hotel was wrapped in a dense haze. Gordon stood in the woods behind the garden shed, pissing into the matted leaves that steamed at his feet. Shaking the last drops from his cock, he stowed it back inside his shorts and zipped up the fly. The loose tongues of his boots flapped as he hopped through the wet undergrowth back to the shed.

He paused at the doorway. A patch of yellow floated across the foggy lawn, unfocused, condensing slowly, resolving itself finally into a bright rain slicker above a pair of long legs. One of the waiters, returning to the dorm along the path that curved by Gordon's shed. The figure stopped and stared cautiously in his direction. "Hello?"

"It's me," said Gordon. "The gardener." Hugging his bare arms, he leaned forward to get a better look at the other. He recognized him now: the tall one with the shoulders, and the wandering eyes. Gordon tensed slightly, and shivered.

"Oh, hi." The boy peered at him. "Aren't you cold, without a jacket?"

"Yup, sure am." Gordon grinned. "I just ran out to take a leak." He looked the waiter up and down. His black dress shoes were scuffed and muddy. "You just getting off work?"

"I finished about an hour ago." Stephen stepped towards Gordon with a curious formality, as if to begin a delicate dance step. "I've been out walking along the shore. I got as far as the next cove, but I got cold and decided to head back." As if to emphasize his point, Stephen sneezed.

Gordon gave the boy an appraising glance. "Come into the shed," said the spider to the fly. "It's warm in here." Gordon held the door open, close enough that Stephen's shoulder brushed against his arm as he stepped through. The shed was larger than it seemed from the outside. Stacks of wooden lawn chairs, painted a dark glossy green, were stacked to the rafters. A sitting space had been cleared in the far corner beside a greasy window. A frayed blanket was sliding off a wicker armchair, wisps of straw poking through the holes. On a wooden crate beside the chair a coffee mug jostled an ashtray overflowing with butts. A shiny paperback lay face-down beside it. Stephen stepped carefully around the handles of the wheelbarrow to peer at the cover. *Howard's End.* A space heater hummed in the corner, casting an orange glow in the gloom.

"Stick this on that shelf over there, would you?" Gordon handed Stephen a shallow tray of sprouting bulbs. The gardener cleared a space on a metal deck chair, rusty steel tubing cushioned with padded vinyl. Blue and yellow printed flowers had been cancelled with dark Xs of duct tape. Gordon brushed away the worst of the dirt and patted the upholstery. "Have a seat," he said.

Stephen sat gingerly and stretched his hands towards the heater. The flaps of his slicker parted to reveal his rumpled uniform. His black bow-tie spanned a muscular neck. Orange light underlined a shapely jaw. Within the sleepy boyishness of Stephen's face, the features of a handsome young man were awakening.

He returned Gordon's gaze with steady blue eyes.

"My name's Stephen," he said, holding out his hand.

"Gordon." The gardener's rough fingers brushed against Stephen's wrist. The younger man's skin was icy to the touch. "You *are* cold. Let me warm you up."

Without breaking the link between them, Gordon swung over to sit beside Stephen on the deck chair. He rubbed the younger man's fingers carefully, kneading warmth back into them. Stephen was acutely aware of Gordon's strong but gentle grasp, of the gardener's leg brushing against his own. Another male body was aligned to his, radiating heat. A sweet hardness rose in his groin. His cock stiffened, straining against the cloth of his slacks. The gardener eyed the thick protrusion and smiled, guiding Stephen's hand to his own crotch, cupping Stephen's fingers around the warm bulge in his trousers. "That's nice," Stephen said. He leaned towards the gardener and kissed him on the mouth.

Gordon's chin was prickly against his lips. So this is what it is like to kiss a man. A rough tobacco taste against the tongue, a strong smoky flavour like wild game. He felt the gardener's arm curl around his shoulder as his fingers explored the older man's crotch, tracing there the outline of a hard cock like his own.

Their sprouting erections necessitated some adjustment of clothing. Stephen peeled off his rain jacket and loosened his tie. Gordon pulled the blanket from the wicker seat and spread it over the deck chair. Then he grabbed Stephen and pulled him down on top of him. Hoisting up Stephen's shirttail, he ran rough fingers up his back. They wrestled in the cool half-light of the shed, legs intertwined, mouths and groins pressed together.

With a shy grin, Stephen wriggled down to Gordon's crotch and pressed his palm against the hard lump in the gardener's pants. Tugging gingerly at the stiff zipper, he peeled away the flaps of Gordon's trousers and slipped his hand inside his underwear. Such treasure buried there! A man's cock, in its lair of cotton. The tip emerged above the waistband, red and shiny. Stephen tasted salt as he took the long shaft into his mouth.

Gordon was engulfed by warm lips and a wet tongue tracing the hard vein that ran the length of his cock. He abandoned himself to that voluptuous pleasure for a while. Then he grasped the younger man by the shoulders and pulled him up until their mouths met. Stephen pressed Gordon's cock against the bulge in his own pants. The gardener loosened Stephen's belt and freed his dick from the constraining fabric. Stephen's young cock sprang up from the open V of his fly. They embraced, cocks hard against each other, rubbing together in the warm space between their bellies. After a few moments of joyful writhing, Stephen gave a small cry of pleasure and dismay. Gordon felt a wet warmth gush over his stomach. The young man lay panting in his arms.

"I'm sorry," he said. "I couldn't stop."

"Shh," murmured Gordon. "Nothing to be sorry for. That was beautiful." He thought of Stephen's face in the moment of release, the mouth open, the startled eyes.

While Stephen's breath broke raggedly against his ear, Gordon dipped his fingers in the slippery puddle on his belly and wrapped his wet fingers around his own cock. Soon his own breath grew tight, his back arched and he erupted in hot urgent thrusts.

In the quiet of the shed they lay together, Gordon's lips buried in the musky turn of Stephen's neck. Muffled in the distance, he heard the foghorn moan. Stephen was falling asleep in his arms.

A damp chill was seeping in from the window. Nuzzling him behind the ear, he roused his sleeping beauty with a kiss.

In a green wood, Stephen dove in a deep clear stream. Golden water slipped over his nakedness and that of the other boy. Their arms and legs intertwined as they twirled through space. Their cocks were hard. Their lips brushed . . . Bubbles burst like tiny bells chiming . . . Bursting in his face . . . Slapping him in the face. A giant fish splashing him in the face, splash, splash, *splash*.

Wake up!

Go away, Stephen said. Can't you see I'm dreaming?

Wake up, the alarm clock shrilled. Time to go to work.

Stephen reached out a groggy hand and strangled the rattling machine.

With one foggy eye he considered the window. Judging by the glare through the curtain, it was going to be a scorcher. Stephen's cock made a hard ridge under his stomach. He moaned and pressed against the sheets, imagining another cock beside his own, and nuzzling the pillow to catch the lingering scent of his dreams. Water . . . another boy . . . Stephen imagined scenes of romance: walking on a beach, snuggling by a fire, making love in a four-poster bed. The identity of the loved one remained open to interpretation. He might be a man he had seen on the street; in the window of a bus or train. He tried inserting Gordon's face, but the fit wasn't right. The dream had been of someone younger, like himself . . .

A knock at the door jolted him awake. Shaking himself out of bed, he scrambled for something to put on, knocking over the clock in his fumbling and restarting the alarm. With one arm halfway in the sleeve of his bathrobe, the other groping under the bed for the jangling clock, Stephen heard the knock repeated, more emphatic this time. "Jesus, Steve, aren't you

up yet? First setting starts in half an hour." Sounded like Andy.
Since when did he provide wake-up service?

Stephen responded to chaos by becoming methodical. One
thing at a time. Stop the alarm. Put the clock back on the table.
All set? Gather your robe together so your hard-on won't be
quite so obvious. OK, open the door.

"Hi Steve. Did I wake you up?" Stephen shook his head
blearily. The boy in front of him was halfway between dressed
and undressed. A clean white shirt billowed open around his
bare torso like petals framing a smooth stamen. His cuffs hung
open, revealing lean forearms forested with shiny dark hairs. A
deep V-crease in his black trousers framed his groin. Stockinged
feet, rumpled hair. Andy looked like he was falling out of, or
into, someone's bed. "You got an extra tie I can borrow, Steve?
I can't find mine anywhere."

A tie? Does he think I run a haberdashery? Stephen grunted
non-committally. Andy interpreted this as an invitation to enter.
He viewed the dishevelled sheets with interest, as if they were
the scene of a crime.

"Boy, you sure are a messy sleeper!" Stephen ignored the
comment. He dragged his old green vinyl suitcase out of the
closet and started rummaging for a spare bow-tie. "You're lucky,
getting your own room. I've gotta share with Little Ricky. He's
always playing his fucking ghetto blaster." Stephen nodded.
He had heard the dulcet tones of Queen shaking the walls as
he passed their room.

"Here's the tie," said Stephen. "Don't get it dirty."

Andy pouted temptingly as he took the soft black strip of
cloth. "Don't worry, Steve. You'll get it back."

"Stephen. People call me Stephen."

Andy turned to face the mirror on the back of the closet door
and began to button his shirt. His reflection stared at Stephen
as he slipped the tie under his collar. "You still sore at me? I
wasn't making fun of you the other day, you know. I was just
laughing at Ricky." His buttocks tightened with concentration
as he knotted the tie. Stephen suppressed a desire to wrap his
arms around the busboy's small sturdy frame, to taste the fine,
almost invisible hairs at the nape of his neck. He shoved his
hands in the pockets of his bathrobe and stared at the floor.

"No, it's OK Andy. I'm just grumpy because I'm not awake yet." Looking up, he saw the other boy admiring himself in the glass. Andy's eyes flickered and met Stephen's gaze. The busboy smiled.

"Thanks for the loan of the tie. Gotta run. See you at the hotel." With that, Andy stepped out and bounded down the hall. Stephen jumped to the door and called after him.

"Ask Monica to cover for me, OK? Tell her I'll be there in a few minutes." The busboy flashed a friendly hand and veered into his room. Loud music spilled into the hall. Thump Thump Thump. Another one bites the dust.

There was a fly in the shed. Somewhere. Stephen could hear the tiny drone weaving in and out of the shadows, nagging the hot sullen silence of the afternoon like an unanswered question. There it was – a flash across the dusty sunlit surface of the window. It bashed against the glass with small stubborn thumps.

I suppose I should kill it, Stephen thought. But I don't want to get up. Stephen lay with his head in Gordon's lap. The gardener was stroking his hair with one hand while holding a book with the other. The hand paused. Stephen heard a page flip.

"Gordon?"

"Mmnh." The gardener continued reading.

"I have to talk to you."

"Ooh, that sounds serious." Gordon leaned over and kissed Stephen sloppily on the nose.

"No, really, I mean it." Stephen sat up. Gordon sighed, closed his book carefully and set it down.

"OK, baby, what is it?"

"Well . . ." Stephen paused, suddenly uncertain. "I don't know how to say this exactly. I mean, I really like you. A lot. You know that. Only . . ." Oh shit, he thought. I'm really going to screw this up.

Gordon rubbed his hand soothingly up and down Stephen's back. "You think you'd like to see other people, too."

Stephen looked at Gordon. The gardener smiled back. "Is that what it is?" Stephen nodded, and added, "You aren't upset, are you?"

"Why should I be upset?" Stephen looked a little disappointed with this response. "I like you very much, Stephen. But we're not married, are we?" The gardener kissed him gently and smiled again. As if to signal that the subject was closed, he stood and pawed the shelf above the chair for his pouch of tobacco. Silhouetted before the window, he rolled himself a cigarette, the sun lighting the fuzzy surface of his old cotton shirt. Now don't be foolish, he scolded himself. They come and they go. No one has a claim on them, least of all you. Gordon grinned to himself. You old whore. Lining the brown leaves along the fold in the rolling paper, he ran a light tongue across the gummed edge. But you have to admit, this one's been pretty special.

The gardener turned back to resume his seat, but it was occupied. Stephen had stretched out across the deck chair, his pants pulled off, his shirt hoisted above a sweet round pair of buns, long bare legs spread teasingly. Gordon moaned and sank to his knees, running a wondering hand across the smooth skin. He slipped a finger along the warm crevice of Stephen's ass and touched the small pursed opening. Stephen stirred and pushed back firmly into Gordon's hands.

"You're sure you're ready for this?"

Stephen grinned over his shoulder. "I'm sure."

Gordon rummaged in a drawer and retrieved a shiny foil package and a half-crushed tube of lubricating jelly. Stephen heard a Zip! as the gardener peeled off his pants and a Rip! as he tore open the condom. With a crinkly noise, Gordon unrolled the safe down the length of his hard-on. The lubricant spread light and slippery between this fingertips and around his prick. He dabbed it along the crack of Stephen's butt and into the tight asshole. Pulling the cheeks apart with his thumbs, he straddled the younger man's back and prodded with the tip of his cock. Resistance. He pressed a little harder and the head moved in about an inch.

Stephen gasped at the unfamiliar sensation. A flash of burning pain made his sphincter contract against the intruder. Gordon held perfectly still. "Are you OK? Do you want me to pull out?" He stroked Stephen's back reassuringly.

"No, it's OK. Just go slow."

Gordon pressed in a little deeper. The sensation was not so much painful, Stephen thought, as disorienting. He experienced it as an urgent need to shit. He countered that with a mental picture of what they were doing. A man has his cock in my ass. A man is fucking me. Stephen's cock stirred and his ass relaxed, allowing Gordon to enter further. He wriggled about, as an aroused heat began to glow in his bowels. He was discovering a whole new body, a new source of power. The gardener's prick buried in his gut seemed to fill him with masculinity, swelling his own cock with its hardness.

Gordon began to hump him, at first slowly, then faster, his balls slapping against Stephen's ass. His beard scratched the back of Stephen's neck, his breath hot against Stephen's ear. And then the long agonized groan of release. Deep inside, Stephen felt a bubble of tension dissolve and flood him with liquid pleasure. At the same moment, he realized with surprise that warm come was streaming from his own cock.

The sound of their panting filled the shed. Gordon sprawled across Stephen, pressing him to the blanket, his cock slipping slowly out of his ass, bringing the condom with it. One furry arm clutched Stephen's chest from behind, another hand tenderly cupped his balls. Stephen stretched a leg cautiously to ease a cramp.

"I have to go. Next setting starts soon. I need to get washed up." He gently eased himself out of the gardener's embrace, and looked around for his underwear. The two men climbed shyly back into their crumpled clothing. Stephen stood and brushed cobwebs from his hair.

"This must be yours." Gordon handed him a small black strip of cloth. The waiter shoved the tie in his pocket. With his free arm he hugged the gardener and held him close for one more kiss.

Stephen ducked through the doorway and squinted in the hot spring sun. Around him, shiny branches bristled with thorns. A thousand buds were opening, unfurling the green flags of summer.

It was only later, back in his room, that Stephen realized it was not his tie.

*   *   *

"Coming in, one hot chicken."

Stephen pushed through the door into the kitchen, holding it open for Andy behind him. "Thanks, Steve." The busboy rolled his trolley in with a clatter of dirty dishes. His pretty butt danced about as he juggled plates and silverware. Stephen fished in his pants pocket.

"Say, Andy, is this your tie?" The busboy looked up, startled, and then took the tie from him. "Yeah, great. Thanks a lot, Stephen. Now I can give you back yours."

"Oh, Andy. Monica's boyfriend is visiting and they're going to the late show in Bar Harbor after work. You want to go along?"

Andy looked at Stephen cautiously. "I dunno. What's playing?"

"It's called *Sweet Bird of Youth.* Paul Newman's in it. The young Paul Newman." Stephen ran his tongue lightly over his lip for emphasis.

Andy's mouth was partly open, trying to formulate a response. Monica bustled by on her way to the dining room. "Hi, Stephen. You led that boy astray yet?"

Andy flushed a deep, becoming shade of red. Then he squared his shoulders and grinned. "Sure, Stephen. I'll see you after clean-up."

"Picking up, one hot chicken!" Balancing his tray high above the heads of the other waiters, Stephen turned to give the busboy a wink. Then he sailed through the swinging door into the crowded dining room.

TRUST

Jameson Currier

I DID NOT come to Washington that weekend in 1987 with an agenda. It wasn't important for me to march, wasn't important for me to scream or shout, wasn't important for me, either, to feel as if I were a part of a larger community, a community still dueling with illness and death. I came to Washington because Nathan wanted me to spend some time on my own, to be away from him for a few days, to see how it would feel, how I would handle it, if it were possible for me to exist in the world without him, or, rather, to imagine my life without him. Death hung over us like a cloud that year, as it had ever since the day I learned of Nathan's diagnosis; I knew there was the possibility that Nathan might not survive this epidemic and I hated that realization. And so did Nathan. And as much as either of us wanted to disbelieve the fact that Nathan might die, we knew we had to confront the possibility of it, and the possibility of my life existing without him – what it would be like for me to live without him, alone.

Was there a way of my avoiding the pain, avoiding the impending sorrow and the grief? I knew in my gut that that wasn't so, and maybe the trip was my way of forestalling it as long as I could. Was there, perhaps, any hope for us? Was there, somewhere, a meaning to all this? In the last few weeks

I had seen Nathan grow weaker and weaker; at night he was unable to sleep because of nausea or fear. I had even heard from Dora that Nathan could seldom finish his work at Grove House, often slipping away from the kitchen to lie on one of the empty beds in the upstairs rooms of the house. Every time I heard something like this from someone else – someone confirming my own fears about the state of Nathan's health – I would slip into a silent mood of hysteria, believing that our time was up, and that Nathan was now approaching the end of the line. My hysteria would soon fade into a furious hatred – a hatred that I kept so checked and silent within myself, however, that I often thought I would some day explode.

Even though it was Nathan who suggested I go away for a while, I decided to come to Washington that weekend to try and find the desire to want to return to Nathan, to want to continue being with him no matter what conditions the future held for us, to find a way to keep my fear and hatred and anxieties in check.

I spent Saturday afternoon wandering through the museums of Washington – the various wings of the Smithsonian, the Air and Space Museum, the National Gallery of Art. I wasn't really interested in connecting with anyone; I wanted, instead, to accept my solitude. It felt good to be looking and moving, flowing, like a documentary film, in and out of the rooms, pausing before an Impressionist painting or touching, briefly, a rock brought back from the moon. The tourists at museums, however, are often more interesting than the art itself; everywhere I went that day was full of cruisy good-looking guys. It was hard not to notice them, hard not to wonder what it would be like knowing just one of them in any sort of permutation: friend, lover, trick.

The day was not without other anxious moments though. I never know what to do with my hands in a museum, feeling often like a bull in a priceless china shop, and for most of the day I walked with my hands shoved into the front pockets of my jeans, my shoulders hunched forward and my elbows jutting away from my body. The posture, I believe, pushed me into too pensive a mood – more so than normal. What I thought about as I heard my boots slap against the polished tile floors was

how small my life was in the grand scheme of the universe –
a tiny speck, really, in a large building in a large country on
a large planet in a big solar system in an immense universe.
I wondered how much my life mattered beyond the meaning
I myself gave it. Would, for instance, a simple encounter with
another man recharge it? Or change its direction or meaning? A
young man wearing black jeans and a white turtleneck fascinated
me as we hovered around each other while viewing a series of
French sculptures: from the rear I was awed by the way the
thin cotton fabric of his shirt stretched taut at his shoulders
and then billowed out like a skirt at his narrow waist; beside
me I noticed his strong profile; in front I studied the auburn
bangs and large brown eyes. I lost sight of him sometime later,
scared, I think, by the fact that I could *let* him change my life;
that I could bestow on him that power.

After a few hours my eyes and legs were tired and I walked
back to the hotel near Dupont Circle where I had found a
room for the weekend. I read for a while, then fell asleep
in front of the television, much as I had done for years with
Nathan. I was up early Sunday morning, however; I showered
and walked to a deli just off Connecticut Avenue. There was an
air of expectancy about Dupont Circle at that hour, everyone
seemed so electrified and purposeful. I could sense it in the way
the guy at the cashier handed me my change, could feel it in
the line that formed in front of the instant banking machine,
see it in the soulful eyes of a man setting up a T-shirt stand
by the subway exit. I walked for a while, following the flow of
the other walkers, down Connecticut to 17th Street and over to
the gates of the White House. I did not expect to feel anything
there, and I didn't, ignoring, I think, the President the way he
had thus far ignored the epidemic.

Those were the days that AIDS activism was just beginning
to germinate; there had been a protest on Wall Street against
the Food and Drug Administration and Burroughs Wellcome
over the high cost of AZT; there had been, too, the vigil in
San Francisco outside the old Federal Office Building. There
had been, of course, angry voices since the beginning of the
epidemic, but those were the days that we were first finding a
collective voice. The purpose of the march that weekend was

to demand increased funding for AIDS-related projects and to insist on an end to federal laws that discriminated against gay men and lesbians. But I had not yet found an outward, vocal expression of my anger; I was, really, still moving through both denial and sorrow, sorrow over the way things had changed, the lives that had been lost, the ones to lose ahead.

Nathan and I had never even marched in the gay pride parades in Manhattan, but we had, for years, watched from the sidelines, cheering, laughing, and applauding. Watching did not mean we were any less proud to be gay than anyone marching, any more closeted than the men and women in the middle of the street. We were, by nature, watchers, I think; our pleasure came from finding people in whom we saw ourselves. We did not, for instance, dress up for Halloween; neither of us preferred, either, to promenade in front of the other men at the beaches on Fire Island and the Hamptons. In many ways I'm sure that some of our trendy gay brethren would find us boring; our lives were no longer focused on parties, clubs, fashions, or trends. We defined ourselves on what we did *together – being* together, whether it was as simple as cooking dinner or watching a movie on television. That was why it was so important for me to be alone that weekend in Washington – to find a meaning to myself.

Which is why I think I felt Nathan's absence all the more that Sunday morning. I walked toward the Washington monument; it was the most obvious thing to do, of course, towering above the skyline. Washington has always reminded me of some unknown European city, the buildings so low and federal-looking, the wide boulevards, the memorials and monuments. The lawn around the Washington monument was bright green and cushiony, the sky so vast and open above me that I felt, once again, like such a minute particle of the cosmos. As I came up over the hill I looked out at the mall which stretched down to the Capitol building. A crowd had assembled around something that was covering the lawn, and I walked in that direction, full of curiosity.

I had not heard of the Names Project Quilt then; now, of course, it is widely recognized as an ever-growing AIDS memorial, but that day it took me a few moments to comprehend what I was seeing: panels, six feet by three, stitched together into blocks of eight and then 32. Volunteers, dressed in white, stood at the corners, handing out programs, brochures and maps. That day, the quilt contained 1,920 names. Spread out, it was larger than two football fields and included the names of brothers, fathers, sons, mothers, daughters, babies, lovers and friends. Even then, at its inception, it was the nation's largest community arts project.

What began as curiosity quickly changed into awe as I read the first few panels. The colors seemed so bright and saturated to me, charged like neon by the morning sun. I followed the white canvas walkway which bordered the perimeter of the panels on the ground. Some panels were simple, containing only a painted name on plain fabric. Others were more elaborate with hand-stitched designs or needlepoint, or names spelled out in sequins or bordered by feathers. Some were personalized by clothing: a plaid shirt, gym shorts, boot laces, a leather vest, one, even, displayed a jock strap. Others held record albums, photographs and quotes. The hardest for me to look at though were the ones that contained only first names, the ones that read Mark, Bill, Mike, or Steve. Those were the names I collected years ago on scraps of paper at parties, bars, gyms and beaches; the very same kind of scraps Vince had kept in the fish bowl in his apartment, dolling out for me to call when I needed a date. Standing there I couldn't help wondering if I had known the man behind one of these names. Could it be a friend I haven't spoken to in the past few months – someone, perhaps, I hadn't even known was sick?

It was hard not to keep my eyes moving from panel to panel, the same way, I believe, it is hard to look away from the aftermath of an accident. When I finally looked up I noticed I had not even made it a third of the way down the quilt. I was surrounded by other viewers; not surprised to discover that they were mostly men and women my age, their heads bowed, motionless, as if in prayer. The tableau reminded me of one of those large cathedrals Nathan and I visited not long ago on our trip to Europe, the ones with plaques and epitaphs lining the walls of the transepts where people are buried beneath the floor. But what, in Europe, was viewed with a calm sense of reverence, was here magnified with anger, shock, compassion, and grief. Here, footsteps moved so slowly and carefully their sounds could not be detected, the silence broken only by the amplified voice of a woman reading a list of names somewhere in the distance. Ahead of me a young man in a blue polo shirt and jeans sat cross-legged on the walkway in front of a red silk panel that spelled David with silver block letters, his head buried in the palms of his hands. Though I strained to hear, I could not detect any sounds from him, but I knew by the way his back heaved with short, jerking breaths that he was crying. Behind him, I was suddenly astounded by the sight of a woman pushing an empty stroller; beside her a man carried a baby, less than six months old, in his arms. On the other side of the panel an elderly woman with a cane touched the frame of her eyeglasses and leaned to read a name. This was something, I realized, that had hit us all.

Behind each name is the story of a life, someone who struggled with this disease and lost. Behind each panel there are many stories: Who made it? Who helped? Why this color? This fabric? What does the design remember or represent? Who cried when it was finished? Who recognizes the name as they walk by? Each of us brought our own stories to the quilt that day, our views, opinions, knowledge, and experiences with the disease. We were suddenly and unexpectedly united, sewn together as it were, by our thoughts of families, lovers, friends and co-workers: some dead, some sick, some worried. This had become our Gettysburg, our Vietnam Wall, our tomb of the Unknown Soldier. Yet those wars were over; this one continued. The horror I felt that day was knowing the quilt would grow larger every day.

And then I could not look at it any more. Something this moving, this beautiful became unbearably painful, painful at the thought that Nathan or I could one day be a part of it, our lives reduced to a name on a piece of fabric. I found myself gasping for breath and I walked away from the quilt, out of the crowds assembling on the mall, over to the sidewalk, pushing myself through everyone, headed, I felt, in a direction no one else was going. I found my way eventually to the tidal basin beside the Jefferson Memorial, looking out at the reflection of the sun against the water, trying to find some sort of tranquillity within myself. But my head still felt thick and dulled and I walked around the waterside and sat on the steps of the Memorial, wanting only, at that moment, to find some space of my own; no one else was seated in that portion of the park.

The workboots I wore that day made walking feel so ponderous and as I unharnessed the knapsack from my back and sat it on my lap, I felt my feet swell and relax into the boots. I opened the knapsack and drank water from the canteen I had filled at the hotel, then unwrapped the bagel I had bought this morning and began to eat. The butter had melted and seeped into the pores of the dough and it gave the bread a sweet and salty taste. What I did to calm myself was to focus on the elemental things – the walking, the stopping to rest, the eating bread and drinking water.

Two girls, arms entwined around each other's waist, sat behind me and I watched them fall into a kiss. Suddenly, this corner of the memorial, which a moment ago had seemed so empty, was now populated with little cliques of tourists. A stocky young man lingered around the steps, then sat down beside me.

"Smoke?" he asked me, indicating the pack of cigarettes he grasped in his wrist.

"No thanks," I answered, watching him use the lighter which hung around his neck on a cord. He had that lumbering high school football player look – thick neck and chest, pale doughy skin, brown hair cropped into a crew cut; if the time and place had been different, I would have felt sure he was waiting for some buddies to show up to harass the crowd. Instead, he took a long drag off his cigarette, then pulled at his tongue with two fingers as if to remove a flake of tobacco, and leaned against the fountain ledge.

"Water?" I asked him, tilting the canteen I held in his direction.

He nodded and took the canteen, resting it on his bottom lip and pouring a quick, thick, drink into his mouth. He wiped the lip of the canteen off with the bottom of his T-shirt when he was done.

"I noticed you on the other side of the lake," he said, as

he handed me back the canteen. It was here that I caught his glance, his dark brown eyes wide and fiery with expectation. "Chris," he said, angling his body toward me and stretching out his hand, not into a handshake, but to place it firmly against my thigh.

"Robbie," I nodded back to him, realizing his brash contact was that of a boy. I looked at him again, searching for the lines on his face, but there were none, and I wondered at that moment if he had even made it out of his teens. His hand, flat against my leg, balled into a fist and he lightly tapped my thigh.

"I've had about an hour of sleep," he said, somewhat proudly, moving his fist now back to his own thigh. "I went to a club last night that was somewhere near here I think," he added, and looked out at the bridge in the distance. "The music was wild. *Real wild*. Lot of hot guys here."

"Yeah," I answered. "Lots to look at."

"I came all the way from Arkansas. *Fucking Arkansas*. I just told my sister that I was going. Not to stop me. I *had* to be here."

I watched him take another drag off of his cigarette, and then looked out at the water and the trees planted along the bank, aware, acutely, of all the places we travel because we are gay – to different towns and different bars, hoping to meet someone, to find someone like ourselves. Hoping to find ourselves, too – another journey, really – traveling inside ourselves to try to figure it all out.

"You ever have a girlfriend?" Chris asked.

"*Girlfriend*?" I answered, a little too loudly, realizing Chris's question had suddenly knocked me back to a mental image of Marcy Telford, a smart, flirty girl I had been attracted to in junior high school. "Long time ago," I answered, wondering, briefly, what Marcy's life was like now. Married, driving her husband crazy with her nagging, I decided; she was always chiding me for never bringing her presents.

"She like really flipped out when she found out I was seeing this guy," Chris said, stubbing his cigarette into the concrete of the fountain. "He's really hot. Paul – that's his name. But he's married. Gina went and told my parents and then the fucking high school gets involved. And then his wife files a restraining order – against me. She's a jerk. He's a jerk. Gina's a jerk. I ended up staying at my sister's, only her husband gets real nervous having me around." And it was here he looked at me again, testing me, I believe, tapping his fist against my thigh once more. "Why is it everyone gets nervous while I'm around?"

A young ball of fire, is what I thought, but didn't say. A boy wound up with expectation and desire. He was wonderfully distracting from my gloominess at that moment. I wondered if I would allow myself the opportunity of fooling around with him if it was presented. Could I do this? Would I do this to Nathan? For a moment I thought about asking the boy for a cigarette, just to keep the contact going, but instead, I reached for the canteen and took another sip of water.

"You come here by yourself?" Chris asked.

I nodded.

"I bet you could probably get any guy here you wanted," he said.

I felt myself flush from his flattery but found my smile somewhat weary. "I have someone."

"Oh," he said, in that of-course-you-do-and-I'm-so-disappointed tone. "Figures. All the hot-looking guys are all taken. Or they're jerks."

I realized that I was now attracted to him, impetuously, simply because of his dismissal of me. Suddenly, he was the unattainable one. "He stayed in New York," I said.

"New York?" Chris answered, his eyes catching fire again. He looked me over again, as if able to see me in a brighter light. "I thought about going to New York. You ever go to the Saint?"

"*The Saint?*" I answered, once again jarred into a memory. "Not in a while," I answered.

"I heard the Chelsea Gym is really hot, too. And the Spike. You ever been there?"

"A couple of times," I answered. Why is it that people in other parts of the world know meticulously what the scene is in Manhattan – more so, sometimes, than those who live there? How is it that the pulse of New York – fashion, art, theater, music, gay life – is more apparent once you are off the island? I

was so concerned about Nathan's health and mood, scanning
the newspapers for possible new drug treatments, that I paid
no attention to theater reviews, celebrity interviews, or gossip
columns. I did not know what the next big musical was due
to open on Broadway, did not know what Harvey Fierstein's
next project was, could not tell you who sang "I Want Your
Sex" on MTV, could not tell you, either, what the fashionable
gay club was, or, even, what the guys were wearing when they
went out. "You'd do real good there," I said to Chris, pushing
myself into flirting with the boy. "The guys there would go wild
over you. You have that look, you know?"

"Yeah?"

"Oh yeah, you could probably get any guy in the place," I
said, playing the young boy's game now but feeling rather old
at doing it. "I know some guys I could fix you up with, too, if
you're ever in New York."

He flipped out a cigarette. "They as hot as you?" he asked,
then lit the cigarette. He took a drag and exhaled to the side of
me and gave me a wry, half smile. "Don't know how someone
could let a guy like you out of his sight," he said, and again his
fist was on my thigh. "He crazy, or something? He a jerk?"

"No," I said. "He's not feeling well." I felt, then, whatever
charm I had been able to muster, instantly vaporize.

"Oh," Chris answered tensely, then looked down at the
canteen he had drunk water from. I watched the blood drain
from his face, a light sweat formed on his upper lip as he took
in the fact of what I had just said. "You should have stayed
with him," he said to me, with a chill that iced the air between
us. I don't think he intended to make me feel repulsive for
coming to Washington. He stubbed his cigarette out briskly.
"See ya," he said, and slipped off the steps and headed away
from the memorial. I felt, then, an overwhelming frustration
settle in my shoulders, till it was replaced by an anger burning
across my chest so bitter I thought I had been slashed by a
knife. Who, here, would be accused of homophobia – him of
his fear of me – or me of the hatred of his insincerity? I felt
myself moving slowly now, as if delayed by the stop-action lens
of a camera: replacing the canteen in the knapsack, brushing
the crumbs off my jeans, slipping the handles of the knapsack

through one arm, then another. Standing. Walking. Crossing the street. I never made it to the march that day. I went back to the hotel. And into the bar just off the back of the lobby. A few drinks later I made it up to my room, armed with a bottle of scotch I had coerced from the bartender.

Later that evening the phone rang in my room. "Robbie?" It was Nathan.

"Hi," I said, somewhat lightly, glad, really, to hear from him, trying to snap myself as well into some sort of sobriety.

"How was the march?"

"Good," I answered, but in a tone of voice that meant I did not want to discuss it any further.

"Are you alone?"

"Of course."

"I miss you," he said, and all at once I again felt my misery of being away from him. "Remember when we were in Rehoboth Beach a few years ago?" he asked.

"Yeah," I answered. I felt the blood return to my body. Nathan had handcuffed me to the bed in the hotel room we had rented.

"You couldn't move," he said. He had tied my legs, too, with rope to the bed frame. I had stayed that way for hours, Nathan kissing me, tickling me, rubbing lotion into my skin, jerking me off. This was not long after we had gotten back together, and it was his way, Nathan had explained to me, of making me trust him again. Outside the room was the beach. It was summer and we were only inches from the nests of single gay boys scattered atop the sand on towels.

"Don't move," he said now. "My lips are against your chest. Feel them?"

"Yeah," I answered. "Nice."

In my mind we were back in the hotel room. Nathan had gotten me hard with his mouth, pulling away just as I was about to come, then suspending his ass just above my erect cock, teasing me by sucking on my nipples, till he slowly eased himself onto me.

"Hard?" he asked me on the phone.

"Yeah. You?"

"Feels good," he said. "You feel so good."

I had stayed in Nathan, that day, what seemed like hours, with an erection so hard I had often measured other ones against it. He held my balls in his hands, squeezed them, pushed them down between my legs so that the skin of my cock was tighter inside him. The smell of him, the sweat of us together, hovered around the room all day.

"Remember what you did," I said.

"Yeah," Nathan answered.

"Do it again," I said. "Let me taste them." Nathan had squatted on my face and I had licked his balls, then sucked on them like candy.

"Feels good," he said again.

"Don't come yet," I said.

"I won't."

"I want to play with your cock."

"Go ahead."

"Making you squirm?"

"Yeah," he answered, with a nice, heavy sigh. "You?"

"Yeah."

"I want to kiss you," Nathan said, and I imagined, now, the odor of him, the press of his face against the stubble of my cheek. Nathan had not left me alone that day at Rehoboth Beach, tied up in bed. He had washed me with a cool rag, lifted my head up to help me eat a hamburger, helped me piss into a glass to relieve myself. He denied me nothing that I had asked for – within reason, of course, and which he could willingly accommodate me with – a different radio station on the stereo, a pillow to prop up my head, relieving an itch on my foot. I knew when Nathan and I got back together that he was out to make our relationship work; he didn't have to *prove* anything to me. Still, I enjoyed the luxury of the demonstration.

"Remember when I let you go?"

"Yeah," I answered. When Nathan untied me I had remained in bed, hoping to prove to him that I would not leave him, that I was not anxious to get out of the bed or away from him. "Fuck me," I whispered into his ear, my arms slipping around his back. His eyes widened and we slipped into a kiss, and then I pulled away and lay again on my back.

Nathan knew I did not *prefer* to be the one fucked. But that day, lying free, finally, of the bindings, what I wanted was to be fucked by Nathan, testament, I felt, of a double-sided trust that existed between us, that I knew Nathan would not abandon me, and that I, too, would not give up on him. Nathan started, first, by lifting my legs and pressing his lips against my ass. Then he rolled me over on my stomach and told me to relax, and he started kneading my buttocks, working his hands gently and firmly into the crack of my ass. He covered his fingers with lotion and then began to slowly part the lips of my ass, rubbing the lubricant against the hole, slipping first one finger into my rectum and then another. He did this again and again, pulling his fingers out and kneading my ass, getting me to relax so that there was no tension, no shock, every now and then slipping his hand around my balls and squeezing my cock. He rolled me over and set the heels of my feet against his shoulders. He continued working his fingers into my ass, making sure I was still relaxed; then, deftly, he slid his cock into me.

"Remember how it felt."

"Yeah," I said. "Do it again."

I had become so relaxed that there was not the slightest discomfort when he entered me, my body drawing his cock in like a warm gulp of air. A man who has never been fucked has no idea how pleasurable the sensation can be, but a man in love fucked by the man he loves finds the exhilaration one of the reasons for being alive.

"Nice," Nathan said. "It feels so right."

He began sliding in and out of me, in and out, slowly and smoothly, and I kept the rhythm going between us. Then he paused, leaned down and kissed me, and I could taste his smile in my mouth. And then he began again, slowly and smoothly. I was already on the edge of coming but I held it back, tensing the muscles of my ass to feel Nathan inside of me more sharply. Nathan gasped and I could feel sweat beginning to thicken the cells of his skin. He leaned further into me and his motions took on a harder, firmer thrust. And then I felt the shift go through him – the transformation a man can go through from simply performing the physical act of sex to having sex with someone he loves. The clear skin of Nathan's chest blushed, his neck tensed and his breathing hollowed out;

he moved inside me now buoyed by a desperation. I felt, then, that same passion overwhelm me as well, that shift occur within me; we stayed that way, in and out, in and out, till I felt the jagged spurts of his come travel up from the base of his shaft and spill inside of me.

"Robbie," he said, and that was all. We were never big talkers or moaners in bed, nothing like the rough-and-tumble boys in porn videos at all. I could tell how Nathan felt about me simply by the way he looked at me, the way he touched me, the way, too, he held me when we had finished making love. Silence meant everything between us. We rolled over to our sides – he was still in me – and we just lay there for a bit, entwined. I didn't want him to pull out. And I made no attempt to leave the bed.

"Did you?" he asked me over the phone.

"Yeah," I answered, rubbing the meager result of my orgasm into the hair of my groin. "You?"

"Yeah,"

There was, now, another a gap between us, neither of us wanting to let the other go.

"I need you back," Nathan said into the phone, the same thing he had said, too, that day in Rehoboth.

"I never left," I answered, feeling, though, that day in Washington, the geographic distance between us.

"I'm not giving up," he said.

I knew he wasn't talking merely about the two of us. "And I won't let you," I answered.

"Robbie," he said with a sigh. "I have a problem."

My body stiffened from worry.

"What must I do to make you happy?" he asked.

An unprepared gap fell between us and I moved the phone from one hand to another to give myself a second to think.

I let out a sigh, not a sigh, really, but more a disgusted breath of air – disappointed because my voice could not articulate the rapid thoughts of my mind. "Nathan," I said slowly. "I want you to fuck me. *Again.*"

Now it was his turn to fumble, but he answered more quickly than I expected him. "You can't ask me to do that," he said.

"I'm not asking you to," I answered. "I *need* you to."

That weekend in Rehoboth Beach happened in 1981, shortly before we began to live together. There was no such thing as safe sex in those days, condoms were used for birth control and besides, anything presented as an obstacle – crabs, amoebas, gonorrhoea – was treatable. That was the weekend that Nathan and I launched ourselves into a monogamous relationship, monogamous in a very loose sense of the word, really, more emotionally committed to one another rather than sexually exclusive; we began to call ourselves lovers, and what indiscretions either one of us entertained, we kept to ourselves. Unlike my first lover Will, Nathan had no desire to bring other lovers into our bed, no desires for threesomes or for comparison lists of who had had the better tricks or hotter sex. What was monogamous about us, though, was a psychological bonding, a combination of companionship, friendship, love and sexuality. The way I made this work was to root my trust in Nathan much deeper than my need for sex from him, knowing he wouldn't walk away from me or give up on our relationship. What Nathan wanted, after all, was for us to work as a *couple*, something that would extend beyond the perimeters of sex. Jealousy or disappointment, in sexual matters, was therefore not allowed to consume us.

Nevertheless, I found it impossible to remove the guilt I felt when I had sex with someone else while I was in love with Nathan. Temptation, of course, is a daily force on the streets of Manhattan. On any day, at any hour, it is possible to pass a handful of desirable men at any place in the city – Manhattan, after all, is a smorgasbord of different types of men – a boulevard of beautiful immigrants, really, from places such as Iowa, Ireland, Italy, and Israel, for instance. How one handles temptation of each one of them – I believe, at least on my part – depends on the state of contentment and fulfillment one had achieved with their primary partner. But we were also young men, then – *young*, young men.

I remember the first time I tricked on Nathan after we had gotten back together – it was in 1981 and shortly before we had gone together to Rehoboth Beach – and even though we had been professing an open relationship for months I was consumed by the guilt of my deed. I had been working in an actor's loft on the Bowery and the guy – a tall, handsome well-built man who had had some soap opera parts – had spent the day parading in front of me in various states of undress, and throwing out suggestive remarks as I worked. I knew from Alex that the guy also worked as a hustler. I could tell that this guy was so eager for sex that it made me nervous while I worked – I had made a rule of never doing anything while I was out on a job and I kept my check throughout the day, deflecting his remarks as I boarded the wall he had wanted to create a walk-in closet. When I left, untouched but somewhat erotically rattled, it was still daylight outside. I walked down 8th Street and over to the park, where I sat on a bench on the south side. A young guy who looked a lot like Nathan passed me once walking a cocker spaniel, then passed me again, and before I knew it we had struck up a conversation and I was headed with him back to his apartment.

That trick was quick and ultimately unsatisfying. As soon as we had both come he was ready for me to go – he wasn't even interested in any sort of conversation, let alone an attachment; I had hoped at least for some sort of dialogue between us in which I could differentiate him from Nathan, make me want Nathan even more, really, than the want to fool around on him. Ironically, the lack of dialogue between myself and my trick had that same effect, for back out on the street I was instantly sorry for what I had become, and I decided, then, that day, that I would just let Nathan think I was fooling around on him, wanted other sexual partners, that my desire for other sexual partners had been realized, even though it was one I would no longer pursue.

Ironically, I believe, it was the course of the epidemic that pitched us deeper into monogamy. I sensed, somewhere around 1983, I think, that Nathan was looking for other sexual partners. I remember, too, the first night I put on a condom before entering Nathan, or, rather, Nathan slipped a condom over my cock; I felt, then, so ashamed of myself, uneasy that I might be carrying something inside that was potentially harmful to another person. Sex between us in those days had become quite passionless; anxiety accompanied every orgasm. We were, however, comfortable and content enough in our relationship to not need sex to define it. How we recaptured sex, though, was through recreating our romance. Nathan called me up at work one afternoon and asked me out on a date. We were both in such deep psychological ruts, I had just heard that Wes had died, that I thought Nathan, going through one of his fits of anxiety, had finally flipped. He persisted with the ruse of asking me out and then asked me to meet him at his apartment – our apartment – and he gave me the address, which I absurdly wrote down on a scrap of paper and folded and put into my pocket. I arrived home without shopping beforehand, without checking the mail. I rang the buzzer and announced my name, fingered the scrap of paper in my pocket as I climbed the stairs. When Nathan answered the door of his apartment – our apartment – he had candles burning on the tables and bookshelves. We ate dinner, which he had cooked, and listened to the stereo, making out afterward on the couch, still fully clothed, like two boys meeting on a first date might do. We danced a bit, taking turns leaning our heads on each other's shoulders, then kissed some more in the candlelight, till finally neither of us could bear the weight of the clothes on our bodies. I suppose in a way we locked out the rest of the world that night; our escape from the epidemic was an escape into our relationship. After that we tried to keep at least one "silent" night together – unplugging the phone, no talk of friends dying, just the two of us, in bed, holding each other.

When Nathan was in the hospital with pneumocystitis, I made an appointment to see Dr Jacobsen; I wanted to be tested for HIV – I had not been tested, myself, when I was hospitalized the year before, or, rather, my results had never been revealed to me and my reasoning was that if Nathan and I were both sick, or both to be sick, then maybe we should just go out together – leap off a building or jump in front of a subway car, or take, concurrently, a bottle of pills. I felt certain that I could discuss the possibility with Nathan, or be ready for a reply, myself, if he were ever to broach the subject. It took two weeks to get blood test results back, and as I shuttled between the hospital and the apartment – not wondering about the result, just suspended, really, until the verdict was to fall – I was convinced that I had done this to Nathan. I had infected him. I was the cause of his illness.

There was the idea, then, that passive partners were the ones that were easiest to be infected, and I had spent most of our relationship – years – fucking Nathan, before the concept of safe sex had been introduced and assimilated.

So I was stunned when I returned to Dr Jacobsen and he announced that I had tested negative. How was it possible that I had been spared this? Nathan and I had shared combs, razors, silverware, sheets, lubricant, clothes, and toothbrushes. I had tasted his saliva, his skin, his hair, his cum, as he had mine. I found out my result the day before Nathan was to be released from the hospital, but I did not tell him that evening. I waited a few days, till we were settled back again in the apartment. Nathan had gotten up from a nap and was sitting behind his desk, checking some figures his secretary from his office had brought him, when I walked into the room and said, directly, "My test came back negative."

I hated myself for the way I had said it so casually, hated myself for waiting the few seconds for him to understand what I was talking about; when he did, I watched an angry fire overtake his eyes. He did not say anything to me, and I didn't allow him a comment. I left the room and went back to the kitchen, where I had been reading the paper, ashamed and guilty because I had brought up an issue we had carefully avoided for weeks. A wall had been thrown up between us, a barrier neither one of us had had any choice in building, but one I was desperate to see knocked down but didn't know how. I wished, then, I had tested positive – and it occurred to me that maybe things would be easier if I were to become infected too.

"You have to be careful," Nathan said, coming into the room. It was then, at that moment, that I knew I would someday have a life without Nathan, and I put down the newspaper on the table with a deliberate movement, feeling censured because I had somehow been spared this virus. Why does one man carry antibodies and another man doesn't? Why does one man's immune system collapse and another does not even contain the virus? Not even science could answer those questions then.

Nathan and I did not stop having sex after he became ill. Sex, or, rather, making love, became redefined for us. The simple fact, however, was that I was negative and he was positive; he was infected and I was not, an identity that I carried with me throughout my day – when I shaved in the morning, took a glass of juice from the refrigerator, brushed my teeth in the bathroom at night. Even when we both had had colds, years ago, Nathan and I had never stopped kissing one another – deep, ardent kisses full of tongues and lips and breath and saliva colliding and mingling with one another. For a while, after he first became ill, Nathan would not kiss me on the lips, afraid of infecting me, and I, too, kept my passion in check, afraid of passing on some other kind of germs into him. Sex, then, became holding each other's hand as we watched TV, hugging one another in the bathroom, kissing each other on the forehead when coming into a room. Sex, too, was still the climax of an orgasm, but there was a division between us, a separation between him and me, a sort of hands-off-while-I-get-myself-off-and-you-just-help-me-a-bit-by-just-watching type of attitude. Nathan had become too protective, too worried. We no longer had anal sex; no longer had oral sex, either. Everything, really, distressed us too much.

"It would be immoral for me to do it," Nathan said when he met me at Penn Station when I returned from Washington. Seeing him for the first time after an absence of a few days, I noticed, now, the darker skin around his eyes, the stiffness in his walk, the tilt of his head as if it were too heavy for his body.

"No it wouldn't," I had answered. "It's only immoral for you if I was unaware of the potential consequences. I know what can happen. I understand the risk."

As daring as my words sounded, when we reached the street I was suddenly afraid of everything: crossing the street too soon, the traffic moving too quickly, even our weaving around a cluster of businessmen wearing name badges. I lifted my hand in the air to hail a cab, but felt, instead, like a man drowning and waving his hand wildly for someone to help.

"Why?" Nathan asked me when we had reached a restaurant in Chelsea where we had decided to go for lunch before returning home.

"Why?" I answered. "Why not? What's wrong with a man wanting his lover to fuck him?"

Fear clung to us like cigarette smoke, the smell of it seeping into our clothes, our hair, underneath our fingernails. In our past, when two men fucked, there was no concept that a virus could be passed between them, lay dormant, undetected for years, then suddenly erupt and send the body into panic. Fear was consuming our relationship: my fear of Nathan becoming ill, possibly dying, fear of myself, as well, becoming infected. Fear. Fear. Fear. And more fear.

"Is sex that important for you?" he asked when our food came, though he did not eat much, moving a pile of shredded carrots around his plate.

By then I had grown annoyed with our conversation, angry that we had to keep talking about it, over and over, that everything in our lives now was tinged with such complexity. "No, you know that. I don't want to be afraid of you, Nathan. I don't want to hate you. I want to trust you – I *have* to trust you." I threw my fork against my plate in frustration. "Don't you understand, Nathan? I accept whatever happens. If the condom breaks, the condom breaks. I don't blame you. You're not to blame." I had worked myself into such a restrained public rage that I could only breathe through my mouth.

Nathan dropped his jaw to speak, looking as if he were going to scream. "Robbie," he said, with an irritated force. "I don't blame you for any of this. What kind of man would I be if I did?"

And so the days passed between us respectfully; Nathan was never one to ask for help and I tried to believe there was a normalcy to our lives together, that picking up medication from the pharmacy was something that anyone would do, that calling Ben Nyquist to check his opinion on a blood transfusion for Nathan was not motivated by some unchecked hysteria. And then one morning in early November we lay in bed together, the sun breaking through a thick bank of rain clouds that had drifted over the city. A thin chill hovered in our bedroom and I slipped myself around Nathan to find more warmth. Patches of rainbows fell on the bedspread where the sunlight refracted through the small crystal prisms which Nathan had hung on the window grating years ago when we had first found the apartment.

In bed Nathan moved in closer to me and as I embraced him, I slid a hand down his stomach and realized he was hard. I held his cock for a moment, feeling the heat of it, then I slipped away from him and opened the dresser drawer beside the bed.

"Two," Nathan said. "I want to use two."

I pulled out the lubricant and two condoms, but he took them from me before I had returned to his side of the bed. He found a T-shirt on the floor and slipped it on to keep the chill of the air off of his back; I slipped between his knees and pressed my lips against his balls as they dangled above me. He slipped first one condom on and then the second one, then took the lubricant and rubbed it on his covered cock. I lifted my heels and placed them against his shoulders and he took the lubricant and rubbed it gently with his fingers into my ass. Our eyes met here and I could see, vividly, his were full of fear.

"Relax," he said, and we shifted our position a bit. I tilted my head back, and my eyes, at that moment, were suspended in a rainbow of light. I held myself there feeling the colors burn into my eyes. I believe, then, I had a glimpse of heaven. I closed my eyes, relaxed, and felt Nathan move himself slowly into me.

"Robbie," Nathan whispered. "I'll take care of you."

Then I let go of heaven. And he did.

THE ROBBER BRIDEGROOM

James Ireland Baker

THE BAR WAS dark and stunk of yeast and I wondered if the man by the window was a killer. I believe that you can tell a man who murders through a science called phrenology, which is based completely on the skull. The shape of a man's head will tell you whether or not he has the capacity to kill. This man in particular was wearing a baseball cap, so I couldn't tell much about him. Even when I wiped the film from my eyeglasses, I could see only that he was biting his fingernails and looking intermittently at me. I wanted to see his head, though, so I concentrated on it. In those days, when drunk, I truly believed that all I had to do was concentrate enough on something and it would happen.

The jukebox, which was famous, began playing a song that stuck in an irritating mental ridge. It was a familiar song, but I was drunk and couldn't tell where I had heard it before, or what it might have meant once. I was looking toward the jukebox, as though the sight of it would trigger a memory, when I felt a finger on my shoulder.

I turned around and saw that he'd arrived, a minor marvel. He was wearing that cap, strands of stringy blond hair dangling from its brim, spilling onto his forehead. He slouched and he was tall and bony and his ears were far too big. He had acne. He bit his fingernails. He was wearing jeans and sneakers. He looked like an awkward adolescent basketball player. He looked like a cartoon character. He seemed nervous.

"Can I buy you a drink?" he asked.

"Sure. A shot of Cuervo."

"You drink *tequila*?" he wrinkled up his nose in tentative disgust.

"Something wrong with that?"

"It makes my heart hurt. I call it *to-kill-ya*. Listen, I'm Abraham."

"Owen."

"Nice to meet you. Live around here?"

"On 20th Street. West 20th Street."

"Nice place?"

"Not really. It's messy."

The truth was that I lived in one room with a shower in the kitchen and a bed in the kitchen and a table in the kitchen. I lived in a kitchen, in fact, or a living room or closet, whichever you chose. The truth was that I had one room and this one room seemed to stand for everything that had not worked out the way I felt it should have.

"Well," Abraham said, "I don't really *care* how messy your apartment is, or anything. It's better than where I live, which is namely with my parents, who live in New Jersey. So that, you know, in order to get home, I have to catch a bus."

"Why do you live with your parents?"

"I'm in rehab – which is also why I look so young, you know. It has a preserving effect on you, junk. You don't ever age."

I did not want to go to New Jersey with a recovering heroin addict whose skull I wasn't sure of. But before long there was the warmth of him and the look of his smile and the feeling of the Cuervo in my stomach, which soon spread to my spine and made me feel less awkward. I reached up to take his cap off, but he stopped me, his hand grabbing mine as swiftly and with as much force as if he were catching a fastball. So I smiled and moved my hand against his belly instead. It was warm and flat. I left my hand there for a while and then I slipped it past his waist, under his belt, felt his bristly moist pubic hair, the warmth of the skin, the place where his penis was attached to his body. He didn't seem to mind. Why he let me feel the root of his sex and not his scalp I do not know – unless, of course, he had something to hide and could sense that I understood the science of phrenology.

"If I go to New Jersey with you," I said, "will you kill me?"

"What?"

"Are you Eddie?"

"*Who?*"

"The man who lives in the hole with his family?"

"I don't know what you're talking about."

A killer was drinking in Manhattan gay bars, I explained, taking young men home and killing them, and he called himself Eddie and said that he lived in a hole with his family. Abraham didn't believe me. Either that, or he felt that perhaps I was playing a game.

Port Authority after midnight is like one of the seven doorways to Hell. More than a doorway, it actually *is* Hell, or at least an *antechamber*. I saw scabby whores with bottles of MD 20/20 and bums reeking of piss and of something far fouler and I stood there with Abraham, near Gate 201, watching these people lurch past us like zombies, or sit, like starving children in Biafra, flies and maggots crawling around the edges of their mouths, masturbating in the corners.

Abraham put his hand in the pocket of my winter coat. It was an alpaca I had purchased at the Salvation Army just one month before. There was a package of saltines in the pocket. I used to steal saltines from restaurants, as well as packages of ketchup and soy sauce. Abraham pulled the saltines out. He looked at me as if to ask, mind? and then unwrapped the package and put one stale saltine in his mouth.

"It'll settle my stomach," he said, blowing cracker dust. "I'm nervous."

"Why?"

"About you. Wondering what you will taste like, for instance, or what we will do." He handed me the second saltine, which I declined. "You sure?"

"I'm sure."

"Can I kiss you?"

"Here?"

He nodded, removing the residue from his molars with his tongue.

"Let's wait until we get to your parents' place."

He grinned at me, all muckle mouth and eyelashes. I could see the film of salty saliva on his front teeth. He cupped his right hand and fitted it gently against my left ear, then leaned into me and whispered, "You'll eat me, won't you?" and it wasn't *what* he said so much as the feeling of his breath and his lips against my earlobe that made the impression.

The bus arrived and we boarded. I spent the first few minutes of our journey touching Abraham's fingers, interweaving them with mine, feeling his nails, which were bitten down to blood. I put my right hand to the glass of the window and made heat impressions in the frost. I looked through the impressions and saw fires blazing atop gas drums. I saw a factory with a large orange-red "A" (and a horse) as its logo. I saw skeletal radio transmitters that looked like Japanese monsters. It was dark in this wilderness and my fingers were cold. I was beginning to feel impatient. I didn't have a watch, but I figured we were on that bus for probably an hour before it came to its final stop, outside a garage in the center of a small town. I felt, suddenly, sober enough for regret.

"You live all the way out here, and you don't have a car?"

"Of course not."

"What were you doing in the city so late?"

"Looking for you."

"Everyone off," the driver said, turning around in his seat. "Last stop, folks."

We emerged into the winter air, plumes of breath mixing with exhaust from the bus as it disappeared, its brake lights flashing. The night was still and cold, the sky low. You could hear sounds – trains, dogs, cars on gravel roads – from miles away. The stars were so bright and they sparkled so intensely I was almost surprised to discover that they themselves did not make noise, like the ringing of crystal or spinning of glass. Abraham looked around, trying to orient himself. Now I wanted to see, not his skull, but his forearms. Were there needle tracks there? I wondered. He led me through the snow, past the ancient Rexall Drug store with its dim blue-green lights, past the post office on the corner, past the birdshit-covered statue of some foreign war hero, until we reached a series of side roads that seemed to lead nowhere, except back to the center of that small town. We were traveling, it seemed, in circles and I was beginning to believe that we were utterly lost when Abraham finally stopped, silently pointing to a lightless, two-story, yellow Colonial with two dormer windows and a small garage abutting its right wall.

He walked up the drive all the way to the garage. A dog began to bark inside. He pressed his face to the window, cupped bare hands around his eyes and stared. He nodded and walked across the front lawn to the stoop, where he stood like a spectre silhouetted against the white front door as he searched through his front pockets for a chain of keys. He muttered something, tried his back pockets.

"I left my keys at the bar," he said loudly. "You go find a rock, okay? I'll see if there's a way to get in through the back."

"Don't you think –?" I began, but he wasn't listening. He jumped over a picket fence and walked into the backyard, leaving me alone on the frozen grass of the front lawn. I looked dumbly around at the neighboring houses, thinking of the people who were lying in their beds, perhaps sitting up, insomniac, staring out the windows at the solitary figure who was standing, without gloves or jacket, in the yard next door. I felt cold and suddenly scared and very worried.

The last dead fag had been found two weeks before in the back of an abandoned truck along Manhattan's West Side Highway. He was last seen alive at Five Oaks with a person some witnesses described as a man and some as a woman. The fag went home with people frequently. He was promiscuous, if not an actual prostitute. What was the difference between him and me? I wondered. He was wearing his best clothes, but even his best clothes had holes in them. He was trying to find in alcohol the hope or glimmer that life itself had ceased to provide. He was trying to make up for the fact that the rest of his life was not what it probably should be. He went home with the man because he, too, was embarrassed by the rented room with the holes in the walls and a bed and a shower in the kitchen.

He was tortured, raped and strangled. There were ligature marks around his neck and heels. Cuts were left in the soft flesh of his belly, spelling out words the police would not release. There was a rust hole in the side of the truck. Above the hole, someone – the killer, perhaps – had scrawled in black magic marker:

MY NAME IS EDDIE. I LIVE IN THIS HOLE WITH MY FAMILY.

"Hey!" I heard a tinkle of glass, followed by the dog's increasingly frantic and menacing barks. I looked up and saw Abraham emerge from behind the garage. He stood on the cement of the front drive, rocking back and forth upon his heels, as though testing the surface, clearly pleased with himself.

"I broke a window," he grinned.

I followed him along a sidewalk that led to the back of the house, where a small, ground-level window had been broken. He kneeled on the dirt before the window, wrapped his bare, white and bitten-down fingers with his scarf and began gingerly, intently picking jagged pieces of glass from the rubber weather stripping. I watched the concentration in his face as he pulled the pieces back and forth. They loosened and popped out. Then he pushed the screen in.

"It's just like we're breaking into someone's house, or – "

"It is."

"It's just like it doesn't really belong to my parents, or something."

"It's remarkably like that," I said.

He stretched out on the ground and inched his legs through the window, body scraping the bottom rail as he lowered himself into the basement room, which must have been the laundry. He turned on the dirty, dangling overhead light bulb. I could see bottles of Tide, cartons of Bon Ami, six-packs of Diet Rite and Fresca, piles of clothing in large wicker baskets.

He walked from the laundry into an adjacent room, disappearing from my view.

"Come on in!" I heard him shout, suddenly screaming: "It's safe! The dog's locked upstairs!"

I hesitated for a moment before I grabbed the edges of the window, pulling myself through the frame. It wasn't until I looked around, however, and saw that I was standing on the top of a white metal dryer that I realized that my hand had been cut deeply and that I was bleeding.

"Oh, look what I found," Abraham crowed as he walked in from the other room, carrying a small wooden box from inside of which a strand of something shiny – necklace? – dangled. When he saw the black blood dripping from my hand, he panicked, putting the box down on the dryer and picking up a silk slip, ripping off a long piece, reaching for my flesh.

"What are you doing?" I said. "That's dirty. Where's a bandage? Where's the bathroom?"

"There's no bathroom down here. I checked."

"What about upstairs?"

"I don't *want* to go upstairs."

"Why not?"

"The dog's . . . it's my dad's new attack dog, a pit bull. He doesn't know me. He's locked in the kitchen, which is caged off. If we come up through the basement, he might attack, and – "

"What's its name?"

"Hunter," he said, defensively. "*Why?*"

The warning signs in gay bars read: "Make sure you know the man you're going home with," which is a little like telling bees to know their flowers. If you don't know the man you're going home with, the flyers added, make sure you introduce him to your friends before you leave. But I didn't really have any friends. The only precaution I was taking was touching scalps. That way I could feel pretty certain what these men were up to. But I couldn't feel this man's scalp and I didn't know anything about him, except that he was a liar.

"It's not really your dog," I said, "is it?"

He looked at me, pale mouth drooping.

"It's not your *father's* dog, either. You don't really live here, do you? You're probably still a junkie, right? Breaking into people's house – "

"I haven't stolen a thing." He dropped the silk slip and walked, eyes flashing, into the next room. I turned to the dryer and saw the box he'd left behind. I opened it up and saw a white piece of cardboard covered with multicolored rocks; half a wishbone; a few large marbles; an agate; a plastic windmill from a Cracker Jack box, and a lime green rabbit's foot on a metal chain.

"If I die in the mouth of that goddamned dog," I heard Abraham's voice from the base of the stairs, "it's all your goddamned fault." I heard him walk forthrightly up the stairs. I heard him open the door. I heard the dog, whose name was perhaps Hunter, begin to whine. I heard Abraham cooing and talking to him. I heard the whine of the electric can opener and the continued thumping of the dog's tail on the floor. I heard Abraham empty the can into a dish.

"Coast is clear!" he shouted.

There were plywood-paneled walls in the next room, along with a large red overstuffed reclining chair, a globe, a map of the world, a sea chest. To my right was the staircase. I walked, trailing blood, up the stairs into the kitchen. The dog, a golden retriever who smelled wet, looked from his food and stared indifferently at me.

"That's no pit bull," I said.

"Bathroom's down that hall and to your left."

The bathroom looked like someone had just left it. There was an open compact on the toilet tank and an tube of Colgate on the sink. A long string of bloody floss hung over the side of the wicker waste basket. I opened up the medicine cabinet, found KY, Johnson & Johnson Baby Powder, a dirty jar of Vaseline, Bactine, Valium, bandages. I disinfected and wrapped my bleeding hand in cloth and wondered what was next. Ligature marks? Cuts on my body reading PIG, FAGGOT, WHORE? A hole in the wall? This man named Abraham had clearly broken into a random house somewhere in nameless New Jersey and I had followed him. It was still possible to cut my losses. It was still possible to leave and avoid criminal charges, or oncoming death, by simply opening the bathroom window and jumping out.

But it was one of those nights where you feel that what is

happening is *supposed* to happen, like it had happened before or had always been there, waiting.

The sound of Frank Sinatra's "In the wee small hours of the morning" came from the living room and I followed it down the hall. Abraham was sitting on the couch. He had unzipped his pants and had pulled out his cock. He was idly toying with himself, watching a movie on the VCR. I could hear the dialogue:

"Can you see her now?" An adult male voice. "Can you see her face?"

"No!" The voice of a young man, boy. "Wait a minute!"

"You can see her hair, though, can't you?"

"Who?"

"You can see her hair."

"It's way too close."

"But you can *see* it. Can't you?"

Abraham turned to me and, still stroking, grinned.

"Come here," he said.

"That dog – "

"Won't hurt you. He's very nice. Would a drink make you feel better?"

"No," I said. "Take off your cap."

He was still wearing his cap.

"What?"

"I want to see your head. Take off your cap."

"I don't like my hair. Come here," he patted the space on the couch between himself and the dog. He held his flaccid penis in his hands and waved it at me. "I have something for you." I sat down next to him and he took my glasses off and I couldn't see a thing, couldn't see his ragged beauty, but we grazed each other. I felt my nose against his nose, felt my lips against his lips. I felt the completeness of his mouth as he opened it, then, and it was warm and sticky, like milk slightly soured and tasting of hay. His tongue was moving along my teeth and I felt excitement. He could tell I felt excitement and he was happy about it. He put his hands on my neck. He was touching my neck. He was pushing me down.

"*Pig*," he said, experimentally. "You're a *pig*, aren't you? You like that, don't you?"

I opened my mouth.

"You like that, don't you? I *want* you to like it."

I shut my eyes. In the back of my head I saw images of the bodies as they might have looked. The eyelids were always cut off, usually before death. Items of clothing, sometimes pieces of flesh, were stuffed into the victims' rectums. The dicks and balls were cut off. The lips were blue. Once, a twig of pine had been jammed within a victim's urethra – while, it was later determined, the man was still alive.

"Close," he said. "I'm close."

I could feel him quickening. I could feel his pelvis thrusting, meeting my rhythms, adding his own awkward and almost peristaltic counterpart. I could feel his hands against my skull, forcing me downward, choking. I pulled away, sat up and put my glasses back on. Saliva, mixed with pre-cum, drooled from my lips, making me feel like an epileptic in the throes of a fatal seizure.

"What's wrong?" he asked with puzzled tenderness. He touched my mouth where my wet and soiled lips met, as if to wipe away the bruise. I felt covered with bruises, like my mouth was now stained with the purplish hues of his mottled, spotty penis. "I thought you liked that kind of stuff."

"*What* kind of stuff?"

"The roughness. You asked if I was going to kill you."

"No," I said, rocking back and forth. I was feeling sort of seasick. "A friend of mine took me not long ago to a place where you can have sex with another man just by looking at him. My friend was going to this place all the time, having sex with other guys, getting fucked by them, sometimes even when he wasn't sure what they looked like. And then I found out that he sometimes was having sex with older guys for money, which upset me. I mean, you like me and I like you and we can have sex together, but when you get paid to get fucked, I don't want to know about it."

"I don't pay to get fucked." He paused; then: "Do you *want* me to fuck you?"

"No."

"I'd *like* to."

"I don't just *do* that."

"Do you want –?" He pointed to his chest, looking at me questioningly. "I wouldn't mind."

This was not his house. I was not his boyfriend.

"I'm a little messy," he said. "I'm going to take a shower, OK? You coming with me, Owen?"

"I'll be right. There."

On the VCR I could see a young man staring into the camera, shrugging his shoulders. He was lying on a bed with a woman who, with flourishes, was tying him to the posts with silk handkerchiefs. The color was bad and the tape was blurry, as if it were a second-generation copy. In time, I could not even see the images I was supposed to see; I was seeing only the grain, the way the scratches in the film shifted and made patterns on the screen. The skin looked discolored and green. The lighting was bad.

The shower water started with a *hisss* in the bathroom and, above the Frank Sinatra music still playing on the stereo, I heard Abraham singing a plaintive, tuneless song of his own in the shower. I walked to the bathroom.

The shower curtain was closed, but it was translucent. He had finally taken off his cap and his thin hair was pale yellow and it clung to his head irregularly, as if he'd been tarred and feathered. He was going bald. But it wasn't his hair that I cared much about. It was the sight of the skull that mattered to me, the sight of his skull that caused me to step, fully clothed, into the spray.

I grabbed his head and felt his bones.

"Does it bother you?" he asked sheepishly.

"Huh?"

"That I don't have much hair?"

"No," I said. "I think you're fucking beautiful."

He had a *huge* knob at the back of his skull, at the very top of the spine, which signifies "Emotiveness." Emotiveness is a nice word for lust. I could see his dick and I could see bad, infected needle marks all over his arms. I turned him around and bent him over, saw his pale and spindly, zitty ass. I unzipped my pants and pulled them down. I took my dick out of my underwear and covered it with hair conditioner, which washed off in the shower water, but I didn't care.

"My name isn't Owen, Abraham," I joked. "Did you know that?"

I could hardly hear his voice. It was muffled in the water. "No."

"My *real* name is Eddie. I live in this hole with my family."

"What's that supposed to mean, for crissakes? Ow!" he said as I wrapped my hands around him. That was it, then: self-defense. I watched his pink scalp get pinker and redder. And suddenly my life seemed suspended in this moment: Warm water and wet clothes, Frank Sinatra and pornography, my balls contracting, Abraham catching his breath in the shower.

EXPERTISE

Felice Picano

WHEN HIS THIRD lover walked out the door, Alex decided he'd had just about enough of gay romance.

Bradley had been as beautiful as an old Arrow Shirt ad model, as delicious as Entenmann's chocolate-chip cookies, and alas! in the final evaluation, about as nourishing. How long could love go on with the perpetually wounded vanity of one partner and the adoring selflessness of the other? Yet it had happened to Alex before: with Tim, with Lenny, and now – most disastrously – with Brad. Enough times, Alex concluded, to qualify as a *bona-fide* self destructive syndrome.

What he needed was to look after himself for once in his life. Yes, to cultivate selfishness: an enlightened selfishness.

So, after the requisite day and a half of tears, the usual two weeks of increasingly bored sympathy from friends, and the necessary month of depression and self recrimination, Alex decided to turn a new leaf.

He would transform himself into a sex object; and as this sex object, he would seek out none but other sex objects. They at least would have the realistic insecurities of their humble origins, the confidence of their developed narcissism, and a healthy respect for anyone who'd accomplished as much.

In a city like New York, Alex knew that taking this step

would soon assure him of: (1) innumerable one night stands, (2) invitations to all the hot parties in town and on Fire Island, (3) as a result of those parties, more one night stands of even higher quality than before, (4) memberships in private discos, discriminating baths and sex clubs, (5) as a result of those, invitations to even hotter parties in the city and even more distant – to Los Angeles and San Francisco, and (6) as a result of all that, extreme, intense, non-stop, mindless self-gratification.

Alex inspected himself in the full-length mirror hanging in his bedroom and thought, well, it's worked for people with far less raw material than I have to start with.

His evaluation was born in that total objectivity that often follows despair. His face was attractive enough – although scarcely magazine handsome. At least it had the character that accompanied ethnicity (Greek-American) without a hint of immigrant to it. Large, light-colored eyes that some had called hypnotic. Dark, straight hair that required little care. An obvious but rather nice nose. Cheek-bones that could only become more prominent with age. Of course his body could use some work, he thought. But mostly detail work. Five-ten, fairly lean and well proportioned, his limbs weren't apelike like some porno-stars people jerked off to, not cutsey doll short either. His back was straight, his posture and walk fine. Detail work: a few months swimming and playing on the rings at some gym; a touch of weights to build up his pecs, laterals and deltoids. As for dress – that all important system of codes and invitations to the knowing – Alex already knew what he would need to buy, what he would have to discard, what he would have to pre-age and partially destroy to achieve that particularly casual look. True, Alex wasn't a natural knockout beauty. But then, how many current Living Legends around him had been before they went to work on themselves?

He began the next day so that he wouldn't have time to find excuses. He phoned Jim Maddox who cut all the hottest and most highly paid models in town and set up an appointment. He joined a local health club with a great pool, extensive athletic equipment and few sisters to distract him. He went through his closets and cut his wardrobe in half, then shopped in the

Village, blowing about $600 in plastic that he would be sorry about next month.

He could already picture himself, 11:30 on a Sunday morning, his lean, tanned body half wrapped around some dropdead number he'd picked up at the Ice Palace and necked with at the afterhours party at a Bayside poolhouse, sweeping down the boardwalk at the Pines, past an astonished Bradley.

It would be heaven!

And, six months later, it was heaven. But for one, tiny, yet all important fact he hadn't taken into consideration months before when he'd begun his transformation plans – a fact that provided Alex with a rather icy awakening.

Henrik turned over on the double bed and seemed to brood. Brooding, Henrik looked as breathtakingly handsome as Henrik seductive, or Henrik comical or Henrik intensely following the progress of a spotted beetle across a beach blanket. His golden blond hair shimmered in the champagne haze of the ocean afternoon. His skin glimmered in the venetian blinds' mottled light, now red, now pale blue, now the faintest hint of green against his deep tan, and against the striking diamond white on white pattern of the designer sheets.

Henrik had gone limp once more, however, which was why he was brooding; and all of Alex's tactics to revive the flagging erection proved failures. Alex knew it was his fault without being able to say exactly why it was his fault. They'd started off so well on the beach, doing a *From Here to Eternity* number in the swirling surf, despite the passers-by, despite the critical commentary from surrounding beach blanket occupants, even despite the two little tots who insisted on playing with beach pails only three or four feet away. Started off so well, so hot, so frantic, Alex and Henrik had finally stood up, rearranged their hardons in their tiny Speedo bathing suits and trekked back to the house. Where they had continued hot – until they'd fizzled.

"I guess I turned you off?" Alex said, knowing it wasn't a question at all.

"Oh, no," came the gloomy, polite, deep voiced bed lie.

"What was it I did wrong?" Alex persisted. "What didn't you like?"

"Nothing. Nothing at all," Henrik insisted, looking at Alex with eyes of the bluest depths of a fjord in summertime. Then those eyes seemed to widen and narrow, as though Henrik were trying to gauge Alex's capacity for truth, vulnerability, and all the connecting links between. He must have decided Alex could stand more truth than flattery, because in the next minute he slowly said, "I suppose my problem is that I'm more used to, well, to experts."

"Experts?" Alex asked, then realized what exactly was being said; he became embarrassed.

"It's what American men are best at, you know," Henrik said, gently, firmly, decisively. "All over the world it's known. I have a Finnish friend, Ole, who comes to America two weeks a year on vacation just to get American blowjobs. He saves up all year for it. He hasn't missed a vacation here in 11 years."

Alex surveyed Henrik's pale, long, flaccid cock and thought, well, I did the best I know how; no one else ever complained. Not good enough, the little voice within him replied. Not good enough for beautiful Henrik. Not good enough for the other beautiful men you want. Not even good enough for your goddamn country! What kind of patriot are you, anyway?

Because Alex was silent, listening to the little voice, Henrik took this as encouragement to go on. He described the five best blowjobs he'd received: their circumstances, setting, the other person, the techniques employed, any other interesting little details. Then Henrik described Ole's travels across the country by train, plane, car and Trailways Bus in search of the perfect blowjob. He mentioned the small, out of the way towns where Ole had been astounded; the times he found himself suddenly surprised by luck on the backseats of buses, in the lavatories of jets, at truck stops, at public toilets – places he'd returned to again and again.

Every phrase reproached Alex; reproached and shamed him. They also excited him. He wondered if this was because it was Henrik, beautiful, sexy Henrik telling it, or if it was because such anonymous, mechanical sex must of necessity be more exciting.

"Here," Henrik said in conclusion, reaching for Alex, "let me show you how it should be done."

The neighbors two houses down the beach must have heard Alex when he arrived at that orgasm.

"Now that," Henrik said proudly, "was what Ole would have called a blowjob."

Alex too. But he was afraid to try it himself, fearing his lack of expertise would cause yet another, and even more embarrassing, failure. Handling the Swedish Adonis' now own splendid erection, he asked in what he hoped was him most enticing tone of voice:

"How would you like to fuck?"

It was a turning point. For the next few months, Alex continued to go to Fire Island, to parties, to the baths, to bars and orgies. He continued to meet handsome men anywhere and everywhere, and to get them into bed with little or no trouble just about whenever he wanted to. And, though it was all undoubtedly more satisfying than having to put up with Brad's moods or Tim's tantrums or Lenny's falling asleep on him whenever he wanted them to make love – something was missing. As though for all his new rugged looks, his posed stances, his rehearsed words of seduction, he'd still not made that last final step in his planned transformation.

During these months however, he began to realize that one group of men completely eluded him. Not a real group, more like an amorphous assemblage; but a distinct one. They weren't the best looking, nor the best connected, not the most talented or talked about – but they were the most desirable. Alex seldom saw them at bars or baths or orgies, and whenever he did see them they were always with each other, always being private, obviously together, without any attempt to hide it, or more to the point, to include anyone else in. They dressed no differently from Alex or thousands of others, yet they had an altogether distinctive aura. Their flanks looked longer and flatter, their asses more delectable in denims or bathing suits, although they wore the same button-fly Levi's and Speedo's he wore. Their chests seemed more defined, less pumped, more natural. Their mouths looked more sensuous, their hands more eager and experienced, their crotches more . . . more everything! Alex didn't know what it was they had, but they knew they had it. And they knew he didn't. He never once received even a half curious look from one of the group, never mind a cruise, never mind the hint of a pick-up.

"It's really only a matter of expertise," Jeff said. He and Alex were sitting at a formica-topped table in a booth in a coffee shop of utterly no distinction across the street from a shoddy, abandoned gas station bathroom where Alex had followed Jeff's offhand cruise a half hour before and where Alex had gotten the best blowjob of his life.

"You simply have to be committed," Jeff went on, "to want the best, and then to practice until you are."

Jeff (no last name offered) was about ten pounds overweight – around his waist where it showed even in a loose T-shirt. He was balding at the back of his curly-haired head. He was prematurely grey in his beard, at his temples and on what Alex could see of his chest. He didn't dress well, nor was he more than ordinarily good looking (certainly not in Alex's class!); yet Jeff was one of that group Alex lusted after. He was always among those seen sleazily grinding their hips into each other at eight-thirty in the morning at Flamingo, and always amid those seen leaving the Ice Palace for a private morning party where who was excluded was more important than who was invited. So, when Jeff cruised Alex on the street, Alex knew he would be late for the movie date he had with a woman friend: he couldn't pass this up. He followed Jeff into the bathroom, and gave himself up to Jeff's expert hands.

Now, however, Alex had to know why he and so many others desired Jeff or his ilk so much, so hopelessly. That was why, after the blowjob, he'd talked to Jeff, asked him to this hepatitis dispensary, why he made himself completely miss the film he was supposed to see, why he sat here with Jeff, why he could bring himself to ask the embarrassing question Jeff had answered so succinctly.

"Practice!" Alex said. "I practice all the time."

"Where?"

"The backroom bars, the clubs, the orgies, the parties, the bushes, the baths, at home, in bed. Everywhere!"

"Too many distractions," Jeff said, all-knowing. "What you

have to do is find a place where distractions are at a minimum, where you can concentrate on what you're doing, where face, body, personality, character, past history, social connections, none of it can get in the way. You need a still, intense focus. It's an art, you know, and like all arts must be practiced purely!"

When Alex paid for the coffee and pastry, Jeff reached into his own wallet and pulled out a tattered, yellowing card.

"Go here. Use my card until they get to know your face. It's very private. Not anyone is allowed in."

Alex stared at the card, defaced by wear to a few lines and cracks. "What is it?"

"Blowjob palace. Two fifty and all you want."

Alex thanked him, wishing he could bring himself to say something about seeing Jeff again. After that lecture, it seemed entirely out of the question, unless Jeff brought it up.

"I hope this works," Alex said.

"It will. Oh, take my phone number. When you think you're really ready, give me a call."

Alex waited a month before going to the place. He put off going week after week, telling himself he wanted to be certain he would go there in the right frame of mind – horny, experimental, perhaps slightly frustrated, perhaps somewhat detached.

Even so, when he did finally go to the club it was more by chance than by design. He'd had dinner with some old friends in the neighborhood, had drank a bit more than usual, had smoked more grass than he usually did and was feeling – if not all he wished to feel – at least horny and bored with the prospect of trying to pick up someone in one of his usual haunts this late on a weeknight.

The club was two floors of what had once been a storefront years ago. A small foyer led to a large, high-ceilinged room, surrounded on three sides by small, closet-sized rooms, divided by wood planking. In the middle was another free-standing series of closets. Each one locked on the inside by a simple latch and was unfurnished except for a low, rough-hewn stool. All very ordinary, except for the obvious irregularity of large holes at lower-torso level in each partition: more oval than round: not big enough to put your head through, but sufficient for most genitalia. Alex supposed they were made that way to accommodate men of differing heights.

Inspecting the almost empty club, he discovered that most of the closets had similar layouts except those located on corners, which only had two holes. Later, he would discover that the two middle rooms within the free-standing group were large enough to hold two or three people, with six, seven and even more holes hewn out of their partitions. Evidently these rooms were favored by couples, groups, teams and insatiable singles.

Aside from the closets were only the most primitive amenities: a sort of waiting room with two benches and floor ashtrays, a cigarette and soda machine, a small bathroom. It was all moderately lighted – not as dark as most of the discos and backroom places he frequented. Disco music of the funkier sort was played over six speakers on each floor, the records spun by the same guy (youngish, cutish) who took your money at the door and gave you a coat check.

As Alex wandered exploring, several men came in, making him feel more cautious. He went into a booth, locked the door, sat down on the stool, and lighted a joint. He smoked, hearing the sound of doors opening and closing around him. None of the three booths that opened up to his were occupied. It must be too early in the evening. Here I am, Alex said to himself, all ready to practice. He didn't feel drunk, or woozy, or overstuffed from the meal, nor even sodden from the grass, but as he always felt while cruising, oddly extra alert. He tapped his feet lightly on the wooden plank floor to the beat of the music, leaning back against the door.

Before the song was over or the joint in his hand half smoked, the door in the booth to his right opened and Alex made out someone come in and saw the figure turn to lock the door. Now something Jeff had said before was clarified: unless the other man bent down, Alex couldn't see who he was, could only see part of him, certainly not his face. Alex leaned forward to get a better look and a longish semi-erection was immediately pushed through the hole in his direction. Alex took a final toke of the grass, smashed its embers out on the floor and began to idly fondle the erection.

Practice time, Alex said to himself. No fooling around tonight.

The guy must have been really horny – he got stiff instantly and came in about three minutes flat. Hardly enough time to be considered anything but a warm-up, Alex thought, turning away to find that roach he'd dropped and relight it. He was somewhat pleased with himself, even though he knew this had been too simple to be any different from his past experiences – certainly not different enough to place him on Jeff's level of expertise. By the time Alex had located the small piece of joint and lighted it, he found two more erections facing him from the previously unoccupied booths. One was olive skinned and thick with a fat head, the other smaller and red on top as though bruised. Choices, choices, he thought, playing with both of them for a minute. Then he decided to take turns, jerking off one while blowing the other and then switching it around. He got two more rather quick orgasms, and was soon facing another erection from the other hole. Was this beginner's luck, or was it like this every night, he wondered.

When Alex emerged from the booth some two hours later for a soda and a rest he'd given more blow jobs than he could keep count of. He'd also received the third and fourth (after Jeff and Henrik) most spectacular orgasms of his life, thanks to guys on the other side of the partitions.

He still had a long way to go before he could attain Jeff's seemingly effortless degree of expertise, he felt, a lot more practice before he could begin to be comfortable with Jeff and his group.

Having found his first experience painless and fun, Alex began going to the club more often: first a night a week, then two nights a week, then three nights a week, clear weather or foul, from midnight to three in the morning, sometimes staying later.

He also began to experiment with moods and mood altering agents to see if they helped or hindered him. Some nights he'd merely have a vodka or smoke some grass before going: that always made him horny and seemed to turn on the other men. Sometimes, if he were feeling a bit tired, he'd sniff a bit of coke before leaving his apartment. Other times, he'd drop half a Quaalude, which definitely made him feel looser, sleazier. But that could also prove counter-productive to practicing, as he would be swinging on a really nice large cock while high on a down and decide he'd really rather take it up the ass, which was cheating. He almost always supplemented whatever mood he had designed with poppers. So did everyone else. He tried heavier drugs once – Mescaline – but it wasn't as good: he became too distracted by the music, lacked alertness, forgot what he was doing, got overly imaginative about the man attached to the cock.

In less than a month, Alex encountered more different cocks than he'd ever imagined existing, even though he'd had his share before. Maybe it was because they were so emphasized here. In one night at the club, he would bring off long ones, thin ones, thick ones, lily-white ones, flaring purples-headed ones, angry red ones, black ones, tan ones, fat ones, flattened ones, bent ones, squarish ones: some with tiny little pointed heads, others consisting of almost nothing but head: several had a network of bulging veins, some had no apparent veins on the shaft at all: some smelled of colognes and powders, others of wintergreen (athletes?), some of urine, others of perspiration – ranging from metallically acrid to sweeter-than-butterscotch: most smelled of nothing at all.

In those early months, Alex practiced on each one that came his way. Even if it were small and thin, even if it were so large he could scarcely encompass it with a hand, never mind get his lips around it. He made it a point with each to find the right angle of approach, much as one does when first meeting a person socially, as though the cock were the entire individual encapsulated, personified. Some were to be handled gently, others more roughly. For some, he had to drop onto his knees, squat and angle up; others had to be gotten at from the left side, or the top.

Alex naturally also observed others: the holes in the partition provided enough room to view. Between increased practice and observation, he learned how not to gag, how to use the top of his palette, how to tongue the sensitive vein-rich shaft bottom, how to titillate the area beneath the head. He learned how to stroke, caress, lick, grasp, grip and fondle each scrotum. He even learned how to hold both genitals – if they weren't too large – together in such a way that he could blow both cock and balls simultaneously.

These technical matters aside, Alex also discovered there was a right attitude and a wrong attitude to take in sucking a cock. Demanding orgasm was meaningless – even wrong-headed. If he were relaxed, in time with the music, and thoughtlessly sucking away, he became nothing but an internal muscle – the ideal state. Often, he'd be without a thought in his mind, almost oblivious of where he was, what he was doing or how much time had passed, when the telltale sign of a sudden new thickening in the head told him he was about to get another little explosion.

One night, he stood up from one of the larger, center booths and saw a handwritten scrawl that read:

BROUGHT OFF TWENTY GUYS HERE TONIGHT

Alex laughed. Only a tyro would bother to keep count – or to crow about it.

He'd become comfortable in the club. He got to be known to the two guys who alternated at the door and spinning records. He started to know almost instinctively the minute a man walked into the foyer whether he'd be good for one orgasm or more. He even began to size up cocks from how their owners walked, from how they played with themselves through their pants.

Soon, men were flinging their bodies against the partitions, moaning and calling out in orgasm when Alex had hold of them. One night someone fell backwards against the door of the booth. Another forgot to lock his booth and fell right out – into someone passing by. Alex became sought after in the club. Booths on either side of his were seldom empty. He began to feel easy, casual, confident, effective.

After not too long, he felt ready for anyone: anyone.

When Jeff walked into the club, he must have been stoned: he walked right past where Alex was sitting on the waiting-room bench without noticing him.

Jeff had lost weight and his grey hair had spread to an even salt-and-pepper over his beard and curly head. He looked terrific.

Alex followed him around a bit, trying to get his attention, but Jeff still didn't recognize him, and finally entered a booth flanked by two occupied ones. Alex stood against the wall, lighted a joint and waited until one of them emptied or Jeff came out again.

Alex had progressed from being completely promiscuous to being utterly selective. He didn't need practice anymore. Now, whenever he stepped into a booth, it was to give someone he'd chosen a special treat. He usually stayed out in the waiting area until someone exceptional arrived – someone attractive, well remembered, or simply new to him. He would then follow the man around, cruise him, watch until his intention was clear. Most guys he cruised, cruised back pretty fast, picking up on his supercharged sexuality. Most of them remained outside a booth until they could find one adjoining to his. But there were times when the place was so crowded only one booth was available. Alex would open the door, and invite the guy in. All of them entered, and all of them stayed.

Afterwards, sitting on the front benches sharing a Seven-Up, a cigarette and a desultory chat, most of the men offered Alex their phone numbers and a few asked for his. It didn't take him long to make a good sized collection. But the few times he called up guys he'd met at the club, there always seemed to be a lot of talk, and endless grass smoking and interminably long foreplay before they got down to what interested him. After a few turn-offs like this, Alex still took phone numbers and said he would call, but he never did.

But he was known now. Whenever he went out to parties or bars or discos – all the most attractive, most desirable men knew him. Some fondled his nipples as he passed, others groped him or patted his ass. All at least nodded or said hello; including most of the men in that group he wanted to know so badly before. Especially them.

Finally a booth next to where Jeff had entered flew open and a tall, good-looking guy stepped out. Alex went in, sat down and looked. Jeff was sitting down too. He needed a little motivation.

Alex had evolved a little ritual which seldom failed to interest. He would walk into a booth, lock the door, play with himself through his denims until he was hard, slowly unbutton his fly, open up, draw it out hard, play with it a little, take out his balls, rub them a little, unloosen his belt, slowly push his pants down to his knees, all the while turning his cock to various angles for differing views, then he would unbutton his shirt, pull off his T-shirt, let them look at his lean, muscled abdomen, then kneel down and present his face. It was as certain as a spider web: and most guys stayed not only to reciprocate, but often for a second blowjob.

It worked with Jeff too. It took Jeff a while to extricate his cock from his shorts and then a bit longer to get the studded cockring untangled, but finally it was free – still flaccid, but large, with exactly the right-sized balls, exactly the right color, the head just thick enough, the cockshaft exactly the right degree of veininess. His lower torso was perfectly muscled. Even Jeff's pubic hair had a shape that excited Alex.

It took Alex a while to get the thing stiff, but when it was, it felt so right in his mouth and hand, that he gave it the benefit of every trick he had learned: the palette rub, the hand slide, the ball tug, the sideways shaft lick – he pulled out all the stops. When Jeff finally came, he lunged against the divider so hard, he even banged his head. He emitted a low guttural sound and spurted a long time. Then he staggered back, dropping onto the stool like a bag of beans.

Alex had caught the substantial load straight down his throat – no more messy moustaches for him anymore – and it still tingled with heat and a slightly alkaline taste. He stared at Jeff, hoping he wasn't having a heart attack.

Jeff's stunned look met his, and there was a momentary smile and mumbled thanks. Jeff still didn't recall him. It must have been over a year ago they'd met. Then Alex was hard and pushing himself through the hole. After a few minutes of that, he asked Jeff to join him in his booth.

There, Alex stripped Jeff, necked with him, sucked him hard again, turned him around, and fucked him. All the while, hands from other booths were sticking out, caressing them. Mouths, faces, eyes were pushed up against them through the holes, wanting to share. When Alex came inside Jeff, it was a moment of total triumph. He'd never felt so good in his life. He'd outdone an expert.

On the bench in the waiting room, Jeff put his arm around Alex's shoulders.

"I was pretty downed out when I came in. I'd only come an hour before too. I sure didn't expect to find anyone like you here tonight."

Alex smiled. Then he reminded Jeff of their meeting in the gas-station bathroom and their conversation in the coffee shop. He enjoyed Jeff's surprise, the grey eyes narrowing in sudden recognition, then widening in satisfaction.

"Well, I'll be damned," Jeff said, and pulled Alex closer.

People came and went around them. They could hear doors opening and closing in the large room.

"Tomorrow's Saturday," Jeff said. "You don't have to work, do you?"

"No, why?"

"Why not come home with me. We'll get some shut-eye, then take up where we left off tonight. All day tomorrow if you want."

Alex suddenly didn't want to. He felt cold, distant. A year before this would have been perfect. But now . . . well things had changed in a year: he had changed.

Jeff went on to talk about the big disco party the next night. He and Alex would fuck and sleep, fuck and then go out to the party, dance sleazily, make out, get each other and others hot too, then go home and do it all again on Sunday. Jeff was amusing, offhand about it. All Alex could read was Jeff's eagerness: his uncool eagerness: his desire to possess Alex alone because he was just as good.

"Well, how about it?" Jeff asked.

"Maybe another time," Alex said, trying to soften it. "I have to see some friends tomorrow night."

"Well, how about tonight then?"

Alex read even more eagerness in Jeff's eyes.

"Don't think so," Alex mumbled. "I'm sort of beat. Got a dog to walk when I get back. Dishes in the sink . . ."

He felt Jeff's arm slide off his shoulder. They sat next to each other for another awkward minute or two.

"I sort of like you," Jeff offered: all casualness gone.

"Me too," Alex said. It came out wrong, hard, wrong. Alex decided to let it pass. He didn't care.

After another few minutes during which he was afraid Jeff would do or say something even more tactless, Jeff stood up, straightened out his pants and said, "OK. Another time."

That was better. "See you," Alex said.

The minute Jeff left the club, Alex realized he hadn't even offered Alex his phone number.

What a phony, Alex thought. All he wanted was a one-night stand. All he wanted was me fucking his tired old ass.

He angrily lighted a cigarette and smoked it, thinking what a phony shit Jeff was. It was three-thirty now. He ought to go home. Why stick around. Nothing but pigs here.

He was just getting up to go to the coatcheck when someone walked in: a lanky blond with full, darker beard and denims moulded so that every inch of his heavy-headed cock could be made out.

Alex exchanged a cruise with him, then a heavier one, and watched his sultry, slightly bowlegged walk to the booths. His jeans were so rubbed around his ass, they looked white. They looked as though they needed spreading.

Alex could probably get him off by eating through the denims.

He got up, went into the room, cruised him again, then found a booth next to another empty one. Inside, he went through his ritual body showing. His cock never looked as ready, his rippled stomach more touchable. He knelt and faced the open hole, and saw the erection push its head at him. He began to fondle it till it was really stiff.

He suddenly remembered Jeff walking out of the place after the best fuck of his life without even offering his goddamned phone number. Fucking phony!

Then a fat, warm cockhead was brushing against his lips. Alex opened his mouth. And was pacified.

TATTOOED LOVE BOY

D. Travers Scott

"Tattooed love boy's out working on his truck," Steve announced. He nodded toward his living-room window.

I looked up from my makeshift studio/bedroom: Steve's living-room sofabed and a card table. Steve stood by the window, a river of sweat soaking the back of his red tank top. He sucked back his bottle of Weinhard's Dark Ale and leered out the window.

"Who?" I asked, capping my no 23 Deep Black art marker.

"Neighbor's kid," Steve said. "Pretty hot." He looked back over his broad shoulders. "Take a look."

I was lucky to be staying with Steve. When my new boss had told me they could cover my relocation to Seattle but not a temporary apartment, only rooming with someone else from the agency, I'd expected to get dumped in the 'burbs with some dumpy art director, her sullen husband and bratty kids. But Quicksilver was a hot independent agency, a rising star in Pacific Rim advertising with progressive benefits – exactly what I wanted to escape the Chicago suit-and-tie trenches for. So I'd accepted.

The biggest surprise of my first-day tour was finding my humpy host-to-be hunched over an artfully arranged palette of silk boxer shorts, his corner of the photo studio plastered

with Bruce Webber and Herb Ritts beefcake posters. Seattle
was enduring a rare hot day; the muggy August temperatures
had already made my dress shirt stick to my back and pits. Steve
worked in cut-off Army fatigues and a Red Hook Brewery-shirt,
both barely clinging to his massive frame. He was like a brick
wall with legs and a light meter.

Looking up with a dazzling grin, his thick, sweat-slick fingers
locked mine in a solid handshake.

"You're my new roommate, huh?" he said. "Great! My place
is kind of a dump, but you can't complain; you're not paying
shit for it!"

He laughed loudly, running his hand through thick, glistening
curls, jet-black and matted with sweat.

"I'm sure it's fine," I said, feeling stuffy in my jacket and
tie. "I lived in lofts and garages all through design school."

"There you go, see? Roommates in a dump, it'll be just like
college." His green eyes beamed merrily. "And since you're
the new art director – we'll be working together!"

He smiled broadly and jerked his thumb at the pile of boxers.
"Maybe between the two of us we can get tightwad here – " he
nodded at my boss, patiently standing beside us, "– to get some
models for these ads. Makes the job a little more interesting!"

My boss cleared his throat. "Uh, Steven, I don't – "

"Oh, relax, Irv, Dan here's a red-blooded fag like me. Least
you can do is send a little skin our way in between all the
pastamakers and cordless phones."

I had to laugh. Steve's easy-going confidence was infectious
and I was impressed by how quickly he'd read me.

His eyes narrowed, studying me while retaining their spark.

"Well. How nice," my boss said. "Then I'm sure you'll both
– ah – get along." He sounded woefully disappointed, as if he'd
just discovered a big mistake.

"Yeah, well I gotta get back to my panties," Steve said,
slapping my shoulder. "Come by when you're done today and
I'll give you directions to the dump."

That had been a week ago. We were getting along great, but
not near as great as I would have liked.

Watching Steve idly stroke his tight, hairy abdomen as he
stared at the neighbor boy, I thought maybe the dumpy gal

would have been less frustrating than this hunk who, despite his bawdiness on our first meeting, seemed absolutely uninterested in getting anything on. He wore big beach towels to and from the shower, changed clothes in his room and disappeared back up there every night, leaving me alone with an aching hardon and "Bohemia After Dark".

"C'mere, you gotta check this guy out," Steve growled. I could see his asscheeks clenched beneath nylon shorts. I set down my T-square and walked over to the window.

All I wanted to do was close my eyes and inhale the sweaty funk he brought home everyday cycling back from work. But my gaze followed his, and I saw the boy.

At the front curb, six lanky feet muscle were stretched under the hood of a beat-up '52 Chevy pickup. His neighbor's son wore nothing but a ragged pair of Levi cutoffs, slung low and barely hanging onto his hips. His taut dog-body supported wiry muscles, not overdeveloped gym-damage, just naturally tight and ripe, bulging beneath his skin without a trace of fat. They flexed and glistened in the rare sunshine. A dust of golden down curved and flowed down the arching currents of his lower back, converging at his tailbone and sliding down into the ass-cleft that peeked above his threadbare shorts. Two diamonds of unfaded denim, deep ocean-blue patches, branded each supple cheek from where the back pockets had been ripped off. The shorts disintegrated into white tatters mid-thigh, from which emerged the slopes and curves of his knees, lashed with stripes of sweat and grime begging to be tongued away.

After those delicious oases sprouted thick calves, pumped from the Seattle hills, each covered with a coarse forest of stiff brown hairs which continued down to raggedy red hi-top sneakers.

"Not bad," I gasped.

"Fuck yeah," said Steve, and swigged on his ale. "Wait til he turns around."

As if on command, Tattooed Love Boy pulled himself out from under the hood and turned facing us.

"Can't see us," Steve said coolly. "Glare's too bright on this window."

Whether he could or not, he put on a perfect show. The Boy

turned around, a square, jug-eared face blinking against the sun, which dazzled off his amber-brown buzz cut. He scowled and folded lithe arms across supple pecs, each capped by a tiny nipple ripe for the chewing. Ridges of abs followed, his V-shaped torso descending down across ribs and obliques, rising and falling like waves of sand dunes, punctuated by a shadowy, dark navel. A sprinkling of golden hairs trailed down into the curving lip of his jeans. I cursed mentally those baggy fashions which obscured any hopes of seeing a basket.

As if reading my thoughts, he raised his arms high above his head in a sensual, cat-like stretch, arching his whole torso and flashing moist clumps of armpit hair. His stretch pulled the cutoffs taut against his thighs, the faded denim wrapping around them without a wrinkle – except on his right leg, where they now outlined a thick bulge snaking down the inside of his thigh. It was at least the size of the smoked kielbasas I passed at the Polish butcher's each morning, and tapered down a mere inch from the shaggy hem of his shorts. Judging from the basket, he owned a hefty set of nuts stuffed up there as well.

He grinned dreamily, savoring the sun's tingle on his flesh. He leaned back against the rim of his truck bed, pinkish-brown skin framed against grey primer coat like poached salmon on a pewter chafing dish. As he stretched, the source of his nickname peeked from his shorts: a dark blue tattoo inscribed along the abdominal plains, sloping down toward his crotch.

"What is it?" I asked.

"Never been close enough to tell," Steve growled.

Sweat trickled down the boy's upper lip. He licked it off, slowly.

A screech from inside the house next door cut short his reverie.

"Donnnn-neeee! You get in here and watch your brothers so I can go get Taco Bell!"

The boy slumped against his truck with a sneer.

"Don-neee!"

He looked up and down the block, disgusted.

"Donnnnnneeee! You out there?"

He slung himself into the truck's cab. He gunned the engine and took off down the street as a large woman stormed out of the house. She sighed angrily, hands on the hips of her glittery "Sweet Honesty" T-shirt.

"Boy turns 19 and thinks he don't have to answer to no one," she muttered.

Steve turned away from the window. "Get used to that sound if you're going to be here a while."

"Yeah, um . . ." I was still stunned by the bronze. "That's why I'm looking closer to work. Damn. What a guy."

"Mm-hm. Too bad he'll be fat from Moon Pies and Funyuns in a couple more years." Steve wandered around into the kitchen, preoccupied.

That night, as usual, Steve disappeared mid-way through the news, going to the bathroom when the sports came on and slipping from there upstairs into his room. I turned off the set in time to hear his door lock shut.

Hours later, I heard something else: a loudly whispered "Fuck!" that pulled me out of my attempts at sleep.

Tattooed Love Boy was back outside, taking out late-night frustrations on his truck. He stood beside it, sucking a cut on his wrist in the halogen-orange light of the street lamp. He still had on nothing but those shorts. As he moved around from one side of the truck to the other, I saw the hairy trail of his crotch pubes and the start of his asscrack creep from his jeans, each curve of his lanky body perfectly illuminated by the overhead light. My dick sprang to full attention.

The new job and apartment-hunting hadn't given me any time to go search for relief, and Steve's continual presence was salt in the wound of my lust.

It was pitch black inside the house, so he couldn't see me. I sat up in bed and listened carefully. The living-room window was wide open in hope of a breeze, and in the night's stillness I could hear the Boy's rattling tools and curses.

Whipping off the sheet, I grabbed my rock-hard cock and fisted it fiercely. I slept naked every night, hoping to catch Steve's attention, and the night air made my skin's every nerve ending super-sensitive, tingling all over my body. My left hand crawled up my abdomen and chest, tracing the washboard I'd worked so hard in Chicago to develop. Still banging my tool,

I gripped my left pectoral with my full palm, digging my nails around and under the bursting muscle. I contracted my grip and grabbed my nipple tight, twisting and pulling hard. My hips rocked up and down to meet the pounding of my fist, and I had to toss my blond bangs out of my eyes to keep a clear view of Tattoo Boy. He stayed in the spotlight, tinkering around the truck, cursing and scratching himself.

I let go of my tit and reached down, pressing a finger behind my balls. My whole ass was clenched like a vice, flexing me up and down on the futon. I slid my finger along the ridge behind my ballsack to my asshole, pressing against the tight muscle-ring, teasing it painfully. I breathed in deep and grabbed my prick tight at the base of its smooth, nine inches and squeezed, watching the neat circumcised head swell red and purple.

The light came on.

I nearly shot my load right then to see Steve standing there, aiming one of his photo floods in my face like an inquisitor. I hadn't heard him come downstairs, and he'd circled through the kitchen. He stood beside the window, facing me with nothing on but a deadly scowl. Every inch of his body was as perfect as I'd imagined, the thick mat of black curls covering his chest and rolling down to his thick, beer-can cock, not as long as mine but huge in circumference with a fat, mushroom-shaped head. It stuck out, engorged with blood and curving downward from its own weight. Two hairy nuts swayed behind it, dark and purple and the size of plums.

Coming through the kitchen, he'd kept his back to the window the whole time and didn't realize what I was staring at or who now had full view of us.

His meaty fingers gripped his fuckpole behind the nuts. He shook the whole monster set of balls and dick up at me.

"You been making things really fucking difficult, Dan." he growled. "I don't believe in screwing around on the job, especially at a small place like ours, and I've been trying to be real professional about all this . . ."

He breathed deep and stepped closer, waving his blimp-dick in my face. "But then I get stuck with you and your pretty-boy little haircut and baby blue eyes and that perky little butt peeking out at me every morning. And don't think I've haven't seen you ogling me every chance you get. You've probably gone through and sniffed my jock when I wasn't here, right?"

I nodded, dumbstruck. . . .

He shoved me against the wall. He hacked loudly and spit a huge wad of saliva onto my chest. "Well, I'm sick of trying to be 'professional'," he said, smearing the slimy goo across my chest. "You're gonna get harassed big time; and I don't think you'll have much to complain about."

He reached behind and grabbed my ankle, yanking on it hard so I slid down until flat on the bed. He climbed above me, firmly planting his knees on either side so they pinned my arms down tight. He waved his piss-can in my face, hanging directly above me. The acrid musk of his crotch filled my nose and burned like smoke.

"Suck my nuts," he said quietly. I looked at the fat balls above me and wondered if I could get them both in my mouth at once. I hesitated too long.

"I said *suck 'em*, punk!" he shouted and grabbed my hair, yanking me up into his crotch. "Suck up or I yank out all this pretty hair!"

I stretched my jaws wide and curled my tongue around the base of one massive meatball, grabbing and sliding it into my mouth. It stuffed my cheek full but I managed to open wider, and kissed the remaining nut, sucking against it until the suction pulled it, too, into my mouth.

The two fat balls rolled around under my tongue and across the back of my throat. Their curly hairs rasped against my lips and gums. All I could see was Steve's engorged prick and his fist slapping it against my eyes and face. His other hand had reached around to grab my tool and was giving it a workover as brutal as that it had just received from me.

"Yeah, I like that dick of yours," he said. "You're one nice package, little fuckboy." His hand crept lower, pressing hard against the bone beneath the base of my cock. He grabbed my nuts and held them tight, pulling upward on them so I couldn't move or buck my hips without ripping them off.

"Now don't let up, boy; you're doing a good job sucking on those nuts, so don't get lazy now." I kept sucking, circling and caressing each ball with my tongue, pressing them back against the inside of my teeth. I jutted my chin out and pressed it hard against the base of his ass, rubbing my evening stubble against the thick mat of his furry crack.

"That's enough," he said suddenly, letting go of my hair and nuts and pushing me back down on the bed. He crawled off and stepped down onto the floor.

"Stand up," he ordered. Shakily I pulled myself up. He grabbed my nuts again, twisting the ballsack, pulling it down tight. His smile grew as he watched me wince and writhe. My arms fell back to support myself against the wall. He leaned forward, taking one of my nipples in his mouth, sucking on it hard and chewing the tit.

"Jesus," I groaned, eyes rolling back in my head. He yanked harder on my nuts; I gasped and my eyes snapped open.

I was looking straight into the eyes of Tattooed Love Boy, standing inside the rhododendron bush to the left side of the window. He crouched, silhouetted from behind by the golden streetlight, and there we were, under the hot glare of Steve's photo light. Enough light bounced back to dimly illuminate his face and front. The boy stared hard at us, unblinking, expressionless.

Steve worked across my chest, licking and sucking hard on the salty hairs and muscles of my armpit. The boy watched silently. The window frame blocked my view of him from the waist down, but his chest rose and fell with deep breaths; his right arm ground in slow circles.

He's into this, I thought. He's whacking off while he watches us!

Steven's head sank lower and I plowed my fingers into his sweaty mop of hair, gripping the back of his skull and grinding his face into my crotch. His tongue slavishly covered my crotch, running up and down the inside of my thighs, circling the base of my cock and suckling my nuts.

The boy stood transfixed at the sight of a hunk like Steve worshiping another man's sex. Keeping my hand on his head, I stared straight at the boy. Our eyes locked, and he looked neither scared, disgusted nor angry, just fascinated, like he was sleepwalking in a dream he'd only ever imagined.

Have to make this good for him, I thought.

"Get up!" I barked at Steve, yanking his head back. Startled by this sudden role-change, he looked up from my crotch with surprise, but quickly broke into a lusty smile.

Steve fell to his knees on the floor. I stood up on my knees on the bed and angled slightly to give the boy a full view of my rigid dick, twitching and bouncing in front of Steve's face. I wanted the boy to clearly see everything: his butch neighbor begging for dick.

"Tell me what you want," I ordered Steve in a steady voice. "What do you want right now more than anything?"

"You know what I want," Steve said breathlessly, licking his lips, frantically yanking on his purple beercan.

"Stop touching yourself!" I shouted. "Put your hands behind your back!"

He obediently did so and hung his head, ashamed. I glanced back at the boy, now pinching his right tit. If only I could see his cock!

"Now, asshole, tell me what you want to do."

"Let me suck your dick," Steve muttered, barely audible. I was sure the boy couldn't have heard it.

"Say it so's I can hear you, fuckhead!" I yelled and slammed my palm against his cheek. Steve closed his eyes, swallowed.

"Try that again," I said gravely.

"I want to suck on your dick, sir!" he barked. "Please let me taste your cock in my mouth, please!"

"This cock?" I said, whacking my meat against his face.

"Yes . . ." he sighed. "Yes, please."

As slow torture, I dragged my crimson, bullet-shaped head across his cheeks, forehead, eyes and along the stubble of his chin. His mouth twitched, wide open, begging like a baby bird for the meat it lived on. I held my dick millimeters from his steamy mouth, so close his breath burned on my quivering piss-hole. I looked over at the boy. He breathed heavily in anticipation. I gave him a big, wide grin.

"Then take it," I growled and plunged my aching dick deep into Steve's mouth, pulling his head forward. My meat slid in easy, and he gulped my full length down till his face was buried in my blond bush. I held him there, cock throbbing deep inside his throat.

"Smell that," I said. "Smell that good stink." Steve inhaled deep. I kept my eyes locked on the boy he sniffed his hand, spit into it. I eased Steve's head back, sliding him up and down as his face got fucked good. Steve's tongue ran all over the surface of my shaft, circling it lovingly, tracing around the ridge of my head. He pulled and sucked with his hot throat muscles, ran his tongue up to the head and poked his greedy tip in and around my piss-slit. I groaned loudly and watched the boy suck two of his fingers.

"Very good," I said, pulling Steve away and stepping off the bed. "But now you got me all hungry." I pulled Steve up to face me. He smiled broadly, holding his fat prong, and began to turn around, saying, "I can guess what you want – "

"Not exactly!" I said, spinning him back around to face the wall. I didn't want him to see his neighbor – yet. I pushed Steve forward and he fell against the wall, holding his arms out for support.

"Spread your legs," I said, falling to my knees behind him. "Now spread your ass."

Steve did as he was told, prying back the furry melons to reveal a tight, hot-pink hole of muscle, twitching and winking in anticipation. I glanced over my shoulder at the Boy. He wasn't going anywhere. I buried my nose in Steve's ass, rooting around like a pig for truffles, lathering his hairy crack up and down with my tongue-juice. The hot hole spasmed with every lash of my tongue and Steve obliged by bending further back, thrusting his ass into my face. Spreading his cheeks further, I shoved my tongue deep into his boiling tunnel, feeling the flesh-rings contract in ecstasy around my darting probe.

"Oh God," Steve groaned. "Oh, man!"

I pulled on his nuts, twisting and turning them in my fist while jamming my whole face deep into the skunky recesses of his hole. Soon I was ready for this show to go to the next act.

I pulled back and leaned beside his thigh, looking back at the boy. My right hand worked back to Steve's ass. I pressed against his tight sphincter with my thumb, massaging it in circles.

"You got a pretty hungry box there, Steve," I said, working my tool with my spare hand. "I don't think my tongue's enough for you," I said, and popped my thumb inside his writhing hole.

"Oh, no," he moaned. The boy and I stared straight at each

other. I smiled broadly as I shoved a finger, and then another into Steve's insatiable sex pit. I waved my cock in slow circles at the boy.

"You want a big, stiff dick up your ass, don't you, Steve?"

"Yeah, please, man," he groaned. "I need it bad."

"I think I know just the one," I said and looked at the boy with deadly seriousness.

"Please hurry."

"Let me just – get it ready," I said, slowly removing my fingers and standing up. "But, Steve, you have to stay right there and wait for it, OK?"

I kept talking to cover my sounds as I moved toward the window.

"You stay right there, bent over, with your hot ass ready and waiting. Don't turn around and don't open your eyes until I say so."

I stood right at the screen, my cock jutting out directly in front of Tattooed Love Boy's face. He stared at it, mouth open. I reached down and pulled back the locks on the screen.

"I'm getting a big ole' dick for you, Steve," I said, "you want that? Tell me how you want it!"

"I want that cock inside me till I bust! I want you up my gut!"

I slid up the screen. The Boy needed no further invitation and reached inside.

"Yesss . . ." moaned Steve, now busily fingering his hole.

I grabbed the Boy's arms and pulled him the rest of the way in. He was completely naked, his tattered cutoffs hanging loose around one ankle. The tattoo stood out clearly now: a dark blue-green goat's head, grinning wickedly above his chestnut-colored pubic bush. His dick was more than I'd even imagined – it swung out from his brown bush like an firehouse, heavy, thick and a good ten inches – and uncut.

"Well, I think I've got a dick that just might do," I called out, grabbing hold of the Boy's boiling prong, working the loose skin up, down and around as I led him over to the bed. He looked at me, his pale-blue eyes open wide. I put a finger to my lips and smiled.

"I'm getting it dressed for the occasion," I told Steve, and reached into my bag beside the bed to pull out a condom and lube. I squirted the slick juice onto the Boy's awesome tool and he began slicking it up. The goat's head seemed to nod up and down as it rippled with the undulations of his abdomen. I tore off the plastic and placed the tight latex against his ruby-red head, glistening and sticking out through the foreskin.

"You ready now?" I pulled back the condom and pressed the head of the Boy's monster dick against Steve's tight hole. "You feel this?"

"Oh, man, c'mon, fuck me good!" Steve cried. I slapped the boy hard on his clenched ass and he drove it home, spreading the hairy globes wide as he plowed into Steve's gut. They both groaned loudly, the Boy biting his lower lip and scowling his freckled face in ecstatic concentration.

Carefully I climbed up on the bed beside them, standing with my feet on either side of Steve's back, but not touching. The Boy worked him over good, pounding his ass furiously, his balls slapping against Steve's butt. Relentless, he slid in and out like a piston, tearing open Steve's hole wider and wider, filling his ass deep with fiery cock.

Now I was positioned with my dick aimed directly at the boy, and it yearned for more action. I grabbed his buzzed head and pulled him close. Without a pause, he opened wide and dove right down on it, covering the head with his lips and slowly pulling it in deeper and deeper, until I felt my snake go all the way down into his throat.

We all three bucked like a well-oiled machine, the boy plowing in and out of Steve with the same rhythm as I fucked his face. His cheeks bulged with dick and his eyes were clenched shut. Steve's ass galloped up and down like an angry bronco.

"Oh, shit," Steve called out. "Man, I want to see you going into me!" With that, Steve began to lift up and roll over. He moved slowly, careful to keep himself skewered on the raging fuckrod he thought was mine. I quickly slipped out of the Boy's mouth and leapt off the bed to stand beside him, my hand cupping his ass and gently probing his tender brown hole.

"Holy–?!" Steve gasped as he rolled around. His eyes bulged, looking from my smiling face to Tattooed Love Boy, whose shit-eating grin beamed proudly back at his neighbor while he kept pile-driving his ass. "Shit!" he moaned and fell back onto the bed, too enraptured to care. He began furiously pounding his meat. I stepped up beside the boy and beat my own.

"Aw, fuck, man!" the Boy growled and jerked out of Steve's ass. I yanked the condom off his throbbing rod and beat his meat with the same force as my own. Steve sat up and we all pressed close together, Steve sucking and chewing on my nipples then the Boy's. I hunched over his shoulder and the Boy bucked his hips furiously.

"Ugh – damn!" the Boy shouted and thrust his hips forward with one final buck. A hot geyser of jizz shot between my fingers, splattering on the wall beside my bed, dribbling onto Steve's chest and shoulders.

The hot juice made Steve lose it as well. He fell back down on the bed, globs of hot cum shooting into the air, falling onto the black fur of his chest and crotch with loud splats. The boy collapsed beside him, their slimy-slick bodies sliding against one another. I stood over them both, pumping out the final seconds on my boiling nuts as Steve and the boy kissed hard and deep, their salty, yeast-smelling loads gluing his smooth, tan chest against Steve's black fur.

They looked up at me and Steve reached for my dick, pumping away on it with his own meaty fingers. The boy reached under and slid his finger in and out of my ass as I fucked Steve's fist.

"*Fuck!*" I shouted and hosed them down with scalding spunk. I kept thrusting as it filled Steve's fist and ran over the Boy's arm. They pulled me down on top of them, adding my sweaty, spunk-covered body to their heap.

We lay there panting, a sticky pile of smelly man-lust. Finally Steve chuckled.

"Well, ah, nice to finally meet you there, son," he said.

The Boy looked us both over slyly. "Just bein' neighborly," he said. "You live here, too, now?" he asked me.

"No," I said, licking the sweat off my upper lip. "But I'm definitely looking for something in this area."

USED TO DREAM

C. Bard Cole

1

"I'M HUNGRY," says Billy, clawing at my face. "You awake?"
I spit hair out of my mouth. Our bed smells like piss. I'm in a
T-shirt, my underwear lost somewhere near my ankles in the
tangle of sheet. He's got one hand around my cock and the
other up by my ear. "You wanna go get some pizza?"

"What time is it?" I say. He's naked, up on one elbow,
looking at me, knotted reddish-brown hair hanging all in his
face. "My watch is on the floor there," I say.

He reaches to pick it up by the strap. "It's one-thirty."

"In the afternoon?" I ask.

"What do you think, at night?" he says. Then, "You
wanna fuck?"

I'm like, "I thought you were hungry."

"Oh I am but I thought you might want to fuck first."

"Well I don't," I say, "my ass hurts. I haven't had a solid
shit in days. Because of all that fucking pizza."

"It's the perfect food," he says. "All of the food groups:
Bread, Dairy, Vegetable, Meat."

"Grease," I say.

"I thought you were tired of cooking," he says. I find a pair of underwear, pull them on. I turn on the television. "What do you want to eat then," Billy says.

"I don't know," I say, "why do I have to make all the decisions for everybody in the world. Why can't someone make decisions for me for a change."

"How about a couple of bagels," Billy offers, "from the deli?"

"Would you? Get me one with butter and a slice of cheese, toasted?" He nods OK. "Well, you'll have to get out of bed to do it." He stands up, snagging a pair of jeans laying across the floor: they're the ones with no ass, just a couple calico patches held together with string. He pulls them up over his thighs, walks on his knees across the mattress to me. "Give me a kiss before I go," he says, his cock sticking out the unzipped fly. I hold it like I'm playing a video game while I kiss him, rubbing its tip with my thumb. Tucking it in with two fingers, he zips up when he stands to go. He puts on a T-shirt that was hanging over the back of a chair, grabs his brown jacket, and searches through the change on the counter top.

"Can we get one with bacon?" I ask.

"No way," he says, "we don't have enough. Besides their bacon is a gyp. They're jews about bacon."

My first boyfriend Jesse was a straight boy who killed himself to fuck with my mind. That's what he said in the note he left, half-crumpled on the mattress we'd dragged together up three flights of stairs: *I never loved you; I've planned this for months; I only did this to make you feel bad. You think I'm joking? Fine. I'm as serious as a heart attack, OK.*

Anyhow, I'm over it. I'm dating Axl Rose now. William Axl: Billy. I know what you're thinking. You know better. Imagine being a 16-year-old hustler in West Hollywood, getting plugged by Pasadena businessmen. Guys who had to slap you around and call you a punk whore while they stuck you with their fat middle-aged cocks so they wouldn't remember their wives or their kid who was maybe about your age. Words like fucking faggot would fall pretty trippingly off your tongue too. Anyhow, I don't need platitudes. Billy's my boyfriend, not yours.

And he loves me too. He called me a fag the other day and I

slapped his face. I mean, it's my cock he's been sucking, wasn't it? And he breaks the end off this beer bottle like you want me to stick you with this? And I'm like: yeah, right, grind it into my face, you fucking queer, I'd like to see that. And he puts it down like he's gonna smile and be nice, and fucking backhands me instead. When I go to wing him back, he sits his ass right down on the glass. All of a sudden he's tears and arms around my neck and he's all sorry. I'm looking down the curve of his back, the planes of his shoulder blades and ribs and just where it starts to curve and sprout hairs right about his ass, a couple gashes dripping red across his paste-white butt. He's holding onto me, and I'm thinking, do I trust this? I kind of don't.

One of the things I do is I go to this bar on Twelfth Street I like. I go there with my friends. Some of them I know from school, some I just know from around. Billy says I should watch how I dress when I stay out late and I say I'll dress as I please, he never worries about me when he fucks me, and that's as likely to kill me as anything else. I think he just doesn't like seeing me in a dress in the first place. It's not drag, really, just a dress. You should see me, in my beige dress with the rhinestones. In my docs and my leather jacket. It looks nice, 'cause I've got pretty legs. I don't shave them. Don't wear makeup either. I used to want to be a girl, but just when I was real little. I mean like six.

I'm meeting my friend Dan. A school friend. He knew me when. "So you don't want to be a writer anymore?" he says.

"Well, I am," I say. "I'm writing something now."

"That's not what I mean," he says. "I mean, you should be doing something else besides. You have a job now?" he asks.

"Oh I got a job, you bet. I sell art supplies at Pearl Paint. Besides, it's all research," I add. I just thought of that one.

"Research?" he says, all snide. He's got a job working for a man who makes movies. "You've got a degree. Have you looked for a better job?"

"I don't need this in the slightest," I say. "Look at me, Dan. I'm a flaming fag. I've got seven earrings in my ears. I got dyed black hair down to my chin. I'm wearing a dress. Can you see me in some office somewhere?"

"Well, you could take out the earrings," he says. Then:

"Never mind, it's not important, I don't mean to be an asshole."

"Besides, I help Billy with his music," I say. I really do, too. I'm good at coming up with words if he's already got the music down. I wrote a couple of the songs he does.

"Well, that's something," Dan says. "You've just got to keep up with it. You can't let it stagnate, you've got real talent."

"Yeah, talent," I say. "I've got just about so much talent," I say, holding my hands about three inches apart. "Maybe more than some people, but this is New York."

"What you have to do," Dan says, "is meet people, that's how you get places. You let them see how good you are, and they'll help you out."

"Maybe when I'm 40," I say. "I'm no child prodigy or anything. Maybe I thought I was once, in a different place. It's easier to be smarter than a bunch of dumb kids in high school. It's hard to be smart on your own."

"Life's hard," he says, "but Art's fun. Vita Brevis and all."

"Oh bullshit, absolutely don't start with that crap. It's life that's easy. I don't even think about it. But Art – man, I'm writing something, and it's even good, maybe, and I'm listening to a tape while I do it, and some line, one stupid line, will jump out of the song to tell me I'm a loser, that I'm never going to be able to write anything that'll make people feel something."

"Like what line," he asks.

I know them by heart, these fucking lines from stupid pop songs that hang around my neck like millstones: You search babe at any cost / but how long babe can you search for what is not lost – Bob Dylan, as sung by Nico. Approaching fifty, Nico got off drugs and got hit by a truck riding her bike down the street.

"It's not just the lines, it's the music that really gets you. That's why I like helping Billy. But even that doesn't seem as good to me."

Dan's on his third rolling rock and I can sense he's getting a little uneasy around me. "You look at me thinking what went wrong," I say.

"No, not what went wrong." He kind of shakes his head, leaning it on one shoulder. "That's what happens when they send you to these artsy-fartsy schools. You don't really learn how to do anything except stuff that people don't need. It's a perfect education, as long as you grow up to be famous."

"I haven't given up on that," I say, though I think we're talking about two entirely different things. "It takes more time than you'd think. Lots of great artists didn't make it big until their forties. Most, I'd say. Oscar Wilde. Beethoven, Dennis Cooper," I say.

"Oh he's not in his forties," Dan says.

"Close enough," I say. "Too old to be writing about punk teenagers."

"I met him once," Dan says.

"You didn't," I say. I mean that. I don't believe him.

"Yeah I did too. The guy I work for was friends with him when he lived in New York."

"Why does he write those stories," I ask. "All those stories about teenage boys getting chopped up. You think he beats up his boyfriend?"

Dan's annoyed. "It's about alienation. The dehumanization of modern culture. Why do you play dumb?" He goes to the bar, gets two more beers. I'm not dumb. I prefer to take things literally. Anyhow, alienation's a stupid-ass thing to write a story about. I can't believe anyone would go to the trouble.

"Dan," I say, "Don't get pissed, I'm not trying to stiff you. I'm completely broke."

"I got it," he says, "don't worry about it. You're smoking like a fiend."

"Am I?" I say. We've both been smoking from my pack and there's like three left. "Yeah you're right." I tap out two onto the table, one for me, one for him.

"You still living with that junkie?"

"C'mon Dan," I say, lighting my cig. "We've been over this."

"I just worry about you, man."

"We both used to do a lot of coke and that can give you a heart attack. We're both drunk. We're both chainsmoking."

"As long as you're okay with it," he says. It gets like this; he's watching me like he's real, real sorry for me, like he knows something I don't.

"You're starting to act like my dad," I say.

"So what is it that you're writing anyhow," he says.

"What I'm doing now," I say, "is I'm preparing the unauthorized biography of Axl Rose."

"Are you now?"

"Billy's probably starting to worry," I say, even though he doesn't.

"Want me to walk you back? It's on the way. I've got to catch the green line."

"Nah," I say. "No, I'm OK." I leave him sitting there. I'm about three blocks away, halfway home, when I stop into the deli and buy myself a new pack of cigarettes and a 40-ouncer.

Billy says "I'm in here" when I pull on the bathroom door. It's locked. "I know what's going on here," I say, banging on the door. "All right mister," I say, "open up."

Switching the latch from his seat on the toilet, Billy pulls the door open a crack, enough for me to see his face. "What? I'm on the toilet." And I ask why is the door locked if he's just taking a shit. He says, "Maybe I just felt like taking a shit with the door locked."

He narrows the crack again, and when I hear the latch click, I smack the door with my open palm.

He takes a slug of my beer when he comes out finally, tugging the left arm of his long underwear shirt way down over the crook of his elbow, like I'm too stupid to know where track marks are. He looks up at me. "What's the matter," he asks me with vomit breath, "what are you being a bitch about now?"

"What do you mean, what's the matter, you asshole," I say. "You think I'm retarded in the brain?"

"Nuh-un," he says, "I'm not on junk man. It's always the same with you isn't it? You have to know what I'm doing every fucking second."

"Don't you have anything else to do besides sit around on your lazy ass shooting up? Aren't you supposed to be some sort of musician or something?" I say.

And he says, "Don't you have anything better to do than get up my ass?"

"I used to be a nice boy. People used to say I had a future. Then I met you." That's what I say to him. He's just sitting there picking strange crud out from underneath his fingernails. "Aren't you even going to look at me when I'm talking?" I say.

"I'm getting a new tattoo," he says to my back as I turn away from him, fixing my gaze out the window. "I'm getting a big red Q right over my heart with your initials in it. 'Cause I'm queer for you, baby."

"And what're you gonna do when we break up finally?" I ask.

"I'll run it through with a big black line and put the next guy's initials underneath."

There's a bunch of Puerto-Rican kids hanging out in the light of a stoop across the street. There's a grey dog tied to the fence and one of the kids is making him bark. He knows how long the leash is, and is standing right at the place where the tip of the dog's nose reaches. He grabs the dog by the snoot and shakes its head and laughs. The dog jumps and snaps its jaws. The boy leans his head in, making noises back at it. He squats down, rests his hands on the knees of his khakis, curling his lip at the dog. The dog's not really mad. I can see that. It's the boy's dog.

"You're getting lost out there," says the asshole on the couch. "Baby, why don't you sit down here with me?"

"Oh, Billy man. Are you gonna stop this?" I say.

"I only did a little. The first time in days almost. My legs were twitching."

"This isn't why I went to college," I tell him.

"Put your head on my stomach," he says.

2

Billy and I are lying down watching the television. I'm upright at one end of the couch, with Billy stretched out between my legs, his head on my folded arms. The news is on, and down in Kileen, Texas, some guy has just driven his car through the front window of Luby's cafeteria and shot a whole bunch of people. He must have been something else because his neighbors didn't act like the usual mass murderer's neighbors. The lady next door told the TV-reporter in a confident voice:

"He was crazy. I always knew he'd pull something like this one day."

Maybe the people who say, "He was a nice guy, kept to himself mostly," just don't know the signs to look for. Personally, I think I'd notice a guy dressing in fatigues, collecting military-style riflery, and barricading his house with high fences and shrubbery. Billy snorts, shaking his head, "If that were true, every adult man and three-fifths of the teenagers in West Texas would be mass murderers."

"The way you talk about it sounds like they were."

"No. Not mass murderers," he says, flipping the channel with the remote. "Just rednecks."

"I grew up in the country," I say, mildly annoyed.

"Hhmph," Billy says.

"You know I did," I repeat, shoving him off me. He catches himself from falling by bracing against the floor with one arm. When I say "Fuck you," he cracks up and, laughing, rolls to the floor with a thud.

He sits up on the carpet, spitting strands of hair away from his face, still giggling. "Where you come from," he says, "doesn't count. You grew up in a fucking Norman Rockwell painting."

Which is more or less true actually. When I say country I mean a place with fields and cows and trees. Creeks spanned by one-lane bridges with green railings. I have seen pictures of where Billy grew up. With all that big, deserty space spreading to the horizon you wonder why they build the houses three yards from the highway.

The city and the country are similar enough, is what I've discovered in the five years since I moved to New York. Three elements – property, strangers, and guns – keep the two apart. I think Billy and I both feel pretty much at home. You go to the grocery store and the clerk knows what you want. You say hi to your neighbors on their stoops. It's the suburbans I don't get, their half-communal, half-defensive mindset a complete mystery. When they live in the city they go to every bodega within a five block radius just so the clerk won't get to know their habits. They like having dozens of acquaintances they hate and they like to gossip. Most of my friends grew up suburban and they like to say things like, "I hope you aren't being sucked into paying his way," and "Maybe you're like my friend Jodie. She doesn't think she deserves to be happy," or "I'd think you'd like being with someone who shared your interests."

My friends and I read a lot. Reading is an interest. Every time I go to a party, in the Village or in Soho or in Park Slope, I look at bookshelves. I have found five titles which everyone in the whole world who's been to college in the last three years has copies of, even if the spines aren't always cracked. When I want Billy to read Discipline And Punish or Gravity's Rainbow, I'll know where to find copies.

Billy's favorite book is the dictionary. It's how he learned most everything he knows, having finished with school when he ran away from home at 15. The best one, he says, is the one with essays in the front, one by William F. Buckley who admits maybe that language can change theoretically, but that rules must be obeyed until the right people decide otherwise, and another by a guy who says Buckley's full of shit, that we can't do anything but study and write and think about the ways people use their language. That using it makes it real. Whatever people do is real. This is what Billy agrees with, and he talks about William F. Buckley sometimes as if he were a very persuasive and dangerous man. Purely because of his dictionary essays, not because of the tattoos he wants on our asses and on Billy's left arm.

I guess I took words for granted because all I ever did with a dictionary when I was a kid was look up dirty words. Sexual words like penis or vagina and slang terms like shit, fuck, asshole. Words with secondary dirty meanings like cock or dick or screw buried in lines of stuffy definitions – *Booby: (1) a species of aquatic fishing birds, usually black-feathered* – before they'd finally concede "a woman's mammary." Hump was my favorite: (offensive slang) to copulate. Hump means to have sex like a dog and sweat and grunt. Hey Billy, wanna hump?

When I was a kid all I fantasized about was what my life would be like when I made all this money. I guess that's normal. No kid fantasizes about working hard, coming home with a headache, taking a nap, then watching TV before initiating some perfunctory sex. I never dreamed about walking down a city street at four-thirty in the morning, drunk with bloody snot balling up in my nose holes. Who knew there were reasons to get so fucked up?

I asked Billy, once, what his childhood fantasies were. They were more practical than mine, I guess, depending on what you think fantasies are for. "I used to dream," he said, "that one day I'd be big enough to kick my dad's ass."

I remember telling my friend Daniel that Billy had told me, "I have issues," the first week he was staying at my place. He wouldn't remove his clothes with the lights on. He pretended to fall asleep while we watched Letterman, and I guess I was supposed to touch him then. He had to move my hand onto him.

"He has issues!" Daniel rolled his eyes with delight. "That's cute."

Billy was the most beautiful boy I had ever slept with. It didn't bother me that no one else could see it. Beneath the dirty black clothes he wore his skin was cool and smooth, the color of milk; beneath his defiantly tangled long hair he had the face of a renaissance Gabriel. "I like issues," I said.

After two weeks, Billy took off his shirt so I could put it in the laundry. A number of dense, straight white scars ran from his stomach to underneath the waistband of his sweat pants. I touched one, imagining he might flinch. Instead he said, "I like you. I really like you. But some things are none of your business."

He used that line a lot. None of my business: where he was the night before when he said he'd be home at seven but didn't come home till twelve, obviously fucked up. "I wasn't screwing anyone else, OK?" what happened to the twenty bucks I gave him yesterday? When did he get that card for the Needle Exchange? None of my business.

"Was he like a strict disciplinarian? Was it spanking or was it hitting? Did your mother try to stop him?"

Some things are super none of my business. "What is it? You want hillbilly stories with a woodshed out back? Why don't you let it drop?"

"My dad had an alcohol problem too. Billy, it's not like we're so different."

"Listen." He seriously leaned into my face, startling me. "I don't fucking want to hear about we're not so different." I stepped back, gasped. I guess maybe I snorted. He didn't like the sound of it. "If I smacked you now you'd fucking remember it for a long time."

The doorway where Billy and I first had sex is only about two blocks from where we live now. I got a bloody knee from the broken glass in front of him. He gripped me by the hair above the neck. Shoulders pressed against the brick wall, he arched his back. "Yeah, get me off, cocksucker." I stood when he let me loose, my numbed nose dripping. He laughed and I was scared. Then he grabbed my head again, pulling me towards him, and sucked his sperm out of my mouth.

Three and a half years ago now. We're in love now, so sex is different. We know what to expect, mostly. Jack off and go to sleep mostly. We even eat brunch now. There are occasional bursts of excitement. "I am an ugly piece of shit with nothing going on and you are a sick fuck for wanting to have sex with me," or "You're getting fat, when you sit on my dick you crush all my guts and I can't breathe."

"I love you," I protest, slobbering over him and prolonging the act forever. When we used to use rubbers, sometimes he'd stay in so long afterwards the thing would come off in my ass.

I still feel like I want to know everything about him. I hate that there are things still off-limits. I'm leaning against the sink in our bathroom brushing my teeth, watching Billy take a shit. We can do that now. It doesn't bother us. It's not supposed to.

I spit out the foam and slurp some cold water directly out of the faucet. But instead of leaving then I decide to stay and see how Billy's project turns out. "Tell me what it feels like," I say.

He's sitting limply forward on the pot, his hands dangling together between his knees. The reddish hair on his shins is bristling, standing on end above the inside-out legs of the jeans pooled around his ankles. "You're a freak."

"How's it feel?" I repeat. "Big? Small? Is it going to come out in one log, or two? Clean or greasy?

"It's soft," he says, eyes closed, like a medium channeling a hesitant spirit. "I'm going to try and push out all I can. It'll need wiping."

"No it won't," I say. "You're not going to wipe it."

I kneel down on the linoleum in front of him, resting my hands on his naked thighs. I stare up at his face. He's keeping his eyes sort of closed but I see a flicker of iris through the pale lashes. Grabbing his cock and balls, I lift them to one side so I can see the poop coming out.

"Don't it feel good up there? A cock feels better than that, even."

"Stop," he says. "You're getting me hard." The poop breaks off, splashing water on the underside of Billy's legs; on my chin.

"I want to pee on you," I say.

"No," he says. "Don't. I mean it."

"Just a little."

"Don't."

"I'll just aim between your legs, all right?" He doesn't answer me, so I kick my shoes off against the side of the tub, pull down my pants and underpants, taking them off by standing on one leg with one foot, extracting the other, then repeating. Naked from the waist down, I sit across Billy's lap and direct a stream of piss towards his cock. It ricochets onto his legs, his pubic hair, the tails of our shirts. He slides his hands up my chest, underneath my T-shirt, and exposes one of my nipples for him to chew on. His dick brushes my leg as it comes to life on its own for once, a hard-on of desire instead of the usual mechanical response I only get from a good quarter-hour of deliberate attention. "It's alive," I say, and he laughs, and says, "I'm gonna fuck you in the ass," because we've talked about it and agreed that fucking "in" the ass is dirtier than fucking "up" the ass.

"I'm gonna fuck you in the ass," he repeats as he pulls my chest to his face, drumming his fingertips along my butt crack. He scowls and winces as the toilet handle pokes him in the back, and I have to brace myself against the sink to keep from falling off. The broad head of his dick is being rubbed against my asshole and I feel a hot jet of piss glance off the side of my butt.

"You're an idiot," I say. He'd been trying to pee on my asshole and missed. I bite his throat, stand up on the slippery floor, and poke my dick at his mouth. He refuses to take it, shaking his head "no" so his bottom lip rubs me the way I like. "Suck it, bitch."

"You're the bitch," he says with two fingers inside me.

I know this boy from the inside out. I've felt the rumble of an unborn fart travel inside his body and the pulse of the pale blue veins glistening under his thin skin. How he works beyond the physical I don't even pretend to know – we've just thrown our chips together, agreed to put our eggs in the same basket, our tongues up each other's asses. He'll kiss me afterwards, as I sit down on his dick, my ass loose and wet. He'll tell me I'm a pig but he'll kiss me. "This is the way our relationship's gonna end," he says. "You're gonna walk out on me, and I'm going to hunt you down and kidnap you and bring you back here and stab you, and while I'm watching you bleed to death, I'm going to shoot myself in the head." Billy's cock is harder than it's been in months; I am on the brink of an orgasm bigger than God. I hope that the neighbors hear the floorboards squeaking, the couch banging against the wall. I hope it corrupts their children. "Or else, you're gonna have to kill me. I'll be fucked up and come at you and you won't have a choice."

"You're only saying that because you love me," I tell him as he licks curds of cum from my chest hair. "You won't always think I'm worth killing."

Smoking cigarettes afterwards, drinking coffee in the kitchen: "I've been lying to you," he says.

"About the heroin?" He told me he's stopped. I know he hasn't, but he's been trying. He's been copping methadone off the street but sometimes you can't find it.

He shakes his head. "They got infected," he says. "My scars. I did it with a razor blade. They weren't that deep. I guess I couldn't stop picking at them."

He sighs and lets his hair fall into his face, turns away slightly and with exacting casualness performs the act of refilling his coffee cup from the pot on the stove.

"I didn't run away because my dad hit me," he says.

And one night he whispers in my ear, "Would you want to fuck me? I mean. Should we try?" I let my hand drop from the small of his back to the cleft of his butt.

"It hurts," he says, when I spread his legs and get in between them, pressing my way in.

"I'll stop."

"No, please don't." I keep my weight off him as best I can and try to slide it in gently. He looks at me timidly, nodding his assent. I lie down on top of him and poke it all the way home and he gasps, horrified. Cringing.

"Billy," I say, pulling out.

His hands dig into my shoulder blades, legs locked around my back. "No. Stay in. I want you to."

I don't dare move, hard inside him as he breathes heavily into the side of my face. "Oh Christ," he mutters. "Jesus fuck."

Billy is crying.

"You're the only man that's done this to me, do you understand? No one else ever. I saved this for you my whole life."

My Billy boy.

He says, "This erases everything else, OK?"

from THE SWIMMING-POOL LIBRARY

Alan Hollinghurst

AT ABOUT DRINKS time I began to want to do something. I wrapped up my trunks in a towel, flung them in my sports bag with my goggles and soapbox and an American "gay thriller" I had been loaned by Nigel the pool attendant, and trotted off out. The pavements and gardens were exuding their summer smells, and as I approached the Tube station I walked against the current of people coming home, youngsters in pinstripes from the City fanning out from the gates, jackets here and there hooked over a shoulder, smart clippety-clop of old-fashioned City shoes. They were quite handsome, some of these boys, public-school types with peachy complexions and contemptuous eyes. Already they commanded substantial salaries, took long, overpriced lunches, worked out perhaps in private City gyms. In many ways they were like me; yet as they ambled home in the benign and ordered vastness of the evening, as I fleetingly caught their eye or felt them for a moment aware of me, they were an alien breed. And then I was a loafer who had hardly ever actively earned money, and they were the eager initiates, the corners of the power and the compromise in which I had unthinkingly been raised.

My disaffected mood persisted in the sweaty train. *Goldie*

was one of the poorer accessions of the swimming-pool library. It was not, alas, about the Cambridge second eight, but about rent-boys, blackmail and murder in Manhattan; Goldie was the gay police officer who got to buy the favours of the chief suspect, and seemed bound to fall in love with him before the sorry end. The book's formula was to alternate blocks of fast, bloodthirsty action with exhaustive descriptions of sexual intercourse. Nigel, night-sighted in the pool's subterranean gloom, had said it was a good one; but I resented its professional neatness and its priapic attempts to win me over. The trouble was that, as attempts, they were half-successful: something in me was pained and removed; but something else, subliterate, responded to the book's bald graffiti. "Fuck me again, Goldie," the slender, pleading Juan Bautista would cry; and I thought, "Yeah, give it to him! Give it to him good 'n' hard!"

As we slowed towards stops I looked around at the other passengers, wary slumpers and strap-hangers who never met each other's eye for more than a fraction of a second. Half-heartedly playing the game James and I used to play I tried to select which person in the carriage I would least object to having sex with. Occasionally the choice could be made difficult by the presence of too many scrumptious schoolboys or too many dusty-handed navvies. Normally, as now, the problem was to choose between that businessman, regular and suited but with a moody something about him, and the too-tall youth in the doorway giving off a tinny, high-hat patter from his headphones, and looking flightily around through a haze of Trouble for Men. It was James's theory that everyone had about them some wrinkle at least of lovability, some peculiar and attractive thing – a theory which gained poignancy from the problems in applying it.

Consoling and yet absurd, how the sexual imagination took such easy possession of the ungiving world. I was certainly not alone in this carriage in sliding my thoughts between the legs of other passengers. Desires, brutal or tender, silent but evolved, were in the shiftless air, and hung about each jaded traveller, whose life was not as good as it might have been. I remembered for some reason a little public lavatory in Winchester, a urinal and a couple of cubicles visited by bandy-legged old men going to the market and at night by ghostly fantasists who left their traces. It was up an alley where the College turned one of its high stone corners against the town – not a place for boys, for scholars, though I went there once or twice with an almost scholarly curiosity. The cistern filled for ever, the floor was slippery, there was no toilet paper, and between the cubicles a number of holes had been diligently bored, large enough only to spy through. Talentless drawings covered the walls, and wishful assignations, and also, misspelt in laborious capitals, long unparagraphed accounts of sexual acts – they had her together . . . 12 inches . . . at the bus station'. In between these were fantastic rendezvous, often vague to allow for disappointment, but able sometimes to touch you with their suggestion of a shadowy world in which town and gown pried on each other. I had read: "College boy, blond, big cock, in here Friday – meet me next Friday, 9 pm." Then: "Tuesday?" Then: "Next Friday November 10" . . . I had thought almost it could have been me, until I just made out, bleared and overwritten, the date "1964": a decade of dark November Fridays, generations of College blonds, had already passed since those anonymous words were written.

At the Corry life was going on full blast. I swam more joylessly than usual, hoping I might catch Phil, starved of him, longing to have and to hold him: I wanted the solidness of him in my arms, and for a moment excitedly mistook another swimmer for him as he lounged at the shallow end. He had trunks on just like Phil's and when I surfaced grinning in front of him he gave me a bothered look before pushing off in a panicky, old-fashioned sidestroke. I felt keenly about the discipline of swimming, and then was suddenly bored by it, and by the taste of chlorinated water. When I hopped out I had a few words with Nigel. He was sprawling in those viewing seats erected long ago for matches and galas which never now took place.

"Hullo Will – good swim?"

"I'm not in the mood, I'm afraid, today. I can *do* it, you know, what's the point?"

"Mm, still, good for you. How are you getting on with that book then? Good one, isn't it?"

"I'm a bit disappointed by it, actually. You've lent me better."

"Mm, but that Goldie, is it, I'd like to meet him. He can give me a taste of his truncheon any time."

I shook my head sorrowingly. "He doesn't exist, love. It's just a silly book."

"Get out," said Nigel, tutting and turning his head away.

"I could show you something really sexy – and true," I said, in a sudden treacherous bid for his interest – he who didn't interest me at all, handsome and idle though he was. "I've got some private diaries of a guy" (Charles a guy? some affronted guardian spirit queried) "with amazing stuff in them. It's even got things happening here – years ago . . ." I had doubts and petered out.

My true come-uppance came not from a fascinated insistence I should tell more but from a deliberate lack of attention, as if to endorse my self-reproach. "You still going with that Phil?" he wanted to know.

"Yup." I squared my shoulders and tried to appear worthy.

"He's looking good." Nigel smiled at me slyly. "He was down here earlier on, splashing about, diving and that. Showing off. I wouldn't mind a bit of that, I thought. Gave me a really fresh look too."

"You little slut," I said, and flicked at him with my towel as I darted off. But I was reassured by how he had got it wrong, for though Phil was taken with his own body he almost stubbornly never tarted. His love was all bottled up and kept for me.

I thought of him with such tenderness in the shower and the changing-room that I was hardly aware of the bustle around me. I had not been good enough to him. I had often been sarcastic, and used him as a kind of beautiful pneumatic toy. He was the only true, pure, simple thing I could see in my life at the moment, and I wished I was with him, and wanted to thank him, and say I was sorry. I decided I would go up to the Queensberry and hope to catch him before he went out. Then I would go to James, who was true and pure too of course in his way, and worrying about his looming court appearance.

I went through the deeply familiar streets and squares through the equally intimate cooling and soft-fingered evening. Then there were the high plane trees and the bold splashing fountains – my mood escaping all the while from its bleak morning pacings and ambling into a more romantic melancholy. I became somehow picturesque to myself, prone as ever to the aesthetic solution.

I was about to go round to the side of the hotel, where I was well enough known now, but I was suddenly tired of my laundry-man's-eye view of life, and swung up the main shrub-flanked steps and into the hall. I had become so used to the back stairs that I was quite surprised to see svelte couples coming down for pre-dinner drinks, others checking in, their anxieties melting as uniformed boys magicked their monogrammed luggage away. One or two people, waiting to meet friends, half-concentrated on the lit showcases where scarves, watches, perfumes and china figurines were displayed, or revolved the squeaking postcard racks, soothed by the customary London views.

I loitered too for a minute, charmed – or at least amazed – by all this bought pleasantness. And then I saw a wonderful young man, perhaps about my age, and with just that air of bland international luxury about him, come from the lift and saunter towards the cocktail bar. He was tall and graceful but gave the impression of weighing a great deal; as he approached I was startled by his deep-set brown eyes, long nose and curling lips and his trotting, swept-back hair; as he walked away I took in his maroon mocassins, his immaculate pale cotton trousers, through which the shadow of his briefs could be seen, the cashmere slip cast around his shoulders. I felt he must belong to some notable Latin American family.

It hardly required thought to follow him, though I gave him a second or two to get settled. I feared he might have gone to sit at a table or have joined his diplomat father and ragging, adoring younger brothers and sisters. But no, he was perched at the marble curve of the bar, and I was able to greet Simon – all in braid and tumbling his cocktail-shaker – as I took up a convenient high stool.

"What are you having?" Simon wanted to know. He was a skinny Lancashire boy who loved fucking girls and should ideally have been following a career as a pianist. He played extremely well, and had a long, long tongue with which he could easily lick the tip of his nose. He knew all about my little ways.

"What's *he* having?" I said, as I watched the wild pink liquid rattle from the shaker into the inverted cone of the glass.

He raised an eyebrow and murmured disgustingly, "Cunnilingus Surprise."

"Mm. Not quite my kind of thing perhaps."

Here the notable Latin American said: "It's really good. You should try one." And then smiled immensely so that I went funny inside.

His lips curled back in a friendly primitive way, and gave an unexpected animation to his dully beautiful face. I realised he reminded me of one of the sketches of Akhnaten on Charles's stele – not the final inscrutable profile, but one of the intermediate stages, half human, half work of art.

I watched incredulously as the various ingredients, some exotic, some European, were measured into the shaker. Simon gave me a smirk of lewd surmise as he agitated it. Mr Latin America and I glanced at each other and then found it proper to look around the lofty bar, with its concealed lighting, reproductions of Old Masters and vulgarly gathered blinds half down against the westering sun. Across the road were the boles of the great trees in the square into whose upper branches I had so often gazed; and that did remind me of Phil, and how I must not take long over this drink.

"Perfectly revolting," I pronounced after taking a sip. "If that's what cunnilingus tastes like, I think I've done well to stay away from it."

"You like?" said my new friend.

I nodded, as if to say it was nice enough.

"You are staying in this hotel?"

"No – no, I've just come in for a drink. After my swimming."

"Oh you like swimming, I am a very bad swimmer." I smiled politely; perhaps in his country, which I believed to be poor and old-fashioned, there were few swimming-pools. Even in Italy there were few: hence the fondness of the language children for hours of bombing and showering. "Do you have a girlfriend?" he asked.

"No, no," I said, actually slightly shocked at his naive forwardness. I let a minute or more pass in silence, but had to grin when Simon started humming *Tristan*. I wasn't sure what to do. The boy was undoubtedly a find. I swivelled on my stool so that we were sitting with our legs apart and knee to knee. He looked frankly at my crotch before meeting my gaze and we smiled enquiringly at each other as he ran his finger up the back of my hand where it dangled from the bar.

"If you come to my room, I will show you something very interesting," he said. "Do you want to finish your drink?"

"Um – no." I started to reach in my pocket for change, but he stopped me with a firm hand.

"Number 205," he said curtly to Simon.

"I must have got the name of that one wrong," said Simon perplexedly as I followed my conquest – my conqueror? – out.

Room 205 was a small but grand suite – a sitting room with a flower arrangement in front of a mirror, a gloomy bedroom looking on an inner well, and a neon-bright bathroom with a roaring extractor fan. The thick double-glazing on the front gave the rooms a strange feeling of remoteness. I walked around in them for a bit before Gabriel – as he was fetchingly called – said, "Hey, Will, look at this," and flung open a suitcase on the bed. It was stuffed with pornography – videos and magazines, many of them still in their rip-off cellophane wrappers. The buying had been prodigal and indiscriminate.

"You like it?" I was asked, as if it were a triumph of his own.

"Well up to a point – but I thought – "

"In my country these things, these dirty pictures, do not exist."

"I should be highly surprised if that were the case. What is your country anyway?"

"Argentina," he said, with a neutrality of tone which showed that this news was likely to have some effect. It made me want to apologize to him; at the same time I could have castigated him for buying up all this trash. Surely if any British self-esteem could have been thought to have survived the recent war it must be something to do with our . . . cultural values? The top magazine in the suitcase was a tawdry old thing I could remember from schooldays, called *Latin Lovers*.

"But what about the war?" I said dismally, seeing a TV news map of the Southern Atlantic and imagining too the customs-check at Buenos Aires.

"That's all right," he said, putting his arms around my neck. "You can suck my big cock."

He stood patiently while I unbuttoned his trousers and slid them down over brown hairy thighs. The black briefs I had glimpsed before turned out to be leather. "I suppose you bought these today as well," I said; and he nodded and grinned as I prised them down and saw the studded leather cock-ring he was also wearing. He had clearly wasted a small fortune in some Soho dump. His assessment of his cock had not, however, been wrong. It was a sumptuously heavy thing, purpling up with blood as the cock-ring bit into the thickening flesh. "I'm not a size queen, but . . ." would have been my classic formulation of the affair.

I hadn't had anything like it all summer, and gorged on it happily. But Gabriel's own performance was becoming off-putting. Every few seconds he would make some coarse exhortation, some dumbly repeated catchphrase, and I came to realise with dismay that this trick too he had picked up from crudely dubbed American porn films. "Yeah," he would croon, "suck that dick. Yeah, take it all. Suck it, suck that big dick."

I took a pause to say, "Um – Gabriel. Do you think you could leave out the annunciations?" But it wasn't the same for him without them, and I felt unbelievably stupid appearing to respond to them.

"OK," he said brightly, as I abandoned the job. "You like to fuck with me?"

"Of course." There was after all some charm in his childlike openness. "But in silence . . ."

"Wait a minute," he said and kicking off shoes and tugging off trousers and pants, ambled into the bathroom, his dick bouncing with a kind of mock-majesty before him.

I slipped off my own shoes and jeans and lay playing with myself on the bed. Gabriel took his time getting ready and after a couple of minutes I called through to ask if he was all right. He came in almost at once, now completely naked except for his cock-ring, the pale gold wafer of his watch and – which I should somehow I suppose have expected – a black leather mask which completely covered his head. There were two near little holes beneath the nostrils, and zipped slits for the eyes and mouth. He knelt on the bed beside me and was perhaps looking to me for approval or amusement – it was impossible to tell. Close to I could see only his large brown pupils and the whites of his eyes, blurred for a split second if he blinked, like the lens of a camera. It was hard and disturbing the way the eyes could not vary their expression isolated from the rest of the frowning or smiling face. I felt that childhood fear of rubber party masks, and of the idiot amiability of clowns who you knew, as they bent down to pinch your cheeks, were fearful old drunks.

Gabriel held my head to look at me closely, and I unzipped his mouth and breathed in his hot breath and the expensive smell of leather. His body was supple though slightly gone to seed – but I liked it and bit it. There wasn't much he could do in his mask, and when I had nosed around him for a while he hoiked me over and pushed my legs apart. I was anxious not to take all that raw, and had begun to complain, when I felt something cold and wet, like a dog's nose, trailing up my thigh. I looked over my shoulder to find that from somewhere this madman had produced a gigantic pink dildo, slippery with Crisco. I heard him giggle tensely inside the mask. "Do you want to smell some poppers?" he asked.

I rolled over and sat up and spoke in a strange tone of voice which I seemed to have invented for the occasion. "Look pal, I'd need more than poppers to take that thing." It was all very well to be violated as I had been last night by Abdul, but I did not like the idea of inanimate objects being forced up my delicate inner passages. He turned and walked across the room – angry, hurt, careless, I couldn't tell – and threw the great plastic phallus into the bathroom. I imagined the maid finding it there when she came to tidy up and turn down the bedclothes. "OK, so you don't like me that much," he said, thickly, from inside the leather.

"I like you very much. It's just the moving toyshop I can't be doing with." And I decided I had better go, and reached for my jeans.

"I could whip you," he suggested, "for what you did to my country in the war." He seemed to think this was a final expedient which might really appeal to me; and I had no doubt he could have provided a pretty fearsome lash from one of his many items of luggage.

"I think that might be to take the sex and politics metaphor a bit too seriously, old chap," I said. And I could see the whole thing deteriorating into a scene from some poker-faced left-wing European film.

When I was dressed and had my bag again slung over my shoulder Gabriel was wandering around the sitting room, his huge erection barely flagging, but somehow no longer of interest to me. I stood and looked at him and he gasped and grunted and writhed out of his mask. His hair was moist and standing up, and his clear olive complexion was primed with pink – as it might have been if we had just simply made love. I went over to him and kissed him, but he closed his teeth against me, kept his hands at his sides. I left the room without saying goodbye.

Well it served me right, I thought, as I wandered with a vague sense of direction along uniform carpeted corridors – Phil's terrain, where he did his job. All this had certainly got me in the mood and now I would be too late to catch him and the uncomplicated solace he could give. Surely hotels must be hotbeds of this kind of carry-on, easy encounters at the bar or unlocking the doors of adjacent rooms. My little Philanderer could make a fortune out of escorting truly glamorous men – and not all of them would turn out to be as weird as the eye-catching Gabriel. It was quite likely, wasn't it, that Phil had already caught Gabriel's eye?

I found the corner by the service lift and the steep flight of stairs up to Phil's attic. It was a drab, cheapjack little area, unambiguously removed from the public, and yet I had come to love it in a way I never could the rest of the monstrous edifice. The little room – and above it the lonely roof – was nothing really, but like the lovers' cottage in "Tea for Two" it had been wonderfully sufficient for our romance. I knew there was no chance of finding him in – he would be well off on his laddish booze by now – but it would be comforting to sit there for a bit with the window open and surrounded by his empty clothes. When I put my key in the lock, though, there was a muffled call of surprise, I thought, from within.

Phil and Bill were kneeling face to face on the bed. Bill's hand rested on Phil's shoulder, and it looked like some College jerk-off job. Their tilting dicks, alert as orgiasts' on a Greek vase, withered astonishingly under my expressionless stare. Not for them the witless priapism of Gabriel; but there was enough defiance in their confusion for them not to blabber excuses – not to say anything at all. And I couldn't think of anything much to say. I know I swallowed and coloured and took in, as if I needed to satisfy myself, the circumstantial details. Certainly there were no signs of passionate haste. Bill's trousers were neatly folded and his vast smalls were spread like an antimacassar across the back of the chair. I nodded repeatedly and slowly withdrew, closing the door as if not to disturb a sleeper. Before I had reached the top of the stairs I heard a gasped "Oh my God" and a loud frightened laugh.

And so to James's. By the time I got there my anger, hurt, care were welling up under the frigid discipline I had instinctively assumed. I smeared away stupid tears. Thank heavens at least no crass, unforgettable words had been spoken. "Darling, whisky" was my own first utterance – and I thought, none of your namby-pamby Caribbean aphrodisiac nonsense.

James was eating scrambled eggs standing up and listening to some fathomlessly gloomy music. "Bad day dear?" he enquired maritally.

"The last twenty-four hours have actually been quite extraordinarily hideously awful."

"Oh darling."

"I thought I was just about managing it until half an hour ago, when I went up to Phil's room at the hotel – I don't know why, just on some sentimental whim, I thought I'd put on some of his clothes and lie there for a bit and just *be* him, you know – he having arranged to go off drinking with some of his appalling friends. Well they may not be appalling, I've never met them. I say we couldn't possibly take this music off? It's driving me insane."

"It's Shostakovich's viola sonata," said James pettishly.

"Exactly . . . That's better. And the drink?" He poured a

generous Bell's. "Dearest – thank you. So I opened the door, to which as you know I have a key, and find Phil in there with old Bill Hawkins, from the Corry, messing around stark naked, etc, etc."

"Fucking hell."

"I do find it very terrible actually." I flopped on to the sofa and gulped at my drink. "I mean, I absolutely hate the thought of Phil going with someone else. But one would understand if it were just some spur-of-the-moment fling – some sexy guy staying in the hotel or something. To go with Bill, who is anyway a pal of mine and what? three times his age . . ."

"No?"

"Well, just about." I stared at James, through him, as I realized how slow I had been. "You know, I should have been on to this. I've seen Bill hanging around near the Queensberry before now – and of course I knew he was sweet on Phil, sweet on him before I was. Indeed it was really Bill's interest in him that got me going, made me see how good he was. And then last week, when I took Phil to the Shaft, I knew something funny was going on. We were sort of horsing around outside the BM and I realized someone was watching us from across the road. I don't think Phil saw him, but I'm convinced it was Bill."

"Kind of creepy, n'est-ce pas?" said James, wandering off and looking out of the window. He was my only friend but I knew that he would take a kind of wistful satisfaction in things having at last – at last: it was what? two months? – gone awry. "This needn't mean it's all over, though, surely?" he said.

I stared some time into my glass. "I don't know. No, it needn't. It will, I think, mean that whatever's going on between those two is all over. What you don't know, and what Bill doesn't know I know, is that he has already been inside for interfering with young boys." But these were the kind of real-life details that never shocked James: it was only on the fantasy level that one got to him. "He'll be pretty scared about all this."

"Well, you're hardly going to shop him to the police, are you?"

"Ooh, I don't know," I said with a rueful laugh, finishing my drink and getting up to splosh in another half-tumbler full. I walked over and hugged him from behind, resting my chin on his shoulder. "It's like one of those frightful seventeenth-century epitaphs: I've had my Will, I've had my Fill, and now they've sent in my Bill. Or something like that."

"Do you want something to eat?"

"I think I'll just stick on the booze, actually. Darling, can I stay here tonight? I just don't fancy going home – and I'm sure he'll try and ring up and it will all be too appalling."

"Yes, of course you can." I sensed his nervous pleasure at the certainty of companionship. He turned round in my arms and gave me a tight squeeze and a kiss on the blunted bridge of my nose.

SCRATCH

Patrick Carr

Birds and busted hearts. Crucifying trees. Arch baby devils. Desperate clawing panthers. Photonegatives for the flesh. She stood among them: emerald green and anatomically impossible: long and lithe and buxom beyond belief. A head-on drunken gaze capped by floating hair that finished in living weedy ends. The scales of her tail were set close, like jewels. What had he been thinking?

SPIKE AND I grew up with each other, in opposite houses on a small suburban dead end. Hamilton Street was a comfort and a curse to us then – a small, protective enclave at times, a cramped, restrictive jailyard at others. The street's six houses sheltered families who had lived there for as many generations as the town allowed; everyone's great-grandfather seemed to have abandoned New York for little Pinehurst at the same time, carving our tiny block out of the woods and rocks that had kept the place a wilderness for so long. The idea that land only 20 minutes outside both Newark and Manhattan had been untamed as recently as the turn of the century struck no one as odd or unbelievable. Not even me and Spike, who frequently wished Nature would spontaneously overrun the whole place again – *sometime real-fucking-soon*, he'd say.

A lot of the things Spike did were, I think, inspired by an actual fear of that place, the micro-community where everyone knew him since he was that-high. He wanted desperately to not belong, pushed himself, really, to stick out as much as humanly possible. He was exceptionally bright, and respected for that – but cautiously, for he countered it with a taste for solitude that many people – chiefly worried parents, like mine – found "weird" or "not quite right." I was the only person Spike let in regularly, and our being thick as thieves and exclusive of almost everyone brought me no end of questioning at home. But Spike inspired in me a kind of loyalty I have not experienced since; no argument concerning him was ever conceded: not to my mother, who worried that he was a "bad kid"; not even to my dad, who'd initially admired him as a "boy's boy" but seemed to come to his own concerns regarding our friendship. I can only guess at what they were.

I can say now that I was smitten with him, and when I think back to him then, he pretty much retains pride of place in the Perfect Young Man category. Even in that town, where boys seemed largely interchangeable.

Pinehurst was, until my late 'teens, a predominantly Italian town, with a small section unofficially labeled Polishtown. Spike was unusual in that he was of mixed blood, which of course meant half Italian, half anything else that had the nerve to exist. His otherhalf was Irish, and it was that half that marked him by name – Benjamin Brogan – even while leaving him to appear the ultimate guinea kid. He was strong and agile, with an olive skin that tanned to a deep berrybrown in the sun; his eyes and hair were the same shadowed ebony. In short, his features were my features, were every boy's features in that town, but with an added grace of proportion, and an extra intensity in the eyes as he sought out his privacy.

The only real obstruction to our friendship was high school: I attended Pinehurst, while Spike was sent to St Simon's in the next town. Its academic reputation was held in high esteem, and it was considered the region's best springboard for acceptance to a better college. I personally had resisted the idea of St Simon's, thought it far too elitist and altogether unnecessary, and so was initially surprised at Spike's willingness to attend. But gradually

I came to see his decision as the only natural one for him: here was his first real chance to leave his stifling neighborhood behind, a break, however minor, with the people amongst whom he'd never felt at home.

High school came, happened and went in much the same way that high school seems to do eternally; in Spike's absence I found myself obliged to make new friends, at least in school related activities. I was tickled to find that Spike had become part of a somewhat arty circle at St Simon's, but that too made its own sense. It was a small circle, set to the side of the larger social setup, and prone to respecting what they took to be his moody side. He was redubbed Ben, and allowed to be the resident dark, introspective young man.

We stayed in touch, to my mother's slight chagrin, and came to feel as comfortable as possible moving within the others' circle of friends. But we did that rarely. We came to have separate lives in addition to each other, and when we spent time together – and we did, regularly – we did so alone. While I could never have been embarrassed by him, I felt uncomfortable and exposed with him around others.

It was on his eighteenth birthday that he first hit me with the idea. A June night, and we sat smoking up on the roof outside Spike's so very typically secluded attic bedroom. Graduation was a week away for me, two for him, and we were talking with uneasy excitement about college. Spike had chosen the State University, while I, for a change, opted for the alien glamour of Boston. We were talking about how, sure, of course he could come up and visit, whenever. At which point he said *you know what I want, what I really want to do before I go*? No, I didn't know. *I want a tattoo.*

Well that was a surprise. I asked if he didn't want to wait till he went in the Navy, and he *tsked* me. *No, no not something like that*, he said. *Something to mark me, something to mark me before I disappear into college.*

I looked at him a little quizzically, wondering how in hell he thought he'd ever disappear into anything, much less something so mundane as college. All I could see was perhaps the most handsome person I had ever met; really, truly so remarkably beautiful. As he matured his face had lost its round cuteness, become more angular and striking. His medium frame was sinewy and balanced, while still covered with the exotic olive of his youth. He had let a trace of black hair cover his upper lip, with the result being a mouth that, over the last year, had me thinking odd things. And as I eyed him that evening, I felt that oddness, that nervous excitement hit me hard, so hard that I didn't care what it meant anymore. I let my mouth hunger for him, let myself admit what I wanted between us.

I asked him what made him think he'd ever disappear. Went a little further and said I'd never let him.

Yeah, he said. *But I don't know.* He seemed somewhat disappointed in my response, so I tried to make up for it. It'd be cool, I told him; you know, sexy.

He smiled, brightening at me. *Yeah? You think so?* Looked away from me – too quickly, I wondered? – and nodded slightly, then more vigorously. *Yeah, I mean I think it would be sexy too. I mean, I don't know. I really want one.*

He sat and smoked silently, blowing clouds out in front of him like spells. I thought of gypsies and sorcerers, and called him a crazy gypsy boy.

Yeah? Really? He was suddenly intrigued by that. *You know when I was a kid*, he said, *I'd tell myself, like pretend, you know? that I was this gypsy prince who'd been kidnapped and sold to some American family.* I had to smile at how much sense that made, in its fairytale way. *And that somewhere*, he continued, *there was a mark on me that would reveal me* – he stood suddenly and grabbed his hair in a mad, regal gesture – *as heir apparent to the Gypsy throne.* His grandeur fell into giggles. *Or whatever it's called.*

So that's what you want, I explained. Your long-lost gypsy royalty tattoo.

And god he just crowed at that. *Yes! Yes! By which I will distinguish myself from pretenders to my throne.* He sat down laughing, and leaned so, so close to me in intrigue. *Do you want to see it?*

See what, I asked, a little startled. I got a sudden rush of . . . something, I can hardly recall what, thinking he was going to peel to some recently inked nudity in front of me.

The picture I want to have done, he said impatiently. *Pay attention*.

I said sure, but he had already scrambled through the window. I could hear him rooting around in his disheveled room. Heard him bounce once, twice on the bed before he tipped himself back through the window to me. He handed me some kind of nautical book, some big library book about Legendary Sea Monsters or something. *It's in there — I marked the page*. Where? I didn't find any pagemark. *Shit. Here . . .* He took the book from me, very excited, and flustered through its pages.

I asked what his mother would think.

I don't have to worry about my mother, he said, with a little superiority, *I am 18, I don't have to ask anyone anything*.

I reminded his highness that I hardly caved to the desires of my mother, either.

Really, he agreed. *Or you'd stop talking to me.*

Forget it, I smoothed. Spike had always been a little hurt by my parents' coolness to him.

Like I'm this evil, horrible influence, he continued. *Like I'm trying to steal her baby away —*

I cut him short with a laugh, hoping I wouldn't flush at the thought.

Here, he said, and handed the clumsy book to me.

It confused me. This? What he'd pointed out to me seemed to be an ancient rendering of a mermaid, a luridly green mermaid at that, as naked as she could get without taking off her tail. Her breasts were really rather overwhelming, if not too terribly realistic. She had wild kelp-hair, and stared blankly from the page with opium eyes. Fellini meets Jacques Cousteau.

He had apparently kept speaking: *. . . and I like that it's a really old kind of thing, you know? With history, and everything. And it's like you said, you know, it's like . . . sexy.*

Well, he had me there. She fairly screamed sex, could hardly have been more livid with it if she had been holding a torch that burned real flame. But her sexual language was different than the one I'd come to speak to myself, the one I realized I'd been listening for behind Spike's words; I felt myself sink like a stone dropped into his mermaid's watery world.

So, do you want to come when I get it done?

Sure, I said. I went home that night wondering if I'd dream of gypsies or sea monsters, knowing well which I preferred. But my sleeping mind was thankfully still.

A week went by, during which I teased myself to how many mocking orgasms with the mental picture of my best friend. With the memorysmell of him. The imagined taste of him – salty, with, for some reason, the dry tang of baker's chocolate. I didn't know why he'd taste like that, and felt certain I'd never know the truth of him on my tongue. As near to where he lived as ever, I was watching him move far, far away.

The day of my graduation arrived. Spike pulled me aside at the after-party, and said *I want to do it tomorrow*. I wondered if my parents had been serving him alcohol, then thought it unlikely. Tomorrow? What's the rush, I asked. Why tomorrow?

Because next week I'm going to graduate a gypsy prince, he said, a little more seriously than I might have expected.

I really planned on being hung-over tomorrow, I replied.

So fine, be hung-over. It's not your arm they're nailing it to. He smiled: *Did I tell you? I want it on my arm*.

For the whole world to see, I thought. For me. But what could I say to him, when he stood there all hopped up like a child, his eyes – his eyes reading me so carefully through the long thick fringe of his hair.

Yeah, sure, tomorrow, I said. Anything to cut my welling desire short. To keep from grabbing him, shaking him, squeezing the idea of me into him.

The following afternoon we drove up and down Farragut Avenue two dozen times. I didn't know what Spike's hesitation was, considering the mania that insisted we go then, absolutely that day. I said listen, if you're having second thoughts don't worry about it. I'm not gonna think you're scared or anything.

No, no second thoughts, he said. And that was Spike, a hundred percent.

We drove past Rage Gallery again. *Is it even open?* he asked a little doubtfully. The sign says "Open," I replied. Why don't we just park and go to the door. He seemed worried about something, as though something weren't going right. *I'm feeling awfully casual about it*, he said out of nowhere, *when, you know, it's going to be a forever thing. I mean, when it's done that's it. That is just fucking it, man. I don't know why I'm being so casual about it.*

The fact of his being anything but was getting on my nerves. I don't know why you're putting it off, I snapped. Just fucking go do it if you think it's such a great idea.

He drew back a little, and knit his brow trying to figure out what he'd done wrong. I apologized. I was, as I'd predicted, hung-over, and just kind of out of it. To myself I admitted that being near Spike was beginning to seem painful to me; a strange, sad anxiety.

All right that's it, he blurted. *That car's pulling out. We're parking there on the street and going in.*

And that was that.

It was a small, white studio trying hard to stay clean. The tattooist was on the phone, said hold on, he'd be right out. Spike slowly scanned the walls, all covered in designs, photos, blueprints for life. I sat down and lit a cigarette, took a deep drag that made my head pound and watched Spike trying to keep himself busy.

Suddenly: *Hey! Look!* I got up and walked over to where he stood. He'd found his mermaid, or a damned good facsimile, right there on the studio wall. She was gracing the rather flabby arm of an older man in a torn-out magazine photo.

How about that, I said blankly, and sat back down.

The tattooist came out and talked to Spike a little about what he wanted. I saw Spike point to the picture on the wall, after which the man just studied him for a second. Then he looked at me. Asked: you too? Uh, I think not. The tattooist seemed to consider that, and me, for a moment, before asking Spike, you're sure that's what you want?

Spike said *yeah*, a little vaguely. He seemed confused about having to convince the guy. The tattooist finally said all right, told Spike to take a seat for a minute, and walked into the back of the shop.

Spike came over to the seat beside mine, picked up a

loose-leaf binder from the small coffee table and started
leafing.

I thought he looked nervous, like a bad kid just before some
piece of delinquency. With a clairvoyant's precision, he asked
me for a cigarette, completing the picture of a bad, bad boy.
He smoked absently, worked his jaw back and forth some as
he pretended to look at the 100 colored-skin pictures. Finally
he snapped the book shut and laid it aside. He turned to
me with a comic little pout that just drew attention to his
damned pretty mouth. My eyes were starting to drift over his
face when the cavalry came, just in time, and told Spike he'd
have to come in back to the actual studio. *Wanna come?* Spike
asked me quickly. No, I didn't. *OK. I'll be back.* No doubt, I
thought.

I waited sullenly, and remarked to myself how very long
it seemed to take before I heard the angry hornet of the
needle begin.

Did it hurt? I asked.
I felt it, he said. *But I had to. I had to feel it, to make sure he
scratched through enough.*
Through enough what?
Nothing. Skin. My skin.

After dinner that night, I crossed the street to see if Spike was
up for a movie or something. His mother let me find my way
to his room, as usual. She seemed a little less than pleased to
see me, so I figured the afternoon's field trip had bombed big
time. I disappeared up the stairs quickly.

I found things dark, and Spike asleep. I entered his room
slowly, looked at him for a moment just lying there in what
light dusk provided the tiny room. He was laying on his left
side, so his bandaged right arm was exposed.

I figured to wake him, and leaned in toward his sleeping.
He had apparently knocked loose the gauze that covered his
arm, and I saw a trace of jet black peer out from beneath the
makeshift bandage. A dark sort of filigree appeared on his skin,
disappearing again beneath the surgical fabric. I struggled to
piece the skin design together with the picture he'd shown me,

but couldn't. I stared at it for how long, trying to decode him. Then he moved, rolled to his back. I hadn't any idea how long he'd been watching me.

Do you want to see the rest? he asked quietly. *I have to give it some air eventually.* Of course I wanted to see it. I had to.

He pulled gently at the surgical tape that held the gauze to his arm. *Look,* he said, *come here in the light.*

He moved toward the nightstand lamp. I sat beside him on the bed.

And saw it, a swirling maze of blackness: its center a hurricane's eye that sent baroque-primitive tendrils swirling out and about each other.

What happened to Our Lady of the Waves, I asked.

It wasn't right, he answered. *The guy made this one up when I told him why I wanted it, how I thought it should feel on me.* Damn if the guy hadn't scratched deep enough after all.

Spike tried to turn his arm to show me as much of it as he could, and as he skitched around I saw that he'd been sleeping naked beneath his thin summer bedsheet. How could I have forgotten that about him. If indeed I'd forgotten.

He looked over his arm at me unsurely, expectantly. *Do you like it?*

I moved my face a little closer.

Don't touch it.

I won't, I said. But the thrill of his being so sensitive to my nearness set me off, and I started breathing so hard I was pretty much panting on his arm.

It has to heal. He sounded somehow closer, and I could see his eyes grow cautious and canny.

I stared him back, matching his silence with my own.

I let my lips open very slowly. And then my teeth, slightly, so slowly. I sent my tongue out to touch the raw, healing flesh.

No. He jumped up so suddenly I scooted back in alarm. And fell off the bed on my ass. I propped myself up on my elbows, laid there with him standing over me, forbidding, giant. *I said don't touch it.* I just laid still, staring at his eyes, so they wouldn't.

Travel.

Down his face to his dark lips. Chin. Down his neck. Hard, jutting collar bones. Down. His chest: wide, smooth, smallish nipples just a little then more and more defined, pointed, rigid. Babyish hair between them, like a shallow scorched valley. And down, along the feathery meeting hairs to his belly to.

His cock.

I didn't know what to make of it. Hard? Halfway maybe. Yes – or was it just highlighted by the pitch of the hair around it, set off by the obscured balls that hung behind it.

He knelt down fast over me.

What? What? Over and over he asked what? Pushed his face in mine. *Huh?* Grabbed my hair. *What?*

I'd let out a hiss of pain when he grabbed me, arched my spine up so we met between his legs. Growled a little in my throat so that he just closed his eyes and pushed his forehead to mine with a little whimper.

I felt it first: a surprise dripping running through my T-shirt. Watched his eyes widen and brows fold together when he realized what he'd done.

It turned hot, and the reek traveled to my nose right away. My head filled with the thick salty smell of him, and I answered his initial surprise with a moment of my own confusion. Then, as if I had been holding my breath unwittingly, I exhaled hotly toward him, let my mouth fall open. I pushed against my bottom teeth and my tongue bellied up over them.

I watched his face move from shock to careful fascination, and knew that I, in turn, was being watched and marveled over for my response to what he'd done. He pissed himself dry on me, flooding my navel, soaking my belly hairs and dampening my crotch with its rivulets. He finished with a familiar little shudder; neither one of us had moved.

And so I was careful about it, moving as I might with a skittish animal: eye to eye, and so slowly. I reached down and felt for my last bit of evidence – yes, there it was, like cooling blood on my skin. And again by degrees, moved that hand up. Up toward our faces. To my mouth, that licked the bitter urine away, and opened wider when he met it with his own.

He lowered himself to me, so we met where both our cocks had grown hard. He moved over me, pressing them together, hump rubbing them slightly.

Hey, he said.

What?

You OK?

Yeah, I'm all right. He rubbed on me faster, a little harder.

Does that feel good? he asked.

Yeah.

You want me to keep going?

I didn't say anything, but brought my pelvis up to meet his motion. And he smiled his big gypsyboy smile, closed his eyes. He went at me harder, rubbed us roughly against each other so it almost hurt – so it tickled so deep it tortured. I reached around to pull him toward me, to hold our groins together in their slippery mess.

Spike reached between us to pull at the buttons of my now soggy jeans. I pushed his hands away to do the job quicker myself. While I worked my pants down, he pushed my T-shirt up, tugged at it, giggled in trying to get it over my head. A couple wiggles more and I was' as undressed as either of us seemed to have patience for.

Spike whispered, *Baby*.

What? Whaja say?

Nothing. Just baby is all. Just baby is how I think of you.

He started with his cock on me again *baby I swear I swear that feels* and I ran my hands up over him Yes *yeah yeah* over and over *you know I think about you baby you know that right yeah? yeah, like this gimme c'mon* yeah? what? what do you want *me? me do you want huh?* yeah *I want you I really you know* that I want that *ha hah yeah? that thing there? ha haha* c'mon *give me your mouth baby* Spike c'mon let me *do it baby huh?* please? *you want me baby?*

I rolled him off me, onto his back. Laughing nervous both of us. Him sweet smiling bluely somehow. Me jumpy as shit when I saw his cock, raging hard. It curved a little to the left, and bobbed as he kept speaking, reaching toward me with his legs

baby huh? *babyboy c'mon c'mon* I want *I want you to so bad c'mon,* man Yes *do it, do it with your mouth* c'mon *don't you want me, prettypretty*

I never had, but I wanted to so badly I . . . I didn't really know how or

*c'mon and suck on me, man, c'mon just take it, take it in
your mouth baby, just lick don't you think I want you baby
don't you believe*

I decided to improvise.

He gasped, and gulped air as I wrapped my mouth around
the head of his dick, licking fast around its swollen ridge with
my tongue, sucking the tip, feeling the slit of it with my lips, my
tongue. I wanted more of it, and made a swallow that brought
him deep to poke at my soft palate lightly, stubbornly.

He'd fallen silent but for heavy dragon breathing. I felt his
hands meet at the back of my head, where they pushed me down
on him. I choked a little on him, heard him groan deeply with me
far down on his cock. He pulled himself out, and I breathed, but
for only the second before he reversed the labor, and pushed
himself up into the head he now held still. Pushed hard up into
me, pulled out bringing slick spit over my lips, before back in,
far far back gagging in he went on fucking my mouth with soft
grunting and relentless push in push in deeper. Filling, empty,
wet, breathless from his cock, his gentle impunity. He moved
into me faster, sounded hoarse in his gasping breaths. Plunged
into me with a deep wordless sound, pulled back, coming on
my tongue, spilling all about my mouth his bitter hotness.

He pulled out of my mouth with delicate quickness. I brought
my lips together but *nono nono*, he pulled my face toward him,
planted his mouth on mine, and fished it for what he had left
there. He kissed me deeply for so long with his calmly unyielding
tongue.

You little baby, he finally said, so softly, as if I slept. He held
me hard where he lay, one hand sometime rubbing down, up
my back. I asked how he was doing.

Me? very gentle smile. *I'm fine, I am very very fine. And how
are you, huh?* And he reached down to my cock, hard as steel,
and ran his hand over it, first like a feather, then a little harder.
Grabbed the head in his palm and squeezed a little. Slid back
down the shaft.

Huh, baby, how are ya?

Came back up to the head, his hand sliding its way along
the piss that was still damp, if cooler on me.

Can't tell me?

He gripped my cock tighter, and pistoned it hard once. Twice.

Don't you know you can tell me anything?

He started pumping steadily, pulling at me, jerking me off with strong strokes as he smiled like the devil.

C'mon. Come. Please. Come for me . . .

It was happening very fast now, him stroking my dick so fast, and the way I felt behind it, somewhere first back behind my balls then the tickle of electric through them, through my balls, the base of my cock that he was pulling at working so hard ruthless now pounding on me pulling it, drawing that electric up my cock out of me.

You know what you are to me?

My jaw shocked open as I came, as I shot so hard from his hand that I saw him flinch, grinning, from a droplet flying up to his face. I poured out onto him, and he said *yes, yes, yes* felt every muscle give way at once so that I collapsed onto him.

He wouldn't let me wipe either of us up, but calmly, insistently rubbed against me. He rubbed the cum into our skin like ink in an old cut pattern, like ash into a bleeding skin design, and said *that's the mark I'll know you by, when I come back to get you.*

We stayed still except for Spike's kissing: kissing my head quietly. I slowed down. Until I finally slept; indeed, very much like a baby.

I think about him whenever I leaf through a gaudy tattoo mag at the newsstand – which I do, of course, to think about him. About the way he tastes halfway to what I'd expected; about the altogether unexpected sight of him standing over me suddenly that night, about the needy way he plunged himself into me, spilled into me. And of course his long-lost gypsy royalty tattoo, that he did for a kind of love, for the in-the-bone hurt of his foreign loneliness.

When he writes, he always begins with Baby –; when he visits, we meet as if starved.

In memory of David, who knew it first

JOHN

G. Winston James

As USUAL, THE room was dim and I refused to lie down. Would not pretend to be comfortable. I preferred the feel of carpeted floor against my socked feet to the softness of my therapist's couch. Especially when leather sofas reminded me so much of my mother's softness when I was young. The way she would embrace me in her bed just moments after she'd beaten me, all the while asking me why I was crying.

". . . and the mirror cracked!" I yelled.

"But so what? Break through it," my therapist urged.

"My mother would never let me hold a knife in my hand. I lived in a world of spoons. Don't you see?"

"No. I don't," he said, probing.

"She cut up everything that wasn't soup," I cried. "Everything! Then she would just sit there and watch me."

"Why?"

"Because she thought that evil little boys couldn't be trusted not to hurt other people along with themselves," I whispered.

After a brief silence, my therapist turned on the lights and allowed me a moment to stand there, two steps from the wall – facing it.

"Do you really listen to me when I rattle on?" I asked.

"Of course I do."

"Then why do you let me come back when we never accomplish anything?"

He thought for a moment. "Because I think I can help you. Help you to break through this wall and get at what's really keeping you and any possible life partner apart." He touched my shoulder. "There's something here, John. It's deep, but we can get to it."

"Maybe," I stuttered, "but I don't know if I can pay you anymore. I'm kinda broke."

"You're not coming back?" he asked.

I just laughed – not fully sure whether he'd asked a question or made a statement – then slowly put on my coat and left, reminding myself that I had a friend's piano recital to get to. With the mood I was in, though, I knew I would need to stop somewhere else before I could possibly sit down to listen to Bryan render the many moods of Liszt's "Transcendental Etudes." I was restless and more than a little depressed, as often happened after my sessions. I told myself that I needed to unwind. To loosen up a bit.

So I walked out of the therapist's office and back into the shadows of my life. Heading directly to where I knew I should not go. To that place where I would be for the next two, three or four hours. I'd end up bored, but trapped. Caught by little desires that would hold me like good sleep, while other pitiful men scurried around me like rats. I'd go there all right. To 42nd and 8th. There.

I walked with very deliberate steps. A tall black man with a straight back, regal neck and a warrior's gait. I exuded so much self-confidence, I think, that I had none left inside to help me fight my own internal demons. Even now, though, I'm not really sure that self-confidence would have any effect against monsters that are the self. So maybe my outward display was more important. At least I could convince others that I was not ashamed.

"Clean under there!" my mother screamed. "I'm not touching it."

"It's foreskin, Mother," I said to myself as I walked. I could name it now, but I never knew then.

"You think Janie and the other kids are gonna play with you with that nasty thing?"

"It's a penis, Mother. My penis. But it is dirty, isn't it?"

"Damned disgusting. Just like your father. Thank God his shiftless ass ain't around no more."

"Don't worry, Mama. I won't show it to Janie. I won't show it to anybody that knows me. I ain't gonna embarrass you."

Sidestepping people. That's what I was doing as I walked. If there was someone directly ahead of me, I moved. Someone too close to my shoulder, I turned. Thank God there was always some room at the side, and that most people seemed to decide a block back that they would not walk the same line as I.

But I looked them in the eye. All of them. I took pleasure in intimidating people like a black man. Especially as I walked to my little hell – it was like practice. There, in hell, you were supposed to look into people's eyes, but only deep enough to discern which perversion had brought them. It was important to be able to distinguish the size-queen from the sadist, and the pederast from the simply lonely man.

Everything else in those eyes was ignored, especially the unmistakable look of guilt. Guilt at the fact that so many of us were there at the expense of spending quality time with others – our wives and boyfriends and children. Loved ones who waited like my boyfriend used to as the hours passed and the bed grew cold beside him where I should have been instead of dropping quarters into the abyss.

For those other men and me, the peep shows were a temptation we could seldom resist. In various ways, we led ourselves to believe that it was only in places like this that we could be true to ourselves – to our sexual natures. Avoiding everyday questions of protocol and morality to be free to explore one another's lust.

"Where you coming from? When did you sneak outta here?"

"Nowhere, Mama. I was just playing around with Bryan."

"At eleven o'clock at night. Boy, there ain't that much playing in the world, especially if you gonna get your knees that dirty."

"We was just – "

"Gimme them keys and shut your mouth."

I arrived at the Show Palace in a short few minutes. By then, hardly remembering the supposed reasons why I'd come. Sometimes three or more times a week I made similar trips.

Some longer some shorter, depending on where I'd left from. The destination, however, was always the same. There. Drawn by the apparently simple compulsion to see other men's dicks and to see just how far I would go with them.

Walking through the door feels the same every time: there's that rush of expectation. The hope that maybe I'll see a big dick soon, so I won't have to waste too much time or too many quarters. But it's not often that I leave in under an hour, all the same.

The ground floor was all straight porn. Racks and racks of magazines with bulging breasts and blonds' darting tongues. I passed them with hardly a glance as I headed somewhat purposefully towards the stairs – dim, with little mirrored tiles forming squares on the walls. Posters of naked men were hung above, below and between the tiles, filling the stairwell with reflections of sex, such that by the time any man reached the bottom of that single flight, he was necessarily resolute in his pursuit of smut. Walking through the lower door and into the men's shop I put aside any lofty thoughts and became someone simply base.

"Get the hell into your room if you gonna cry! Nobody don't wanna look at you!"

"Why'd you hit me then, if you ain't expect me to cry?"

"Shut yo ass, Boy, before I take off them clothes and beat the devil out of you! I don't want to hear about your feelings."

The shop was almost empty except for the attendants who sold quarters and supposedly enforced the store rules against loitering and public sex. Worse still, there was no one attractive who was free. Most of the six or seven patrons there were hustlers – homeboy rentals dressed in the roughness they knew would sell, to someone, even if sex appeal failed them.

Every so often as I walked by, one of the hustlers would enter a booth and take out his dick for me to see. I would look up into the Hispanic or Black face, down to his trade, then I would smile and just walk on. The fact is, I'm reluctant to pay for sex. There's something about the payment, I think, that reminds me of a contract – of a responsibility that I'd owe to someone in return for their service to me. The exchange seems like some warped relationship. One in which giving love is replaced with the exchange of money. I find the idea distasteful.

So, for the most part, I avoided them for what felt like an hour. I ducked into booths next to the occasional Black man, Hispanic or white, pressed the "Up" button and waited for the buddy shade between the booths to rise. For that to happen, though, the other man would also have to press the "Up" button in his booth. It was another dreadful waiting and hoping game. I wanted to look full on at my neighbor as I masturbated. I was hoping to see that humongous dick that would make me grab mine harder and jerk it and pull it faster until I came, eyes closed and lips apart.

It didn't happen, though. The pieces I saw were mediocre at best. At one point, five of us were looking at one another as the entire row of booths had raised its shades. We looked back and forth across the panes as we yanked on our dicks to get them hard, but there were no sculpted monoliths in the lot, not even a muscled body or handsome face. So after half a minute I pressed the down buttons on each side of my booth and left.

"Whas up?" a muscular teenager asked. He was wearing baggy black denims and a tight-fitting shirt that read BOY across his chest. The B and the Y emphasized his nipples as he stroked his stomach with the hand that was not on his crotch.

"Nothing much."

"You wanna watch a movie?"

I ignored him, and looked around as if to remind him that this was not a Loews, and that he could never invite me on a date so easily. I was hoping that he would read my silence as lack of interest and leave me alone, but he just stood there looking more deeply into my eyes than I should have allowed him. I wanted to walk away as I had with the others, but his undeniable sexiness held me.

"You got any quarters?" he asked.

He was persistent. In spite of myself, I moved the quarters between my fingers. Counting. Wondering if I might spend much more on this young man.

I glanced at my watch before looking back at him, and realized with undisguised shock that what had felt like an

hour had actually been two, and that I had missed the first
half of Bryan's recital. Panicked, I moved to leave, but then
my young friend reached for his crotch. I watched as his hands
pressed into the oversized denim and then gathered up the
material around his trade. He squeezed it gently. I felt it as
if he were touching me. His erection reached and stretched. I
looked up to find him peering into my eyes with his head tilted
slightly to the side. His lips were as wet as his smile.

"So you wanna watch a movie?" he asked. "You obviously
already late."

"Are you hustling?"

"Nah, man," he said, with his hands making spirals in the
air. "I'm just tryin to get some money. So I can get somethin
to eat and, you know . . . for the bus back to Jersey. Can you
help me out?" His hands landed on his crotch.

"How much would this help run me?" I asked.

"Le's go watch a movie. I'll show you my thing and you can
tell me how much you willin to pay. Don't worry, it won't be
much for all you gonna get."

He stepped into the nearest booth and stood against the far
wall. With one hand he rubbed his swollen crotch and with the
other he beckoned me to come in.

"What you and Bryan doin in that room with that lock on?"

"Nothin, Mama."

*"Get the hell out! I don't know what you'd wanna be locked up
in some room with some little boy on a hot day in the summer for
anyway. Get out!"*

"All right, Mama. We'll go to the park."

I closed the door behind me and took a moment to let the
peculiar intimacy of being with a stranger in a three-by-three-
by-seven booth settle into my quivering bones. It was like the
privacy invasion of being jammed in a crowded subway car
with someone's hand caught on your crotch. You wanted to
say excuse me, but you could see that there was nowhere for
either of you to move until the next stop. I reached over his
right shoulder and dropped the first quarter of our interlude.
The overhead light went out as the movie came on. Men
humping and sweating and gyrating. It was almost sexy. But
mostly violent.

"So how much you got?" I asked.

"Ten inches. And fat. Come here."

He took my hand. "You like that shit, right? Yeah. Yeah."

I was rubbing his dick through his jeans. The top of my head fell at the bridge of his nose. Suddenly I wondered why I'd ever thought of him as a boy when there seemed to be nothing about him that spoke of youth or innocence. Then I looked down again at his shirt.

"Das it. Yeah. Take it out."

After pulling the shirt from his pants, I unzipped his zipper, and searched for the opening of his boxers. But I was fumbling, so he undid his belt and pants himself and lowered them over his buttocks. His penis pulsed toward me in his underpants. I reached for it as it took the initiative to part the slit in his shorts.

"Yeah! Pull on it, Little John. Uh hum."

"Why?"

"'Cause that's what it's there for."

"But what if your wife sees?"

"Little John, she won't. Just put it in your mouth and shut up."

"But – "

"I'll take you back to play with the other kids later."

"How much you want?" I asked the hustler.

"Just ten dollars. That ain't much right?"

"All right." I was starting to want it now. In my head, I hesitated only slightly as I imagined Bryan looking up from his piano to search the audience for me. The guilt was building, but I was used to it.

"Wha's your name, Man?" he asked as if he wanted to know. He opened his legs and moved his feet farther forward.

"I don't want to talk" I replied.

"Ah 'ight. Then maybe you wanna suck my dick."

"Mm."

I went down on him and forgot he was a hustler, maybe because he hadn't lied: he was at least ten inches. And I rationalized that each one of them was probably worth more than a dollar, so he was just about giving it away.

I sucked hard and fast.

"Ah yeah. Yeah, Boy. Suck that shit!"

But I felt like I couldn't get enough of it into my mouth. It was great to find a dick that was a challenge. I took it to the back of my throat, let it rest on my gag reflex, lull it. Then I opened my throat and pressed forward until my upper lip brushed against his pubic hairs and my lower lip was crushed up against his balls.

"Motherfucker, suck that shit!"

I gagged.

His hands were on my head now that he knew that I'd learned to deep-throat the way most black men thought white guys did it naturally. He rocked his hips back and forth. He began to sweat and I smelled it. Strong. Like an aphrodisiac. Then I forgot that he was anything but a dick.

"John, you never say anything when we make love."

"I know. I'm just quiet."

"Well, sometime maybe I'd like to hear you grunt or call my name while you're cumming so I don't think I'm wasting my time."

"Oh yeah. How do you know I won't call somebody else's name?"

From the sound of his moans, I thought he would cum. I didn't want him to ejaculate in my mouth, and not yet. I raised my head. "Wait a minute." I fumbled in my inside coat pocket to find the little GMHC envelope with the condoms and lubricant. "I want you to fuck me. OK?"

"Just turn around."

I pushed my behind at him as he applied the lubricant with two of his fingers. He shoved them into my ass and held them there. Wiggling them.

"You like that shit? Right?"

"Uh hum," I smiled.

"Well, I'm a fuck you lovely. Ah'ight?"

"Yeah! Mmmm!"

He plunged into me immediately. It was all I could do to remain quiet in the tiny booth. It felt like the first time all those years ago when I met a 20-year-old man who said he wanted to "fuck" me, but I somehow heard the word "love."

"I thought you said I had to let you do it? Or else you'd leave?"

"That's right."

"Then why are you leaving me? I thought we were boyfriends."

"We are. Kind of. But virgin ass ain't all it's cracked up to be, Boy. And I can fuck anybody I want. Including you."

"I thought I was yours."

"Shit, we both know you are."

I lost count of the strokes he levelled into me. It was damned sweet. He seemed to be able to hold out forever. But maybe that was because we had to stop every so often to drop another quarter.

"Fuck me, you no-named motherfucker," I thought. "You've got a dick like God!"

"Ah yeah! I'm gonna come."

"Yes. Yes. Do it!" I panted. "Is the condom all right?"

"I guess so. It should be fine. I ain't wearing that shit!"

"Oh no," I muttered. "Oh no!" I could hardly get it above a whisper for a second. I struggled to turn around, but his strong hands held my hips as he buffeted my ass.

"Mmph" he stroked, arching his body to send his dick into me like a wave. The new position sent his trade into a part of me that before then I didn't know existed. It sounded like success. "Oh shit," he said. "Yeah. Who ass is this?"

"Stop! Take it out." I was whispering what should have been screamed. I couldn't raise my voice, though, because it was against the rules to have more than one person in a booth. I wanted it to stop right then, but inside it felt so good. I felt trapped. I may as well have been bound and gagged because it was useless to struggle against something, love it and try to be quiet all at once.

"Why are you driving so fast, John?"

"Because I'm in a hurry."

"But if we crash we won't never get there."

"Yeah, but we won't have to worry about gettin' anywhere else either."

"At least buckle your seatbelt."

"Why? I'm not afraid."

He pulled my torso closer to him, put one arm around my neck and covered my mouth with his other hand as he fucked, humping upwards into me.

"Take this dick," he whispered into my ear like a lover. His tongue caressed my earlobe as he breathed. "It don't matter now, anyway, Guy." He fucked. "This gonna cost you more, by the way. Acting like you ain't know I ain't put that shit on."

I pushed him back against the far wall with a thud, as his head struck the screen. Still he held on – not even missing a stroke. He choked me. "You like it like that, right? That rough shit."

It did feel damn good. But then I knew this fight wasn't about the feeling – it was about the fuck. He forced me forward again into a corner of the booth so that my left eye looked out through the gap between the door and it's frame. I could see people gathering. He kicked my feet outward and rammed even harder. I could hardly breath.

"Ah yeah! Here it cums. Hold on, you motherfuckin cocksucker. Yeah! Yeah!"

I tried to push his hips away, but found my hands sliding on the sweat of his smooth skin.

He squared his feet and pressed my pelvis against the door as he sighed, "Mmmm. Daaamn."

I bit his hand and gasped. Frantic, I finally found the courage to scream, "No!"

"Now how you gonna raise your hand to your mother?" she asked as her hand fell across my face.

"I'm sorry, Mama."

"You ain't sorry yet. Go get me that belt so I can beat your ass!"

He tightened his arm around my neck and punched me in the head with the hand I had bitten. His hips surged forward a few more times. He shivered, then pushed my face against the door, yanking his dick from my ass.

"Ouch," I thought. "Don't you know you never pull your dick out that fast?"

"You gonna pay me my money, Man," he said. "Look at this. I should make you suck this shit off my dick," he added, as he started reaching into his inside coat pocket. Cum was shooting from my penis onto the pants at my ankles while he talked. My heart raced with orgasm and fear. I saw violence in his eyes. As he withdrew his hand,

I heard the click-click of a utility knife. "Now motherfucker, you – "

In a moment of desperation, I kicked him in the groin, pushed him back, and quickly turned to open the door. I tried to run out, but sprawled face down in the aisle because I hadn't thought to pull up my pants. I looked up and just saw faces. Men who'd gathered around because of the commotion they'd heard inside the booth. There were a lot more of them than when I'd gone in. And now there were some real beauties.

Above the clamoring, I heard, "I'ma fuck you up." And I looked up to see my trick walking proudly out, wiping his hands on a kerchief that he threw in my face. "You gotta come out sometime, right?"

"Caught in the parking lot at school with some man! Who the hell is he?"

"I don't know."

"Get the hell out my house. Get out, you faggot! You don't belong around decent people."

"Where am I gonna go, Mama?"

"Straight to hell!"

I tried to pick myself up gracefully. The older men had managed to contain their laughter. The young boys, however, were holding nothing back.

"Get out!" the fat shop attendant yelled. His hair was jerry-curled and turning orange at the edges. "There's only one person per booth. Take yo stupid ass on outta here!"

"Can I fix my clothes first?"

"Fix yo damn clothes at home," he said loudly as he adjusted the waist of his dingy sweatpants, and pulled his T-shirt down to cover his protruding stomach. "This ain't no boutique. Now, let's go."

"Shut the fuck up!" I yelled at him, trembling.

"What? Boy, I'ma call the police. We'll see how – "

"Go ahead. Call. Just leave me alone." The way I was feeling, I just wanted to squeeze my butt cheeks together and pray.

Then from within the small crowd, I heard, "John?"

I kept quiet. Sometimes when I'm in distress I think that simple things like ignoring people will make them think that I'm not really me. That maybe I'm just a look-alike.

"Talk to me, John."

I knew the voice. "Hello," I said. It was my most recent ex-three-month boyfriend, Peter. He was standing there staring at me, trying to pretend that the situation was not peculiar.

"I won't ask what you're doing here, John. I guess I already know."

"Good," I said as I buckled my belt. "And I won't ask you. You know, don't ask don't tell."

He started to sort of tisk and hah, nodding his head as if he was confused.

"You left me for this?" he asked.

"You'll never understand why I left you," I said sharply. "And I'm certainly not going to stand here trying to explain it to you. Shit, did I leave you to this?"

"I don't know," he answered, throwing his hands up. "But, good enough. Have a nice life, John."

"Fuck you," I murmured, angry at so many things, including the fact that I knew I could love this man, if I weren't compelled to drive him away. I felt lubricant and the hustler's cum oozing from my ass. I needed to leave.

"Maybe what they say is true then, John – that some people just don't appreciate what they get for free. And that seems to include love, huh?"

"Whatever," I said slowly, stepping around him to leave. "Maybe I'll call you when I figure it – "

"Didn't I tell you to get your tired black ass outta here!" the attendant burst in. "You must think you special because all o' New York know you got fucked by a ho. Well, you ain't. Upstairs!"

"Yeah right. You'll call me." Peter dismissed me with a frown. He almost had to yell to be heard above the screaming attendant, whose loud voice was his only real weapon. Hoping to embarrass people enough to make them scatter. "Don't bother. I'm not about to wait on you. And I don't need to." He hesitated, then said, as if in triumph, "I'm gonna go watch a movie."

"Get out before I put you out!" the attendant rushed closer. "You ought to go douche if you know what's good for you. And you," he turned to Peter, "if you ain't spending no quarters you can take a hike, too. Port Authority is across the street. Don't no buses come here."

"Don't do anything I wouldn't do," I said to Peter.

"You're sick, John."

"I know," I said loudly, as I turned away from him. "Even I can see that. And I'm out of quarters."

"Get into that closet! Tryin' to kill yourself again in my house. After I let you back in here."

"No, mama!" I screamed, wishing she hadn't grabbed the knife from me. As she slammed the closet door shut, I heard the mirror on the door crack. "Don't leave me in here!"

"This ain't your life to take, Boy."

"Then you take it, mama. I don't want it," I cried in the dark.

"I love you, but you wrong. And always been wrong. You ain't gonna die no time soon, you damned sissy. God'll keep you alive — to punish you."

I picked my cum-stained coat up from the floor of the booth and left. Looking at my reflection in the mirrors on the walls of the stairs. I wanted to go home, though I knew my young stud was waiting outside.

"Where's my money, Man?" he asked threateningly.

I smiled. "Here," I said. I gave him 35 dollars and my telephone number.

"Yeaah," he crooned. "You musta really like the jimmy, huh?" He covered his mouth with one hand and cupped his crotch with the other as he laughed. "Yeah, buddy." He came closer and put his arm around over my shoulders. "So you want some more of my shit?"

"Yes," I said, looking him directly in the eyes. Our lips a breath apart. I noticed immediately that his eyes held no guilt. No shame at the cum and God knows what else he left in my ass. Making my underpants slippery in my crack, and causing me to be cautious of passing gas. I hardly wanted to admit it to myself, but my eyes couldn't have been holding any guilt at that moment either. Bryan and Peter had become distant thoughts when I came face to face with the truth again. This B-O-Y. Somehow this young hustler had known exactly what I'd wanted: finally to be taken advantage of by someone who hadn't hinted otherwise. Not to be loved: to be fucked. I liked him and hated him, but told him to call me anyway, excited about what he might do with that dick and his concealed box-cutter in my house. Knives my mother no longer had the strength to take away.

As I walked along 42nd Street, past the porno theatres, I remembered slowly emerging from my mother's closet that night with every intention of running away. But as I closed the door, my own reflection in the shattered mirror frightened me. I stood before myself broken, segmented and afraid. I'd heard that reflections didn't lie. So I went back inside and waited for my mother to let me out. She never came.

"I know you ain't out that closet!"

"Uh uh," I yelled.

"I tell you what: You'll stay in there if you know what good for you."

"I know, Mama. I know."

SEX IN THE SEVENTIES; OR FADE TO BLANK

Michael Denneny

ONE MORNING WHILE Mingus was stumbling around in the dark trying to get ready for work, the current ex-lover stirred and said, "I want to watch *Nightcrawler* with you tonight. I want to see what you think of it."

"The one that's subtitled 'A Leather Sex Fantasy'?"

"Well, it sure isn't that. Not really. It's about sex in the seventies."

"Oh, good. A historical film. Put a pillow over your head, I've got to turn the light on to find my shoes," said Mingus. "OK with me. But I'm going to the gym and then stopping by the hospital to see Tink, so I'll be home late. See you tonight."

So, after a surprisingly good dinner prepared by the current ex – Mingus is still surprised because eight years ago the lad didn't know how to boil water for tea and once Mingus found him eating cold ravioli straight from the can – *Nightcrawler* was put on the VCR.

The film opens with the camera panning along parked cars at night, lots of blue light and noisy crickets giving atmosphere, until we see a guy in a black leather jacket with a day's growth of dark stubble getting a blow job from a boy kneeling in front of him. Total silence except for the crickets.

"This sequence is very real. It brings back memories for me," commented the current ex as the camera plays with the scene. "Does this guy have a big cock, or no? It's hard to tell with these camera angles."

"That's the point. But how can he make those sounds with his mouth full of cock?" wondered Mingus as the kid cums and then black leather shoots his wad onto the ground.

Suddenly a security officer is playing his flashlight over the cars, demanding to know who's out there, and it's time for pulling up pants and running through the car lot. The chase and escape is an unusually nice piece of film editing for a porno flick and when Pierce Daniels, the hero of this epic, jumps over a fence and reaches safety, a satisfied, sexy, cat-like smile slips over his face. This man really does look like an alley cat, a randy Tom who prowls the by-ways of the night.

"Now it gets tacky," predicted the current ex as the film cuts to a smoke-filled gay bar where one Cassandra, who evidently thinks she's in *Cabaret*, is doing a strip on a small stage.

"Can you imagine a bar having a transvestite strip like that?" demanded our boy.

"Sure," Mingus said. "I used to see things like that all the time at the G.G. Knickerbocker. Of course, that was ten or twelve years ago. It was nice. You would have liked it. The G.G. sort of worked like a clubhouse for the TV's and hustler boys working 42nd street. A bit bizarre, but real friendly. Of course, then it got famous, Andy Warhol started coming and it all went to hell, especially after they opened the Barnum Room."

"God, how tired!" complains an aging queen at one of the small tables. "Where is Jock, anyway?"

"Downtown, at the trucks, or the piers," answers his companion.

"That's dangerous! Why doesn't he grow up? And why's he always late?"

"You know Jock. Wherever the action is, that's where he is."

"Oh, please. He's just a faggot like the rest of us."

"Jock's no faggot, and he's certainly not like the rest of us," replies his companion as Jock walks in and apologizes for being late. Sitting down, Jock (Pierce Daniels) catches the eye of a sexy guy in the corner (J.D. Slater) who nods toward the back door, but Jock just smiles and turns to his companions.

"Honestly, Jock," says the querrulous queen, "you're not getting any younger. Don't you think it's time you did something serious with your life?"

"Like you have?" Jock asks as he catches the eye of young Chris Thompson, who is walking to the door. Laughing, Jock rises and follows Chris out into the street and then into an alley, not noticing when J.D. Slater also rises and follows them both.

"I didn't like that bar scene," said the current ex. "The friends were bitchy and that was just motivated by jealousy. No brotherhood there."

Looking back over his shoulder, Chris weaves his way to the back of the parking lot, uses a pocket knife to jimmy open a car door, and is sprawled on the back seat, pants down, cock out, licking his lips, when Jock comes up to the car. Jock goes in, closes the door and slides his mouth over Chris's cock. Chris slips off the black leather jacket while Jock is sucking his nipples, then kissing him, as Slater lurks outside watching them and rubbing his crotch.

"That's awfully hot," said the current ex, as Chris opens Jock's pants while sucking on his nipples.

"That car has the biggest backseat I've ever seen," said Mingus. "They ought to do car commercials like that."

"Maybe it's a limo," suggested the current ex distractedly as J.D. Slater pulls his cock and balls out of his pants, showing us he's wearing *four* steel cock rings.

As Chris gets himself up over Jock, the better to fuck his face, Mingus was amazed, "There's more room in this car than you would believe."

"What are you, Consumer Reports? This film is about sex, not cars."

Chris comes over Jock's face, Jock comes all over himself and J.D. Slater comes – spectacularly – over the ground, emitting a loud grunt that nobody notices while slapping his ass and spitting a large wad – a disgusting but oddly sexy gesture.

As our Jock walks back through the parking lot and down an alley, Slater follows him – a creepy scene done well by someone who has learned something from Hitchcock. Suddenly Jock jumps out and grabs Slater around the neck from behind: "All right, what do you want?"

"It's a gift, boy, a gift," says a struggling Slater who manages to pull a card out of his breast pocket and runs away when Jock takes it. "Paradise" reads the card, "Private".

"That's a private sex club he goes to later," offered the current ex helpfully.

But this night Jock just goes home. Home is a tacky, temporary room which is a mess, cheap furniture and imitation wood panelling covered with porno pics and, leaning against the wall, the kind of "full length" mirror you buy at Walgreens for 12 dollars. Jock takes a beer out of the fridge, shucks his jacket (he wears no shirt underneath) and starts massaging his basket while looking at a magazine which features Tom of Finland. When the phone rings he drops the magazine and flops onto the bed, murmuring into the receiver while working his cock.

"You want to hear it? I'll let you hear it," he says and holds the receiver close as he spits into his hand and starts working his cock and balls, occasionally slapping his cock against the phone.

"This is weird," said Mingus.

"No it's not," replied our boy.

"What could you hear?"

"If you do it loud enough you can hear it. On the other hand," he added, "it *is* a bit like putting a dog on the phone. 'C'mon, Fido, bark!'"

Going over to the mirror, Jock puts the phone on the floor and continues to jerk off while watching himself. Some clever camera angles distort what is already a big cock until it looks huge; very effective camera work.

"*That* wouldn't work, however; the phone's too far away, even if you were loud and sloppy. There are so many things you could do with hot phone sex, but they're not into hot talk in this film really. I'd have hung up by now, wouldn't you?" the boy asked as Mingus looked at him hard.

Just then Jock comes on the mirror, some of it splattering onto the receiver on the floor. After smearing his cum around the mirror with his cock, Jock picks up the phone and says, "Hey, talk to you later, OK? Bye."

"*Talk* to you later? There are some things that pass my understanding." Mingus commented.

"You said it, I didn't."

Mingus was about to reply, but Jock is holding up his Paradise card to a peephole. After the door is buzzed open, he walks into total darkness, a spot shining on him as he comes to a halt. Three naked guys surround him, two on their knees, taking off his clothes and adoring his body.

"For the first time in this film, he's got a shirt on under the leather jacket," commented the current ex. "That's funny; he's going to this sex palace and he wears a shirt."

"Formal wear on the west coast," offered Mingus. "This is obviously supposed to be the ultimate bathhouse. Funny, it reminds me of the first time I took Tink and Johnnie to the Continental Baths in the early seventies. You know Johnnie, you've met him at the hospital. He and Tink have been boyhood buddies since they were both three, I think."

"By the way, how was Tink tonight?" asked the current ex.

"He was sleeping when I got there, so I just read for an hour or so. Then he woke up and I fed him some of the protein shake you brought him this morning. Then he fell asleep again. He looks so young when he's sleeping, like a little boy. He and Johnnie were so adorable when they were teenagers. They'd never been to a bathhouse before and they begged me to take them, but they were very nervous. I walked them to the door and made them go in alone. But I waited outside smoking a cigarette and, sure enough, fifteen minutes later they tried to sneak out, thinking I'd left. So I marched them right back in. Later on, they came by my house to tell me their adventures. They'd had a wonderful time. Babes in Toyland. They told me they'd met this nice older guy who invited them to come out to his house in The Pines the following weekend. But they had no intention of going. I think they were afraid they were going to be kidnapped into white slavery or something," Mingus said smiling.

"How old was this older guy?" asked the current ex.

"Oh, thirty-two or so; your age," Mingus answered laughing. "I asked too."

Having removed Jock's clothing, one of the ephebes slips a

cockring on our Jock, and all three disappear into the darkness as another door buzzes open. Jock walks naked into a long hallway, loud echoing sex noises coming from the cubicles that line either side.

Looking into one of the rooms, Jock sees a Paul Bunyan clone, naked except for socks and boots, sprawled in a chair watching himself jerk off in the three mirrors that surround him just as if he was trying on a suit at Brooks Brothers. They both (or rather, all four) jerk off *at* each other for a while, then Jock walks on.

Next he sees a naked guy in a cubicle, facing away from the door and squatting down, with an enormous dildo up his ass. Slowing standing up, he works the dildo in and out, half squatting again to get maximum leverage, for all the world reminding Mingus of a demented spider.

"That's Chris Burns, I think," offered the current ex. "That's his specialty. It really looks weird. Why don't they show his face?"

"It looks even weirder reflected in the window," said Mingus, pointing across the room. "Its downright bizarre superimposed on the buildings across the street. Looks sexier, actually."

Chris Burns cums and Jock walks on down the corridor, pausing and then entering a room where there is a small orgy going on: one guy is laying on his back getting fucked up the ass and down the throat while another guy stands behind him jerking off.

"The young guy getting fucked is Michael Cummings, I think. And Chris Thompson is fucking his mouth," said the current ex. "Don't know who the third one is."

"You're a regular tour guide tonight," commented Mingus.

This is a very hot scene, in its way a vision of the perfect seventies sex – with all its shortcomings: while everyone is goodlooking and hot, they all somehow look the same and there is no erotic psychology to distinguish one from the other. These guys are clones, although they're certainly sexy clones. It made Mingus reconsider the much decried impersonal sex of the seventies; somehow there's just no room for personalities here. This is generic sex; like the generic food section in the supermarket, names have been stripped away and you're left with the basic stuff. In the market it's cheaper; in the seventies, generic sex was cheaper too – it cost less time, less trouble, less involvement of the self. And was it just as nourishing? Mingus wondered as the kid cums on his belly and then everyone else cums on him, the last being Jock who sprays his seed on the kid's chest and neck, bringing a warm grin of satisfaction and triumph to the kid's face as he fondles Jock's cock and balls lovingly.

Soon Jock is back prowling the halls, weaving his way through the moans and groans of sex until his attention is stopped at a new door. Looking in, he sees one guy wearing black leather studded straps and black boots, sitting on what looks like a modified toilet seat, under which a guy is licking his ass and balls.

"Is that a contraption for eating shit? I've never seen such a thing," said Mingus.

"Yeah, it's supposed to be, I think. Chris Thompson is on top. I can't quite see him as a top."

"He has a pretty face."

"Yeah, but he's not what I'd consider a top. They're sort of confused about that stuff in this film."

In any event, the spectacle gets Jock excited and he's working his cock with pleasure when first Chris Thompson comes over the kid's chest and then the kid gets off.

Now the film cuts to cars driving down a dark street. Jock drives up to "Paradise", flashes his card and is buzzed in; Jock walks the halls assailed on every side by moaning, groaning, and shouting; Jock back home; Jock walking the corridors again; Jock enters a room with a stool and two gloryholes, big dicks pushing through them; he squats on the stool sucking first one then the other till both come all over him and he wipes their cum across his chest and leaves.

Meanwhile back in the gay bar, where Cassandra is still bumping and grinding, Jock's friends are nattering away, but the camera focuses on a new kid drinking a glass of beer sloppily. The camera comes in for a close-up as he puts down the empty glass; along comes a crotch, hands pull out a cock, and the glass is filled with piss as the kid smiles. If this is supposed to be Jock, he is clearly beyond the activities of your usual gay bar.

Suddenly we're back in the corridor with Jock who looks in

on a kid in a sling, a remarkably large dildo being shoved up his ass, much bigger than your average muscular forearm. Another guy in a black leather hood is oiling up his forearm – sure to be disappointing, Mingus fretted – as Jock watches and jerks off.

Back in the gay bar, Jock's friends are talking dispiritedly.

"I don't know what we saw in this place."

"Jock came here and any place Jock was was exciting."

"You haven't seen him here lately, though, have you? It all goes flat like the wine," complains the bitchy one. "This fucking cheap wine."

"How 'bout Jock? How does this story end?" asks the other guy, as the film cuts to Jock getting a blowjob in a toilet, then prowling the hallways, then we see two guys pushing their cocks into Jock's mouth, then a flashback to the empty table at the gay bar, then back to an orgy scene in "Paradise" where another hunk (Melchor) is getting his ass plugged by the piss-guzzling boy from the gay bar.

"You know, this is really hot fucking, but they don't show enough of the faces." complained the current ex. "A longer view would be a lot sexier."

All the while Melchor is lying on his back getting fucked while also sucking Jock's cock as Jock holds Melchor's legs together, and it's a tribute to this very sexy man that, even while he reminds you of a turkey getting trussed, the scene is *still* hot. Soon Melchor rolls over onto all fours and Jock fucks him hard and fast while Melchor takes another cock down his throat; then Melchor lifts up, Jock's cock still in him, and sprays cum over the black shag rug as the rest of the gang jerks of onto his body and Jock cums on his ass. Quick cut to the kid with the dildo cumming, the Paul Bunyan clone cumming, the guy in the sling cumming; faster and faster they gallop through every cum shot in the movie, the visual equivalent of the climax of Tchaikovsky's *1812 Overture*.

"Is this supposed to be the answer to how Jock's story ends?" asked the current ex, dubiously.

"No, I think there's more," said Mingus, and we're back again in the gay bar, Cassandra still bumping and grinding away. Could she be trying to tell us something about the imminent fate of Troy?

"Don't be silly," scoffed the current ex, "they don't get that literary in porn flicks."

Jock, sitting alone, glowers at a young boy, then gets up, goes over and gives the kid the card, walks away, turns and looks one last time and walks out into a dark street.

"That's it?" cried Mingus. "What was the *point* of this film? That he passed the card on to a new, younger guy?"

"I don't think they were particularly trying to make a point," said Mingus' current ex-lover, "I mean, it *makes* a point, but I don't think it was intentional. But what I particularly didn't like was that bar scene, how bitchy the friends were. You know, yesterday was a breezy day and I was in the Village just walking around and I went past the Ninth Circle and Julius' and I remembered when I used to hang out in those bars, and I remember the sex and the friendships, and it wasn't like that. In the movie those friendships were vicious and yucky, sour grapes basically, like the reactions of some people to Fire Island or pretty boys. And those are the only friends you see him with, period. I thought it was pretty heavy-handed in showing his life was only sex. A very moralistic, anti-sex movie."

"OK, OK, but I still don't get the point, the *unintentional* point of this movie." Mingus complained.

"Passing on the card to Paradise," the lad said, "Like your generation passed sex on to my generation. I mean, every 14 years is like a generational change."

"You're not 14 years younger. Don't exaggerate."

"OK, 13. But I think that's what it was all about, passing on the key to Eros," said the current ex-lover as the final credits came to rest with the standard disclaimer, not often seen in porn films, that "any similarity to persons living or dead is purely coincidental."

For once Mingus was completely silent and he stared at the blank television screen, as the tape expired and white nose filled the room.

THE BARRACKS

Stan Persky

IN THE SAN DIEGO US Navy boot camp barracks one night shortly after "lights out," one of the four of us (not me) suggested that we jack-off to see if the chemical (saltpetre) that was allegedly put into our food to reduce our sexual urges really worked.

We happened to be billeted at the end of the barracks, afforded some privacy by a wall of lockers, in two double-bunk beds, slim Donnie from New Mexico above me, and in the next double-bunk over, beefy Bruehl from Arizona on top, and in the lower bunk, a boy from somewhere in the South, curiously named Richard Richards. Although he tried to get us to pronounce his surname "Reichart," we simply dropped the "s" on his last name, and subjected him to the accusation that his hillbilly parents were so dumb that they couldn't think up another first name for him. "Richard, on the double!" the company commander or drill sergeant would call out. "That's Reichart, sir," he would plead, in a doomed effort at correction.

Name-play was crucial in the ongoing daily struggle over the barracks pecking order. I was relatively inept at accomplishing the tasks that constituted our training, and yet, the distinctions made were fine-grained enough that I was nonetheless considered a real, if mediocre, guy, and spared the contempt of being consigned to the category of the lowest-of-the-low, occupied by a whiny, uncharmingly awkward kid named Gorney – who was instantly dubbed "Horny Gorney" – and who was eventually actually dumped, head-first, into the metal barracks garbage can. Whereas I, for all my failings (unable to swim, not very good with guns, etc.), managed to elicit the sympathetic attention of one of the barracks' tough guys, a kid named Harsh, also from Arizona, who invited me one day to do some practice wrestling with him, thus publicly demonstrating that I wasn't to be considered a complete wimp.

The companies were assembled in random fashion, on the basis of the coincidental arrival of busloads of recruits from various parts of the country. We were a group of midwesterners, bussed out to the Coast from the Great Lakes Naval Training Station near Chicago; a gangly, giraffe-like, but prematurely sober guy from Milwaukee named Brinkhoff was named our recruit company commander, a position he retained once the whole company was put together. (I remember him offering me some "buck-up, kid" fatherly consolation once when I was feeling homesick.) We arrived in the middle of the night, were issued blankets and some other gear, and bundled off to the barracks.

The next morning, on the "grinder" – a vast, asphalt-paved, sun fried marching area in the centre of the San Diego boot camp – we sleepily met our company-mates, a group of boys from the American Southwest, mainly Arizona, and were marched off in raggedy order to the messhall. I'm not sure how Richards (or Reichart) got to be with us; maybe he was from Tennessee or Kentucky and got lumped in with the Midwesterners.

In the semi-darkness, perhaps illuminated by some stray moonlight pouring in from a nearby window, we reached into our underwear (there was a Navy word for them, what was it? – now I remember: "skivvies"!) or maybe pulled our skivvies down to mid-thigh, and began to masturbate. Although it didn't occur to me at the time, the proposal (whoever made it) had the function of alleviating our embarrassment about the problem of secretly jacking off. To the sounds of the gentle ship-like creaking of the metal double-bunks and our own increasingly excited breathing, we entered eternity. I came easily.

Then there occurred the moment that further changed my life forever. While Bruehl and Donnie were privately occupied above, Reichart – though we refused to call him that, as he wanted, I always *thought* of him as Reichart – whispered to me from his bunk. In memory, our bunks are shoved closer together – only inches apart – than they could have been in actuality. I can't remember his precise words, though from time to time, I'm still able to see him in memory, not so much beautiful as sexy, freckles across the bridge of his snub nose, skinny hips. It went something like, "Hey, I can only get it up half-way," and then he asked me to help him, to jack him off a little with my own hand. I refused. "Aw, come on," he said, in his sly, cajoling, half-promising, persuasive way that no one in their right mind could refuse.

Or at least I couldn't. I reached out from my bunk to his. His hand took mine and placed it around his velvety, but hard cock. I remember feeling, just before being overwhelmed by other emotions, an instant of confusion – he had claimed to be only semi-erect, but his cock in fact felt pretty hard to me – innocently unaware that his small fib was in service to his seduction of me.

Guiding my hand with his own, Reichart moved it up and down the sheath of his foreskin, instructing me in the motion he liked, hoping that once I learned the movement I would continue it on my own. I was in ecstasy, terrified ecstasy, ecstatic terror. But instead of continuing to masturbate him, I withdrew my hand. He tried to coax me. I wasn't to be persuaded.

He would have his revenge the next day, saying to the guys at our table in the messhall – to Bruehl and Donnie immediately, but others were also within hearing, "Hey, you know what Pussy did to me last night when we were jacking off? He played with my dick," thus, not only confirming my lowly status, but raising the prospect that I was also a "fruit." Naturally, I furiously, but carefully – not wanting to excite further suspicion by protesting too much – denied Reichart's charge.

Meanwhile, above us, in their respective bunks, oblivious to the whispered drama below, Bruehl and Donnie carried on. Shortly after I'd come, Donnie triumphantly declared, "I came!" He was a teenager with fine, delicately shaped facial features, almost feminine in his beauty, and had, by way of self-protection I suppose, developed a slightly nasty, pugnacious edge to his personality. "I don't believe you, you're shitting us," Bruehl said. "Here," Donnie replied to the challenge, stretching out his cupped hand containing his cum in the direction of Bruehl's nose. Bruehl took a whiff. "Pee-uuu!" Bruehl reported, confirming Donnie's success. At which point, memory breaks down, dissolves, but that's not at all the end.

What if I hadn't refused Reichart? What if I'd continued, on my own, to slide his foreskin up and down the column of his dick? What if I'd brought him off, his cum running over my hand as he unclenched his thigh muscles and sighed in contentment, would he have then told the others at "chow" the next morning? Or would he have kept it a secret, using the secret to get me to do it again (and again), whenever he wanted? Would he have kept me for himself?

I had another scenario, which preserved the original scene. Reichart tells the others, and they begin mildly teasing me. I get him aside, and urgently appeal to him, "You've gotta stop telling them I touched your dick, you're going to get me in trouble." As he smiles that lazy smile of his, I make my proposal: "Look, if you tell them you were just kidding, I'll jack you off." He knows he has me, but sizes me up with his shrewd, narrowed, farmboy eyes. "How do I know you will?" I look around hastily, see that there's no one to see us and, taking a chance, grab his dick through his denim workpants ("dungarees," they were called), and then rub and fondle it just long enough to convince him. "You better not chicken out," he warns me.

But he promptly brings off his end of the bargain. We're at lunch in the messhall, and one of the other guys, maybe Bruehl, is ribbing me. "Pussy, did you really play with Richard's dick? Did you?" At which point, just as it's about to get nasty, Reichart intervenes, in a slow half-drawl, "Boy, you-all sure are hicks. You didn't believe all that stuff, did you?" And now the spotlight shifts to Reichart, chuckling and ducking his head as Bruehl tries to whack him with his sailor's boater. "You dumb shithead!" Bruehl grumbles, as Reichart sends me a telling glance.

That night, Reichart's on guard duty, and I make my way out of the barracks to the little shack outside of which he's standing watch, passing through the concrete area where we do our wash, and where clotheslines are strung up, on which we hang our sheets and cambray shirts and dungarees. In the night, the whites move slightly in the breeze, like sails, strangely glowing. "It's me," I say, before he ritually asks, "Who goes there?" "Hey," he says, pretending to be a little pleasantly surprised. "I said I would, didn't I?" I say, mock-offended that he might've doubted my word.

Inside the dark shack – we know when the patrols come by to check that the watch isn't asleep, so we're safe for time – I unfasten the buckle of his Navy-issue cloth belt, undo his fly, and take his skivvy-covered cock in my hand, then reach into his underpants, and hold it directly, intentionally, consciously, impressed by the heat of its flesh. His body involuntarily leans against, into mine, and I put an arm around his waist as I jack him off.

There's an elaboration of my fantasy of his seduction of me. His dungarees and skivvies are down around his ankles, and as I lean over, my shoulder against his flat belly, jacking him off with my hand, Reichart suggests, gently touching the back of my neck, "Why don't you put it in your mouth?" "No," I refuse. "Aw come on, just a little. You know you wanna," he drawls. It's the last sentence – "You know you wanna" – his making explicit his knowing of my knowing, that's the clincher.

Now, I make my counter-offer: "I will if you'll jack me off." "Sure," he agrees, increasing the pressure on the back of my neck. "How do I know you will?" I ask, lifting my head up to look into his blue eyes. "What if I do it and you just go and tell the others I sucked you off?" Without hesitation, he reaches into my pants, takes hold of my already hard cock and jacks me off enough to prove to me that if he said anything to the others about what we're doing, I'd be able to tell on him, too. "Just put it in your mouth," he urges, continuing to hold my cock, and returning his other hand to the back of my neck. I slowly bend my head toward his erection, looking at it with awe as my lips get closer to its tip.

This fantasy operation proceeds in stages. Now he's playing

with my butt, wants to fuck me, offers to suck my dick if I let him, etc.

Reichart knows everything about sex; we urban kids were astonished to learn that Southern farmboys regularly fucked barnyard animals; they casually assured us that fucking a cow's ass or a lanolin-smooth sheep's vagina was "the next best thing." When our marching instructors ordered us to close our ranks to "cornhole distance," they knew all about shoving corncobs up asses. Apparently that was a favoured farm product for anal stimulation – in fact, I once saw an ear of corn so used in a porno flick about French rural life. Eventually, "cornholing" became a general term referring to anal intercourse. And in assembly and marching terminology, "cornhole distance" jokingly meant close enough to fuck the guy in front of you.

In one version, in which Reichart now has me trained, and admitting that I like it, he turns up one night with Donnie in tow, generously prepared to share me with his mates.

In this masturbatory scenario played over so many times, persistant for so long, fantasy has come to seem almost indistinguishable from memory; the importance of distinguishing the two seems increasingly less important. Though I have a memory, I've little sense of it being a memory of myself. If Reichart, Breuhl and Donnie are still alive (now men in late middle-age – married, divorced, fathers, failures, successes), they've most likely completely forgotten that trivial, boyish, incident. I once imagined or dreamed about Reichart in his late twenties, living in a trailer park with his wife and a kid, maybe talking up the waitress at the coffee shop in town where his work crew take their breaks.

Though the boy I was, aflame with desire, seems like someone else, nonetheless, his desire continues to influence me at this remove, shapes my pleasures, my sorrows. I think, So, that's what I'm left with; and more important, That's what I've been given; that's what I've got.

GHOSTS

Paul Russell

THEY SAT IN an uncrowded First Avenue bar, their fourth or fifth in a chilly October evening of exuberant wandering, and watched, during the occasional lapse in their conversation, two short-haired young men play a game of pool. Dressed identically – jeans, black boots, gold rings in both ears – the two players could have been brothers, even twins, though the way they touched each other suggested they were lovers.

For some moments Tracy gazed their way in wistful contemplation. To be back in New York was to feel haunted. Though he had been away only two months, teaching upstate at the Rifton School for Boys, the city he had loved and perhaps inexplicably fled and now returned to for a weekend visit seemed strangely unreal compared to the brave new life he had elected for himself in Middle Forge, that town of quiet desperation some miles up the Hudson. Turning his attention back to his friend Tracy said, "Basically I'm staying one step ahead. I teach all day, then rush home and try to figure out what to do tomorrow. It's exciting, I guess, but exhausting."

Devin Shimaburo toyed with the cigarette he'd extracted from the Marlboro pack that lay between them on the table. "You can't fake it?" he asked.

"They're smarter than you think," Tracy said. "They give me a run for my money. But they're fun that way."

"Want one?" Devin offered the cigarette.

"Why not? I've been living like a saint. It's driving me off the deep end."

"I'm sure you love it," Devin said. "You always had saintly tendencies."

"Get out." Tracy slapped playfully at him from across the table, into which countless patrons had carved their names, frustrations and longings.

"Which I personally have tried to encourage," Devin went on. Flicking his lighter, he held it out. Tracy leaned over to touch the flame with the tip of his cigarette. Devin drew another one out of the packet for himself.

Tracy had always been crazy about the way Devin handled his cigarettes. If he could manage cigarettes half that well, he'd smoke all the time too.

Tilting back his head, Devin blew a plume of smoke from his thin lips.

"You're watching me," he said.

"I know. I can't help it."

Devin half shut his eyelids and smiled at him langorously. His father was courtly Japanese, his mother a fierce Jew from Chicago. The mix had spawned an extraordinary beauty. At twenty-five he was boyish and aloof. An edge of wear was just beginning to show itself in the fineness of his features. He took up his empty glass and turned it forlornly upside down. One or two drops fell into the ashtray. He made his mouth into a theatrical pout. "Another beer?" he wondered.

"You do encourage me, don't you? My head's practically spinning. I'm out of the habit. I'm going to have a splitting hangover tomorrow."

"That's what bloody Mary's are for."

"You," Tracy chastised him fondly.

One of the pool players had moved near them to prepare a shot. He checked over his shoulder to make sure his cue would clear them. Tracy gave himself over to a momentary study the young man's denim-sheathed buttocks. Did his companion fuck him? He found himself picturing it: the young man bent over the pool table, cheeks spread, pink, puckered hole ready to receive his partner, the one pumping away inside the other with brilliant abandon. Desire flickered in him, thirsty and dry. The player tensed and shot, his buttocks clenching in sympathetic spasm. The ball ricocheted against others with a succession of sharp, satisfying clicks.

"I am *such* a bad shot," he sighed. Resting his hand on his partner's shoulder, he leaned a close-cropped head into the other's neck, and Tracy felt in himself such an uncomplicated outflowing of goodwill towards these lovers or brothers or both that his sudden, inexplicable proximity to tears startled him.

When he looked back at Devin, his friend was watching him curiously. Tracy rummaged in his memory to recognize that stare.

"What?" he said quizzically.

Devin continued to stare at him. His voice was casual and matter-of-fact. He might have been saying anything in that tone of voice, but the dreamy look that stole over his features betrayed him. What he was saying was, "Let's go home and have sex."

"I'm enjoying being out like this," Tracy told him. "Let's have another beer. Then we can go home."

Devin's smile showed his acceptance of that. He stretched his legs out under the table and rested them on the seat of Tracy's booth. He wore pointed Italian shoes so fashionable they were practically ugly.

Tracy didn't resist the invitation. Reaching out his hand, he stroked Devin's thin ankles through his socks. Ankles could excite him. He shook from himself a sudden torpor of desire.

"I have to go piss," he said. "You order."

In the bathroom, the urinal was occupied and the stall also. The man at the urinal seemed not to have relieved himself in a week, his stream was so copious and unending. A photo collage of men so young they were scarcely out of adolescence adorned the walls. They were all naked, all smiling as broadly as toothpaste advertisements, they all had erections some bit of trick photography had doubled or tripled in size. The effect, more comic than arousing, was finally, Tracy decided, more depressing than comic. With some relief he turned his attention to the condom dispenser whose bulk on the wall hid at least some of that relentless display. He fished in his pockets for change.

"That's the idea," said the man of the endless bladder as he zipped and moved over to the washbasin. "Have fun. Play safe. Getting lucky tonight?"

Tracy pocketed the condom and positioned himself in front of the urinal. "I'm visiting an old friend," he said as he extricated his penis from his jeans.

The man considered him frankly. "You wouldn't want to liven things up, would you?"

Once upon a time he'd obviously been quite handsome. Now, stranded in his middle forties, some bright urgency in his gaze betrayed the desperation with which he sought to hold back the ticking clock.

Tracy was almost apologetic. People fell for him. His smile won them over, his brown eyes. He'd never gotten by on that, but it was something he carried with him. And he was still young. He had no doubt how much that counted for. "I haven't seen this friend in a while," he explained. But in spite of himself he felt the unsought stirrings of an erection; his piss came in fitful spurts.

"Old times' night," the man said. "I understand."

He took a slip of paper from his wallet and wrote out a phone number. "You never know," he sighed, and boldly slid the folded paper into Tracy's shirt pocket. "You have, by the way, a very beautiful cock there," he mentioned as he walked away.

From the stall, still-occupied as it turned out, came a snort of laughter.

Disconcerted, Tracy zipped up and returned to the booth without washing his hands. Devin had ordered not only beer but shots of whisky as well. "I'm still celebrating your return to the *cité radieuse*," he explained. He held Tracy's hand in his and stroked it fondly. "You've been away from us down here far too long, lamb chop."

"Who'd have thought I'd end up in exile?" Tracy told him. "I guess it's my own damn fault."

"Upstate," Devin sighed. "I hear there're a lot of prisons upstate."

"Prisons and prep schools."

"Youth must be educated," Devin said. "One way or another. No one said it would be easy, or that the cost would not be great. Some might even consider you a hero, slaving away to make the future safe for . . ." – he paused and threw up his hands – "well, for whomever."

"Safe for the rich," Tracy told him disgustedly. "I'm working my butt off so some super-privileged spoiled brats can get into college and not fuck up their lives too much. The Headmaster was quite frank about that when I first took the job. We're making sure the little darlings don't embarrass themselves too much when they step into Daddy's business, which is probably some corporation that ruins third world countries with the stroke of a pen. Only he didn't quite put it that way."

He was surprised to hear himself sounding so sour. He'd perhaps been talking too much to Reid Fallone, whose mordant epithets for his students were legion and, in their way, contagious.

"Face it," Devin told him, "Everything's a compromise. We all do it. You think the fashion industry's a vision of socialist utopia? Rich people all over again. They control the world and there's nothing you or I can do about it."

"Let's don't talk politics," Tracy said. He took up the shot glass and downed his whisky in a stinging swallow. "I'll get too depressed. And actually – some of the kids at Rifton aren't too bad."

"Here's to ignoring reality." Devin raised his own glass. "Or at least softening the edges. And to the boys of Rifton, at least the ones who aren't too bad. So tell me – any cuties in your classes? Hot little numbers itching for the teacher to bring them out?"

"Please," Tracy prodded Devin's ankle. "Don't be prurient."

"I'm always prurient," Devin told him. "But I can afford to be. I don't teach them. To me they're just tight little theoretical bodies to be drooled over from afar."

"Yeah, tell me about it," Tracy said. "They're just kids."

"Be honest," Devin cajoled him. "Don't you find there's something really attractive and, well, *moving* about a 15-year-old boy?"

"Let's not continue this little discussion," Tracy said.

"But I think I'm onto something."

"You wish."

"I don't know," Devin teased. "I can imagine things getting to be very difficult."

"I think," Tracy told him, "you let your fantasies get a little out of hand. Teaching isn't what you think it is. Anyway, let's get off this subject." He reached in his pocket and took out the condom. "See what I got?"

"*Pour moi?*"

He laid it on the table between them.

"*Pour* whoever."

"Only one?"

"You're incorrigible," Tracy told him. He took up the foil pack and replaced it in his shirt pocket. "It's the thought that counts. I'm depending on you to be well stocked. Now let's go home."

Out in the streets, a fine chill rain had begun to fall. "I'm so happy to be here," he had to exclaim. He took Devin's arm as they walked west toward the apartment. "It's just so stultifying up there. Everybody's so straight, they all have wives and kids. Can I tell you? I actually got so desperate I went to a meeting of the county's gay and lesbian group. Sort of a support group with volleyball games and square dancing on the side. It was in the basement of a church. So depressing. There wasn't anybody in the room I'd touch with a ten foot pole. They all looked so lumpy and depressed, and such bad haircuts. It's from living upstate. It does something to you."

"Get out while there's still time, girl," Devin said. "I didn't want to mention your haircut. I didn't want to hurt your feelings."

Devin's apartment was above an Afghan restaurant. Pungent aromas of cumin and lamb and eggplant pervaded his rooms. His roommate Frank was out for the evening.

"My *selfish* roommate," Devin said. "You'll get a kick out of this. The other night I'm lying in bed jerking off before I go to sleep, and I can hear that Frank's jerking off too. So I say, 'Hey Frank, why don't you just come in here and fuck me while you're at it?' And you know what he says? 'I need to spend some quality time alone.' And it's not like he was making a joke."

"Frank's sweet," Tracy thought he should say, though he agreed: Frank tended to be depressingly earnest. He wondered if he too could seem like that at times.

"He *is* sweet," Devin affirmed. "And look: he left us flowers. He's such a homosexual."

Frank had arranged a gather of lemony gladiolas in a vase on the coffee table.

"Well," Tracy had to observe. "I feel very welcomed."

"Though the place is just a mess," Devin apologized. In a manic burst of energy he moved about the room straightening the pillows on the sofa, the magazines on the coffee table. He took off his thin black tie and unbuttoned the collar of his white shirt. "What a day it was at the office," he vamped. "That is, before I met you."

Tracy stood and watched. They were both at a sudden loss with each other. He hadn't expected to feel awkward – and neither, apparently, had Devin, who busied himself with putting away the dishes in the dishrack.

"Hey," Tracy said decisively. "Calm down. Come here."

He held out his arms; an excitement surged in his chest.

"Hello," Devin said gently, as he came into his arms. Imitating the boy in the bar he'd observed earlier, the pool player, Tracy leaned his head into Devin's neck. He did that sometimes: adopted a gesture, a tone of voice or turn of phrase he admired. There was a pause in music called the *fermata* – that eye with its raised eyebrow that commanded: *Stop here, linger, take a deep breath before moving on.* Louis Tremper had introduced him to the word during one of those sessions of after-dinner music-listening that had become something of a weekly ritual. Suddenly he had to laugh, not so much at Rifton's headmaster intruding on his thoughts at such a moment as the urgent pressure he had become aware of in his bladder. "I don't know why I've got to piss so much," he told Devin, releasing himself from their embrace. "I must have the world's smallest."

The walls of Devin's bathroom were painted black, and there was no mirror over the basin. As Tracy pissed a clear heavy stream he considered how easily, and with what a sense of relief, he'd taken up the Rifton School's strict regimen. His life there was bare, uncluttered, and if he'd stayed away from Devin's *cité radieuse* – all that aimless energy that was Manhattan, specifically gay Manhattan, its clubs and restaurants and gyms, its ceaseless striving for the chic and the buffed, under the guise of which one's real life, whatever undiscovered thing that might be, frittered itself away – his exile wasn't unintentional. Even now, inside this not unpleasant *fermata*, all he secretly wanted was to be back in Middle Forge reading a book and sipping a cup of tea. With a shiver of longing that was a little surprising, he found himself missing his dog Betsy, and the lovely, clarifying emptiness of his rooms.

He'd arranged for one of his students to house-sit; given him keys, instruction on feeding and walking the dog, free run of the place. Noah Lathrop probably wasn't the best choice, but it was a gamble Tracy'd felt he wanted to take. He'd made light, to Devin, of Louis Tremper's welcoming words about Rifton, but the truth was that he had actually taken them to heart, and he was trying to earn his students' respect, their trust. With Noah, from the very first, Tracy had felt an unspoken challenge that was also, perhaps, a call for help. Here was a kid more chased by trouble than most. His father was the one Tracy had been thinking of earlier, the man who ruined third world countries with the stroke of a corporate pen.

At the thought of Noah, a pang of emptiness spread through him. He saw the boy as he had last seen him, standing in the doorway, having shed the slightly soiled Rifton sweatshirt he'd been wearing when he arrived, gym bag in hand, for his weekend of house-sitting. Pulling the sweatshirt over his head had caused his sky-blue T-shirt to ride up as well, revealing an expanse of flat belly, the sweet flaw of the navel inset tautly in smooth flesh. Noah rolled the sweatshirt into a tight ball, kneading it thoughtfully as he absorbed one or two last-minute instructions. As the taxi waited at the curb, Tracy resisted the urge to attempt some casual bit of affection – a hug goodbye, perhaps, that light peck on the cheek Europeans found so unobjectionable. Instead he registered only the immense gulf between teacher and student as Noah, turning, mumbled "See you when you get back," and disappeared inside.

Tracy found Devin already stripped and in bed. Unbuttoning his shirt, Tracy folded it carefully and placed it on top of his overnight bag. Of course there was the matter of that Halloween present Noah had sprung on him before he left. It lay, even now, in his overnight bag, and he didn't know what to make of it, or what he would say about it on his return.

He sat on the edge of the bed to take off his shoes and socks. It was late; almost certainly Noah was in bed, his body curled under warm covers; probably he was fast asleep. Tracy shivered in the apartment's chill air as he stood and removed his pants. With comical eagerness his cock pointed straight out in front of him.

Devin's smooth body was warm as Tracy snuggled in next to it. He put his arms around his treacherous friend of many years and pulled him close. He could smell, not unpleasantly, the whisky and cigarette smoke on his breath. Someone had once remarked to him, "Kissing is like eating a peach," and Tracy thought of that whenever he found himself in the sweet, wet surprise of a kiss with a man.

A little stunned with the luxury of touching another body after so long, he slid his hands along slim, boyish hips till he found what he was looking for. Tracy always teased Devin that his parents had given him the best of both worlds: the slender body of an Asian, the cock of a Caucasian. In the dark of desire, this substantial offering he grasped might almost belong to anyone he chose to imagine. His desire was specific and urgent. "Go on," he told Devin huskily, "I want you inside me."

Devin laughed. "He's passionate tonight," he observed to no one in particular. "Mary, where's that condom?"

Disentangling himself, Tracy reached over to find his pile of clothes. Devin's thumb traced the crack of his ass. His shirt pocket was empty, his pants pockets too. "I can't find it," he said.

"Did it fall on the floor?"

"Why does this always happen? Can you turn on the light?"

But the light that suddenly illuminated the room illuminated no condom anywhere. Tracy lay back on the futon with a sigh, and folded his arms across his chest.

Devin reached over to tweak a firm nipple between thumb and forefinger and said delicately, "Honey, you know I'm not going in there without a rubber. I tell you what. Frank keeps a bowl of the little darlings by his bed. You go in there and borrow one. I'm sure he won't mind."

The air was cold on his naked flesh, and Tracy felt a little ridiculous, traipsing around with his still-aroused cock jutting out in front of him. For a moment there with Devin he'd felt the most delicious anticipation, as if, somehow, it wasn't Devin beside him in the darkness but the pulse of a certain mad possibility. Now all that fantasy was gone, but nonetheless a strange elation still worked in him. On the nightstand beside Frank's bed sat a dainty antique bowl incongrously filled to the brim with foil squares. As he plucked out two for good measure, he heard a noise, an opening door, footsteps in the hall. He turned around to find himself face to face with a quizzical-looking Frank.

"May I help you?" asked Devin's roommate, not so much deadpan as simply earnest.

"Um, hello," Tracy told him, conscious of the gaze that was eagerly taking him in. "I was just, um . . ." He waved the condoms forlornly in front of Frank's face.

"Oh," Frank said mildly, "you're welcome to them."

"A saint," Tracy told him. "That's what you are. A saint. I definitely owe you one."

"Anytime," Frank said. His tone was warm and sincere. "And you and Devin have a good night."

Tracy found Devin pressing a pillow to his face and heaving with suppressed laughter. When he uncovered his eyes, Tracy made a fright face at him – open-mouthed, wide-eyed – and fell into bed beside his companion.

"Perfect," Devin gasped. "Perfect. Now where were we?"

"Jesus Christ," Tracy moaned. "How do I live that one down?"

"Oh," Devin told him as he moved in closer, "we'll fix that in no time. See, I'm all ready to go. Roll that thing on down me. That's good. Now how do you want to do this?"

Usually he wasn't quite so voluble. "Shh," Tracy said. "Just let me turn out the light." He was surprised by how swiftly desire once again overtook him. Anybody can be anybody, he told himself as he eased his body down onto Devin's lovely Caucasian cock, the blunt pain of a beautiful pleasure wedging him open, filling him up – for all the world, he thought, grasping Devin's bony shoulders and rocking himself sweetly back on the hips that surged to meet him, like a delicious flower of fire blossoming inside him. No one was anyone, he told himself as the flaming flower bloomed and unbloomed rhythmically in his flesh. No one was anything, and Noah Lathrop was just a troubled boy he happened to know, a problem student he taught, an odd stray flicker of yearning, a phantasm to be banished – and what better way to banish it than with such rough exorcism as this?

After such exertions, Devin always dropped off to sleep with admirable dispatch. He had left the radio on low, tuned to a classical music station, which he claimed helped him sleep better. Like the rumblings of an uneasy stomach, thunder obscured its background murmur now and again with its more urgent demands. From the next room came the unmistakeable sounds of Frank spending some quality time with himself. Tracy lay awake, trying to listen to one set of sounds but not the other, or to both together, or to neither, but his bladder was full again and his mind as wide awake as it ever was. Sex did that to him: opened some part of his brain that usually was still. He could never find sleep till hours afterward. In a kind of alert stupor he lay motionless, unable or unwilling to hoist himself from the futon and stumble through the dark to the bathroom. Once, long ago, he and Devin had woken in the morning to find someone – they never knew who, and though both playfully accused the other neither would admit it – had pissed the bed. Another chord of thunder added its voice to the quiet business of a piano concerto. He thought about getting up to turn it off, but some bit of tenderness toward Devin made him refrain. At least one of them should sleep restfully.

For years Tracy had played what he called the memory game. Whenever the present, whether through anxiety or insomnia, became too present, he'd consciously cut some cord that bound him to it, and allow his mind to drift, rudderless, within a memory he thought of as potentially oceanic in its unexplored reach and depth.

Mostly he remembered the storms from that one summer, blistering squalls that broke out across the landscape every late afternoon, gray curtains of rain shot through with blue-white snaps of lightning, heartstopping eruptions of thunder. Then the clearing aftermath, sunsets of fantastic drama. Nearly a decade later Tracy could no longer recall the exact details of his initial meeting with Eric, nor trace the slow degrees by which, over two months, they became friends. He couldn't even remember Eric's last name, an omission of memory that plagued him until he decided he must never have known it in the first place – as if it were possible to be so preoccupied with a person as to miss so fundamental a thing as that.

What he could never forget was the wondrous shock of falling in love. He had just graduated from high school, and in the fall would be heading south to William & Mary for college. Emotions he'd glanced at on other occasions and then shunted nervously aside coalesced around this lanky, 27-year-old costume designer and wouldn't dissipate. August found them together every noon on the lawn in front of the theater where Tracy worked as a summer intern. Shirtless, they'd stretch out in the long grass and take the healing brunt of a noontime sun that gave no clue of the thunderheads it already, in secret, had begun to breed.

"It's because we're so close to the ocean," Eric told him. "The sea coast of Connecticut is famous for its storms." Like much of what Eric said, it was enchanting if dubious. Hailing from Kansas, Eric was an *afficionado* of violent weather, its vagaries, its cruel wonders. Once a tornado had passed directly over him as he lay prone in a ditch by the side of the highway – sparing him, but he'd never forgotten the cyclonic roar, the sudden ear-thumping dip in pressure, the eerie feeling that some ghost of enormous force was treading across his back. He talked vividly and nonstop – they both did, it seemed, in their daily respite together before their tasks took them separate ways, Tracy to help in building a great stage ark for *Noye's Fludde*, Eric to the cramped little costume shop to fashion shining robes for the patriarch and his sons, or elaborate heads of papier mâché for the fabulous animals the ark would bear to safety.

One thing Eric let slip, early on in their voluble friendship: how he suspected, despite his girlfriend in Manhattan, whose praises he freely sang and whom he went every weekend to see, that he was probably, all things considered, a bit gay. He reported it casually, the way you might report "I'm a Libra" or "I graduated from Oberlin," both of which were in fact the case. But unlike those other facts, this one possessed Tracy completely. His own fledgling secret, never before uttered, perched on his tongue, tested its newfound wings, but then, despite everything, refused to fly. Before he could say it, they'd somehow moved on to other, safer things, and then day after day passed, the subject didn't come up again. They talked about Shakespeare and Tennessee Williams and the weather in Kansas and he began to wonder whether Eric had ever confessed such a thing about himself, or whether his own less-than-reliable imagination hadn't spawned those words, the way tornadoes appeared out of nowhere in the heartlands.

Each evening Tracy drove home to his parents' house nursing the unaccountable certainty he would never see Eric again, that some mysterious reckoning would take him suddenly away, no message left, no goodbye. Storms passed over the house, an old maple in the backyard came down, once he saw lightning dance like a sprite along the telephone wires. Then the reprieve of blue sky to the west. Tracy flung himself out of doors, walking for hours, solitary, his heart storming without any end in sight.

Nights in particular were torment: no sooner had he shut his eyes than Eric's after-image, as if imprinted by lightning, swam before him: the loose, vibrant ease with which he carried himself, his teasing smile and liquid eyes, the way he wore his blond hair, fine as midwestern corn silk, pulled back tightly in a pony tail.

By day Tracy found some furtive consolation in studying Eric's half-naked body reclined next to him in the grass – his featureless navel set in a flat belly, the trail of dark hairs that disappeared past the waist of his gym shorts. Often Eric wore an earring in his left ear, a tiny blue-green stud you could miss if you didn't look closely. Other days there was just the hole where his lobe had been pierced, and that was worth examining closely as well.

Every morning Eric brought a duffel bag with him to the costume shop, and at the end of the day he reclaimed it, hoisting it over his shoulder and sauntering off to wherever he spent those nights Tracy would have given his soul to share with him. Small things made the boy desperate. One morning they stood at the mailboxes, and Eric read through a note he'd received.

"You're frowning," Tracy told him.

"Oh," Eric said, "it's just from a guy I ran into last weekend at a party. It's nothing." And folding the piece of paper, he stuck it into his bag. But the words made Tracy burn. That afternoon he excused himself from his stagework and hastened to the costume shop. Eric had told him he and his assistant had to drive into town after lunch to buy some things. No one was around. Sick and excited, Tracy found the duffel bag stashed in a corner. Loosening its cord, he slid his hand inside. His fingers touched soft fabric, underwear and socks and T-shirts. Resisting the temptation to spill the contents onto the floor, to smother his face in communion with all that secret, sweat-sour fabric, he instead extracted the folded-up slip of paper and read breathlessly.

"You're right," was all it said. "I was an asshole. I'm sorry."

Anything was possible, of course – but nonetheless he felt utterly, despondently sure. Something had happened that night, or hadn't happened – but whichever it was, a terrible sense of loss accosted Tracy. With unsteady hands he replaced the note in the duffel bag. In a fit of frustration, he made his way back to the stage. He had the beginnings of a headache, and the incessant banging of hammers as they built the ark seemed to nail the lid on the coffin of all his hopes.

As a child Tracy had been fascinated by an hourglass that sat on the desk in his grandfather's study. Whenever he visited their house in Connecticut, he would sneak into that hushed room, redolent of old books and leather armchairs and pipesmoke (his grandfather and namesake had retired from a New York law firm of legendary prestige). When he inverted the glass, at first nothing seemed to happen. Though a steady trickle leaked through, the level on top hardly changed. Only at the end did all the sand suddenly appear to run out at once.

For a week of performances, *Noye's Fludde* sailed through its deluge to reach safe shore. Who could have guessed, in advance, its odd relevance? When the audience joined in for a final, heaving hymn, tears came to Tracy's eyes. The month had been the most important of his life. Helpless, he watched the vortex open as Eric made ready to return to New York, where he and his girlfriend would be looking for an apartment together for the coming winter which would, Tracy felt sure, be never-ending.

Those lunches on the sundrenched lawn turned gray with anxiety. Each day he trembled on the verge of that bold confession he'd spent sleepless nights rehearsing. But each day slipped from him. Then at the last possible moment he found himself speaking. They had shared what was to be their final lunch together; they lay on their backs, shirts rolled up underneath their head as pillows. No breeze blew; the air was sultry and thick.

"I want to sleep with you," Tracy said. The words sounded dull and impossible. Silence swallowed them up, and Eric only laughed.

"Do you have any idea what you're saying?" Eric wondered aloud – as if they had both been napping, as if Tracy had spoken incoherent words in his slumber.

"I want to have sex with you," Tracy said. This time the words were clearer; they hung there and refused to disappear. He felt as if he were swimming up from some great drowning depth. His heart beat so furiously in his chest, it seemed impossible the whole lawn didn't hear. When he dared look Eric's way, Eric had turned on his side and propped himself on one arm. He was watching him with a soft and unfocused gaze.

"Hey, Tracy," he said gently, perplexedly. "Don't you think you're a little too young for me?"

Tracy was on his side now too, facing Eric across mere inches of space, a gap both negligible and infinite, and Eric was shaking his head slowly. "I should have realized," he went on, as if in bemusement – or perhaps it was wonder. "I guess I should've noticed."

Boldly, Tracy reached out his hand. Lightning did not strike. He touched, tentatively, then with growing assurance, his friend's lightly stubbled cheek. He ran his fingers along the jawline he'd longed for a whole month to caress.

"No," Eric told him after a moment, taking him by the wrist and pushing his hand away.

"I thought you liked me," Tracy said.

"Stupid," Eric told him. "Of course I like you. I'm fucking crazy about you."

It seemed impossible they could be here like this. Tracy couldn't contain himself.

"Then what's the problem?"

"So what's the problem?" Eric laughed bitterly. "You're priceless. The problem is, either way, I'm going to regret this, whatever I do."

"Then there's no problem," Tracy said quickly, afraid to give either of them time to think. He knew all about time. "Better to go ahead and make it with me than not make it with me."

"We both know that's not true," Eric said simply. He sat up abruptly, and clasped his arms around his bare knees. Tracy watched him in profile: that ponytail of cruelly pulled-back hair he'd never seen unloosed, blond sideburn fading out into stubble, the jaw his fingers, unbelievably, had grazed. The space around him, the silence, was inviolable. Tracy had never been so conscious of the sky above the earth, the dangerous clouds that gathered there, the way humans lived beneath such grandeur and threat every moment of their lives. Eric, too, seemed intent on figuring up some incalculable sum.

"What the fuck?" he said at last. "Come on, let's get out of here. And just remember," – he paused in slipping his T-shirt over his head – "you're the one who started it."

Tracy's erection made it painful for him to stand up. When he tugged at his crotch to rearrange himself, he saw Eric's gaze flicker there for a moment, darken, and then dart away.

Wordlessly, they walked – past the theater to the edge of campus, then along a busy street lined with student bars and bookshops. They were radiant criminals, unafraid, untouchable, bringing off the greatest caper the world had known. And the world, oblivious, let them pass right by.

Cutting through an empty lot they entered the woods. It was a place Tracy would never have thought of going. A path took them alongside an overgrown field whose edges were thick with blackberry brambles. On the far side an abandoned house hid among young trees that had crowded up around it. The porch sagged, the windows were broken out, despite the relentless procession of summer storms the roof still held. It solved a mystery.

"Totally illegal," Eric said, "but what can you do? The rent's unbeatable." His mood had lightened, he reverted to his familiar, carefree self – the self who'd gotten drunk on vodka at a party in high school and let his best friend Charlie pierce his ear with a hot needle.

"You're crazy," Tracy told him. "Wasn't there any place else you could stay?"

"Really, it was lots of fun," Eric confessed. "At night there was an owl I could hear. Heather absolutely freaked when I told her about this place."

But Tracy wasn't freaked. He saw the difference between himself and the hated Heather quite clearly. To live like this seemed, at the moment, nothing less than heroic. To roam the world with only a knapsack of belongings; to sleep in fields, in the woods – even in abandoned houses. He himself had longed for great adventures. To visit India, Nepal, Tibet. To meet the friend who'd go anywhere with him, do anything.

"I want to kiss you," he told his new friend of the wide world. Already he could sense the heady air of the Himalayas. He moved toward Eric; their embrace was clumsy. It tumbled them down in slow motion onto the floor. Tracy lay on top and explored Eric's mouth with his tongue.

"You're certainly the precocious one," Eric laughed and pushed at him playfully. But Eric gasped as Tracy felt his way inside his gym shorts. "Hey," he warned. His cock was long and thick and lazy. Freed from his shorts, it lay flopped over his thigh like a big snake sunning itself on a rock. Tracy raised it up and kissed its bulbous head. He breathed its sweet reek. His lips rested against hard beautiful flesh.

Then he felt Eric take both sides of his head and firmly lift him up. "I can't do this, Tracy" he said. "You're a kid. I can't change that."

"I know what I'm doing. I'm not a virgin," Tracy lied.

"No," Eric said. "I'm not doing this."

It seemed too wildly unfair only to get this far. "Please," Tracy heard himself say. He hated the unmistakable pitch of desperation in his voice. And he was amazed to see there were tears in Eric's eyes. The young man curled his mouth. His brow furrowed up. Unable to speak, he simply shook his head. He took Tracy in his arms and held him, rocked him back and forth for the longest time in silence, tears streaming down his face, Tracy dry-eyed but pressing his cheek to Eric's cheek in his hopeless attempt to make those tears his own.

It was seven years before Tracy saw him again. On a sunny day in June thousands marched down Fifth Avenue beneath banners and placards. Tracy stood on the sidelines and watched. And there was Eric, whose last name Tracy had either forgotten or never known. He beat a hand drum and shouted slogans of desperation and defiance. He'd lost his looks, he was gaunt and bright-eyed, terrible signs Tracy had grown, over the years, to recognize. His ponytail had vanished, all that gorgeous silky hair Tracy had never seen loose now sheared so short Eric looked practically bald. Tracy was sure it was him: something in the limber way he moved, the loose way he threw his shoulders back. His lips had kissed those lips – even, for a moment, that big lazy cock that had never gotten entirely hard for him. The sun shone fiercely. Black and white balloons filled the sky. The sidewalks were mobbed with cheering onlookers. Eric banged relentlessly on his drum for the whole world to hear.

Tracy stood on the sidewalk in front of the address he'd been given and tried to find a front door, or a least a buzzer. To his surprise, only the slightest of headaches had chosen to settle behind his eyeballs, in the stiff back of his neck. His anus felt raw from the previous night's adventures.

There was no door, no buzzer. To the side of the little building, a locked iron gate led into an alley, and perhaps that was the way in.

"Arthur," he called out in frustration, and at an open second-floor window Arthur appeared, smiling impishly, his head wrapped in a maroon bath towel.

"Oh, young man," Arthur called down in falsetto. "Yoo hoo."

"I bet you spend hours leaning out that window," Tracy told him.

"My elbows've worn a bare spot on the sill. See, there's this old Italian woman lurking in my ancestry. Now don't run off. It'll take me a minute to come down and let you in, honeypot."

Someone had hung a bird feeder from one of the spindly street trees, and little gray birds hopped nervously from branch to branch. The overnight rain had caused most of the leaves to drop all at once; they formed a bright yellow skirt on the sidewalk. He was sure he didn't feel the least bit nervous. You're not obligated to go, Devin had counselled him.

Appearing behind the gate, Arthur fiddled noisily with the lock. "Maybe it makes some people feel secure," he said, "but me, I feel like I'm in prison."

"At least the Jehovah's Witnesses don't pester you," Tracy told him.

"No," Arthur said as the gate swung heavily open. "The Jehovah's Witnesses definitely do not pester me."

"Well, they actually came to my door," Tracy said. "They brought children and pamphlets."

"To sell? To give away? What did you do?"

"I was rather proud of myself. They asked me, Do you read the Bible? And I said yes, as a matter of fact I do, and I'm appalled by what I find there. How anybody could worship such a cruel and bloodthirsty God is beyond me. Well, they just turned and ran." Wishing he could have drawn the anecdote out a bit more, he concluded, "I don't think they'll be back anytime soon."

Arthur watched him curiously. "Just hope lightning doesn't burn your house down," he said with a seriousness that caught Tracy off guard. He took Tracy in his arms and planted a big wet kiss on his lips. Tracy let himself be gripped tightly for a long moment; then, as Arthur turned to lead him into the building, he surreptitiously wiped his mouth with the back of his hand.

With a flourish, Arthur threw open the door onto a very small, wood-panelled room. "It's, well, charming," Tracy judged.

"Cosy, I like to think of it as. But my own. Domestic bliss at last. I have no furniture – but then, I have no room for furniture. So it's fine. At least I don't have to put up with roommates. And there're only five steps to negotiate. For that time when stairs start to be a problem."

There was nothing in the tiny room to conveniently engage his attention – no books, no CDs, no personal artifacts at all – so he sat down on the step that led up to Arthur's alcove bed. Regal in his maroon turban of a bath towel, Arthur took the room's single wooden chair and seated himself grandly: hands on his hips, legs crossed at the knees. He'd always been such a queen. For an awkward silence they both studied the extremely worn Turkish carpet on the floor. "You like?" Arthur said at last. "I'll put it in my will. Rescued from a garbage can. You could say I felt an affinity for it."

There'd been Arthur's phone call a year ago, after several months of lapsed contact between them. In answer to Tracy's somewhat surprised "So how've you been?" he'd said mildly, almost apologetically, "I'm afraid I've been having a little health problem" – a bad cold he hadn't taken care of until one afternoon he collapsed in the editorial offices of the women's magazine he worked for and had to be spirited to the emergency room. Diagnosing pneumonia, his doctor had remarked tersely, "I suppose you realize what this means."

"Whatever you are," Tracy said, unwilling to take his eyes from the relative safety of the carpet, "I wouldn't call it moth-eaten."

"Always the diplomat," Arthur told him, reaching out across the narrow space of the room to pat him on the knee.

He'd been unsafe with Arthur. In a moment of unaccountable madness, he'd let Arthur fuck him without a condom. They couldn't find any in the apartment, it was late, it was cold out, they were both a little drunk, a little stoned, they were both feeling carried away. "Go ahead," he'd said, "put it in me," and then felt, after a few deep thrusts, Arthur's semen spurt inside him. Afterwards they didn't talk about it; they pretended not to notice it had happened.

Tracy had always tried to be careful. He could count on the fingers of one hand the times he'd swallowed another man's cum. Only twice in his life had he let himself get fucked without a condom, and that other time had been years ago. The thing to do, of course, was to get tested. But it wasn't that he wouldn't do it – he couldn't. Knowing for certain, losing for good the far-fetched possibility that there was nothing to worry about, it was all in his head, the psychic terror and lifeline of that game he played nightly with his own darker thoughts – all that paralyzed him. Look at it this way, he argued to himself: If your dad, who never smoked or drank, died of liver cancer at 49, then you, who've been fucked in the ass by a cock loaded with deadly virus, could very well live to be 100.

He didn't believe that for an instant.

"Let me get dressed," Arthur said, "and we'll go out. One does tend to exhaust, rather too quickly, the meager charms of my new abode. Are you hungry? There's a lovely little restaurant around the corner, which I've managed to make my home away from home."

He stood and slipped his bathrobe from his shoulders. He'd always been skin and bones, but now the skin stretched over those bones was translucent as the parchment on which monks had copied out their hymns to the God Tracy professed to deny. He was wasting away. His ribs really were a cage. Only his cock, that formidable organ, remained undaunted. Horsedick, Tracy had used to tease him. All that was four years ago – in between Tracy had spent a year in Japan, he'd gone trekking in Nepal, he'd read nearly half of Proust, and built houses in the Hamptons. The virus didn't care about those things. If it was going to hunt him down it wouldn't matter how far he ran or how many bargains he made.

For an instant he thought about just giving up: why not surprise them both and go down on that cock with all the abandon he used to muster when they were going out?

Who would that joke be on? he wondered as Arthur, oblivious to all that desperate fantasy, selected from his closet a red-and-black flannel shirt. He pulled on khakis four sizes too big and cinched them together with a broad belt. Unwrapping the towel from around his head, he shook out the longish hair he tinted with a henna rinse.

From the very first it had been madness. Swept off his feet:

that was the only way to describe that feeling of being caught up by the wonderful whirlwind this talkative rail of a boy from south Texas, met at a dinner party through mutual friends, turned out to be. At 22, Tracy had never met anybody quite like him. Three years older and a decade more experienced in the ways of the world, Arthur was game for practically anything, as Tracy found out later that night. He'd heard of a wild time, but he'd never found himself encountering such primitive unfettered energy as Arthur brought to bed with him. Naturally cautious to a fault, Tracy had found something inside him whispering yes, and despite his better judgement plunged in.

It turned out to be way over his head. He was disconcerted to discover exactly how much sex Arthur had had in his short life – on the docks and in backrooms and with strangers he'd brought home from the street, anonymous and dangerous and obliterating sex. He loved getting slapped around, or pissed on; he loved, as Tracy would squeamishly learn, taking a fist up his ass. Accosted by two men in a doorway on his way to meet Tracy one evening after work, he'd followed them upstairs and smoked crack, reporting afterward, cheerfully, "My hair felt like it was on fire." His one regret: those two shady characters hadn't fucked him. He'd thought that was on the agenda, and sex on crack, by all accounts, was supposed to give you a truly life-expanding perspective on the world.

Tracy, who'd waited for an hour at the café before finally giving up and going home, listened with something very like terror to this man he'd made the mistake of confessing his eternal love for only two weeks before. Arthur, who was all for love, albeit of a more temporal kind, had confessed back that he himself, unfortunately, wasn't in love at the moment, wasn't sure he *wanted* to be in love right now, didn't think, in fact, he quite had the time for it. Which wasn't to say there wasn't lots of truly fabulous stuff that could happen between the two of them. Tracy hid his hurt and soldiered on, but in only a further matter of weeks he was ready to understand quite clearly the ways in which he couldn't, whether through cowardice or just plain prudence, rise to Arthur's challenge. At the same time he began to glimpse in this love of his life – beyond the charm, the sweetness, the wit – a certain cold desperation lurking. He'd understood he had to bail out of this particular whirlwind.

"So," Arthur said, regarding himself in the mirror (he ran a bony hand through his hair to muss it), "do I look gorgeous these days or what?"

"Gorgeous is as gorgeous does," Tracy told him regretfully.

The little restaurant around the corner was the kind of place that had made Tracy love New York. It threatened, in fact, like so many small moments this weekend, to make him fall in love all over again. Hardly bigger than the railway car he'd ridden down in, its tables huddled close. An elbow's length away, three women carried on a lively conversation in Italian.

Their waiter was too quietly beautiful to be either an actor or a model, just one of those boys who, like moths, find their way to Chelsea. He handed them their menus with lovely presence. "So how's your sex life?" Arthur asked. "Oh, not you, honey," he told the waiter. "I mean this one. By the way, Tracy, you should order the trout with pepper bacon."

"I'm a vegetarian," Tracy reminded him.

"Well, I have to tell you, it must be this disease, but all I ever want these days is meat, meat, meat. I think *I'll* have the trout, and with extra bacon if that's possible. *You*, my dear," he went on, "should order the yummy sweet potato pancakes. And for dessert," Arthur smiled beatifically at the waiter, "we will both have double helpings of you."

Tracy could only marvel at their waiter's truly wonderful self-possession. Arthur was a regular here, after all.

"See?" Arthur tapped him lightly on the wrist. "You *are* hungry. So back to my question. S-E-X. And you'd better tell me you're getting it on somewhere, somehow, with someone up there in your new home. Otherwise you're just taking up valuable space on the planet."

Tracy laughed uncomfortably, though something like this line of questioning was presumably what he'd come to Arthur for. "Sorry to disappoint," he sighed.

"Well, I at least thought you and Miss Devin-Eleven would still be getting things on."

"Oh, that," Tracy said, his memory of last night now bleakly clear. *Your typical all-night convenience store* was how Arthur had once described Tracy's friend from college. Between those two there existed a fierce mutual animosity that Tracy afforded himself the luxury of believing had everything to do with him. "Did you know Devin's got a real boyfriend these days? Apparently I'm the last to know. He only told me this morning. It's serious with a capital S. They're thinking of buying an apartment on the upper west side. I find out all this, I might add, only after we'd done it every which way. So much for serious."

"My dear, if I didn't know better, I'd say you sound bitter. And anyway, never, never apologize the morning after for what your hormones were telling you last night."

"You're right. It's his serious relationship, not mine. Devin and I have been this way with each other for years. I can't imagine it's about to change any time soon."

"The old friends syndrome," Arthur said. "Tell me about it. What is *with* gay men?"

But Tracy didn't know what was with gay men.

"Surely, though, you're at least *interested* in someone?" Arthur pursued.

"You know," Tracy said brutally, "I don't know if I've ever been all that interested in anybody, to tell you the truth."

Arthur was above being wounded. "Now, now," he consoled. "You always say these extreme things, even when you're not under duress. Or *are* you under duress? There are five gazillion gay men your age out there casting about for husbands right now. It's a seller's market, as far as I can tell. Don't you think," he asked their waiter grandly as a whole trout, smothered in bacon, was set before him, "that this gorgeous man sitting across from is extremely eligible?"

"Of course," said the waiter without blinking an eye. "And would you like for me to debone your fish?"

"Any time, anywhere," Arthur told him, and sat back in his chair to allow the young man room for that delicate procedure.

Tracy waited in silence, studying the waiter's beautiful wrists, his hairless forearms, the fingernails that were bitten to the quick.

"You do that very well," Arthur complimented when the task was complete.

"And it's not even my greatest talent," the waiter told him. Now here was somebody you could fall in love with. Though the young fellow didn't seem particularly interested in anything except doing his job. Tracy had been through all that before. He'd dated beautiful waiters, and they were all the same. Why were the beautiful ones always so vacant? What did beauty matter, anyway? As the beautiful vacant waiter bore away the bones on a saucer, and Tracy and Arthur both followed his progress longingly with their eyes, Tracy complained, "Does everybody always have to be on the prowl for love?"

"Well, as a matter of fact, yes," Arthur said with great certainty. "Everybody does have to either be in love or be on the prowl for it. It's a rule. I, for example, think I am absolutely in love with this trout. Don't you want even a taste?"

Tracy the vegetarian wasn't, after all, above consuming a bit of fish – or even, God forbid, bacon – now and again, as Arthur knew all too well.

But Tracy shook his head. Suddenly his hangover, which had mercifully been lying low, welled up in him. Feeling not the least bit hungry, he stared at his orange pancakes, so prettily and fatuously decorated on their blue plate with slivers of orange, strawberry, pineapple. "I don't think any of that's for me anymore. I'm not talking about eating meat. I'm talking about other kinds of hunger. Desire. I want to get clear of it all. Maybe it's just the times we live in."

"You mean AIDS?"

"Not just AIDS. This whole gay thing," he said. "Or not even that. This whole relationship thing. The need to be involved with someone else, like you're not complete unless you are. Isn't that a great word, *involved*? Makes me think of puppets with their strings all tangled up together. Sometimes I almost find myself wishing, I don't know, that I'd never gotten into any of it. That I'd stayed on the sidelines and just watched it all."

"What an odd thing to say," Arthur remarked coolly. "You haven't gone and tested positive, have you?"

Tracy's chest constricted in familiar panic. "No, no," he said hastily. "Nothing like that. I'm completely healthy. I'm probably too healthy."

Arthur was still watching him closely. "Meaning what?" he said.

"I don't know. I don't know why I said any of that."

"I see," Arthur told him.

"Meaning, I don't even know what I'm talking about." Tracy drummed his fingertips restlessly on the tabletop. "I'm just totally confused about myself right now."

He needed, he felt obscurely, to show Arthur how unhappy he was, even if that unhappiness wasn't exactly true. He needed, more than anything else, for Arthur simply to ask, "Do you regret having had sex with me?" He needed to erase the simple fact that, despite of his best intentions, he and Devin had fucked last night, that he'd lost his head, allowed it to happen when for the past two months he'd been celebrating his clean break from the city, the entanglements it had come to stand for. That he'd enjoyed it immensely.

Was it possible Arthur knew him well enough to guess all that? Spearing a last piece of trout, Arthur studied it for a moment on the end of his fork. "So you're going to stay out of trouble for a while. Well, good luck with all that. As for me, I'm going to stay where I belong, which is smack dab in the middle of trouble. It's the only place that's halfway interesting."

"I don't feel very satisfied with how I've managed to express myself here," Tracy said.

Contentedly, Arthur pushed his empty plate to one side. "Don't worry. You school teachers always have a way with words. I personally think it's been good for us to have this chat. In fact, I would go so far as to say that, these days at least, I think good conversation is really the best form of sex. And we haven't had conversation in so long, you and I. One of those proverbial blue moons. Can I confess something terrible? For a while, before you moved away, I had the misguided impression you were avoiding me. Now wasn't that just plain silly of me?"

"Completely," Tracy lied. "I was incredibly busy with stuff. You know how it is."

"And can I confess something else while I'm at it? Maybe it was for the best if you were avoiding me, because, see, I have this suspicion that you, of all people, have no idea that I, of all people, graduated from the Rifton School. Isn't that a hoot? Now don't look so shocked. It was years ago, nine to be exact."

For a second time in their conversation Tracy felt that tightness around his heart. He wasn't the least bit superstitious. Still, an itch prickled along both his legs, an icy finger ran down his spine.

"You've hardly touched your pancakes," Arthur noted.

"I'm really sorry I didn't call," Tracy told him.

"It wasn't like I had anything really to tell you about Rifton. It's not a bad place, really it's not. What does Quentin Compson say to that peachy roommate of his? I don't hate the south, I don't hate it. But tell me," – his voice grew reflective – is somebody named Louis Tremper still teaching there?"

Once, years before, as Tracy was about to step into an elevator he had had the strange premonition the elevator was going to get stuck, and that he shouldn't get on. But that was ridiculous, and he'd gotten on anyway, and the elevator did in fact get stuck. He was trapped there, alone, in the stifling dark, no way out, for nearly an hour. Tracy spoke with some care. "Actually, Louis is headmaster there now."

"Too bad," said Arthur. "For him, I mean. I was so hoping he'd moved on. Does that mean that Herr Professor Doktor Gestapo von Emmerich finally retired?

Tracy felt the elevator begin to move. "I think Dr Emmerich died," he said. "I'm not really all that clear on the details, but I get the impression that Louis became Headmaster all of a sudden – you know, unexpectedly. I haven't really talked to him about it. I do know that he thought extremely highly of Dr Emmerich."

"Well, I personally hope it was a gruesome death," Arthur said. "Pardon my compassion, but that man terrorized poor Louis. Had him under the heel of his jack boot from the word 'Go'. But anyway – you should say hello from me. I've completely lost touch with Louis Tremper over the years, but I'm sure he remembers me. He was a very important presence in my life there for a couple of years."

How Louis and Arthur might have managed to get along Tracy couldn't even imagine, though all at once, before his eyes, he saw Arthur as he might have been at 15 or 16 however old he'd been when Louis was his teacher, and what he felt was a longing, a loss. Louis had known Arthur when he was still just a kid. Though Louis, on the other hand, would have been exactly the same dapper fugitive lurking behind his sunglasses, life's secret agent.

Smiling at that thought, Tracy found himself suggesting, entirely against his better judgement, "You should come up for a visit sometime. I could invite Louis over for dinner. God knows I've been over there often enough."

"Louis's famous evenings. Let me guess. After dessert he makes you listen to classical music. See? Nothing changes. I'm glad he still does that. I remember when I was a sophomore, he played me Pachelbel's Canon. It was before that delicious little piece got turned into such a cliché. We sat in the dark and just let the music do its thing. I have to say, it was a beautiful moment. We never had any music like that in South Texas."

For a moment he was quiet, they were both quiet. "I've never forgotten it," he said. Then, after another pause, in which Tracy tried to fit together the various, faintly troubling pieces of a puzzle whose overall shape he wasn't in the least sure of, "Here you've gone and put me in a mood. So is Louis still married to that dyke?"

"Arthur!" Tracy had to protest. "Claire's been very kind to me."

"Oh, she's very kind to all Louis's young men. Believe me. They're a very devoted couple."

Tracy remembered the day he'd had to wonder, afterwards, for the briefest of moments before dismissing the thought as ludicrous, whether the headmaster's wife intended to try to have an affair with him. "When I was in Japan," he said, perhaps a little testily, "the rumor went around that I was a monk. Like, I mean, they thought I lived in a monastery back in the states. Slept in my coffin and everything. Took a vow of silence. Students get strange ideas. You can't trust everything you hear."

Arthur stared at him intently. "You're not out to anybody at Rifton, are you? Not even to Louis."

"It's never come up," Tracy defended. The circumstances under which such a subject might come up, especially with someone like Louis, weren't immediately apparent to him. "I mean, I've only been there a few weeks. It's not like I wear a sign around my neck. When the time comes, I'm sure the right people will know."

"I think," Arthur observed, "this is part of what's got you worried. The teacher's a fag. You hadn't thought about that beforehand, had you? It was different in Japan. Now you've got all these yummy American boys on your hands. I'd say you're in a bit of a delicate situation."

"No." Tracy was adamant. "I can assure you that that's not it."

All the Metro North cars had names: John Cheever, Thomas E. Dewey, James Fenimore Cooper. Maria Mitchell, whoever she was. He boarded the Washington Irving.

Coming out of the long tunnel from Grand Central into the sun, he felt a pang of loss so keen it took him by surprise. Forget Tokyo. No matter how you felt about, Manhattan was still the center of the world.

Around the edges, though, it was fraying. The train glided through a no-man's land of looted automobiles, mounds of rubble, whole streets of abandoned buildings, their windows boarded over with sky-blue plywood. At the base of bleak apartment towers sycamores struggled in bare earth, their limbs draped in shredded plastic bags tossed from the stories above. And then in an asphalted lot, five shirtless Puerto-Rican beauties were playing basketball in the mild October sun.

There was no denying it. Boys grabbed him. Their loveliness tore him apart. The world was a wonder after all.

For a while he tried to sleep, but that was no good. His brain seethed with the weekend's sensory overload – the spent condom lying on the floor next to Devin's bed the morning after, Arthur's cheerful enumeration of his various symptoms and the array of pills he was taking. In the seat behind him, a man and woman talked back and forth to one another with dull, mechanical constancy. Their voices weren't loud, but as if having haplessly discovered the frequency of their broadcast, Tracy couldn't seem to tune them out. He hated couples who'd been married so long their lives had settled into what

amounted to little more than a stupor. Did anything mean half
as much to them as a momentary glimpse of boys without shirts
playing basketball meant to him? What would they make of his
razor-sharp ecstasies – or, for that matter, the terrible anxieties a
25-year-old gay man these days had to fight down every minute
of his existence? All the probabilities were that he'd be dead at
half their age.

For a moment he was on the verge of remembering something
important, but then the couple behind him resumed their dreary
exchange of nothings, and the memory, whatever it had been,
went behind a cloud. Desperate to sever himself from their
voices, Tracy rummaged in his bag and pulled out *A Separate
Peace*. He was surprised anybody still taught it, but there it
was on the syllabus Louis had given him at the beginning of
the term for English II. He could barely remember a thing
about it. A prep school kid with a crush on his best friend.
Kind of suspicious, really. But it might prove interesting to
teach – the challenge being, of course, to get his students to
think about all that without it seeming too suspicious on his
part. The last thing he wanted, at this early point before he'd
sufficiently settled in, was for his class to be able to write their
teacher off as a fag.

Though maybe, he thought, he should give them exactly
that chance. Maybe it would do them some good. They were
so terrified of being little faggots themselves that they were
afraid even to touch one another for fear of their motives being
mistaken. That was one of the things that had surprised him
about Rifton. Told that he'd need to supervise some athletics,
and remembering his own high school days, he'd looked forward
to the innocent pleasure – well, maybe not so innocent – of the
lockerroom, only to discover that virtually none of the boys
would even set foot in there. After the period was over, they
hightailed it back to the privacy of their dorm rooms to shower
and change.

Suddenly the memory that had failed him earlier returned
at full wattage. Funny what difficulties the mind, left to its
own devices, could hedge on. He'd managed to forget about
Noah's so-called gift for most of the weekend.

"Something to entertain you on the train," Noah had

said, presenting him with what seemed to be a partial roll of toilet paper wrapped loosely around an unsharpened pencil whose eraser end was capped by a rubber jack-o-lantern's head. "And Happy Halloween," he'd continued awkwardly.

Seeing there was writing on the toilet paper, Tracy had started to unroll it; but Noah grabbed his wrist. "It's for the train," he admonished with a nervous, inadvertent laugh. "No unfair peeking."

He had an unhumorous way of smiling. His eyes would narrow to slits, the corners of his mouth pull back tensely. He looked more grim than amused, and it worried Tracy. He knew so little about this boy, his inadequacies, both academic and emotional, the various troubles that dogged him. What he did know, or at least had come, during the last month, to sense with some certainty, was that Noah represented a special kind of challenge. But the nature of that challenge, and whether he would prove at all adequate to it, completely eluded him. Certainly his Japanese students, those well-behaved and inviolable girls, all giggles and at the same time possessed of a really sublime earnestness, had been straightforward compared to this American boy who offered him toilet paper and a pencil.

He hadn't waited till the train. Deposited some half hour early by the taxi – Louis had warned him they were highly unreliable – he'd sat on a bench in the bleak Metro North waiting room and unscrolled his present. On the individual sheets of toilet paper, one sentence per sheet, Noah had written in felt-tipped pen that bled almost illegibly:

> i wonder what he looks like when he's asleep
> i wonder what he'd look like with a beard
> i wonder if he likes it here
> i wonder what he was like in high school
> i wonder if he likes us
> i wonder if he lets anybody get to him
> i wonder if he ever gets depressed
> i wonder what he'll be doing in ten years
> i wonder what he thinks he's doing now

Following was a crude caricature of an alarmed face – wide
eyes, open-mouthed, hair on end – along with the cryptic
caption, as if he'd been reading ahead in his assignments
(though that seemed rather uncharacteristic of him):

help me finny i'm drowning

Out over the rippled river, shale-gray clouds were moving in
from the west. The surrounding hills grew somber, the waters
darker. He would not think anymore about Noah. Though
Tracy had this sudden, distressing feeling. The word floated
in his head: *subcutaneous*. It was so sudden, so unexpected.
How had he let someone get under his skin like that? Devin
had been almost too right: there was something moving about
a 15-year-old boy. Not so much the individual boy himself, but
rather some quality that attached itself to him, the simple fact
of his youth, the territory he was passing through. Some light
that shone about him that made him, for a moment, crazily
special. How strange that you could fall so hard for that trick
of light. And what, when you fell, did you want from it?

Idle thoughts. There wasn't anything he wanted from Noah
– unless, and this was the startling thought that occurred to him
as he watched the sullen plain of the river out the window, what
he wanted was not to be seen through. He paused, testing that
discovery, its plausibility. *i wonder what he thinks he's doing*?
Noah had written with sly aggression. Was it true that that
was precisely what Tracy feared – some threat by Noah to see
through him? To catch him unawares at something he himself
was too dense to see. To unnerve him. From the very first his
casual glance had said, almost contemptuously, I know you.
Tracy had been attracted to that. Yet what did it mean – to
be known? And why on earth should he care?

Once, when he was in college, a boy had stopped him on a
path and given him just such a look. He was only a kid, 13
or 14, but Tracy, suddenly, was uncannily aware that sex, its
hunger and lure, lay somewhere in that look. Unnerved, he'd
hurried on, gaze averted but spookily certain that if he paused
to glance back, that boy would be standing there looking after
him. Safely in his dorm room, he'd flung himself on his bed

and, in a fit of desperation, saying to himself You're crazy, you're crazy even as his imagination spun thrillingly out of control, masturbated furiously.

Shifting uncomfortably in his train seat, he tried to concentrate on the landscape passing outside the window – the river's flat shallows where birds skimmed in the dimming light. Painters had sought these shores. On the wall of Louis's office hung a very minor production of the Hudson River School: a limpid twilight, oxcart fording a broad stream; the Catskills drowsing in the pearly distance.

Out in the river, an oddity caught his attention – a series of ramparts and crenellated turrets set on a small wooded island. He'd seen those ruins on the way down, they caught his imagination, an inexplicable romantic folly out there interrupting the ordinary run of scenery. Who built it, and why? He'd craned his head to catch as much of it as he could before it passed by. And this time too: flitting past the train windows, in an instant it was gone. But it had broken, thankfully, his somber reverie. He re-entered the droning frequency of the couple behind him.

"Somebody," the old lady was telling her husband, "really should get out there and tear that thing down. It's a terrible eyesore. And somebody might get hurt."

Betsy's boundless enthusiasm ambushed him at the front door. Drooling and slobbering, deliriously happy, she desired him as no one, it seemed, had ever desired him. She kept leaping up to put her paws on his stomach. "Hey," he told her, "I missed you too." In the empty living room he could see Noah rousing himself from what appeared to be a nap on the sofa.

"Jesus, what a racket," Noah complained.

"Fit to wake the dead," Tracy told him.

"Well, I guess that would be me." Noah stood and stretched. His drab short hair was dishevelled from sleep, and he combed through it with splayed fingers, to no particular effect. Barefoot, he wore gray sweatpants, a blue flannel longsleeve shirt, untucked and half buttoned. Used as he was to seeing his student in regulation blue blazer and red tie, this casual dress – mufti, he supposed it was – struck Tracy as oddly intimate. "Your dog, by the way, is a whore," Noah observed matter-of-factly. It took Tracy, still puzzling about *mufti*, off guard.

"How so?" he asked seriously.

"Well, the instant you were gone, she transferred all her affections to me. One hundred percent." Kneeling, Noah encircled Betsy in his arms. "Didn't you, girl? You didn't think about him one bit."

Where his shirt fell open, Tracy couldn't help but register smooth skin. Still thrown a bit by Noah's antics, and half hoping, guiltily, for a glimpse of nipple, he asked, "How do you know what goes on in her head? She may have been secretly pining for me the whole time."

"You can believe anything you want," Noah said. He held Betsy's head and peered into her eyes.

We're not really fighting over the affections of a dog, Tracy thought. We're doing something else. But he wasn't exactly sure what that something else was.

Tracy felt a pulse not unlike nausea. He didn't really know Noah at all. He wasn't sure he wanted to know him. He wasn't sure he even liked him.

But the die, it seemed, had been cast. He'd made his overture of friendliness – in the form of Betsy he'd handed Noah responsibilities he couldn't now easily withdraw. To draw back now would be a gesture of cowardice.

Abruptly dropping the subject of Betsy, Noah leapt to his feet. "I have to tell you," he said excitedly, "I think this house of yours is haunted. Have you noticed that? I thought there was this old woman hiding in the closet. She was all covered in blood, and there were these bloody fingerprints all over the house. I was sure I'd find them on the walls, but I didn't."

"Get out of here," Tracy told him. "What on earth did you have for dinner?" Kneeling down, he in turn nuzzled with Betsy – who did seem promiscuously eager for any affection that came her way.

Noah only shrugged. "I'm just telling you," he insisted. "I think something bad happened in this place."

Shaking his head in bemusment – he'd never lived in such a welcoming house – Tracy tried to humor Noah. "Did Betsy notice anything?"

"She's just a dog," Noah said.

"Well, dogs have incredibly fine hearing. There's this whole world out there that only dogs know about."

"I think Betsy's maybe not the smartest dog," Noah judged. "By the way, you got some messages on your machine."

He was disconcerting, the way he veered abruptly from this to that. Attention Deficit Disorder, according to his files. He took ritalin for it. They were a remarkably doctored-up bunch, these Rifton students. Still, as Noah glided over to push the button on the answering machine – Tracy was about to say, "That's OK, I'll listen to them later," but it was too late, the tape was already rewinding – something in his movement, the purposeful way he sailed through space, chest out, head bent, gripped Tracy with surprising force. There was a moment in late boyhood when shambling awkwardness and long-limbed grace came together in tune. Noah rang with that clear pure pitch, and Tracy felt, gazing at the boy who stood by his answering machine, shifting his weight from one foot to the other as the first message began, something very much like awe.

"Oh, hello there." A tentative, cultivated voice spoke from the tape. "Louis Tremper calling. Claire and I wondered if, perhaps, you might care to come round this Friday for drinks and dinner, but I see you're not in. Well, I'm sure we'll run into one another on Monday, but I hope you'll be available."

Noah watched him. He had presumably heard all this already. The machine beeped and the next message, which Noah had presumably also already heard, began to play.

"Hi sweetie," a high, musical voice sang out. "It's . . ." There was a pause, in which Tracy hoped, absurdly, the machine would cut off. But it didn't. ". . . Arthurina. As in . . . *Queen* Arthurina. So lovely to have seen you. Hope you had a fabulous trip home. You know, I've been thinking, and I would definitely really really love to come see you, the sooner the better. And good luck with staying out of trouble. So many ephebes, as they say. And so little time. Call me soon."

In other circumstances the coincidence would have been interesting, even propitious, but Tracy felt himself redden as if an accusing finger had been pointed his way.

But what did it accuse? Noah was nonchalant. "That's all," he said. "Only two. Do you want me to save them?"

"Yes," Tracy said, "I mean, no." Did he owe an explanation? "An old friend," he said lamely.

"So will he come up and visit you?" Noah asked. It was impossible to tell whether he was interested, or only making conversation. He was inscrutable that way. Then, without waiting for an answer, he change the subject. "You should buy a television. I went crazy without a television here. How do you stand it? What do you do at night?" He paced restlessly up and down the bare room.

"Oh," Tracy said (thank God, he thought, for Attention Deficit Disorder), "there's this bloody old woman who comes out of the closet, and we sit and talk."

"Fuck off," Noah said lightly. "You're too weird."

"Me?" Tracy said in mock surprise, both relieved and disappointed to leave the subject of Arthurina safely behind.

It made Noah smile; this time there was even a hint of humor in his eyes. "You're weird because you've got nothing in your house," he proclaimed. "There's a ton of things you need to civilize this place. I should've made you a list."

As if to show the extent to which his house-sitting had gained him some stake in the house, he flung himself back down on the sofa and, grabbing a pillow, held it to his chest. "Before your friend comes up to see you, we should go shopping," he said. "I'll help you fix this dump up."

"I sort of like it like it as it is." Though he wondered if that only meant there was something depressingly lacking about his inner life.

"You mean – empty," Noah told him. "Ghosts *love* empty houses."

"Oh yeah?"

"Well, I mean – wouldn't you, if you were a ghost?"

"I have to think about that one," Tracy told him. There were perhaps worse things to contemplate than spending some Saturday afternoon at the shopping mall with Noah, looking for various furnitures that might keep away the ghosts.

Though it might also move things a next step in a process he should perhaps call a halt to while he still could. Before him flitted the crazy image: Noah and Arthur meeting one another. It was simply impossible. He had way too many different lives going on at once.

"By the way," he said distractedly, to get his mind off that troubling thought, "thanks for your Halloween gift." Releasing Betsy from his attentions, he looked forthrightly at his house-sitter. He hadn't thought he was even going to mention it.

Noah squeezed the pillow as if he wanted to force life into it. "I guess I was kind of bored," he said. "I'm great at procrastinating."

"Well, it was very, uh, creative."

"Yeah, yeah," Noah said flatly. "About as creative as my asshole."

Tracy scrambled to conceal his surprise. "You kids have such foul mouths these days," he joked, though inwardly the words sent a sharp thrill through him.

"Sorry," Noah apologized, as if it were a belch or fart that had slipped out. "It's just a saying."

What could Noah possibly know about assholes? Except that he had one – whose secret particulars Tracy, in spite of himself, had no choice but to inwardly contemplate.

"Kids these days are stupid as dogs," Noah went on. "But then you know that. You're the one who has to teach us."

But Tracy was unwilling to pursue any of that any further. "Look," he said, for fear of spoiling the acute, unlooked-for pleasure he'd already got, "I think you've gone and hurt Betsy's feelings" – a betrayal that wasn't strictly obvious from the way she lay, content, on the bare floor between them.

"Aww . . . Betsy," Noah crooned. "Light of my life." He released the pillow he'd been hugging to his chest and reached down for the top of her head, stroking her delicately for a minute. Her tail wagged madly and Tracy thought about all this affection – for the dog, the pillow. But none, apparently, for him.

Instantly he chided himself for that stupid thought, even as Noah said, relinquishing Betsy with a regretful sigh, "I should probably be getting back to my dorm. Believe it or not, I have to try to do some homework tonight."

"That's the spirit," Tracy told him heartily. But as Noah

disappeared into the guest bedroom to gather his things, he felt both relief and disappointment. He was suddenly, depressingly conscious of invisible lines circumscribing him all around, unmarked boundaries it was unwise, even downright dangerous to cross.

"So now," he said as Noah, hair newly combed, shirt buttoned, sneakers the size of motorboats on his feet, reappeared in the doorway with his gym bag of belongings, "tell me honestly. Did you really see a ghost in my house?"

GEOGRAPHY

Philip Gambone

I PRINTED OUT the invoice for our last patient of the day: vaccinations for Hep A and Japanese encephalitis.

"So, you're going to Vietnam?" I asked, handing him the sheet of paper and smiling. It was a question and a smile that could be interpreted as just a bit of friendly customer relations, though if he was game to flirt, so was I. An American, 28 years old, his medical history form said. And cute as a cornfed farm boy, which he might have been, since his permanent address (also noted on his history) was Kansas City.

"Yeah, Hanoi." He glanced at the bill, handed over his credit card and waited while I processed the transaction.

"I hear it's really beautiful there," I said, smiling again as I passed back his card and showed him where to sign . . . His hair was the color of wheat on a high Kansas summer afternoon. "When are you leaving?"

"Tonight," he said distractedly as he folded his copy of the transaction in half. "I've got reservations on the soft sleeper. Two and a half days from Beijing to Hanoi." He looked up, shook the doubled over paper at me in a kind of farewell salute – "Take it easy," he said – turned and left.

I placed the office copy of the invoice on the pile to be processed tomorrow. "Brian O'Rourke," I whispered to myself. I tried to imagine what it would be like to cuddle up with him in the loft bed of a soft sleeper, the train gently rocking us through the Chinese countryside.

From my desk, across the waiting room and through the window, I could see the first phalanx of workers peddling home. As they maneuvered their bicycles through the traffic, the expressions on their faces remained as focused and obedient as Buddhist monks in meditation.

Just then, Mrs Chen, the *aiyi*, came over and carefully set down a covered cup of tea.

"*Xiexie*. Thank you, Auntie Chen, thank you," I said, tripping over myself with politeness. Although I didn't want any more tea, I still hadn't learned how to graciously decline our auntie's ministrations. I took the lid off the cup, sipped, then nodded to her approvingly. "Very good, very delicious. Thank you, thank you."

She bobbed her head, her approbation equal to mine, then stood there, waiting for I didn't know what.

"How is your son, Mrs Chen?" I asked. It was the first thing that popped into my head, anything to break the awkwardness of the moment.

"He very good, very good," she said. "Thank you."

In truth, Mrs Chen's son, Xiao Cai, was a knockout. In his mid-twenties, he stood slightly taller than the average Chinese, had a face that was somewhere between boyish and butch, broad shoulders, and a modified crew cut. As he had done on the night when he met me at the airport, he favored open-collar jersey shirts that showed off a smooth, hairless chest. Xiao Cai was the first Chinese I met when I came to Beijing. He was – should I be ashamed to admit this? – the first Chinese man that I thought of as hot.

"Please tell him hello for me," I told Mrs Chen.

"Yes, I say hello." She nodded to me again, backed away and disappeared into the staff kitchen. I took another sip of tea and looked out the window again.

It had turned into a beautiful late-September afternoon, the sky finally blue and smog-free. Since I'd arrived in Beijing, we hadn't had many of these days. The pollution all month had been heavy, casting a dusty, pallid light over everything. I thought of

Provincetown, of how clear and clean and sparkling the light is there, especially in September.

I'd been thinking about Provincetown a lot lately, about my first summer there, eight years ago now, and how disoriented I'd felt. I was 37 that year; never been to a gay resort before. But *that* I was ready for. No, what had really unnerved me was the turned-around geography of the place. I couldn't get it into my head that what the locals called the West End was really on the west side of town. There I'd be, every Friday afternoon, driving east on Route 6 all the way from the Sagamore Bridge, and the next thing I knew I was entering the village from the East End, headed *west*. It was as if I'd passed through some bizarre geographical warp.

The explanation was simple, of course: how the Cape gradually turns in on itself like a conch shell, curlicuing around – east, then north, then west – an almost imperceptible shift. Still, that was just information in my head. Somehow my body, my sense of where the sun should be, refused to cooperate with my brain.

Flying west to China had been a little like that. I'd passed through several time zones, each one putting me an hour earlier in the day until, somewhere over the Pacific, we crossed the International Date Line, and suddenly it was a whole day later. It didn't stand to reason: that I could have been traveling earlier and earlier into Tuesday, only to end up in a place where it was already Wednesday.

I took a last gulp of tea. Jasmine. I wondered why I hadn't noticed the flavor before. Was I actually getting used to not having Earl Gray? I flipped on the clinic's after-hours answering machine, fit the dust cover over my computer and walked to the staff room. Tyson McCallum, one of the clinic's young doctors, looked up from where he was washing his hands at the sink.

"Tyson, I still don't get it," I said. At lunch, I'd been telling him about my disorientation. "What if I'd flown *east* instead, across the Atlantic?"

"Then you'd have lost hours, Mate."

"But I wouldn't have crossed the International Date Line."

"Right." Tyson pulled a paper towel from the dispenser and dried his hands.

"So it would still be Tuesday?"

"Depends on how early in the day you set out, Mate."

Tyson's Australian. I'd always thought that "Mate" stuff was just a cutesy tourist industry gimmick, but Tyson really talks like that.

"All right. Think of it this way," I suggested. "Two people leave New York really early on a Tuesday morning, one eastbound, one westbound. They both arrive in Beijing twelve hours later."

"That'd be a mighty fast flight," Tyson said. "You can't do it in twelve hours." He took off his white doctor's jacket and hung it on a peg, next to which was a large framed poster of the Sleeping Buddha at Fragrant Hills Parks. He'd hung it there a week ago after visiting the temple with his girlfriend . . .

"But what if you did it in a supersonic plane or something?"

Tyson put his hands on my shoulders and looked me straight in the eye.

"Time moves on, Matey. Yes, hypothetically I suppose you might arrive earlier than you left, but in reality it doesn't work that way."

He went on about the sun and the earth's rotation and why the International Date Line runs down the least populated area in the world. But all I could focus on was his gorgeous blue eyes and the fact that it couldn't be both Tuesday and Wednesday in Beijing, though it seemed to me that, depending on which direction you traveled in, it might be.

"I'll have to think about it some more," I told him. "I need to sit down with an atlas."

"There you go," Tyson agreed. "Well, now. How about a beer? We haven't had a proper conversation since that time we went out for drinks – what's it now? – I make it the week you got here."

I wish I could imitate the way Tyson says things like "there you go" and "well now" and "I make it." It's the Aussie accent – one of the things I fell for when we first met – but every time I try to mimic him, it just comes out sounding British or stagy or goofy sounding. I'm afraid I haven't much of an ear for the nuances of sounds and language. Which is why, after almost a month in Beijing, I still hadn't mastered the four tones of Mandarin.

"I'd like to join you, Tyson, but I can't tonight." I took off my tie and tucked it far down into my backpack.

I'd come to Beijing in August, the new office manager for the Western clinic. It's the kind of work I'd done back in the States – managing a health center. Back there it was a gay health center, which seemed to me, at the time I interviewed for the Beijing job, excellent experience for this new undertaking. As I saw it, in both situations I was serving a minority population.

"Gotta date?" Tyson asked. He meant a gay date. I'd come out to him a few days after we'd met, over those first beers and conversation. I'd assumed Tyson was gay, and was kind of hoping that he'd prove to be boyfriend material, but it was only his boyish looks, the amazing blue eyes, and his interest in Buddhism that I'd picked up on. Tyson was one of those sensitive, "new straight guy" types and definitely okay with my being, as another Australian friend of mine puts it, a "poofter."

"A date?" I repeated. "No, not exactly." This was, I saw, my opportunity to give him more details about my life as a gay man. "I'm going cruising."

Without missing a beat, Tyson said, "So I'll come along to your pub, Matey. I've been to gay bars before."

I laughed. "Tyson, where I'm going they don't sell beer." I told him about a park I'd just learned about, a place where Chinese gay men hung out.

"Dong Dan?" he said. "It's notorious. A lot of money boys traipsing about there, mate. I didn't suspect you'd fancy that."

"I don't, and it's not Dong Dan." Before I spoke again, I wondered if my friendship with Tyson would ever be comfortable enough to tell him about the time I'd picked up a money boy – a "hustler," as we Yanks say – back home in Boston. "No, it's a park just north of the Lama Temple. This American I met at the Ta Ta Club showed me where on my map."

I used to hate that name – the Ta Ta. It sounded so prissy-faggy. Jesus, I thought, is *this* the image of homosexuality we're exporting to China? Then someone pointed out to me that in Mandarin "ta ta" just means "he and he." Nothing effete about it.

"What goes on in that park?" Tyson asked.

"Oh, the usual." I tried to sound like the worldly gay American who'd seen it all, done it all. But, in fact, I had no idea what a Chinese cruising park was like. In fact, I hadn't had much gay contact at all – sexual or otherwise – since coming to Beijing. At the Ta Ta Club, most of the Chinese guys stuck to themselves. The one guy I'd tried to pick up there had been an American. It hadn't worked out.

"What's 'the usual'?" Tyson asked. In the short time that I've known him, his curiosity about gay life has never seemed perfunctory or prurient. He's truly interested. Tyson is 28. When I was his age, I was in therapy about my homosexuality.

"It's like this," I explained. "You either pick someone up and take them home, or you do it right there."

"That *is* an advantage of male-to-male sex, isn't it?" he offered. "A lot less fuss and bother about it all. You and your mate have a lovely mutual wank and then straight off you go, back to whatever it was you were doing."

"Very efficient," I agreed.

I'd learned that kind of efficiency during my summers in Provincetown. My friend Michael, with whom I shared a season-long rental for three years, called those summers "David's Second Coming Out." Michael was blond and beautiful, and for one brief, cold February before we became friends and shared the house in P'town – the winter he turned twenty-six and I was 35 – he'd been my lover. Those three summers at the tip of Cape Cod, Michael taught me how to dance, how to cruise, how to dress to pick up men. He taught me to ride my bike fast through the dune trails, and that it didn't have to be lovemaking every time I had sex with another man. He taught me how to work the tea dances at the Boatslip and what brand of briefs to wear for the underwear parties at Back Street. These were things I needed to learn, Michael used to say. I once told him he was the most dangerous friend I'd ever had.

"Thank you," he said. "If you don't live dangerously, you

just end up a frightened old queen. What's great about being gay, David, is that we're free to invent ourselves. Girl, you work it," he'd tell me. "Whatever you've got, you work it."

What I've got is not the classic American Guy look, but Michael taught me that my features – I have black eyes, a Roman nose, a heavily chiseled Mediterranean face: my "ethnic" look, he called it – would draw its share of admirers. That's what I learned to work. And then, after a while, it didn't work any more, or I couldn't get it to work, or I didn't trust it to work. Maybe, after Michael died, I got frightened again. Or maybe there's another kind of living dangerously, one Michael never knew about, that I wanted now. All I know is that when I saw the ad for the job in Beijing I jumped at the opportunity to get away from a life that was going nowhere. The next thing I knew I was flying over the Pacific, gaining and losing time simultaneously.

"Well, Mate," Tyson said, "Doesn't sound as if there's much at that park for me." He slipped into his sports jacket, a beautiful silk and linen blend. I laughed.

"You know, for a Buddhist and a straight man, you dress better than half the gay men I know."

Tyson looked at me, the Aussie joviality momentarily gone from his eyes. "Good fashion, David, is a kind of paying attention, too."

"Well, you'd be a big hit at the Ta Ta. I almost wish we were going there tonight."

"Not too late to change your mind," he suggested.

I zipped up my backpack. "No, I've been planning this little excursion for a while now. I want to follow through with it before I get cold feet."

"Sounds like a project," he said.

"Is that bad?" I asked. Sometimes I wondered if Tyson was going to take Michael's place as my life teacher.

"No, it's not bad. It's just a project."

"Well, then," I said, "a project," and hefting my backpack onto my shoulder, I went out to fetch my bike.

I rode along the canal that parallels Liangmahe Nanlu and then, when it intersected with Dongzhimen Street, kept going west through a district of old gray-brick quadrangle houses. I'd spent my lunch hour with a map of the city, memorizing my route to the park. I didn't want to be stopping every half mile to check directions.

The streets were heavy with traffic – cars, taxis, bicycles, trishaws piled to toppling with goods. What always amazed me on these bike trips through the city was how few accidents I saw. It was as if the Chinese rode around with a sixth sense, an acute, intuitive awareness of everyone else within a 20-foot radius: where they were, their speed, their direction, their likelihood of doing something unexpected. Perhaps in a culture that's 5,000 years old, you develop an instinct for avoiding trouble.

At Gulou Street, I turned north. In the two months that I'd been in Beijing, Gulou had become one of my favorite streets. It's quieter and narrower than Dongzhimen, a bicyclist's haven. The alleyways, those side streets the Chinese call hutongs, feel more inviting, less secretive. Tall grasses have sprung up on the gray-tile roofs, rooted in the chinks and crevices like a living thatch. In the crisp September air I could smell the forestry aromas of roasting chestnuts and smoke from the charcoal braziers. To my right, the sway-backed roofs of the Drum and Bell towers rose above the squat houses and shops. The whole district had a cosy, villagey feel, a respite from the noise and fumes and speed of the Second Ring Road not far away. Even the light seemed to fall more gently here.

I was aware of all of this – remembered how much I'd delighted in all these sights on previous bike rides this way – but today Gulou attracted me only as an idea: a postcard, a photo in a guidebook, a series of picturesque images rushing by. Elsewhere is where I wanted to be.

Be present to what is, I tried to remind myself. Those were the words Tyson was always telling me.

I got to the Second Ring Road, at this hour a tidal wave of motor vehicles and bikes. The blaring and beeping of horns, which the Chinese lean on like a second accelerator, quickened the air, making me think of noisemakers at a New Year's party. I waited for a break in the traffic, then, along with the hundreds of other cyclists trying to get across, walked my bike to the other side. Everyone else who was crossing was Chinese, but at this hour no one bothered to stare at me.

In America, a man makes eye contact with another man not of his acquaintance, and it means only one thing. That's what it had felt like my first weeks in Beijing: as if every man in China were cruising me. I couldn't distinguish one look from another. And though I've gotten used to the stares now, as I pushed my bike along, I told myself that going to the park today was just a way to learn what real Chinese cruising looked like. *Be present*, I thought.

Once across the street, I took out my map and rechecked my bearings. The park was a small one, my friend at the Ta Ta had told me.

"Look for an iron fence," he'd said. "Just to the other side of the canal that runs along Second Ring Road. You'll see a pagoda-like gazebo up on a little hill. There's a gate in the fence. Can't miss it."

I walked my bike over the bridge that arched the canal, then got on and rode west again under a canopy of poplar trees. I'd been surprised to find these formal allées in Beijing. Long, straight lines of trees were something I expected from the French, not the Chinese. This and the expatriate district, with its cafés and bistros and frame shops, reminded me of Europe. When I first got here, I kept looking for more of Europe in Beijing, kept wanting this place to be an Asian version of London or Rome or Madrid. Now I'm trying to let Beijing just be Beijing. Tyson says that's "very Buddhist" of me. I'll have to ask him if there's a very Buddhist way to pick up boys.

In a few minutes, I found myself at the gate to the park. Not knowing the custom, I decided to get off and walk my bike. I didn't want to be stopped for breaking any rules. I wanted to be as unobtrusive as possible. My heart was beating fast, the way it used to when I was just starting out in the gay world.

I followed a winding path that led past rocky outcroppings and plantings of trees – evergreens of some sort, hemlocks they looked like. I wondered if these groves functioned the way the trees and bushes and banks of reeds functioned at the various outdoor sex areas I'd tried back home. My friend at the Ta Ta had not been explicit about what exactly went on here. A bit farther along, I saw the hill with the pavilion, just as he'd described. A man and a woman were sitting inside, holding hands. I walked on.

The next bend in the path opened onto a large pond choked with lotus pads. At one end some old men were fishing. I strolled around the lake, stopping to listen to a band of percussionists – about a dozen men who, with amazing precision, were keeping up a tricky syncopated rhythm on their cymbals and drums. They'd attracted maybe 26 onlookers, most of them elderly people who had paused from their Sunday strolls and exercise groups to gather around and listen. A few children, too, standing close to their *nainais*.

I was making my way around the other side of the pond, when I saw a young man coming toward me on a bicycle. As he passed, he looked at me, but in a way – there seemed to be more intention in it – that was different from the stares I usually got in Beijing. I walked on a few feet, then turned around. The guy had stopped and was twisting around on his bike looking back in my direction. There was something about him – but what was it? – that made me feel his curiosity went beyond the mere fact that I was a Westerner.

I walked my bike over to a rocky hillock across from the pond, parked it, then leaned casually against a boulder, pretending to listen to the percussionists across the water. The guy on the bike stayed put, continuing to stare in my direction. Then he turned around and slowly rode toward me.

As he passed, we made brief eye contact again. A subtle nod from me. Nothing from him. He pedaled on, then stopped again. He might have been listening to the percussionists, too. Or trying to appear as if he were listening. Being able to distinguish the "as ifs" of gay cruising from genuinely innocent behavior is crucial, Michael used to tell me.

Casually, as if I'd had enough of resting, I walked away from the boulder toward the boy on the bike. He looked 18, but was probably in his mid to late twenties. His black, lusterless hair was rough cut, somewhere between the length of Mrs Chen's son's crew cut and the long silky bangs of so many Chinese guys his age. It was an unstudied haircut, so different from the careful grooming of so many of the boys back home, which made him all the more exotic in my eyes.

As I passed him, we made eye contact again. I wondered if there was a phrase for "cat-and-mouse game" in Chinese. Cat and mouse seemed like it might be a direct translation of *something* Chinese.

I was walking away from the pond now, over toward another arrangement of boulders. The Chinese seem to like these rugged settings: piles of rocks, clumps of trees, meandering paths. Such manmade landscapes, evocative of the harmonious contours of nature, are also, Tyson once told me, "very Buddhist."

I perched myself on top of one of the rocks. A few minutes later, the boy strolled by. I was glad I'd worn my baseball cap. I think it makes me look younger. We made eye contact again.

"*Ni hao*," I said.

He stopped, then smiled. From my perch atop the rock, I looked down at him. He seemed to be waiting for me to make the next move. The way he just passively stood there – was he frightened? demure? tongue-tied? – it seemed a little subservient, an Oriental stereotype. I wanted to tell him he didn't have to relate to me that way. Instead, I smiled.

In silence, we continued staring at each other. He was wearing a dark blue suit, a white shirt buttoned at the collar, a pair of soft white leather loafers. Except for the loafers, this might have been the Sunday strolling outfit my Italian uncles would have worn in the forties and early fifties.

"*Wo*," I said, pointing to myself, "David. *De Xiang*." I used the Chinese translation of my first name. A last name didn't seem important at this moment. He told me his name, but my ear didn't catch all the sounds. "*Hen gaoxing jiandao ni*," I said. Very pleased to meet you. I hoped I'd gotten the tones right.

A faint smile appeared on his face again and he repeated the phrase. It's something I've found the Chinese do a lot – repeat what you've just said. I still haven't figured out whether this is for clarity's sake or simply out of politeness. I motioned for him to come join me on the rock. He knocked the kickstand down, stabilized his bike and scurried up the embankment. I extended my hand to pull him up. I wanted to touch him. He took it. His hand was thicker than

I'd expected. Coarser, too. A worker's hand. He squatted next to me.

"*Ni hao*," I said again. I only had a dozen phrases at my command, half of them useless in this situation. In fractured Mandarin, I tried to explain that I could only speak a little Chinese, and asked if he knew any English. No, he told me. We fell silent again, but he kept looking at my face – to say scrutinizing it would not be an exaggeration.

"Slanted" is the way I'd learned, as a child, to describe Chinese eyes. But his were softer than that. Almost dreamy in the dark, unblinking gaze he fixed on me. Though not as stunningly beautiful as Mrs Chen's son, he radiated a calm, quiet peacefulness that was fast melting my heart. I thought of that soft sleeper to Hanoi.

I eased off my backpack and rummaged around inside. There was a pack of gum in the small pouch. I offered him a stick. (Hadn't I seen this gesture in Second World War movies: the GI befriending the native children with sticks of gum?) He shook his head no, then said something in Chinese. I shook my head. We both laughed.

"You're adorable," I told him.

He said something like "*dou bu le*," and I realized he was trying to repeat my words.

"Adorable," I repeated, slowly.

"*Dou a bu*," he said.

I pointed to him. "You. You adorable."

"*Yu dou a bu*." He didn't have a clue as to what I was saying.

I pulled out my tourist's phrase book and flipped to the back, the dictionary section. The dictionary was only about 20 pages long, confined to touristy vocabulary like "hotel," "restaurant," "aspirin." It did not list the word for "adorable."

I looked up at him. "Just as well."

He said something else. From his inflection and the few words I could pick up, I understood that he wanted to know where I was from.

"America. *Meiguo*."

"*Meiguo*," he repeated and nodded his head approvingly.

I flipped more pages of the phrase book until I got to the section titled "Introductions and Occupations."

"*Wo*," I began, pointing to myself again, "*wo shi*" – and then I scanned the list with my finger, looking for something that came close to "office manager." "Secretary" was the best I could do. I wondered if secretary was a gender-specific occupation in China and what this would tell him about me. He motioned for me to pass him the phrase book. When I gave it to him, he pointed to a word on the list: *gong ren*, a factory worker, a manual worker.

I wanted to ask him what kind of manual work, but my phrase book didn't go in for that sort of detail. I smiled at him. "This is going to be very slow going, isn't it?"

"Slow," he repeated.

We continued passing the phrase book back and forth, "talking" in tourist phrases. So much of what it had to offer was useless here: "How much does it cost to send a letter to the United States?" or "What time does the train leave for Shanghai?" I considered showing him the sentence that said, "Do you have a room with a private bath?" but decided not to risk it yet. Sometimes, as I held the phrase book with him, I let my fingers brush against his. He seemed oblivious to this.

When we had exhausted the resources of the book, he motioned for us to walk a bit. Perhaps up that hill, he indicated, toward the little pavilion? I looked. The couple who had been holding hands were gone.

"Up there?" I asked, nodding and pointing. "You want to go hold hands up there?" It was weird being able to say such seductive things, knowing he wouldn't understand a word. I thought about the months after Michael died and how I'd wake up in the morning, clutching my pillow, whispering intimate things into its soft belly.

We climbed up to the gazebo and sat on the railing. I leaned against a post. He sat straight up without any support for his back. This seemed very Chinese to me. For a minute we didn't say anything.

"*Nide mingzi*?" I asked. I wanted to get his name again.

He repeated it, three syllables, but I still couldn't catch all the sounds. I reached into my backpack again, this time pulling out a pencil and a small notebook. Making scribbling gestures in

the air, I motioned for him to write down his name. He took the
writing equipment and started jotting down some characters. I
eased away from the post, leaning in closer toward him as if to
get a better look. I was close enough to smell a faint trace of
cheap, overly sweet cologne. That and the Sunday suit made
me realize that he'd tried to be at his best for this excursion in
the park.

As he wrote, I looked at him again. His hands, though
coarse, were neatly manicured. Unlike Auntie Chen's son,
my new friend was not sporting the long pinky fingernail –
an affectation dating back to the days of the Mandarins – that
seemed so popular with certain guys I'd seen in Beijing.

When he'd finished writing, he turned the book back to me:
three square, neatly aligned little ideograms. I looked back up
into his eyes. I tried to imagine what it would be like to lay my
lips gently on his eyelids, press my tongue into the corners of
those almond-shaped eyes.

"*Pinyin*?" I asked, and mimed the scribbling again.

He hesitated, then took up the notebook again and laboriously
began to write the Romanized version of his name. I moved
closer, my thigh touching his. He didn't seem to notice.

"Chang He Bin," I pronounced.

A smile blossomed on his face and he repeated his name.
His tones were different from mine – rising where I'd fallen;
level where I'd raised the inflection. I tried again. His smiled
widened.

"Do I call you Chang, or He Bin?" I asked, touching his arm.
"Huh? Which is friendlier? I still haven't got that straight." He
continued to stare at me. "Let's go with first names, OK? OK,
He Bin?"

"*Ni*?" he asked.

I said my first name again, enunciating the two syllables,
Da-vid, then the Chinese version of my whole name: Ma De
Xiang. He repeated it. I pulled out my wallet, took a business
card from the slip and handed it to him.

"*Wo*," I said. "That's me."

He Bin tried pronouncing my name in English. The "vid"
part gave him trouble, as did my last name – Masiello. As
we both laughed, my attention momentarily went to one of

the posts that supported the roof of the little pavilion. Like so much architecture of this ilk, it was painted Chinese red. There on the faded, peeling surface of that russet post, I noticed how former visitors to this little love temple had left various messages scrawled in pencil, the first graffiti I'd seen in China. I wondered what these characters said. Were they love notes? pornography? subversive political slogans? Maybe all three?

He Bin took my pen again and wrote out a sentence of about ten characters. I recognized two of them – the characters *Zhong guo* – Middle Kingdom. That was China or Chinese. And the last character, *ma*, the word that means you're asking a question. Curiously, in a sentence that otherwise ran from left to right, he had written one character – it looked like the character for "man" – above another. I looked more closely. The signs for man and woman, *nan* and *nü*. He was asking me something about Chinese men and women. No, Chinese men *or* women. *Which one?* he was asking me. Which one did I like?

"Men," I said. "*Nan, nan.* I like men. Oh, God, do I like men!" When I laughed, he let out a little demure chuckle.

That's how I'd always been with Michael: to his uproarious laughter, I'd always respond with a diffident chuckle, never ready to go as far as he.

"So now what do we do?" I asked. I wanted to run my hand along the sleeve of He Bin's blue serge jacket again, but whenever I'd touched him before he hadn't responded. "What are *you* ready for?" He Bin said something else. I shook my head pleadingly. "Darling, I wish I could understand you. I wish you could understand me."

Back in the States, I'd had many encounters with guys where neither of us ever spoke a word. Where neither of us ever *wanted* to speak a word. Late nights under the dock in Provincetown, wandering through a maze of men who were silently masturbating each other, the only sounds the sloshing of the tide and the slurping noises – exaggerated, it sometimes seemed – of fellatio. For a long time, I'd savored all that, too.

I looked at He Bin again.

By now, the sun had fallen below the tree line and the air was beginning to turn chilly.

"I think it's getting late," I said, nodding toward the hazy orange glow bleeding through the leaves of the poplar and sycamore trees.

I fingered the phrase book in my lap and thought about that question again – "Do you have a room with a private bath?" I'd been in China long enough to know that the answer would be no, but I figured it was the closest I could come in Mandarin to suggesting that we sleep together. I figured He Bin would get the point and that somehow we could negotiate the details.

I looked up again. His face radiated the still, unruffled serenity of a peasant waiting for . . . well, what? Flood waters to recede? A sow to give birth? His luck to change? Almost more than his body, I wanted him to give me that serenity, too.

And then I noticed the graffiti again. Up until now I'd never imagined that the Chinese, whom I'd thought of as respectful and full of self-control, would ever engage in even this mild a form of vandalism. I tried to picture He Bin furtively scrawling some pornographic message on one of the posts. I tried picturing what it would be like to have him in bed with me, to feel hot flesh again, to forget about the quest for serenity. I felt my penis stiffening. Surreptitiously, I glanced down at his crotch to see if I could detect any similar stirrings. The blue serge pants were baggy. Again, I thought of my old uncles.

He Bin was still holding my business card. I slipped it from his fingers and wrote down my Beijing telephone number.

"*Wode*," I told him, pointing to the number and handing him back the card. "Mine."

He studied it, looked up, smiling and nodding, then said something in what I knew to be simplified Chinese. I caught enough to know he was telling me he didn't have a telephone.

"No problem," I said. "You call me." And then, looking up, into the painted canopy of the pavilion, I chuckled. "It'll be a dandy conversation, won't it?"

We sat there another minute, looking out over the park. I knew that if I didn't make a move now, didn't do or say something, that we'd part and I'd never see him again. There was no way that He Bin and I could arrange a second meeting through a telephone conversation.

One summer, Michael kept a jar in which he deposited scraps of paper with the telephone numbers of all the tricks he'd picked up. "When it's about sex, the second time is usually a disaster," he once told me. "One look and you wonder what it was you ever saw in each other." Michael also used to say, "Never postpone a trick you can have today until tomorrow."

"It's not that I'm shy, Michael, not this time," I said into that painted canopy. All blue and green and white, chevrons and diamonds and zigzags, it looked like an intricate, geometrical heaven. "I guess I'm looking for something else now."

He Bin cocked his head toward me. I think he knew I wasn't speaking to him. "A ghost," I said. "I'm speaking to the ghost of my little brother." I reached over and touched his hand. He let me caress his knuckles, but didn't reciprocate. What was this? Chinese reserve? Working-class shyness? I decided the name didn't matter: I'd just be present to whatever it was.

"*Zaijian*," I told him. "Goodbye."

I left the park, not turning around, and biked along the canal that parallels the Second Ring Road. I was headed west, into the fast descending sun, and soon it was dark. Even the light from the few street lamps was obscured by the overhanging branches of the leafy poplar trees. But I knew my way. Beijing is an easy city to travel in. Everything's arranged on a grid — that Chinese passion for orienting their environment along a north-south, east-west axis. That, I suspected, was Confucian, not Buddhist. How those two ways of being ever managed to coexist I still didn't understand. Maybe in the morning I'd ask Tyson. In the meantime, I just tried to savor this new, very un-Bostonian geography.

And once again, I thought of that first summer in Provincetown, and how the sun never set where I thought it should. Every time I would try to show visitors where home was, I'd get it all wrong. Three summers — that's what it took for me to get the hang of that curlicue, to get it firmly in my bearings, to not be surprised at where the sun was rising.

NEW YORK 1942

Christopher Bram

LATE ONE MARCH afternoon in 1942, Seaman Second Class Hank Fayette entered the Lyric Theater on 42nd Street.

The war was four months old. Hank was 20. Tall and blond, a black pea coat buttoned over his uniform, he climbed the steps to the balcony two at a time, grinning like a kid at the gold ceiling, brass rails, and fancy carpet. There was nothing like this place back home in Beaumont, Texas.

Two sailors stood off to one side of the upstairs lobby and watched him pass. One nudged the other; the other shook his head. Hank wondered what they were considering, but he wanted nothing to do with them either. This was his very first day of liberty after two months at sea and he was sick of the navy. It was his first time in New York City and he wanted everything to be new. He'd spent all morning and most of the afternoon riding trolleys up and down this concrete beehive, getting a crick in his neck. There was something wonderfully unnatural about a place where buildings dwarfed the tallest tree. The city was straight out of the Planet Mongo in the funny papers.

The inside of the theater was as big as a circus tent, but the movie looked the same as movies in Beaumont, only taller. This was another one about the boy from the radio who talked through his nose. Hank almost turned around and went back out again, only he'd paid his four bits and there was no harm in staying long enough to see what happened. He stood at the back of the balcony, behind the partition, took off his bulky pea coat, and draped it over the partition. There were plenty of empty seats up here for the matinee, but theater seats never gave Hank enough room for his lanky legs. He tugged at the scratchy dress blues that pulled too tight across his butt and wondered if the guys had been only ragging him about this place. It was just a big old movie theater.

There was a sudden smell of cologne, sweet and boozy. Then the smell faded. Hank looked left and right. He saw the back of a man sliding off to the right. The pointy crown of the man's half-lit hat was turning, as though he'd been looking at Hank.

Hank glanced back at the movie – Henry Aldrich was getting scolded by his mother – then looked around the sloping balcony. Someone got up, walked up the aisle, then sat down again. So many Yankees wore those funny shoulders that Hank wasn't certain which were men and which were women in this light. He looked up at the staggered windows of the projection booth and the beam of light that occasionally twitched inside itself.

The smell of cologne returned, and hung there. Hank waited a moment. When he turned around, he found himself looking down on the spotless brim of a hat. The man stood only a foot away. Like most people, he was shorter than Hank.

The man looked up, his face slowly appearing beneath his hat. He had a smooth, friendly face and a red bow tie. "You're standing improperly," he whispered.

"Beg pardon?" said Hank. "Sir?"

"If you want to meet people, you should stand with your hands behind you."

The man sounded so well-meaning and knowledgeable. Hank automatically took his big hands off the partition and placed them at his back in parade rest.

"And you're quite tall. You should hold them a little lower."

"Like this?"

"Let me see." The man stepped up behind Hank and pressed his crotch into Hank's hands.

The wool was ribbed and baggy. Hank cupped his hands around a loose bundle inside before he realized what he was doing. His heart began to race.

The man lightly cleared his throat. "Uh, you interested?"

Hank let go and spun around. He snatched the man's hat off his head so he could see him better. Strands of light from the movie flickered in the brilliantined hair while the man anxiously reached for his hat. He wasn't so old, maybe 30, and not at all effeminate. Hank let him take the hat back, then reached down to feel the man's crotch from the front.

"Oh? Oh." The man pulled his brim back over his eyes, glanced around, reached down and touched Hank, tweaked him through the cloth. "I see," he whispered. "I don't suppose you have a place where we can go?"

Hank closed his eyes and shook his head. It felt so damn good to touch and be touched again. The cologne wasn't so strong once you got used to it.

"I live with my mother, you understand. But I have some friends downtown with a room we can use." He removed his hand and used it to take Hank's hand, rubbing a smooth thumb across the wide, hard palm. "Do you mind going downtown?"

"Hell, no!" Hank cried and pulled loose to grab his coat.

"Shhh, please. Discretion." But the man was smiling to himself as he nervously glanced around and nodded at the curtain over the exit.

Hank followed him out to the balcony lobby, where the two sailors still waited. "What did I tell you?" said one. "Trade."

The man didn't look at Hank, but walked quickly, trying to keep a step or two ahead of him. So even in the big city people were shy about this. Hank buttoned up his coat so he wouldn't show. He buried his eager hands in his coat pockets to stop himself from grabbing the man's arm or slapping him on the ass, he was so happy. His shipmates hadn't been teasing him when they joked about this movie house, laughing over why they wouldn't want to go there and why Hank might.

Out on the street it was almost spring, but a city kind of spring, just temperature. The other side of 42nd Street was deeper in shadow now than it had been when Hank went inside, the penny arcade brighter. Gangs of sailors charged up and down the sidewalks, hooting and elbowing each other over every girl they saw, not understanding how much fun they could've had with themselves. Hank had understood since he was 4. Thumbing around the country or working at a CCC camp, he had met plenty of others who understood, too. There had to be others on the *McCoy*, but living on a destroyer was worse than living in Beaumont. You had to live with them afterwards, which could get sticky if they started feeling guilty or, worse, all moony and calf-eyed. It should be as natural as eating, but people were funny and Hank did his best to get along with them. Most of his shipmates thought Hank was only joshing them or playing the dumb hick when he told them what he liked.

That Mongo skyscraper with the rounded corners stood at the far end of the street like a good idea. Hank's man stood at the curb, signaling for a taxi. The traffic was all trucks and taxicabs, with a lone streetcar nosing along like an old catfish. Finally, a square-roofed taxi pulled over and the man opened the door and signaled Hank to get in. "West Street and Gansevoort," he told the driver.

The man relaxed. He smiled at Hank, offered him a cigarette, then offered the driver one, too. "I thought our homesick boy in blue deserved a home-cooked meal," he told the driver. The men smoked cigarettes and talked about all the changes the war had brought about. The driver asked Hank all the usual civilian questions about home and ship and girlfriend. The man smirked to himself when Hank mentioned Mary Ellen, but he didn't understand.

They drove along a waterfront, the low sun flashing gold on the dusty windshield between the high warehouses and higher ships. It looked just like the area around the Brooklyn Navy Yard, where the *McCoy* was in dry dock. Suddenly, there was a long stretch of sunlight, and Hank saw the rounded metal ridge of a ship lying on its side in the river. "Poor *Normandie*," sighed the driver and said it was sabotage. The man said carelessness and stupidity; the two began to argue about how much they could trust the newspapers. The driver mentioned a house that had been raided in Brooklyn, where there were Nazi spies and all kinds of sick goings-on, but how the newspapers had to hush it up because they'd caught a Massachusetts senator there. The man abruptly changed the subject by asking Hank if he had any brothers or sisters.

The driver let them out beneath a highway on stilts, in front of a yellow brick warehouse whose cranes were loading another zigzag-painted ship. The man watched the taxi pull away, took Hank by the arm, and led him across the street, away from the river. "Almost there," said the man. "How long has it been? Two months? Oh, but this should be good."

"Hot damn," said Hank.

They walked up a cobblestoned side street, a long shed roof on one side, a snub-nosed truck parked on the other. Whatever the place was, it was closed for the day. Hank smelled chickens. There was a stack of poultry crates against one wall, a few feathers caught in the slats.

"Not the nicest neighborhood," the man admitted. "But what do we care, right?"

The street opened out on a square, a cobblestoned bay where five or six streets met at odd angles. Two flatbed trucks were parked in the middle. The entire side of a tall warehouse across the way was painted with an advertisement for Coca-Cola, the boy with the bottle-cap hat wearing a small window in his eye. There were houses on their side of the square, three of them wedged together in the narrow corner. The man went up the steps of the white frame house that needed painting and rang the bell. Hank stood back and wondered what the man looked like without his overcoat, then without any clothes at all.

A little slot behind a tarnished grill opened in the door.

"Hello, Mrs Bosch," said the man. "Remember me?"

The slot closed and the door was opened by a horse-faced woman with a nose like a pickax. "Uf course I ree-member you. Mr Jones? Or was it Smith? But come een, come een." She spoke in a weird singsong as she ushered them inside and closed the door. She wore an apron over her flowered housedress and smelled of cooked cabbage. "And you breeng one uf our luflee servicemen. How happy for you."

Hank was shocked to find a woman here. The women back home knew nothing about such things, which was only right. But Yankees were strange and this woman was foreign. Hank had never seen an uglier woman. She and the man weren't friends, but she seemed to know what they were here for.

"And you are smart to come earleee." Her voice went up at the end of each sentence. "There is another couple before you, but I think they are looking for courage and will let you go in front of them."

She took their coats and hats and hung them on a rack. The man hiked his trousers and winked at Hank. He looked nice and slim.

The woman opened a door to the right of the narrow stairway and Hank heard a radio. The man stayed back but Hank leaned forward, so he could see what was in there. It looked like an old lady's parlor, with a red-faced, bald man and a pale boy sitting side by side on a flowery sofa. They kept their hands to themselves, demurely folded in their laps.

"How arc wc doing, Father? I mean . . . Mr Jones," said the woman. "Will you mind if these two gentlemen go ahead and use the room?"

The bald man consented with a polite bow. He held up an empty glass. "Is it possible, Valeska . . .?"

"Uf course. For such a constant friend as you, anything. I will tell Juke." Pulling the door closed, she mumbled, "Drink me out of house and home, the hypocrite. So it is all yours. Leaving us with only one thing."

"Quite so," said the man, taking a billfold from inside his jacket. He handed her a bill while he looked at Hank, as if the money proved something. Hank was used to money changing hands for this. Sometimes people paid him; now and then, Hank even paid them. Money made some people more comfortable, but it was of no matter to Hank.

"And it has gone up a dollar since the last time," said the woman. "The war, you know."

The man smiled, shook his head, and gave her another dollar.

"Fine." She opened a door across the hall from the parlor and waved them inside. "I will be seeing you later. Enjoy."

The room was small, with scuffed linoleum patterned like a Turkish carpet, and cabbage roses on the wallpaper. It looked like any room in any boarding house, except the bed had no blankets, only sheets. When Hank heard the door click shut, he spun around and grabbed the man.

His hands were all over the man, inside the beltless trousers, under the shirttail, over soft cotton drawers and stiffening cock. The man kept his teeth together when Hank kissed him. He laughed when Hank got himself tangled up in the suspenders. The man unhooked the suspenders, stepped back, kicked off his shoes, and shed his trousers, then insisted on undressing Hank himself. He was already familiar with the uniform's complicated fly and 13 buttons. Hank couldn't keep still; he touched and grabbed, undid the man's bow tie and shirt, yanked the man's drawers down so he could get a good look at him. Hank often had sex with clothes just opened or rearranged, like when he was hitchhiking or making do in a storage locker or the bushes, but what he really liked was stark nakedness, the way it had been those first times, when an aunt's hired hand had shown him what they could do together after their swim in the pasture pond, squirreling around in the warm, wet grass while cows watched. Girls were for marriage and families, guys for getting your ashes hauled.

In heaven and naked, Hank lay back and grinned while the man loved him with his mouth. Because he was paying, the man still seemed to think it was up to him to do everything, but Hank didn't mind lying still for this, a cool mouth and tongue admiring his cock. He held the man's crisp, brilliantined head with both hands, then stroked the man's neck and shoulders. Hank's hands were callused, so the man's skin felt very smooth. Hank slipped a bare foot beneath the man's stomach and brushed his leathery toes against the wispy hair and hard cock. With his other foot he stroked the man's bottom.

Hank wrestled the man up to him so he could feel more of him. After Hank's cock, the man didn't mind Hank's tongue in his mouth. He still wore his socks and garters, which Hank pried off with his big toe. The man had a city body, spongy where it wasn't bony, but the patches of warm, cool, and lukewarm skin felt good. Hank hummed and moaned and laughed without fear of who might hear them. They were safe here.

When Hank spat into his hand and reached between the man's legs, the man shook his head in a panic and said he didn't do that. So Hank got up on his knees, straddled the man, spat into his hand again, and did his own ass. The man watched in blank bewilderment, said he didn't like that either, then laughed and said, "You'll do anything, won't you?"

They ended up on their sides, curled into each other, their cocks in each other's mouths. Sucking while getting sucked was like having two people talk to you at once, but Hank enjoyed the game of doing to the man what the man did to him and, even upside down, the guy knew how to suck cock. The man was cut, so there was a round head with eaves and a smooth stalk to tongue. Hank pressed his foot against the cold wall and rocked himself into the man's mouth, his own full mouth murmuring and moaning around the man. Hank still wore his dog tags and they were thrown over his shoulder, jingling and rattling while the bedsprings creaked. When it was time, Hank pulled his mouth back and let go with a string of yelps as it flew out of him. Before he finished, he was back on the man, twisting around to work his tongue against the best inch. The man was spitting and swallowing, trying to breathe again, but then he gave in to Hank, closed his eyes, and lay very still. Until the weight in Hank's mouth became harder than ever and, simultaneously, seemed to turn to water. The man finished with a shudder, gritting his teeth and sighing through his nose.

Hank wiped his mouth, climbed around, and stretched out beside the man. "Whew!" he said. "I needed that." He lay his leg over the man's legs and took a deep breath.

"Well," said the man. "You certainly seemed to enjoy it. How old are you?"

"Twenty." Hank gazed gratefully at his cock and the man's.

"I see. You've clearly been around. Uh, could you please let me up? We should be getting dressed."

"Naw. Let's stay like this. Wait a bit and have another go."

But the man was done for the day, maybe for the week. Beneath his politeness, he was slightly miserable. Still, better that than goo-goo eyes. Hank let him up and watched him wash off at the pitcher and basin on the dresser. His backside looked like dirty dough in the light of the bare bulb in the ceiling. Hank sprawled on the bed, hoping to change the man's mind, but the man didn't look at him until he was back in his suit.

"Is my bow straight?" he asked. There was no mirror in the room. He approached the bed and held out his hand. "That was thoroughly enjoyable," he said, shaking Hank's hand. "Good luck to you. Take care of yourself overseas." And he went out the door.

Hank smelled the brilliantine on the pillow one last time, then pitched himself out of the saggy bed. Yankees were no stranger than anyone else. The room was suddenly cold, the wash water colder. Hank quickly dressed, wet his hand, and flattened his hair. He wondered if there was time to find someone else before midnight, when he reported back to the Navy Yard.

There was nobody out in the hall. Then Hank saw a colored boy sitting on the stairs with a bundle of sheets in his lap. The boy slowly stood up. His hair was as straight and shiny as patent leather.

"You took your sweet time, honey," said the boy, only he sounded like a girl. He batted his eyes at Hank like a girl, and curled one corner of his mouth. "Miz Bosch!" he hollered. "The seafood's out!" He went into the room muttering, "See what kind of mess you and your girlfriend left me."

The horse-faced woman came out from the parlor. The radio was louder and someone inside was laughing. The woman grabbed a handful of sleeve at Hank's elbow. "Your friend is gone but you are welcomed to stay. I have a visitor who is having a paaaardy." She pulled Hank down so she could whisper, "You do not have to do anything. Just stand around and act like you are having a good time. There is food and beer. Yes?"

Hank didn't want to leave. He let the woman drag him through the door and heard her announce, "Look what I have. A saaaylor."

The bald man and pale boy still sat on the sofa, but there were new faces here. A laughing, fat man with a mustache arranged food on a table: piles of sliced meat and cheese on sheets of delicatessen paper, a loaf of machine-sliced bread still in its wrapper, a handful of Hershey Bars. "Yes, welcome, welcome," the fat man boomed. "The more the merrier." Behind him stood a thin man with violet eyelids, hennaed hair, and hands like spatulas. He eyed Hank and smiled.

A soldier in khakis sat with one leg over the arm of the armchair in the corner. He seemed quite at home, and bored. He glanced at Hank with the same cool arrogance soldiers always showed for sailors.

"Yes, sir, a good time is worth all the ration stamps in the world," said the fat man. "Hey, Valeska. Where's that beer you promised?"

The horse-faced woman closed the door behind her, then immediately opened it again to tell the bald man the room was ready. The man and boy walked out, one behind the other, without a word.

"Thank God!" said the thin man when the door closed. "Now we can let our hair down."

"Now, now," said the fat man. "It's not her fault she's a priest. Just another victim of life's dirty tricks. Here, son. Help yourself to some of this fine salami. A growing boy like you must keep his strength up," he told Hank.

"He can help himself anytime to my salami," said the thin man.

Hank made himself two sandwiches while the men teased and flirted with him. Sex always left Hank hungry. He liked the men's friendly noise, but he didn't feel like touching them. The soldier, on the other hand, looked awfully good, even if he looked like the kind of guy who pretended to do it only for the money. Hank remembered how much money he had left and wondered how much the woman charged for use of the room. That would be a hoot, if he and the soldier went off together, leaving these two with their chocolate and salami. But the soldier only sat listlessly across his armchair, rocking his raised foot to the jingle that played on the radio.

The colored boy came in, carrying glasses and a pitcher of cloudy beer. Hank watched him more closely this time. He didn't mind the boy being colored – he liked that; it reminded him of home, but Hank had never seen a colored so womanly. The boy moved like a willow and swung his hips as he walked. Hank thought only whites, like the thin man, could be that way. The boy moved so gracefully he seemed boneless.

He set the pitcher on the table and caught Hank watching him. He did not look away but stared right back at Hank. He straightened up and perched the back of his hand on one hip. "What's the matter, Blondie? You a dinge queen?"

The fat man began to laugh.

"A what?" said Hank.

"If you ain't, don't go eyeballing me, Willy Cornbread," he sneered.

Uppity northern niggers: Hank couldn't make head or tail of them. He meant no harm by looking at the boy.

There was another program on the radio. New music came on, click-clickety and South American. It snapped the soldier to life. He jumped up and began to jerk his knees and butt in time to the music. "Hey, Juke!" he called out to the colored boy. "Samba, Juke!"

The boy curled his lip at Hank and sashayed toward the soldier, already stepping with the guy as he approached him. They danced without touching at first, then the soldier actually took hold of the boy's hand and put his own hand on the boy's hip.

Hank couldn't believe it. The soldier looked Mexican or maybe Italian; he probably didn't know any better. But the fat man and thin man were amused, not shocked. And the two were good dancers, there was no denying that. The colored boy's baggy pants shimmied like a long skirt as he twitched inside them. The soldier's khakis tightened, went slack, then went tight again around his butt and front as he stepped to the music with all its extra beats.

"It must have been a sister who designed your uniforms," said the thin man as he passed Hank a glass of beer.

Hank watched the soldier and drank. The beer was homemade and tasted like wet bread. The soldier's hair was black and curly.

The song ended and the dancers finished with a twirl. Hank applauded with the fat man and thin man. Colored or no, it had looked like fun. Hank wanted to be able to dance like that. He set his glass down, wiped his mouth, and stepped in front of the soldier.

"Can you teach me that dance?"

The soldier was grinning over his samba. He grinned at Hank, then burst out laughing. "You, swab? I'd sooner dance with your cow, farmboy."

Hank was used to being taunted by Yankees, and there was nothing to gain by slugging the guy. "I can dance. Honest. Try me."

"No thanks, bub. I don't want my tootsies tromped on."

"You can dance with me."

It was the colored boy, looking up at Hank with a brazen smile.

He couldn't be serious. He was mocking Hank, sneering at the hick. His brown face was full of fight.

"This I gotta see," said the soldier, stepping back to the radio, tapping it as if that could hurry the program to the next song.

Hank just stood there.

"What's wrong, Blondie? You afraid you'll get soot on your hands?"

"No. Where I come from, whites don't dance with coloreds, that's all."

"Do tell. But do guys jazz with guys where you come from?"

"Sometimes." Hank didn't see what that had to do with it.

"But yeah. I know. You don't talk about it. While coons is something you talk about all the time. And that's all the diff. Come on, Blondie. Time you broke another golden rule."

More samba music was playing.

Juke did a box step to it, wiggled in a circle to it. "White dance. If this nigger can do it, you should too."

The boy was needling Hank, and Hank didn't like it, not in front of others, especially the soldier. Maybe the soldier would like him if Hank showed he could dance with the boy. He moved his feet like Juke moved his.

"There you go, baby. Ain't so bad, is it?"

It wasn't, so long as Hank kept his eyes on Juke's two-toned shoes.

"Now move that tail of yours against the music. And step light. Shake that cowshit off your brogues. There you go, Blondie. Ain't you fine. Just like you and me was wiggling between the sheets."

Hank stopped dead.

Juke continued dancing. "What's the matter, baby?" No matter how sweetly he talked, his eyes had never lost their fight. "Oh, sorry. I forgot. You don't dig dinge. That's okay. I don't dig crackers."

"You're crapping me!"

"Am I ever, honey. And it feels so good."

Hank grabbed the front of Juke's shirt, but the boy was too small for Hank to hit. "Why you riding me like this? What did I do to you?"

Juke only pinched a smile at him, cool as ice.

The soldier rushed over. "Let the kid go," he said as he pushed his way between them. "Get your hands off him, you damn hillbilly."

"This is none of your damn business!" But Hank didn't want to hurt the boy; he only wanted to find out why the boy had it in for him. He released Juke, but Juke just stood there, not bothering to step behind the soldier.

"You want to pick on somebody your own size?" The soldier threw his shoulders back, pulling his uniform taut across his chest.

He was shorter than Hank but looked tough and muscular. He stood so close, Hank felt his breath when he spoke. Hank wanted to hit him and find what the body felt like. "Maybe I do. You want to step outside?"

"Maybe I do. Sucker!"

"Two big white boys," sang Juke. "Fighting over little old me."

"Shut up," said the soldier. "This is between me and him. Time you learned your lesson, hillbilly."

"I ain't no hillbilly, spick."

"I ain't no spick. I'm a wop, and proud of it."

"Oh, boys," said the fat man. "I do love it when the trade gets rough, but let's not go flying off the handle." The man stood beside them, gingerly patting the soldier on the back. "We're here to have fun. Juke? Bring these boys some beer."

Juke rocked on his hips a moment, then stepped over to the table.

The soldier opened his fists and wiped his palms against his pants.

"And food? You haven't eaten a bite, Anthony. I know when I'm feeling ornery, there's nothing like a sandwich to calm me down." The man turned away to make the soldier a sandwich.

Hank and the soldier stood there, facing each other, catching their breath. Their bodies were still jumped into gear for a fight. Hank's muscles were humming; he ached to use them.

"You want to go off somewhere?" Hank whispered.

The soldier's jaw was still locked, but his eyes narrowed, surprised by the whisper. "To fight?" he asked.

"Nyaah. Not to fight." Once, it actually started in a fight, then, drunk and bruised, went one step better. Tonight, Hank wanted to skip the fight.

The soldier stared, then glanced at the others.

The thin man whispered and giggled something to the fat man.

Juke brought them their beer. "You're not going to let that fat queen talk you out of a fight, are you?" he whispered.

"Juke, fuck off," said the soldier.

The electric bell out in the hall rang. "Juke! The door!" the woman shouted in the distance.

"Shit. Ain't no Joe Louis here," sneered Juke and he left to answer the door.

"Oh, God," said the thin man. "Will it be more possibilities or more competition? And just when I made up my mind, too."

The soldier drank his beer and looked at Hank. "You're nuts," he said, but kindly.

Hank grinned. "What's that lady charge for a room? I'll buy."

"Yeah? Sheesh." The soldier shook his head in disbelief. "Like I was your whore? Uh uh. I'd go halves with you. Only I don't think the witch'll let us do it. She doesn't want to piss off her regulars."

"Is there somewhere else?"

"Maybe."

The two looked at each other and thought it over.

There were voices out in the hall, then something fell.

The door had been left open. Suddenly Juke was standing there, mouth and eyes wide open. He had already screamed, "It's the Shore Patrol!"

Hank wheeled around, but the only door was the one where the boy stood, and an arm with an armband and club had grabbed the boy's collar.

"Dammit to hell. Dammit to hell," the thin man hollered at the ceiling. "I'm sick of this."

"Fucking mother of God," the soldier shouted, jumped on the sofa, and tore down the heavy curtain. Hank jumped up beside him to help push up the window.

Someone grabbed Hank's ankles and yanked him off the sofa.

Hank jerked around and saw Juke gripping him while a Shore Patrol man pulled Juke backwards with a billy club across the boy's chest.

"Help me. Please," Juke pleaded. "I can't go back."

A woman screamed in the back of the house. The thin man stood there, cursing and spitting. The fat man stood with both hands raised over his head.

Hank swung his fist at the patrolman's face. The guy could not block the punch; his head jerked back and he let go of one end of his club. Juke scrambled over the sofa and jumped out the window the soldier had opened. The soldier had already jumped. Hank had his hands on the sill, a single light flared over a warehouse dock outside in the darkness, when someone grabbed the back flap of his jersey. Hank swung his fist and elbow behind him without looking.

Something hard banged his head. All at once, he was thinking every thought he had ever had: the excitement and burn of his first taste of liquor; his need to get through the window and back to his shipmates; his Baptist preacher's egg-smelling breath; his blinding anger during a fistfight with his father.

The thoughts slowed enough for Hank to notice he was on the floor now, sitting against the sofa. Everywhere were the canvas leggings of the Shore Patrol. Cold air poured through the open window behind him and there was scuffling outside. A man in a trench coat led the thin man, still cursing, out the door to the hall. And another man in a trenchcoat stood above Hank, a thin mustache across his upper lip, the hand at his crotch holding a square blue pistol.

Hank reached up to touch the pain on one side of his head.

"Don't move!" said the man, pointing the pistol straight at Hank's face. "You stinking fairy."

THE BLUE DRAGON

Michael Thomas Ford

THE FIRST THING I noticed about him was his hands. The fingers were long and thin, the nails rounded and cut short. He was rolling a rice ball, scooping the sticky white grains from the big heated pot at his side and then shaping it in his palm until it was a perfect oblong. When he had it completed, he took a sliver of fish – pale pink with an edge of yellow fatty skin – and laid it over the waiting bed. He leaned over the counter and placed the fish on the small wooden board in front of me.

"Tuna," he said simply. "You will like."

I nodded my thanks and picked the rice up with my chopsticks, lifting it carefully to my lips. The fish was fresh, with a hint of sea still on its skin, and melted into the smooth taste of the rice. It was delicious, and I smiled.

"It's very good," I said to him. "Tastes wonderful."

He nodded his satisfaction and went back to his work. I enjoy sushi, especially when it's made correctly by an experienced chef who knows his work. Many people shudder at the idea of eating raw fish, but sushi is one of the most pleasing of the Japanese art forms, requiring as much skill as a delicate water and ink painting or the three perfectly worded lines of a haiku. It takes years of practice to learn just how to roll the rice into a shape that is not too small or too large and how to slice the fish correctly so that it fills the mouth with a subtle taste, hinting at more but not overwhelming.

Because of my work as a journalist with an international investment magazine, I travel frequently to Japan. My favorite city is Osaka, on the southern side of Honshu, the largest of the Japanese islands. Situated on a beautiful bay surrounded by green mountains, Osaka has one of the largest outdoor fish markets in the world. The tuna, mackerel, sea trout, and octopus are lifted in great dripping nets from the holds of the boats that crowd the piers and dropped, shining and flopping, onto the decks, where fishermen and merchants buy and trade until the catch is gone. Minutes after the buyers disperse, the fish are seen in the countless stalls that line the water's edge, laid out on beds of crushed ice for buyers to inspect.

The best fish end up in the sushi bars, the traditional meeting places of the Japanese. There the sushi chefs slice and arrange the day's catch into simple, beautiful shapes eaten by the customers that crowd the rooms heady with thick smoke from the hand-rolled cigarettes popular in the city. Over steaming cups of green tea, diners point with their chopsticks to what they want, watching as it is prepared in front of them, nodding their approval when something pleases them, frowning when it does not.

Whenever I am in Osaka I make a point of going to the sushi bars, trying the specialties of the different chefs. I had never been to this particular bar before, but the concierge at my hotel recommended it, saying that the service was the best in Osaka and that it had some special offerings available nowhere else in the city. It had taken me some time to find it, wandering through the crowded streets and asking directions several times before finding the doorway, unmarked, between a discount electronics store and a brothel offering to fulfill my wildest dreams for only 4,000 yen.

The concierge had been correct; this was the best sushi I'd ever had. The fish was hours old, the rice grains sticky and sweet. And the chef was a true artist. He handled the knives flawlessly, deftly peeling slices from the pieces of salmon and tuna and chopping the cucumbers and seaweed into ribbons translucent as the thinnest paper. He moved quickly and fluidly, finding his way around the table without hesitating. He made a roll of eel, wrapping everything up in a slip of crisp seaweed paper and slicing it into six pieces. He brushed the pieces with the thick, sweet sauce used to bring out the subtle flavors of the eel and then laid them in front of me.

He watched my face as I ate, waiting to see if I liked his creation. When I nodded my satisfaction, he broke into a smile. Waving the bartender over, I asked him to bring a bottle of the chef's favorite beer, a traditional way of thanking him. When it arrived, I toasted him with my own glass.

It was quiet in the bar, so we began to talk as he worked. His English was very good, he told me, because he had once spent a year at the university. His name was Kamo, and he had been studying the art of sushi for over ten years. Like many Japanese, Kamo was slight of build, with delicate features and a fine-boned face. His black hair had been cut short on the sides but left long in front so that it hung down over his forehead and nearly covered one eye. His dark blue robe was tied in front with a sash of white.

As the evening progressed, Kamo prepared many different things for me – treasures dipped from the seas, like soft folds of urchin rich with the taste of salt, and the firmer pieces of conch, the flesh pinkish-gold and sweet on my tongue. Most of the things I had had before, but he also presented me with several things I had never seen, and for which he knew only the Japanese words. Each time he gave me something new he watched expectantly until I nodded my delight, then his face broke open in a happy smile.

As I watched Kamo work, I began to wonder what it would be like to make love with him. His movements were very sensual, controlled and fluid yet at the same time expressing great pleasure from doing his job well. I imagined him moving his hands over my body in that same attentive way, and felt a stirring in my groin. The more I thought about Kamo, the more worked up I got. I envisioned sliding against his smooth, naked skin, feeling the hardness of his cock pressing against my leg as I kissed his soft mouth. I could almost feel his thick dark hair beneath my fingers as I pictured his head moving up and down my prick, his lips warm and welcoming, his tongue teasing.

The Japanese are generally very reserved, and I knew that asking Kamo straight out to come back to my hotel with me was out of the question. Besides, I didn't even know if he was at all interested. He had been friendly all evening, but for all I knew he had a wife and three little kids somewhere. I decided the best thing to do was just enjoy the great food he was placing in front of me and be grateful for an evening of the best sushi I'd ever had. But the more my growing hard on pressed insistently against my pants, the more I thought about rubbing my hands over his smooth ass, and the more I wanted him.

It was almost midnight, and the bar had pretty much emptied out. I was drinking a cup of tea and wondering if I was going to end up shooting my load into my hand in my hotel room when Kamo asked me if there was anything else he could get me. I was just about to say no when I decided to go for broke. "Well," I said, hoping he wouldn't see how nervous I was. "I understand there are some very special things to see in this part of town. I'd sure like to see them, and I was hoping that maybe you could show them to me."

Kamo looked at me, a strange light rising in his eyes. He smiled slightly and nodded his head. "I thought that perhaps you would be interested in something special. I see by the way that you enjoy what I make for you that you appreciate the unusual."

I grinned back at him. "Yes, I do," I said. "The more unusual the better."

Kamo wiped his hands on a wet cloth. "You wait here," he said. "We will go where I will show you something I think you will like very much."

Kamo went into the back of the bar. As I waited for him, I started imagining all of the things that I could do to him. My cock was rock hard, and I couldn't wait to free it from its prison in my pants and let Kamo go to work on it. I felt Kamo's hand on my shoulder, and turned around. He had put on a dark robe over his clothes. "We will go now," he said.

When we exited the bar it was raining, a strong downpour typical of the coastal towns. Because it had been clear when I left my hotel, I had foolishly not brought an umbrella. Luckily, Kamo had one, and I held it over us as we scurried through the narrow streets. While I could hardly tell where one street melted into another, Kamo moved us swiftly through the maze of buildings that make up the area near the wharf. Despite the umbrella, we were both soaking wet by the time he led me up a narrow stone stairway and stopped in front of a big red door.

Producing a key from the pocket of his robe, Kamo fitted it into the hole and turned it sharply, pushing at the same time. The door swung inward, and we entered. Inside, I shook the rain off as best I could and looked around. We were standing in a small entryway with a stone floor and bare white walls. Directly across from the one we had entered was another door.

"Is this your house," I asked Kamo.

He nodded. "It is a very old place, once used by Shinto monks. Now it is home."

Kamo led me to the other door, stopping first to remove his shoes. When I bent to remove my own shoes, he stopped me. "I will do it for you," he said as he knelt in front of me. "You are my guest."

He quickly untied my laces and pulled my shoes off, holding my foot in his hand. His fingers grasped my sole gently, rubbing slow circles over the skin for a moment before releasing me. Placing the shoes on a small mat next to the door, he rose and opened the door. Stepping through, I found myself in a large room filled with soft light that came from several oil lamps that burned with golden tongues of flame. There was no furniture but for a low wooden table surrounded many large pillows thrown over thick carpets that covered the floor.

The only other thing of interest was a large fish tank that stood in one corner. About four feet long and three feet high, it was filled with green plants and a single piece of white coral. The water shone with pale light, and bubbles rose from one corner. I could see shadows darting amongst the waving leaves, but they never stayed in one place long enough for me to see what they were.

"You are wet," Kamo said. "Come with me and you can dry yourself."

He led me behind a large screen at one end of the room and into another, smaller space. From the futon on the floor, I guessed it was his bedroom. Kamo opened a small chest and removed a white robe. He handed it to me. "You may change in there," he said, pointing to the bathroom.

I went into the bathroom and shut the door. Removing my wet clothes, I hung them on a hook behind the door. The rain had temporarily sent my boner into submission, and my dick hung limply between my legs. But once I started thinking about Kamo's body, it jerked back to life. I tied the belt of the robe loosely around my waist and went out to see what Kamo was doing.

He wasn't in the bedroom, so I checked the living room. Kamo was arranging pillows around the table. While I had been in the bathroom he had himself changed into a white robe. When he saw me, he waved for me to come sit down. Confused, I walked over and sat where he pointed. I wondered now if we'd both had the same thing on our minds when we left the bar. While I was aching to sink my prick into his ass, he had laid out plates like we were having a dinner party.

Kamo went over to the fish tank and scooped something up with a net. Returning to the table, he placed in front of me a small bowl. Inside it was a fish. About three inches long, it was a strange blue color, with two yellow stripes on either side of its head. Kamo disappeared again and returned with a round bowl, about a foot across, and a bottle. Putting both on the table, he sat across from me. "You are going to see something very special," he said.

Still puzzled, I watched as he poured a clear liquid from the bottle and filled the bowl almost to the top. Then he reached into the smaller bowl, lifted out the fish, and dropped it splashing into the other one. For a minute the fish sat at the bottom of the bowl, not moving. Then it began to swim in circles, its mouth opening and closing rapidly. It moved faster and faster, as if running from something. As it did, its blue color began to brighten, as if it were being lit up from the inside.

Finally, after circling the bowl madly for several minutes, the fish stopped completely, its mouth open wide. Kamo waited to make sure it would not begin swimming again, then reached into the bowl and lifted the fish out. Picking up a long, sharp knife, he sliced the fish quickly, peeling away the electric blue skin to reveal the bright pink flesh beneath. Cutting two strips, he placed them on a small white plate.

"What is it?" I asked.

"Very rare," Kamo said. "Fish is very poisonous. If cut wrong, it can paralyze you instantly. But done correctly, it can bring great pleasure."

I looked at the thin strips on the plate. "What was it swimming in?"

"Saki and herbs," Kamo answered, lifting one of the slices in his fingers and raising it to my lips. "Eat quickly before its power fades."

Reluctantly, I opened my mouth. Kamo placed the fish on my tongue, his fingers momentarily brushing my lips. I waited to feel my body becoming motionless. But when nothing happened, I concentrated on the taste that was filling my mouth. A sensation both hot and sweet was soaking into my tongue and traveling into my throat. I swallowed the fish, and felt the warmth move with it into my belly. It was like nothing I had ever tasted before. As I tried to pinpoint exactly what it was like, I felt my head begin to swim. My mind began to cloud over, and I shook my head to regain my focus.

"No," Kamo said through the veil that was falling over my mind. "Do not fight it. Let the pleasure come."

Relaxing, I felt my head clear again, leaving behind a sense of heightened awareness. At the same time, my arms and legs began to feel heavy, as if a great weight were pressing on them, and everything around me seemed brighter and warmer. I looked at Kamo and saw him pick the other piece of fish from the plate and eat it. He closed his eyes, and when he opened them again a few moments later, I saw again the brightness I had first noticed in the bar.

He rose from his seat and came around to my side of the table. "Come," he said, holding out his hand. "We are ready now."

My body refused to move on its own, and Kamo had to help me rise. With slow steps, I followed him to an area of the room where the floor was thick with pillows the dark blue of midnight. Kamo pulled at the belt at my waist and let my robe fall open. He slid his hands underneath it and pushed it off of my shoulders, letting it fall to the floor so that I was standing in front of him naked. Because I was held in the grip of the strange fish's drug, I could only stand while he looked at me, feeling like a statue being perused by a museum visitor.

Kamo reached out and ran a hand lightly over the dark fur of my chest, my skin tingling where his fingers crossed it. "You are very beautiful," he said. "I like your hair very much."

I laughed, knowing that the fact that he did not have hair was exactly what I liked. My voice sounded low and far away, like someone calling through a rainstorm. As if pushing my way through water, I reached out to remove his robe, but he stopped me by taking my hand and pulling me down onto the soft pillows. I sank easily into their softness and lay back, letting myself fall into them so that I was reclining with Kamo positioned between my spread legs.

He ran his fingers down my belly and to my waiting cock, which was hanging half-hard across my thigh. His long fingers circled the thickness of my stiffening shaft and squeezed lightly, stroking it to life. "It is big," he whispered appreciatively, as my prick filled to its full nine inches.

I closed my eyes, the feeling caused by eating the fish filling my head, and waited to feel my cockhead slip in between his lips. But Kamo seemed content just to keep jerking me off. While his one hand kept up a steady rhythm on my dick, his other hand went under my balls, cupping my big nuts in his hands. "They are like the fruits of the lemon tree," he said, smiling up at me. "Round and firm."

Right then I didn't care what he thought they looked like. Although I found it hard to move, the rest of my senses seemed to have intensified. His fingers brushing my balls were sending bursts of excitement through my belly, and I just wanted to have his tongue on them. "Suck them," I whispered as best I could, putting my hand on his head and using what was left of my strength to grab a fistful of his black-blue hair in my fingers. Wrapped in my grip, his hair was soft and thick. I spread my legs wider and pushed his face between them until I felt his nose at the base of my cock. His tongue snaked out and tickled my aching nuts, licking in slow circles around first one and then the other.

Kamo worked his way under my sac, and lifted my legs so

that he could get at the sensitive area above my asshole. His mouth moved over my skin slowly and deliberately, covering every inch of my flesh with kisses that burned like cold fire. His delicate movements were making me crazy, and I couldn't wait to see what he had in store for my cock.

All of a sudden I felt him put one of his fingers, wet with spit, at the opening of my hole. I opened my mouth to ask him what he was doing, but nothing came out. After pressing gently but insistently for a moment, his finger slid inside, my ass muscles closing around its thin length. Kamo fingered me for a minute while his mouth worked on my balls, then he pulled out. Reaching into the pocket of his robe, he removed a string of silver beads. Each one was about half an inch in diameter, and the string was about six inches long.

I thought he was going to tie it around my balls like a cockring, but instead he took the first bead and placed it against my hole, pushing it inside easily. He did this with each of the other beads, until the whole string of them was inside my ass and all that was left was a short length of string hanging from my pucker. I didn't know what the hell he was doing, but it sure felt good. I could feel the balls inside me, moving back and forth as I rocked against the pillows.

This whole time Kamo was still wearing his robe. Now, he knelt with his back to me and let it fall off of his shoulders. My eyes went wide as I saw what he had kept hidden from me. The pure white skin of his back was covered with a tattoo of a dragon. It's head was centered between his shoulders, and it's body stretched down towards his buttocks and then disappeared, it's tail sweeping around to his stomach. The dragon was covered in thousands of tiny scales, each one shaded in perfectly in blue. The fine lines were etched on his body like veins running just below the skin. The detail was amazing, and looked as though it had taken months to complete.

Kamo turned to me, his eyes oddly bright. "You wished to see something special," he said. "It is special enough for you?" he asked.

I stared back at him, unable to move my lips. The dragon's tail curved around his waist and down his groin, the end disappearing under his balls and circling back up the other side so that the base of his prick was encircled by it. His entire body appeared to be shaved completely smooth, not even a single hair marring his pubic area.

Kamo stretched himself on top of me, his mouth finding mine, and I pushed my tongue roughly between his lips. Kamo kissed me back, his mouth drawing me in. As he sucked at my tongue, I felt him grind his stomach against my cock, his hairless skin sliding along the pulsing shaft. Reaching down, Kamo moved my hands so that they were cupping his ass, the fingers closed around the curves of his buttocks so that I feet their roundness against my palms. Kamo pressed back against me, and ran his mouth over my neck in a rush of hot kisses. His white skin shone out against the sea of blue pillows we were floating in like a strange, delicate fish.

As I lay under him, the strange paralysis holding me tightly, Kamo moved over my chest, biting softly on my nipples and rubbing his cheek against the hair that covered my pecs. The fact that I could not move my hands to touch him through the fog that had enveloped me increased the longing in my balls, and I wanted to cry out for him to satisfy me.

Finally, he moved down my belly towards my anxious cock. Without touching it, he placed his lips on the tip, sucking only the head and caressing it with his tongue as he lapped up the stream of sticky fluid that had begun to flow from my slit. Slowly he moved down the length of the shaft. I was amazed that he could get such a thick piece of meat into his small mouth, but he had no trouble. Soon his lips were pushed into my bush, and I was throbbing deep inside him. He moved back up my cock, his throat pulsing around it like a warm hand.

Kamo began to move quickly up and down my dick, his lips sliding easily over it. Every motion of his mouth felt like a thousand tongues caressing my cock. I felt my balls starting to tighten, and knew that if he kept it up I was going to lose my load down his throat before I had a chance to fuck his beautiful ass. Kamo seemed to sense it, too, because he stopped sucking me. Moving up, he straddled my chest, his smooth legs holding me tightly between them.

His cock was hard now, jutting up and away from his body. Although it was only about five inches long, it was perfectly formed, the sculpted head round and tapered atop the straight shaft. His balls hung neatly in a sac of smooth skin, and the dragon's tail curled perfectly around them both. Kamo moved forward so that I could suck his exquisite prick. It slipped in easily until not only the shaft, but the balls as well, were filling my mouth. I sucked hungrily, eating up the delicious flesh that slid in and out of my throat with each movement of Kamo's thrusts. I let Kamo's balls slip out of my mouth so that I could feel them against my chin as I blew him.

As I sucked his cock, Kamo fingered the tight slit of his asshole. He moaned as he slipped one finger in, pushing roughly to get through the small opening. Pulling himself from my mouth, he moved back until his ass was resting against the head of my prick. Feeling the smooth flesh of his buttocks against my aching piece, I almost washed his back with a wave of cum, but I was able to hold back. I didn't think my big tool would ever get into his tight hole, but he pressed against me until the head of my prick pushed between his asslips. Slowly I entered him, my head parting the walls of his chute like a boat moving through the sea. I groaned loudly as he surrounded me with his warmth, his tight ass swallowing my meat greedily.

I looked at Kamo's face and saw that his eyes were shut tight, a smile crossing his face. He had his hands on my chest, and his fingers tugged gently at my tits while I slid into him. When I was fully inside him, he began to slide back and forth slowly, fucking himself with my dick. I lay beneath him, unable to lift my hands to touch his skin but filled with intense desire as I watched him pleasure himself with my tool.

As Kamo pumped my cock, something caught my eye, and I noticed for the first time that there was a mirror behind and to the left of where we were lying. A big antique frame sat on the floor, and in the large glass I could see the shadowy form of Kamo riding my prick. It moved up and down with him, my cock disappearing into his tight hole and reappearing as he devoured inch after inch of me. Above me his face was a mask of delight, his eyes and mouth reflecting the pleasure he was feeling deep inside him.

Looking again in the mirror, I caught my breath. While the outlines of our bodies were barely visible in the shadows, the dragon tattoo on Kamo's back was sharply defined. Just like the skin of the fish we had eaten, the dragon radiated with a luminous blue light. Each line and curve shone as though coursing with strange blood, seemed in fact to almost to move across Kamo's back. I watched as it pulsed and flowed on his back, the claws scratching at his shoulders, the mouth opening in a silent roar. Kamo seemed to take no notice of what was happening beneath his skin, rising and falling along my prick in heated strokes, his cock slapping against my stomach as he moved.

I wanted to run my hands over his back, to see if I could feel some of the movement I saw reflected in the glass. But I was still bound to the floor by the mysterious weight. Whatever was happening to Kamo didn't appear to cause him any pain, so I watched silently as the dragon twisted and turned over his flesh. The harder he thrust against me, the harder the dragon writhed in the mirror.

As fascinated as I was with the strange events, the rising heat in my groin was a stronger attraction. Kamo began to push my cock deeply into his tight ass. As he did, he reached behind me and grasped the string that was hanging from my hole. Still riding me, he pulled on the string, and the beads slipped one at a time from my chute. The feeling was unbelievable, and sent me into a shuddering, out of control rush of pleasure like nothing I'd ever felt before. This seemed to break the invisible chains that wrapped around my body, and I cried out, my voice echoing through the room as all of the passion that had been building up in my throat spilled out at once.

Now that I was able to move again, I plunged one last time into Kamo's depths, my load crashing into him in a shuddering wave as I squeezed his ass in my hands. I could feel the cum gushing from my prick as I pumped more and more cream into him. Kamo continued to work my prick with his ass muscles as he came, too, long ropes of ivory squirting from his bobbing cock, falling on my chest and splashing my neck. At the same time, his eyes flew open. They glowed with the same mysterious blue light as the dragon, and appeared to see nothing. His lips were stretched wide, mouthing but not voicing his ecstasy.

Then he shut his eyes, and when he opened them again they

were the same black color they had always been. He collapsed against my chest, my cock still inside him, and lay still. I ran my hand over his back, tracing the muscles from his shoulder down to where I could feel my cock enter his asshole. I half expected to feel the dragon's scales under my fingertips, but touched only warm skin. Inside the mirror, the glass was dark, the only reflection that of Kamo's body on mine.

A MATTER OF TASTE

Dean Raven

1

THE FIRST THING he asked was: "Do you have any protection?"

Which was quite ironic, really. I mean, sitting atop a wind-blasted sand dune, with only a few scraggly bushes to hide us from prying and potentially dangerous eyes, my immediate thought was that if I had wanted protection I would have stayed at home. But he was so cute and sincere I found it impossible to be facetious.

"No," I replied bluntly after a suitable pause. "I don't screw on the first date."

His smile was enough to cause sunburn.

"Well, we're in luck," he enthused. "I've got one left."

I don't know if it was his affected innocence or simply my unabashed lust at the sight of his youthful, silken body that did it, but it wasn't long before he was on his knees in front of me and I was easing myself into him.

But, truly, I meant what I said about screwing on the first date. In fact, I hardly ever screw at all. What made this different was his wide-eyed willingness to be taken – it was so damn sexy. He had that kind of high-pitched groan which is unique to teenagers and Tom Cruise. And his hedonistic pleasure at engaging with a stranger under the reddening sun, with the surf pounding out its beat just metres away and seagulls looking on like affronted old ladies, was almost enough to make me come straight away.

When finally I was harbored deep inside his warm, clenching body, I paused, experiencing a feeling so profound it was almost religious. I was suddenly, unaccountably, bewildered by exactly where I ended and he began. His smooth, unmarked body had become part of me, and when I stroked the hardening muscles of his back it almost felt as if I were touching myself.

Slowly I began moving in and out.

And, surprisingly, despite my initial fears, grains of sand did not wriggle into the KY and rip his bum to pieces.

Roy is one of those guys who, when they come, want the world to know. As my cock surged and burst, discharging its disappointed cargo of semen into the little latex bag, Roy reared up and grunted deliriously, apparently forgetting we were virtually on public display. I looked around in fright. I had this mad image of a little old lady coming along and emptying a bucket of cold water over us, and then finding, when I tried to withdraw, that we were stuck together. Fortunately, though, little old ladies did not tend to hang around secluded sand dunes at that time of the year.

After a protracted groan, Roy came. The spurts of thick white fluid torpedoed out of his penis, volleyed into the air like rabid seagulls, and finally landed in the branches of a small bush on the other side of the clearing. I was astounded. Roy stared for a few seconds, then collapsed in convulsions of laughter. Neither of us made a move to disengage.

"That was fan-tastic," he said at last. "You've got a great dick."

"You've got a great . . . everything," I replied lamely.

He rolled away from me.

I'm one of those people who become slightly dysfunctional in the few minutes after coming. As soon as we were no longer in contact my interest in Roy took a nose-dive. Suddenly I was viewing his looks very academically, and all I could think was that it would probably be quite nice if I saw him again at some indeterminate time in the future.

I peeled the sticky rubber bag off my slowly deflating member, said sorry to the teeming millions trapped inside and dug a shallow grave. I saw a disturbing image of hordes of little tadpoles, all with my face, begging for mercy, before dropping the condom into the hole and covering it up for eternity.

The way I felt then, I could just as easily have done the same with Roy.

Instead, we said quick goodbyes and went our separate ways.

2

The human body is a strange, wonderful and exasperating thing. It was less than an hour later, just as Endora was banishing Darren Stevens to a life on the other side of the mirror, that an overwhelming sense of loss assailed me. I panicked. It was if the air had all been suddenly sucked out of the room.

What if (I was thinking) I never saw Roy again?

Whereas before I couldn't have cared less if Roy had floated out to sea never to return, my dick had now recuperated, and in its infinite wisdom had decided it liked Roy more than anyone it had ever before encountered. And, of course, my mind tagged along like a lost sheep.

My thoughts went into overdrive. They swarmed across several scenarios:

(1) Maybe I'll see Roy at one of the Clubs.
(2) If I hang around the city centre long enough he's bound to pass by sooner or later.
(3) Maybe if I mention his name to one of my friends, someone might know someone who knows someone who knows someone who knows him.

The most likely scenario, however, was that I'd catch him again at the beach.

3

I was engrossed in squeezing the bananas when I caught his eye over the top of a precarious stack of watermelons.

For a split second I was thrown: he looked so different with clothes on. In fact, I think it was my dick that recognized him first; it began straining against my fly as soon as it realized that hidden within the folds of those rugby shorts was the scene of its most recent excursion.

I smiled quickly and, I must admit, rather too eagerly. However, by that time he had already moved on.

My heart pounded. I felt faint. My next reaction was to flee.

This time, though, things were different. This was no embarrassing fuck-in-the-dark I now wanted to avoid. I had made love to this guy in the splendor of a sunny spring afternoon, with fresh sea air and Nature swirling around us, and I knew he was as close to perfection as I wanted or could expect. I determined to follow him and somehow let him know that my intentions had become honorable.

I peered at him over the zucchinis. I squeezed more bananas. I even fondled the ox tongue while gazing wistfully at him bending over the chocolate rack. He feigned disinterest.

Eventually I could stand it no longer. I sidled up beside him, grabbed the same packet of Toblerone as he and looked victoriously into his amber eyes. Adeptly he let go the Toblerone and chose a Milka. He casually dropped it into his trolley and sauntered off.

I was livid. I considered chasing after him and causing a scene in the middle of the meat department. However, common sense quickly prevailed. I mean, how could I broach tactfully my charge that after screwing his hot little butt atop a windswept sand dune he would dare ignore me, as if I were some perfect stranger?

At the best of times my thought processes work rather slowly. By the time I had resolved to follow him, take down his car registration number and somehow convince some burly policeman at my local station to give me his name, address and telephone number, he had gone.

And, predictably, I never saw him there again.

4

Roy is amazing.

There he was, sitting astride me, bucking like a cowboy and gasping uncontrollably, his handsome face contorting with pleasure. After what seemed like hours, his distended penis erupted in his hand like Mount Vesuvius, sending buckets of semen shooting over my head, splattering me in the face and riding up my chest like driven snow. I have never seen anyone like him.

Afterwards he collapsed on top of me, spent. One hand trailed in the sand and the other almost imperceptibly caressed my hair. His soft cheek rested against mine. His warm body insulated me against the sting of the cold air. His weight was like a promise. I fantasized for a time that he was my lover.

And for a while we lay there, his hot semen rapidly cooling on my goose-pimpled skin. I dipped my fingers into the glittering pools and drew mysterious patterns across my chest. I wanted to drown in it. I raised my fingers to my lips and licked.

I read somewhere years ago that if you eat a lot of oranges your semen begins to taste sweet. Well, if that's true, then Roy must be a committed citrus lover. I tasted more. He looked up.

"Could I have your phone number?" I asked.

"I'd better not," he replied apologetically. "I live with my parents and they don't know about me."

"Oh," I responded with a nod of understanding. "Well how about I give you mine?"

"Yeah, sure."

"Remind me later."

Gazing at his blushing lips, I wanted badly to kiss them. However, I resisted the urge, thinking it might scare him away at this point in our relationship.

"Do you ever go out?" I ventured.

"To gay clubs? Not very often."

"Did you wanna go out with me sometime? Say this weekend? I mean, not to a club, just to a movie or something."

"Yeah, I suppose. I'll ring you."

I smiled. He reciprocated. Love suddenly grabbed me and dragged me under, like a sand lion ensnaring a hapless ant. I found I had no desire to struggle. The incident in the supermarket became like the memory of a bad dream.

"Are you ready for some more?" I asked.

He sat up and showed me his stiffening cock.

And five minutes later, as I knelt in front of his thrusting body, my hands on his hips, the silken head of his penis sliding back and forth across my swollen, eager lips, it struck me that there was nothing I would rather be doing, no place I would rather be, than right here with Roy, engaging in this ostensibly senseless act of mutual pleasure.

5

It's a typical Saturday night, and I'm leaning against the wall at The Club, surveying a less-than-inspiring crowd.

Although my contact lenses are dirty and viewing is obscured by the clouds of acrid vapors emanating from the overactive smoke machines, I recognize Roy immediately his face appears at the top of the stairs.

Despite my angry frustration with him, I rush to his side. My heart is pounding and I'm experiencing an almost ecstatic light-headedness. I feel like an infatuated schoolgirl.

"Hi," I say with a smile.

"Well, hell," he replies with apparent pleasure.

"Strange seeing you here."

"Well, I'm on holidays and I've just been out with some friends, so I thought, what the heck."

"You haven't called."

"Yeah, sorry about that. I lost your phone number. It must have been in my pocket when Mum did the laundry."

"Oh."

I look around the room, pretending it doesn't matter.

"I'll have to give it to you again."

He nods.

We exchange small talk for a few minutes. The lights are dazzling. I ask him to dance and he replies to the effect that he doesn't generally engage in that type of activity. I offer to buy him a drink and he quickly accepts. I touch his arm and make my way to the bar.

Twenty minutes later I'm still looking for him. The beer in my hand is getting warm. A song is proclaiming, "Baby doncha leave me, Baby doncha leave me this waayyy . . ." Suddenly, he appears at the top of the stairs and makes his way towards a dark corner. Intrigued, I follow.

As I watch, I can see his eyes scanning the room, alighting every so often on an anonymous face in the crowd. Maybe he's looking for me. Just as I begin to make a move towards him, he starts conversing with Roger, the languid glass collector and well known despoiler of innocent young men. For 15 long minutes I stand there, glowering at them like a jealous lover. I consider dobbing in Roger to the Manager. When they part, I quickly move in.

"Here's your beer," I say, as if I haven't noticed his disappearance.

"Thanks," he replies, as if he's been waiting there all the time.

He takes a swig and wrinkles his nose.

"It's a bit warm," he says with affected nonchalance. He looks at me expectantly, probably hoping I'll buy him another.

I count backwards from ten. It's amazing how an ideal face and body can excuse such megalithic rudeness. As I count I concentrate on the movement of his tongue as it flicks across his lips. I can feel the rising tide of my hormones. Maybe a more direct approach is required. It certainly works at the beach, and maybe that's the only way Roy responds.

"How about we go back to my place for a while?"

He looks suitably regretful.

"Nah, I'd better not. I have to go soon."

"But it'll be a lot more comfortable than down the beach. Just think what else we can get up to."

"Maybe some other time."

I panic. Blood rushes to my head. It's time to go all out.

"I can give you a massage; I've done a course. And we can screw all night. I've got heaps of condoms. I'll even let you come in my mouth. I can drive you home afterwards. Come on, Roy, please. You won't regret it. We'll have fun."

I know I'm sounding desperate and pathetic but I can't help myself. He shakes his head.

"I'll give you a ring," is all he will concede.

"Well how about we see a movie on Tuesday night?"

"I'll give you a ring."

There's nothing more I can say or do. I write down my phone number again. He takes it, folds it carefully in two and places it in the back pocket of his jeans. I picture him throwing the jeans into the dirty washing basket as soon as he returns home, conveniently forgetting that a part of me has been quietly nestling there close to his backside.

Suddenly he steps away and says, "I'm just going to the toilet. I'll be back soon."

I gaze at him as he's consumed by the crowd. I try to think of what else I have to offer.

He doesn't return.

6

Roy and I were grappling in the surf when he kissed me.

It was quite unexpected. One minute he had been looking strangely at my mouth, and the next his lips were suddenly pressed against mine. Waves washed over us. His tongue forced its way between my teeth and roughly licked around the inside of my mouth. He hugged me fiercely and groaned, the vibrations of his jaw setting up sympathetic vibrations in my own. I lapped up his saliva greedily.

It was clear to me by then that Roy only functions at a certain level at this stage in his sexual career. I've always believed that sexuality is simply a matter of taste, and it just so happens that Roy's taste at the moment is for unencumbered sex in wide open places. Who am I to judge him and proclaim that that is wrong?

And instead of blaming him for leading me on and turning me into an emotional cripple, I decided it was best to just accept what he has to offer and hope that one day he'll turn around and offer something more. After all, ten per cent of something is better than 100 per cent of nothing.

As the sun completed its slide into the boiling sea, we said our goodbyes.

"Will you be here tomorrow?" he asked. "Same time, same place?"

I looked into his clear, eager eyes. I could still feel his rough tongue moving around the inside of my mouth.

"Sure," I said. "It's a date."

TO/FROM

Matthew Rettenmund

I'M 31 YEARS old and I've probably slept with about two men for each of those years. Since I didn't have much sex in my pre-teens or even my teens, and didn't start doing men until I was 25, that two-per-year average sounds a lot better than the reality. The truth is, I've slept around in the past six years. I've slept around.

I'm not one of these silly, sex-absorbed, flashy queers who brags about his conquests and treats sex like Oreos, one after the other. I've slept with every man who's shown interest in me – old friends, dudes met at parties, men who pressed up against me on the subway – for one reason only: I'm looking for a lover, and I'm worried that if I pass some guy up for sex, I might be missing out on one.

I've racked up dozens of sex partners, but only one lover, and I was right; Craig probably never would've become my lover if I hadn't jerked him off within the first two hours after we met.

"Daddy, how did you and Daddy no. 2 meet?" A postmodern question I'll fortunately never have to answer. "He was visiting his friend, a neighbour of mine, and after making eye contact, he slipped into my door for a tawdry handjob and the rest is history, Pumpkin."

I know there are arguments against blending into straight society, against accepting monogamy as natural, normal, and our ultimate goal. But as long as I can remember, that's all I've really wanted. I get sick of introducing myself to guys at bars, playing cat-and-mouse, luring them home or being lured to their homes. Lured? It's more like sixth-grade square dancing – you just mechanically choose partners based strictly on physical desirability and hope that your peers don't laugh at your idea of a first-round draft.

"I love your apartment."

"I love your chest . . ."

The worst time to be alone is not, as some people will tell you, Christmas. Christmas, I can handle. I just hate not having a lover when I do something spectacular. I'm not a Nobel Prize-winner, or a published author, nor have I pulled some clumsy waif from a well. My accomplishments are considerably less newsworthy, but that doesn't make them any less exciting to me.

Last week, I challenged my boss. Nobody challenges Ms Ha. Ms Ha is devoid of conscience. She has been known to fire people at staff parties simply because she knows she'll find them there and because she doesn't believe in cordiality, sentimentality, or, well, kindness. Ms Ha is a reptilian woman with dull brown hair and cold green eyes who somehow managed to convince a perfectly charming, almost jovial Korean guy to give her his name. If you were to cut her finger off – just theoretically – you can be sure there'd be a new one in its place in the morning.

I've been with Bright Idea for over five years, and my work has always been solid. I've never had a client outright reject my plans for an ad campaign; at most, I've had some express doubts or ask for minor revisions. But most of the time, I'm dead-on. I did that slapsticky Elizabeth Taylor commercial where she tells the guy his wife stinks and offers him a jug of her perfume. I know it's hard to watch every ten minutes, but that scent has doubled its sales in a little less than six months. Liz hasn't been this happy since she got her second brand-new hip.

That was my ammunition in getting Ms Ha to give me a raise. She told me I had an inflated sense of self-worth and I told her either I got a raise or I walked. She studied me carefully over an imaginary pair of librarian's spectacles (she doesn't wear glasses and is rumored to have better than 20/20 vision), pursed her upper lip, and – stop the presses – relented. I got an $8,000 raise. It was unprecedented. Unimaginable. And almost completely ignored.

None of my friends could truly appreciate this achievement because I only spoke to them once a week or so, and rarely talked about Ms Ha like I would to a lover. They had no idea that I'd just landed on the moon. So Ms Ha had the last laugh – I may have beaten her, but I'd done it anonymously.

But I have to let that go; I didn't have a lover to excitedly talk to my raise about, so I'd just have to get one before I did something else kind of cool.

It was about ten degrees outside and I'd actually passed a snow drift that had once been my neighbor's jeep on the way in, so I didn't much feel like going out to a bar or for Chinese-for-one. Yet I didn't have anything in the house, either. I could have had spaghetti, but I was sick of the stuff, sick of supporting Paul Newman or his charities or whoever he gives his sauce profits to . . . Joanne Woodward?

I was about to give up and order a small pizza when Craig called. We do that nineties' thing, where you stay friends after you break up. It had been so long since we were intimate – three years – that I could hardly remember what had attracted me to him in the first place. Maybe it was the dark hair and intense eyes, the Rock Hudson jaw and shoulders, or the way his ass ski-sloped off his lower back. Maybe it was his hairy arms, his erotic, Speedsticky musk, or his singleminded determination when he used to fuck me. Or maybe it was his voice, that after-hours dj tone that made him so popular on a.m. radio – yeah, actually, that was it. "What are we eating tonight?" he asked. He always did that – just started talking about the way things would be before asking. It was our little joke, like he was constantly trying to put one past me. I crinkled.

"Nice try," I said, "What? You get stood up?"

He snorted. "Never. Just by you that one time." I silently rolled my eyes at the man with the memory of Operation Dumbo Drop. "I just had this intuition that you would be free on this particular night. You told me you had no plans last week, and if you don't have Ex-mas Eve plans the week before, you don't have plans at all."

"You're takeeeng the Christ out of Christmas," I whined playfully. I'd forgotten – it was Christmas Eve and all through my house, not a creature was stirring, not even – well, no, I'd actually been greeted by the sight of a teensy brown mouse sitting in the middle of my sofa when I came home that night. I started thinking about glue traps and animal rights protests and rabbits with Obsession-scented eyes and almost forgot about the matter at hand.

"Oh, mmm, the thing is, I really want pizza on Christmas Eve this year," I said, "I have my heart set on pizza." I knew that would drive him away since he usually went in for fancy sit-down meals.

"Fine. Want me to pick up a couple pies and maybe show up in an hour?"

I was surprised that he was up for anchovies over the hors d'oeuvre, surprised and unexpectedly . . . pleased. I almost felt like we were courting, which was a newsflash to me, and would be the same to his current datemate, Peter. Peter couldn't be called a boyfriend; I take that word too seriously, in the way some people take "lover." When I think of the word "lover," I think of what an aging Gabor calls a one-night stand: "He is vone of my luffers."

"Great," I said. "Come on over. And, uh – we're not exchanging gifts this year, are we?" Hoping against hope since it was too late to grab him anything.

He laughed. "I guess we aren't, but I'm giving one to you. You'll like it. It's nothing major. Relax."

When that voice says to relax, your shoulders listen before your mind does. My mom used to sing me to sleep, and Craig used to talk me to sleep.

"And don't expect Peter to come, too. He's history."

I made a sympathy sound and said, "Sorry." He had no reply, so I had a suspicion that Peter had done something Major and wasn't even going to be discussed as a human being any more.

We hung up and I immediately started pacing about, looking for something I already owned that I could wrap up (in magazine tear sheets? newspapers? an A & P bag?) and present to him as new. He'd been over since I acquired my latest batch of books . . . he worked at a radio station so CDs would be pointless. I settled on a small antique frame I'd found at a flea market, into which I put a photo booth shot of him and me together. I gingerly sliced it from a strip of four, then stopped to recall the day it was taken. It had been our third anniversary, right before he left me because he was too young and wanted to make sure he wasn't passing up other opportunities. Yeah, I know, I know. Might as well be a woman dating a straight guy.

We'd just made love that day, and I remember it because it was a rare mutual orgasm. We'd been lying on the bed, frantically working each other over, stroking chaotically, until I had the sensation that my hand was actually stroking my own prick, and that sent me over the edge. When I opened my eyes, I saw both our ejaculations arcing in the air at the exact same moment, and that sent another, even more powerful burst through my balls. I wound up with a faceful of somebody's jizz and Craig walked away unsoiled. The bed was worse off than my face. But it was one of those sexual peaks you think about forever.

I hadn't come close to achieving that since. My next runner-up was the time I let two drunk bartenders take turns poking me, and the only reason I came so hard then was from having my prostate battered; it was hardly an emotional or psychological thrill.

It was snowing like mad outside when I sat down to watch TV, and to await Craig's arrival. Dusk made the city look lavender, which was a nice thought, politically, and which looked pretty neat, too. I didn't bother to shower since I didn't expect anything to happen. Except the fact that I was even aware I wasn't showering meant I was at least thinking about letting something happen.

I wondered if I could stir up the same passion from our mutual O, or maybe even rekindle some of the fun we'd had our first Christmas together. We'd been so very good, so safe for a whole ten months, and since we were both negative and both positive that we weren't going to cheat (I was naive), we'd decided to start having unsafe sex. I don't know if I'd expected something momentous that night, but I never thought we'd be so giddy, or that I'd find giddiness such a turn-on.

I was lying on my bed, trying to look hot and bothered. I hadn't shaved (he loves – loved – my scruff), I had my shirt off, I was wearing a pair of white briefs fresh out of the package, and I was sitting back so my legs were bent at the knee and my crotch clearly spread toward the door. My hairy balls were half-hanging out and probably a hunk of my cock was, too. That always got Craig hot, the illusion that he was sneaking a peek. He was always fascinated with my balls – firm and round and low hanging. I'd shaved them when he kept commenting favorably on the hairless balls of his favorite porn stars, and that had driven him wild.

He came in for bed wearing a huge grin and his padding-around-the-apartment running shorts, very tight and very old. The kind that has sheer, built-in support so you don't wear underwear. We both have jock fetishes even if we are couch potatoes outside vain trips to the gym. "You want some action?" he teased, gathering the material at either side of his cock and tugging until his erection, trapped, was outlined as clear as nudity.

I let my knees drift further apart, reaching under and around and tugged on my nuts like I had an itch. "Always."

He came up to me and pulled his shorts down and off, flinging them across the room. He was totally naked except for his beat-up running shoes, which he left on. There was something in that gesture that turned me on, something about his unselfconscious libido, about just how certain he was that he could fuck me; I felt my boner stretched in my briefs, pulsing so hard it felt pretzeled.

His cock was pointing straight toward me – out and slightly down, like it was a divining rod seeking H_2O. He's got a big one. I have no clue about inches since I never had occasion to measure it. It's just . . . big. It's fatter than it is long, with a mass of dark hair I used to love to sniff. I'm a sniffer. I like the way men smell, and I love the way Craig's crotch smells. The peculiar odor that his body decides to emit about six hours after a shower is like a truth serum to me, forcing me to admit I'm horny, which I always am, but which I usually mask.

"Get me ready," he said in a normal, conversational tone. No whispering or shame. But his voice is so sexy that it had the same effect as another man grunting, "Suck my cock." I got up on my knees and grasped him at the base of his cock, my fingers braced against his sensitive balls. I started by licking up and down the length of him, getting him wet, so that when I closed my lips around the tip of his wide, flared head, it was simple work sliding down his slippery prick.

I did what he liked best: I gave my face over to a fastpaced bobbing, working almost – but not quite – friction-free up and down, up and down. I knew my curled lips were rubbing wetly against the flared head of his cock, and I knew that that made him almost uncontrollably hot.

"I like that," he growled, "Fuck – I like you on my cock, baby."

I did it so fast I didn't have time to gag as his massive meat tickled the back of my throat. I did it totally for him, but I'd be lying if I claimed not to love the taste of dick.

"No, stop," he begged, and backed half off me. My mouth followed, pinning him against my dresser. I reached behind him and felt his plump ass pressed into the handles of the drawers. He had a great ass, big and pliable, like straight guys have. So many gay guys have those perfectly sculpted buns, but I prefer the fleshy feel of Craig. I squeezed and spread his ass, feeling his moist, hairy crack, working my way toward his hole.

"You want to eat my cum?" he asked as a warning, but then he remembered we were going to be unsafe and he shut up. Of course I did.

When my fingers reached his puckered hole, I rubbed it furiously, making it hot and wet. He loves that kind of stimulation – all on the surface, no insertion. I rubbed his butthole and continued suctioning his prong. If I'd had a third hand, I'd have reached up and smacked his pecs for him, that other little peculiarly Craig thing he likes guys to do to him.

"I'm so close," he said through clenched teeth. I kept at it, made my sucking even more deliberate. I was so hard myself it was a chore to keep from reaching down and bringing myself off. But first I wanted to eat his cum.

"Oh, man," he said raggedly. "Oh, fucking suck me – yeah!"

I felt a well of juice pouring onto my tongue as soon as he said, "Oh, man," and then had to make room in my cheek for the six or seven spurts of spunk that followed. It felt like I was holding a mouthful of live crickets the way his shots pulsed in my cheek . . . and it tasted a shade worse. I'd discovered that I didn't really like the taste of cum after all, but it had been a noble experiment. I blocked off my nose (and my sense of smell) inside and avoided tasting any of his ejaculate, just kept siphoning it into that reservoir until he was done. Then I took a deep breath and swallowed it, staring directly up into his eyes, never allowing myself to show any distaste.

"How was it?" he asked eagerly, no afterglow at all.

I cracked up and smacked his ass. "Just shut up and fuck me."

He was always good for two loads in a row before his cock got hyper-sensitive, whereas with me, I can sometimes have sex and feel great without coming at all. Not that night, though.

"How do you want it?" he asked.

I pulled my underwear down to my knees, got on my belly, and raised my ass to him. "Like this."

I get turned on by that position so much. Something about the restraint of keeping my knees together, but offering my butt up. It makes my asshole feel so tight, makes every passage through it burn. It's like that position makes me feel every fucking inch.

For once, we didn't lose valuable time and enthusiasm with a condom. Craig hunkered down on top of me, straddling me with his cum-slicked dick poised at my hole. I felt it ease between my half-clenched cheeks, squirmed when it sank snugly into the small area just before my sphincter. It was wildly hot, that anticipation. I couldn't wait, and so I reached back and pulled my left cheek roughly away; his hardness was sucked into the beginnings of my hole and I felt like the happiest slut on earth.

"Knock yourself out," I panted, pushing back on him, trying to make do with almost no lube. He started wiggling his cock in circles, slipping it around in the last few drops of his cum. When it was finally in me to the hilt, he just started banging me like a convict.

It hurt without lube, but after a few minutes, my hole felt

pretty slippery and there was no stopping him. He fucked me so hard the wet smacking noise on my ass sounded like I was being stropped. His balls banged against mine, and my dick rubbed against my mattress until I started blasting cum involuntarily, and with no warning.

My hole spasmed frantically around his big tool, and Craig stopped his pumping and came loudly up me. It felt surreal, like ribbons being drawn upward into me and then through my dick.

I didn't feel right down there for days.

The doorbell rang and I felt real regret at not having showered and changed into something sexy. I realized that all I wanted for Christmas was that first Christmas we'd had together.

Craig came in with two small pizzas and his gift. He looked really handsome. He seemed older, but in a good way, and he hadn't shaved either.

We hugged, which I prolonged, as if we were still together and he was just back from a business trip or from seeing his folks at Easter.

"You'll love my gift," he said proudly.

Later, I was relieved at how touched he was at my thoughtless gift. He remembered that day at the photo booth with a little story about how reluctant I'd been to sit for those shots, in contrast to my over-enthusiasm in the resulting photos. Sitting on his lap always put a big grin on my face. I think he felt like I was reminding him of our last day together, our mutual orgasm – our relationship – which I hadn't been doing at all. Or had I?

I opened his gift. It was not, thank God, a Rolex. It was an ornament. I studied it and read the girly script on it, and realized it was an antique ornament he and I had once been given by his best friend. He'd taken it when he'd moved out. It said, "Our First Christmas Together."

I had a brief flashback to our first condomless fuck and glanced up at him. He was grinning like a wolf, but his eyes were smiling sweetly, nostalgically.

I didn't know right then if his gift was an invitation to reignite our relationship or just a really terrific way of getting into my pants, but I decided not to look a gift horse in the mouth. If we were about to get back together, it'd happen. If not, I'd at least be spending an intimate Christmas Eve with a friendly face and the hottest cock I'd ever met.

"You shouldn't have," I said, and we took off for my bedroom. On my way, I grudgingly went to the medicine cabinet for some condoms and lube. Let's not get carried away with reminiscing, shall we?

BLOWING HOT AND COLD

Barry Lowe

"ANSWER THE PHONE, will you?" Wally shouted while attempting to stuff our thermal underwear into an already bloated suitcase.

"Why can't Adam do it? I'm busy."

Indeed, I was. Searching through a pile of books to see which would be interesting enough to read on the plane but innocuous enough to get through Chinese Customs.

"He's putting on his face."

I groaned inwardly as visions of our devastated bathroom flashed before my eyes. For Adam, a young man with whom Wally and I shared communal sexual favours on an irregular basis, putting on his face meant virtually rearranging the bathroom, using every available towel, smearing make-up over the vanity basin, scrunching the bath mat into the most grotesque shapes, and spilling enough water on the floor to keep the Snowy Mountains hydro-electric scheme going for years.

I picked up the phone.

"Wanna wank?" the voice on the other end panted.

Putting my hand over the receiver I yelled to Wally, "You got time for a wank caller?"

"Come off it, we've got to be at the airport in half an hour."

For a split second I was going to call Adam but I noticed he was struggling with his eye-liner and thought better of it.

"Sure," I breathed huskily down the mouthpiece.

At first I could not make out what was going on at the other end but then I realised it was a well-lubricated hand going to town. I waited patiently for him to put the phone back to his ear before launching into some heavy breathing.

"Rub the phone through your pubes," he mumbled hoarsely.

About this time I realized I was not in the mood for all this carry on and that I had to ring my mum to wish her a merry Christmas and all that festive shit which we were doing our best to escape.

Anyway, I was still fully clothed.

Rubbing the phone through the hair on the top of my head I wondered if it had the authentic sound. I was rewarded with groans of ecstasy from the other end.

"Tell me what you want to do to my body," he whispered.

"I want you to leave your front door open. . ." I was beginning to get turned on as Adam could see as he looked up from fishing for his eye liner in the basin.

"You're disgusting," he sneered as he applied another layer of pancake.

"Oh, yes please," came the whisper. "What would you do to me then?"

"You'll be spreadeagled over your coffee table and I'll drink about a gallon of water in the half hour or so before I arrive . . ."

By now things were straining at the leash and I attempted to push the bathroom door closed with my foot so Adam could not see or hear what was going on. He merely swung it open again. There was going to be no privacy.

"What would you like me to do to your body?" I asked in my huskiest voice hoping to avoid some of the embarrassment of Adam listening to my telephone technique.

The voice began to babble on and I put my hand inside my jeans. It was uncomfortable – but pleasant.

Just as he got to the part where I was standing above his face on the coffee table I heard a knock at the door. I looked pleadingly at Adam but he merely shrugged and went on with Ramboing the bathroom. And there was no use calling for Wally who was cursing having to pack winter clothes for China when the temperature in the room would have fried an egg.

Good manners dictated I couldn't interrupt my caller's fantasy so I carefully cradled the phone on the kitchen Laminex and went to the door.

It was Jordan.

"Just dropped in to say goodbye and tell you about last night at the baths."

Ushering him in I motioned I was on the phone. He busied himself fishing in his oversize bag for cigarettes while I picked up the receiver.

". . . and then I want you to really go to town . . ."

The caller had not even noticed my momentary disappearance.

"Oh yea, what a turn on," I muttered.

"Wank call?" Jordan enquired without looking up.

I nodded and motioned to him to continue his story. Adam waved from the bathroom.

"That guy I was supposed to meet last night at the steam bath . . ." Jordan continued.

I struggled to remember while trying to retain the thread of the phone conversation – Jordan had so many dates and so many stories.

"It turned out a disaster. I met him there but he was a novice. Fascinated by the shaven crotch and the ball stretcher but wouldn't let me lay a hand on him, and here was your sister prepared for all sorts of mischief. Had the bag full of toys and condoms. It was so heavy I almost needed a removalist van to get to the city."

Nodding, I wished my ears were ambidextrous.

". . . and then you can tie me to the coffee table and I'll open my mouth really wide . . ."

"Well, naturally I dumped him as soon as I could and went wandering. Let me tell you, your sister fell in love a hundred times but nobody was reciprocating. Until, that is . . ."

Jordan paused. "Why are you rubbing the phone through your hair?"

Adam shouted from the bathroom, "The wanker's into pubic hair."

Jordan looked closely at the hair on the top of my head and merely said, "Oh," before going on with his story.

"I passed one room and there was this number with tattoos all over his arms. Normally I'm not into tattoos but he had on all the paraphernalia – the tit clamps, the cock ring, the ball stretchers, the works. Well, your sister threw herself into the room with the bag full of goodies . . ."

"Help me with the bags, will you!" Wally griped as he struggled past.

Adam put the finishing touches to his new retro-Grace Jones hairstyle and wandered out, grabbing one of the suitcases.

"Love your hair," Jordan flirted.

"I had a lawn that looked like that once," Wally quipped as he hustled the bags to Adam's car.

". . . then I want you to turn me over and part my cheeks with your rough, callused hands . . ."

Callused? My hands had never seen a hard day's work in their life.

"I looked at all the things he had attached to his body and I was too embarrassed to get mine out so I just felt under the towel for the meat and . . ." fanning himself with his hand ". . . I wasn't disappointed. It was about . . ." he mimed a size which would have looked interesting on an elephant but which, on a human, must have looked grotesque. But then Jordan's entire reading list consisted of Tom of Finland drawings.

"Are you close to coming?" the voice from the phone asked.

"Uh, yeah," I lied.

"Tell me about your fantasy with me," he begged.

"Look, at the moment . . ."

"I can leave if you like," Jordan leered.

I motioned Jordan to stay put and he continued with his tale while I mumbled into the phone.

"After I've spread your cheeks I'll lube my fingers and . . ."

"His gear was so co-ordinated, so Gucci, I wasn't about to show him my BBC Hardware make do's. I gave him a few yanks on the chains he had all over his body and he screwed up his face in pain. He looked like one of those statues of the saints being done to death with spears . . ."

"Will you hurry up!" Wally was getting impatient.

"Look, mate," I said sharply into the phone.

"Oh! You've made it go down interrupting like that."

"Are you close to coming? Because I've got to get ready."

"Why don't I ring you back in a few minutes when I'm in the mood again?" he whined.

"He loved every minute of it and got a kick out of the condoms too. He hadn't realized you could do so much with a piece of flaccid rubber. Not that anything else was flaccid."

"OK," I sighed, "Hear from you soon."

"Rub the phone through your pubes one more time."

I put the receiver on top of my head for a few perfunctory rubs and then hung up. Jordan managed to retrieve a grey hair from the mouthpiece.

"I don't think you're listening," he sulked.

"Your S/M gear didn't match so you were too embarrassed to use it," I huffed, madly searching through my books to find the still elusive suitable title.

"Anyway, gotta go," I said grabbing the novel closest to hand, pushing Jordan toward the door, Wally and Adam were both in the car beckoning wildly.

"Is the answering machine on?" I asked.

"You'll be gone for ten days; that's an awful backlog of calls," Jordan pointed out.

"Adam's looking after the house while we're away," Wally cut in. "Now get in the car."

"Well, your sister's off on a date. I've got all my goodies," Jordan displayed a 12-pack of condoms and a vicious look-ing studded dildo. "Have a good time," he waved as he headed off.

I was opening the back door of the car as the phone rang.

"Darn," I said. Or expletives very similar.

"Get in the car!" Wally demanded.

"Could be my mum," I said as I unlocked the door to the house just in time to hear the answering machine beat me to it.

I listened for a while and it was a few seconds before I could make out the distinctive sounds of a phone being rubbed through pubic hair. This was followed by the slurping of a well-lubricated wank. I closed the door laughing.

"Who was it?" Wally asked.

"Wrong number," I smiled.

"Are we ready to go?" Adam wondered.

"China here we come!"

A few days later we rang Adam from our hotel in sub-zero Beijing. He informed us the weather was great and that he had developed quite a tan at Lady Jane. "Oh, and the phantom wanker called back."

"Did he leave a message?" I asked remembering our machine worked on a 30-second cut-off cycle.

"He dialled 14 times before he had an orgasm," Adam said.

All I could do was marvel at his stamina.

CHRONIC MANAGEABLE ILLNESS

James Hannaham

MY MOTHER USED to tell me never to let my hand write a check my ass couldn't cash. Not only didn't I listen, but my hand must have a mind of its own. It can't stop scribbling my signature at the bottom of blank checks for accounts long overdrawn. I realize I've written another one as the drugs set me down for a moment of clarity. I'm lying in bed with these two guys. I never got their names. Names aren't that important, especially since so many of them turn out to be false. My real name is Elverett Jordan, but I told these guys my name was David. David is a name that no one asks me to repeat. I'm not sure they even heard it over the loud music at the club, or if they remember it anyway. Or care.

We've just ruined their expensive-looking duvet with ribbons of sensual lubricant and five and a half loads of cum. I say five and a half because they each came twice, and I came once, but I'd come so many times already that day that my second load was a dribble of clear liquid with a tiny opaque rivulet of sperm in it – the population of a small midwestern town, maybe. The guys – lovers I think – have turned over and twisted their limbs together, lost in that gray area of consciousness where they're either going to fall asleep for good or suddenly snap to attention and kick me out. The candles are still flickering, dousing the air with a heavy perfume. Outside, the black sky is turning blue.

I lie there for a few moments, and rather than raid the closet for a towel, I massage the sticky semen into my skin, where it has splashed on my chest, neck, and face. My own body turns me on. I've always considered that one of the advantages of homosexuality. If you're looking for a dick, you can always find one between your own legs. I've spent enough time sculpting my torso in abs class after abs class that when I run my hands along my bumpy stomach I get a feeling somewhere between a sexual thrill and a sense of accomplishment. This is enough of a turn-on to get me slightly hard again. My lust barely forces itself through all the ketamine I've snorted.

I notice a phone on the nightstand, and, wiping my hand on the duvet – Not my laundry bill, I think to myself – quietly raise the receiver to my ear. I dial carefully, so as not to wake my partners.

A deep, masculine voice answers. "Thank you for calling 1–900–MAN–2MAN, New York City's ultimate man-to-man action line. To leave your own personal message, press –"

I press three, as usual. Another voice appears on the line.

"Hey bud, what's up?" the voice says.

"Feeling real horny tonight," I drawl. "Where you calling from?"

"Brooklyn," the voice says, and before he finishes the word, I've pressed the pound key and moved on to the next voice.

"Hey buddy," I say.

"What's up, guy," he responds. "Where you calling from?"

"Chelsea."

"Oh, cool, me too. Where in Chelsea?"

"Twenty-fourth between ninth and tenth."

"Eighteenth and eighth. You?"

He sounds sexy, and more importantly, geographically promising. I want more. "Whadda you look like?"

"I'm about five-eight, Italian, 160 pounds, black hair, smooth, work out five times a week, extremely good looking, tattooed, pierced, hot guy. Submissive bottom. What about you?"

"You sound hot. I'm a Black guy, six feet tall, 185 pounds, work out twice a day, extremely good looking, shaved body,

into kink and raunch, light B&D. You won't be disappointed."
One of the lovers next to me starts snoring, so I cup my hand
around the mouthpiece.

"Black men are hot, that's cool," he says. I don't think it
applies to every black man, but I'm not going to look a gift
horse in the mouth. "Top or bottom?"

"Top," I say, because I know that lying makes me more
marketable.

"Oh yeah, I'd really love to get fucked by a hot black guy
right now. What's your address?" He says. I'm stumped for a
moment.

"Hold on."

Afraid to wake the lovers up, I look around the room for a
piece of mail with their address on it, or an address book, but
there's nothing. Except for the duvet, the room is immaculate.
No newspapers, no bookshelves, just sleek furniture made from
maple and gun metal, red candles and framed snapshots of
gorgeous white men on tropical beaches with their arms around
each other. They're smiling brightly. They have crimson dots
in their eyes from the flashbulb. There isn't a single piece of
paper in the apartment.

"Still there?" I ask.

"Yeah, what's taking so long?" he says. I don't answer. I
lightly nudge the closer of the two guys. He slowly turns his
blond head toward me.

"What's the address here?" I ask. Confused, he squints at
me.

"410 West 24th Street no. 5D." His head falls back onto his
boyfriend's shoulder.

I repeat the address into the receiver. "Be there in ten
minutes," the guy says. "Is it OK if I bring a friend?"

"Yeah, sure, that'd be hot," I reply. I put down the phone.

I tiptoe out of the room. My temples are pounding. My
eyeballs are so bugged out they could scare Marty Feldman. My
head feels like there's a junior high school chemistry experiment
going awry inside it. One of those sulphur volcanoes, probably.
I grope my way to the kitchen through the darkness. I've left
my duffel bag on the couch, unzipped.

I fumble through and find a clear ziploc bag with two white

plastic bottles, one marked "Motrin," the other "Advil." The container marked "Motrin" is where I keep my Crixivan, so no one knows I'm positive, and the one marked "Advil" is for the Zoloft, so no one knows I take anti-depressants. Or is that the other way around? Good thing I don't have a headache. The only cup I can find is a dirty martini glass toppled over in the sink. As I attempt to wash it, my hands turn slick again from all the dried sperm and lube. I have a difficult time holding the glass.

As I'm gulping my medications and drinking multiple glasses of lukewarm tap water, the buzzer sounds. Most of the apartments have been renovated in this complex, a block-wide Tudor monstrosity, but they haven't changed the obnoxious doorbell since 1929. It startles me so much that I drop the glass and it shatters in the sink. I find the doorbell and buzz in the guys from 1–900–MAN–2MAN.

A few moments later, there's a knock on the door. I open it. The hot Italian guy is there, dressed in a leather jacket and no shirt. He is not as attractive as I imagined he would be. His assessment of me ends with a similar resolve – my body is much hotter than my face, due to a battle with acne in high school – so we're even. He is accompanied by a much larger, fatly muscular man wearing a striped tank top and athletic shorts. The Italian guy, seeing the contours of my naked body in the dim light, falls to his knees and takes my dick into his mouth. The harder he licks and sucks in an attempt to get it hard, the softer it feels to me. He is not concerned. I grasp the nape of his neck with both hands. His leather jacket squeaks as he moves. Behind him, the man in the striped tank top pulls a thick semi-hard cock out from one of the legs of his shorts and gives it a few tugs.

Suddenly the lights go on, and I turn to see that one of the lovers, the dark-haired one, is standing naked in the doorjamb of the bedroom, frowning at the scene. I feel like a roach, but lacking a crevice to scurry into, I just stare.

"What are you doing? Norman!" he exclaims.

The Italian guy slides my flaccid member out of his mouth and looks at the dark-haired lover. "Oh shit . . . Joey . . . I thought this address sounded familiar." I realize the broken glass has cut my right hand and I've been bleeding profusely down Norman's back. I rush to the kitchen and wrap the bleeding appendage in a dishtowel. The man in the tank top hasn't stopped jerking.

"How many times do I have to tell you to stay the fuck away from Brad," he spits.

"I'm not looking for Brad . . . that black guy gave me this address and I thought maybe you moved out or something or it wasn't the right address. You can't find anyone's apartment in this anthill anyway."

"Like hell you did. Do you really expect me to believe that you just 'forgot' that this was the address? After you spent all fucking week across the street spying on us? Mary, you're tripping."

"Fuck you, Joey, I wasn't spying on you. I was house-sitting. You're such a paranoid asshole."

"Why don't you just get the fuck out of my apartment!"

"Why don't you just leave us the fuck alone and go back to bed," Norman says. Then, to my complete shock, he defiantly replaces himself in front of my crotch and starts licking my balls. Joey grabs a small fold-up umbrella from the hall closet and strikes Norman repeatedly across the shoulders.

"Oh, come on, Joey. You can do better than that," he says, and then plants his tongue in my navel. He slips off his leather jacket to reveal, in addition to a large tattoo of a dragon with its tail wrapped around one of his arms, that his back is covered with scars and burn marks. "You know I've had worse than that. Don't fucking be a sissy about it."

Joey stops hitting Norman and violently tries to pull him away from me. Norman grabs my thighs. Joey pushes me backward, and I fall on top of the garbage can. I grab Joey's hair, trying to steady myself before I fall, and the three of us pile up in the space between the free-standing counter and the sink. Joey starts punching Norman. I intercept Joey's hand to restrain him. Norman slips out from under him and holds back his other hand. The guy in the tank top, who I now recognize from the gym, sneaks into the bedroom during the commotion.

"I hope you don't think I'm not aware of what this is really about, Joey," Norman says contemptuously.

"What is it about, Mr Know-it-All?" Joey fires back. Without a second thought, Norman brutally pinches Joey's right nipple with his free hand, grabs him by the back of the neck and kisses him full-on. Joey struggles for a few moments, then his body goes limp. He wraps his arms around Norman's waist. He plants kisses all over Norman's face. His hands travel around Norman's body like it's a fetish.

"You fucking love me, you piece of shit," Norman growls. I've never heard anyone sound so arrogant. "Suck my cock."

Joey fumbles with the button-fly of Norman's leather pants, and within moments is hungrily worshipping his manhood. At the same time, I feel two of Norman's fingers penetrate my butt. He goes too fast, and without lubrication it hurts. He doesn't care. Soon he is pressing his fingers as deep as they will go, mauling my prostate gland. This turns me on, to be with a dominant guy who uses me without inhibitions. I guess Joey feels the same way. Norman removes his fingers, shoves them into Joey's mouth, and laughs.

Norman rises and forces us into the bedroom, where we can already hear the bed creaking in the rhythm of sex. He closes the front door to the apartment. The huge guy has removed his tank top. It is now wrapped around Brad's neck. Brad looks like he's unconscious, his head moving freely back and forth with the shaking of the bed. Suddenly, Norman grasps the back of my head and shoves a small amber vial into my one of my nostrils. He holds the other nostril closed and knees me in the stomach, practically knocking the wind out of me. I take a huge breath. I realize he's just done this to Joey while I watched Brad get fucked. Joey is doubled over, his head swelling with blood from the heavy hit of amyl nitrate. In another moment, he parts Norman's buttocks and plunges his face between them, like a hungry pig at a trough. Norman places the vial under each of his own nostrils and snorts vigorously. He grins at me and takes a little swig from the bottle.

"Numbs the tongue," he comments as he screws the cap back on.

The next time I get a peek into full consciousness, I'm lying flat on the sticky duvet, keeping my nostrils just above the line where the down would suffocate me. My intestines gurgle painfully, as they do regularly now. I must still have a stomach ache. There's a consistent pressure and release in my abdomen. If the tank top guy were not in front of me, his member poking at my cheeks, I would think he was fucking me. But the object invading my body feels too big to be him anyway. When I groggily turn my head sideways, I catch a skewed glimpse of Norman behind me. He's spilled vegetable oil down my back. My ass glistens like an eggplant. His elbow positioned like a lever at my thighs, he pushes his naked fist between my buttocks and penetrates me.

Joey arranges a trail of clothes pins across my back. They ripple in succession, like dinosaur spines, every time I inhale or exhale. Joey looks like someone I went on a date with once, an architect who stuck his napkin into his collar and kept fixing his hair in the mirror behind me while he thought I wasn't looking. He couldn't stop talking about the tiny painful dots on his tongue. He couldn't figure out what they were. Maybe they were cold sores, he said, maybe he'd burned his tongue, maybe they were an allergic reaction. He never mentioned herpes. But I don't think Joey is the same guy. Brad is underneath me, inverted, biting the inside of my thigh. I'm clinging to his waist, drawing his shaved crotch up to my chin. The tiny hairs brush against my cheeks.

I always thought activities that edged into S/M like this would hurt, but my body is so relaxed and the drugs so powerful that I can't experience it completely. Everything seems two-dimensional: I know it's happening, I know it causes some kind of trauma, but it doesn't affect me. Instead, I only find it interesting and mildly uncomfortable, like watching one of those TV shows where the cameramen follow the police on raids. I'm safe at home, while the guns blast away on the screen. I wish I could feel this way every time I ask my younger brother for money, or when captains on my infrequent catering jobs fire me in front of the guests, or when I go home with an ashen, pimply old man just to have a place to crash and the guy starts begging me to urinate on him and then forces me to leave right afterward. Or when I think about what might have happened to me if my doctor friend Charles hadn't gotten me into a clinical trial for protease inhibitors, or at the gym when I run into Bryan, my last boyfriend, who convinced me to fall in love with him and then stopped returning my phone calls once I did, or when I get so depressed thinking about how far away from my goals I've strayed and how futile life is that I consider giving up and going home, and then I remember that I'm not welcome there either, and I start wandering around the city playing "What if" – "What if I jumped in front of the F train?" "What if I stepped off the platform and touched the third rail?" "What if I shut my eyes and walked across the West Side Highway?" Then the game of "What if" tuns into the game of "I should."

Just as Joey releases the last clothes pin, I come. I am immediately returned from my mind trip. A sharp stinging pain starts in my left arm and shoots into my chest cavity. It lodges in my abdomen and radiates outward. My legs flop from under me and I convulse like a marlin on a line. My penis aches as it shifts and bends in a failed attempt to reach full hardness. It is raw and bruised from excessive friction. My balls heave, yielding only a glistening spot of seminal fluid at the opening of my urethra. My teeth clatter. My arms flail uncontrollably. One of them knocks a candle over. It hits Norman in the stomach. The hot wax drips into his crotch and he moans. My eyes roll up into my head.

I can't stop screaming, "Yes! Yes! Yes! Oh fuck! Yes!"

After a few minutes, the tremors subside. We collapse. Joey, Brad and I lace our limbs together on the duvet, the tank top guy slumps into the chair by the bed, and Norman gradually comes to rest on the floor. The breeze pushes a tree branch up against the window. There's a long silence, then the tank top guy clears his throat. "I'm starving," he says. "Anyone feel like brunch?"

After much squabbling, we wind up at Étude, a small, slightly too-expensive country Sino-French bistro with a limited yet eclectic menu – goat cheese won tons, *pain perdu* with lychee syrup, bamboo crêpes. We sit at a round table in the corner of their backyard garden, in front of a stone wall topped by a row of potted petunias. Gay men make up about 99 percent of the clientele here, but calling a place like this a "gay restaurant" sounds silly, as if homosexuality were an ethnicity. It's a beautiful day. The sky seems artificially blue. The sun turns all the tablecloths a brilliant white and spangles the ice water.

"Has anyone else seen *Describing the Arc*?" Brad says while splitting a corn muffin with his knife. Brad is one of those fortyish blond guys whose physical charms made him the center of attention in his twenties. Now that deep creases have set into his cheeks and the sun gives him more wrinkles than freckles, he overcompensates by dominating conversations.

"The new Angelika Philmore movie, you mean?" tank top guy asks.

"Guillermo Calabresi directed it, right? What about it?" Norman remarks with a mouthful of bread, staring at his menu. "He used to be so good until he sold out. That movie's a fucking piece of trash."

"I can't stand Angelika Philmore," offers Joey.

"Yeah, I keep meaning to go see it," I say casually, so as not to appear moronic. "Everyone's talking about it." I readjust the new, more efficient gauze bandage around my hand. I found it myself in Brad and Joey's medicine cabinet. They didn't know they had it.

"Do you remember that scene at the end, after she kills her abusive husband and she's standing there in the kitchen in that dress –" A series of groans travels around the table.

"I don't know what possessed the costume designer to put her in all those fleur-de-lys."

"It was a Versace, I think."

"I knew the best boy on that shoot."

"I'll bet you know all the best boys," Norman slips under the wire.

"Anyway," Brad continues, "She's standing in the kitchen, in that horrible dress, about to wash the dishes, and she's still got all the dirt on her hands from burying him in the cornfield about a half hour before . . ."

I wonder if I should see the film now that I know so much of the outcome.

". . . and the house is, like, totally immaculate, with the

gingham drapes and the boxed tablecloths and she's just about to wash all the blood and dirt off her hands and do the dishes when—"

Tank top guy, throwing his wrist in the air, suddenly barges in and squeals, "Did you notice how even after she's just hacked her husband to bits and dragged him for four miles, like, the makeup is still perfect, the hair is still like, not a single strand out of place?" Everyone laughs.

"And you know there wasn't a bloodstain to be found on that Versace, honey!"

"I'm hoping I can still look that good after I throw Brad in the Cuisinart!" Joey exclaims.

Brad is gesturing with his buttery knife, trying to recapture everyone's full attention. "And then the phone rings!" He chuckles as he stuffs more muffin into his mouth.

"Right, right. What about it, Brad?" Norman inquires after a moment.

"Nothing about it, I just thought of it for some reason."

"What made you think of it?"

"I don't know, I guess I was just thinking about it for some reason."

"Yeah, but what was the reason is what I asked," Norman replies. He crushes an ice cube with a rear molar.

"Does there have to be a reason for everything? You're too analytical for your own good. Always analyzing stupid subway ads and television shows to find the 'hidden politics' or whatever. You thought Mr Peanut was a Nazi or something, didn't you? That's why I knew it would never work out between us."

"Brad, if I didn't know you were dumb enough to think that Gore Vidal made hair care products, I'd punch you right now."

"It was an honest mistake, fuck you very much."

"Anger anger anger!" Joey remarks with mock perkiness. Brad's jaw clenches. He brushes a petunia away from his ear. Now I can hear people at the adjacent table discussing a New Yorker article about the behavior of spotted snails off the coast of Bimini. "It's too long," one of them says, "But I always feel like that's the point." They laugh.

A slender, beautiful waiter appears as if out of nowhere.

"Are you ready to order, guys?" he asks. I don't even hear what anyone else wants. I can't stop staring at his tautly muscular, tanned bicep twitching under the flimsy white sleeve of his form-fitting shirt as he scribbles down the shorthand for all those elaborate dishes. A sexy vein bulges at the edge of the hem. I'm an impulse away from leaning over, kissing it gently, letting my tongue travel into his armpit. Just to see what happens.

I only notice that he's speaking to me the second time he addresses me.

"Hello?" he says, waving his pad in directly in front of my eyes. "I said, do you know what you'd like? Maybe I should come back when you're ready."

"I'm ready," I declare. "I'm always ready."

Brad fans himself with a napkin. "Whoa, Mary, I'm sweating over here." I silence him with a stern look.

"Well what would you like . . . for brunch?"

He's caught me off guard. I attempt to glance at the menu without losing eye contact. I wonder if he has a big cock. People always say you can tell by looking at a guy's hands and feet, but I think it's the lips. Aren't the lips and the dick formed in the same way, when the two halves of your body come together? He has unusually full lips, too soft and thick for a white boy. I'm already imagining them sliding over my prick.

"I'll have the, um, General Tso's frog legs," I say unsteadily. My gaze, however, is unflinching. I let my jaw stay slack as a challenge. My tone of voice remains all business and 100 percent butch. I'm almost doing a James Earl Jones impression. His breathing goes ever so slightly irregular.

Maybe it would be better to wait, just to get his phone number and save this morsel for later. After all, who am I kidding? I'm chafed, tired, and ruined. I'm supposed to go to a movie with a friend later this afternoon, so technically, I don't really have time to have sex with him. But what was it that movie with all those hot preppy boys in it used to say? Carpe diem? Seize the day? Seize the dick is more like it. Maybe once I get him to confess that he wants me, we can just shake hands, he'll congratulate me, and we'll and part ways in a matter of seconds.

"Excellent choice," he says, reinforcing his opinion with a

long glance down my torso. He turns toward the kitchen. Even though his black khaki pants hang relatively loosely around his waist, they grab his thighs provocatively. I involuntarily tighten my stomach muscles.

As he leaves, I twist around in my seat to watch him. He tears off our order as he enters the hallway that leads back into the main part of the restaurant, where there's a small window into the kitchen. He delivers the order to the chef and then turns to face the garden. Though I'm a few yards away, our eyes lock. His shoulders heave.

Brad and tank top guy have just begun to discuss the reasons why it's much easier to meet men at the Strap than at Maneuvers. "The music's so loud at Maneuvers," Brad says. "You can't even hear yourself think!"

"You'd have to listen pretty hard for that anyway, Brad," Norman snipes.

"Excuse me, guys," I say, still fixated on our waiter. As I rise from the table, I notice that Norman and Joey are holding hands under the table.

The waiter turns and begins marching toward the kitchen. The hallway is lit like an underpass, with only the reflected sunlight from the dining room and the back garden. I accelerate, hoping to stop him while the darkness can hide whatever transaction needs to be made. Instead he outpaces me, bursting into the anteroom just as I arrive at the end of the tunnel. I stop by the bathroom door and watch as he approaches a table full of massive bodybuilders, all wearing baseball caps and second hand team uniform shirts. If it weren't for the beard growth and the absence of grass stains on their kneecaps, they'd look like a blush of boys just in from little league practice.

The waiter chats with them, his back erect, his chest thrust out slightly. He pauses to push a strand of reddish-brown hair out of his face. His skin is smooth, his eyes set slightly forward like those of a wet clay bust. His face is sensuously rounded, his nose substantive, his cheeks full without being fat. The combination gives him a hare-like appearance, but not one without guile. I notice the swarthy bodybuilder closest to him is laughing. He smiles and grabs the waiter's forearm. The waiter gently removes the guy's hand as he takes their order.

Sensing that he will have to return to the back garden, I open
the bathroom door outward so that it can block the hallway if
necessary. He leaves the table of guys and approaches the trap
I've set for him. His shoulders are hunched over. He's staring
toward the ground. As I watch him, I slowly pull the door
toward me. Just before we collide, he stops abruptly. He's
more confused than startled.

"Um, hi . . ." he says. His voice is low and masculine, it
glides out of his mouth like a radio announcer's. There's a
sardonic hint trapped in it now. "I was just going to the back
garden, to, you know, do my job and stuff. Do you mind, um,
stepping aside?"

"Yes," I say. "I do mind." I grab his slim waist and, using
the door for leverage, shove him into the bathroom. I place
my body between him and the door. He's mine now. I turn
on the lights.

The interior is painted pink, with shiny white mouldings
that look like birthday cake icing. A potpourri in a basket on
the toilet tank spills the scent of roses, cloves and sandalwood
into the air. The fixtures are all gold plated and shaped like
curlicues. The sink faucet stretches up from its oval base, regal
as a swan's neck. A small plaster cherub does an arabesque in
a niche above the sink.

"Hey, what are you doing?" he asks.

"Nothing," I say, my eyes traveling up and down his
body, "Yet."

"What do you think you're going to do?"

Before he can finish asking the question, I loop my arms
around his waist, securing him against me while my hands
vigorously maul his gym-streamlined butt. I fasten my lips
on top of his. He tries to turn away, but he can only turn as
far as the wall allows. In a moment, he has parted his lips in
surrender. I stop kissing him, now that he wants it.

"See, you fucking want me, don't deny it." He nods and
pushes his head forward. His warm, slimy tongue enters my
mouth and begins to explore. I move my head forward to
accept it, pushing my own lips under his. I suck his tongue
nearly to the back of his throat. He groans. I push my hand
up his shirt. His skin is flushed, his chest stubble chafes my

hand. He's practically fat free. He must be doing steroids. Good, I think.

Suddenly he pushes my hand away. "I have an um, well I have kind of a boyfriend . . ." he mutters.

"Is he going to see us?"

I kiss him again. The finish makes a smacking sound that reverberates against the bathroom walls.

"I really shouldn't be doing this," he says, unhooking my belt and hiking my pants down to mid-thigh. "I really shouldn't . . . oh man." He kneels before my semi-erect member. A crucifix on a necklace falls out of his shirt.

"Are you Catholic?"

"Good guess. Hey, what's that?"

"What's what?"

"It looks like blood or something."

I examine my inner thigh and discover a spider-leg of dried blood traveling from just behind my nuts, running down below where my pants have fallen. There is a discoloration I hadn't noticed on the inside of my pants leg. My Calvin Klein boxer briefs are covered with a brick-red stain. A crimson droplet suddenly falls on the cloth with a tiny slapping noise. We stare at each other for at least ten seconds, neither of us knowing how or whether to proceed.

"Here," the waiter finally says, unraveling toilet paper from the dispenser by the handful.

"I got fisted last night. It was pretty rough. I'd never done it before. Dude should've clipped his fucking fingernails." I laugh nervously.

He rises and steps past me. "I'd better get back out on the floor."

"Say, can I get your number?"

"Just call the restaurant," he tells me, carefully clicking the door behind him.

I wipe off my leg and pad the inside of my underwear with the remaining bathroom tissue. I pull up my jeans and refasten my belt. I smooth out my hair. I unwind the gauze on my hand. I'm starting to heal, the wound is pink and sticky. I wrap it up again. I wash my hands and face. I tuck my shirt into my jeans. I smooth out my hair again. I turn my back to the mirror and twist my neck to make sure that the extra padding in the seat of my pants is not showing. I hurry out of the bathroom and dash across the terracotta tiles of the back garden.

As if to celebrate the first warm day of the year, no one is wearing a sweater, although the air is still chilly. It's a beautiful sight, like a June wedding: all the tablecloths flapping like sails, ivy stretching up the stone wall beyond the petunias and covering the brownstone next door, and at every table a group of beautiful men, all having lively conversations. Just this hint of summer seems to promise them all to me, one table at a time. For a moment or two I can't distinguish our group from the rest. I find it just as the busboy sets down our brunch. Norman raises his knife, and it flashes in the sunlight.

"What's the phone number here?" I ask the busboy.

WRESTLING WITH AN ANGEL

Larry Duplechan

I HADN'T EVEN wanted to go to Bronco and Louie's. Like, I really need to leave the West Side, where the blessed Pacific breeze keeps it relatively cool even in the depths of summer, to go to the Valley, where it was sure to be hotter than the devil's butthole before noon. What I'd wanted was to maneuver Joe Callahan into my house and into my bed, where (if I had anything to say about it), we'd likely spend the day, the night, and maybe the following morning, emerging only for the bathroom and maybe the occasional meal.

But I'd told the boys I'd try to meet them at Throb Saturday night, which I didn't, and heaven knows those guys take it so personally if I don't go out and shake it with them until the wee smalls – especially Big Tim, who seems to consider the experience nothing short of religious. So I thought the least I could do was to put in an appearance at the traditional post-Throb Sunday afternoon aftermath pool party at Bronco and Louie's. And I do mean put in an appearance – howdy-howdy, a little laugh, a little talk, maybe a dip into the shallow end of the pool, and then back to Plan A, involving me, my king size four-poster bed, and Joe Callahan – ay-kay-ay Joey King, though I was obviously the very last man on the planet to get wind of that one. But I'm getting ahead of myself here.

I'd just met Joe the Saturday night before the Sunday afternoon of the broken highball glass. I met him at the Comedy Corral over on Sunset in Hollywood. I don't generally frequent comedy clubs – I can get more stand-up than I can stand in my living room on Comedy Central, and besides, the drinks are better at my house; but I had kind of a gig at the Comedy Corral that night. Now, there may be uglier places for a black, queer jazz singer to play than a comedy club, but I can't imagine where (except maybe opening for some thrash band with big hair and a name like Severe Tire Damage at the Troubador on a Saturday night). I only agreed to do this one little 20-minute set at the Comedy Corral as a big, fat personal favor to Robert Franks, who's a stand-up comic, and gay – but deep in the closet, I mean the smell of moth balls precedes him. He's also an old friend of mine (okay, we also tricked once, it was not pretty, and we will not go into it here).

Robert was putting together an industry showcase at the Comedy Corral and needed an opening act. Now, the last thing a stand-up comic wants as the opening act for an industry showcase, is another stand-up comic. It's like, Mother of God, what if he's funnier than I am? Which pretty much leaves singers, dog acts, and those guys who spin plates. Robert, Lord love him, had once been instrumental in getting me a relatively decent gig at a relatively decent jazz club in Redondo Beach, and he decided to call in the favor. Which is how I found myself onstage at the Comedy Corral, belting out a few of the quirkier numbers from my cabaret days, accompanied by a seemingly palsied piano player with sunflower-yellow teeth and an amazing inability to keep a steady rhythm.

As comedy club audiences go, this one was better than average – at least half of them actually acknowledged my existence, some of them even seemed to comprehend that I was singing. True, I had tailored a set all but devoid of jazz sensibility and unusually high in novelty material. It was definitely not a "Night In Tunisia" -followed-by-"Goodbye Pork Pie Hat" kind of an evening. So, I pulled out "Lydia the Tattooed Lady," "Come To The Supermarket In Old Peking," and my "Rock and Roll Death and Dismemberment Medley" composed of "Teen Angel," "Leader of the Pack," and "Tell Laura I Love Her". No scat breaks, no ballads, no George-and-Ira-Gershwin, just wham, bam, gee-thanks-you've-been-great, and I'm outta there.

So, I'm right in the middle of "Black Demin Trousers and Motorcycle Boots", when I suddenly notice this beautiful little man perched on a stool at the bar, which is way in the back, behind the tables. I noticed this man because, even with the house lights down and a follow spot bearing down on my face, I can tell he's one of the handsomest men I've ever seen. And because this handsome little stud is watching me intently. Not chatting up the babe he came in with, not ordering a second vodka gimlet, not sucking on a Marlboro as if his very life depended upon it. Just watching me work. And smiling one of the widest, toothiest, most incandescent smiles ever to light up a small, smoky roomful of slightly drunken humanity.

Generally speaking, it is not a particularly good idea to focus on the attractive lips, teeth, and gums of an audience member while performing a fast-paced, wordy patter song, as one is apt to lose one's place – which I did, somewhere in the middle of the third verse.

I laughed a good, long one, staggering back a couple of paces, then stepped back to the mic, as the audience laughed with me and/or at me.

I did a big, vaudevillian shoulder shrug and said, "So sue me, already." Glancing across the room, I could have sworn I made eye contact with the guy, the one with the smile.

I turned to the piano man, who sat staring up at me with eyes full of question marks.

"Third verse," I said, counted off a loud, "Five, six, seven, eight!" and finished the number to loud laughter and even louder applause.

America loves a come-back.

I closed the set with "Lydia the Tattooed Lady", which has never been known to fail, and what's-his-name played me off to a round of applause that likely stuck terror into dear Robert's heart – I mean, one would prefer one's warm-up act to warm the audience up, but one generally doesn't want one's warm-up act to kill.

I made a genuine bee-line to the rear of the room, where –
God is good – there was a conveniently vacant bar stool right
next to Mr Flawless; who, I discovered upon approaching, was
even better looking up-close than from across the room; and
who greeted my arrival by tossing me that smile of his and
saying, "You're wonderful."

"Thanks," I said, grinning like the Cheshire Cat on Ecstasy.
"Very much." I motioned toward the empty stool and said, "Is
somebody sitting here?"

"No," he said, and I sat down next to him. "Joe Callahan,"
he said, offering a smallish, square-fingered right hand, which
I readily accepted.

"It's a pleasure," I said.

Joe said, "The pleasure's mine. You were wonderful," he
added, our hands still clasped. "I said that already, didn't I?"

"Say it as many times you'd like," I said, finally relinquishing
Joe's hand.

He turned to the bartender (a squat, muscular fellow with
a rapidly receding hairline and a handlebar mustache) and
lifted an empty Calistoga bottle. "Another, please." Then to
me, "May I buy you a drink?"

"You may," I said. "The same," I said to the bartender, and
back to Joe, "Thanks."

We clinked our little bottles together, toasting nothing in
particular.

"You sing here a lot?" Joe asked.

"No," I said. "This is my first and, pray God, my last
engagement at this little venue. This was a favor for Robert
Franks."

"You're friends with Robert?" Joe asked. "Me too."

And suddenly I thought, Shit – is this guy Robert's
boyfriend?

"Are you –?" I began.

"Oh, no," Joe cut me off. "We're just friends."

"Good," I said. "I mean –" Well, there was no graceful way
out of that one, so I just shrugged and said, "I guess I mean,
Good." Which earned me another smile. I quickly found Joe
Callahan's smiles to be dangerously habit forming. I already
couldn't wait for my next fix.

There followed a brief conversational lull, during which Joe and I sat, sipped, and grinned at one another. I was about to ask him how long he'd known Robert and from where, just to keep things rolling, when the M.C. came onstage to introduce "a very funny guy – ladies and gentlemen, Robert Franks!"

I joined in the applause for Robert's entrance, whistled once, did a few Arsenio Hall whoop-whoop-whoops, and shouted "Go, Robert." And for the ensuing 40-some-odd minutes, I did my level best to focus my attention on Robert's set. I knew most of his material already, which was generally amusing, if not spectacularly original, covering the usual sort of late-Baby-Boomer-comedy subjects – dating (and I mean male/female dating, thank you very much), old television shows ("Didn't you ever wonder about Gilligan and the Skipper? I mean, really!"), people who bring 11 items to the 10-items-or-less checkout – that sort of thing.

But try as I might to pay attention to the man on stage (and I did try), I spent the duration of Robert's showcase set preoccupied – nay, utterly consumed by the young man seated next to me. Sensing the heat of his arm near mine. Enjoying the way his pumped-up pecs and perky little nipples pushed out against the black T-shirt he wore. Warming myself in the glow of that smile. And sporting an incessant boner as I imagined loving Joe Callahan in every room of my house, my back yard, my front yard, and the fully reclining passenger seat of my '91 Honda Accord.

Robert said, "Thanks, you've been great, I mean it, goodnight," and I joined the applause as Robert took one, then another shallow bow from the waist, blew a kiss off his fingertips into the audience, and left the stage. I was all set to make some relatively vague inquiry into Joe's plans for the rest of the evening, hoping I could convey my interest in him without seeming too forward or too needy, when he turned to me and said, "I'd like to give you my phone number."

"I'd like to have it," I said. "What've you got going for the next few hours?"

He made a frowning little face and said, "I've got this thing I've got to go to."

I just said, "Oh." I could feel my face fall. My basic insecurity came careening around the corner, bringing with it the thought that Joe might be planning to scribble down the phone number for Dial-A-Prayer, just to placate me long enough for a smooth getaway. I'm sure I must have looked like a poster child for abject disappointment.

"I'd love to ditch this thing," Joe said, touching my arm lightly with fingertips that seemed to paint my skin with goosebumps, "but I really can't. What's your schedule like tomorrow?"

"Free," I said, a smile returning to my lips. "I'm totally free tomorrow."

Joe smiled (turning my ankles into bread pudding) and said, "Great. Do you have a piece of paper?" And to the bartender, "Could I borrow a pen?"

I retrieved an old automatic bank teller slip from my wallet and handed it to Joe.

"Call me tomorrow, anytime after 11 or so," he said as he wrote on the back of the slip, which he then offered back to me. "May I have yours?" he asked.

"Of course," I said. It had actually not occurred to me to offer him my number. For some reason, powerful attraction to a man tends to produce in me something very like dementia.

I accepted the bank slip from Joe and handed him one of my business cards, feeling somewhat giddy at holding this beautiful young man's phone number between my fingers.

"Where're you parked?" Joe asked.

I stood at the curb, side by side with Joe Callahan, waiting for one of a crew of small, brown men in ill-fitting black pants and too-short neckties to return with my car from wherever it is valet parking guys leave three-year-old Hondas. Joe stood close enough for me to smell his cologne (I couldn't place it, but I liked it). Close enough for me to brush the back of my right hand softly against the back of his left, which made my crotch swell like bread dough in a warm kitchen.

"So what is this thing you have to go to at this ungodly hour?" I asked. It was just after midnight.

After a moment, Joe said, "It's kind of a gig. I dance."

"I should have guessed," I said. "You have a dancer's behind."

"So do you," he said.

"Actually," I said, leaning in toward Joe, "I have what a buddy of mine likes to call a BBB."

"A what?" Joe said.

"Black boy butt."

Joe laughed, a deep husky laugh to match his speaking voice. "Somebody said that to you?" he said.

"Yeah. What was I going to do? Deny it?"

I felt a touch at my shoulder. A nice-looking 30-something blonde in a jumpsuit, towing her nice-looking 30-something date by the hand, paused just long enough to say, "Really enjoyed your singing."

"Thank you," I called toward the two retreating backs. "Thanks very much." After a short beat, I said, "So – may I go and see this gig of yours?"

"It's really not something I'd care for you to see," he said. "Really. I'll tell you all about it tomorrow, OK?"

At which point, a short stranger drove up in my car.

"This is me," I said. I held my right hand toward Joe.

"Call me tomorrow," he said as we clasped hands. He took a half step toward me, smiled, and said (so softly I nearly had to lip-read), "I promise – I'll be worth the wait."

I smiled back. "Like Janet?"

Joe nodded.

The valet swung my driver's side door open so wide I feared a passing vehicle speeding toward Beverly Hills might wrench it free. I tipped the man a couple of dollars (I was feeling pretty darn good), slid into the driver's seat, and executed my trademark finger-wiggling wave as I left Joe Callahan, his dancers ass, and, Lord-have-mercy, that smile, curbside in front of the Comedy Corral.

Heading west, I briefly considered stopping by Throb, where things would just be getting off the ground, and shaking my BBB for an hour or two. I'd already told Big Tim I'd probably be exhausted after my gig and might not make it, so I was basically off the hook. But my excitement over having met Joe had added to the adrenaline rush I always experience after a gig, so it would likely be awhile before I slept; besides, I'd pass right by the place on the way home.

Which is exactly what I did – passed right by. I just wasn't in the mood.

On a complete whim, I stopped at Circus of Books to pick up the Randall Kenen now that it was in paperback. One thing West L.A. could use is a good open-all-night book store. I pulled into the 24-hour-monitored, quarters-only-metered parking lot across the street from the store, which (since it was Saturday night and the lot not only faces the book store but backs up into the Gold Cost, a friendly neighborhood beer-pool table-and heavy cruise bar), was completely full. In a rare stroke of luck, someone was pulling out of a space, and I pulled in.

I walked through the lot, past a man leaning into the driver's side window of a parked car, making hushed conversation with the man inside; a husky, very black man leaning against another car, wearing only a pair of sneakers and some spandex shorts in which was clearly outlined a set of genitals which would not have seemed out of place on a bison; and a pair of healthy young specimens in jeans and no shirts, engaged in what I will tastefully term a public show of affection against the hood of yet another automobile. The smell of booze and cigarettes and the sounds of clinking glass, bartalk, and the Pet Shop Boys' "You Were Always On My Mind" poured from the open front door of the Gold Coast as I crossed the street.

Entering the bookstore, I paused in the doorway, my glare-sensitive, contact-lensed eyes blinking against the sudden brightness of the room. On my way to the gay fiction section, I paused in front of the rack of gay slicks, where my eyes immediately fell upon the current issue of *Advocate Men*, from whose cover smiled a handsome young man bearing a resemblance to Joe Callahan far too striking to be mere coincidence.

I was sitting cross-legged on the TV-room sofa, slurping up a bowl of granola and soy milk, and watching *Ren and Stimpy*, when the cordless phone made the high-pitched, electric purr that was its version of ringing. I moved the bowl and spoon into my left hand, and with my right I just managed to punch the Mute button on the remote, followed by the Speak button on the telephone before the fourth purr, at which point the machine would have answered.

"Wha's up?" said a husky, instantly familiar voice.

I said, "Joe," as if it were a complete thought.

"So, were you gonna call me, or what?" he said.

"I was just about to," I said. Actually, I had promised myself I wouldn't call Joe until after *Ren and Stimpy* was over at 11:30 – the man had said call after 11, and I didn't want to appear anxious, despite being plenty anxious.

"So what of you got going today?" Joe said.

"Jack nothin'," I said. "I'm free." And then I remembered. "No," I said, "I lied. I almost forgot, I've got to go to this pool party this afternoon. In a couple of hours, in fact. In the Valley."

"Can you bring a friend?" Joe asked.

"You'd go?" I said.

And he said, "Ask me."

I spotted Joe climbing out of a black VW Rabbit just as I pulled up to Bronco and Louie's house, a pretty two-story traditional in one of the nicer sections of Northridge (roughly twice the size of my house for roughly the same money, but of course, they're in the Valley). I'd offered to drive Joe to the party, but he'd insisted on taking his own car. I'd argued that it was on my way, but Joe had countered (and correctly) that heading from the West Side to the Valley, West Hollywood is something of a detour.

He turned at the sound of my car door and I watched that damned smile spread across his face.

"Good to see you," he said, walking toward me. I offered my right hand; Joe took it and pulled me close, kissing me softly on the lips, right there on the sidewalk in front of Bronco and Louie's. It was as sweet as it was unexpected, like a little gift-wrapped present when it isn't even your birthday. Having been kissed right out in public, I felt free to take Joe's hand as we walked up the driveway.

Despite the techno-funko-disco blasting from the outdoor speakers and the somewhat weary grins on the faces of the boys (Louie very much excluded), one could cut the tension around that pool with a cross-cut saw. One look at Louie and a wee-small inner voice told me the better part of valor was definitely retreat. I later made a mental note to listen to that voice the next time it came a-calling.

It quickly became obvious that Bronco and Louie were either having a fight, about to have a fight, or crawling through the wreckage of a very recent fight. Which is hardly an unusual occurrence for Bronco and Louie. It isn't just that they argue – all couples argue. But Bronco and Louie argue almost to the complete exclusion of all other forms of communication, verbal and non. If Louie says the restaurant is south of Santa Monica Boulevard, Bronco will tell you it's north. If the jacuzzi is just right for Bronco, it's entirely too hot for Louie. Disagreement is the *leitmotif* of their relationship. I think it was the Tims who nicknamed them The Bickersons.

So we're sitting around the pool, pretending to have a party, sipping cold drinks making the most frivolous of small-talk (even for a bunch of queens), when Louie, who'd been paying far too much attention to his cocktail (and I'd have bet dollars to doorknobs it wasn't his first), suddenly hurls his glass to the ground and stomps away into the house. Which pretty much stopped the party dead in its tracks. The remaining five of us – Bronco, the Tims, Joe and I – just sort of stared gape-jawed at one another for a long, infinitely uncomfortable moment. It seemed to me someone ought to go see if Louie was OK. True, we'd all seen Louie make hasty exits before, but this looked particularly unpleasant. Bronco made no move toward the door. Aware that I might well have been making a grave mistake, I got up and followed Louie into the house.

I quickly checked the kitchen, living room, and dining area, then started down the hall, gently opening doors (the bathroom, the guest bedroom) and calling Louie's name. I found him in the master bedroom, lying face down on a jagged diagonal across his and Bronco's massive oaken king-size waterbed. The image made me think of Betty Anderson, the teenage daughter played by Elinor Donahue in *Father Knows Best*, who, when angry, hurt, or otherwise upset, invariably ran upstairs to her room (taking the stairs one at a time in small but rapid, ladylike steps), threw herself across her bed, and cried.

Pausing in the doorway, I rapped lightly on the doorframe and said, "Louie? You all right?" When Louie didn't reply (or move, for that matter), I said, "Would you rather be left alone?" Still no answer from the figure on the bed. In my best Lucy Ricardo, I said, "Are you tired, run-down, listless? Do you poop out at parties?"

I heard a laugh sputter between Louie's lips, and knew I'd made contact. I entered the room and closed the door behind me. Louie rolled over onto his back, hid his eyes in the crook of an elbow.

"Johnnie," he said, as if it were a complete thought.

"Wanna talk about it?" I said.

Louie took in a phlegm-rattling breath and said, "He doesn't love me anymore."

And I thought: Oh, shit. I had, in fact, made a grave mistake. I had walked into a pile of emotional doggie-doo so fresh and pungent my nose wrinkled. I was ready for, "Bronco's being such an asshole." Or even, "Bronco and I are having a knock-down-drag-out." "He doesn't love me anymore," had definitely blind-sided me. The urge to flee was nearly overwhelming. Unfortunately, graceful exit was by now quite out of the question. I had no real choice but to sit myself down in the bedroom's only chair (an old high-backed wooden dining chair, a hand-me-down from Louie's parents) and do my best to comfort the obviously distraught Louie while trying not to appear to be taking sides in a domestic drama – rather like maneuvering a mine field on crutches in the dark.

"I'm assuming you mean Bronco," I said, just to buy myself a few seconds. I mean, who else could Louie have meant? The mail man? President Clinton? RuPaul?

Louie nodded, sniffed noisily.

"Did Bronco tell you that?" I asked. "That he doesn't love you anymore." No one knows better than I that, when one is in love, anything from one's beloved forgetting the anniversary of your first date to that beloved's failing to give one's cheese soufflé due praise, can be taken as proof positive of the Death of Love, and more than worthy of public drunkenness and at least one good cry.

Louie lifted himself up onto his elbows into a semi-seated position. He looked at me with red eyes (each eye toting its own bag) and said, "He wants to see other people."

"Oh?" I said, feeling somewhat relieved and hoping it wouldn't show and be mistaken for a lack of concern. "So he didn't actually say he doesn't love you anymore."

"No," Louie said. "Not exactly."

"What did he say," I asked, "exactly."

Louie sat up against the massive, bookshelves-built-in headboard, wiped an arm across his eyes and said, "He doesn't feel any passion for me." He gave me a look I'm sure meant, The prosecution rests.

"How long have you and Bronco been together?" I asked – rhetorically, since I'd attended their sixth anniversary party a couple of months previous.

"Six years," Louie said.

I left the chair and climbed onto the bed with Louie, causing one of those seasick-making tidal waves I so dislike about waterbeds. I sat cross-legged (sneakers and all) facing Louie, touched him softly on the shin, allowing my fingers to slide down Louie's sun-warmed, sunblock-slick skin and rested my hand a moment on the top of Louie's high-arched foot.

"Louie," I said, "I know you're upset, but you've got to believe me when I tell you that love and passion are two very different animals. Love lasts. Passion – it waxes, it wanes, it comes, it goes, here it is, there it went. Believe me. I know."

"Did it happen to you and Keith?"

"Yes," I said. "We were together ten years. And I know for a fact there was a will year there – four or five years in – when Keith felt like the thrill was gone. He told me about it, years afterward. But the point is, he stuck with it. Hung in there, you know. Because the love was still there. And in time, the passion came back. It does that."

"During that time, did he . . ." Louie paused for a moment, probably looking for an appropriate euphemism, and then did without one. "Did he fuck around?"

"No," I said. "It just wasn't his way. We still had sex, Keith and me, even then. And maybe it wasn't the best sex we ever had, but the fact is, even when nothing else in the relationship was up to snuff, the fucks were still good."

"If he'd asked you for an open relationship," Louie said, "what would you have done?"

"I don't know," I said. "I really don't. We were monogamous. I mean we just were, it was never even a question. Of course, we also split up for two years, so it's not like it was ten years of non-stop monogamy, either. But now, when I think about the possibility of being in another relationship, I can't imagine asking anyone else to be monogamous. For one thing, I don't think very many men would do it. I'm not sure it's the nature of the beast to be monogamous."

"It's the nature of this beast," Louie said, and sniffed another wet sniff.

"I know," I said. "Me, too. And then there's Bronco."

Louie leaned back, knocked the back of his head against the headboard.

"He wants Wednesdays off," Louie said.

"Boy's night out?"

"Uh-huh." Louie's lower lip trembled and he wasn't quite successful at blinking back a couple of fat tears. He sniffed, pushed at the tears with his hands. I yanked my handkerchief from the tiny hip pocket of my shorts and held it toward Louie. He stammered a refusal, but I insisted. "Please," I said. "I've always wanted to be there with a clean hanky when somebody really needed one."

Louie accepted the handkerchief and blew a long Bronx cheer into it, then crumpled it tight in his fist.

"Thing is," he said, "he's getting it anyway. At Throb, mostly. When I don't feel like going, or after I've had enough and gone home. I'd been doing a pretty good job of convincing myself he just liked to dance." He laughed a bit, or maybe it was just another sniff. "So what do you think?" he asked. "Think I should give him his damn Wednesdays?"

"Louie," I said, giving one of his thumbs a little tug, "do you have any idea how much I don't want to take sides in this?"

"I'm not asking you to take any sides," Louie said. "I just want your opinion. Please."

I hesitated a moment, then said, "All right. Yes. I think you should let him have this."

"Why?" Louie said. From his wide-eyed face, I could tell Louie hadn't expected a yes.

"Because," I said, "I think once Bronco's no longer sneaking around behind your back and feeling like some kind of sexual outlaw, the whole thing will lose a good deal of its glamor."

"Really?"

"It'll become just another routine, like going to work or cleaning his contact lenses. You'll see."

"I hope you're right," Louie said.

I said, "So do I." And we sat smiling rather weak smiles at one another for a moment. Finally, Louie said, "Thank you," and leaned in toward me and kissed my mouth, first with his smallish lips and then just the very tip of his tongue, taking me quite by surprise.

"Any old time," I said, tasting the flavor of Louie's kiss, salty with snot, just a trace of bitter sunscreen. I climbed down off the bed. "And if you need to talk," I said, "you know the number. I think it's time for me to gather up my fella and go."

"That Joe's quite the little studmuffin," Louie said.

"You got that shit right," I said.

"Have you had him yet?"

"No, but the day is young – even if I'm not."

Louie smiled. "Have fun."

"Count on it," I said.

"Your place or mine?" Joe asked as we approached the curb outside Bronco and Louie's. My arm was draped loosely about his shoulders, a position I liked quite a lot.

"Where do you live?" I asked.

"West Hollywood."

"I'm in Mar Vista," I said. "So your place is closer."

"My place it is," he said.

Joe Callahan lived in perhaps the smallest apartment I'd ever seen – a single with kitchenette and three-quarter bath, not unlike an apartment I'd had in Santa Monica immediately post-college. You could have put the entire apartment into my walk-in master bedroom closet and still have room for all my shoes. There was a single bed covered with a light-blue chenille bedspread against the far wall, and a CD-player boom-box set atop a lumber-and-cinder-block home entertainment center, with maybe twenty-five CD's underneath it on the well-worn hardwood floor.

The entire place was filled with angels.

A flock of baby-faced, birdy-winged, bodiless cherubs in terracotta, glazed ceramic, wood, papier-mâché, pink plastic, and construction paper cut-out, circled the room just below ceiling level, nailed, thumbtacked or Scotch taped to walls in some need of paint, walls decorated to the point of clutter with post cards, Christmas cards and magazine clippings of winged ones. A battalion of angel Christmas tree toppers stood in formation atop the chest-high semi-wall separating the kitchenette from the rest of the apartment. A framed poster of the Broadway production of *Angels In America* hung above the bed. A framed poster hung on the wall above the boom box: an arty black-and-white photograph of a pointedly homoerotic angel – a beautiful naked man with largely superfluous superimposed wings, his lips, pecs and tumescent penis highlighted with some sort of make-up or body paint – a picture I remembered from a coffee-table book on male nude photography, and which I now recognized as a picture of Joe.

I stood in the doorway beside Joe and took in the room.

"So you like angels," I said. "Me, too."

"Yeah?" Joe said, shutting the door behind us.

"Not quite to this degree," I said. "But I've always had a thing about them."

"They're all around us," Joe said, turning to face me. "They watch over us; take care of us." He hung his big arms over my shoulders. My arms encircled his waist. "I just wanted to express that visually," Joe said, just before our mouths met. We kissed a warm, wet, sloppy mess, Joe's mouth tasting so sweet that I smiled as I kissed, and a little sound of satisfaction erupted in my throat and escaped from between my lips; I passed it to Joe from the tip of my tongue to the tip of his.

"There's something I need to tell you," Joe said, his face suddenly gone serious.

"Are you sure you want to talk now?" We stood with arms around each other's waist, the hard lump of my crotch pressed against the hard lump of his.

"It's important," Joe said.

"All right," I said, and licked a squiggly little stripe up the bridge of Joe's nose. "Talk." I strummed my thumb around the general vicinity of Joe's left nipple until I felt it pop up like the built-in timer on a Butterball turkey.

Joe clapped his hand over mine, looked into my eyes and said, "I'm HIV positive."

I removed my hands from Joe's chest and cupped his beautiful face.

"Thank you for telling me," I said. "But the fact is, I assume every gay man I meet is HIV positive and conduct myself accordingly. Whatever level of risk I decide is acceptable, I take on that basis." All of which was quite true. What I didn't mention was that I couldn't help wondering just what all of Joe's ever-watching angels might have been doing while some stud was pumping him full of HIV-infected spooie. Do angels take coffee breaks?

I kissed Joe's lips, softly, my lips barely brushing his. "OK?" I said.

Joe nodded. "OK."

"Could we get back to the kissing part now?" I said.

Fortunately, we were able to pick up exactly where we'd left off.

"I want to make this good for you," Joe said.

I sat naked at the head of Joe's single bed, my back against the headboard. Joe sat facing me, his big-muscled, smooth-shaven legs outstretched over mine, wearing only his Calvin Klein briefs (the official underwear of the West Hollywood gay boy), his hard-on overcrowding the front of those underpants, and leaving a dollar-size wet spot, in the bargain. Joe was smiling with lips slightly swollen from several minutes of rather athletic kissing. He was prettier than anything I could imagine. He was stroking my hard dick with both hands.

"This is good for me," I said.

"No," he said, making a motion like a socket joint with the hollow of one hand and the head of my dick. "I mean, I really want to give you something special. Like you gave me last night."

"What did I give you last night?" I asked.

Joe let go of my penis, leaving it feeling cold and not a little bit lonely.

"I've seen you onstage. You can give yourself to a whole roomful of people. You have talent. All I have is this body."

"Joe," I said, reaching out with one hand and running my fingertips lightly down Joe's torso, just touching his clavicle, his heavy, perfect pectorals, the finely delineated ripples of his belly. "Lots of people can sing. Relatively few mortals can boast a bod like this one."

Joe smiled. He said, "Thanks. That makes me – I'm glad." He swung his legs over the side of the bed and pushed himself to a standing position. He turned his back to me and lowered his underpants, bending forward from the waist and pulling the briefs down over his thighs, revealing the most beautiful (without question) ass I had ever seen.

While I spent my entire ten-year relationship with my late husband, Keith, doing a better-than-average impression of a bottom (deferring to Keith's superior size and nearly insatiable desire to pound my butt), the fact is, I'm a top by nature. I harbor a fondness for the male derrière bordering on fixation. And Joe Callahan's ass was prettier than many men's faces. High and round and nearly obscenely protuberant, it was the sort of behind usually found on African-American track runners and dancers, seldom on white men of any ilk.

I may have cried out, made some involuntary noise of utter amazement and awe, because Joe turned and looked into my face. His smile spread. Somewhere in the back of my head, Janet Jackson started singing, "You want this."

I slid from the bed and onto my knees: this wasn't just sex – this was religion.

I nuzzled Joe's ass, my eyes closed, humming a soft, one-note, wordless song of praise deep down in my throat. I rubbed the cheeks of my face against the cheeks of Joe's butt, kissed each cheek and then gave it a secret name; licked a long line up each (first left, then right) with the flat of my tongue, then bit the left one just hard enough to leave hot pink scalloped marks on the soft, hairless skin. Joe bent low from the waist, grasping his ankles like a Catholic schoolboy preparing for corporeal punishment, exposing the tiny pleats and gathers of his asshole. And a rosy rosebud it was – the exact color and gloss of a cherry-flavor Tootsie Roll Pop. I'd never before seen an anus so ruddy and (like some stud baboon sighting the scarlet haunches of some baboon babe in heat) I found myself excited nearly to the point of trembling. I traced the perimeter of Joe's anus with a fingertip, then touched it (tap-tap-tap) like a friendly neighbor at the back door. I watched Joe's asshole opened up and out like a red rubber rose at my touch. And as my lust-muddled mind struggled to formulate the words to ask, to request, to beg for that ass, if it came to that, Joe whispered, "Johnnie."

I made an odd, grunting sort of sound, the power of speech having apparently deserted me for the moment.

And Joe said, "Please fuck me."

Please, he said.

Who could refuse such a polite young man?

I rubbed my knees raw on the well-worn wood of Joe's floor, with Joe on all-fours, rocking back into me, shouting (in that balls-deep, husky voice of his) encouragements so nasty I shivered. I tested the muscular, bone and connective tissue strength of my legs, arms and back doing Joe standing up, Joe (just over six feet and probably upwards of 175 pounds of Joe) up in my arms, his fine, big legs wrapped around my waist, his arms around my neck, bouncing him against my pelvis. I lay back on Joe's bed and took it easy for awhile, watching Joe raise and lower himself on my painfully engorged, latex-encased dick, Joe's head rolling back, his cock hard as the headboard, curved back against his belly, its shiny red noggin painting his tummy with little sticky-wet stripes.

Joe's eyes closed and his lips curled into a little smile. He said, "Oh . . . yeah," as his dick spurted and then flowed like a flesh fountain, and the sight and sound of it all spurred my own orgasm. I imagine that the noise I made (an uncharacteristic beastly growl-and-roar that left both my throat and chest feeling raw) was heard throughout Joe's apartment building, and perhaps throughout West Hollywood in its entirety – rattling the glassware at Café d'Étoile, rustling the pages of the boycake magazines at A Different Light bookstore, pricking up the ears of the dudes slurping Margaritas at Mickey's.

Later, I lay on my back, Joe lying on top of me, sticky belly to sticky belly, big and heavy and hot, his breath warm against the side of my face; my breath still ragged, pulse pounding in my temples.

Wondering what day it was. Wondering if I'd ever be able to walk without crutches, or play the balalaika again. Wondering if perhaps this was how Jacob had felt after having spent a long, hot night wrestling with an angel.

BURNING BRIDGES

Lawrence Schimel

THE BED WAS on fire! I jumped up, pulling the blankets with me. Reflex made my fingers shy away from the heat. By force of will, I grabbed the burning linen, flipped them over, and smothered the fire.

My heart was racing as I sat naked on the floor amid the smouldering bedding. The smoke detector still cried overhead. I forced myself to stand and reset it. I looked at the bare mattress and burnt sheets and stumbled into the living room, where I flopped down on the couch. I winced as I landed on my stomach; I still had a hard-on from my dream and had bent it in my landing. I wondered what I had been dreaming as I rolled onto my back and tried to fall asleep. In the early-morning light, I could see smoke still drifting from the bedroom.

I have a spark, a tiny flame inside my mind, like the spots that dance before your eyes after you've looked at the sun. Sometimes it gets loose.

I closed the lid of the toilet and sat. The ceramic brought goosebumps to my skin as I leaned against the tank, pressing up against it to absorb the cold into my shoulderblades, the small of my back. October and it was still as hot as August or July, the sun blazing during a drought. They promised me it never got this hot when I was thinking about moving to San Francisco from New York City. But then, a lot of promises had turned up empty, I reflected, as I stood and turned on the tap. I dipped a wash cloth into the sink, soaking up the cool liquid. Elliott . . . I held the cloth up to my lips, letting it drip against my neck and chest, cold. Elliot . . .

I hadn't seen him in months. I had given up all that was familiar so I wouldn't see him at our favorite haunts in San Francisco. I know I didn't get very far (Oakland) but I couldn't bear the thought of being away from him. I was still madly in love. He had my new address and phone number, I knew, but I hadn't heard from Elliott since the night I walked out on him, when I found him in bed with another man.

I ran the towel under the tap again, and pressed it against the back of my neck, reveling in the feel of the cold, wet cloth.

My rage knew no bounds that night. It welled up inside me, a searing pain in my gut, burning like I was on fire. And suddenly my anger burst free, setting fire to items at random as I ran from the apartment. The thought of someone else making love to Elliott, other hands running across his body . . .

I leaned forward and stuck my head under the tap, but the image of Elliott's body stayed before my eyes. I imagined they were my hands pressed against his flesh again and opened my mouth to nuzzle one of his large, dark nipples. I bit down on my shoulder, running the cold cloth down my body, between my legs. I cupped my balls, remembering the feel of his mouth on my cock, our bodies pressed together in ecstasy.

I grabbed the bar of soap from its dish and pressed it to my groin, rubbing it back and forth along the length of my cock until it had produced a lather. I remembered when Elliott and I had showered together the first night we slept together. He was in New York on a business trip. Was it two years ago, already? I remembered every detail: our first lovemaking, deliciously awkward as we explored each other's bodies, uncertain of everything but our desire for each other. I let the soap slip between my fingers into the basin, and reached for my swollen, lathered cock instead. I remembered the taste of Elliott's skin, the salt of his sweat under his armpits, his balls, the sweet flesh of his cock. I remembered the feeling of being inside him, the half-closed look on his face as he lay below me, his hands on my hips, pulling me towards him.

I could not hold back any longer and sat down, hard, on the toilet as I began to come, shooting pale white arcs against my chest and stomach, legs. Beside me, the roll of toilet paper burst into flames. I ignored it, stroking my cock as it spasmed with pleasure.

I am lying in the top bunk. They are the bunk beds I had as a child. I look about me and find that I am in my room at home, except everything looks odd. I step on the ladder to climb down, when the rung snaps under my weight. I fall, snapping each of the rungs as my legs push towards the floor. Am I grown so big, since last I slept here? I catch my breath, then lean down to pick up one of the broken ladder pieces. They are candy canes. I lick one to prove by its peppermint taste that I am right. This is what is odd: everything is made of candy.

I walk into the hall and hear noises downstairs, follow them into the kitchen. My mother is cooking. She is dressed all in black and has a big wart on her nose. On her head she is wearing a large, black witch's hat. "Good morning, dear," she says. "I'm making myself some breakfast." She points to the corner near the stove. "Would you like some?"

Elliott is chained to the refrigerator. He is naked, gagged, his hands and legs cuffed. I cannot help thinking he looks like he's ready for a B&D session, even as I open my mouth to protest. "You can't eat him," I say.

"What's the matter?" my mother asks, cackling like I have never heard her do before. "Don't you want to share with your mother? His flesh is sweet enough for you to eat, isn't it?" She crosses to where Elliott is bound. He tries to shy away from her, but the chains prevent him. She turns to look at me and grabs him by the balls. I know it hurts, because Elliott stiffens, his back suddenly hunched. "You eat his meat, don't you?" She shakes his flaccid penis for emphasis, violently tugging it. "You eat his meat all the time."

Suddenly, my mother throws open the door of the oven. It is enormous, like a huge, gaping maw. Inside, the coils are so hot that flames leap up from their orange filaments. I rush forward to stop her, but she throws Elliott into the oven and shuts the door. I try to open the door, but it will not budge. The light is on inside, and I press my face against the glass, desperate to at least see him one last time before he burns. Behind me my mother cackles on and on, her voice as high and nasal as a smoke detector.

I was choking, and bolted upright, coughing. A blanket of smoke covered the room. My spark must have gotten loose again, during the dream. Frantically, I looked about the room, wondering what was burning, and for how long; was I too late?

The smoke detector cried angrily overhead and I felt I just had to get out of there. I struggled into a pair of jeans, thinking as I did that this was no time for modesty, and ran down the stairs. Fire raged up and down the street. I cringed from the heat, awed and overpowered by the strength of my anger. What a dream of Elliott I had been having! Everything was on fire, from my block all the way to the Hills!

I felt my insides suddenly wrench with guilt. I had to make sure everyone got to safety. It was my fault if they died!

I heard shouts for help to my left. The neighbor's house was on fire, the roof crumbling in. I rushed into the building without hesitating, following the shouts. The heat was incredible, like standing in an open furnace. My jealousy-induced pyrokineses was no help in protecting me from fire. All it did was cause damage, cause harm.

Even with Elliott. Elliott was afraid of my anger's spark. Afraid of me. That's why he hadn't called. He was too afraid to face what it meant, my love for him.

The shouting woke me from my memories. I rushed upstairs and into a bedroom filled with smoke. "Over here!" a voice shouted, "Help me! Over here!" I stumbled towards him. He was trapped beneath a fallen beam. I struggled to push it off of his legs. Come on, I berated myself, *Lift!* You caused this fire! Adrenaline surged within me and I managed to lift the beam, holding it on my shoulder as he scrambled out from underneath. I reached out with one hand to help pull him free.

"Get your hands from me, Faggot," he shouted, swinging a fist at me.

I dropped the beam, ducking the blow. I felt a chill

in my bones, as the adrenaline burning along my muscles froze.

"You're disgusting. Take advantage of a man trapped in a fire." He stumbled toward the door, turned and spat. "Pervert," then slammed the door behind him.

I was in shock. Why had I bothered? I had saved his life, and all I got in return was hatred. I wished for a moment that I had left him trapped beneath the beam.

No. This was all my fault! As full of hate as he was, I wasn't ready to kill him, wasn't prepared to be responsible for his death.

His, and how many others?

I saw Elliott's face before me, inside the oven. I tried to reach him, but the glass was in the way. I banged against it with my fists, but it would not budge. I cast about me blindly, looking for something, anything, to break the glass. My fingers closed on a pipe, and I swung it desperately at the oven, hoping I wasn't too late.

I choked suddenly, as I gulped in huge lungfuls of smoke. I stared blankly at the wooden door in front of me.

Elliott? Where had Elliott gone?

I was in the burning house. Elliott wasn't there. He hadn't been there at all, but was safe from the fire, miles away.

But I still heard his voice, calling for me.

"I'm coming!" I shouted, my voice tearing my throat. Panic surged through me; I had to get to him, save him from the fire. My spark burst forth, incinerating the door. I could feel the intense heat as I ran through the now-open frame, but I didn't care. I had to find Elliott, I had to save him. I ran down the stairs, out into the street.

Where was he? I heard shouting to my left, turned towards my own apartment. I saw the man I had saved, ignored him. I could still hear Elliott calling my name; where the hell was he?

Suddenly, the door to my building flew open and Elliott was there, shouting for me. I rushed to him, practically threw myself at him. He held me in his arms, arms that were so comforting and familiar I couldn't help but believe he was real.

"You're safe," he said, hugging me so tightly my chest hurt. "I'm so glad you're safe."

I began to cry, an overflow of fear and frustration and happiness, and then passed out.

I could feel the flames licking at my skin. I was on fire burning up but I had to go on I had to save them this was all my fault I had to find Elliott I had to save Elliott!

And suddenly he was there with me, holding me, cradling me in his arms, shielding me from the flames. His hands were deliciously cool, draining away the heat.

"But we have to save them," I said, trying to push him away. "This is all my fault!"

"Shhhh," Elliott crooned. "You're safe now. Nothing is your fault. It was an electrical fire. Up in the hills. You had nothing to do with it. Because of the drought, it got out of control."

I stopped struggling. Electrical fire? Not my spark. Not my fault at all. I wanted to laugh with relief! I thought of the neighbor I had saved. Did I regret it? Risking myself for the sake of preserving his hatred?

No, I realized. I didn't.

I opened my eyes and looked at Elliott. His concern was obvious as he stared down at me, as he held me against him. I never wanted it to end, wanted to remain frozen in that moment, forever the object of his full attention. I was afraid that if I looked away, even for a second, everything would fall apart and I would suddenly wake up from a smoke-induced hallucination and find that I was still trapped in a burning building.

I could feel cloth beneath me, and finally I tore my eyes away from him to look at my surroundings. I was in Elliott's bed. In our old bed. Everything was as I remembered it. He hadn't changed a bit. I even pressed myself up onto my elbows to peer into the corner by the closet and laughed when I saw his dirty socks and underwear in a pile.

I lay back against the pillow again and closed my eyes for a moment, simply for the pleasure of opening them again to find Elliott before me. He really was there, holding me, running his cool hands along my body, draining the heat away. We were both naked. I wondered what had happened between the fire and waking up here, wondered if perhaps the last few miserable months had been nothing more than a nightmare. But then I coughed, my throat still raw from the smoke, and I knew that Elliott had found me in the fire, had brought me home and nursed me until now. I knew that he still loved me.

Tentatively, I reached out with one hand and pressed it against his chest, over his heart. His skin was as cold as marble, or perhaps I was burning up. I let my hand drift, luxuriating in the cool feel of his body as I explored its familiar planes, in the feel of his hands along my body, my chest, arms, thighs, draining away the heat. It was as if he was absorbing my spark, all my built-up anger and frustration. I surrendered to the sensation.

I sat up, pulling him towards me. My tongue was stone-dry as it entered his mouth, but he didn't care and, after a moment of kissing, it was soon wet. My hands ran up and down along his chest, which felt like a Grecian pillar, solid and safe; I clung to him. He pulled away for breath, and I kissed my way down his smooth neck and chest to his nipples, those large, dark nipples that had haunted my dreams. I ran my tongue around them, moving from one to the other in figure eights. Small tufts of hair grew in rings at their edges, the only hair on his smooth chest. I let my hands fall into his lap to his cock, swollen with desire and anticipation. His hands ran through my hair and down my back. I licked the strong muscles of his abdomen, working my way towards the sweet flesh of his cock. I felt his mouth wrap around my own cock, moist and tight. I wanted to consume him with my passion, to devour every last piece of him.

Unbidden, my mother's voice from my nightmare echoed in my mind as my tongue was about to touch his cock: *His flesh is sweet enough for you to eat, isn't it? Don't you want to share with your mother?*

I shook my head, trying to clear the voice from inside my skull.

Elliott sat up, concerned. "Are you OK? Did I hurt you?"

I looked into his face, at his loving concern and felt there could be nothing wrong with the world. I pulled his head towards me, kissed him deeply, my tongue pressing far into his mouth. "I love you," I said, grinning like a baby from happiness.

He smiled back at me, and winked. "Likewise."

I laughed out loud. He hadn't changed one bit!

I turned and eagerly buried my head in his crotch, licking my way down his shaft to his balls. My tongue thrilled at the familiar taste of his skin. I could hear Elliott's catch of surprise as I took one testicle into my mouth, which turned into an almost-purr in his chest as I began to suck on it gently. I let it drop from my mouth and rubbed my face back and forth along the length of his wet cock, letting it slide against my cheeks, eyes, chin, neck. With one hand I reached for his nipples, teased them with pinches and twirls. With my other hand I lifted his cock to my lips. Even his swollen, throbbing cock felt cool, inciting my own desire as the heat of my spark drained away.

I felt Elliott's mouth on my own cock, pumping up and down its length, his lips tightly clamped. It felt like he was going to suck the fire from me! We fell into a rhythm, in unison in sex, life, everything. I tried to hold back, to make the moment go on forever, but I crested over into orgasm, crying out in pleasure. A moment later, Elliott came, too, cum shooting up at me; I bent my face to catch his warm seed on my nose, eyelids, chin. He shuddered, and I felt an intense fulfillment that was soured by only one thing.

I looked about me nervously, wondering what my spark had set on fire. But nothing in the room was burning. I smiled, turned around towards Elliott, kissed and held him tightly.

We walked down to the Embarcadero and stood together at the water's edge. The Oakland hills were glowing like the coals after a barbecue.

I kicked off a shoe, let it drop, splashing water onto the reflected image of the flame. I stepped from Elliott's embrace and dipped a toe into the water, to prove to myself how cool it is, how wet it is, orange and red from the fire and the lights. I had to prove to myself that I had escaped the flames as I had finally escaped my anger at Elliott.

I thought of my life on the other side of the Bay, in Oakland. I was perfectly happy to step back into the life I had left behind when I ran away instead of staying to talk. Life seemed so perfect right now, I never wanted it to end. It didn't have to, I thought. All I needed to do was forgive Elliott. He had proven himself when he came searching for me in the middle of the blaze. And he had forgiven me, for leaving him, for my anger, my dangerous spark.

To my left, three people conversed in French, leaning against the rail and smoking. Ash drifted before me, dropping to the water. One of the tourists laughed loudly and I began to shake.

Elliott put his arm around me and turned my face towards him. "Likewise," he said, and kissed me deeply.

When we came up for air, I focused on the tip of the tourist's cigarette, and let go of my anger, forever.

Our arms around each other, Elliott and I turned our backs and walked home.

THE SILENT STAR

David Evans

"NAME?" BARKED THE chesty, short Greek-Cypriot girl behind
the counter at the dry cleaners.

"Stokes," he mumbled. "Are they ready?"

"Should be," the girl remarked, off-hand, "usually are, aren't
they?" she added as she rifled through the rail of plastic-bagged
garments which hung like so many chrysalises in a deserted
time-ship. "You come in most sat'days, don't you? Stokes,
y'say?"

"Yeah," he agreed.

"Jeans, isn' it?" She stood, as though in deepest consternation
and drew her stubby fingers through her lank, shoulder length
dark hair.

"No," he sighed, shaking his head, beginning to be agitated,
"sort of a boiler suit."

"You mean like overalls," the girl countered, "them things
with straps over yer shoulders?"

"Not really," the man said. Curt. He resisted further
enlightening her.

"Oh, 'ere they are. Behind this long dress. Or is it a dressing
gown?" She pulled out the plastic film wrapper, crackly with
static, which held his khaki coveralls. "Bit trendy for you in'it,
this?" she remarked, saucy, attempting a joke. "Y'know. Bit

way out. Thought you was a most conservative gentleman. Still, I spec you wear 'em for cleanin' your car, don'cha? Or gardenin', p'raps? Do a lotta gardenin', do ya?"

The man pointedly ignored her overtures. It was obvious that he couldn't even bear to look at her, this damp, steamed and pressed blouse of a drab. "I am in a bit of a hurry, see."

"You're always in a hurry, people like you," the girl cautioned. "An' people in a hurry can end up gettin' nowhere, y'know."

"Well I am going somewhere," the man muttered, suddenly angered. "How much is it?"

She told him. He paid. She gave him his change and he left the shop, folding the overalls in two, thus halving their length, making them look like trousers. The girl shook her head, irritated at the reproachful absence of comeback, frustrated by her failure to elicit the information, thwarted by the lack of decent, everyday badinage resulting from her efforts to find out more. Her customer who, melding, now almost unnoticeable, in the pedestrian stream outside her window, had always puzzled her. So terse, so ungiving, so private.

The man, Stokes, relieved to get away, hurried down the soggy, Saturday afternoon high road, the pavements like chip paper, vinegared with a light drizzle, through the shuffling knots and bottlenecks on the pavements caused by the throng of damp shoppers. Late February. Not a lot to look for as far as the weather went. Would it stay the same? Alan Stokes hoped very much that it would clear up just like the weather forecast had said.

He shook his head as he remembered the Cypriot girl's remarks. Cleaning the car . . . Gardening! Going nowhere, indeed! It was, after all, only what *she* used to say. He caught a glimpse of himself in the window of the betting shop at the end of his street. Well, maybe that's what he did look like, he admitted. A bit of a tweed in his sportcoat and bagging beige Marks and Spencer corduroys. Bit boring, probably. But there were other places than wet Walthamstow. You got somewhere, he reminded himself, just by getting in your car and driving out of Walthamstow.

He pulled his peaked cap, one of those give-away hats that advertise things, further over his face. He walked quickly up his street, a quiet turning, a terrace. His was number fourteen. In the middle. It didn't stand out in any way. There was no shining, no blue plaque. Unassuming. Self-effacing, almost. In all, not unlike the first impression that a casual caller would have struck of its owner occupant. Alan Stokes was the most retiring of stars. The most unlikely. Private. He invited neither censure nor infamy, neither applause nor vilification. Alan Stokes, to Alan Stokes, was just another man.

Alan Stokes lived alone. He had no family now and only a few friends. Occasional. He was uniquely self-sufficient. What friends he had were mostly work colleagues from his job as a supervisor in the accounts department of a middle-sized distribution company in Dagenham but they would rarely, if ever, have been to this unassuming terraced house. Dagenham of course is Essex. Not a lot out of the ordinary in Dagenham. Not that Alan Stokes had discovered, anyway. Not a lot out of the ordinary in Walthamstow either, nor in the house he had inherited when his mother died five months previously.

Alan had been a good son; he'd done his duty, cared assiduously for her in her long days a-dying, along with the social services and along with the local health centre. All very kind. All very understanding. All except her. Though she'd never thought so, Alan'd always felt that he could have got somewhere. He felt that he could have proved her wrong. But not, of course, whilst she was alive. For, he reminded himself as often as he felt comfortable, where did she get, in the end, but dead? What use is somewhere if you're dead, mother?

Things should have been a lot different now, he reminded himself as he let himself into his house with his drycleaning. Life should somehow have been more attractive. Especially now he was free. He was only 46. Neither old nor young. He exercised. Always had done. The gentle one-two, up-down sort like they'd done in school. In PE. And it had worked. He didn't drink much either and so there was not one ounce of fat on him. Trim, still with the body of a young man, he fancied, although he would have preferred some muscle. Just a bit. He would have preferred, too, to be at least a little hirsute. On his legs, maybe. On his chest even. But there wasn't much. Nothing to make him into anything like a bear. He sometimes fancied being a bear. But Alan felt no nagging lack. He didn't agonize over what he didn't have. He never had been a man of to regret, neither to complain. It was why he was now quite content to change so little. After all, he would remind himself, he'd now been somewhere, been something, and he had that somewhere to return to whenever he chose.

Alan hung up his coveralls on their hanger from the back of the lounge door. Where there had only been a television, he had now installed another video recorder, a newer model from the one he had always had in his bedroom. Now, on the shelves which he had had installed behind the electronic stack, there were his short row of video tapes. Unpredictably perhaps, he had not expanded the collection since her death. Previously, he had kept the precious few he'd been able to amass stashed in a disused stained pillowcase beneath the bottom boards of the Edwardian wardrobe.

He'd watched these few tapes lovingly, over the years. All but worn them out over some eight or ten years. So very few tapes but, like a favourite child's picturebook, so lovingly lingered over and rediscovered, something new each time.

However. . . . The sound had always been muted. He couldn't risk waking her as she lay so long a-dying on the other side of the wall. Or the nurse. Or his aunt who often came and sat beside the dying all night in the bedroom next to his. A vigil. Years of vigil.

Alan had rarely, if ever, heard the voices on the tapes, seldom heard the sounds the actors made or listened to the repetitiousness of the music. He had lived the performers' exquisite agonies in silence. Of course, now . . . Now, although he knew different, he could have lip-synchronized by heart the litany of moans and cries and yells but now, at root, he knew that there need be neither sound nor fury for him to achieve his pleasure. Sound wasn't important. Unnecessary, even. They didn't have to talk. He didn't have to talk. What was there to communicate? Who was there who would be interested in listening to his pleasure?

So, he had stolen silently to the phenomenon of his own pleasuring. How he wished, as he had lain in bed watching the unreality of the flickering images on his bedroom television . . .

How he had wished, long ago, for the reality of it. How he had wished he could become one of those actors.

And such actors. Lithe young men, of course, no more than thirty years old in their prime. Physical acme. Exemplary perfection. Unattainable beauty. He knew of course that he didn't look like them, would never be like them. He knew his body was merely ordinary. Pleasant was the most both it and his physiognomy would ever rate on a scale of handsome.

But through all these silent dreams, there had emerged an arena in which he could score. Maybe even a ten. A stage on which he could shine. Almost become a star, even a star like those golden boys on his television screen, those macho men of sexual iron who bounded incandescent from the darkness of his video tapes to shine in the movie in his mind.

But it was not going to be easy. Not as difficult as stealing a man into his house, smuggling a real flesh-and-blood lover into his bed. To begin with it had been almost insuperably difficult. For Alan Stokes, whilst his mother was alive, sharing his life with his aunt and, later, the night nurse, the district nurse, the home help, all those strangers who could, might, maybe did invade the privacy of his room whilst he was out at work was a threat. Uncomfortable, unsettling, nerve-racking.

So he had begun in a rather trivial way, like an apprentice, walking before he could run. Sensibly, as everyone thought he was, Alan started on his quest for the grail of ultimate pleasure merely by means of whatever humble devices came immediately to hand, whose presence in the house caused neither worrisome flurry nor undue curiosity.

He simply used what he found in the larder.

So the refrigerator, the wheezy, juddering old Kelvinator, became for Alan a harem; for days he would eye the occupants of the crisper drawer, fondling their shape and ripeness, licking his lips in anticipation of their taste at body temperature. Food shopping in the street markets became almost obsessive and set him loose in a plunderland of root and vine vegetables which he would stalk with all the stealth of a hunter tracking down his prey. This prey, when secured and borne home to await maturity and transubstantiation, when wrapped in a towel from the clean laundry or a pile of socks, would be undetected should he be apprehended by any of the strangers as he went, late night, to his room.

And of course, the bottle of olive oil was nothing more than standard apparatus in the medicine cabinets of most households in the land where one resident was of pensionable age. Amongst other things, one rubbed it onto one's chest, didn't one?

For years, Alan lay in his bed, carefully positioning himself on a very old towel after he had anointed himself gently but thoroughly with digital applications of the olive oil, watching his on-screen heroes, mimicking their movements, their gestures, copying their attitude whilst all the while embracing their silence, sharing their dumb, muted ecstasy as he teased himself, initially, with a carrot.

Then, when emboldened by experience, he found he could gorge on the tumescence of a perfectly, subtly curved courgette before undertaking the quest of quests, the assault of a firm, unpeeled British cucumber.

The need for the real thing, the props which the actors used in the films, overtook him rather slowly. He realized after a wonderful half-hour spent with a more than adequately proportioned baby marrow that the size was not the problem. The lubricant was all. The lubricant and the . . .

He found himself purchasing the first of his varied collection of manmade aids the day after he had scattered her ashes, as she had directed, on Hampstead Heath. Alan had performed the ritual, as he had always performed rituals, rather covertly. Making a song-and-dance about emptying the gritty contents of a bronze-coloured plastic container would mean that he might be observed. Questions might be asked. Authorities alerted. So, Alan went nonchalantly behind a tree and, as inconspicuously as he could, looking this way and that to ensure that he was not being observed, he returned ashes to ashes and ensured that dust once again became dust. What to do with the container? Alan stuffed it in a crevice formed by the roots of the tree which would now draw either sustenance or suffering from the eternal presence at its foot of the paradise-bound Mrs Stokes.

With his mother finally taken care of, Alan felt huge relief and went and sat on a tree stump, not ten yards away.

It was a kind tree stump, the sort that remains after a great oak or, in this case, a hornbeam had been blown over and the greater part of the trunk sawn and removed by foresters. The stump had a comforting curve to it, almost like a natural arm-chair, in which Alan reclined on that late October day. He closed his eyes, feeling what warmth there was still to be enjoyed from the weak sun soothing his face like an ointment, an unadulterated celestial balm. His sensation of loss caused by his bereavement was not one of pain but there was an emptiness which nagged at him, rather like a hunger pang, a reminder that somehow he'd missed his lunch.

Instinctively he pulled his legs up and found that, at waist height, the trunk sported woody outcrops on which he could rest his feet, his knees pulled up in the most comfortable position he had ever encountered. He rested there, sometimes moving slightly to improve his position and felt curiously weightless.

And he felt a strange empowering realization creep over him, a feeling suffusing his pliant body with an energy so rich and deep and powerful that as he tentatively parted his knees wider, he discovered his niche. He finally found his somewhere. It was a feeling both sexual and intellectual, a confluence of both instinct and experience, a carnal apotheosis. His nipples became suddenly sensitized beneath his shirt and he daringly allowed himself to press the palms of his hands against his coat so that the touch of the layers of fabric rubbed and inflamed the heavy buds of flesh which he had so courted during his video nights. He could feel, too, where his underpants pulled at his crotch and where they snugly encouraged erotic sensations, a visceral expectation in that mysterious area sited between his all-but-hairless balls and the eager smoothness of his well-tempered asshole.

And thus it came about that he knew what he was going to do. About it. About him. About everything. He knew that from that moment on he had somewhere to go. That, contrary to what she and everyone else might have thought, he had got somewhere, after all.

He had not acted impetuously and did not. To do so would have been un-natural. Alan had waited until the following Saturday afternoon, until after he had done his chores in the, now, comfortingly empty house. Alan was not an innocent.

He had, after all, sufficient knowledge of how to buy video films. He knew about gay newspapers freely available in certain pubs. He had supposed that it was just that he had neither been particularly interested nor found it particularly convenient to be part of what the newspapers purveyed.

However, *in extremis*, Alan knew exactly where to go for his accoutrements. He was neither awed nor excited and behaved as though he were going to a car accessory supplier for a special kind of tyre or a kitchen equipment dealership for a special rolling pin. He wasn't surprised at what he found behind the black doors and neither was the shop's sales assistant surprised to see him come in. To Alan's tweedy well-composted punter, the shop-boy's sharp 'n' shiny punked and pierced attitude was the equal, though opposite, in laid back unconcerned transactionalism. Alan was there to buy; Guy, for that was his name, was there to sell.

Alan had first looked at the selection of video films and almost immediately decided that he wasn't going to bother with any new ones. Why should he, he argued to himself, be an onlooker when it was more than more enjoyable to be the looked-on. Indeed, he reminded himself, as Mae West once observed, it is better to be looked over than overlooked. Alan had a feeling that his plan would render him unmissable although, possibly, in front of an audience a mite smaller than Miss West's. He therefore eschewed this minor temptation and progressed comfortably to the toy department.

He reminded himself, carefully and logically, that he could now buy whatever he wanted. There was no one to hide from, no one to discover any hidden secrets beneath the bottomboards of the old wardrobe. No more lions, no more witches . . . No need for Narnias no more. And, certainly no more 'nanas.

But Alan was careful and considered. He was immutably cautious and so, reminding himself he could return later for more, he chose, simply, a super-realistic rubber casting in black latex. It was not merely huge, it was monstrous. Unbeknownst, the young salesboy behind the till looked over and blinked. What Guy saw was a man making up his mind. Guy saw Alan say, "Yes!"

It would more than do, Alan decided, with an emotion akin

to pride, weighing the gargantuan fabrication in one hand as
though he was an angler judging the weight and girth of a
superbly landed eel.

Alan took his catch to the pay desk. There were only two
other browsers that afternoon. If they looked upon him, they
looked. Alan was unaware of them.

"That it, then?" the youngman drawled as Alan deposited
his priapic booty on the counter.

"Yes. Thank you. You do accept a credit card, I presume?"
Alan replied.

"Oh, sure," Guy replied carelessly. "You wan' some lube
with that?"

"Lube?" Alan murmured.

"Yeah," Guy smiled, amused. "You wasn't gonna try and
get that up ya without none, was you?"

"What would you suggest?" Alan countered, declining to
share any information he might have possessed concerning the
properties of pharmaceutical, doctor-prescribed olive oil.

"Jar of this, mate. I would. An'a dispenser," Guy said, selling
helpfully, pulling out a container of lubricant and a pump action
dispenser and offering them for Alan's inspection. "An' while
you're at it, you better 'ave some poppers," was the young
man's final exhortation.

"Poppers?" Alan murmured, finally, having nodded his
acceptance of the extra purchases.

"You're 'avin' me on," Guy said, confidentially as he totted
up Alan's purchases to date. "Hey, you ain't no copper,
are you?"

"I certainly am not," Alan remarked with a wry grin. "Does
it look like I'm a policeman?"

"Well . . ." Guy said doubtfully. "You never know, do
you?"

"I suppose not," Alan replied. "Now, what do you do with
these poppers? Where do you put them?"

So Guy told him. Relaxing, heightening, limbering . . . Not
too much, mind. And careful, with 'em . . . Made some people
giddy, he'd warned.

After agreeing that he would be careful and that, no, he
wouldn't hold Guy responsible for anything that might happen

to him, Alan left the shop and drove home to Walthamstow.
On the way, he became annoyed that he hadn't taken more
advantage of the helpful young man in the shop and enquired
what clothing he should wear for the ritual. He wanted something
easy, not too fiddly. Something he could spoil with impunity.
Something that didn't matter. He settled on a pair of army
trousers which he had worn as a boy at school. In the corps.
He was somewhat pleased his figure had changed so little for
the pants still fitted him. So did the boots which he polished
up for the first time in 30 years. He combined these items with
an anorak and a thermal vest which she had bought for him
once to wear in the winter and which he had ignored.

And so, with his arsenal packed in a Safeway plastic carrier,
off Alan went that first Saturday night, expecting nothing other
than the recreation of that feeling. That signal feeling. It had
remained as fresh in his three-day-old memory as it been bright
when new.

He parked the car in a side-street, locked it carefully and
retraced his three-day-old steps. He found the tree stump. He
thought of the discarded urn. He should tidy it away. He should
have taken it with him. Several shadows moved in the dark.
Ghosts? No. He didn't believe in ghosts. There were, however,
mortal rustlings in the lately fallen leaves, heralding the approach
of night-cloaked strangers who came near to him, looked closely
at him, and then moved away. Alan returned their gazes all of
which he noticed turned almost immediately to disinterest as
each nightwalker in succession moved away, further into the
wild area where Alan had no interest in exploring. Alan knew
exactly where he wanted to be.

He removed the bottle from his pocket and unscrewed the cap
and inhaled. He had tested the notion earlier, found himself rosy
from it, felt himself pink with the flush of heart-pounding energy
which he had deemed not unpleasant. It made him neither giddy
nor ill but rather intoxicated. He put the bottle on the tree stump
and then removed his jacket, shirt, and boots. He decided that he
would put his boots back on after removing his trousers, which
he folded along with his other clothes as an extra luxury for
the comfort of his back and head in his naturally sculptured
chaise-longue du bois.

The phallus he unwrapped, which together with the dispenser, he placed reverently on the tree beside him. He then assumed his position.

And there it was.

The feeling.

Warm, even though the night was chilly. Supportive even though he was alone. Exciting even though he was quite calm. The silence beneath the trees was deafening. At home, in bed, there had always been the buzzing made by the television, the creaks and groans of a house settling down for the night. Pipework contracting. Out here, there was nothing but a huge, velvet drift of silence on which he had set himself afloat.

Through this peace, he heard the rustle of leaves, sensed a presence. He was neither afraid nor alarmed. He felt leather-gloved hands, cold in the autumn night, brush against his hard nipples. He enjoyed the caress, moved slightly but did not open his eyes. His legs parted, allowing his stiffened dick to spring upright. His was a cock to be neither ashamed nor boastful of, but Alan had little interest in massaging it or having it touched by another. It would serve, when time came. It always had. It was merely a tool. A conduit.

The hands left his chest and he heard the visitor walk away. Then he remembered the . . . the . . . He had forgotten what the young man in the shop had called it. Oh, yes. Lube. He had forgotten. He gently raised himself on his elbows, leaned across and pumped several squibs of gel into his palm. He lay back and massaged the new product into his hole, into it, around it, inside it as deep as his fingers could probe.

Then he wondered about allergy. He had never had an allergy and so he dismissed the thought as irrelevant. Alan wiped the excess of the lube onto the head and the shaft of the virgin black dildo which stood waiting, like the black monolith at the end of *2001*, he fancied, full of knowledge and purpose but useless without a civilization to accompany it.

Alan relaxed back into recumbency; he did not count minutes or seconds or wonder why time was ticking on. Another presence settled at his side and, almost immediately, another. This time, he opened his eyes and was surprised at how light the night was. At how much there was to see. The man's head seemed to be shaved bald. He looked at Alan with a steely, unblinking intensity. Alan saw that he wore a leather jacket, the sort that Marlon Brando wore, the sort the actors in the fuck-films wore when first they appeared on set, before they stripped to achieve their script, to play their roles. Alan wondered whether the man too, like the actors, would at some point remove his jacket.

Alan felt other hands feeling his body, straying over his cock, roughly examining his asshole and, finding it wet and moist, quickly withdrawing and turning attention to squeezing and pulling his enlarged, excited nipples. But these flutterings were of no consequence, like the flickering wings of moths against a lighted glass. It was the solitary strength of the intent of the bald man which fixed Alan's attention, even more so when he saw the man reach down and pick up the massive rubber manufacture and rub the watery gel which Alan had deposited there all the length of the foot long shaft. Slowly, the man nodded at Alan, who responded merely by shifting slightly in his posture and parting his legs. He thought he should maybe close his eyes but then, no . . . Of course. Like watching the films, he had to see. To Watch. He must not, he decided, close his eyes; he must look into the eyes of the stranger.

He heard another two sets of footsteps and then a third arrive at this open-air studio. His place of exhibition. Then a third. Then more, too many more to count.

"Give it to him," he heard one remark.

"Put it up there, go on," urged a second.

The man nodded again to Alan and Alan felt almost immediately the pressure of the giant rubber head against his sphincter. Was it like the marrow? The question flickered like a celluloid frame through the gate of his mind only to be replaced immediately by the rest of the film, by the enjoyment of the sensation of the texture of the material as it pushed ever deeper. His hands gripped the bark of the fallen tree, his fingers found the rough texture compatible, opposite to the sensation of total smoothness which emanated from the zone of his anal canal.

Someone held something under his nose. Oh, yes, Alan remembered. The bottle. Was it his, he worried for a moment, and then forgot to worry any more as he felt his asshole being

spread like the ripple of groundwaves of a mighty atomic
explosion. He inhaled deeply. Whooshing upwards like the
onrush of the vertical cloud, he felt the length of the dildo
taking him in its vanguard. No, he quickly decided, better
than the marrow. Better than any cucumber. Only once had
he seen Scott O'Hara, one of his favourite actors, assimilate
a conveniently poached zucchini. No wonder. No wonder the
other actors used these rubber things. So much more . . . and
more . . .

"Fuck him!" a brash voice announced. "Fuck his hungry
fuckhole, man!"

Onwards and upwards . . . Slowly, the feeling engulfed him,
as the stranger twisted the apparatus slightly, easing it through
the atmosphere inside Alan's asshole like the shuttle craft twists
and curves on its way from America to the outer limits.

"Yeah!" voices exclaimed as the front of the unyielding
rubber scrotal sac came to rest against the dark mouth of Alan's
yawning hole. The stranger allowed himself a smile as he began
to withdraw the devilishly clever piece of shagcasting and begin
to pump Alan again and again, his fingers of his other hand
tracing as though in wonder the line of the interface between
flesh and rubber as the dildo slid in and out, up and down.
Other hands followed suit. Alan made no remonstrance. He
had no objection. For a moment he allowed his eyes to leave
the stranger's and he looked about him. Ten, twenty men
stood around, either playing with their own cocks or shifting
slightly as two or three other men, on their knees, entertained
the crowd of onlookers even further by varying displays of oral
expertise of their own. Alan neither smiled nor spoke, neither
murmured nor moaned as his body shook with the pounding
which was being administered. He was quiet. He remained so
– quite, quite silent for the remainder of the succeeding few
minutes. Some spectators left, some new ones arrived. Old
ones returned. Alan was touched, several times, by hands
which reached out almost unbelievingly, incredibly, hands
that touched his flesh as supplicants would touch that of a
martyr, as pilgrims would brush their fingers over the surface
of a reliquary. To gain strength, to be similarly empowered, to
have some of the idol-gilding rub off onto them.

Alan looked forwards again, for the last time and saw that the stranger had unzipped himself and that, as well as continuing to pump the dildo in and out of Alan with his left hand, was stroking the length of his own prick, faster and ever more firmly. The man's eyes opened momentarily wider, only to relax, then to widen in a cycle of intent leading up to what Alan recognized from the films was going to be the climax.

"Yeah, yeah, yeah!" the man panted though clenched teeth as he left the rubber cock embedded to the hilt in Alan's ass, pushing his thigh against the flattened end of the dildo, holding it in position as he spurted a stream and then heavy gobs of his cum over Alan's torso. And, just as he had known, Alan produced his own orgasm in concert, his cock releasing a stream of thick soapy cum without his hand ever coming near.

The man, panting and laughing, stood over Alan as he flicked the residual cum off his fingers onto the ground. He wiped his hand on the rough bark of the tree and then against his jeans, which he zipped up after flipping his cock back inside. Alan lay back on his tree stump. Silent. Satisfied. The throng of people had moved away. It was, after all, all over.

"Thanks," the man said as he too made to move away. "Hope I see you again. You're a fuckin' star, man!"

PLAYING BITCH

Chris Leslie

ONE NIGHT I was, again, pretending to be a hustler in a Times Square peep show. I was mostly hanging out and talking to one young man in particular, a tall skinny guy named André from the Bronx. As you might guess, André is a straight guy who tries to make a few dollars in these places after work to help make ends meet.

It was a very slow night, and only a few freaks without money were milling about, checking out the short line of hustlers on the back wall. "This shit is not happening," André told me. I didn't say anything because it was true. I was thinking of breaking out when he asked me for a dollar.

André is one of the few people I've met who will borrow a dollar and pay it back. He probably did have money, just not a dollar bill needed to use one of the booths. I nodded my head and he asked me if I wanted to come with him. We waited until the coast was clear and ducked into a booth that was relatively clean.

André is a good-looking guy, a little rough around the edges and a little fuzzy about the face, but we share the unaffected street style that allows us immediate friendship without intimacy, the kind of relationship I have with my cousins.

I put a dollar into the slot as André sat on the bench. We surfed the 64 triple-X channels, hoping that there was something on. André stopped surfing on a lesbian movie.

"Look at those girls, man," he said.

"They're crazy," I agreed. There were three girls and a half-dozen dildos; the movie was practically a farce.

I really don't understand what André's story is. He quizzed me thoroughly when we first met to make sure I was real a hustler and not a police officer or a con artist of some sort. He was a tough one to convince, but when he made his decision he stuck by it and never questioned me again.

I didn't think that André wanted to have sex with me, but he was much too curious about what I got into and the sick explicit details of the jobs I had done. I figured he just liked to have guys talk dirty to him and I was more than happy to oblige. But on this quiet night at the peep show, André revealed his intentions to me.

"We should try to get a few dollars out of here and go over to the hotel," he said. "They got girls there."

I looked at André carefully. He didn't know, but I figured I knew the hotel he was referring to: a place that rented rooms for ten dollars an hour. You have to be kind of aggressive – it's not legal to rent rooms by the hour, and they pretend to uphold the law – but if you hold your ground they will bring you up the back stairs to the special section of hourly rooms.

The guy bringing you up will try to sell you other stuff like drugs or prostitutes – "Do you want fries with that?" – before unlocking a room and letting you take care of your business. I had been there before, but that's a different story.

I never thought of making a party out of it. I wouldn't mind doing a girl with André, in a way – and yet, I didn't quite trust him. It could be a set up. André could see I was uneasy and he didn't want to press the issue. The dollar ran out in the machine.

"Let's get out of here." André followed me downstairs. We stood outside the peep show and shared a cigarette while watching the hookers and the tourists come and go on Eighth Avenue.

"What do you got planned tonight?" He always asks me that, and I'm never sure why.

"I'm going to break out in a few and get some Zs, I guess."

"You live in Brooklyn, right?"

"Yeah."

André was quiet; three good-looking female tourists were passing by. He caught the eyes of one and said hello. She smiled uneasily but kept walking. "Now there," André said confidentially after the women were out of earshot. "There is some good clean pussy."

I thought a lot about André's offer, and working over someone else seemed a good compromise: we both could maintain our fronts while having sex. His idea came to mind the next time a hood approached me on the street. I had been hanging out with Bard in the East Village and was on my way to the subway when out of nowhere this guy stumbled in front of me and asked me for a cigarette.

I gave him one, and he told me he was looking for a movie theater that was supposed to be on the block.

"I know where it is, but do you know what goes down there?" I asked. I stopped in a shadow of a van so we could have some privacy.

"I hear they got some freaks up in there," he said.

"What's your name?"

"Joe," he said, as if he didn't believe it. I wondered at this thing we call banjee; Joe saw me on the street and knew that he could ask me about this sleazy gay movie theater and didn't have to worry about what I would say. If I was for real I would tell what I knew. If I wasn't for real, he wouldn't have to worry because he could take me with a hand tied behind his back.

"It's true. They got plenty freaks in there." We were standing on Fourth Street between Second and Third avenues. "You got ten dollars?"

"Yeah."

"I can take you."

"You gonna take my money just to bring me there?" he asked suspiciously.

"Naw, you gotta give it to the man. I don't need your money."

I started walking and Joe trailed behind, not sure if he was going to go through with it.

"What's your name?"

"Chris."

"Chris," he repeated. "What's it like in there?"

"You'll like it fine."

"You don't know shit about what I like."

"Are you horny?"

Joe looked away and I decided that that was a yes. "Don't worry about it." I opened a door that lead to a stairway to the basement of a restaurant and held it open for him. He looked at my face carefully as he passed and ambled down the stairs.

We gave the cashier our money and we were buzzed inside. "I'm going to the bathroom. Walk around."

Joe didn't want to look scared, so he nodded his head and started down a dark hallway. I went to the bathroom and washed up, and when I came back to the main room Joe was standing in a corner. He walked over.

"There ain't nothing going on here," he said. He sounded disappointed.

"Not yet there ain't," I said. "We just got here." I started down a hallway lined with dark booths. Men were standing around, some in the booths and some in the hallway. Joe followed me as I checked things out. I found a likely candidate sitting in a booth. I made a space for me an Joe on the wall across from the booth and we waited.

Joe looked at me for an explanation but I didn't look back. Joe decided that none was coming and slunk back, despondent. Perfect. The man in the booth took the bait. He motioned to me to come into the booth. I didn't move. He motioned for me and Joe to both come into the booth. I didn't move. Joe was looking at the floor.

The man waited. He was agitated. Having two hoods in front of him made all sorts of fantasies play in his head. He motioned again, but I pretended not to see.

The man finally got down on his knees in the back of the booth. I let this get my attention. He pointed at his mouth, and I grabbed my dick. Joe watched with his mouth open, too. The man motioned again, and I took a step forward.

Joe started to sneak away, but I snagged him by the utility loop on his trousers and he stood by. I looked back and forth, pretending to be nervous. Joe was genuinely nervous but stood still. The man licked his lips and we entered the booth.

I had just begun to close the door when the man fell on Joe, trying to unzip his pants. Joe didn't quite understand the scenario I guess and pushed the man away. I locked the door and said quietly, "It's alright." I unzipped my pants and the man reached inside, pulling out my raging dick and jamming it into his mouth. "Yo, yo," I said, more loudly. "Take it easy."

The man eased off and sucked my dick with more respect. Joe had his mouth open again as he watched. The booth was kind of small, but there was room enough for us to stand shoulder to shoulder. I pushed Joe by his ass until his crotch lined up with mine. I whispered in his ear, "Take it out."

Joe looked in my eyes as he unzipped his pants and freed his boner from his fly. "Now tell him to suck your dick."

Joe licked his lips and cleared his throat. "Give me some of that," he said. The man looked up at him. "Yo, suck my dick." The man hadn't noticed Joe's dick, even though it was kind of hard to miss. But with a quickness the man was off my dick, his sucking just a wet memory as he turned on Joe. The man with two banjee dicks was in heaven.

I was in heaven too, and I don't know what Joe was feeling but he sure wasn't complaining. He tried to stand close to me but his arm was in the way, and finally he reached behind me and stuck his hand in the waistband of my boxers as he got his cock sucked. We stood, touching from shoulder to hip, bracing each other for the pending explosion.

When he got close to cumming Joe tried to pull his dick out, but the man wanted it all and wouldn't stop. "I told you to stop," Joe said evenly, pushing the man off with a firm pressure. "I ain't ready."

The man wiped his face and started back on me, working to take all of my dick into his throat. Joe pressed his lips against my neck and I closed my eyes. I was about to come and pushed the man off. He knew what he was doing now; he obediently turned on Joe who started to moan lightly, a light whine that only I could hear.

This continued for a time before we couldn't take it anymore. I noticed Joe close his eyes, getting ready to bust it off. I put my lips to his ear and whispered, "Let it go. Let it go." Joe grabbed one of my butt cheeks and shot.

The man, not stopping even to spit, turned on me. Joe whispered, "Yeah punk. Bust a nut." The man held my crotch closely to his face so there was no room to escape. Joe turned and pressed his dick against my hip. It was still throbbing and I could feel the goo spread on my skin. Joe took my ear between his teeth and bit, and I came.

We stood in the booth quietly. The man pulled some tissues from his pocket and wiped off my boot; I guessed that he had come too. He tried to stand but he felt a little dizzy, so I grabbed him by his shirt and set him against the wall until he got his balance. Joe and I zipped up and I kissed the man like he was a good boy before opening the door.

Joe followed me out of the basement club and back onto the street. I was walking toward the subway; I didn't know where he was going. "I came in that guy's mouth," Joe said.

"Yeah me too."

"Yeah?" Joe smiled. "That was crazy."

We were standing on Houston Street. I gave him the secret banjee handshake and broke out before he did something corny, like give me his number. Even the hardest boy can experience moments of weakness.

I wanted to tell the story to André the next time I saw him, but when the time came I didn't really feel up to it. I didn't know if I was supposed to know about such places, for one thing, and for another the story was only good if I described what Joe looked like and I was pretty sure that I was not supposed to have noticed. So we just hung out as usual until this guy walked in.

I was to find out that this guy's name was Matt. He was very uncomfortable being in a peep show with male hustlers, but I knew that he was no stranger to the darker side of Manhattan. I had often seen him tooling around Times Square. I was pretty sure that he was a drug dealer, but since I hadn't actually seen him deal I figured he was a supplier and not a street dealer.

Matt didn't look at all like a street dealer to be sure; he had more of a tourist from the suburbs style. Of course, while this made him unattractive at the same time it made me curious about this "real" dealer.

Matt's head was shaved tight on the sides, not faded but just taken down to the skin, and he pushed back the longer hair on top. He was wearing blue jeans and a T-shirt under a black leather coat. His sneakers were colorful and clean. Too clean. His teeth were white and lined up in a row. Even though he was a drug dealer he was, in fact, also a dork from Jersey. A good-looking, clean dork – not much of a hood at all.

André caught Matt's eye first. I couldn't hear their conversation, but André kept on shaking his head no so I suspected that Matt was asking him if he sucked dick or liked to get fucked. Finally, André said yes and they shook hands. André stood quietly while Matt checked out the surroundings and approached me.

"What's up?" he said.

"Chilling," I said, not looking at him. Hustlers don't talk to young guys; they're either other hustlers with bad aim or kids looking for a freebie.

"What are you looking for?"

"Some ends, just like everyone else," I said. I prayed he wasn't cop; you were supposed to make sure before you say anything like that.

"Are you a cop?" he asked.

"I ain't a cop."

"Do you like coke?"

I shook my head.

"Do you live around here?"

"Naw I live in Brooklyn."

"That's a shame. Do you know somewhere around here where we could smoke a blunt?"

"Yeah," I said. "What's your name?"

"Matt."

"Chris." I realized I had been shaking my head no, then said yes and shook his hand, just like André. What was this guy up to?

"Do you know my boy Ralph?" He was pointing to André.

That ain't your boy, I thought. "Yeah, I seen him before."
"Do you mind if he comes with us?"
"Naw, he's cool."
"Good. Let's go." André took the lead and brought us to
the sleazy hotel. Just what he had been waiting for, I suppose.
But things were not going to happen the way I had thought
they would.

André grabbed Matt's arm as we went inside the hotel and
told him to give the man ten dollars and ask for a room. Matt
obeyed, and when the clerk said they didn't have any ten dollar
rooms anymore Matt looked at André, who nodded his head.
Matt turned back to the clerk. "Come on man, we just need
a room for an hour. We won't be any trouble."
    The man motioned to the guy outside the booth, who took
us upstairs. He paused in the hallway to see if he could sell us
more. "You guys need anything? Coke? Girls?"
    I was about to say no when Matt spoke up. "You guys want
to get a girl?"
    André, to my surprise, shrugged noncommittally. "What
have you got?" he asked the man.
    "I've got some real pretty girls," the man said. "You'd like
them. But you'll need at least two, don't you think? I don't
want anyone to get hurt."
    This made me snort, but Matt ignored me. "Where are they?
Do we get to pick?"
    "You can tell me what you want, and I will send someone
down. You have more money, right?"
    Matt shook his head. "I want to see first."
    "Why? Go relax in your room and I will send up whatever
you want. What kind of girls do you guys like?" We were
standing in the hall with the rooms. André was picking his
teeth, looking bored. Matt looked at us and decided. "Maybe
later. You going to be out here?"
    "You let me know. I'll be right here."
    Matt whispered in my ear as the man unlocked our room,
"I bet you will."
    We closed the door behind us and Matt started to complain
about the man. "He wants us to take girls sight unseen, and

you know that we'd have to pay whether we wanted her or not. That's fucked up, right?"

André sat on the bed and Matt took a chair near the window. I decided I should use the bathroom and went back into the hall. There were two stalls, a sink, and a condom machine. When I came back Matt was still talking about prostitutes.

"They got some fine hookers out there in Taiwan, son. You should see. Really beautiful girls. And you can trust the pimps too. They won't bring you anything wack cause it's bad for tourism."

Matt pulled a cigar out of his pocket. "Do you know how to roll?" he asked me. I admitted that I did not.

Matt started licking the cigar, using his spit to loosen the tobacco leaf. "Taiwan's not like here at all," he said, between licks. "In New York you gotta check out the merchandise first. You're just as sure to get a busted crack-head with herpes if you're not careful."

Matt pulled a strip of leaf from the cigar. "Either of you got a blade so I could cut this?" he asked. He didn't need a blade to make a blunt; it's just a good thing to find out what people are carrying before you get too open. We both shook our heads, even though I knew that André was usually carrying one.

Matt took a breath and turned to me. "You ever been to Taiwan?"

I told him I hadn't been much of anywhere.

"Let me know if you want to go sometime," Matt told me, as if we were old friends. Matt wasn't watching André, who was almost laughing. We're always talking about how tricks get so familiar so fast, and then wonder why they get hustled.

The sex, when it finally happened, was not much to get excited about. Matt jerked off with us standing in front of him. He sucked our dicks quickly, trying to will the cum out of us. We weren't really turned on. We stood silent with our thumbs in our pockets, like good street hustlers should.

Our indifference did not please Matt. He stopped sucking dick but continued to jerk off as he complained. "You guys are bricks. Ain't you ever had sex with a man before?"

"I don't do this much," André said. "I'm kind of new to the scene."

I was going to make a smart remark but André gave me a look that told me to keep my smart remarks to myself.

Matt was sucking on my dick, stopping only to whisper, "Come on guy. Let it out. Give it to me." I really didn't think I could come. I had already jerked off that day, plus had embarked on another adventure that I don't want to mention.

"It's kind of backed up, man. You got to do it better," I told him. I grabbed Matt's head and gave him more of what he wanted. Ramming my dick until it slipped into the fleshy part of his throat, I talked dirty to him in the street slang that he admired but could not master. Matt shot his load on the leg of my trousers and apologized.

"Come for me," Matt demanded. He grabbed my dick and jerked me off as he sucked. I closed my eyes and held my breath.

It was a long time coming, but it was a big load nonetheless. Matt was pleased and paid us both 20 dollars for letting him play bitch. Not bad considering the low rates in the area. André and I got a beer and found a secluded loading dock to chill for a few before breaking out.

André dug half of a blunt out of his pocket and lit it with a butane lighter. Not the torch kind used to heat crack but an all-weather type used to build a fire in arctic conditions. André styles himself as is something of a paratrooper, ready to rock in any environment. The sharp blue flame set the blunt blazing, and after a toke he handed it to me. "I'm glad you showed."

I took a puff and handed it back. I was still buzzing off of Matt's weed. André sucked down some more. We attracted the attention of a hooker, but André told her we didn't have enough to go around. After she left he handed me the blunt but I waved it away. "I'm done," I said.

André poked me with a finger, pretending to stick a fork in me. "Yeah, you're pretty well cooked," he said. He spit on the end of the blunt to put it out and resumed poking.

I pushed his hand away. "Cut it out," I said.

"What's the matter? You don't like to get poked?" André laughed at his own joke.

"Not by punks like you."

"So now I'm a punk?"

"You were always a punk."

HOW DO WE COMMUNICATE LOVE?

Aiden Shaw

SOME THINGS ALWAYS seem to happen at night. People live their daily lives which sometimes, often, differ from their nighttime lives. This may be out of practicality, concerning the conscience, which doesn't like to be seen by day. It's a little like not wanting to have sex with the light on, only less about the body and more about the mind. Souls come together to explore their dark sides, their usually hidden-away sides. Slapping bottoms and pinching titties isn't what this is about, nor naughty but nice. This is the realm of fear and trust. Master and Recipient. There is no play-acting here.

A fluorescent strip lights this space, a dungeon or play room. There are contraptions, toys, that have been created especially by the Master, who wants very particular responses from the recipient.

A figure is strapped onto a table, which is cushioned slightly like the ones used in operating rooms. There are numerous straps that fit snugly, keeping the recipient perfectly in place. Running through the center of this table is a pivot so that the whole thing can spin 360 degrees on that axle. A person could lie with their face up and then turn right over so the whole of their body weight hangs face down. The sensation can be anything from an exciting ride at a funfair to being securely held like a baby.

The man in this contraption has a latticework of leather straps – over 40 shiny, silver buckles crossing his body – keeping him in place. Through the squares and rectangles they form, his flesh is naked and hairless, his body having been shaved in preparation.

Removing your clothes can make you feel vulnerable enough. Add to this a blindfold. Then, the knowledge that you are going to be shaved from neck to foot with a cut-throat razor. You have been told to keep still. So you do. Very still. Even when the blade maneuvers around your nipples, then your arse and balls. Imagine what goes through your head as the sack of your scrotum is lifted up, and gently pulled, so that all the hairs can be reached. There would be no point in saying, "Enough!" You are here to push yourself, to stretch yourself.

Over this landscape of black leather straps, pits of skin and highlights of metal, something protrudes. Sectioned off, in an area of its own, a dick and balls splendidly sit. A focus point perhaps, but there are other ways to think. And, other things to experience before the deadening event of an orgasm.

The table is turned three times in succession. Slowly, so that the blood can adjust. A strap covers the eyes but the mouth is left free. It is important that the submissive be able to give an indication when they've had enough. It could be anything. For example, three grunts in a row could be serious and mean "stop." The mouth could be covered, but this Master has chosen to allow more complex communication. To hear exactly how things feel, how anxious or exhilarated the responses are. On the last turn, the table is left at an angle just past the vertical. The body hovers, as though at any moment it might plunge. The body neither rests on the cushion nor on the straps, but sits comfortably between the two.

"I'm going to begin by putting a mild acid on your skin, it won't disfigure or permanently harm you in any way. Do you want me to do this?"

"Yes."

There is no room here for indecision. No questions – like,

"What kind of acid?" or, "What strength?" or "Are you sure it won't harm me?" – are allowed. There is only one answer. It must be said clearly and with a confidence that shows you believe in your master, beyond all else, for this moment in time.

It may be clear, how wonderful this could be for the Master: How far someone will let you take them? How much belief and even love they show for you during this sacred process?

"Are you ready?"

"Yes."

No indication is given where the acid will be poured. Would it be on the sensitive nipples, or worse, the face? The fluid is squirted from a plastic bottle, spraying lightly over the crotch. There is a loud scream. Through this, a voice is heard.

"Tell me how it feels."

With the promptest of replies, "It burns, Sir."

"Do you trust me?"

"Yes."

Invisible to the naked eye, a stirring takes place deep in the gut. Not like an erection or a cramping. More like the place where the physical sex of a person links with their thoughts, not their emotions. When the brain releases chemicals, the blood arouses and desire responds.

Blowing gently over the crotch, the burning stops. How could this be?

"It's only alcohol, there's no need to worry. Unless this flame . . .," you hear a lighter being lit, ". . . comes too close." The master lights a long thin piece of wood and passes it over a sweaty chest, singeing the odd stray hair that escaped the blade, leaving fine wisps of smoke.

"Do you trust me?"

"Yes."

If you could enter the thoughts of a submissive at this time, you would be very aware of the sounds. The creak of leather and your own stammered breath. You would be acutely conscious of your Master's movements: the turning of gritty soles, footsteps walking away, stopping, then returning. Guessing at actions and possible consequences. All the time, reassuring yourself and trying to relax. It's only when you give in, when you abandon yourself completely – it's only then that barriers can be crossed and true enjoyment gained.

You feel heat on your neck, around your chin, over your lips. You needn't flinch, your Master knows the right distance. Then, there is complete silence. So you listen. And; because there seems to be nothing, you stifle your breath and you listen extra hard. At this point, you hear something you now recognize. The sound of the alcohol being picked up again. Your mind races forward. You forget to control yourself by trusting your Master and you say, "Stop!" and you fail. You know in an instant that you are pathetic, that you don't deserve to belong to anybody. Especially, not to someone who treats you so well, who's kind and careful and so meticulous in meeting your needs. You knew that your master knows your fears, that fire was one of your deepest; and yet, you fail. So lost in all your other fears, you fail.

When these thoughts subside, you begin to think about the blindfold. Your focus is so small. It's on that one strap of leather. You obsess, because you know that when the blindfold is removed you've got to face your Master. Such shame. You've failed. There is no other way of looking at it. When you leave you replay the scene time and time again. Rewinding, then dissecting every single moment. When you were strong. When you were good. When you still had some self respect. Before you gave in and became nothing in your mind. Would you even be allowed to try again?

THE QUALITIES OF LETTUCE

Paul Allatson

VINCENT IS REMOVING words from Don's magazines. It is delicate work, requiring a steady hand and an eye for detail. Scissors, including Vincent's fine-armed, stainless-steel pair for nails, prove inadequate for the task. No amount of careful trimming rectifies the initial fraying penetration of paper. Razor blades are preferable. They create clean-edged rectangles, windows which open onto other words. Sometimes those windows direct Vincent's gaze to colours and hints of flesh and muscle and skin when a photograph fills the following page. For the moment, hints are all Vincent desires.

Vincent does not know why he ended up with Don's collection of pornography. Earlier on this bright summer day, after he dragged the box into the hallway, after he found the typed note which read "from Don", Vincent thought a mistake had been made. He hadn't known Don all that well. Vincent had never been intimate with Don while Don lived. The fact was, Don used to smother conversation. For example, he had a tendency to recite from memory the street names of suburbs chosen randomly from the Sydney metropolitan area. He would proceed from a boundary road and work his way in from T-junction to intersection only ending when the street or avenue or crescent ran into a neighbouring postcode. Long before this, Vincent would have found an excuse for flight.

Such memories come to Vincent as he reads and occasionally cuts out words that Don must, that Don may have read. The words refer to the body, the male body, in moments of ecstasy, moments that Vincent has always presumed were outside Don's range of life experiences. Vincent would never have said Don oozed availability. Or at least, he never responded to Vincent's subtle signals. And in spite of the evidence at his fingertips, Vincent is still inclined to doubt. Some of the magazines have not been extracted from their shrink-wrapped covers. The rest remain in what a collector would call mint condition. Vincent comes across no bent corners or telling stains. He does not have to prise pages apart. None of the magazines open automatically onto the ardent sections of the story, or the photographs of the washboard stomach or the waxed-smooth arse or the engorged dick Don would have turned panting to, again and again. They are a dead man's magazines. Don's magazines. Magazines that look as if no hand before Vincent's has touched them.

When Vincent begins, just after midday, he has no sense of where Don's words will lead. He does not anticipate a logical climax, or expect to uncover a pearl of wisdom, the foretaste of a flood of indisputable revelations. He removes about one hundred words. At ten to two he breaks for a coffee and a cigarette, and returns to push Don's words around the polished surface of his desk. Vincent categorizes them so that it will be easier to form phrases or sentences. He cannot explain why he wants to make sentences from the words he has sliced from Don's magazines. In fact, he does not form any that make much sense, probably because he is not yet interested in such useful conjunctions as "and" or "but", or even coherent combinations like "it", "was", "a", "bright", "summer", and "day". Vincent is much more attracted to parts of speech that evoke the splay-legged men of dreams. Vincent has a pile of adjectives, one of nouns, and yet another of verbs, richly connotative, active verbs like "thrust" and "strip", "ride" and "clamp", "cum", and of course, "fuck". Eighteen "fucks", for example, from three quite vigorous stories in the first two magazines. Eighteen versions of the same doing word, the word he has not yet encountered, this word in the story he has so far preferred above all others, a story he has carefully pulled from the magazine without ripping it at the samples. A story about . . .

the tussle-haired boy from next door, his grease-smeared torso rippling between sunlight and the shadow cast by the raised bonnet of his ute. The lad is engrossed in his engine, his singlet damp with sweat, his movements around the bonnet revealing a dick barely constrained by a skimpy pair of Levi cut-offs.

Vincent concentrates on the stories. He accepts, too, that he will eventually want to do something with the photo spreads, but he does not think he has the stamina to contend with the advertisements or classifieds, the few columns of readers' letters or the video reviews. Vincent's choices provide him with a workable framework. He concentrates on the two or three stories in each magazine. He applies himself to those pages with the diligence and the longing for the clear-cut that might otherwise be swamped by the rich abandon of material on display. Vincent is methodical as he removes and arranges Don's words, as he reads, as sweat appears on his forehead, and he lubricates his dry lips with his tongue.

Of course Vincent will never know about Don's passions. However deeply he probes, he will always be immersed in conjecture. He could be making connections between words that turn out to be undesirable scribble. One word may or may not lead to Don. One Don may or may not be a Don who may or may not turn out to be Don. And so on, until the moment Vincent collapses because he cannot bear his desk-framed interests any longer, until other matters distract him, until frustrated or enraged or completely spent, he sweeps Don and Don's words from his desk into the rubbish bin, until he recognises that even in death Don eludes him, that Don will always leave Vincent unsated.

But for the moment, Vincent has Don's magazines and his piles of words. In some of those words Vincent has actually found Don, or Dons of sorts. Those Dons form his fourth pile, eleven Dons lurking in "don't" and "donut", "donger", "donation", and "done." Just after two o'clock, Vincent begins to hallucinate more Dons. He thinks he sees Don in the preponderance of "abdominals". At quarter past two, Vincent attributes those false Dons to the lapse in concentration that occurs when

the lad lowers the bonnet of his ute and peels off his singlet to reveal a chiselled chest, nipples fringed with curling hair, and an armpit pale as milk. He leans over to retrieve a sponge from a steaming bucket and begins to clean the ute's black panels with slow, circular caresses that relay tremors through the sinews of both arms, across the shoulders, and down the v-shaped back to where his butt begins its impressive curve.

Vincent feels rather foolish when placing those deceptive "abdominals" on top of the bulging pile of other nouns.

Vincent cannot recall Don mentioning either lovers or anonymous tricks, but he had lived two blocks away from KKK, a coincidence which for a while lent itself to some half-hearted speculation. Apparently he once placed an advertisement in the *Star Observer* for a flat-mate. At the time he desired a university student, preferably a fee-paying South-east Asian with an interest in permanent residency. Nothing came of it. He lived alone, for the three and a half years Vincent knew him, in a rented, grey-carpeted flat in Randwick. The living Don played the occasional set of tennis and was fond of word games. In fact, it was during a game of dictionary that Don provided the false definition of "cresset" which, for those present on that otherwise unmemorable occasion, encapsulated his very existence. From then on, with his pale skin emerging from the insipid clothes he favoured, with his town planner unobtrusiveness and his tendency to wilt in the summer heat, Don would always have "the qualities of lettuce." Those scattered facts, Vincent realizes, are all he knows of the Don before death.

After death, however, Don has surprised Vincent. An altogether different Don revealed himself at the memorial service held in the stone church on Alyson Road. The service was held there after Don's cremation the week before somewhere in greater London. Don had died from meningitis, a day after the first symptoms appeared, on the third day of his first overseas trip. While Vincent was taken aback to learn of the rapidity of Don's extinction, he was even more astonished on overhearing the whispers as he sat in the pew closest to the church door, whispers of a cover-up, insinuations that in the 1990s there was no way for a gay man of 37 to die of anything but AIDS. Most perplexing of all was Vincent's discovery that he was merely one of a hundred people who had known the living, breathing Don. A Don poles apart from, but once upon a time as real and palpable as the one

standing shirtless, his left hand slowly caressing the left nipple on his taut, expansive chest, his right hand grasping the hose and directing a spray of water across the gleaming surface of his ute.

Vincent's incredulity was echoed by speaker after speaker who drew attention to the size of the crowd Don had managed to pull in death. Many had only experienced Don in one to one encounters. None had contemplated the possibility that Don would have had at his disposal so many erotic inspirations. Of those men, Vincent had suspected nothing.

Just as Vincent never suspected the day would come in which he sits with a pile of Don's words, and spread before him, three of the more typically alluring centrefolds from Don's magazines. Vincent is sure that no one in the world can envisage him imagining Don

buffing chrome with a pale-yellow chamois,

while he transforms Chad and Diego and Bobby by pasting Don's name over their faces. Vincent sits at his desk staring at a Don who is at once a blond and body-waxed, muscle-tightened preppie, jerking off as he reclines in hay, a swarthy, hirsute Mediterranean type soaping up under the shower, and a massive-thighed navy cadet, caught in the process of pouring baby oil onto a scimitar erection that almost reaches his grin. Don's grin. A splendid grin below the letters "D" and "o" and "n".

Vincent is pleasantly surprised by Don's transformations, and now, at two-twenty in the afternoon, he laughs. And

he looks out of his window at Don who has heard him, and who, smiling back, is waving a right hand in recognition, their eyes locking and the colour rising in

Vincent's cheeks. Vincent is convinced that somewhere Don most surely is privy to his thoughts. Somewhere Don knows what Vincent is doing with the magazines, with Don's words, with the three Dons that have caused the unthinkable, a fantastic link between Vincent's bulging crotch and a Don

who turns to pick up his bucket and sponge, his chamois and can of turtle wax, and heads towards his front door.

Vincent looks at his centrefold Dons. His left hand lingers in Don's words, while his right moves inside his fly. Vincent is contemplating a scenario that will alleviate throbbing ache, when

he hears knocking at his front door. "Just a minute," he yells, but at this moment on this bright summer day, open door admits both the expected and unexpected into his home. "Hello there." "Hi," he says to the figure filling the doorway of the room he sits in. "Listen mate, I've been cleaning my ute and I've locked myself out. Could I climb over your back fence into my back yard? I'm sure the back door isn't locked." "No problem, go ahead," Vincent replies, his right hand caught inside his unzipped fly, aware that Don's eyes are flicking from his crotch to the sprawl of bodies across the desk and down to the pile of magazines on the floor. Don grins. "You look like you're having fun. Mind if I take a look?" He steps closer. He stands behind the chair, his bare torso almost touching

Vincent's back. Vincent tries to calculate the number of millimetres that separate them. He tries to concentrate on the letters across Don's three faces. He reads "Don" three times, but his eyes keep scanning Don's three cocks. His

heart thuds, and he moves his shoulders backwards a fraction, and a little more, until they rest against a hard wall of sun-warmed flesh in the very moment that Don's breath ignites the zone behind his right ear.

Vincent undoes his belt buckle and rises just enough to manoeuvre his jeans down to his knees. Thumbs spread, Vincent's hands slide down his chest and stomach until they reach the bottom of his T-shirt. Where shirt meets hips, he takes hold and starts to drag the fabric upwards. As the finger tips touch his slowly revealed skin, goosebumps emerge in their wake. Now unencumbered by his shirt, Vincent sucks each thumb and begins to massage their moisture into his nipples. He lifts his feet to disencumber his legs of his jeans, and as they fall he

hears a belt buckle clink and a zip, the slide of cloth and the smack of a bare foot on the wooden floor. Behind him, Don is naked. "I've been aware of you all afternoon," he says. A floor board creaks. "Looking is not enough, is it?"

And Vincent cannot help himself, he wonders if looking was ever enough for Don, he is trying to conjure up Don's cock, but the words fail him and his effort falters when Don

places a hand on each shoulder and presses his erection against him, assailing Vincent with the pungent mixture of sweat and motor oil and turtle wax. Vincent breathes, deeply. "Relax," Don says, rolling his heavy dick along Vincent's right shoulder to the base of the neck. Vincent smells the precum ooze and hears the squelch as Don's dick slides towards Vincent's right ear, as Don lets it hover there for a few seconds, then moves it over Vincent's cheek. Don says, "move around to your right." Vincent shifts. His dry lips part. He lubricates them with his tongue. Don rests the head of his cock on Vincent's lower lip. He stops all movement. The dick sits there, oozing until Vincent can't bear the suspense any longer. As Vincent sends the first tentative probe of his tongue out to circumnavigate his prize, his Don, he drops his hands to his lap, lifts his buttocks and pushes his jocks down past his knees and feet, liberating his dick from its moist discomfort.

"My Don," Vincent thinks, but he has little time to register *the revelation of Don easing more of his pulsing dick into his mouth, as Don's right hand drops to massage the precum around Vincent's swollen glans, as Vincent's toes curl, as Don glides his right hand up and down Vincent's cock, as Don twists Vincent's right nipple, as Vincent's eyes follow the sparse trail of hairs from Don's pubic bush and up across the abdominal ridge, as Vincent's eyes linger on the smears of grease mingling with the wisps of dark, curling hair around the nipples on Don's chiselled chest, as Don slicks his dick in and out of Vincent's mouth, as Vincent and Don moan.*

"My Don," Vincent thinks,

without releasing Don from his lips. He runs his hands up Don's hefty thighs. Vincent's finger tips linger over the white skin on Don's hips. Don quivers. Don's hands abandon Vincent's nipple and cock to grab the sides of Vincent's head, to align Vincent's head with his undulating pelvis. As Vincent slurps on Don's dick he drops his right hand to grip his own, and moves his left hand over the smooth mounds of Don's arse, searching for the sweaty, hair-lined crack. Don pushes in and out of Vincent's mouth, Vincent curls his tongue around Don as he withdraws, and sucks as if thirst-obsessed. Vincent inserts a finger into Don's arsehole, gyrating it in the warmth, kneading the button, building a finger-fucking rhythm, preparing to push in another. He fists his cock in time with Don's thrusts, up and down, tight, fast, then slowly, pulling the foreskin back until the purple glans begins to ache, and again, up and down, furiously. Don groans with each fuck of Vincent's face. Vincent's hand-on-dick is a blur. His fingers are clamped in Don's arse. Don tenses, his body steeled for this moment, a final lunge into Vincent's throat, holding it there, pumping out a searing flood, gasping, his eyes glazed.

Vincent's eyes narrow until he can no longer read the script, until he can no longer connect the letters "D" and "o" and "n", until the three Dons blur into each other in a swirl of colours, until Vincent's whole being is centred on the pressure in his balls and the tingling along his shaft, and the indisputable proximity of eruption supplants all the truths and suppositions of his world. Vincent's dick swells in his frenzied hand, the slit hole widens, and cum arcs upwards and spatters over his desk, over Don's words, white globs across Don's three bodies, as Vincent gulps at air, before Vincent's spent body sags.

At two forty-five, Vincent stretches. He stares at the three, cumspattered centrefolds, already curling, and at the soggy piles of Don's words that litter his desk. He crumples the words into sticky balls, and one by one, tosses them into the bin. He wipes his cum off the three Dons with a tissue. He sticks a floating "D" back on the face of the Don reclined in hay. Vincent puts Don's three bodies in a manilla envelope which he slips into the bottom drawer of his desk.

TOURIST TRAPS

Jim Provenzano

IT MUST HAVE been the atmosphere, the moisture in the air.

The Cape. I had five days to escape New York. The plane from Newark to Boston was fine. Smooth, uneventful. The ride from Boston to Provincetown, however, provided an appetizer for my week and a harbinger of things to come. I was not prepared.

In the back of the bus, three hunky young guys sat in separate seats, their long legs sprawled across the cushions. I could tell they were friends, probably straight, since gay boys aren't wierd about sitting next to each other. I took the two seats in front of a big longlegged blond, who sat alone on one side, two up from the bathroom. A quick glance as I sat down revealed that he wore a grey college T-shirt, blue nylon shorts, and Weejuns, no socks.

I let the journey proceed without cruising this guy. Plenty of adventure lay waiting in P-town. The possibility of snaring one of these guys in the company of his friends was next to impossible anyway. I read an old copy of John Rechy's Numbers for inspiration and settled down for the ride.

Once we'd been traveling a while, I remembered the hunk seated behind me. I slipped my bus seat back a notch. Peeking between the cushions I saw the lanky blond asleep. His muscular body was curled up sideways, so that his right thigh was inches from the crevass between my cushions. I looked down his leg into the blooming cave of his baggy shorts, where his skin became pale and smooth, almost hairless. Looking for an outline of cock proved difficult. Not only were his legs crossed, but he had a strong down-covered arm placed protectively between his legs.

I found it difficult to continue reading with this big dozing stud to gaze at only inches behind me. Putting down my book, I decided to enjoy the sight of him. He slept fitfully, occasionally waking. He may have noticed my glance through the seat, but he made no protest. I did gaze at him looking out the window a few times. His eyes were a deep turquoise. His features were sharp; a well defined aquiline nose, full pouting lips and a day's blond stubble coating his tanned face and jaw. As he slept, he seemed quite vulnerable. The bus jostled his resting figure. He resembled a fallen soldier awaiting an attending physician.

I'd heard him speak with his friends briefly, who both lay sleeping. He had a slight accent of Northern Ireland, but Americanized, as if he'd been in the States for school the last few years. His grey shirt hung loosely from his chest. As he shifted to his side I admired the outlines of a well defined pectoral and a semi-erect nipple.

The pile of newspapers the blond Celt had discarded lay in a rumpled pile between him and the aisle seat, and was arranged in an intentional vertical stack to hide his lower torso from his buddy across the aisle. I had the only view of what had become a slow and gentle rise and fall of his arm between his legs. He must have been rubbing himself with his forearm, all the while feigning sleep.

He ceased for a bit as we pulled into a shopping mall for a stop and were jostled about, the driver taking the bus through a few sharp turns. When we were back on the road again, the hunky Celt seemed to sleep again before resuming his rubbing. His blond-haired thigh lay only inches from my face, the padded seat our only divider. I inched my fingers between the sides of the crevass and grazed my hand over his small forest of down. A moment after I softly pressed my palm on the warmth of his resting thigh, he twitched up to sitting.

He glanced over at his sleeping buddies, rearranged the papers to further camouflage what was about to happen in his seat. He brought his feet down and sat straight forward, his muscled legs relaxed and parted wide.

Whether it was me or his dreams, he had indeed become aroused, and no doubt had been so for a while. Bus rides have a tendency to give guys hardons. His legs were parted wide like two solid branches bearing fruitful treasures in the center. As large as two grade-A brown eggs, his testicles bounced and jiggled in the thin blue shorts. A good bit of pale scrotum skin peeked out from the left side of his crotch. His two thick-fingered hands, crossed supplicantly over his shorts and above his balls, rubbed up and down slowly along the columned outline in his shorts. His balls jiggled again from his furtive tugs. I'd never seen a guy jerk himself off so discreetly, fingers crossed as if in prayer. Perhaps he'd learned this method in parochial school, a sort of simultaneous Act of Contrition/Perdition. Pray while you Play.

We came upon a long bend in the road. As the afternoon sunlight arced and spilled into the bus window, the Celt's jerking became quicker. Sunlight fell across his body, giving his ringlets of hair a golden angelic glow. More shafts of yellow light fell between his legs. In response, his hips rose to meet it. A spurting wet stain emerged on his shirt from beneath. Then another, which spread over the shirt. He held his hips up for a moment like a diver poised over a cliff. A short grunt escaped his throat.

He relaxed and settled back to rest. At a loss for what to do about the pools of cum on his T-shirt, he lifted the shirt up to his face, exposing his just spent dick, bent to the side and glistening with sperm. Quite nonchalantly he brought the dark wet stains to his mouth and sucked the cum out of his shirt.

With his chest exposed, I noticed another pool of white liquid clung to his belly hairs. He scooped that up and slurped it off his index finger and thumb.

I turned to face front and gazed out the window. Quite stiff from the excitement, I considered popping off myself, but decided against it. The sun angled over to the other side of the bus as we turned again down a winding Cape Cod road.

Evergreens and sand dunes rolled into hills for miles. The tinted bus window gave the landscape an artificial green cast.

By the time the bus pulled into Provincetown, it was about six-thirty. As the passengers stood in the parking lot waiting to retrieve luggage or board, I pulled my duffel bag from the underbelly of the bus, nearly jostling the lanky Irish blond, who merely smiled at me. Glancing down at the still-moist stains on his shirt, I thought of chatting him up, as I would have in New York, following proper courting procedure.

But something in the air of P-town, with its crisp salty flavor, mellowed me enough to let this stud pass. If anything more were meant to happen, we'd see each other again. This was a small town. Why chase one apple on your way to an orchard?

I was charmed by the small size of Provincetown when I literally bumped into Bobby, my host for the week. Having last seen him in full ACT UP clone leather at a demonstration in New York, I was surprised to see him tanned, in elegant summer white shirt and pants. He looked great but seemed unenthused about meeting me.

"Sorry I'm not peppy. We just got rid of Claude's sloppy Quebequois guests. The place is a mess." He gave me a hug and told me to go on to the house and drop off my things.

"You hungry?" he asked.

"Yeah."

"Meet us at Old Reliable. It's a great restaurant just down the street."

"OK. What was your address again?"

"Twelve Cottage Street." I found the house with no difficulty. The number 12 was set above the white picket gate that opened into a fence surrounded yard. The house was a bit messy, the floor itself on a crooked slant, but on the whole the place had a quaint openness.

I put my stuff in Bobby's room, which was barely big enough to fit the trundle bed and dresser, then cleaned up and headed back out into the warm inviting streets.

Being in the midst of so many slow-moving tourists reminded me of summers with my family at Rehobeth Beach, 14 years old and gazing longingly at handsome lifeguards and waiters, expressing these desires to no one.

As I headed down the street in my Avias, jams, Read My Lips T-shirt and black plastic Mardi Gras beads (all the rage that summer), young boys with McCarthy-era crewcuts looked back at me, curiously connecting, my past of self doubt and unfocused heartache reflected in their eyes. They would return in a few years. We travel in circles.

The streets of Provincetown (or rather street, since the aptly named Commercial is practically the single shopping/dining/cruising thoroughfare) are small and quaint with a Disney aura. Restaurants and shops are full of gays and straights, but mostly in different shifts. There are obvious differences. At night, the bars close promptly at one a.m. The boys, men and some women descend on Spiritus Pizza, which compliantly stays open late. The tiny avenue that in sunlight was flooded with dazed families window shopping for yet another whale T-shirt or seagull refrigerator magnet is nightly sprinkled with cruising men of handsome shapes and sizes. Frequently a bike rider will whiz through the darkness, or a slow-moving car will make its way through the crowd like a tourist jeep at Busch Gardens.

The first night I couldn't deal with the Spiritus crowd. Bobby had to go home and rest for his breakfast shift at Cafe Blasé the next morning. I was alone amongst a very closeknit crowd of queers and felt very foreign.

Deciding to walk home, I followed a very tall crewcut man who could have been an Olympic water polo champ. I was quite pent up from the afternoon's escapades in the bus, and damn near wanted to walk right up to the guy and talk him up. Being a tourist gave me a very determined, arrogant feeling. But he walked quite fast, his long legs not wanting to be cruised. As Commercial Street parted, he went right. I left.

Walking toward the water, I passed a small firehouse with a red light glowing over the garage door. As I passed by the circle of rose-glowing asphalt, a cute skinny guy on a bike passed me. He looked back twice before heading through an alley and down to the water. His hair was closely cropped, his face pale yet open and honest. I followed.

The relaxing surges of surf on the dark beach led me to a small area of broken wood and logs where a dock once stood. A craggy salty smell of rotting fish kept the scene from being too sublime. I saw the guy's bicycle leaning against the wooden breakfront. He stood about ten yards away, looking out at the distant glowing lights of dingies and buoys. I walked up to him. He heard my sneakers crunch in the sand and turned.

"Hi," he said. In the dim light, I saw a warmth in his eyes.

"Hi," I answered. Quite simple and openly, we made some small talk about the ocean.

"How long you been in Provincetown?" I asked him.

"Three months. You?"

"Six hours."

"Boy, fresh off the boat."

"Bus."

"You ever been here before?" We began to walk closer to the tangled remains of wooden dock. It seemed to lead us to it. I felt the sexual romps of hundreds of men like us taking the same small adventure.

"You staying with anybody here?"

"Yeah, a friend just a few blocks away. It's nice."

"I work in a restaurant just up the road. You should come by." We were both in near darkness and holding hands.

"That'd be nice." I brought my face close to his. I was absolutely sure of his attraction to me. What was it, my newness to this place? The air? The ocean? Or was I so casually determined to make love with a guy that it was recognized and appreciated by him? Maybe it was just because the moon was full and the town was full of queers. Pretty good averages for anybody.

We kissed, then proceeded to feel the warmth under each of our T-shirts, the hardness growing between our legs, and the wet softness in each other's mouths. He was very nice and affectionate, and I was quite surprised to meet a guy so quickly.

We played it safe, kissing all over, occasionally a little sucking. His cock was thick for such a thin guy. His smooth skin was clean as if he'd just showered. After we fumbled with each other's shorts and got them down around our ankles, he knelt down to suck my rigid dork. I looked around through the canopy of rotting wood and saw three men approaching from different directions. Like dark apparitions, they were quickly under the dock with us, making out themselves, occasionally touching and grabbing our asses. Mike stood and we smiled at each other.

"Wasn't expecting company. Were you?" he whispered in my ear.

"No. It's like a Tom of Finland cartoon," I replied. And so it was. Two more guys mysteriously appeared. I felt a pair of hands on my butt, a finger nudging its way up into my asshole. I squirmed away, still kissing Mike while we tried to hold on to each other. It became a bit difficult, so many hands pumping on different cocks. At one point, some chubby guy greedily pulled my dick from Mike's grasp and aimed it at his pale bent over ass. I was suprised, then disgusted. Here in the darkness, some squatting idiot wants a strange cock up his ass, without so much as a hello.

I put my morals aside and smacked the anonymous ass. "Not without a rubber, big boy," I growled and turned back to Mike, who smiled while we resumed kissing. But the greedy fucker wouldn't take no for an answer, and turned around to kneel on the sand. He grabbed my dick once again from Mike's warm loving hands and clamped his wet lips around it, jamming my rod down his throat with a hungry ferocity.

"Watch the teeth, man," I hissed while I jacked Mike's dick and resumed licking his armpit. But once again the chubby sex fiend pulled me away, practically wrenching my dick from the root.

"Jesus!" I shouted, once again destroying the coersive silence of this seaside seven-man orgy. I pushed the face away, noticing thin blond hair and piggy little cheeks. The creature crawled over to a tall black-haired guy behind Mike and apparently got what he wanted, since he left me and my newfound buddy to finish each other off.

"You ready?" Mike whispered before licking behind my ear where my closely cropped hair brushed against his tongue.

"Yeah," I answered. "You?"

"Yeah," he said, leaning over to give me, near ready to burst, one last slurp. I did the same to him, then we both stood, pumping each other's spit-slicked gear shifts. I shot on his stomach. He spurted down between my legs. A droplet of my cum flew up between us and landed on his shoulder. We finished off while the other guys frantically jerked off to accompany the sight of us. I slurped another wet kiss on Mike and licked my own cum off his tanned chest. We held each other a few moments, while the rustled pumping of four other men surrounded us.

After the frenetics were dispensed with, the other men slunk off into the darkness. I held Mike's hand as he led me out from under the dock.

"Well, that was different," I commented. Mike smiled in a way that told me it wasn't so different if you lived here long enough. We walked up to the street, him holding his bike by the handle bars as the gears clicked.

"Well, you should come by the restaurant sometime," he repeated.

"I will," I said.

We kissed goodnight. I walked up Commercial Street as he rode off.

The next day I rented a bike. I went window shopping, rode around the park and the dunes, expecting to see scattered men fondling themselves in the bushes. No such luck. The boys of Provincetown were, for the most part, creatures of the night. Many were out in the day, but it seemed almost inappropriate to pursue them in the happy sunny streets littered with screaming children and potbellied parents.

Having gotten into the habit of P-town life, I did the usual things; went to the beach and watched the boys, swam, read a few chapters of *Eighty-Sixed*, then headed back into town and bought groceries for a light dinner. I showered. Sand gathered at the tub's basin. After drying off, I rubbed down with Aloe lotion, something I'd never tried before, but which later turned out to help my skin from becoming a serpentine nightmare of post-vacation flakes and peels. I ate, napped, and listened to a Callas greatest arias CD while Christopher, Bobby's lanky and cheerful roommate, and I cleaned up around the cottage.

That night we went to the A House, got a beer and quite agreeably split up. I didn't find anyone I wanted to meet, not that I was in hunt mode. After closing time Christopher

and I headed over to a party with two quite short and cute
Quebequois friends of Claude, their invisible roommate. We
smoked a joint on somebody's back porch. Jean Pierre, the
cuter and shorter of the two, shotgunned the joint and brought
his thick, quite kissable lips to mine. I couldn't help but meet
his lips quite lustfully, whereupon he removed the joint, gave
it to Christopher, and gave me a long wet kiss. He mumbled
something in clumsy English, thickly accented. I attempted to
respond in French.

"Excuse me?" he said. My language skills proved ineffectual.
His deep brown eyes glazed with a light pink tone from the pot.
He waltzed ahead of us, drunk and stoned, more a muse than
a good conversationalist.

"Ee says ee as a boyfrein, an das all ee can give you," the
other Quebequois explained as we walked through the darkened
streets. Other groups of gay men walked by at a distance in
giggling clumps. An occasional "Sister!" was heard above the
night quiet.

The party proved to be a bore. No beer and a very catty
crowd. The star and loudest guest was the local celebrity and
Marilyn impersonator, Jimmy Jolly, whose blaring Southern
Belle cadence ripped through the post-Edwardian rooming
house like an insane matron. As he waltzed past me, ignoring
our crowd in favor of a pair of drag queens with 45 records as
earrings, I felt something oddly familiar about him.

My thoughts were dashed when a tall boy in a "Shut up and
Dance" T-shirt tripped over someone's foot and spilled a beer
on me. No one offered to assist. Christopher had disappeared
and the Montreal twins were smoking cigarettes in the foyer.
I bid them adieu before storming out the door.

Walking down Commercial Street, I passed the last remnants
of the cruise circuit. This Disneyland had begun to resemble
Pinnochio's Playland, and all the boys were swiftly transforming
into jackasses. I was about to be run over by a jeep when, instead,
the guy slowed down and drove beside me as I walked.

"Hi," he said.

I looked. He wore black boots, jeans, a leather jacket, and
no shirt. Just what the doctor ordered, I thought, a quick fix
of purebred clone.

"Hi," I responded, leaning into his Jeep. We kept moving. His chest muscles perked under the jacket. One nipple displayed a small silver ring.

"I'm Ron. Where you going?" he asked.

I hopped into the passenger seat. "With you."

Thank you, John Rechy, wherever you are.

"It was awful what they did."

"They don't live here. They don't have to account for it."

". . . bringing in so much anger and leaving us to pay the damage."

The sign.

The god-damned wonderful sign.

Unfortunately, no party discussion excluded the events of the previous week's gay and lesbian pride march. Shops in the heart of Provincetown sold a variety of vulgarities:

"FUCK OFF, I'M ON VACATION!"

"IF YOU DON'T LIKE MY ATTITUDE,
DIAL 1-800-EAT-SHIT!"

The town authorities had no problem with the commercialization of profanity. But one sign, held up near the front of the parade by a lithe and serious young man, read "LEGALIZE BUTT-FUCKING." On the flip side he'd scrawled "LEGALIZE CLIT-LICKING." All factions of this queer Disneyland were swept into an uproar.

At three separate gatherings on three occasions I was cast as defendant of the very group I had come to vacation from. By the third encounter, I'd wrapped my defense up in a few words.

Bobby and I sat with Greg, our shaggy-haired overtanned host, on the porch of his rooming house. He, like many others, was outraged. I defended yet again.

"Anger that should have been focused on the creep who shot a guy with a BB gun was instead raged against someone using the march as a platform for an outspoken assertion of rights," I explained to Greg, who was on his third Cape Cod. Dozens of people casually walked by on the street in front of us.

"I don't care what they think," Greg asserted. "People here don't want us to be outspoken. They want, they want . . ."

Bobby broke in. "They want us to be entertaining or dead."

Greg glared at him, a picture of casual radicalism. Bobby's loose "READ MY LIPS" T-shirt disguised his quite muscular chest. The frayed edges of his white cutoffs daringly exposed a good deal of upper thigh. The best and most incongruous for P-town, his black army boots, were perched on the bannister, dirty with beach sand.

Bobby sipped his beer. "It's true. They want us prancing around like queens or nothing but statistics. Don't you get it? A guy was shot and you're whining about a piece of paper with a naughty word!"

"But it was the way they did it." Greg winced, sipping again at his pinkish cloud of a drink. "It was so tacky. Without any style."

"Do you like to fuck?" Bobby dropped his boots down off the porch railing. A gay couple on the street looked up at us.

"Well, yes, with the right guy," Greg nervously admitted.

"Do you know how many states you can't fuck in?"

"Honey, I can fuck wherever I want. You should see my little black book."

"Twenty-five," Bobby insisted. "Half the country makes it illegal for you to fuck. Do you give a shit about that?"

"No," Greg protested. "We've lived outside the law for this long. I'm just gonna live my life."

"When are you going to demand your rights?"

"After I get another drink," Greg sashayed off to the kitchen. "You need another?" he called out.

"No, thanks." I answered back.

Eager to change the topic, Bobby whispered in a low voice, "So, didja get lucky last night?"

I blushed. "Well, I guess so."

"Who was it?"

"Some guy in a jeep."

"Tell me, tell me," Bobby insisted.

"He took me back to his trailer park." I recalled the evening. His mobile home had displayed his warm and ordinary taste, like something out of Urban Cowboy. We'd spent a good time experimenting, Ron initiating me into a few bondage games.

"Ooh, how butch."

"Very. So were his toys," I preened.

"Such as . . ."

"Handcuffs."

"Ooh. I didn't know you were into that."

"Neither did I. But I couldn't resist."

"Was he really tough?"

"Pretty much. But it was all kind of ruined when I woke up the next morning and he made me breakfast in bed."

"He didn't."

"Well, he wanted to, but I told him I preferred to use a table."

Bobby laughed as the screen door slammed. Greg sat down in his lawn chair. His refilled glass tinkled with ice. "What's this gossip I'm missing?" Greg sniffed.

"Our guest is regailing his S/M adventures from last night."

"Aw, c'mon, it wasn't like that."

"No?" Greg queried.

"No, I expected to be tied up for two days and fucked beyond consciousness."

"You'd like that," Bobby chirped.

"Well, maybe not," I wondered. "But what was so funny about it, I was really in control the whole time. He did nothing but please me. It felt . . . like a play. Like, he kept telling me to react, and then I started making up all this silly, yessir, and no, sir, and it was just like being in a play. Performance doesn't get me off."

"But you got off."

"Oh, yeah," I admitted. "I released a lot of sexual hangups by finally trying it out."

"My, my, our city boy is getting his dance card filled right up."

"Must be the sea water," I yawned.

I came to Provincetown to have fun, get a tan, and get laid. I didn't expect to fall in love. But Bobby helped make it happen.

Wednesday we went to The A House about midnight. Although Bobby had to work that morning, he wanted to come with me for a quick beer. We went to the back bar, a tacky enclave decorated in fishing floats and nets. Cheesy blue and red lights gave the few men standing around a murky glow. Then I saw him, the bartender.

"Oh God. Who is he?" I whispered as we headed to the bar. He saw Bobby and smiled in recognition.

"His name's Mark. He has a boyfriend," Bobby murmured back to me.

"Shit."

We sidled up to the bar. I locked gazes with this tall brown-haired man – early twenties, probably. His eyes were clear, brooding like a soap opera star, with what seemed an Italian panther-like quality. His skin was clear and lightly tanned. A clean-shaven jaw did not disguise a dark outline of beard. His cleft chin below thin lips made my stomach flutter. But even his thick hairy arms and macho stance, his sturdy frame and brooding good looks could not disguise a quiet vulnerability under the strong frame. I wanted him.

"Hi, Mark." Bobie played Yenta. "Meet my old friend."

We shook hands over the bar. His palm was warm and thick.

"Hi."

"How ya doin?"

Chat and more chat. I forget what we said. Bobby kept it going so well. I could have kissed his feet for dodging my shyness, keeping this stud entertained by our silly conversation. It was after only a few minutes that Bobby said he had to get up in the morning.

"Well, I'm gonna stay a while," I said, sneaking a glance at Mark.

"Okay," Bobby relented, sensing my predatory claws at work. "See ya later."

It was near closing time. Happily, few guys came to Mark's bar while we talked. I felt like a schoolboy. He seemed nervous with me near him.

"So, you probably get hit on a lot, being a bartender." I said.

He paused, embarrassed. "I guess so."

"I do some bartending work when I do catering jobs."

"What, in New York?"

"Yeah. It's kind of awkward getting hit on. Especially when the guy's wife is at the other end of the room."

Mark's smirk grew into a laugh. There was a long pause. Go for it, I told myself. Go.

"So, how long are you here?" Mark asked.

"Till Friday."

"Not much time left."

"No. I better move move fast." He smiled. All systems go. "So, would you consider it rude if I asked to see you later?"

His mouth opened slightly, and before he answered, I saw him considering, weighing one of two options.

"No, not at all."

"I don't wanna push you." Except completely over the edge.

"No, that's OK. I just have to meet some friends."

"Oh, well, I could just come back tomorrow and bother you then."

"No, no."

Bobby had told me of the boyfriend. So what? Where was he? LA. Any real boyfriend wouldn't let this man out of his sight for a minute. Mark seemed resolved and looked about with an air of espionage. This was going to be fantastic, I could tell.

"You going to Spiritus?" he asked.

"If you are."

"See ya there?"

"OK."

It was closing time and the bar poured out with men eager for a match not yet made. I raced home on my bike, cleaned up and brushed my teeth. Christopher kindly lent me a pair of jeans for the cool weather.

I rode back to the center of the gay crowd around Spiritus Pizza. I stood straddling my bike, trying not to let my desperate anticipation show. A pair of hands touched my back.

"You changed." It was Mark. On the street I realized how much taller than me he was. We stood next to each other a few minutes, breaking up the awkwardness with a few moments of chat. He held a white plastic bag with some small package. "Tips." Mark explained. "All quarters."

As I smiled, I felt the whole crowd watching us. One after another of Mark's friends approached, filling us with useless banter. Go, I thought. Leave. One especially persistent guy, a small sandy-haired painter, made a lot of chat and for a long moment stared deeply into Mark's eyes, willing him to go with him. I saw a long history pass between them. Two weeks, maybe. Go away, I meditated while staring at the space on his forehead between his eyes.

He did leave, long enough for Mark to casually say, "So, ya wanna meet up later?"

"Sure," I chirped a bit too eagerly.

"What's yer address?"

"Twelve Cottage Street."

"How 'bout two-thirty?"

"Fine."

"I just gotta go to this party."

"Right. See ya then."

"I can't tell anybody. My boyfriend's flyin' into Boston day after tomorrow."

"I understand. See ya in a bit?"

"Yeah," he said, his hand grazing the back of my neck. I rode off. The wheels barely touched the ground.

Under the glow of the nearby streetlight, I waited in a lawn chair on the front porch. At two thirty-five I considered retreating to bed. I imagined what I would do if he didn't show up. Probably rent the entire cottage for the winter and grow dust like Miss Havisham. Why was I so crazy about this guy, having met him only hours before? Did we have anything in common? What was it, just his absolute beauty? I was a mess. My nervous mood, however, crested and settled as a tall lanky figure walked up the street in silhouette.

"Hi." It was Mark.

His body was a solid footballer's. I correctly figured him as a center. "Guess I always liked bending over for guys," he joked as we lay in bed afterward. Mark's torso was a solid muscular trunk, not at all gym defined, but made muscular naturally through sport. He said he hated the beach, the lazy aspect of it. "Haven't been sunbathing more than twice." Yet Southern Italian roots gave his skin a light olive brown color. His hands were strong and wide but soft from years of business school and summers bartending. His back was smooth and freckled, his chest was hairy. His legs and ass were a veritable forest, but smooth and dark, thick and shiny, unlike any man I'd loved. Use Tony Stefano in The Pizza Boy, He Delivers as a reference point. Searching through the dark areas around his thigh and butt for the tight ring that made him hum with pleasure, I realized how many years it had been since I'd wanted to get so intimate with a man. It was because he was clean and so responsive and, I don't know, because he was him.

A great part of Mark's charm was his naivety. He didn't know when I was quoting Oscar Wilde, and didn't care. But he knew how to make love. He knew how to kiss.

"You've got a wide mouth," he smiled, our spit shiny on his lips after he'd been burrowing his tongue down my throat. "You, too," I agreed and resuming intensely sucking face.

"I wanna fuck you," he said, his middle finger slipping in and out of my ass. "Then I want to you to fuck me. Hard."

"Got any rubbers?" I asked.

"Nope. Sorry."

"I'll have to go shopping."

"Nothing's open at five in the morning."

"Later, then."

We did want to fuck without rubbers. We even went so far as to give each other an unprotected jab up the ass, just to feel it.

"Tempting, isn't it?" he sighed, perched atop me, my jutting dick aching for him to sit on me again.

"Uh huh," I moaned, my cock nestled between his furry buns. He hovered over me and growled. A tiny part of his left green eye was flecked with yellow.

It must have been the impossibility of our continuing any love that made him so attractive. We rushed through 12 hours together, knowing that his boyfriend's arrival and my departure loomed over, separating us with its shadow.

Something else connected us while cultural differences left

chasms. He licked my body exactly the way I wanted and I responded to him. There was none of the fidgeting and fighting for positions. We fit each other like two baseball gloves.

By eight the next morning, we hadn't slept. We talked a lot, about the gay and lesbian pride march, about politics, being out. Mark was quite comfortable being "discreet" about his sexuality back in Boston. Perhaps his conservative exterior helped enliven his bedroom behavior. It was his major form of release.

He'd sucked my dick like it was the last popsicle on earth. Then we'd kissed like newlyweds, jerking each other to moaning crests of orgasm. I'd come three times, he four. We took showers and walked down to shore.

We didn't leave the house til noon. Near the docks watching a few motor boats set out to sea and separate, I leaned my thigh against him as we sat on an overturned dinghy. We ate peaches for breakfast. I watched the juice dribble down his chin. His profile was an amalgam of dozens of men I'd fallen for from life and the movies, most of them straight. Was it the thought of having some top-shelf-before-unreachable pleasures that made him so attractive? He knew football better than any man I'd ever kissed. He was the objectified jock made real. I imagined us sharing a house somewhere in Gay Family Land. He invites his buddies over to watch the game. I try to comprehend a pass interference. That night we go to a multimedia performance art show and I explain to him the uses of Decontructivism in Post-Modern art. Then we hop into bed and hump like rutting buffalo for hours upon hours.

We sat in silence by the water. A fisherman pulled in, finishing his day at sea. It should have been October. I was that melancholy.

"What are you thinking?" Mark leaned toward me. The yellow fleck in his eye was lost in water reflections.

"I'm thinking I miss you already," I admitted. He blushed and looked down, putting his hand on my thigh a moment. It seemed a brave move for him, being gay in daylight. He looked out at the water. I glanced up at his face, the combination of musculature, bone structure, Italian and Polish blood that gave him the burden of stunning good looks. Given another night with him I would experience a special bliss, the removal of which mutates into tragic obsession.

"Let's go get some food," one of us suggested.

We sat across a wobbly table wolfing down omelettes and home fries. "This is good," I commented.

"Yup. Best breakfast in town."

"Outside of you." He blushed and gulped down his orange juice.

I looked over at a small herd of children arguing over the last piece of toast. Their mother, at a table on the other side, glanced at her kids and mumbled to her husband, "If we sneak out quick, do you think we can lose them?"

We paid and left a healthy tip. I wondered what gorgeous creature would have emerged if between us our love could procreate.

"So, ya wanna meet up again?" Mark asked. My stomach flipped.

"Sure!" I said a bit too quickly. He had to work for a few hours getting beer and booze set up at the bar. We agreed to meet at four near his house. Once again he had the opportunity to say goodbye and had instead invited me back into his arms.

"We're gonna have to try and sleep. I gotta work tonight."

"Right. Sleep. I remember that."

"Well, where have you been?" quizzed Bobby as I snuck into the cottage by the side door. He sat at the kitchen table spooning jelly out of a jar and onto a piece of peanut buttered pita bread while chatting into a cordless phone. The Indigo Girls crooned from his CD player.

"Guess," I said slyly.

"No!" he gasped.

"Yes." I assured him.

"Mark Gentile?" he cried in mock astonishment.

"Don't tell anybody." I warned.

"How was he?" he queried. For lack of appropriate words, I simply mock-fainted to the floor, lay on my back, and stretched out my arms, ready for crucifixion.

"Are you OK?" Bobby peered over the table at me.

I lay spent. "I'm in love."

"How horrible." He spoke into the phone. "Amanda's invited us to dinner."

"I can't. I'm seeing someone."

"Mark?" Bobby exclaimed.

I nodded.

"Again?"

I nodded.

"Oh, nothing," Bobby told Amanda over the phone. "He just bagged the P-town god hunk-in-residence."

The moment I finished locking my bike on the corner street, Mark was standing behind me. It must have been the sea water.

Once again entering his rooming house, I felt a strange comfort. The lumbering white building began to feel like home. Mark pointed over to a clump of plastic bead necklaces in several colors. They hung on a wooden hat post connected to a hall mirror.

"Got those from all the parties at the A House. Different color each week."

"What color is this week?" I watched his fine ass press against his jeans as we headed up the stairs. I reached out and squeezed him.

"White." I'd seen the posters around town. Elizabeth Taylor in a black and white beach still from *Suddenly Last Summer*.

I closed his door after we entered his room. "I'm gonna be gone, though."

"Really?" I asked, unfastening his jeans. I peeled the denim down to expose his white Jockey shorts and hairy muscular thighs. His hardon pointed out through the fly.

"Meeting my boyfriend in Boston."

"Oh. That's right." I lay back on the bed. The sheets were stained with the previous night's joys. I looked up at him.

"What's the matter?" he asked.

"Nothing. Nothing. I just have to take as much of you as I can, right?"

"Yup," he said as he fell down over me on the big bed.

We didn't sleep this time either. We went further. As I began to lick and caress his body, he responded with abandon, at least within the AIDS-imposed limits.

"Guess what?" I murmured between kisses.

"What?" His lips smacked my cheek, then my neck.

"I went shopping."

It took him a moment to get the joke, but he did, broke into a wide smile, and leaned over to rustle into my bag for the rubbers. I looked at his firm furry butt and thought of the hundreds of hours I'd spent watching TV football games, cherishing the moments when the quarterback's hands dug into his center's bent over ass. I didn't know it then, but months, even years later, I wouldn't be able to watch a single play without thinking of Mark.

As he bent over the bed searching for my newly bought condoms, I was reminded of a poster of Burt Reynolds, whose ass was damn near as furry as Mark's. Something about the anticipation of fucking is almost as good as the act itself.

For the next few hours, we burrowed into each other with absolute passion. Him first in me, then me in him, wrong way on the bed. His head kept knocking against the wooden foot board, but he didn't seem to mind. I was close to coming when I slipped out and the awful smell of shit took over the room. Embarrassed, he tossed me a towel and we headed off to the bathroom, tiptoing naked down the hallway, wary of his nosey landlord. The sight of me tagging after Mark, my shitty rubbercoated boner bobbing about, would have no doubt sent her into shock.

Clean from the shower, we returned to bed and lay down. We lay quietly, me on top of him. He continued his occasional humming purrs while we shared more post-fuck kisses. The sounds he made were of pleasure, but also somewhat removed, as if he were surveying the situation and it met with his approval.

His clock alarm buzzed. Eight-thirty p.m. "I have to get ready for work," he said. I felt a pang of dread. I was drawn back to his age of 22, of the painful crushes and waves of obsessive love that I thought I had since conquered.

While he went to the toilet, I dressed and scanned the room; so simple, almost like a set. Sunlight bled through the shades of the bay window with an artificial bronze.

I snuck a look into his bedside drawer. In a Photo Hut envelope were pictures. I took them out. Mark standing on a deck. Mark sitting in a lawn chair. In an apartment eating food with two other men. Drinking a beer with one other, obviously the boyfriend, a small darkhaired, slightly balding man with what looked like a built-up gym body. Fine. You can have him. Mark says you're a big record executive. I'll just melt every tape I have with your company's logo on it. I'll just take your picture and curse you with a voodoo doll.

I calmed down and selected a picture of Mark alone with a green bottle of beer in his hand. His eyes looked at the camera, calm, indolent and inadvertently seductive. I dropped the snapshot into my bag and put the rest of the pictures back in the drawer.

He returned moments later wrapped in a white towel. I kissed him again and left my number on a piece of paper. He seemed surprised but didn't offer his number in return. I didn't ask, didn't want to push him.

"Come to New York," I said more like a command than an invitation. He didn't answer. I walked around the bed to the door, backing out. I wanted my last image of him like that, standing like some deeply loved college frat brother, naked but for a white towel. I wanted that to be the end.

But he invited me back to the bar that night. "I'll buy you a beer."

I didn't want to go back, but I couldn't say no. I nodded and closed the door, stepping quietly down the stairs. On my way out, I noticed once again the several plastic Mardi Gras beads hanging on the wooden hatpost. I picked out a lavender one, put it around my neck and stepped out in the sun. Halfway down the block I turned and saw him standing at the window, wearing shorts, watching me like a Bruce Weber model in an Edward Hopper painting.

In the cluttered back bar of the Atlantic House, Jimmy Jolly was fending off a drunken fan. "Honah, go off and partay," he bellowed. Two other queens argued over who was next in line at Mark's bar. As I approached, he saw me and we stared at each other through them all. Near the cash register stood

David, an ex-model, and his cute friend whose name slipped my mind. I'd met them both the previous night. Bobbie called David and his friend Mark's two biggest "groupies." David, whose lean frame made him look somewhat British, remarked about wanting to bear Mark's children. I had laughed, vowing never to go that far for a man.

"So, I come back and you're still here," I joked with them, avoiding Mark until his bitching customers left.

"Yes, a day later and no better," David remarked.

"Twenty-four little hours," I half sang, glancing back to Mark, who winked at me. It was ten to one. A day ago we'd never met.

"You know, you're right about him," David said slyly, glancing to Mark.

"About what?" I asked suddenly vulnerable.

"Children. I want to bear seven of his." He smiled and put his cigarette to his lips. David bummed one. I became clouded in smoke. Before leaving, I said, "I've already considered converting back to Catholicism."

Leaving he and his friend laughing, I sidled up to Mark's bar. He lit an incense to defray the stink of the nearby septic tank.

"Hi there," he said.

"'Lo."

"How are you?" he asked, as if we'd never met. His eyes, however, betrayed a warm sincerity.

"I hear you're giving away free beers."

"For a special few." We spoke just out of range of David and what's his name, but I figured they could tell that the tone was intimate. He handed me a cold Heineken. I gulped it down.

We spoke lightly of plans and plane trips, all of it awkward and superfluous. The blathering of arguing men rose over the Donna Summer music from the dance floor. This time it was for real. I hated being in that bar again. I hated owing the bar for presenting this beautiful man for my too brief indulgence.

I had to leave. Taking a final gulp of his free beer, I set it down. "This hurts too much. I gotta go."

"Oh, well, uh . . ." He extended his hand, which hours before had massaged the most sensitive and private parts of my body. I held it, our last contact.

". . . take care." His eyes brightened.

"Come to New York," I said, now more of an incantation than a command.

He said something as I released his hand. I couldn't hear it over the bellowing of the ubiquitous Jimmy Jolly, who burst into an chillingly precise impersonation of Cher.

I walked out of the bar, bidding David and his friend goodbye. At the end of the sea junk-strewn bar, I turned back. Mark and I shared a last glance through the corridor of drinkers. More men crowded the bar, demanding alcohol and attention. He seemed caught, a life time prisoner in a kissing booth.

That night I dreamt. Mark sat in a long fishing boat, just offshore. The dusk sky burned fiery red with wisps of ripped cotton clouds. I wanted to throw a football I'd found on the beach to him, but stood ankle deep in the water. The rocks were hard and sharp. My feet hurt. I couldn't move. He watched me, raising his arm to catch, drifting out into the bay.

The next night Bobby and I went to tea dance at the Boatslip. Usually the thought of a tea dance made me cringe. Overeager men and women dancing in daylight? How absurd! But I only had one day left, and decided to go for the full P-town experience. Bobby seemed up for it. I was up for anything that could help me start forgetting Mark.

"What time does it end?"

"Six-thirty."

"What time is it now?"

"Five-thirty."

"Let's go." We biked down to the Boatslip, a bland rectangular motel on Commercial Street. We locked up at a fence post next to two other bikes.

"Let's just use your lock," I suggested.

"Well, that's not positive thinking. What if you meet somebody?"

"Please," I assured Bobby. "I'm not gonna need it for quite a while."

"OK." We used Bobby's steel chain lock and walked down the driveway. A donation bucket sat near the entrance. We ignored it. Bobby wasn't drinking, but I got a Cape Cod with too much cranberry juice and nary an aura of vodka. The pink-Izod-shirted waiter skipped off without giving me change, assuming he was worth the 75 cent tip.

We were both tired, but watched the men and women. The hotel boardwalk setting reminded me of Fort Lauderdale; tacky and loud. People purposelessly stood on the boardwalk and danced inside the glass doors while Madonna told us to express ourselves.

"Ya wanna go to the White Party tonight?" Bobby asked.

"I dunno. Maybe not."

"Oh, is it because of Mark?"

"No, no. He's in Boston." I sighed. Probably kissing his rich boyfriend hello right now.

"Oh."

"I just didn't bring those white hot jeans I bought in Montreal."

"Well, you can wear some of mine."

"Really?" I began to cheer up.

"Sure. I've got some hot little white cutoffs." Bobby spotted an especially handsome Portuguese that he'd met before. "Let's walk around."

Men of all kinds stood and leaned in pre-dusk hunt mode. There were less younger men, it seemed. Most were probably still at work, or in transition, between beach and bar, eating or sleeping.

As we sauntered about, a tanned and hugely muscular guy said "Hi" to me. Bobby, once again scenting a mating ritual, was quick to exit. "I'll see ya," he demured as the muscle man approached. He was older, about 35, slightly balding, which added to his good looks. His tight white shirt complemented his deep tan, thick arms and melon-sized pecs. The outline of his penis dangling between the legs of his blue sweat pants seemed more appropriately sized for a small horse.

"I'm John." he said.

Of course you are.

We shook hands. The chat was the usual, if not a bit impetuous on his part. I noticed he began to grow erect, as did I. A New York staying for the summer, John told me I was cute.

"Thank you. You're amazing."

"You here for the summer?"

"Naw, leaving tomorrow."

"Shit. That's too bad. I'm really horny and I wanted to get fucked." My cock tensed in my jams.

"What's stopping you?"

"Uh, I gotta friend I'm supposed to meet. I'll get back to you." And off he went.

The fuck. Probably hits on a dozen guys to get a boner, then just takes the best offer. The direct approach can be charming if you're chosen, but it's another thing when you're dumped like an overripe avocado.

An acquaintance from Jersey City sidled up to me, having just arrived and chatting with enthusiasm. I forgot his name but listened distractedly as he recanted his trek from New York. I glanced over his shoulder as John the muscle man talked up a lanky blond twinkie much cuter than myself. The prospect of plunging into that mass of flesh made me practically reel with excitement. If that horse-dicked muscle man, with possibly the bedroom etiquette of a goat, couldn't help me forget Mark and those damn thumpings in my chest every time I thought of him, then nothing could.

After a few darted exchanges, and after visiting the hotel room of a half-dozen beer drinking macho gays on a balcony overlooking the tea dance (Bobby's extended invitation), I spotted the muscle man hovering near the exit.

"Hey, Hercules, didja find yer friend?" I was already imagining my white sperm jettisoning into the valleys between his tanned pecs.

"Yes," he smiled apologetically, bouncing from a steroid rush, no doubt. I could have punched him.

"Life is full of little disappointments." I glanced down at his crotch. "And big ones."

"Well, maybe I'll see you in New York," John said, flexing his pecs.

"Yeah, right." And you'd probably dump me then, too.

I cheerfully waved him off, simultaneously charmed and insulted.

That night at the White Party I danced with abandon in Bobby's racy pair of white cutoffs. I tried to shake off the hatred thrown at us by a clump of straight kids in a Camaro that had nearly run us over on our way to the bar. One of them shouted, quite simply, "Die!"

I also tried to avoid the back bar and thoughts of Mark. That was next to impossible until Bobby introduced me to a nun.

"This is Sandy."

"Sister Betrell to you," the nun allowed me to kiss his hand. Yet another of Bobbie's dozens of friends from New York, Sandy was planning to win first prize in the costume contest.

"You simply must fly me. Bobby says you're a choreographer."

"Well, no, actually . . ."

"Perfect. Now, let's just get that other hunk over here. Daniel!" After corraling Daniel (who did not know anyone, but was coerced for his well-developed upper body and good looks alone), Christopher, Bobby and I to the back outdoor area by the pool, Sandy/Sister Betrell coached us into lifting him above our heads in a stately fashion. We jokingly led him to the pool and nearly dunked him, but didn't.

"Now, you all just stay here. I'll get you all beers." With that he skirted off into the bar, bopping queer heads with his Sally Field headgear. I ended up sitting on a bench with Daniel.

"He certainly is festive," Daniel said, somewhat amazed by it all. It turned out he had good reason to be amazed. As we talked, awaiting our call for the contest, the facts I coaxed out of him were these: he was a conservative lawyer from L.A. (which prompted some good chat about the TV show, "No, it's not always like that"), he had a strict Catholic upbringing (which prompted more funny jokes about Sandy's Sister Bertrell getup), and he was here for the first time and hadn't been laid ("I'm staying with relatives, so it's a little difficult"). I liked him, and he seemed interested in my radical activities in New York. I craved his impressive musculature, having been recently dumped by John the steroid case and still going through fresh pangs of Mark withdrawal. I was determined that we both enjoy each other's company and bodies later that night. I owed it to Bacchus and Dionysos for showing me such a good time.

The contest provided lots of distraction. The drag queens were done up to perfection. There was a floating wedding cake, a swan that lit up and a white Christmas tree. The swan won first prize, the cake second, and Sandy won third. We whirled him about on the dance floor with abandon. He tried to give us his prize, a gallon bottle of Absolut, but none of us were real drinkers, so he ended up leaving it on the pool table. After a slow dance and another drink, I took Daniel by the hand and led him out of the bar and into the night.

After driving around for a half an hour in his aunt's Lincoln Continental trying to find a place to park and make out, Daniel and I settled for a back road near the beach. It was quite clumsy going. He wasn't small, and our clothes kept getting caught on window handles and door locks. Finally we skulked off to the beach itself, where, without the benefit of a blanket, we made out, kneeling in front of each other, pants around our ankles, tugging on dicks and licking and kissing.

"There's something about you, something devilish."

"No," I corrected him. "The devil is hate. This is love." I licked his buxom and smooth pectorals. "And this is love." I leaned down and licked his penis, hard now and arcing back and forth.

We fumbled through gnats and passing headlights, and finally both came, Daniel a bit furtively. He didn't seem comfortable with the situation, but moaned lightly and bit down hard on my shoulder, almost crying as he came. It was quite messy and terrific, like high school might have been.

He drove me back to 12 Cottage Street and we made out some more in the car. At four in the morning, I let him go, driving slowly down the quiet street. I fumbled in the darkness to the living-room couch and fell immediately to sleep, the smell of Daniel still on my body.

The bus back to Boston was an hour late, so despite the cool weather, I took the boat. On the first deck, over a dozen gay men sat at the polished wood tables and benches. A frail Asian and cute muscled blond sporting a crewcut with a tail compared Boston bar experiences. A trio of three older gay men sat a few benches away, grinning approval.

I had a cheeseburger and a beer, then stood up on the deck, watching the faint brim of P-town disappear in an ocean grey line. A seagull hovered, awaiting scraps. Having packed neither a sweater or long pants, my body shivered. I hadn't come prepared for the cold.

I hadn't come at all prepared.

In Provincetown I made love to four men in five days. After returning home I didn't have more than a date in two months, and he didn't invite me over because he had to "go to work in the morning." Men in New York are like rats: skittish. You have to back them against a corner to get a reaction.

Daniel sends a card now and then. I'm going to LA this summer. I'll see him. It'll be nice. Ron the Jeep leather clone came to New York last month. We had some fun. Bobby and I got arrested together at an ACT UP demo. I saw John the muscle man outside Video Blitz. Naturally he didn't recognize me. He was with his wife.

I sent three postcards to Mark at his rooming house. He never gave me his address in Boston. I called information for a number. Two phone machines and one old guy who could barely speak English. The other was unlisted.

Last week I lost the lavender Mardi Gras beads dancing at Mars.

A LETTER FROM PARIS

Will Leber

Dear M –

Does it sound presumptuous to say that I find Paris boring?

Well, I did until tonight: I have something very exciting to tell. I'm up at one-thirty a.m. writing to you because I just have to tell someone. Perhaps I can inspire a sexy scene in your new novel?

I am still kind of shaking and I'll *never* be able to tell Robert. Mr Investment Banker is still out on the *Bâteaux-mouches* entertaining clients with a fancy dinner while they cruise down the Seine. Honey, take my advice, never marry a businessman – especially a salesman! There – I've called Robert the s-word – well, what does he do but peddle hype?

If you must marry, go for an intellectual professor type, or a union electrician; a man who puts in a day's work and doesn't need to entertain old farts all the night long. Or, marry someone like me, a high-school English teacher with three months of summer vacation.

Robert and I have been coming here – what? – twice a year for the last few years. I feel like I'm almost a Parisian. I no longer want to see any museums, I tend to simply search out the best pastry shops and order up a feast of fat. I can easily consume five of those luscious, lascivious little tarts – raspberry, strawberry, kiwi, chocolate and hazelnut. Even though I do 50 sit-ups every morning, it's a wonder that I haven't ballooned.

After breakfast, I wander and watch the Parisians parade while Robert is off playing at business.

You know, I really don't speak any French. I quit even trying. I've found a couple of words can get me far enough. To order my sweets I need only point and say, "*un, deux,* or *trois.*" And – this may be the most scandalous confidence I've given you yet – I've taken to eating my dinner at McDonald's! Well, the food is always served hot and I can eat as slowly or quickly as I like. There isn't a waiter to deal with and I don't feel out of place. I don't feel lonely at McDonald's.

I digress: where I'm eating in Paris is not nearly as interesting as where I'm doing the nasty.

After promenading by myself down the Champs-Elysées this morning and tramping through the Louvre all afternoon, I felt like – meeting – someone. Of course I knew where to go: I had read in the Spartacus guide about the legendary gay cruising scene at dusk along the banks of the Seine. I exited the Louvre and set off across the Tuileries Gardens toward the river.

As I walked down the gravel path through the garden I passed near a bald man reclined on a bench with a newspaper covering his lap. He stared at me like Rasputin. Strange magnetic powers pulled at me. I fled toward the water. He followed.

Have I told you the French slang for cruising? *Drague* – it literally means dredging, scraping the bottom. I stopped at the river's edge and watched the barges and tour boats glide by. Could Robert's boat have passed at the moment Rasputin came along the pathway and stood beside me? He took my hand; he offered no verbal greeting, just took my hand and pressed my open palm against his hard cock. The heat passed right through his wool trousers. But – dare

I say? – I was not impressed. Was it because he expected me to be?

Men and their dicks. French men and their dicks. French men and their *uncut* dicks. I go into the *pissoirs* and I have the worst time peeing. All the French men check out every other man's equipment. Always. All of them. Their dicks are very important to them. They never just haul it out and piss. They unwrap it, fondle it, stroke it, for God's sake they even talk to it. They hold it cupped in their hand before they pee and admire it, no, they adore it. And they hold it there for the rest of the row to see. Oh, and did I mention that they all wear wedding rings? Even the most fey fags in the gay bars wear wedding rings. I once asked a Frenchman about all the wedding rings. He said that in Catholic-France you must be married by the time you graduate from college, you must.

And they are all uncut; I said that already, right? And I am snipped, a typical and obvious American at the urinal. Anyway, I've seen so many assignations in the *pissoir*. They don't go home to do it – wedding rings mean wives and children – and so often they all live with their inlaws! That's why the river banks and the parks and the dark alleys serve the Pope so well.

So, back to the bald guy. Can you spell j-a-d-e-d? It all felt too predictable; typical urban queer, vapid, pee-pee sucking in the bushes. No. I needed something more intriguing to make me break my vows to Robert. Yes, I know that *you* know I've broken them before. But shouldn't each time be worth it?

I had some hope Rasputin might work out, mostly because I'd never had sex with a Frenchman – until tonight. Read on!

I walked away from baldy toward the Eiffel Tower. Up ahead, I saw a pack of young boys with shaved heads emerge from beneath the shadow of a bridge. I had a brief fantasy about having a *ménage* with them. Decided it might be more of a mugging, so I turned and walked the other way.

I decided to go to happy hour at the most popular gay

bar in Paris – the Quetzal. When you open the door to the place a huge plume of cigarette smoke escapes and if you're lucky a couple of drunks fall out allowing you enough room to squeeze in. It's always packed with the most international crowd I've ever seen. Every language is being spoken around you. Oh, and the beer is total rot-gut, but cheap, and nothing is cheap in Paris. So the beer-bust is extremely popular – mass psychotic consumption, instant brain-death. I struck up a conversation with an Irish guy, named Paddy – tell the truth – who is teaching English in Paris. He suggested we try a video bar nearby.

I bought Paddy a beer and excused myself to use the restroom. It was in the basement and I headed down a rickety spiral stairway. The basement was quite dark. Its only light came from the single bare lightbulb inside the *pissoir* at the far end. I headed toward the light and heard the muted moans and slurps of mansex in the dark recesses beside me. As I peed a dark-complexioned man, perhaps 32 years old (our age!), slid in beside me. I glanced toward him and he smiled. A big smile.

It was the smile that made me hesitate outside the *pissoir*. OK, it wasn't the smile. It was my desperation to be desired. When he came out, he scooped me up and led me off into the dark. He pulled me against his chest and French-kissed me like a vacuum cleaner on high. His full, thick lips cushioned his assault. I searched for his penis, unzipped it from it's confinement and fondled it. I pulled the foreskin back from the head and swirled my thumb in his precum. I was tempted to taste it, but he suddenly swooned and fell back away from me. He wimpered, "Ooh," and creamed in my palm. It was that quick.

"*Pardon,*" I said, as if I had accidentally jostled him on the crowded Métro. I wiped my hands on my jeans, climbed the twisted stairs and left the bar without saying goodbye to Paddy.

I was tanked. I weaved my way to the hotel. I stopped in the lobby bathroom to wash up before going up to our room. I expected to find Robert back from the cruise. It was just after midnight. No Robert. Just that empty room: two chocolates staring up at me from the pillows of the turned-back bed. I sat down and devoured the chocolates. *Fuck him*, I thought. *If he's still out, I'll go back out*. And I already knew where I was going to go: the Banque Club.

The Banque Club's ad in the Spartacus promised "*action sur quatre étages*." Yes, Charlotte, a sex club on four floors!

I was already on the street by the time I checked my pockets for cash. I had only 90 francs. The ad said the admission to the club was 60 francs. I clearly could not afford a taxi. I did, however, still have several tickets for the Métro. I rushed to the subway.

A train pulled up immediately, heading in the proper direction. I jumped on and then began to worry about catching the subway back to the hotel. As you may know, the Métro in Paris is not open all night like in New York. It was nearly twelve-thirty when I got off at the station a few blocks from the club.

I decided to ask at the ticket booth when the Métro closed. At that moment a stalky man came up to the door at the side of the booth. He shook the three large key rings hanging from his belt, searching for the key to the lock in front of him. It made quite a commotion. I'm certain he carried a hundred keys. I took him to be the stationmaster and I tried my sentence of broken French on him, "À quelle heure c'est fermé le Métro?"

He appeared of peasant stock. If most Parisian men resemble baguettes, I'd call him a *bâtard*.

He spoke a couple of sentences to me in French. I launched into a mixture of French and English. He raised his bushy eyebrows and then mustered a bit of English, "You go where?"

"République," I answered, indicating the Métro stop of my hotel.

My answer seemed to please him. He grinned at me. I suddenly imagined myself driving dusty roads, lost in the *campagne*. I saw him walking over to my car from the grapevines he'd been tending before I stopped. Like a good country person, he isn't satisfied with pointing out directions. He wants me to come and rest in the shade with the family, have a glass of wine, before I go on.

The stationmaster laid a hand on my shoulder and told me in French the time the last train to République would leave his station. Somehow I was experiencing a delay in any comprehension of the French language. I stared at him dumbfounded. I remind you, I was drunk.

He saw my confusion and led me over to the clock above the booth's window. Keeping his right hand on my shoulder he pointed with his left to the clock. He actually had to do a little jump to reach the clock and point to the hour hand and the number one and then with another leap to the minute hand and the number five. Each leap was accompanied by an excited timpani of keys, as if to underscore the importance of his gestures.

"*Merci, merci bien.*" I nodded my thanks to him as he let go of me.

"*Plus tard.*" He waved as I left.

The Banque Club did not have a sign out front. I found the street number on what looked to be a closed three-story office building. It had a steel gate before the entrance painted in a black lacquer matching the trim around the windows of the brick walls. Flowering geraniums cascaded from the ground-floor window boxes.

I waited across the street until I saw a lone man with jet-black hair ring the bell and be buzzed inside. I followed right behind him and I too was buzzed in. In front of me was a coatcheck separated from a television lounge area by a little counter atop which sat a bowl of condoms. Obviously, I was in the right place. An older gentleman sat on a sofa smoking and carrying on a conversation with the cute *mec* (that's the French word for fag) who took my jacket and my money. He paid me little mind and I considered asking him if the condoms were free. I thought I could muster the French, but I felt mute. I could have asked in English, I'm sure he'd have understood, but I decided I didn't need condoms anyway. I certainly wasn't going to be doing any fucking. But then, I thought, maybe

I should have some for sucking. I still am never quite sure that it is safe to suck, you know? I also – I am kind of embarassed to say it – thought maybe I should have a condom in case I wanted to suck a French dick. Well, it may be hard to believe, but I'd never sucked an uncut dick before – and well, you know, smegma.

But I didn't ask and I didn't take a condom.

I looked around the dimly lit room for the stairway. It was just beyond the counter and to my surprise it headed down, not up. Now I was getting revved. Three *étages* of basement – how dark, how dirty, how cool!

I headed down to the first level. Walls painted flat black. Dim lighting. I checked my watch. I had twenty minutes. Light flickered out into the landing from behind a set of barroom doors. I pushed through them into a long, eerie room where an American porno video played on a large screen. Empty. I continued down to the *-2 étage*.

A maze of small cubicles clustered in the center of the space. I went down a hallway. Many of the doors were closed and I noticed they had locks. In several open doorways men leaned with erections obvious beneath the tent of their pant legs. Inside one cubicle a fragile young man crouched on his haunches. He stuck his index finger into his mouth to indicate his desire to suck my dick. A bare-chested *mec* stepped into the hall. He resembled Tin-Tin, France's popular kid's cartoon detective: big eyes, a boyish body, and a shock of hair standing in the center of his forehead. He opened his trousers, pointed his dick at me and pulled the foreskin back from the head. It winked at me like an eye.

I now feared any encounter which might require me to speak. I worried that if I entered one of these rooms I might be asked a question. I felt like a tongue-tied tourist, taking in sights but unable to converse.

I descended toward the *-3 étage*. About halfway down the flight of stairs it became pitch black. No light at all. I clutched the handrail and felt with my toes for each step down. Luckily, when I reached the bottom someone struck a match. The room illuminated briefly. The man lighting his cigarette leaned against a wall inside an area bounded by prison bars which could be entered through an open iron gate directly in front of me.

The flare of the match gave me just enough time to reach the entrance before the room returned to darkness. Where the flame had been I now saw the red tips of two cigarettes. I stopped just inside and clung to the bars behind me. Sliding a little farther along the bars, I bumped into a nice hairy, muscled forearm. I froze. There was something scampering across my feet. *Rats*, I thought, and I wanted to scream. But I remained silent. It touched my foot again. I pulled my feet together. One of the smokers struck a match and I looked down at a greasy black haired mop of a head nestled at my feet. The head tongued my boots, hands appeared to caress my ankles. I kicked him away like a noisome puppy.

Back in darkness, a hand landed like a spider on my right tit. Eight legs scurried across my chest. The rat crawled up my leg. A glowing cigarette ember traveled toward me from across the cell. The furry forearm unbuckled my jeans, burrowed into my underwear and wrestled with my hard-on. Fingers snaked along my arms. My T-shirt peeled up from my abdomen. My pants slipped down to my ankles. A mustachioed mouth engulfed my penis. I couldn't decide if this was heaven or hell – if I was being worshipped or eaten. Oh how I wished I'd had a pack of matches!

I pulled up my pants, felt my way to the door, and crawled on all fours up the stairs out of the dark. I felt I had blown my last chance for the night. It was already time for me to go catch my train.

It was a few minutes before one when I entered the Métro. On the opposite platform the stationmaster appeared. Rattling his keys he shouted to the few people waiting for a train. Apparently, they'd missed the last outbound train for he chased them all out of the station. He looked at me briefly and I felt proud that I'd done as I was told and made it back before the last inbound train.

A handful of people waited on my side: a fat woman carrying shopping bags, a stick woman carrying a Chanel clutch and three dark men speaking some Arabic language.

I settled against the wall near the wide hallway that led away from the trains to the escalator out of the station. Behind me I heard the barage of jingling that accompanied the stationmaster as he walked. Then I heard one loud jangle like a tambourine. Moments later, another tambourine hit. I turned around and saw the stationmaster slide behind an open door. I heard the tambourine again. I turned and saw his shaggy head stick out from behind the door. He caught my eye, jerked his chin upward and disappeared again. I knew instinctively what was happening. But it was happening to someone else, not me.

I walked down the hall until I was opposite the doorway. He stood in the jamb and motioned me in. I slipped by him and he shut the heavy steel door.

The stationmaster unbuckled his dirty khaki pants and heaved out a heavy, red, swollen, uncut dick. He stirred his hands in the air, tapped my belt and then grabbed his penis and stroked it. Then he pointed at me and shook his head up and down. I understood and I exposed my dick and began to massage it. I reached out to touch his cock, but he slapped my hand away. He pounded his penis and gesticulated to me to catch up. I got into it – the doing it in a little electrical closet with a man about to go home to the family, a man with a flabby stomach, a wedding ring, an unkempt mustache, an uncut club of a dick and a clattering chorus of keys to the whole place. I got hard.

I wanted to bite his tits so I moved nearer to him. He pulled back, then smiled, pointed to his penis and said, "Suck?"

This couldn't be happening to me, it was happening to someone else, someone willing to kneel and stick their tongue inside the little glove of skin surrounding the glans, someone keen on the smell of a workingman's sweaty groin, someone whose destiny was to live a porn fantasy.

His dick slid down my throat like buttery *escargot*. I swallowed, but it lodged there, cutting off my air. I gagged and coughed it up. He looked down at me with a lurid leer.

He shoved it back in and face-fucked me hard, in a hurry. His keys clashed against my right ear. Unexpectedly, he pulled my mouth off his dick with a hand in my hair. He forced my lips against his salty balls. I watched his foreskin slide up-down, up-down, up-down, over his cockhead as he frantically jerked himself. I awaited my bath, postulant, expectant. But as his penis erupted he aimed it toward the floor; only one hot splatter fell on my bare leg.

His pants were closed instantly and he urged me up to my feet. While I buttoned up he cracked open the door and looked both ways. Then he pushed me out the door just as my train pulled into the station. As I rushed to the platform, I thought, *timing – timing is everything*.

As I entered my train's automatic doors I heard the stationmaster shake his keys behind me and shout the French words I couldn't understand but whose meaning was clear: this was the last train. The station was closing. It was time to go home.

Now I'm sitting on my hotel bed writing this all to you. Does it titillate you – my little escapade? I'm already thinking about chocolate croissants, *café au lait* and perhaps a truffle for breakfast. And did I tell you what Paddy said about the Père-Lachaise cemetery? He tells me it's the hot cruising spot in all of Pareeeee! Oscar Wilde is buried there. You know his famous quote? "The only way to get rid of temptation is to yield to it."

Cruising a cemetery? Weird?

What we'll do to fight a little boredom.

I'm tired . . . off to bed. Robert's still not back. I'm getting cravings for all kinds of French delicacies. It's nice to go to bed with something to look forward to in the morning.

I remain,
your friend,
your confidante.

COUPLE

by Neil Bartlett

IT WAS A full week before they reappeared in The Bar; we hadn't seen them for six nights and there had been much discussion. Someone said that O had not been seen at his job in the video hire shop for the whole week either.

Of course when they did reappear the predictable line "And on the seventh day he rested" was much used.

If Boy had been quiet before, now his quietness had become silence. All he really wanted was to be next to O; and you could see that the whole time he was listening, watching. Also for most of the time at this period in their affair Boy was either slightly drugged, or drunk, or exhausted; and he was in a permanent state of sexual tension, for either he had just come from O's bed or he was on his way to it. He found it hard to think, never mind talk; all he could do was wait. All he could feel was his body, trying to anticipate the next touch.

Boy was of course no virgin, but he had never spent a whole week with one man before. He had never had someone say to him, at half past 11 in the morning, *let's go back to bed now.* He had never been with a man who wanted to take him out at three in morning and stand him up against a wall in a dark street and jerk him off, not because there was nowhere else to go, but for the pleasure of doing it like that; he had never done it again and again with one body. In fact Boy had never done it more than three times with anybody.

We were not surprised to see Boy behaving like this; in the week of their absence, we had decided that their lovemaking would be extraordinary, legendary. Since so many of us had made love to either O or to Boy we felt that by comparing notes we knew a great deal about how they behaved when making love, and so when we saw them reappear so obviously as lovers we were pleased to see that our predictions had been correct. We had assumed that their affair would in some way be a violent one, because O was known to be violent, and because Boy made you feel strange when he gave himself away to you, a strangeness, and a feeling that you always wanted more, that often came out as violence. And now here to prove our thesis was Boy, silent, stunned, clearly exhausted. His eyes glittered. He looked quite extraordinarily tired, ravaged by intimacy, shattered by sex, dazed with sex.

When a young man looks like that you think about the phrase *Still waters run deep.* And also we had our own adaptation of the phrase "She's out to lunch"; in such extreme cases as Boy's, we would say, *Darling, she's gone to the Opera.* "And," added Gary on this occasion, "it looks like she's not coming back."

As well as the silence we couldn't of course help noticing the bruises. We were, let me tell you, impressed. Boy was bruised badly around the mouth, and had red burn marks around both of his wrists. Of course we weren't about to ask, *what on earth has happened to you,* since we knew it could only be O who had done this to him. And we wouldn't even have thought of asking such a question. It was a point of honour, in The Bar, to behave as if nothing, not anything, was extraordinary. No sexual perversion, no possible error of taste in the choice of erotic or romantic partner was considered odd. To cry for no apparent reason was not considered odd. Nothing anyone wore was odd. The strangest of stories (*And of course when I told her that, she just threw me out of the house, my own Mother . . . well, Goodnight Mother, I can tell you*) were treated as entirely credible. So we said nothing, and noticed everything. The bruises on his wrists showed like diamonds beneath Boy's cuff; he was

wearing one of O's white shirts, with the sleeves rolled down.
When someone finally did ask, How are you two? Boy smiled,
and then winced slightly, because his lower lip was split, and
then he took a sip of his beer and he smiled sweetly and said,
In love. What he actually wanted to say was, *I'm struck dumb
with love.* (He smiled, and thought, *I'm just a dumb kid.*) But
he realized that that wouldn't make sense, since a man cannot
be struck dumb and then speak of that condition, so what he
said, when we asked him how he was, what he said was, very
slowly, *In Love. In Love with Another Man.*

They spent that first night of their return to public life just
standing close together in silence, like they were a couple of
lovers; but they weren't, of course, not yet. Six nights together
does not entitle you to be lovers in that sense of the word.
Occasionally O would take hold of a handful of Boy's black
hair, which was still long all over then. We noticed that they
touched each other all evening, shoulder to shoulder, knee to
knee, nothing obvious, although I did see O raise Boy's hand
to his lips once, and later I saw Boy rest his head on O's knees,
just lay it there for a moment like a dog. When I saw that I
wanted to be him, or one of them, or both of them, but anyway
I was just so happy to watch them together. Like several of us
in The Bar at that time, when I made love, or masturbated by
myself, I often used to have fantasies about doing it with either
O or Boy. Now that I'd seen them together like that I started
to have fantasies of being invited to watch them together or
to take photographs of them. My biggest fantasy I think was
to be a sort of assistant, a nurse, holding Boy's hand while O
worked on him. Stroking his brow, holding down a thrashing
arm, holding Boy's precious and sweating head in my two hands
on the pillow and whispering to him, *go on, push, push, breathe,
push, breathe, that's it, push, push, push.*
      We were all waiting for Mother's reaction to the reappearance.
Mother, of course, was allowed to say anything to anyone. She
left it right to the end of the evening. When they went to leave,
having sat in silence all night, O paused to speak to Mother.
She said,
      "Goodnight, O."

And then she turned suddenly to Boy and said to him, very pointedly:

"And what on earth have you done to your eyes?"

This was a trick question, because of course no one does anything like that to themselves; both of Boy's eyes were as black and blue as if he was still wearing yesterday's makeup. And also it was a trick question because Mother knew full well what had caused the bruises; she was just testing his nerve. Boy paused before answering, and looked at himself in one of the mirrors. I think Boy thought about everything he ever said. Then he spoke to Mother, but didn't look at her; when he replied to her question he was looking at O, and O was looking at him.

"It's all right," he said, "I don't think he'd ever do anything to hurt me."

And then they left, hand in hand.

After six nights in a row with O, Boy spent the seventh night on his own; he went to his own place. He slept immediately and deeply, and then got up at six a.m. to turn the television on and make the tea ready for when the man he lived with got in from work. They had their tea, then Boy went back into the living room to watch the breakfast television, which was sport, and then the phone rang. It was O, calling Boy up for the very first time.

The man took the call, in the kitchen.

He was surprised, since for all Boy's nights out, during which, as the man correctly assumed, Boy had sex with many different men, he never received visits, calls, or letters from the men he had been sleeping with. The man did not think that Boy ever gave his address or phone number to anyone. He wondered sometimes if Boy even told people what his real name was.

And now here was someone on the phone saying, *Is Boy there?*

The man dried his hands and took the phone through to Boy, then walked back into the kitchen. Then he heard Boy say "Yes," and then he heard the TV change; Boy had got up and turned it over to a boxing match, which was something Boy never usually watched. Wanting very much to hear (because he was sure that this was a lover calling, from the voice), the man used the boxing match as an excuse, and he came and stood in the kitchen doorway with a wet plate and the cloth in his hands, and looked at the television. And on the screen was a blackhaired, whiteskinned, 19-year-old boxer. His lip was split, and he was bleeding.

What had happened was that O had been at home, not sleeping, thinking about Boy at six in the morning, and he had called up and said, "Are you watching TV," to which Boy had replied, as the man had heard, "Yes," and then O had told Boy to turn over to the boxing; he'd just said, "Get up and change to the third channel. I'm watching it, and I want you to watch it too. It makes me think of you."

Though it was so strange and so cryptic, Boy understood this call, because he began to understand now that there are different kinds of wanting someone. He thought, there is wanting to go to bed with someone, which is really just an erection; and there is the kind of wanting which extends beyond the night into the day, the kind where you spend all day waiting, sometimes several days. Sometimes you are waiting for a phonecall and sometimes for a touch. You think about the person all the time, *I think about you all the time*, that's what you say. And you begin to say things that don't make any sense to people who don't know what's going on between you, but you know that the other person, to whom what you've said is really addressed will know what you mean, even though he may not actually be there.

And also, as he watched the boxer on the television, Boy began to think that there are two kinds of sex: the kind of sex where you say *do this, do that*, or you manoeuvre yourself into position for a particular kind of pleasure; and then there is the other kind of sex, where you want to say, *do anything. Do anything you want to me, you can do anything you want, I give you entire permission over me*. This feeling and especially these words cannot actually be spoken, because the words are too shaming; but for the men I know and for myself certainly I know that it usually comes out as *fuck me, please fuck me*, though that may not be exactly what you mean. I mean it is not necessarily about wanting to be actually fucked this feeling. It's more to do with the way my women friends use the word "fucked", when they say, *I fucked him*, or *I didn't want to fuck him* – for us it still means literally I fucked him, he got fucked by me. What I mean is, sometimes you are on top of him, you have the back of his neck in your teeth, and you still find yourself wanting to say to him, fuck me, go on, go on, even though you are on top of him.

This is all so hard to tell someone, so you try to do it with your body. When you see a man bury his face in his pillow, he is doing it to avoid saying all this; to escape from the words he hears himself wanting to say, to silence himself, because he knows that your face is just six inches from his but still he cannot look at you or say what he means.

You noticed this when O and Boy were out together in public. They were always very close to each other, but would never seem to be able to look one another in the eye, as if afraid of some terrible blush. They avoided each other's eyes in different ways: O would stare away as if checking out some man across The Bar; Boy would often as not still look down at the floor as had always been his habit, as if he were indeed living up to his name, as if he were indeed some young and inexperienced boy who O had just fucked into the ground. As if he was unused to having his body turn on him and shame him by admitting that it wanted these things to happen to it. As if reluctant to acknowledge in public that it was indeed his body and not someone else's body that had done those things the night before or the afternoon before. As if he was not responsible for his actions. As if suddenly he might not be able to help himself and suddenly right there in the middle of The Bar he would say out loud: *Fuck me. Please fuck me, take this body of mine right down into the deep with you, pull me under the earth, drag me under the sea; pinion my arms, put your mouth over mine and pull me under these heavy waves I'm feeling, drown me.*

When O put down the phone at the end of this first call, he did not know how to say goodbye to Boy; he did not know what name to use. He would remember this later, this not knowing what to call him, *Boy* or *Darling* or whatever. One night, later in their affair, O woke up in the middle of one of his long and noisy dreams and lay there for a long time looking at Boy's face as he slept. And then, very deliberately, as if this was what he had decided, O said, very quietly, but very definitely, out loud, *baby.*

ABOUT THE AUTHORS

PAUL ALLATSON is a Sydney writer whose work has been included in the anthology *Hard*.

TONY AYRES is a screen-writer and film-maker, and the editor of two anthologies, *String of Pearls* and *Hard*. He lives in Victoria, Australia.

JAMES IRELAND BAKER is an editor and writer at *Time Out New York* and his journalism has appeared in the *Advocate*, *Out*, *Playbill*, and *Poz* magazines. He lives in New York City, USA.

NEIL BARTLETT is a co-founder of the Gloria Theatre Company and Artistic Director of the Lyric Theatre, Hammersmith, London. His books include *Who Was That Man?* (Capital Gay Book of the Year), *Ready to Catch Him Should He Fall*, and *Mr Clive and Mr Page* (short-listed for the Whitbread Prize). He lives in Brighton, England.

KERRY BASHFORD was editor of *Pink Ink*, *Kink* and *Campaign* magazine and now edits *The Sydney Hub*. He lives in Sydney, Australia.

CHRISTOPHER BRAM is the author of six novels, *Gossip*, *Hold Tight*, *Father of Frankenstein*, *Missing Angel Clare*,

Surprising Myself, and *Almost History*. He lives in New York City, USA.

PATRICK CARR's short stories have appeared in John Preston's *Flesh and the Word* series. He works for Masquerade Books and lives in New York City, USA.

C. BARD COLE's work appears in numerous magazines and anthologies. He lives in New York City, USA.

JAMESON CURRIER is the author of the short story collection *Dancing on the Moon*. He lives in New York City, USA.

MICHAEL DENNENY is the author of *Decent Passions* and *Lovers*. A founding editor of *Christopher Street* magazine, he works at St Martin's Press where he founded the Stonewall Inn imprint. He lives in New York City, USA.

LARRY DUPLECHAN is the author of four novels, including *Blackbird* and *Captain Swing*. He lives in Los Angeles, USA, with his life partner of 21 years.

LARS EIGHNER is the author of the bestselling *Travels with Lizbeth*, as well as the mystery *Pawn to Queen Four*, the collection of essays, *Gay Cosmos*, and numerous volumes of gay erotica including *Whispered in the Dark, Bayou Boy, B.M.O.C., American Prelude*, and *The Art of Arousal*. He lives in San Antonio, Texas, USA.

DAVID EVANS is the author of the novels *Summer Set, A Cat in the Tulips*, and (writing as Ned Cresswell) *A Hollywood Conscience*, and biographies of Freddie Mercury, Dusty Springfield, and Cat Stevens. He lives in London, England.

MICHAEL THOMAS FORD is the author of more than twenty books, including *100 Questions About Aids, Outspoken*, and *The World Out There: Becoming Part of the Lesbian and Gay Community*, and editor of *Best Gay Erotica 1996, Happily Ever After*, and other anthologies. Writing as Tom Caffrey, he is the author of the erotica collections *Hitting Home & Other Stories* and *Tales from the Men's Room*. He lives in Massachusetts, USA.

PHILIP GAMBONE is the author of the collection *The Language We Use Up Here*. Currently, he teaches at The

Park School in Brookline, Massachusetts, and in the creative writing program at Harvard Extension School. He lives in Massachusetts, USA.

JAMES HANNAHAM is a journalist whose work has appeared in *The Village Voice*, *Details*, and *Out*. "Chronic Manageable Illness" is his first published fiction. He lives in New York City, USA.

ANDREW HOLLERAN is the author of three novels, *Dancer from the Dance*, *Nights in Aruba*, and *The Beauty of Men*, as well as a collection of essays, *Ground Zero*, and numerous pieces in magazines and anthologies. He lives in Florida, USA.

ALAN HOLLINGHURST is the author of two critically-acclaimed gay novels, the intensely erotic *The Swimming Pool Library* and the Booker-finalist *The Folding Star*. He lives in London, England.

G. WINSTON JAMES is the Executive Director of the Other Countries: Black Gay Expression artists collective. His work has appeared in numerous anthologies, including *Shade* and *The Road Before Us*. He lives in New York City, USA.

MICHAEL LASSELL is the author of two prize-winning volumes of poetry, *Poems for Lost and Un-lost Boys* and *Decade Dance*, and of a collection of poetry, stories, and essays, *The Hard Way*. He is the editor of *The Name of Love; Classic Gay Love Poems* and *Eros in Boystown: Contemporary Gay Poems About Sex* and, with Lawrence Schimel, of *Two Hearts Desire: Gay Couples Write About Their Love*. A former editor of LA *Style* and *Interview* magazines, he is the articles editor for *Metropolitan Homes* magazine. He lives in New York City, USA.

WILL LEBER'S short stories appear in various anthologies, including the *Flesh and the Word* series and *Flashpoint*. He lives in San Francisco, USA.

CHRIS LESLIE is the publisher of *Dirty* magazine, and his stories and essays have appeared in numerous anthologies and periodicals. He lives in New York City, USA.

BARRY LOWE is a playwright whose work includes *Rehearsing the Shower Scene from "Psycho", The Death of Peter Pan,* and *The Extraordinary Annual General Meeting of the Size Queen Club.* He lives in Sydney, Australia.

WILLIAM J. MANN is the author of the novel *The Men from the Boys* and the biography *Wisecracker: The Life and Times of William Haines.* He is the 1996 winner of the fiction prize from the Massachusetts Cultural Council. He lives in Northampton, Massachusetts, USA.

ROBIN METCALFE worked for the Canadian National Railways before switching to a literary career, writing art criticism and gay porn. His journalism has appeared in the influential Canadian magazine *Body Politic,* among other periodicals, and his short fiction appears in the *Flesh and the Word* series among numerous magazines. He lives in Halifax, Nova Scotia.

STAN PERSKY is the author of *Buddy's, Boyopolis,* and other books. He lives in Canada.

FELICE PICANO, novelist and poet, is the author of fifteen books, including *Like People in History, The Lure, The Deformity Lover,* and *The New Joy of Gay Sex* (with Charles Silverstein), and the founder of the Sea Horse Press and the Gay Presses of New York. He lives now in Los Angeles, USA.

JIM PROVENZANO is a writer whose work has appeared in various magazines and anthologies. He lives in San Francisco, USA.

DEAN RAVEN's short stories have appeared in various anthologies, including *Divertika* and *Outrage 1993.* He lives in Perth, Australia.

MATTHEW RETTENMUND is the author of the novel *Boy Culture,* and the non-fiction books *Encyclopedia Madonnica, Queer Baby Names,* and *Totally Awesome 80s.* He lives in New York City, USA, where he works as a magazine editor.

PHILIP RIDLEY is a painter, screenwriter (*The Reflecting Skin, The Krays*), playwright (*Ghost from a Perfect Place, The Fastest Clock in the Universe*), and author of novels (*In the Eyes of Mr*

Fury, Crocodilia), short stories (*Flamingoes in Orbit*) and books for children (*Meteorite Spoon, Krindlekrax, Kasper in the Glitter*). He lives in London, England.

PAUL RUSSELL, named a *Granta* Best Young Novelist, is the author of *The Sale Point, Boys of Life*, and *Sea of Tranquility*. A professor at Vassar College, he lives in Poughkeepsie, NY, USA.

STEVEN SAYLOR, writing as Aaron Travis, is the author of *The Flesh Fables, Beast of Burden, Slaves of the Empire*, and other volumes of gay erotica. As Aaron Travis, he was editor of *Drummer* magazine. Under his own name, he is the author of the acclaimed Roman mystery series *Roma Sub Rosa* featuring Gordianus the Finder. He lives in Berekely, California, USA.

LAWRENCE SCHIMEL is the author of *The Drag Queen of Elfland*, and editor of more than a dozen anthologies, including *Switch Hitters: Lesbians Write Gay Male Erotica and Gay Men Write Lesbian Erotica* (with Carol Queen), *Two Hearts Desire: Gay Couples on Their Love* (with Michael Lassell), *Food for Life*, and *Kosher Meat*, among others. He lives in New York City, USA.

D. TRAVERS SCOTT is the author of *Execution, Texas* and editor of *Strategic Sex*. He lives in Seattle, USA.

AIDEN SHAW is a porn movie star and prostitute, poet and performer. His books include the novel *Brutal* and the poetry collection *If Language at the same time Shapes and Distorts our Ideas and Emotions, How Do We Communicate Love?* His story in this volume is an excerpt from his second novel-in-progress, *Boundaries*. He lives in London, England.

DON SHEWEY has published three books, including *Out Front*, the Grove Press anthology of gay and lesbian plays. He has written extensively for *The Village Voice* and has taught theater at New York University. He lives in New York City, USA, where in addition to writing he makes a living as a professional bodyworker.

EDMUND WHITE is the author of *The Farewell Symphony, A Boy's Own Story, The Beautiful Room is Empty, Nocturnes for the*

King of Naples, *States of Desire*, and a biography of Genet, among other works. With Adam Mars-Jones he wrote *The Darker Proof.* He has won numerous awards, including the National Book Award, and is a fellow of the American Academy of Arts and Sciences. He lives in Paris, France.